By Kelly Link

The Book of Love

White Cat, Black Dog

Get in Trouble

Pretty Monsters

Magic for Beginners

Stranger Things Happen

The Year's Best Fantasy and Horror (*editor*)

Trampoline (*editor*)

THE
BOOK
OF
LOVE

THE BOOK OF LOVE

A NOVEL

Kelly Link

RANDOM HOUSE

NEW YORK

The Book of Love is a work of fiction. Names, characters, places, and incidents are the products of the author's imagination or are used fictitiously. Any resemblance to actual events, locales, or persons, living or dead, is entirely coincidental.

Copyright © 2024 by Kelly Link

All rights reserved.

Published in the United States by Random House, an imprint and division of Penguin Random House LLC, New York.

RANDOM HOUSE and the HOUSE colophon are registered trademarks of Penguin Random House LLC.

Library of Congress Cataloging-in-Publication Data
Names: Link, Kelly, author.
Title: The book of love : a novel / Kelly Link.
Description: New York : Random House, [2024]
Identifiers: LCCN 2023012774 (print) | LCCN 2023012775 (ebook) |
ISBN 9780812996586 (Hardback) | ISBN 9780812996593 (Ebook)
Subjects: LCGFT: Gothic fiction. | Novels.
Classification: LCC PS3612.I553 B66 2024 (print) | LCC PS3612.I553 (ebook) |
DDC 813/.6—dc23/eng/20230316
LC record available at https://lccn.loc.gov/2023012774
LC ebook record available at https://lccn.loc.gov/2023012775

Printed in the United States of America on acid-free paper

randomhousebooks.com

First Edition

Book design by Caroline Cunningham

To Gavin

Pretty soon I'll write music for you.

—JOHN CAGE, *The Selected Letters of John Cage*

THE
BOOK
OF
LOVE

The Book of Susannah

A GIRL WAKES UP in her sister's bed. "Laura?" she says. No one answers.

Oh, she shouldn't be here. The one who should be here isn't.

The girl's name is Susannah. She is too tall, lamentably tall, and she has bad dreams. Shouldn't her dreams be comforting? Restorative? Shouldn't she see the ones she longs with all her heart to see? But in dreams, too, they are inexplicably missing.

The sheets are half off the bed as if someone has been yanking them. It isn't morning yet. It's the middle of the night. Everything is in the wrong place, except it isn't. Her mother, Ruth, isn't home yet. All those NICU babies with their complicated medical needs, their rashy bottoms and feeding tubes, suffused in ultraviolet light, parents slumped in blistered Naugahyde recliners, nurses murmuring in corners about the bid to unionize, about husbands and television shows and their own children. Do they fall silent when Susannah's mother comes close?

"I'm tired of this," the girl says to the moon in the window, because no one else is there to talk to. "Not knowing. Being in the dark. Being alone in the dark. Don't you ever get tired of it?"

The moon is full. Isn't this proof of something? That things can disappear and then come back again? Eleven months since whatever happened happened, and Susannah knows Laura isn't coming back. If she did come back, she'd say, *What the hell are you doing in my bed, Susannah? Oh my God.*

Susannah can almost hear her say it. She gets up and makes the bed the way Laura would, because Laura isn't here to do the things that Laura ought to do. To keep Susannah from doing the things Susannah shouldn't do. All of Laura's stuffed animals are on the floor. The sky-blue owl and the pangolin in its gingham dress. Everyone loved Laura best. Everyone misses Laura. The threadbare dog with the sewn-up place where the button eye should be has a secret name. Laura would never tell Susannah what she called it. Its name was probably something stupid, though. No one ever keeps a good secret. And now no one knows except for the dog.

Susannah picks up Laura's things and puts them down again. Laura isn't here to tell her not to. So she conjures Laura up in her head. Don't worry, Laura. It's easy to put little things back where they belong. The little circles and marks in the dust on the shelves show where each right place is. If Susannah puts each of Laura's things back exactly where it ought to be, then everything will go back to the way it should be.

The china shepherdess that was their grandmother's. (Susannah has a silver ring. Missing all but one of its seed pearls.) Pictures of Laura and Susannah and their mother. Pictures of Laura and Susannah and Daniel on stage. Laura's romance novels, alphabetically arranged. Her favorite writer was Caitlynn Hightower. The covers of the romance novels, meant to indicate that the attractive people on them will eventually have sex. Fall inextricably in love, which in these books neither lessens nor changes but instead hardens, trapping those who inhabit it as amber preserves the insect. Wistful symphonic music ("Lara's Theme." Céline Dion. That kind of thing.) will begin to swell appropriately while these attractive and imaginary people fuck. Perhaps on a horse! Behind a tapestry. On a boat. On a hill. In the past. Hail fellow kismet. Everything in the right place. Very knock-knock joke. Knock knock. Who's there? Does it matter? You're a person with (a pirate ship) (a dreadful secret) (a good fortune) and I'm a person with (a fortress) (a walled garden) (a stone) for a heart so let's have sex. Let's fall in love. Sure. Why not.

There are so many novels about falling in love and so few about finding a really good and rewarding job. Not that Susannah has read a book in a long time. Books are for kids who go to college. Her mother keeps leaving community college brochures on the kitchen counter. Susannah keeps throwing them away.

Little lines of dust where the spines meet the shelf.

THINGS THAT LAURA liked: Romance novels. Milk Duds. Susannah sometimes. Music.

Laura could make her guitar talk. The guitar saying the things that Laura felt. I'm so happy. Are you happy? I'm happy. Knock knock. Go away, Susannah. I want to go to sleep. I'm sleepy. Are you happy? I'm so afraid. I'm so sad. I'm so sad.

Laura's bed, Laura's closet, Laura's clothes in drawers and behind the closet door. Susannah can borrow them now and Laura won't complain. Knock knock. Who's there? Dear sister, it is I. Your sister. I am here and you are not. Can I borrow your red sweater? Okay. Sure.

Why not.

The jadeite mug on the windowsill holds guitar picks and Chinese fortunes. (*You are beautiful and mysterious to all who encounter you.*) (*Do not fear change.*) (*Every door will be open to you.*) Platitudes and lies.

Susannah stands at Laura's window. Across the lawn is Daniel's house, the yellow rectangle of Daniel's window, a light on in Daniel's room. Does his mother sit there when she can't sleep?

Susannah picks up her sister's old Harmony Sovereign Marveltone acoustic and runs her hand down the neck. "Laura?" Susannah says. "Come back. You should come back or else I'll do something terrible. I need you to come back."

She waits for an answer. Gets none. Actually, this is typical of Laura, who believed in the silent treatment. So, Susannah thinks, let's be typical. She's tried so hard to be good the last few months. Has anyone even noticed? If Daniel were here, he would have noticed. Mo would have noticed even if he didn't say anything. She's pretty fucking sure Laura would have noticed.

If Daniel were here, he would help her figure out how to live without Laura. If Laura were here, she and Susannah could figure out together how to live without Daniel. But it's only Susannah. It will only ever be Susannah again, which means that Susannah can't be Susannah. She doesn't know how.

Laura's first guitar was the Harmony. Its previous owner was careless and left it near a radiator one night. This was their father: someone else who isn't here. If the guitar had still had any value, he'd have taken it with him when he left. Right? Susannah lifts the Harmony over her head and brings it down hard on the corner of Laura's desk. When this isn't hard enough, she brings it down again and again until she has smashed what she can into pieces. With the last blow, a section of the neck splits away and ricochets off the window, and there goes the jadeite mug, over onto the desk. Picks spill everywhere, and the handle cracks right off at the lip. Well, that's a mess. When Susannah crosses the carpet to pick up the mug, she feels something in her heel as if she's stepped on something sharp. She sits down on Laura's bed and examines her foot. Yes, there it is, a splinter. She'll leave it there for now. A reminder of her sins.

What does she feel? The small hurt where a splinter sits. Nothing to cry over, and so she won't cry.

Susannah gets down on her hands and knees and gathers up all the pieces of the guitar and puts them into Laura's closet. She puts the mug back on the windowsill, too, turned so that the crack in the lip where the handle ought to be is hidden.

What has she accomplished? Well, maybe wherever she is, Laura felt a psychic twinge of loss. Next time, Susannah thinks, I'm donating all of your Caitlynn Hightower romance novels to Goodwill. I'm going to throw away your Bed Head shampoo and the expensive face stuff that smells like rotten ginger ale even though you always pretended you liked it. I'm going to accept the fact you're gone forever. Fuck you for being dead or whatever it is that happened. Be a secret. See if I care.

Susannah could go downstairs and turn on the TV. She could tear the pangolin to pieces. Smash the shepherdess. She could go into the bathroom and run water over the tender place where the splinter went in. But instead she lies down again on Laura's bed and pulls the comforter over her head. She'll wake up when her mother gets home; she has to wake up before Ruth gets home because what if Ruth opens the door to Laura's room and thinks that Laura is back? What if she opens Susannah's door and thinks Susannah is gone?

Right up until the hour she disappeared, Laura was the good one, Susannah the counterweight. Now Laura is gone, and so Susannah has had to fill both roles. She's still the fuckup, the one who didn't go to college, but she's also been the good child, the one who does the dishes and lets her mother know where she's going to be and how late she's going to stay out. She contributes grocery money, and she tries not to make her mother any sadder than she already is. She's been so good. If she lies here a little longer on Laura's bed, Susannah can absorb just a little more of whatever it was that made Laura able to be the good sister. But it's so tiring to be good. So exhausting to be sad. Someone should make a Fitbit for being good. For being sad. At the end of the day, you could look at your wrist and see just how sad you'd been. Tomorrow you can be even sadder! She'll just lie here a little while longer, being sad. Then she'll go back to her own bed.

AND WHAT DOES she dream of when she falls asleep? Susannah dreams she stands before a door. She can't figure out how to open it. It won't open. But then it opens. A wind has knocked it off the latch, and it bangs open and shut, open and shut, knock knock. Who's there? Knock knock!

(*Every door will be open to you.*)

Susannah's eyes fly open like two doors, but she isn't truly awake. The pangolin's lumpy snout pokes her wet cheek. Still dreaming, she leaves Laura's room (open the door, shut the door, but this is not the right door) and goes back to her own room (door opens, door shuts, and this door, too, is not the door of her dream) and lies down upon her own bed. There is a splinter in her heel. A thing where it shouldn't be. Susannah drags the covers over her head for the third time this night and continues to sleep as large and small pieces of the smashed guitar in Laura's closet begin to knock together. Knock knock! The guitar neck thumps against the closet door, and the guitar strings, taut again, twang, and the closet door falls open.

A guitar pick sails out from under Laura's bed and up into the jadeite mug, pinging off the cracked lip. The Harmony leans against the wall again. But the handle of the mug is still broken.

The Book of Laura

There were three. Where were they? Someplace they shouldn't be. They couldn't get out. When they found a way out, someone else followed them. Something came along with them.

Something happened. Something had happened to them. What? Something that shouldn't have happened. Had they died? Were they dead? Surely they were not dead. But if they were dead, then what was this place? You couldn't get out. This terrible place. Sometimes together and sometimes apart. There was no comfort in being together, but it was worse to be separated. Sometimes each of them was alone and that was worst of all. And now? Where there had been three, no question about that, now there were four.

They had been in an awful place. A blotted, attenuated, chilly nothingness—how to describe it? Later on, one of them said, "I think I remember a lot of trees. There was a dirty path. And a clearing with someone in it." Someone else said the only way to describe it was that it was like being an ant that had fallen into an Icee machine with only one flavor selection: expired-milk insomniac pushing dirty bad-luck needles through the hangnail skin of an endless, resentful night. Which was poetic, sure, and maybe not inaccurate, but it didn't give you the whole picture. Really, you had to have been there.

They had been imprisoned. Then there had been a seeping warmth, a kind of shiver as if someone you'd once known how to be had walked past a door, and though that door was closed, they had pressed against it until there was the very thinnest seam—Such small stitches, whose hand had made them? Who had hung the hinges on this door?—but *they* were very thin now, too, and slipped through that loose stitch, one by one by one. And one more. Who?

THERE WERE FOUR of them now. That was the first mystery.

The second mystery was where they found themselves. They had been in that other place. And then they dragged themselves out and found themselves in Mr. Anabin's music room at Lewis Latimer Public School. They knew it was his room because there was Mr. Anabin's baby grand. There was the poster of Hildegard of Bingen on the wall in front of them. De La Soul on the wall behind them. (Four is the magic number.) Dark outside the windows, and Mr. Anabin himself, playing a minor scale on the baby grand.

When he saw them, Mr. Anabin closed the piano lid and rested his hands in his lap. "So," he said. The sound of a human voice in a human space was terrible and unfamiliar. "I thought it might be something like this."

None of the four moved from where they were. Muddled together, they occupied less space than one or two would have in their proper state. The cracked linoleum floor was visible to them through the drifty suggestion of their own limbs.

Mr. Anabin approached slowly, as if, should he startle them, they might go flying through a keyhole, a window, the pockmarked ceiling tiles. He stood looking for a long time, and then he said, "Laura. Laura Hand."

He made a little movement with two fingers. And here was Laura Hand (up until a year ago, quite sure of her place in the world) manifested, bewildered, and altogether both less and more herself than she had been for a long time. Her companions eddied around her like conturbations of dust.

"Mohammed Gorch." Mr. Anabin flicked his fingers again. And there was Mo Gorch, who was a grade below Laura and Daniel but nevertheless in Laura's third-period calculus class and fifth-period A.P. history. He was a friend of Susannah's.

"And Daniel Knowe. Of course." His fingers delineating a shape. Here was Daniel, who was dear to Laura. He and she and Susannah had a band, My Two Hands Both Knowe You.

Laura pinched her own arm. She was herself again: the sturdy architecture of her ribs, pulpy heart with its four chambers and the doors that open and shut, open and shut, the hasty blood rushing through, a red mark appearing where she had pinched. And yet something was still missing.

Wasn't she?

"Where's Susannah?" Laura said, looking around for her sister. "Susannah! What did you do?"

It was always Susannah who had done whatever it was. Wasn't it?

But Susannah wasn't here.

Laura's entire skin felt wrong. She felt squashed and stretched somehow, like a piece of Play-Doh in a warm hand, and she felt like the hand, too. She thought, Well, I am a Hand. And then, Perhaps I have been given an experimental drug.

"I'm going to sit down," Mo said. "Just for a minute." Instead of sitting down on one of the chairs, he sat down on the floor and put his head in his hands.

Daniel said, "Someone lost a pencil."

He reached up and pulled a pencil out that had been stuck in a ceiling tile. (For how long? Who knew?) That was how tall Daniel was. The pencil was very short. Someone had chewed on it.

Laura reached out and took it from him. She dropped it on the floor. "Don't touch that," she said. "No one wants it back."

"Something very strange has been happening," Mo said.

"Yeah," Laura said. "But it's okay now. Isn't it?" Mo looked up at her. She held out her hand, and he took it in his own, startlingly warm and solid. She pulled him up onto his feet. Once, in calculus, he'd loaned her a piece of graph paper.

Having established they were all together and in the world again, at last they looked at Mr. Anabin. After all, it was his music room.

MR. ANABIN WAS a middle-aged-ish, brown-ish man. Tall-ish. Terrible posture. His wiry hair was short, and there was just a little gray in it. His hands were elegant, expressive. Manicured nails. Fingers long but not too long. They were, without question, the hands of a music teacher. The previous year, the PTA had raised enough money for the school to offer chorus and band as electives. Hence, Mr. Anabin. He played piano during school concerts. Chose and directed the school musical. Ran detention occasionally. He didn't seem anxious to be anyone's favorite teacher, but neither was he one of the bad ones. He wore blue jeans and T-shirts with affirmational statements on them. There was something in his eyes that, taken in concert with the T-shirts, made students feel vaguely uneasy. It was a certain look. Was it sardonic? Or only a little knowing? After a while, you didn't look into his eyes. But then, as far as anyone knew, Mr. Anabin lived alone. Once, Susannah had said to Laura that sometimes during band practice, she found herself imagining Mr. Anabin's laundry, Mr. Anabin sorting his whites from his colors. After all, no one else was going to do it for him. Folding his shirts: BE YOUR OWN KIND OF BEAUTY. WE CAN ACCOMPLISH MIRACLES IF WE BELIEVE WE CAN. TODAY IS GOING TO BE THE MOST AMAZING DAY AND TOMORROW WILL BE EVEN BETTER. WHEN LIFE GIVES YOU LEMONS SAY THANK YOU. LEMONS ARE DELICIOUS AND REFRESHING. It was pretty fucking depressing, Susannah said, when you thought about it, which Laura didn't understand. Laundry was just laundry. There wasn't anything there to be depressed about.

Mr. Anabin's gaze seemed fixed on something just past Mo's shoulder. Laura, looking where he looked, could not see anyone standing there. And yet she felt sure someone was there.

Nonetheless she said, "Everything's fine. It's all going to be fine."

"Why are we wearing these clothes?" Daniel said.

"They're from *Bye Bye Birdie*," Mo said. He sounded astonished to know anything at all. Laura hadn't ever really hung out with Mo, although of course she was aware of him: his grandmother was Caitlynn Hightower. Laura had all of her books. Other things Laura knew: Mo was gay. His mother was dead. "From last year. I'm Albert. I'm wearing Albert's clothes. I know that because I was Wardrobe. What's with the bare feet? Is that weird? That we don't have shoes or socks on?"

"I wasn't in *Bye Bye Birdie*," Daniel said. "Because of football practice. I don't know why I'm barefoot. I have no idea what's going on right now."

"Looks like you're Maude's Dishwasher," Mo said. "Laura's Rose."

Laura looked down. Her feet were filthy—Daniel's and Mo's were in a similar state—and she was wearing, what? A poodle skirt. She hadn't even noticed.

"Clothes seemed the least of the problem," Mr. Anabin said. "I took what was nearest to hand. Be quiet for a moment. There's one here I don't know. Who or what are you? What is your business?"

Something seemed to move, or perhaps something that had been in motion now grew very still. There was an exhalation, a sigh, as if Mr. Anabin had asked the air a question, and the fine hairs rose at the nape of Laura's neck.

"Something touched me," Daniel said. "I felt something."

They all felt it now. It rushed around them, tugged at their ridiculous clothing, Laura's cheerful skirt. The blue hair ribbon, which she hadn't realized she was wearing, came undone and went whipping around the music room until Mo caught it as it flew past. He gave it to Laura, who tied her hair back with trembling fingers.

Mr. Anabin made that small motion with his hand again, and then here at last was the other one, the last one. But not altogether there, still not entirely. A pair of pale eyes. A mouth. The pencil Laura had dropped on the floor went sailing up into the air, point first, and stuck into the ceiling again.

"The end of the pencil is just as important as the other end," Mo said. Laura had no idea what he meant by that. Mo, she was beginning to remember, said a lot of things that didn't seem to mean anything.

"Speak," Mr. Anabin said. "Tell us your name."

"Oh," a voice like the scrape of an empty lighter said. "That was lost a long time ago. So long ago."

"Then pick a new one," said Mr. Anabin. "Quickly."

"They were all lost," the voice said. "I lost them all."

"Excuse me, but you can't have lost them all?" Mo said. He pointed at one of Mr. Anabin's posters. "I can think of hundreds. Hildegard. That's a name. Aretha. Prince." He pointed again. "Bowie."

"Bowie," the voice repeated.

"Bowie then," Mr. Anabin said. "You'll forgive me if you don't resemble yourself, but time is short and there is very little of you left." He blew on his hands, rubbed them together, and made another gesture, this one more extravagant.

And there was the last of the four, back in the world again. He wore Conrad Birdie's biker jacket and white scarf. Was barefoot and dirty. Laura was certain she had never seen him before in her life. A boy their age. Longish, sandy hair and a white face she was not sure about. Human faces didn't really look like that, did they? Like a box accidentally closed up with something alive inside it. Mismatched eyes like Bowie on the wall.

"Perhaps a bit too much like," Mr. Anabin said, and gestured. And both eyes were blue.

"Can he do that?" Laura said to Daniel and Mo. "Just make a person? Is that what he did to us?"

"I could give you each six pairs of wings, a heart of glass, and poison glands," Mr. Anabin said. "But there would be no point to it. You are as you were. I made you out of yourselves, what you were and had been."

"I have no idea what that means," Daniel said. "And I don't want to know, either. We should go."

Mo said, "Something happened, but I can't remember it. Except that it was bad. We should all go home now before more bad things happen. Mr. Anabin, catch you later."

"No!" Laura said. They all looked at her. The look on Mr. Anabin's face was patient. Interested. His T-shirt gently encouraging. YOU ARE SPECIAL IN WAYS YOU DON'T EVEN KNOW YET.

She said, "I mean, not yet. Mr. Anabin, how did we get here? What was that place, the place we were in before?"

"I'm leaving," Mo said. It was as if Laura were not standing right there, as if her desires, her questions were immaterial, as if she herself were still immaterial. "You coming? Laura? Daniel? Bowie Not Bowie?"

"No!" Laura said. And stamped her foot. "I want to know what happened! I'm not leaving until I know."

"It's too late," Bowie said. "He's here."

"Then tell him to go away," Laura said. She didn't look to see who Bowie meant. (If she didn't look, then no one would be there.) "There are enough people here right now."

"We were dead." That was Daniel. "That's what happened. That's what you remember, Mo. That's what you want to know, Laura. Isn't it? We died. We were dead. Whose dog is that?"

Laura turned to look.

A LARGE DOG sat at the threshold of the music room. Maybe the music room door had been open all this time, though Laura thought it had been closed. (Or had not been there at all.) But then, how had she and the others come in—Through the windows? Like Cathy Earnshaw's ghost?— and where had the dog come from? Laura began to wonder, looking at it, if it was a dog at all. That squashed feeling came over her again, except somehow the opposite was happening, too, as if she were shrinking and expanding at the same time. Her skin suddenly too loose and Laura—the most essential part of her—too small, so small she was suddenly afraid she might slip out of her own mouth or eyes and dissipate altogether, leaving only the emptied sleeve of her skin in a starched froth of poodle skirt.

Daniel had said something she knew she should have paid attention to. He'd said something, made some joke. Had it been funny? She'd wanted to laugh when he said it, but then she'd seen the dog.

The dog in the doorway had white fur, matted and coarse and bristling; a voluptuary's red tongue lolled out. Its ears were latched flat against the prow of its head. It was such a very large dog the room seemed smaller: even Daniel seemed diminished in its presence. What was it Daniel had said?

"Good dog," Mo said in a gentle voice. "Good doggie. Where did you come from? What a big, fucking, terrifying nightmare doggie. Yes. Yes, you *are*."

"It isn't a dog," Daniel said. "It's a wolf."

"It isn't a wolf," Bowie said.

The thing on the threshold regarded each of them in turn as they spoke. It looked at Laura, its gaze reproachful and ravenous. At last it looked at Mr. Anabin.

Mr. Anabin's hand went up as if he were about to make some gesture that would save them all, but instead he scratched his head, shrugged, and said, "You are welcome, Bogomil. As welcome as you ever are."

Then Mr. Anabin turned his back to the open door, facing instead the windows and the night outside.

The thing upon the threshold had begun to shudder all over as Mr. Anabin spoke. It opened its jaws and panted. As Laura watched, it shimmied as if shucking off a too-tight dress, stretching and flexing, emitting little whining noises of discomfort, and then there was a person instead of a dog-wolf-thing, on his hands and knees upon the floor, person mouth split open in an airless yawn. The mouth closed. The person stood up, ran his hands down his face, then held them up to better examine his nails, which were, it was true, very dirty. His hands were filthy down to the wrists, as though he had been digging a hole in a muddy garden. He wore the Mayor's costume from *Bye Bye Birdie*. Despite the dirt and the costume, he was by far the handsomest man Laura had ever seen. (Had she thought this the first time she saw him? Probably not. She could not remember the first time she had seen him.)

He had been a very large dog. But now he was not much taller than Laura. How old was he? Oh, not so very old. There are older things in the world. But still he was very old.

His bare feet like theirs were crusted with dirt. The only one wearing shoes in the music room was Mr. Anabin.

"Who are you?" That was Mo.

But Laura could tell that, like the rest of them, Mo knew.

"Am I really so forgettable?" the man said. He spoke softly enough Laura strained to hear what he was saying. He stayed where he was, leaning against the doorframe. There was something wolflike still in his posture, as if at any moment he might spring. "Quite a surprise, really, you gone from my house, all of you at once without so much as a thank-you note. And I don't mind telling you it's been some time since anything has surprised me."

Laura thought, I've changed my mind. I'd like to leave.

"How?" Daniel said. "He's standing in the doorway." So perhaps she had said it out loud.

"I don't like any part of this," Mo said. His chin was out. "I don't like the part where I'm wearing a costume from last year's musical, and *Bye Bye Birdie* is really not a great musical anyway. I never liked it. There's only one good song. It isn't that good, actually. I don't know if I remember you or not, wolf person, but I don't like *you*, either. And I definitely do not like how I seem to remember some really bad stuff happening—thanks, Daniel, by the way, for reminding me—and I also don't like the feeling I'm starting to get that, in a minute or so, something else bad is going to start happening. Like this is a bad sandwich. A sandwich where the filling is a middle-of-the-night school music room in between two slices of being dead. Who orders a sandwich like that? Nobody!"

"Will somebody please just explain what's happening?" Laura said. "*Please*. Mr. Anabin? Mr. Anabin! Who is this person?"

Mr. Anabin stayed where he was, staring at the window, his back to them. Laura's heart was beating so quickly in her chest she thought she might die. Had she died? Oh, but she was alive now. She had a heart, and her blood moved through her heart, and as it flowed it sang, Oh alive, *oh alive*!

In the window she found Mr. Anabin's eyes. He said nothing. And there, too, was the reflection of the man who stood at the door.

"I'll introduce myself," he said, "since Anabin has no manners. You four left my house before we had much chance to become acquainted. You may call me Bogomil. No need to tell me your names. I know you. You need no names with me."

Bogomil paused. "Except." He pointed a long, filthy nail, and Laura, standing closest to Bowie, recoiled. But Bowie did not move. "I wonder if you could tell me what you are called."

"I don't know," Bowie said. He didn't sound afraid. He sounded in some place far beyond that. "I wish I knew."

"Old wine in a new bottle, I think," said Bogomil. "Or maybe only the dregs."

"His name is Bowie, you freak!" Laura said. Who did this weird person think he was? It was the middle of the night! Everyone should start being nicer and also less confusing. Although now that this person named Bogomil (Really? His name was Bogomil? It sounded like a German breakfast cereal.) was looking at her and not at Bowie, she thought perhaps she had been a little rude. Perhaps the right tack was politeness tempered with firmness. You weren't supposed to show fear with gods. No, dogs. That was what they said.

"Oh, *Laura*!" Bogomil said. He took a step into the room. Then another. "Susannah's lovely sister. Won't you cry for me. Yes. Daniel elo ello hello. Mo who doesn't know, not yet. She died of grief. And this one. There's something familiar about that famine face. No matter, really, how you got out. Just a tick and we'll put everything right again."

He took a third step.

There was something about the sound of his dirty feet on the floor that was the worst thing yet. His expression did not change, but the sound suggested contact with the world was agony. As if whatever Bogomil was made of—surely not flesh?—rejected the contact even as it occurred. Or did the floor, that unremarkable linoleum, reject Bogomil? Yes. The whole room, in a kind of agony, refuted Bogomil. He was smiling. But every footfall was a strike on a bell stopped with mud. A clot of blood trembling on a rusted wire.

Bogomil was close enough now that Laura could not escape the familiar reek of him—roses—and under the roses, something burning. Would she ever get that smell out of her clothes? Her hair? It permeated every pore, every orifice. It was the only real thing in the whole world: oh, how could Laura have forgotten? She could feel herself coldly boiling down to nothingness, a vapor. Every thought she had ever had, every stupid thing she'd ever done. Every song she'd ever figured out the chords to. Every verse. Every lyric, every key change. Every drop of night. Each bright day. Any minute now the person called Bogomil would catch them all up and Laura and the others would be carried away like a handful of loose coins.

Bogomil's finger went up, and just as Laura thought, Do something, oh do something quickly, Daniel said, "Wait. Wait! What do you mean, how we got out? Out of where? And what do you mean, 'put everything right'?"

Weren't these, more or less, the same questions Laura had been asking earlier? Not that Laura wasn't grateful Bogomil wasn't zapping them with that dirty finger, but if it hadn't been the time for questions earlier, it most definitely wasn't the time for questions now. Or the person.

"What is the taste of a soul as it is drawn from between the lips?" Bogomil said. "Who whispers in the darkness? Those are questions for which I have answers. *How—you—got—out* is my question. You will supply the answer to me. Sooner or later or much later or, if you are lucky, much sooner. Oldest brothers should keep true answers in their pockets, Daniel. Why is the sky blue? Why is the moon so full of hate? What costs more dearly, one's first death or the second? In simple words: Your guess is correct. You died. You came through the door and into my realm. And then, through some unforeseen chance, you slipped away from me. You passed yourselves through some knot or hole or oubliette, and here you are. In Anabin's realm. But you know very well you can't stay. This is no place for the dead."

As he said it, Laura knew it was true. They had died. They were dead. A flush of embarrassment crept over her, as if she and Daniel and Mo had been caught sneaking into a movie, stolen candy in their pockets. And with Bowie! Who wasn't even a real person! Real people knew who they were supposed to be, knew their own names and did not have to borrow them. They had their own faces.

Daniel said, "So I was right. We're dead."

Mo said, "Bullshit!" He said it so emphatically spit flew out. He wiped his mouth. "We're here. We're alive!"

Laura thought once again, without knowing why: Susannah! This is all your fault!

She hadn't even made it out of high school, to the good parts. For God's sake, she hadn't even had sex with a girl yet, which meant that as far as she was concerned, she hadn't really had sex at all, unless you were going to count lying on a blanket in the sand dunes while some summer guy with scratchy facial hair and a tattoo of a lobster riding a unicorn with MAGICAL MAINE written underneath it—and no sense of timing—fingered you while he humped your thigh, which Laura did not. Meanwhile, Susannah did whatever she wanted. Susannah kissed people on a regular basis, and now Laura was remembering something that had happened right before they had died, which was Susannah kissing someone during "The Kissing Song." Well, that was what Susannah did during "The Kissing Song." It was the whole gimmick. Except this time Susannah had kissed Rosamel Walker. Which was typical of Susannah. Kissing people you knew you shouldn't kiss, as if that were something you could do and not expect there would be repercussions.

Laura didn't want to be thinking about Susannah. There had been songs that Laura was going to write! She'd had a plan for the next few years. Finish high school. Get a full scholarship at some reasonably good college. On the music side, shitty performances in shitty clubs, followed by better performances at better clubs. Preferably with Daniel and Susannah, but if not, then oh well. There were other musicians in the sea. More songs, more acclaim, more hard work. More life! More!

Finally, if Laura had had any idea she was going to be dead soon, she would have stopped saving up for the Gretsch G5422TG Electromatic Double Cutaway Hollowbody and bought the Epiphone Casino Coupe instead. She'd had enough money for the Epiphone months ago.

"Someone do something," Laura said. She realized she was whispering. So she tried a second time, really projecting this time. It was like being on stage. You just had to make yourself be heard. Even when you were petrified. Even when your audience looked as if they might be planning to eat you alive. Bogomil grinning at her the whole time. "Mr. Anabin! Hello? Hello! Are you just going to let him do this?"

She dragged her eyes away from Bogomil in his borrowed costume, found Mr. Anabin's face again in the window glass.

But then Bowie was speaking. "I don't want to go," he said. "Anabin. We want to stay. We are asking you to help us." He took Mr. Anabin by the shoulder and forcibly spun him. As Mr. Anabin turned, so did Bogomil, so that now Bogomil faced the piano, the blackboard, and the clock upon the wall above.

Mr. Anabin said, as if he had been a part of the conversation all along, "If you wish to stay, then Bogomil and I must come to an agreement. Perhaps a game? Or a set of trials, like the old days. With prizes. Bogomil likes those."

They were all looking now, first to Mr. Anabin and then to where Bogomil stood. Bogomil's shoulder rose, just a little. He sat down on the end of the piano bench beside the blackboard, still facing away, and lifted the lid. So gently! One finger came down on a black key.

Mo said, "Dead or alive, there's no way in hell I'm going anywhere with him. No pun intended."

Daniel said, "Nobody is going anywhere with that guy."

As if we'd have any choice, Laura thought.

"There must be rules," Mr. Anabin said.

A finger on that black key again.

"I'll keep them here," Mr. Anabin said. "You and I to devise the trial. Something educational? Perhaps a series of tests. If they succeed, you will let them go."

They waited, hardly daring to breathe, but the black key did not depress. Instead Bogomil stood up and scraped, leisurely, a fingernail down the blackboard. Laura found she could not lift her hands to cover her ears to block out the sound the whole time Bogomil wrote. Her sides grew wet with sweat where her leaden arms hung down. When Bogomil was done writing, there was a message upon the blackboard in a smear of reddish brown.

2 RETURN
2 REMAIN

"Hold on," Daniel said. "What does that mean?"

But Mr. Anabin was already speaking.

"Done," he said.

Bogomil turned at this and faced them. He was not smiling, but there was something different in his face now. How beautiful he was! He advanced, not speaking, and Mr. Anabin did not speak, either. Bogomil looked at each of them in turn: Daniel, Mo, and then Laura. Laura returned his look, trying to be as brave as possible, or at least to seem so. If she couldn't be brave, then at least she could pretend to be brave. It seemed to her that she looked at Bogomil for a very long time. His beauty only increased, until it became a kind of ache inside her, yet she could see nothing good in him. Only horror. And she knew he could see that she was not brave.

At last he looked at Bowie. But Bowie would not look at Bogomil at all. Instead he stared at the floor.

Bogomil took three steps forward until he stood no more than a foot from Mr. Anabin. Mr. Anabin, like Bowie, would not meet Bogomil's gaze. Bogomil reached out and took Mr. Anabin's face in his dirty hands. He reached up and touched Mr. Anabin's hair.

Mr. Anabin smiled. He closed his eyes. "Bogomil," he said, and Bogomil's hand fell. He began to shiver and shake until Laura felt he would fly into pieces, but the next moment he was not there at all. Instead a black rabbit crouched on the floor at Mr. Anabin's feet. Its long ears flicked back and forward; before anyone could move, it dashed between Mr. Anabin and Bowie, zigzagging toward the very back of the classroom, to the door, then between Bowie and Laura, headfirst into the wall below the window. It hit with a bad sound.

Both hind legs were still jerking spasmodically when Mo knelt down beside it, Laura saying, "Oh, be careful, Mo! Be careful!"

But the rabbit's neck was broken. It was dead. Sometimes things keep moving for a little while after they are dead. The Mayor's costume lay in a flattened, dirty heap where Bogomil had stood. The room stank of roses.

THE FIRST ONE to speak was Mo, which wasn't a surprise. His hand was almost always first to go up in class, as if that ever impressed anyone. He and Susannah at a table at What Hast Thou Ground?, sitting and laughing. Look how much fun we're having. Even his trumpet-playing in band had been showy. He said, "What just happened? Right now? Also, what happened before that? And also before that? What exactly is going on?"

They all looked at Mr. Anabin. He said, "A complicated question with a complicated answer."

"We're smart kids," Mo said. He shot Daniel a malevolent look. Now Laura remembered, too: Mo didn't like Daniel for a reason that, according to Daniel, was a complete mystery. Even Susannah said she didn't know. "Well, most of us."

Daniel said, "All I want to know is if I can go home."

"Of course we can go home," Laura said. Before Bogomil had shown up, she'd wanted to know some stuff. She'd had questions. But it was clear that Bogomil was the answer to every single one. Answers were terrible. "We can walk. Daniel, let's go."

"You may go home," Mr. Anabin said. "You should go home. But there are one or two things you must understand first."

Laura didn't want to look at Mr. Anabin. Instead she kept her eyes on the dead rabbit.

"Oh," Mo said. "Sure. I mean, if you're sure those things aren't too complicated for us to understand."

"You were dead," Mr. Anabin said. "And, yes, what you are now is complicated. Let us put our attention therefore on the most pressing matter. This game, this contest that Bogomil suggests. There will be three trials. Yes. That should suffice. As long as our game runs, and as long as you adhere to its rules, you will stay in the world of the living."

"What if we don't want to play some game?" Daniel said.

"Then there will be nothing I can do," Mr. Anabin said. "By rights you will belong to Bogomil again and he may dispose of you as he chooses."

"You mean we'll be dead again," Mo said.

Mr. Anabin said nothing.

"What does it mean?" Laura said. "What he wrote on the blackboard? Two return, two remain?"

"Bogomil's math," Mr. Anabin said. "An equation that will take some time to solve. You asked if you could go home. Go home. But you must not tell anyone about any part of this. That is the first rule. Do not break it. I will arrange an explanation for your absence."

"How can we tell anyone anything when we don't know what happened?" Mo said. He went over to the blackboard and picked up the eraser and began to scrub at Bogomil's writing. "Take, for example, our deaths. Was it a car accident? Bubonic plague? Did we enter a fried-clam-eating contest and win a bad prize? Does anyone remember? Why won't this eraser just erase? What's the point of an eraser that doesn't do the only thing it's meant to do?"

He banged the eraser against the board and a cloud of dust flew up.

No one said anything. No one could remember, Laura saw. It seemed to her that perhaps Mr. Anabin did not know, either.

"Okay, so table that," Mo said. "I mean, it's not like it's a big deal, how we died. Happens all the time. People die every day getting out of the shower. Checking their email. Making a sandwich. So we died. Who cares how, right? But maybe you can tell us how long we've been . . . not alive . . . ?"

"Where Bowie is concerned, I cannot answer that question," Mr. Anabin said.

They all looked at Bowie, but Bowie appeared to have no opinion or feelings on the subject of how long he had been dead.

"You three," Mr. Anabin said, "died almost a year ago. You died at the start of the year and tomorrow is the fourteenth of December. The year is 2014. When you . . . died, your bodies were not found. There was no trace or explanation of what might have happened. Where you might have gone."

Laura's heart turned over. Mom, she thought. Oh, Mom, poor Mom. Poor Susannah. Poor Mom, stuck with just Susannah.

"A year," Daniel said. His face said he did not believe it.

Mr. Anabin made a gesture with his hand.

"What was that?" Laura said. "You just did something again, didn't you?"

"It's fixed," Mr. Anabin said. "You may go home. There won't be any questions."

"Oh, I have questions," Mo said from the blackboard. "For example, what do you mean 'it's fixed'? What exactly is 'it,' and also, what do you mean when you say 'fixed'? And also, how is 'it' 'fixed'?" You could hear every single quotation mark.

"This year the three of you have been abroad," Mr. Anabin said. "You graduated in the spring after having accepted offers to attend university in Ireland. Full scholarships to a prestigious program at a private conservatory in Ireland."

"Ireland?" Daniel said. "Why Ireland? Did we actually go there? Did we die in Ireland?"

"But I'm a junior," Mo said. "I mean I *was* a junior. When, you know, we died."

"You graduated a year early," Mr. Anabin said. "The scholarship was contingent upon your early graduation. Everyone is very proud of you. The three of you. You returned home yesterday for the winter break. An overnight flight to Boston, where I, as the liaison with your program, picked you up. It's two o'clock in the morning and you are, all of you, in your beds asleep at this very moment. The day that lies ahead is Sunday. Sleep in. On Monday, you will come to this room at two P.M. sharp. I will be waiting."

Laura listened as Mr. Anabin spoke, and some part of her wanted to believe every word. Did believe. She had not been dead. She had graduated! Accepted a scholarship, gone to the DMV, and had passport photos taken. She'd flown from Boston into Dublin, then taken a bus from Dublin to the outskirts of Cork, been picked up by a van from the conservatory. She'd almost left her suitcase on the bus, she'd been so jet-lagged. She'd been homesick, but it had been an amazing experience. She and Daniel and Mo had gone sightseeing. For example, she'd been in a . . . castle? Somewhere dark. Cold. She hadn't been able to get out. The dead rabbit on the floor of the music room said, Remember. Remember death. You were dead. One day you will be dead again.

"What if we don't come to you?" Daniel said.

"I leave it up to you," Mr. Anabin said. "You may come to me. If you do not come to me, then Bogomil will come to you."

While they were thinking about that, he said, "When you come to me, you will tell me what you remember of your death. And here is the first trial. You will accomplish some form of magic. On Monday you will bring me proof."

"Homework!" Laura said. It almost felt normal. "Let's go, let's go. Daniel, *come on*."

"Mo?" Daniel said. "You coming? Bowie? You got somewhere to go?"

Mo lived with his famous grandmother in one of the old Victorian houses on the Cliffs. Way above the rest of the town, where people had the most money and the nicest views and didn't have to worry about king tides or crab migrations or drunk day-trippers in summer wandering out of the dunes and into backyards. Laura had never been inside Mo's house, but once she'd watched an episode where Oprah had actually come to Lovesend, Massachusetts, to interview Mo's grandmother. It was an extremely awesome house. Plus, Mo's grandmother was Mo's grandmother, successful and celebrated and generally amazing. Laura thought, Mo can take care of himself.

And was Bowie supposed to be their problem now, just because he'd come back from the dead with them like a package deal? Buy three dead people, get one free?

Bowie, or whatever his name really was, seemed of a piece with Bogomil and the place they had escaped from. Who knew why he had ended up there? *Death*, she thought, but other people had died—lots of them— and none of those other dead people had hitched a ride back to Lewis Latimer with Laura and Daniel and Mo.

But you couldn't just leave this guy here, in a music room with Mr. Anabin and a grand piano and a dead rabbit. Could you?

Laura said to Bowie, "Ruth would lose her shit if she woke up and there was some strange kid in the house. But you could stay with Daniel, I guess?"

Daniel's family lived next door to the Hands. They'd been neighbors all their lives. What with all of Daniel's brothers and sisters, odds were good his mother and his stepfather would never even notice some strange kid.

"Sure," Daniel said. "I guess."

Bowie said, "I can take care of myself."

"Bowie. What a puzzle you are. Every piece of you a puzzle. Eventually you may remember more of what you were," Mr. Anabin said. "But the world, too, is not as it once was."

Bowie said nothing to this. When he left the room, Laura thought, He doesn't even know where he's going, does he? The thought was so unmooring she bit the inside of her cheek.

Mr. Anabin said, "Mohammed, I'll drive you home. It's a long way for you to walk."

If Laura had been Mo, she wouldn't have accepted. But Mo just hunched his shoulders and nodded.

"Wait," Daniel said. He held out his hand to Mo. "Give me the eraser. Let me try."

Mo said, "Go for it."

But the words on the blackboard wouldn't come off for Daniel, either.

While Daniel was scrubbing with all of his considerable might, Mr. Anabin got a plastic bag from the closet. He put the dead rabbit into this. Who would clean up the smear of blood, the dirt that Bogomil's bare feet had tracked across the floor? The taunting words Bogomil had left upon the blackboard? Not Laura.

Mo went through the door and into the hall, and Laura followed him. Where they had been, there had been no doors, no hands to grasp a doorknob. She would have liked to go back and forth, back and forth through the door like an absolute lunatic, except that there was the prospect of other doors. She could pass through every single one.

Mr. Anabin turned off the lights and shut the door of the music room. On Monday morning, someone would open it again. Doors here could be opened.

Here was also a place where men could become wolves. Did Mr. Anabin? He and Bogomil seemed to do their magic with a kind of gesture language. But it had to be more complicated than simply waving your fingers around, because otherwise if you were Mr. Anabin, you'd have to keep your hands in your pockets all the time. She imagined Bogomil picking his nose and accidentally turning a cup of coffee into . . . something. A rosebush. If Bogomil was evil, did that mean Mr. Anabin wasn't? That he was a good guy? In movies, you usually had a bad guy and a good guy, but in real life, you probably just got two assholes and Bowie, whatever he was.

In Laura's experience at What Hast Thou Ground?—where she'd been a barista for two years—there were a lot of petty assholes out there and not a lot of good guys. Give them magic and they wouldn't suddenly become better people. The reverse, probably.

Nevertheless here went Laura and Daniel and Mo, trailing down a dark hallway after Mr. Anabin like an illustration out of *Make Way for Previously Dead Ducklings*.

But: The shadows in the hallway darkly loomed in the most ordinary way. The high lockers held no wide-mouthed devils; no skinned corpses dangled on hooks. The empty classrooms did not promise passages to worlds you wouldn't want to go to. The neon exit lights did not hold a double meaning. No angel stood holding a flaming sword, against all the school rules, upon the staircase landing.

Daniel and Mo and Laura went down the two flights silently. Would they have talked if Mr. Anabin had not been there? It wasn't normal to talk about important things in front of a high school music teacher, even when the music teacher wasn't whatever Mr. Anabin was. You'd think that a supernatural wizard person would be a supernaturally amazing teacher, but in Laura's opinion, Mr. Anabin had been about average. She'd never come out of band practice feeling that her life had changed or anything, despite his T-shirts. Except, she guessed, her life *had* just changed.

She hugged herself around her own middle. How strange, how discomforting, it was to be alive! It was like getting a haircut, aware afterward of your own head, its lightness, except she felt that newness in every part of her body. She could smell herself: her armpits, the damp warmth of her skin. She had to pee. Why did she have to pee if she'd been dead? She had all sorts of questions again, all sizes and shapes, but could not imagine asking Mr. Anabin a single one. Not while he was carrying the dead rabbit in its flimsy Dunkin' Donuts bag.

And why think about the mystery of Mr. Anabin when they were passing through the double doors of Lewis Latimer at last, and here was the real world, the outside world, the one with a moon and a flagpole; air that moved according to natural laws; the emptied-out lot where teachers and seniors were allowed to park. But Ruth would never have spent money on a second car when it was only a fifteen-minute walk or five minutes on a bike. And Laura hadn't wanted a car. She'd wanted the Gretsch G5422TG Electromatic Double Cutaway Hollowbody.

She was gulping in air. Filling her lungs until it was almost painful, and then there was the pleasure of pushing that air, changed, out again. She was alive and she was in the world. There was the smell of pavement, of the trash dumpsters. She did not smell ashes. She did not smell roses.

Daniel said, "It's kind of warm for December, isn't it?"

Mr. Anabin said, "I expect the weather will be unusual for the next few days. Coming back from the dead has . . . certain side effects."

Daniel and Mo, too, were alive. How angry Susannah would have been if Laura had come back alone. Daniel's chest went in and out. There was stubble on his face, as if he'd gone a few days without shaving. There were goose pimples on his arms, despite the unseasonable warmness. His jaw was clenched, the way it was when he was upset and wasn't going to say anything about it.

It was usually easy for Laura to tell what Daniel was thinking because Daniel's thoughts were mostly not very complicated. He liked people. He liked to be liked. He liked throwing and catching things and dancing and music and sandwiches. He did not like being caught in rainstorms with no umbrella or dirty dishes left in sinks. He hated conflict.

He was such a big guy that usually people assumed he was older than he actually was. Right now he looked very young.

She blurted out, "It was your birthday."

Daniel looked at her.

"The thing that happened," Laura said. "You know, to us. Dying. It happened on your birthday."

"I think that's right," Mo said. "I think I remember it that way, too. Although I don't know why I remember."

Which was a good point. Mo and Susannah hung out sometimes. Mo had plenty of friends. But he and Laura and Daniel weren't close. Mo was a year younger. He'd transferred to Lewis Latimer in the fourth grade. When she was in the sixth grade, Laura had said something to Mo about his grandmother's romance novels (Was it a crime to be a fan of someone's books? Like, at least a quarter of the tourists who came to Lovesend came there to take pictures of themselves on the street in front of Mo's grandmother's house.) and Mo had made a face like Laura was telling him she liked to pour Diet Coke on Circus Peanuts for breakfast.

And Mo had never liked Daniel, even though everyone liked Daniel.

Well, those were things that had been true before they'd all died. Now they were all in possession of the same secret, even if it wasn't yet entirely clear what the secret was. Surely they were all friends now.

Perhaps Mo felt this, too. He said, "Happy belated birthday, Daniel."

"Thanks, man," Daniel said. He rubbed his head with one big hand and dirt fell out of his hair and onto Laura's shoulder.

And Mr. Anabin, all this time? He'd put the dead rabbit into the trunk of his car. Then he stood waiting patiently until Mo got in on the passenger side.

It wasn't until Mr. Anabin and Mo drove off that Laura believed she would truly, actually, be allowed to go home. A beautiful wind, the most beautiful warm wind, was blowing her skirt against her legs and lifting her hair off the back of her neck. The wet patches where fear had made her sweat through her shirt stuck, burning coolly, to her skin. The sidewalk was rough and damp, pressing up on the soles of her feet as she pressed down on it. When she looked up, the moon was perfectly balanced atop the roof of the liquor store where the one clerk never carded anyone. The stars were where they had always been.

There were Christmas decorations in the windows of the Walgreens. Laura counted the months back. Last Christmas her mother, Ruth, had given her cash toward a new guitar. Susannah and Laura had agreed not to give each other anything, but then Susannah, being Susannah, gave Laura a green rock she'd found on the beach because (she said) it was shaped like a three-legged cat. And then had been hurt because Laura had nothing for her: doubly unfair, because Susannah was not easy to buy presents for. And what was so great about a rock?

Laura was so angry at Susannah. For what, she wasn't sure. She couldn't remember. She couldn't wait to see her sister. Maybe she would remember when she saw her.

All through the previous year, before Laura and Daniel had—well, she supposed it was *died,* they had *died,* so say it—died, My Two Hands Both Knowe You had had a once-a-month gig at a local restaurant, the Cliff Hangar. In return they got free fries and fountain drinks. All year Laura and Susannah and Daniel wrote songs and played music together and talked about the future.

Oh, the stars were bright.

Things they had not talked about: The fact Daniel and Susannah were obviously sleeping together again, regardless of whether or not that was good for the band. Which of course it wasn't. About Rosamel Walker, whom Laura had a crush on. Who did not know the way Laura felt or, maybe, even, that Laura existed. But Susannah had known.

Laura and Daniel cut through the parking lot at the 7-Eleven that marked the farthest edge of downtown, then down through the small park where there was a sculpture of Meta Vaux Warrick Fuller, who had been a sculptor herself. Below the statue was a plaque: I SEE THE BARQUE AFLOAT UPON THE EBBING TIDE.

They had always walked home this way, and Laura had always wondered about the person who had sculpted a sculpture of a sculptor. She'd always meant to write a song about Meta Vaux Warrick Fuller, who had not only had the most badass name you could imagine but had apparently been a badass in life as well. Of course, you could be a total badass in life and then in death end up in a little strip of park where people let their dogs shit and didn't bother to clean up afterward. Out the other end of the park were Lovesend's working-class neighborhoods, tree-lined streets prone to flooding in the storm season when all the sewers runneth over. You could, if you liked, try paddling a boogie board right down to the ocean some days. Tree roots had broken the sidewalks into vertiginous territories. Barefoot and only recently alive, Laura and Daniel made their way carefully.

One day Laura would be a star. It seemed proof of this, somehow, that she had come back from the dead. She would make it mean something. She would go as far away from here as you could get. But, oh, it was so very good to be here now. Slipping like shadows past shabby New England triple-deckers. Vinyl-sided toffee Victorians split into two- and three-bedroom apartments; single-family Capes spangled up with state-of-the-art Christmas-light systems. Chicken coops and soccer nets in backyards. Dry taps in maple trees, waiting for tin pails to be hung in spring. The potholed roads all led, meandering, down toward the shore, where out-of-state families spent the dog days of summer in one of Lovesend's two motels or one of the brightly painted cottages along the marsh, sitting in Adirondack chairs, swatting mosquitoes, and watching water creep closer every year. Up on the Cliffs, the rich-beyond-comprehension people like Mo's grandmother.

Laura and Susannah served out-of-staters and townies chai lattes and iced mochas on hot afternoons downtown at What Hast Thou Ground? all summer long. Hot chocolate and hot tea in the winter. Except, Laura had been dead this summer. All fall, too. Susannah, no doubt, had gotten some good sympathy tips.

No streetlights in this neighborhood, but sensors turned on floodlights as Laura and Daniel passed. Each time, Laura rejoiced at this proof that she was alive. A mossy fur of darkness lay over roofs and tree crowns.

Only once, a car went past, a vintage sports car painted the color of fresh milk. The woman driving slowed to look at them, took in their bare feet, the costumes Laura and Daniel wore, and then the car sped off, so quiet it seemed to float above the ground. Daniel moved beside her like a sleepwalker. His face was so peacefully, irritatingly blank, except for that clenched jaw, that Laura stuck her dirty foot out just in front of his next step. He went sprawling, the palms of his hands smacking against the sidewalk.

"Daniel!" Laura said. She was full of mild regret. Everything, even wrongdoing, was proof of life. "Are you okay?"

A few lines of blood were welling up from his skinned palms. But the blank expression was gone from his face.

"I'm fine," Daniel said. He sat cross-legged, rubbing his knee. "Just wasn't looking where I was going. I was . . . I don't know. I was wondering why he didn't give us shoes. Mr. Anabin. Why was Mo hanging out with us on my birthday? Do you remember? 'Cause I don't. All he ever does in band is complain. Like, it's not a performance. Wrong mute, big deal, so what. What was that dog person rabbit thing?"

"Bogomil," Laura said. She imagined, as she said it, Bogomil's ears (wolf ears, rabbit ears, person ears?) pricking up.

Daniel said, "What if it isn't safe to go home?"

"You're worried about your family."

"Yeah," Daniel said. "And Susannah. Bad enough we're stuck in whatever this is. Nobody else ought to get involved. They must have been so angry with me. That I was just . . . gone. I promised Davey and Oliver I would take them to Little Moon Bay and teach them to surf as soon as it was warm enough. And now summer's long past. It's December. And, Susannah, whatever happened to us, what if it happened to her, too? What if she's dead but she didn't make it back?"

"No," Laura said. "Susannah wasn't there. Where we were."

"Maybe," Daniel said. "But what if she was? What if she still is?"

This is what Laura remembered. They'd been in the middle of a show at the Cliff Hangar. They'd been playing "The Kissing Song." At the point in the song where Susannah stopped playing drums and Daniel took over for her, Susannah was supposed to pull someone up on stage and kiss them. She hadn't done that. Instead she'd stood at the edge of the stage, looking out. There had been a lot of people they knew in the audience. Some of Mo's crowd, so maybe that was how Mo had ended up where they'd ended up? Rosamel Walker had been there, in a pink tutu over pink leggings, pink fake fur shrug, and pink lipstick. Plenty of faces, looking up, hoping to be kissed, and Susannah had just stood there. You could tell she was thinking about doing something stupid. And then she did it, reached down and pulled Rosamel Walker up on stage and kissed her. She'd kept on kissing her, and it had been clear Rosamel was super okay with all of it, and meanwhile, the song wasn't over yet, but nothing was going the way it was supposed to, and so it was not a bad thing, the thing Laura had done. Laura had put her Yamaha down and walked across the stage, right past Susannah and Rosamel, who were kissing (still!), and she'd leaned over the drum set and kissed Daniel. Why not? It was "The Kissing Song." And two could play whatever game Susannah thought she was playing.

What had happened next? The audience had made a lot more noise than usual, even though now there was no song, no guitar, no drums. Only kissing. The audience always liked the kissing part of "The Kissing Song." Daniel had gone along with it. There had been a kiss and Daniel's mouth had been open and Laura's tongue had been inside it. When Laura looked over, Susannah was walking off the stage, leaving Rosamel Walker standing there. And now Susannah would always be a point of comparison if Rosamel and Laura ever kissed. Which was gross.

Then Laura and Daniel had mysteriously died. Even more mysteriously, Mo had been there and also died. And then everything else, all of which was also—Laura had to admit—pretty much a mystery.

"Your birthday," Laura said. "That's the last thing I remember. Cliff Hangar, 'The Kissing Song,' Susannah being weird. Are you going to get up or are you just going to sit there?"

Daniel touched his tongue to his skinned palm. "You're leaving out the part where you kissed me. Probably why we died. Susannah waited until we went backstage and then she killed us. My blood tastes like blood," he said. "Stings, too. That's good. You kissing me was against band rules."

"Why is it good?" Laura said. "Anyway, I don't see how it's a big deal. You and Susannah did a lot more than kissing. A lot more than once. We just came back from the dead so I'm giving up on the whole pretense you guys never had your whole weird thing."

"It's different," Daniel said. "You kissed me to piss her off. And it's good that blood tastes like blood because I wasn't sure it was, actually. Who knows what Mr. Anabin made us out of?"

"What do you mean?" Laura said.

"Hear me out," Daniel said. "You know how sometimes at a party someone gets the idea they should play bartender and then they just dump a bunch of different kinds of booze and mixers together? You end up with something terrible most of the time, even though everything's the same stuff that goes into actual mixed drinks. Mr. Anabin teaches music. Not biology. What does he know about bodies?"

Laura said, "So like when there's a cover of a song and they just totally missed the point. Like, why not just photocopy the original song lyrics and tape them to your face? Don't pretend you and Susannah weren't hooking up again. Just because I never said anything doesn't mean I didn't notice."

"The difference is, with a cover, the original song still exists," Daniel said. Clearly he was going to just keep sitting on the sidewalk pretending Laura had never said anything about him and Susannah. Just like he was going to pretend the whole thing had never happened. "And our real bodies, who knows?"

Laura said, "Is this helpful? What you're saying? Come on, stand up. Your legs are brand-new! They work fine!" Her own brand-new arms and legs were growing cold even though the night was so strangely warm. But her face grew hotter and hotter, and she realized to her horror that tears were pouring down her face. When she kept on sobbing, Daniel, still sitting on the sidewalk, pulled her down into a bear hug, her head stuck in his armpit. He rocked her slowly back and forth.

He said, "You can punch me if you want to." It was a thing Daniel did when somebody got angry or sad. He let you punch him right in the stomach. It hurt your hand more than it seemed to hurt Daniel.

In Laura's opinion that took all the fun out of it. "Why did we have to come back in winter?" she said.

"You hate summer," Daniel said. "You hate sweating. You hate wearing sunblock. You don't even like watermelon."

"In summer you can just walk into the ocean," Laura said into Daniel's armpit. "All the bad stuff, it all washes away when you do that." She shoved at Daniel's chest until he let go. "Susannah isn't dead. Stay here, okay? I have to pee."

"Right now?" Daniel said.

"Yeah," Laura said. "Hold on." There was an overgrown mulberry tree one yard down, and she went behind it. Hiked up her skirt and realized she wasn't wearing underwear. Well, fine. She squatted and peed for so long she wondered if she'd been holding her bladder ever since she'd died.

It made her trust Mr. Anabin even less: to have given her a full bladder and no underwear.

Susannah hadn't been there with them. Laura knew that with all of her being. Although, my God, it was almost a shame she hadn't been. Wasn't it? Susannah, with her on-again, off-again flirtation with all things goth. What had it been like? Like goth Disney World, she imagined telling Susannah.

It had not been like Disney World.

"Much better," Laura said when she came out from behind the mulberry. "Now let's go make sure Susannah's okay."

Daniel said, "It used to be a poodle on your skirt, right?"

"What?" Laura said.

"Your skirt," Daniel said.

She looked down and saw the poodle was now a wolf. "You know what?" she said. "That's not scary. I'm not even scared."

"I am," Daniel said. He reached his hand out for hers and she took it. Although the night was warm, his fingers were cold and so were hers. But they had been so much colder while they were dead. They started down the dark street toward home again.

The Book of Mo

Mr. Anabin's car had an interesting smell to it. Not one Mo could put his finger on. (Could you put a finger on a smell? No, probably not.) Vaguely medicinal or herbal or something. Frankincense, myrrh, something like that.

He bet his grandmother would know what Mr. Anabin's car smelled like. She had a whole drawerful of herbal teas. There was even a tomato mint one. It tasted exactly as bad as you'd think it would, his grandmother said. She had seemed almost pleased about it.

Mo looked over at Mr. Anabin. Mr. Anabin ignored him. There was nothing about him that said you ought to pay him any attention.

What he looked like was what Mo had always thought he was: a high school music teacher with embarrassing taste in T-shirts and a haphazardly maintained fade. Which was to say, a standard-issue public school music teacher. Which was different from looking like a musician. There were plenty of musician types in Mo's family tree. His mother had been able to play every instrument she'd ever picked up. And his grandfather, of course, whose name Mo bore. Who might or might not know Mo even existed. Mo's grandmother was cagey about that. He was a semi-famous drummer based in Cairo. He hadn't toured in the United States, though, for decades. Sometimes Mo looked on YouTube to see if there were any new uploads. Concert videos. Sometimes there were. Altogether, there were about two hundred hours of YouTube footage, albeit much of it grainy. Sometimes Mo wrote comments under the videos. But he never posted them.

Like Mo, Mr. Anabin was brown in the way that made white people feel they should ask you where you were really from. Although at the moment Mo really did want to know where Mr. Anabin was from, because surely there weren't a lot of people living in Lovesend who could raise the dead. Right? Mr. Anabin: supernaturally ambiguous. Maybe Mo would ask. Or maybe he wouldn't. Mo: smarter than a lot of white people.

Maybe Mo was thinking about frankincense and myrrh because you used them to preserve the dead.

Moonlight was streaming into the car, so bright it stung Mo's eyes. The tips of his fingers were powdered with chalk dust from the music room eraser. He brought them up to his nose and sniffed. A dusty, neutral smell. The smell, too, of his own perspiration. The sound of his own breathing. The taste of his own saliva. Metallic, as if his palate, teeth, and tongue had been coated in some alloy.

"Thanks," Mo said, "for giving me a ride home."

Mr. Anabin inclined his head. You'd have thought a music teacher would at least put on the radio when he went for a ride. The silence was kind of freaking Mo out.

He said, "Um, so. If you don't mind? I had some questions. Number one, do you know where I live?" He wanted to remark on that nose-prickling smell (and the taste in his mouth, the eye-watering brilliance of the moon, the feel of chalk dust in the ridges of his fingers) but maybe that was kind of personal?

Mr. Anabin came to a complete stop at Walnut Street. For someone with some pretty crazy supernatural abilities, he was a cautious driver. Again, though, Mr. Anabin was brown. Mo considered this. Found it more than a little depressing.

"Yes," Mr. Anabin said. "I know where you live."

"Because you're a supernatural being and you know everything?" Mo said. "Or because of some other reason?"

"Your grandmother had a dinner party for me when I first got to town," Mr. Anabin said. "A fundraiser for the school."

"Oh," Mo said. "Yeah. I remember now. The caterers made little ginger cheesecakes with chocolate treble clefs. You know what? I'm really,

really hungry. Any chance you'd be willing to make a detour? Swing by McDonald's?"

"It's very late, Mohammed," Mr. Anabin said. "They won't be open."

"Then could you make a cheeseburger and also some fries? Like, *could* you make a large fries? With magic?" Asking this, Mo felt very cunning.

"I could," Mr. Anabin said. He did not say this as if he felt it was something to brag about. If it had been Mo, he would have sounded more impressed with himself.

"How old are you?" Mo said. "Like really, really old?"

"Yes," Mr. Anabin said. "About that old."

"And you can do magic," Mo said. "I guess I always thought magic was more of a white people thing, like in books. Like Gandalf. Or Houdini. It would explain a lot about the world if magic was a white people thing. Like hockey. Is it a job? Or would you say it's more of a hobby? Or a condition? Like psoriasis or perfect pitch? What's your *deal*, exactly?"

"Music," Mr. Anabin said. "My deal is music. Music and balance. More or less. Sometimes more and sometimes less."

None of these answers was, so far, Mo felt, very helpful. But he persevered.

"Are you, like, a god?"

Mr. Anabin smiled. He said, "Oh. No. Not like a god."

"Oh, good," Mo said. "I mean, no offense. I'm sure you would be really good at it. Or do you mean that you're not *like* a god because you *are* a god?"

Mr. Anabin said nothing.

The car began the last steep climb past Elm and Cedar, taking them up to the Cliffs where Mo lived with his grandmother. Realm of the Gods, Mo's grandmother called the Cliffs, because wasn't money the thing that made you godlike? Money meant you had friends if you wanted them and plenty of peace if you didn't. Money was religion. Money was magic. But that was only as long as there was no such thing as real magic. Unless you were Harry Potter and had both. Like, that dipshit should have gone around wearing a T-shirt that said YOU CAN NEVER BE TOO RICH OR TOO MAGICAL.

Now you could see the ocean through the guardrails. The extravagant and shameless moon spilling light; the soapy luster of the long, foaming lines of wave after wave; the wet, bleached shine of the beach.

If you looked down long enough at the beach and then back out, the horizon became a black door.

"You have to admit," Mo said—not because at this point he thought he was going to manage to pry even the smallest crumb of information from Mr. Anabin but because he was not a quitter—"it's a little weird how you just happen to be teaching at our school when all of a sudden we die and then come back to life. It kind of begs the question."

"No," Mr. Anabin said. "It does not. To beg the question does not mean to raise a question. It means you're assuming a fact to be correct without giving evidence for the truth of it."

"Right," Mo said. "Right. Thanks for setting me straight on that. This is something I really needed to come back from the dead to learn. Oh, sweet mystery of my do-over life! Jumping off from there, and please do let me know if I'm phrasing this poorly, I'm stating that you had something to do with our death as well as us coming back. Is that begging the question?"

They were almost home now. Here was the stop sign where Maple dead-ended onto the Cliff Road. Before them now was the concrete barricade. For most of the year prior to Mo's death, this section of Cliff Road had been closed because a big chunk of the cliff had sheared off. You had to detour onto Maple and back around. Three houses had had to be condemned. Eventually, maybe a hundred years or so from now, Mo's grandmother's house would also fall into the ocean. But why worry about that now?

Mr. Anabin did not turn onto Maple. The car idled. Far below, the tide was either coming in or going out. Silver clouds took the shape of strange beasts, went racing on.

"I was not the cause of your death," Mr. Anabin said. "But it would not be incorrect to say I have an interest in this business."

"And the other guy? Bogomil?" Mo said.

Mr. Anabin said, "He and I stand in balance." Still the car lingered at the junction.

"Got it," Mo said. "You and Bogomil stand in balance. Anybody else I should know about? Mrs. Paulsen in chemistry, is she a Satanist? All those pewter wolf accessories. The floor-length hemlines. I just think you should tell me if she is."

"I have no special knowledge," Mr. Anabin said, "of Mrs. Paulsen's practices or beliefs."

"Wiccan would be my guess," Mo amended. "Is there a reason why we're stopped? Is Maple Street currently guarded by a fearsome hellbeast or a grue? A zombie horde?"

"No," Mr. Anabin said. He took a hand off the steering wheel and pointed at the barricade. As he did this, the Lincoln began to move forward.

"Fuck!" Mo said. "What the fuck are you doing?"

"The view is better this way," Mr. Anabin said, and the car went through the place where the barricade had been. Mo threw his hands up in front of his face, but there was no impact. The car rolled on with only a series of small jolts as it passed over pieces of debris, across fissures in the disintegrating road. Just ahead, the cracks in the road widened. Beyond that, there was no road at all. The Lincoln moved forward, and then Mr. Anabin braked, put the car into park, and turned off the ignition.

"The fuck are you doing?" Mo repeated, his voice going up and up. They were well past the break where the cliff and road had been sheared away. Out the driver's window was the cascade of fallen rocks, small saplings sticking straight out horizontally from the rockslide.

"You asked for a demonstration of my abilities," Mr. Anabin said. "Will this do?"

"I wanted a cheeseburger!" Mo said.

Mr. Anabin rolled his window down. Air streamed into the car. Air, of course, was moving all around the car, and below it, too. There wasn't anything else. "If you still want a cheeseburger, you may have one," he said. "I can do that as well."

"I don't want a cheeseburger," Mo said. "I do not want it on a plate. I do not want to levitate. I want to go *home*. I want to get there in one piece. I want a road, the kind with a sidewalk and a nice yellow line down the middle. I want none of this to have happened. I want to wake up in the morning and realize all of this was a really weird—an impressively weird—dream, and then I want to promptly forget most of it so when I tell my grandmother about it at breakfast, it's confusing and missing all the exciting bits and all I can say is that I dreamed I died and there was a scary dog and also some people from school and then I couldn't get a blackboard clean and that was the worst part for some reason."

Mr. Anabin put his window back up. "There is one more thing I must tell you before I take you home. I don't know the right way to say it, though." The way he said it made Mo think Mr. Anabin rarely found himself in this situation, but so what? This wasn't a situation Mo had ever been in, either.

"The last time a teacher said that to me, it was the guidance counselor, and he wanted me to know he knew I was gay and if I wanted to talk about anything ever, I should just stop by his office," Mo said. "Which was completely unnecessary because I'm not exactly in the closet. My grandmother gave me a copy of *Giovanni's Room* and an autographed copy of *B-Boy Blues* on my fifteenth birthday because, she said, the classics are important but gay boys need stories with happy endings, too. I have people I talk to already. None of them do magic or supernatural shit and I'm fine with that. Genevieve in band aside, because it's kind of supernatural the way she's consistently and precisely exactly two beats behind everyone else."

"It isn't supernatural," Mr. Anabin said. "It's the most astonishing natural lack of ability I have ever encountered in my long life. Examine your heart, Mo, and see if you can summon some sympathy for poor Genevieve. Who tries. Who goes on trying."

He still didn't say whatever it was that he apparently had to say, so Mo kept babbling. Wasn't this the way things always went? First you think you want to know some stuff, curiosity killed the cat, etc., but then at the point of discovery, you consider your hard-won knowledge (or one-step Internet search) and realize if you had known what you were going to know once you knew it, you'd never have googled it in the first place. Most of the time a cat was sorry he ever asked. Like the yearly roundups that websites do for the worst things online, the kind Rosamel always made him look at. Sometimes all you had to do was type a word or phrase ("why" "Black" "gay" "sometimes I think about") into Google and you saw what other people looked up and you were sad for the rest of your life. Mo had a presentiment that whatever Mr. Anabin was going to say, it wasn't something Mo wanted to hear. And by presentiment, Mo meant a rising feeling of unease tipping over into sheer terror not unlike what it felt like to sit in a car resting on nothing at all over what was basically an abyss.

"Could you do something about that? I mean, about Genevieve? With magic? What's the point of magic if you can't use it to make the world a better place? And why is it you won't tell me any of the things I want to know, but you feel you need to tell me something that I'm pretty sure is not something I want to hear?"

"Genevieve could be helped. Yes. I could help her. The cost would not be high. I don't mean to make you uncomfortable," Mr. Anabin said, "but nevertheless I must tell you the thing you do not wish me to tell you."

"First you drive your car through a concrete barrier, then you park it in the middle of the air, and now you tell me that magic has a cost?" Mo said. "What's the cost of this? A buck fifty?"

Mr. Anabin shrugged. "When I expend magic here, then Bogomil has a little more access to this world. Part of the cost of my magic is more magic for Bogomil."

"Good to know," Mo said. "I'll pass on the cheeseburger." He put his hands on his face and rubbed hard at his eyes. "Tell me whatever it is you're going to tell me. I want to go home."

Mr. Anabin said, "Brave Mohammed. The thing I must tell you is this. Four months ago your grandmother had a heart attack. A neighbor found her on her kitchen floor. She'd died during the night."

Mo said, "That isn't true." His hand found the latch of the car door, as if his body's first instinct was to escape.

Mr. Anabin said nothing.

"No!" Mo said. "No! I'm the one who died! She isn't dead!"

"I'm sorry," Mr. Anabin said.

Mo said, "She's dead?" He pulled his knees up toward his chest. Planted his dirty feet on the fabric of the car seat. Night air was seeping up from the floor of the car, whistling in from Mr. Anabin's window, which he had not rolled up properly after all.

Mr. Anabin said, "Yes."

"Is she," Mo said. And stopped. For a minute he could not go on. Mr. Anabin waited.

When he could trust his voice, Mo said, "Is she in that place?"

That place, that fucking place. Is that where you went when you died? He couldn't imagine his grandmother there. No one made you coffee there. No one opened the lid of the jam jar or reminded you what your password was when you wanted to check your balance online or helped you with the Velcro on your tennis shoes because your knees were bad and so were your hips. But then, who had done those things for his grandmother while Mo had been missing (dead) and she had still been alive?

How irresponsible of Mo to have died. How heartless. He dug his nails into the palms of his hands.

"I don't believe so," Mr. Anabin said. "The circumstances in your case were not ordinary. One assumes. Your grandmother left her life in the usual way."

"Alone," Mo said. "She was all alone."

"She wasn't afraid," Mr. Anabin said. "Your grandmother wasn't a woman who feared trivial things."

"Trivial things?" Mo said. His voice broke on the word "Things." You couldn't trust anything. "You mean *death*?"

Mr. Anabin said nothing.

"Okay. So. My grandmother died. She died while I was fucking dead," Mo said. "You needed to tell me and now you've told me and now you're going to tell me how you're going to bring her back. You have to bring her back."

"That is not a thing within my power," Mr. Anabin said.

Mo said, "But I came back! You put me back in my body and everything! So do that for her. She's more important than me. She's important to *me*! Knock fifty, sixty years off, fix her heart! Or, what did you say, you could give us wings and poison glands? She'd love that! The only romance writer in the world ever to come back from the dead. She'd love having wings and poison glands. Think of the books she'd write!" Was he yelling? Was that him yelling? Yes, it was.

"I gave you a simulacrum of the body you once inhabited," Mr. Anabin said. "That was a thing within my power. I can't bring people back from the dead. You made your own way back from the place where you were."

"Well, maybe she'll come back, too," Mo said. He made an effort.

Didn't yell. Also, he couldn't see anymore. He was crying too hard. He could barely get the words out. "Bring her back. Please. I *need* her. She's the only one I've got. She's the only one. I'm a minor. She's my *guardian*. What's going to happen to me if she's dead?"

"You will go home," Mr. Anabin said. "I promised I would take you home and I shall." He started the car again. Mo went on crying as they drove along the road that wasn't there, through a barrier that was, and much too soon, here was Mo's street, the driveway, Mo's grandmother's house. The porch light came on automatically. There was the cheerful yellow door. A mailer stuck halfway through the brass mail slot. The powdery ghost white of the chalk dust embedded in Mo's fingerprints. As if he had touched death.

"But," Mo said, "I'll be alone."

"Yes," Mr. Anabin said. "You'll be alone."

The Book of Susannah

Honestly, it had always been a comfort to Susannah, how Laura was always Laura. Susannah was older than her sister by ten months, but that was just birth order, which only counted for so much. It was like that Cole Porter song, the one their mother loved. Susannah was a worthless check, a total wreck. Laura was a Bendel bonnet, whatever that was. Not that Susannah would ever have said any of this to Laura because Laura would have just rolled her eyes. Anyway, Susannah thought, was there really any point in saying things out loud that everyone already knew?

Laura was an old soul. Their mother said so, and Cole Porter would have said so, too, had he ever met Laura. Laura was Camembert, a sold-out show at the Coliseum; Laura had a full-color map of her future. Before she was just plain gone, Laura was going places, Susannah the baggage she was dragging along.

Susannah was a new bruise. The world was always pressing on her. She grew angry too easily and for no good reason, went out into the world without brushing her hair and not only because she knew it distressed Laura. There were so many things that Susannah could not see the point of doing. Do them once and you'd have to do them again, no matter whether or not you were ever going to get them right, which, let's face it, you probably weren't.

According to their mother, Ruth, there was a devil inside Susannah. (She was only half joking.)

All the things people did every day, the things that Laura did without complaint, were the things Susannah objected to, and sometimes she hated music most of all, because Laura loved it so very much. Susannah hated music, but sometimes she, too, loved to stand on a stage and watch people dance because of a sound she was making. She hated how the sound was never quite the sound as she'd heard it in her head before it emerged, but she loved Laura's guitar. Daniel's ghost notes. His steadiness, his ability to find the pocket. The way the audience caught the sound and increased it with their attention. She loved picking someone out to kiss and she loved shoving them back out into the audience again afterward.

Susannah and Laura Hand had known Daniel Knowe all their lives. They'd walked home from school down the same block holding hands with their mothers on the first day of kindergarten. They'd learned to swim in the same class at the Y; borrowed unattended boats and gone around Little Moon Bay with only one life jacket between the three of them; endured the separation and divorce of Susannah and Laura's parents as if they had been Daniel's parents, too. (Daniel's father had died when Daniel was so very young that none of them, not even Daniel, could remember him. Daniel's father had been a good guy, according to everyone, and everyone liked his stepfather, Peter Lucklow, too. To Susannah and Laura, this had always seemed like a strange mixture of good luck and bad luck. Bad luck to have a dead father, inconceivably good luck to have had not just one but two good fathers.)

Laura and Susannah had played in Daniel's house and in Daniel's yard with Daniel's half brothers and half sisters; eaten Mr. Lucklow's gloppy spaghetti dinners in winter and delicious barbecue in summer; taped up the windows of their houses and played Risk with Daniel by lantern light during Category 3 storms; swept floodwater and mud-swollen magazines and drowned baby mice out the doors of both houses and down both sets of porch steps when the storms were over; collaborated on perfunctory Spanish and algebra homework assignments with Daniel, waiting for Ruth to come home from nursing school and late rotations to collect them. They'd all gotten stinking drunk for the first time together off shots of Midori and apple cider. Daniel had come over with tampons from his mother's bathroom when Susannah ran out. Buried Laura's gerbil when Susannah accidentally stepped on it. They'd started the band

My Two Hands Both Knowe You sophomore year, played at open mics and beach parties. Susannah with the blunt instrument of her voice, the feel of the sticks and the satisfaction of bringing them down hard. Daniel on bass, Laura on the Yamaha, shaping Susannah's wail into something approximating harmony with their vocals. Laura ought to have been lead singer. She should have been. The band was her idea, her thing. Yes, it was true Susannah could grab attention. Was it bragging if it was true? Once at rehearsal Daniel had said that when Susannah sang it was like she was about to tell you a secret, if you would just keep listening. That had made Susannah laugh. She'd said Laura sounded like she had a secret when she sang, too, but the secret was boring. Then she'd felt bad she'd said it. She hadn't meant to hurt Laura's feelings. Anyway, Laura had always said that what she needed right now was to focus on guitar.

Susannah and Daniel had hooked up back in the Pleistocene era. Before they knew, really, whether sex was an animal, a mineral, or just a really bad idea. It turned out it was a bad idea, they both agreed. (If Laura could go around not kissing anyone at all because she said this wasn't the time in her life when she wanted to be distracted by unimportant things like relationships, then surely Susannah and Daniel could not kiss each other. Find other people to kiss.) And yet, they had done it again, hooked up, kept hooking up. Several times over sophomore year. And then the summer before their senior year, Susannah had on impulse climbed onto Daniel's lap at a boring party and kissed him. She'd had a beer in each hand. It had not been the kind of kiss you write songs about. Which was why Susannah had written a song about it: that was the start of "The Kissing Song." Susannah hadn't spilled even a drop of beer. Sometimes she thought no one should write songs at all. There were already so many songs.

At the same party, Susannah had kissed another guy. Peter Gourney. They'd been in an unfinished basement room where everyone else was dancing, and Peter Gourney was not a good dancer, maybe because he was extremely high. But being stoned gave him a certain amount of focus when it came to kissing. They'd made out until Susannah's lips were numb and most of the people dancing had wandered off to get more booze. So maybe people thought "The Kissing Song" was about Peter Gourney. When, really, "The Kissing Song" wasn't about anyone, as far as

Susannah was concerned. It was more about how sometimes things happen and don't mean anything at all. Or don't happen. Other things happen instead. It had been one of those parties where everyone had been drunk and then they had been drunker. Did anyone even remember? Well, no doubt Laura did. Laura kept a ledger in her head, Susannah knew. Every ridiculous or embarrassing thing Susannah had ever said or done was written down there in Laura's tidy handwriting. What was the point, now that Laura was gone, wherever she'd gone, in doing the things Susannah did? Laura wasn't there to balance it out in the ledger.

And Daniel? He was gone, too. No doubt there were boys in the world who were better looking than Daniel had been. Peter Gourney, for one. On the other hand, no one was taller. No one had a sweeter, better, sillier face. His gray eyes, the way every summer sun bleached his hair, turned his fair skin gold. No one else had ever said "Susannah" the way Daniel said it whenever she was about to do something awful, as if he understood her even when she didn't understand herself. As if, whether or not he understood her, he still, essentially, just plain liked her.

Very early on, when they had begun playing music together in a serious way, Laura had drawn up a list of rules for the band. There were seven. (Rule 1: "Be on time!") Rule 3 was "Susannah doesn't have to sing if she doesn't want to." Susannah's rule, the only one. But she'd gotten up and sung every time. Hadn't she?

IF THERE WAS a devil inside Susannah, then why was she so lonely now? Shouldn't a devil, at the very least, be company? Shouldn't a devil whisper in your ear when you were all alone? If she tried, she could almost imagine what her devil would sound like. It would sound like Laura. *Oh, Susannah. Don't you. Don't you dare.* She and Daniel had gone at it like rabbits, compulsively, secretively, all the previous fall. Susannah's hand over Daniel's mouth when they were in her bed. So that Laura wouldn't hear. Not that Laura didn't know: you couldn't hide a thing from Laura. At least not if you were Susannah. The goal was only plausible deniability. If Laura could manage the pretense that her own sexual impulses were nonexistent, then she could also ignore Daniel and Susannah and what they were doing. Susannah had seen the way Laura looked at Rosamel Walker at parties. During volleyball. So what if Laura, observing Susannah, saw what even Daniel didn't seem to see? A sister knows you better than anyone.

WHATEVER. ONE NIGHT, Susannah stopped singing. Dropped her sticks. This was the part where she was supposed to kiss someone. The devil in her said to kiss Rosamel Walker. And so she did. And even though Rosamel was a good kisser—Laura didn't know what she was missing—Susannah's brain kept asking stupid questions. Like, what was the point of kissing people just for fun? What was the point of singing the same song over and over again? She thought, I'm tired of this. I don't want to do this anymore. No more rules. Laura could walk over and kiss Daniel and really it shouldn't matter at all. No more than any kiss mattered. *Kiss whoever you'd like,* she wanted to tell her sister. *I'm done with both of you.* Only she didn't get to say that because Laura and Daniel disappeared right off the face of the earth. Poof. Mo, too, because everyone Susannah had ever liked was auditioning to be the next star of a true-crime podcast.

YOU KISSED YOUR sister's crush, and your sister, always two steps ahead of you, kissed your oldest friend. You walked off the stage and you never saw your sister or Daniel or Mo again and you never found out what had happened. You'd never know what happened. You just kept on living the same life in the same house with your mother, and neither of you was ever going to get past this. Both of you trying your hardest to be kind to the other person. To keep from putting a finger on the scale. The lightest touch can be a blow. There was already so much pain there. You couldn't expect the other person to carry any more.

She was asleep, she was crying in her sleep. The next time Susannah woke up, Laura was home and Susannah's eyes were so swollen she could hardly open them. She had no idea why she'd been crying, though. Only that it had been the saddest dream. But now it was gone entirely.

The Book of Ruth

Two a.m., moving just a little back in time now, but not far enough back, never far enough, the moon is a little higher in the sky, and Susannah, asleep in her own bed, is dreaming about a white dog. Something in its mouth. Her mother, Ruth, home after her third overtime shift in five days, stands in the kitchen making a peanut butter and banana sandwich. On her way upstairs, she does not see a long, white shape slink soundlessly down the hallway. They don't have a dog. Sometimes after a long shift your mind plays tricks on you. Ruth stops in the dark hallway and opens Susannah's door the smallest crack. Just to be sure there is a girl in the bed. A white shape at the foot of the bed resolves itself into a rumpled blanket. She stands in the doorway of Laura's bedroom longer. As she stands there, leaning her head against the doorframe, no tears in her dry eyes, she does not imagine something in the hall behind her. Nothing makes a sound as it lopes back down the stairs. She's so very tired. And so she goes to her own bedroom and does not even take off her scrubs or brush her teeth or turn on the lights. Night nurse hurrying to catch the (white) (wolfish) tail of night.

It will happen in a moment. We will all be changed.

The Book of Daniel

This coming back from the dead thing might be the most interesting thing that would ever happen in Daniel's life. He wouldn't be able to stand it if something more interesting ever happened to him. He'd never wanted to be an interesting person.

It seemed unlikely any of this was real. But then, Mo was part of this situation and Susannah was not. Daniel kept coming back to Mo and Susannah. If all of this was some kind of breakdown Daniel was having, why was Mo a part of it? Why wasn't Susannah? This was the kind of situation Susannah excelled in finding herself in, wasn't it? It could go right under her picture in the school yearbook: *Most likely to be dead under mysterious circumstances.* * * *Most likely to then mysteriously come back from the dead.*

If none of this was real, there was nothing, really, he could do about that. So Daniel was just going to get back up off the sidewalk and go home the way Laura wanted him to. He wanted to go home.

There was another thing as well. There was the earring. Prior to being dead, Daniel had not had a piercing of any kind. Besides which, once he'd removed the earring and examined it covertly while they were all standing around in the parking lot, the next thing to become clear was that the earring—now in the apron pocket of the ill-fitting costume he wore—was twin to the earring in Laura's left ear. Laura's right ear, on the other hand, had no earring in it. In fact, the ear on the right side of

Laura's head did not seem to be Laura's ear at all. Daniel was fairly sure the ear on the right side of Laura's head had originally been Daniel's ear.

What if it wasn't just the ear? Who knew what this whole coming back from the dead thing entailed? Wonderfully and fearfully made—and that was just the body you were born with, not the creepy special edition someone shoved you in when you came back from the dead.

THE EAR ON his head was not his ear. His missing ear was on Laura's head. But the world? Excluding this business of ears and black rabbits and music teachers with secret powers, the world was the way it had always been. Wasn't it? Houses he had walked by year after year, Laura at his side. Susannah on the other. Look: the moon no bigger or smaller than seemed reasonable. Laura in the dark beside him, so much herself.

The moon changed its shape, was not always the same, but that was only a trick of perception. A change in where you stood. The moon was always the moon, the new moon just as much the moon as the full. Daniel himself in the world of the ordinary had been altered from day to day without even knowing as it happened. The way people looked at you changed when you got tall. And of course you saw other people differently, too. The tops of their heads. The high places in cupboards they couldn't even see, where they had put all sorts of things and never been able to find them again.

Daniel put his fingers in his pocket, pinched the earring between them. Smooth bead, carved grooves of the butterfly, sharp point of the post.

"Do you feel weird?" he said to Laura. She'd been crying off and on for a little while. Sob-gasp-sob. She didn't really seem to notice she was still crying.

"Yeah," Laura said. Sob. Gasp. "I feel pretty fucking weird right now."

"No," Daniel said, trying again. "Do you feel different, like, does anything feel wrong to you? Like, your body?"

"I'm tired," Laura said. "I don't know why our feet are so dirty. It's bizarre. And I'm thirsty. Or hungry. Or something. Are you hungry?"

He thought about it. "Yeah. I guess I am. But look, we're home."

"Home," Laura said. She wiped her eyes. Sniffed.

Laura's mother's Subaru was in the driveway. There were no lights on in the house. The ivy in the window box beside the front porch was dead, soft with decay. You couldn't count on Ruth to water anything. Susannah, either.

Laura rummaged in the window box until she found the spare key, exactly where it should have been. As if you could just find a key for every door. As if every door would open for you. She said, "Do you want to come in? Come in with me and make sure Susannah's here. You know, not there."

Daniel said, "Yeah."

So they went into the dark house and up the stairs. There was Susannah asleep in her bed. "Oh, thank God," Laura said.

"Shhhh," Daniel said. "You'll wake her up." He'd seen Susannah sleeping before, of course. Plenty of times. In the back of a car, on a sofa or a blanket at the beach. Once or twice they'd been somewhere and she'd fallen asleep with her head on his leg. Leaning against his shoulder. He was good at keeping perfectly still. Even when Susannah was asleep, she was in battle-ready mode. Always fighting something. But this, he didn't think he'd ever seen her face like this. So peaceful, so unlike Susannah.

They stood beside the bed, Maude's Dishwasher and Rose. What would Susannah have thought if she woke and saw them? Daniel looked away and saw Laura was watching him and not her sister. She motioned to the door. It was still open so they went through it. But Daniel couldn't bear to close it when they were in the hallway again.

They went downstairs, avoiding the treads that squeaked. Laura said, "Do you want me to go over to your house with you?"

Daniel said, "No. It's okay. It seems okay, right?"

"No," Laura said. "It doesn't. But I'm back in my own house and I'm going to sleep in my own bed for one night before the next terrible thing happens. You go home. We can talk tomorrow."

Daniel said, "I know we just got back, but maybe we shouldn't be here. Maybe we should go away somewhere, not get anyone else mixed up in any of this."

Laura said, "You really think Mr. Anabin and you-know-who wouldn't find us? You think they'd just let us go?"

Daniel thought about it. "No," he said.

"Do you want to be dead?" Laura said. "Because I don't. I want to avoid being dead for as long as possible."

Daniel said, "I don't want to be dead, either."

In the moonlit kitchen, though, Laura looked dead. Why hadn't they turned on the lights? Perhaps they were too accustomed to the dark now. Pale face, dark hair, shadow eyes, and shadow mouth. Wearing the clothes of another century. She said, "We'll figure this out. You and me. Us and Mo. Us and Mo and that Bowie guy. Except, there's the thing on the blackboard: two stay and two return. There's four of us."

"What are you saying?" Daniel said.

Laura said, "Maybe only two of us get to stay alive."

"So two of us don't," Daniel said.

"Well," Laura said, "if it's a competition, you and I have some built-in advantages. We know each other. We know we can work together."

Daniel said, "I'm not sure having been in a band is the only qualification we're going to need."

Laura considered this. "You mean, if we need to do stuff."

"Do stuff?" Daniel said.

"To win," Laura said. "You know. What if we have to do *bad stuff*. Like kill neighborhood cats or sacrifice babies or something?"

"You really think they'd make us kill someone?" Once, when his parents weren't home, Daniel had had to kill a mouse stuck in a glue trap.

"I don't know!" Laura said. "I haven't read the handbook yet, because there isn't one! But when somebody comes back from the dead in a movie, there's always a body count. Do you think you could kill someone?"

"No," Daniel said.

There was a calendar on the kitchen wall behind Laura. It said the year was almost over. They'd have to run to catch up.

Laura had asked her question like she couldn't imagine ever killing anyone, but Daniel had known Laura for a long time. He didn't fancy Bowie's chances, or Mo's—or his own, honestly—if this turned out to be some kind of Hunger Games deal.

He said, "Of course we're not going to kill anyone. Go to bed. I'll see you tomorrow."

Before he was off the porch, Daniel heard her lock the door. He crossed the Hands' yard, heading for the back corner. Something he must have done hundreds of times. Thousands. The chain-link fence was low enough and he was tall enough he could just step over.

Once he was in his own yard, he turned and looked back at the Hands' house. There under the eaves was Susannah's window. Daniel imagined chucking gravel at it. He'd done it before. Wake the sleeper. No harm in such a small act. She'd open the window, and what would he say? Long time no see, Susannah. You'll never guess where I've been.

If he asked her to throw some clothes in a backpack and come out, if he said he wanted to go out to Route 1 and hitch rides without stopping until they'd made it out to the Pacific Ocean and could go no farther, he thought if he dared her, Susannah would do it. She would come with him. But then he wouldn't have to worry about Bogomil. Because Laura would hunt him down and kill him first.

Even as he went on pondering what he should do, whether he should go home at all, he was moving toward the front door of his house. He skirted the various Lucklow bikes, beaters in such variously terrible states of disrepair, who would ever bother stealing them? A half-skinned basketball, a mushy soccer ball and one in slightly better shape, dirt-and-dog-slobber tennis balls. A baby doll, an empty socket where there should have been a head.

Somebody had forgotten to put the spare key back in its hiding place, but when Daniel tried the kitchen window, it was unlatched. He could get his arm through, and his arm was long enough he could unlock the door from the inside. The spare key was beside the sink. He took it outside, put it into its rock.

Would it have been a true homecoming if the Lucklow house wasn't in a state of absolute chaos? His parents both worked their asses off, which left Daniel, the oldest child, as default babysitter, dishwasher, sometime chef, and enforcer of the chore wheel, which, during the period of Daniel's unlife, might as well have been a prayer wheel in a mouse nest.

Someone had started a house of cards on the kitchen table and abandoned it halfway through the third story. Someone (else?) had drawn a smiley face in peanut butter directly on the table. Artistic impulses should be encouraged in children: the philosophy of the house. Or perhaps it was a message from the other side. The jar was still out, and the remains of a sandwich. Daniel picked it up, suddenly ravenous, and took a bite. The stale sandwich was the most voluptuous thing he had ever tasted. There was a gallon of whole milk in the refrigerator, nearly full. He drank straight from the container.

On the refrigerator, magnets held up new school photos. Lissy's hair in Afro puffs, Dakota's in box braids. They would have fought like weasels to have their hair done the same way, they always did, and their mother always said, "Not on picture day. You want to live to be ninety, only to spend your last few years trying to figure out which one was you?" Oliver missing two front teeth, Davey with a black eye. Most likely not related. You could get a do-over for school pictures, couldn't you? But Davey looked pleased with himself. They probably hadn't been able to get him to sit for another.

Here, too, was a picture of Daniel from the year before, unaware of everything about to happen to him. "The pink crayon nobody uses," Carousel had called him when she was younger. "Because he's tall and he doesn't look like us." That had hurt, but she hadn't meant it to.

In the living room, Daniel discovered an impressively baroque cushion fort. There were two blue fleece blankets rucked up to simulate a moat around the perimeter. There was even a flag of sorts that turned out to be a pair of Peter Lucklow's white boxers. A unicorn drawn with a Sharpie across the seat. In the tan seams of the stripped couch—jetsam left when the tide goes out—were a few gummy bears and the head of a doll, no body. An orange hair pick and a small dirty sock. Daniel took in every detail, some anxious organ restored to serenity inside him. It was so unlike where he had been, and so like home.

Here at his feet was a cigar box. Daniel bent over and picked it up. "Oh, you assholes." They'd borrowed his coin collection to play pirate treasure. Here were his Indian Head pennies, a guitar coin from Somalia. Here was the rarest coin in his collection, a Nova Constellatio Copper. He picked it up, ran his thumb over the pointed rays.

At that moment, Fart, the Lucklow greyhound, came up from behind and thrust his cold, wet nose into Daniel's open palm. Daniel dropped the treasure chest. Coins spilled out onto the shag carpet.

When he turned around, though, there was only a white, skittering blur—Fart, a coward all of his long life, dashing for the safety of the kitchen table. He went beneath it and stayed there, making anxious, growling noises even when Daniel crouched down, trying to coax him out again. All that was visible in the dark space below the table was Fart's narrow, ghostly nose, his black-lipped snarling mouth.

"Be that way," Daniel said. "Not like I was expecting a welcome-back party." Even to himself, he sounded sorry for himself.

DOWN THE HALL, he could hear Peter snoring. How did his mom sleep through that? He'd always wondered. All the kids were upstairs, two and three to a bedroom. Only Daniel had his own room. As he passed the bathroom, Carousel came out, mostly asleep. He thought she might be an inch taller than the last time he'd seen her: he felt this like a blow.

"Daniel," she said. "I'm so very angry at you."

"Sorry," Daniel said. "I'm sorry." He knelt down. Took her hand in his. There was a dirty Band-Aid around her index finger. "Why?"

"You were away too long," she said.

"Oh, Carousel," he said. "I'm back now, though. Don't be angry at me."

"'Sokay," she said. "I'll be angry at someone else. What time is it?"

"Late," Daniel said. "It's late."

His sister put her warm arms around his neck and sighed into his ear. The one that wasn't. "Gladyoureback," she said. "It's weird."

"What's weird?" he said.

"What you're wearing," Carousel said. "It's weird." She patted his face lovingly and went back to the room she shared with Dakota and Lissy, twelve years old the last time Daniel had seen them. Now thirteen. Carousel, whose real name was Caroline, ten.

JUST INSIDE DANIEL'S room, there was a half-emptied duffel bag with airline tags on it. A sticker that said HEAVY. It looked unpleasantly like a body bag missing its body. The moon was in the window beside his bed. He had spent such a long time in a dark place, the moon never showing herself.

No sign of his Squier bass. But he thought he was done with all that anyway.

On his desk was his cellphone. Was this really his, or was it, like his body, something Mr. Anabin had enchanted out of air? Wouldn't Daniel have had his phone with him when he'd disappeared? Or had it been found, a clue that led nowhere? Did Mr. Anabin and Bogomil have cellphones? Mr. Anabin must, surely. Did Bogomil know how to text? BE THERE 2 EAT U IN 10. DEPENDING ON TRAFFIC. DRIVING THE WOLF SUIT.

Daniel tried his password and apparently Mr. Anabin had known that, too. To be fair, it wasn't that clever a password.

The wallpaper was a picture he'd never seen before. In it, he and Laura stood in a field on either side of a shaggy black pony, their arms around its neck. Laura was kissing the pony on its hairy jaw, Daniel looking at whoever was taking their picture. The grass was luxuriantly green. The sun shone. It looked like it had been a good day, but of course it had never happened. The more he considered the pony in the picture, the less he felt sure that a pony was what it was. There was a gleam in its eye as if it knew things Daniel did not. Honestly, he could not imagine the circumstances under which he would place his hand upon a pony like this pony. In fact, if he were to encounter a pony like this in a field, he hoped he would run for his life.

What had his wallpaper been before? Susannah and Laura. The day he'd braided their hair together after they'd fallen asleep, a long day down at Little Moon Bay. Daniel was an expert braider of hair. He'd done lots of little plaits and it had taken forever to disentangle them when they woke up. He hadn't really thought it through.

Daniel put the phone down without setting an alarm or changing the wallpaper or looking to see what other photos were there that he had no memory of taking. He reached around and untied Maude's Dishwasher's apron. As he did so, he realized he was not alone in the room. Here, in his bed, under the duvet, motionless, something crouched.

The corner of his desk dug into his thigh as he stepped back. His phone fell onto the floor. In his bed, Bogomil waited, veiled in eternal darkness, eternally patient. The black rabbit or the white wolf. Fur smelling of your own death, muddy claws to hold you fast.

Daniel flattened his hand like the edge of a blade. Raised his arm to bring it down.

Too late to hitch a ride out on the highway. And what good would that have done, anyway? Every road ended here. He yanked down the duvet—but the person in his bed was his brother Davey.

His arm dropped to his side and he sat on the bed. Prodded Davey's shoulder. "What are you doing in my bed, kid?"

"Go away, Daniel," his little brother said. He, too, older. Unsurprised in the least to see Daniel. "I'm asleep." In fact, he did not appear to be awake. Davey often drifted to strange locations during the night. An unoccupied bed was almost reasonable. One morning they'd found him under the kitchen sink. In the fireplace. Squatting like a gargoyle, asleep upon the kitchen counter.

"Okay," Daniel said. "Okay." He bent over and kissed Davey's warm forehead. Then grabbed a clean pair of boxers and a T-shirt out of a drawer.

The bathroom, too, was reassuring, typical Lucklow chaos. Rubbery snail trails of toothpaste icing the counter and wet towels heaped on the floor, the cupboard lacking clean towels of any description. Only a Winnie-the-Pooh cloth diaper, now used as a cleaning rag. Daniel locked the door and stripped down, examining his arms, his legs, the divot of his belly button, squeamishly. It seemed to him he was himself, the face in the mirror the one he'd worn all his life. His dick was no smaller. Every part of him familiar to the eye and the hand, including eyes and hands. All was as it ought to be, but for the ear, which was not. And the butterfly earring.

Daniel left the earring in the soap dish on the counter while he took his shower, turning the water up as hot as could be borne. He couldn't bring himself to pull the shower curtain closed, though he knew he could have seen over it. The thought of something leggy and white crouched down low against the lip of the tub troubled him. He bent to get his head under the showerhead, and black, caked dirt in his hair, on his feet, mixed with the spray of water and clotted the drain. There was gummy dirt under his fingernails, too, and behind his ears. It came off in hard flecks.

Daniel stayed under the water until there was no warmth in it.

WHEN AT LAST he turned the shower off, the bath mat was so full of water it oozed when he stepped on it. He dried himself with the hand towel beside the sink.

He swiped the mirror with his towel and spent some time examining his reflection once more: poking at his chin, feeling the skin just below his eyes, first one ear and then the other. Had his eyebrow always had this scar? Had his nostrils always been this large? His mouth this worried? Could he still touch his tongue to the tip of his nose? He could. The knuckles on his right hand still cracked, and the knuckles on the left still did not.

Clean, damp, possessed of a body mostly familiar to himself, Daniel retrieved the earring and his phone and, with the heap of wet towels, went back down the stairs. He looked for Fart. But Fart was sleeping somewhere else now. Daniel took apart the pillow fort. Got on his hands and knees to pick up the borrowed coins. Wiped the smiley face off the table in the kitchen; completed, carefully, the third floor on the house of cards; and, having accomplished these things, felt more comfortable, more himself than he had since coming back from the dead. Took cereal bowls and glasses back to the kitchen and rinsed them. The dishwasher was full of clean dishes and so he put those all away.

He drank the rest of the gallon of milk and made two sandwiches with white bread and cold hot dogs and ate them. Put the rinsed dishes into the dishwasher and went upstairs to the bedroom Davey shared with Oliver. Oliver was snoring in the upper bunk. When Daniel had died, Oliver was a sunny and easygoing four-year-old, a good sleeper unlike his fraternal twin. Now he and Davey would be five. Oliver's face was less round than it had been.

Daniel climbed into the lower bunk and discovered it was wet and smelled of urine. Which explained why Davey had left it. Daniel stripped the sheets and took them down to the laundry room, where the washer was full of wet clothes and, mysteriously, so was the dryer.

He fell asleep on the downstairs couch to the sound of the dryer, knees hooked over one corduroy arm, feet almost on the floor. He slept and woke and slept again. When a damp, velvety nose pressed into his neck, exhaling ticklish warmth, he groaned. "Go away, Fart. Bad dog."

The remainder of the night was marked by little clicks against the hard surface of the floor as Fart made his slow passage through the living room into the kitchen and back again down the hall, the oscillating tick of a metronome keeping time as Daniel dreamed of music played in a sunny place he could not reach. Susannah walking beside a white dog.

When he woke in the morning, Davey was tucked against him on the couch, and his stepfather, Peter, in a faded pink bathrobe, was making pancakes. Daniel's right fist was clenched so tightly that when he opened his hand, the coin he held there left a perfect impression in his palm. There were six texts from Laura on his phone, and when he checked Facebook, here were messages from all of his friends, the ones back in town for the holidays, wondering when they would hang out. But sometime in the past year, he saw, Susannah had unfriended him.

The Book of Laura

Laura, long an expert—the equal of Susannah, really, even if Susannah would have said otherwise—in sneaking out and in after curfew, avoided once more the steps on the stairs that creaked. She stopped in the hallway just in front of their mother's bedroom door. It wasn't all the way shut. She could see the shape of Ruth beneath the comforter, head under a pillow. Laura inhaled. The smell of sleep and Ruth's lavender neck pillow. How could you be homesick when you were at last returned to home? But oh, Laura was.

Someone should make a fuss over you when you come back from the dead. Party balloons and confetti for the surprise guest. Except that, what? Mr. Anabin had magically long-distance hypnotized everyone? Or something. If you set aside the whole ethical question, it was kind of neat. Imagine you could just *do* that. Rewire people's brains. You could change things for the better. Make improvements, reward the virtuous and gently correct the sinner. The whole world your oyster if you liked oysters, which Laura was still on the fence about.

Susannah was still sleeping soundly when Laura went to check. Laura suppressed an urge to pinch her. Of course she was glad Susannah hadn't died, too. But it wasn't fair. Laura had been dead for such a long time, and what had Susannah done about that? Nothing! Or at least nothing useful. But oh, how reassuring it was to see Susannah's face and feel vaguely annoyed for no good reason at all.

Her own bedroom door was closed. Had police been here? Had they pawed through her jewelry, called up her browser history, gone through her drawers? Better or worse to think about Susannah, her sticky fingerprints on Laura's things? And here was a crumpled Kleenex next to the wastebasket instead of in it, which is how you knew it had been Susannah and not Ruth. Typical Susannah. Crying because Laura had disappeared, apparently much too fucking sad to manage to actually place the Kleenex in the basket.

Oh, she should not be so mad at Susannah. What had Susannah done? She had kissed Rosamel Walker. And Laura had died without ever kissing a girl at all. One of these things could be laid at Susannah's door, but the other could not. Laura set the question aside. There were too many mysteries already that needed solving.

Here was the crappy old Harmony, but her Yamaha Pacifica and her Flamma amp were nowhere to be found. Her fake memories told her she'd left them back in Ireland with the Córdoba Protégé she'd been learning to play classical guitar on, but Laura wouldn't have done that. Not even if Ireland were real.

There, at the foot of her bed, was a suitcase full of clothes she had to admit were the sort of clothes she would have packed for an extended trip to Ireland. There was even a stuffed animal on top, a black lamb. It had soft rag ears, button eyes. A cloth ribbon around its neck bore a name. Bogomil. "Really?" Laura said out loud. She suppressed a shudder. Picked the black lamb up between her thumb and index finger and, after some thought, put it in her closet and closed the door.

There was a passport on her desk. Stamped. Laura wondered if she'd had a good time at this conservatory. What had she been studying, even? And thought, again: classical guitar. There were all sorts of new things in her head: chord progressions, positioning, free stroke. Well, that explained why the fingernails on her left hand were so short. But all of her calluses were gone. That had to be the new-body thing, not classical guitar. Classical guitar! What had been the point of that? And yet, she itched to pick up the Harmony, just to see if her hands actually knew the things her head told her they did. But that would wake up her mother. And Susannah.

Laura undid the hook on the poodle (wolf) skirt and shoved it down and off. Why had poodle skirts ever been a thing? More mysteries. When she took out the hair ribbon, her hair fell in dirty clumps against her neck. She put on a T-shirt from her drawer: first she would set her room to order. Then a shower.

She took clothes out of her suitcase, sniffed them to see if they were clean. Some clothes she threw in the laundry basket against the wall. Some clothes she folded up again and put in drawers. It was an impressive amount of detail to fake, but was packing suitcases with a mix of clean and dirty clothes really what magic ought to be used for?

She knew, of course, that she hadn't really gone to Ireland. She had been: where? Dead. Dirt was still in her hair and under her nails as if she'd clawed her way out of a grave. But it hadn't been a grave and she hadn't had a body when she did it. It had been a room with no door. A forest at night, a path where someone lay in wait. No passport stamp for that place.

She had never packed these clothes, and yet here were dirty socks, T-shirts, cardigans she'd never worn. Mr. Anabin had paid careful attention to all the little details.

There was a caution in that.

For example, on the kitchen counter downstairs was a tea towel with some sort of funny slogan—a gift for Ruth. Laura could picture it there quite clearly, even if the slogan did not come to mind. She'd gotten the black lamb for Susannah.

Apparently if she had gone to Ireland she would have bought for herself a blue sweater made of the softest, warmest cashmere. Yes, this sweater was exactly what she would have bought for herself. The blue made her think of water. She'd been thirsty for a very long time.

There was no glass in the bathroom, so Laura stuck her head under the tap, taking long gulps until her teeth grew cold. She was sitting on the lid of the toilet to take her earrings out and thinking about a shower when Susannah shoved the connecting door open.

"Do you mind?" Laura said. She stood up and flushed. Put the single earring down on the counter. The other had come off somewhere on the walk home. Well, they hadn't been a favorite pair.

Susannah said nothing. Just stood there wearing a *Night of the Living Dead* T-shirt, a mountainous pimple at the corner of her mouth. Remarkable that she had on anything at all, really. Susannah's attitude toward clothes was mostly indifference, but on the subject of pajamas she was an abolitionist. She was reassuringly, annoyingly tall. Possibly taller. Reassuringly, annoyingly annoying.

"Welcome home, Laura," Laura said, since Susannah was silent. It was clear from Susannah's expression she did not remember Laura had been missing, presumed dead. "So glad you're back home safe and sound, Laura. I really missed you, Laura."

"Why are your feet so dirty?" Susannah said.

"What?" Laura said. She looked down. "None of your business. I couldn't sleep. So I went for a walk."

"Barefoot?" Susannah said. Her look was sardonic. "Also there's mud in your hair."

"The weather is unseasonably warm," Laura said. Calmly put toothpaste on her toothbrush.

"I saw Daniel going over the fence," Susannah said.

"He couldn't sleep, either," Laura said. "For God's sake, Susannah. Wake up on the wrong side of the cemetery again? Can you give me at least a day before you try to make some big thing? I'm too tired to fight."

"Whatever," Susannah said. "I'm sure whatever it is, it's stupid. Keep your stupid secret."

"What secret?" Laura said reflexively. But she knew how unpersuasive she sounded. She was practically a gothic piñata stuffed with bone shards, dead rabbits, secrets so secret not even she understood them. Perhaps it was less the secrets that she had and more a secret that had Laura.

Daniel and Laura had both been dead. They knew about Mr. Anabin. Susannah did not. They knew about Bogomil. And Mr. Anabin and Bogomil knew them. All this must have been on Laura's face, the things she knew and would not say. The things she did not know. Susannah must have seen them. She said, "Welcome home, Laura. I missed you every single minute of every single day. So glad you're back. Observe the joy that hangs around me in a miasma."

"Ow," Laura said. She put the cap back on the toothpaste. "Your sarcasm is really wounding, Susannah."

In the mirror she could see her sister trembling with rage.

"You know what I wish?" Susannah said.

"No," Laura said. "Clear skin? A purpose in life?"

"I wish you were dead!" Susannah said. She banged the connecting door shut so hard it bounced back and Laura had to slide it shut again.

Then she was alone. She wished Susannah would come back again to yell at her some more.

In the shower, she began to sing very quietly. Realized the song was "Fairytale of New York." Well, it was the season. Was this her voice? Yes. She thought it was. She scrubbed herself so thoroughly there was not a trace of death or sadness or mystery left on her new body when she had finished. But when she turned the water off, there was the horror, the stain, all over again. Or perhaps this, too, was just part of what it was to have a body again. Just another room without a door.

When Laura had brushed her hair, put on her oldest, most comforting pajamas, and climbed at last into bed, she found she could not sleep. The black lamb in the closet. Mr. Anabin at the piano bench. The dead rabbit, the woman in the shining car, the moon and the sidewalk and Mo Gorch holding the blackboard eraser. Bogomil in the doorway. Susannah at the bathroom door. Laura got out of bed and found her earbuds on the desk beside her Nokia. The battery charge was low, and this was not a realistic touch. Laura never let her phone get this low.

In her music library, though, was a new playlist: Transatl/Antics. So Laura plugged the Nokia into the wall and put on the playlist. She lay there awake, unwilling to turn off the light beside her bed. It wasn't a bad playlist. And there were songs she didn't think she'd heard before. People, she supposed, had continued to make music while she'd been dead.

Whenever she closed her eyes, the sensation came inexorably over her that someone else was in the room. Standing beside the bed. So she kept her eyes open and the room stayed empty. She wondered if Susannah was asleep in her room, if Susannah would mind if Laura climbed into bed with her. Well, of course she would. But Laura could explain the situation with Daniel, explain everything that had happened. She could tell Susannah how there had been no doors. About Mr. Anabin and Bogomil. What would happen if she told Susannah?

This was a stupid question. Susannah would think Laura was a lunatic. She wouldn't believe her.

And if she did?

Laura closed her eyes. Kept them screwed shut. Let music fill up her ears, soft as wax. The pillowcase was cool under her wet hair, all of her stuffed animals on the headboard kept watch, and yet the feeling crept over her again. Someone was there with her, standing just inside a doorway. Bogomil! Laura thought. She sat up in bed and saw her mother standing there instead.

"Mom?"

Ruth said something. Then came inside Laura's room and sat on the bed. She put her hand on Laura's hair, and Laura took out her earbuds.

"Did I wake you?" Ruth said.

Laura shook her head. "I was awake."

Ruth looked as if she herself hadn't slept well in weeks. Months, perhaps. She stroked Laura's damp hair tentatively. What was the last thing Laura had said to her before Laura had died? Ruth said, "Can't sleep?"

Laura swallowed and shook her head again. "No."

"It's the time difference," Ruth said. "It takes the soul a while to catch up with the body when you travel that far. What an adventure you had, Laura."

"I don't think I like adventures," Laura said. She saw the look on her mother's face and hastily added, "I'm kidding. It was amazing. So great. I can't even describe how great it was. I just can't believe I'm finally home."

"There's nothing like sleeping in your own bed," Ruth said. "Although I don't know why I said that, because I was having a terrible dream. The most terrible dream. But here you are!"

"Here I am," Laura said.

Ruth said, "When you get up, I'll probably be gone. There's a meeting about the union vote, but we're being sneaky about it. Meeting in Bridgetree at the Ruby Tuesday. And then I'm taking a double shift because at the moment we're completely overrun with babies. It's like Mardi Gras. NICU babies up to all kinds of things. Everywhere you look the moms all flashing their boobs. All the nurses sneaking off to the supply closet with their pockets full of nip bottles. No, seriously. They caught someone in the supply closet with a bunch of mini booze bottles. So now we're short a nurse."

"Who was it?" Laura said.

"Abby."

"The one who wanted to start the book group?"

"That's Rosemary. Abby's the one who yelled at the grandmother who didn't wash her hands. That was the first strike. But, you know, she was great at finding a vein, even with the micro-preemies. That's a rare and precious gift."

"Oh, I know," Laura said. She and Susannah sometimes caught Ruth looking covetously at their forearms at odd moments, clearly thinking about their lovely, large, and accessible veins.

Ruth said, "There's money for pizza on the counter. I want to hear all about everything when I get home." She leaned over Laura, kissed her forehead. "She missed you, you know. With you away and all the stuff with your father. It's been tricky."

As if everything, everything that Susannah was and did, all of Susannah's nature, could be laid on their father's doorstep, wherever that was. For fuck's sake. He'd been gone for twelve years. You'd've thought Susannah would have gotten over it by now. Laura had. But she said, "I know."

Her mother turned off the table lamp.

BUT STILL LAURA couldn't sleep. She could hear Susannah snoring through the wall. If only Susannah had died, too. Then when she came back from the dead, Mr. Anabin could have fixed her deviated septum. It was a mystery how someone with such a terrible, untuneful snore could sing like Susannah. A crow dropping small rocks on a pile of larger rocks, that's what she sounded like. Laura put her earbuds back in.

What was Susannah's deal, anyway? Couldn't she just be happy Laura and Daniel were home again? If Laura thought about it, she could vaguely recall the way that things had (hadn't) happened. Susannah hadn't gone to Ireland out of spite and pride. After Laura had kissed Daniel, Susannah had quit My Two Hands and turned down the scholarship to Cork. She hadn't even applied to community college. But before Mr. Anabin had changed everything, who knew what Susannah had really thought? What she had felt and done and not done?

And Ruth: she looked thinner and older and sadder. When Laura had been missing, she would have been devastated. Had she thought Laura was dead?

Were Daniel and Mo lying awake now, too? Or were they braver than she? What if she, falling into sleep, woke up in that place again? Was that where you ended up when you died? Because she wanted to avoid that. She was going to come up with a plan to live forever. Live on prunes and honey and never even think about doing anything more dangerous than clicking on a YouTube link.

She turned on her side, toward the window. There was Daniel's house and above it the sky. Still dark, but now there was a wire of burning gold along the horizon, that same burning wire that ran through all living things. The sun would be up soon and it would be safe to sleep then. Wouldn't it? No, because the night came after the day. Every day eaten at its end by the dark. These thoughts—the wire of gold, the eaten day—seemed peculiar to Laura. Their formulation, their vividness, the taste of them in her mouth. She was not sure they belonged to her. Did they belong to her?

No. They were Bogomil's thoughts. Mr. Anabin's. She'd never had these kinds of thoughts before she'd died.

Thinking this, Laura fell asleep with a song she didn't remember playing in her ears. But it was a good song. Next door, Susannah was also asleep. Susannah was dreaming. She dreamed Laura borrowed her head without asking and went with Daniel to see a wolf play the piano. The wolf chewed every key to splinters and that was how the song went. Laura dreamed she was sailing out at Little Moon Bay. Her boat was made of black and white stones and so it fell straight through the water and down to the bottom of the ocean, and Laura was made of stone, too. On the bottom of the ocean, which is where we sometimes go when we are sleeping, Laura dreamed someone came by moonlight down a long hall. They came down the hall on four legs and then stood on two just outside her bedroom door. They stood there waiting for her to wake up. To open the door. To see them and to know them. But she didn't know them.

And what did Laura dream of next? She dreamed Susannah stood before a door. The door was locked, thank God, but Susannah had the key in her hand. "Don't open it," Laura said. "There's something terrible inside." But which side of the door was Laura on? And when had Susannah ever done what Laura said? If there was a thing you knew you shouldn't do, trust Susannah to go ahead and do it anyway.

The door flew open, and Laura went rushing out. Susannah threw up her hands. Too late.

The Book of Bowie

HAVE YOU EVER seen a boy like this? So old, so new. Conjured out of a tattered scrap of air, fizzing and slippery, an oily effervescence that even now, stoppered in its new bottle, seems to make only the faintest of impressions upon the surface of the world. Light takes a moment longer than it should to find the vessel he has been tipped into, and there is so very little light here, only the moon and the strange bowls hanging upside down on poles along the thing he knows is a road. But there is so much more light now than there was in the place where he had been. Tears come to his eyes and it takes him too long to remember he has hands to wipe them away.

There is too much and too little of him: watch his shadow change the contours of its shape as he goes along, as if he might not be a boy at all. So surprised by everything he sees.

There is so much of the world. He cannot take it all in. Words above the doors of buildings that he does not know, and doors, too, so many. He tries every one he passes and they open although they are locked and he does not have a single key. Sometimes when he opens a door, there is a strange wailing noise that goes on until the boy tells it to stop.

He leaves each door open and walks until he comes to a green place where smells emanate from a cylinder made of something he does not recognize. He sticks his hand through a small aperture and reaches down until his fingers close around a promising shape filled with other shapes. What's inside are little pieces of cold, soft food. He eats it all and licks the salt off his fingers. Then he tips the cylinder over and sorts through the mess he has made. There is more. Bits of bread, half-eaten apples, mushy and sweet. As he eats, whitish gray shapes fall out of the sky around him. They ignore him, snapping up things he has rejected or not noticed. Once his stomach is full, he lies down on the grass and falls asleep, his arms wrapped around himself. Gulls settle all around, preening and talking. Some of them, like the boy, doze. Others are keeping watch when the boy calls out in his sleep. A name that the gulls do not know. The body of the boy begins to tremble and then to shake and then there is not a boy upon the grass at all. Now there are seven gulls where before there were six. When the sun comes up, though, there will be six gulls again and a boy, still asleep, in a white scarf.

The Book of Maryanne

Mo's grandmother, in the moment of her death, is more surprised than anything else. Was she expecting a visitor?

Here she is in the kitchen of her house in the middle of the night, holding a mug of Bengal Spice tea. It is late summer, and the roses in her garden are giving off their perfume. There is another smell. Someone has a wood fire going, which is the first strange thing. Who starts a fire in August? She is a sixty-six-year-old woman in a silk head wrap and a housedress embroidered with pink and purple peonies, wondering if she should call the fire department, and then she is her twenty-three-year-old self in an office supply store. Chattanooga, Tennessee. Her blouse is polyester and has a bow at the neck. The tea is too hot and it burns the roof of her mouth. She did not hear a knock on the door. She buys two reams of paper and a secondhand IBM Selectric. She is going to write a novel. It will be a love story. She is in her parents' driveway beside the mailbox, opening a letter. The day so hot she can smell the road as it melts back into tar. The letter informs her she has won first place in a contest run every year by the magazine *Young Miss*. The title of her essay is "Why I Love Love." It is 1967 and she has never been in love. She is holding her newborn daughter. Surely nothing will ever be as hard as this is. But here is her reward. She smells her daughter's soft, clean head. She will never find out what has happened to her grandson, Mo. The band plays six encores. The drummer keeps smiling at her. Afterward, she is at the bar and then there he is beside her. He's still smiling. There are cracks deep in his palms where the calluses have split open. She takes one of his hands in her own to see. She's a recent graduate of Red Bank High School, she has a full scholarship to Baylor. Here she is in the dorm room, only three months later, packing up her suitcase to go home again. She does not want to be in school. She is too shy to raise her hand in class although she knows the answer almost every single time. She is carrying the drummer's child. A daughter. Her daughter, Cara, is dead. Her heart has failed her, the body left behind lying in a morgue somewhere in Lower Manhattan. Can she come and identify the body? Is this your daughter? Yes. This is Cara. Here is your baby. A healthy baby girl. Who will take care of her son? I will. The man she has been seeing for the past few years has driven her down to New York. In two days, he will drive her and Mo back to Lovesend. He carries Mo, who is nine years old and asleep, upstairs to the room that used to be Cara's. He comes back downstairs and lets her cry on his shoulder. Then he says, I don't think I can do this. I'm too old to raise another child. I'm sorry. Oh, she's sorry, too. She has had other lovers, but this man's heart was kind. Sometimes she wonders what it would have been like to grow old with him. To raise a child with him. Maybe in a different life. A kind heart.

Arrhythmogenic cardiomyopathy.

She is sitting down to start work on a new book. What is the year? Oh, a good year, this one. 1990. Her rose garden is spectacular. But dinner is burning. She has forgotten to take the casserole in its ceramic rose dish out of the oven. She was busy thinking about her new book. A romance novel, but the heroine will be a Black girl this time. Someone like her. Only braver, happier, luckier. She will call it *Ashana's Heart*. She has a Brother AX-28 now. It's 1971 and she has a job at the Chattanooga Bakery, famous for its MoonPies. She does not particularly enjoy MoonPies. The flavor is waxy. Arrhythmogenic cardiomyopathy runs in families. When Cara dies, Maryanne and Mo are both tested for the gene. She has it. Mo does not. Here Maryanne is on her lunch break, sitting on a bench on the bank of the Tennessee River. She reads romance novels. She likes the happy endings. Some of them are so bad that she thinks, I could write a better book than this. But even the bad ones are reliable in the end. Love conquers all. Hand in hand. She's a fast reader. She's a fast writer. In forty-two years, she writes seventy-three books. She writes every day. Ten pages every day. Every second book is a book about Lavender Glass, and later she moves on to Lavender Glass's beautiful daughters. Maryanne is in labor. In the twenty-first hour, they cut her open and take Cara out. Sometimes when she is writing, she reaches down and touches the little pucker where a doctor closed her up. Time is a row of small and hateful stitches. No one slips through that door once it has been shut. Here Maryanne is, typing the first sentence of the first Lavender Glass novel on the Selectric. *I would die for love, Lavender Glass thought, looking down at the sea.* Maryanne Gorch has never seen the sea. Maryanne Gorch drives east until she comes to the Atlantic Ocean and then she drives north until she finds a house on a cliff above the ocean. Gulls nest in the cliffs below her house. One day she will have a rose garden here, below the pine trees. She and Cara move into the house before there is even furniture. They have sleeping bags. Cara has a toy ukulele. Every weekend, Maryanne rides the Chattanooga Incline to the top of Lookout Mountain and then walks down the trails in the Chickamauga National Park. She loves high places. The name of the town is Lovesend. *I love love.* The ending is always happy. When Maryanne writes, she is not unhappy. Her mother says, Who will ever buy a romance novel by a Black girl? They won't know I'm Black, Maryanne says. She submits the manuscript under the name Caitlynn Hightower. Who wants to read a romance novel written by someone named Gorch? Write what you know: well, fine, a thing that Maryanne Gorch knows is romance novels. Terrible things happen at the start and in the middle, but the ending is always happy. Hearts are mended. Lavender Glass is a red-haired and not particularly bright firebrand with freckles, milk-white skin, ahistorical and conventional middle-class dreams and aspirations, not particularly shocking sexual proclivities. There is no one in Lovesend whose skin is darker than Maryanne Gorch's. Cara likes to lay her arm along her mother's arm. She asks if her skin will be darker when she is older. Later, when Maryanne reveals that Cara's father lives in a suburb of Cairo, Cara gets a middle-grade biography of Cleopatra out of the Lovesend library. The ending makes her cry. Endings shouldn't do that.

Maryanne Gorch is paid an advance of two thousand dollars for the first Lavender Glass book. It goes back to print five times in six months and sells more than 500,000 copies in that year. The contract she signed is pretty standard for romance novels, which means it's pretty awful. She gets an agent. They work together for almost forty years. The first time they meet, her agent takes her to a famous steak house. Her agent likes her porterhouse well done. The third time she sends it back to the kitchen, it comes back so burnt that Maryanne almost feels ill smelling it. Something is burning. The phone is ringing and her agent calls to tell her sales of *Ashana's Heart* are not what they had hoped they would be. She is sitting with a reporter, a Black woman, in her office. The woman wants to talk about *Ashana's Heart*. About being a Black romance writer before the Black romance genre blew up. I'd rather not, she says. What is the perfume you're wearing? Is that Rose Absolue? Excuse me, I think something's burning.

Mo, where have you gone? Why must I lose my daughter and then lose you, too? She has offered money for information. She has so much money. Perhaps it was a kidnapping gone wrong? But then, why take that girl, Laura, and the other boy? Daniel. Why has there been no ransom note? For a while, suspicion falls on Daniel's stepfather. Because he is not white, she thinks. She is not white, either, but she is famous and old and rich enough to pay for private investigators. Daniel's stepfather is blameless. His heart is breaking, too. It is the hardest thing to lose a child. Laura's sister, Susannah, comes to Maryanne's house. Stands on the porch but does not ring the doorbell. Maryanne does not go out to her. She does not want to grieve with the other families. She does not care if their children come home. She only wants Mo. They have other children. Mo is all she has. She writes every day. The lovers in her book say the usual things. Come back to me. Let the rest of the world burn. Only come back to me.

Oh, there has been happiness in her life. Lovers who made her laugh. Cara putting down one instrument and picking up another. She can play the piano with one hand and pick out a line of melody on her toy ukulele at the same time. Surely her life will be unlike anything Maryanne can imagine for her. There is a kind of satisfaction, certainly, to being the Black woman who gets to make all the decisions about the life of a rich, spoiled white girl who lives an imaginary life in an imaginary castle. There is a queasy pleasure in inhabiting Lavender Glass's white skin. Sometimes when she sits down to write, Maryanne pictures a glass of skim milk. And then, of course, there is the other one. Caitlynn Hightower. Or does she mean Maryanne Gorch? No one knows much of anything about that girl now. Caitlynn Hightower and Maryanne Gorch's partnership as long and complicated as many marriages. Every line of that first author bio a lie. I love love.

Here is her little yellow Datsun with the Greenpeace bumper sticker. She hasn't thought of that Datsun in years. She can afford a new car, but she wants to wait until she gets to wherever she is meant to be. Her new life. The Datsun is in good enough shape to get her and Cara there, but you can barely see out the back window. There are Hefty bags full of clothes, liquor-store boxes full of books. Cara's toys. Everything else gone to Goodwill, all except for the penciled lines on the frame of the kitchen door to mark Cara's height on each birthday. That must be left behind. She's marked up a map of coastal towns above New York City. They have names she likes. Watch Hill. Goosewing. Lovesend. She wants a high place and the ocean below it. The Datsun is on a pretty street in a neighborhood called the Cliffs. Cara is crying in the back seat because she left her stuffed bear in a hotel room somewhere back on Long Island. They can afford a new bear. A bigger bear with brighter eyes and plusher fur. They can buy a whole menagerie, bears and rabbits and wolves, if Cara wants. A house, too, because Maryanne is tired of driving and hotels and Cara is tired of being in cars and Lovesend is a pretty town and if you go much farther east you're going to get your feet wet. Maryanne will have a room for writing and Cara will have whichever bedroom she likes best. Here's a for-sale sign in front of a house as ornamental as a wedding cake. There is a rose garden in the back. They move in before the water has been turned on.

By the time Maryanne has picked out furniture she likes, Cara has spent three weeks sleeping on the floor and roller-skating around the empty rooms. Eating off paper plates on parquet floors. When men bring the bed up to her room, she screams so much she loses her voice for a week. For two whole months, she insists on falling asleep on the floor and not in her lovely canopy bed. Every night, Maryanne picks up her daughter and puts her into the bed, and every morning she comes in to find Cara on the floor again. Secretly she's proud of Cara for knowing what she wants. Mo is such a good child. He climbs into Maryanne's bed at night when he wakes up after a bad dream. He plays with his mother's old toys. Maryanne gets out the coin collection she started when she was nine. Here is a peso from Mexico. Here is a dinar. Where is that from? Iraq. I can't open this, Nana. No, the catch is hidden. Like a piggy bank but just the one coin. Where is it from? I don't know. Egypt, I think. It's not valuable. Just a curiosity. What does that mean? A souvenir. Something you have a question about. Someone I used to know gave it to me. A man.

What time is it, though? There is a man in her kitchen. She didn't even hear him knock. Do you smell that? she asks the man. Something is burning. Mo says, You sit down. I'll open a window. We'll throw this out and we'll get takeout. You feel like pizza or Chinese? A woman has been standing on the sidewalk for almost a half hour now. Maryanne watches her take a picture. She's a middle-aged white woman in a floral print halter dress. She comes up the walkway toward the house and rings the doorbell. When Maryanne opens it, the woman's big smile falters. She has a copy of Maryanne's latest book, *I'd Drink the Sea Dry for You,* in one hand and her camera in the other. She says, I'm sorry. Is this Caitlynn Hightower's house? I thought . . . You have the new book, Maryanne says. Did you like it? The woman smiles uncertainly. She says, Oh yes. I cried so much. You're Caitlynn Hightower? I didn't know you were . . . Black? Maryanne says. The woman blinks several times. Home, she says. I didn't mean to bother you. Maryanne says, It's no bother. Just a surprise. No one's ever come to my house before. Did you want me to sign your book? Yes, please, the woman says. To Bonnie Miller. So Maryanne signs the book. She wonders if Bonnie wanted to take a picture, too, but Bonnie just takes the book back. Studies the signature. She says thank you and goes back down the walkway again, turning to look back at Maryanne still waiting patiently on her porch. How puzzled she looks. Have you read my books? she asks the man in her kitchen. Although he doesn't really look like much of a reader. Surely wolves don't read books.

And now it's morning and Cara is in her bed, and, oh my God, for a minute Maryanne thinks her daughter is dead because she's still in her bed and she's so very still. You can hardly see the rise and fall of her chest. But she's just asleep, she's breathing, and she's slept the whole night through in a bed, and after that, Cara stays in her bed the way she ought to and doesn't sleep on the floor. It takes time, but you get used to things. You can get used to anything except for the things you don't know. The things you don't understand. Sometimes at night Maryanne comes into Cara's room. No, now it's Mo's room. Mo is a restless sleeper. He kicks all the sheets off, so she places her hand against the tender sole of his foot. Tucks him back in again. You aren't Mo, she says to the man. Who are you? He's the handsomest man she's ever seen. So handsome Maryanne knows he isn't a real man at all. Your happy ending, he says. Well. Your ending, anyway. Do you know me? Yes, Maryanne says. Yes, I think I do. But I can't go yet. I'm waiting for Mo to get home. He isn't home yet. Shall I sit with you a while then? the man asks her. Shall you and I stay here? Maryanne thinks about that, and she says, a little sadly, No. I don't think that would be a good idea. No, the man says. It wouldn't be a good idea. It might be fun, but it wouldn't be a good idea. He holds out his hand. Oh, the smell of roses. There is something about her kitchen that is troubling Maryanne. She thinks that maybe it isn't really her kitchen. She is somewhere else now. The investigator says, I'll be honest with you. Something about this stinks. We're missing something here. Something crucial. Do you know where he is? Maryanne asks the man in her kitchen. Is he here? Wherever this is that we are? She can't help asking. The man smiles. Does not say anything. Still holds out his hand. Maryanne doesn't want to take it, but she does. Oh, his hand is so cold it burns! His nails are too long and there's dirt under them. What is that smell? What is burning here? It's better looking at his handsome face than at the hand that is gripping hers so tightly. Tell me about my father, Cara says. His palms were like horn, Maryanne says. Hard as horn. Cracks in the skin. The hard bits peeling back. I could have stuck my pinkie in between. What happens next? Maryanne says. Everyone always wants to know the same things, the man says. But Maryanne, my love, surely you know better. You know how it goes. You don't know how a book ends until you turn the last page. Maryanne wants to argue with this because the ending is always happy and you know that from the start, but now the page is turning and Cara is curled up beside her in bed while they read, and she says, Oh, Momma, this is my favorite part Nana let me read this part he says and surely Mo will be home soon now and Maryanne is in the kitchen in Chattanooga because these days she sits at the little Formica table with the crack shaped like a Y where her daddy once dropped a wrench and writes while dinner is forgotten in the oven and she turns off the Selectric and says to no one at all, Well, that's it. I think I'm

The Book of Mo

Mr. Anabin's car was already pulling out of the driveway when Mo tried the front door of his grandmother's house. He wasn't crying now. He just wanted to lie down somewhere and close his eyes for a long time. That was what his heart wanted. Maybe he could cry and sleep at the same time. But it was hard to ignore how hungry he was and who knew for how long? Who remembered the last time he'd eaten? Not Mo. No sooner did you have a body again than, hooray, you were reminded of the undignified demands the body places upon you.

Caitlynn Hightower's readers came to Lovesend and visited the local bookshop, where all the Lavender Glass books had been signed by Caitlynn Hightower in lavender ink. They walked on the beach and then drove through the Cliffs to take selfies on the sidewalk in front of Maryanne Gorch's house. They left letters and bouquets of lavender and baggies of homemade shortbread on the front porch. Sometimes they rang the doorbell and, depending on how badly his grandmother was trying to avoid working on her current book, she might go sit with them on the front porch swing for a while or sometimes even invite them in. She'd make sandwiches and coffee for adolescent Black girls who loved books, even the books that hadn't thought to make space to include them; young Black women who had read *Ashana's Heart* and never even picked up a single one of the Lavender Glass books; middle-aged Black women who still believed love ought to conquer all in books even if in real life everyone knew love was mostly just hard work. Sometimes they brought her their unpublished novels and she read the first chapter while they sat at the kitchen table. She talked about how to make sex scenes sexier if they asked. She told every single one to keep writing. Mo thought he would have told some of them not to bother. Weren't there already enough books about straight people discovering they liked having meaningful eye contact during sex?

MARYANNE GORCH'S RULE was all baked goods left on the front porch went straight into the trash. There was a fair amount of treachery in the Lavender Glass books. Drugged wines, dirks dipped in poison, mean girls who pushed their sisters into millponds. Mo was so hungry he would have welcomed even the most villainous of burnt baked offerings, but the porch was bare.

His grandmother must be buried somewhere. Probably beside Cara. Here lies Caitlynn Hightower, not her real name, who was famous for writing a series of romance novels set in Scotland, a place she never visited, every one with its happy ending, which in real life are elusive and, even when occurring, only temporary. Love only lasts so long. Sometimes only slightly longer than pastries and shortbread. Though hadn't Mo's grandmother loved Mo all of his life? She'd buried Cara at the age of thirty-nine. Sometimes a heart fails the one who loves it best. His poor grandmother, who only needed to be left alone to write her books. And Mo. To love and fret over and spoil, to help her with the high shelves and stubborn jar lids, with finding keys and glasses and printer cables and misplaced pill bottles. But Mo had not been here, and now that he was back, she would never be here again. No doubt there were little parcels of lavender on her grave. Baggies of shortbread. His mouth was watering, horribly, at the thought.

The front door of the house should have been locked. It wasn't. Maybe that was more of Mr. Anabin's magic. But as Mo went from the darkness of the porch into the darkness of his grandmother's house, someone in the kitchen called his name.

Off the foyer, down the hall, a light was on in the kitchen. Someone had been waiting for him to come home. Lying in wait, licking their chops. The door he'd just come in through was still there, a real door, and Mo could have slipped back through it, only Mo didn't want to run. He was too angry and too sad. Honestly, he wouldn't mind Bogomil dragging him back to hell as long as he got in a lick or two first. Oh, how satisfying it would be to make someone feel, if only for a moment, as awful as he was feeling. He drew his grandmother's cane out of the stand beside the door. Only as he got to the kitchen, cowardice and, yes, common sense beginning to seep in, did he realize he was holding an umbrella instead.

And there, sitting at the kitchen table, was a thing with a nightmare face, all indigo and smeared, a flash of crystalline eyes and a bristling shock of white and purple hair. Mo stuck out the umbrella, ready to deploy it.

"What the hell, Mo?" the person at the table said tartly, and he dropped the umbrella on the floor. Jenny Ping, his grandmother's secretary. The stuff on her face was only a blue face mask. You could even smell it. Lavender and honey. (Or maybe that was the tea.) Jenny wore a pair of cat-eye glasses over the mask. Her feet were bare, her toenails painted purple to match the purple hair, and she wore a threadbare concert T-shirt over a pair of flannel pajama bottoms. Barry Manilow? Mo had never been quite sure how old Jenny was, but he revised his best guess up a decade.

"Jenny?" he said.

"No," she said, sounding quite cross. "Santa Claus. I'm getting Christmas done early this year. Presents for the well-behaved kids and nothing at all for the ho ho hos. Where you been, Mo? And what the hell are you wearing?"

He looked down at his clothes. "Oh," he said. "I don't know. I just . . . uh, these . . ."

Jenny said, "Never mind. I don't want to know. Just, next time you go for a stroll in the middle of the night, would you please take your phone with you? And keep it turned on? I get we haven't talked much about how all this is going to work, but if I'm going to do this guardian thing, then you need to at least pretend I get to tell you what to do once in a while. Maryanne would climb back out of the grave and strangle me with her own two hands if something happened to you. And you know what? I'd let her."

"Yeah," Mo said. "Okay. Okay." To his horror, he felt his lower lip begin to tremble.

"Oh, darling," Jenny said. "Oh, Mo, sweet Mo. Don't do that. Unless you need to! Oh, it's okay. It's okay. Sit down. I'll make you some tea. Do you want tea? A snack? It's the middle of the night, I know. But you're on a different clock. Your body doesn't know what time it is. And to come back and she's gone, I can't imagine. Not that you should feel guilty! No! It was the right thing to stay in Cork. Finishing out the semester. But of course the right thing isn't easy."

Mo still couldn't speak. Jenny went on. "Me, when I'm feeling awful, I eat until it doesn't hurt anymore. Store-brand vanilla ice cream. Or frozen peas. Or tuna. Right out of the can. I'm not particular. Look, we've got stuff. Sandwich meat. Bagels. I've got ground beef. You want a burger? I was gonna do that for dinner tomorrow, but I've already made the patties. I could make you a burger. A cheeseburger?"

"Yes," Mo said, gasping. "I'd like a cheeseburger. I'd like that."

"Okey doke," Jenny said. "Coming up." She became a blue-faced whirlwind of efficiency.

Mo sat at the table. His eyes were full of tears again. Had he always cried this much? Or had he come back changed in some fundamental way? When Cara had died—but what had that been like? He didn't really remember. Everything had been wrong and awful and frightening, and no one would tell him where his mother had gone, and then suddenly his grandmother had been there. She'd sat in the back of a car with him, and it had been raining. She'd told him things about her garden and held his hand until he fell asleep. When he woke up, they were still in a car and it was still raining, but his head was in his grandmother's lap, and she'd put her coat over him. Surely he had cried then. Snot everywhere. Little kids didn't know any better. His grandmother had brought him here and his life had started over again. His new life, his second life.

Now he had another life.

He laid his head down on his grandmother's kitchen table and closed his eyes, and Jenny had to wake him up to eat the cheeseburger she had made. Oh, it was good to eat. He would have licked the plate if Jenny had not been watching. When he looked up, she was stifling a yawn that flaked off bits of her blue face mask.

"You can go back to bed," Mo said. "Or at least go wash that stuff off your face. I promise I won't disappear again."

Jenny just sat there and looked at him. "Something's different about you," she said. "I don't know what, though."

"That was a really great cheeseburger," Mo countered. "Maybe life-changingly good. Maybe that's what's different."

"Maybe," Jenny said. "I don't know. I was going to guess you met someone in Ireland. Or maybe you weren't in Ireland at all. You were on some top-secret spy mission and things went wrong and you accidentally discovered Atlantis but then Atlantis was kind of boring and so you came home."

"I would tell you," Mo said, "but." He tried to keep his tone very light. He had forgotten how smart Jenny Ping was. How long had she worked for his grandmother? Since Mo was very little. Really, she was almost a part of the family.

"Well, if you need to tell me anything," Jenny said, "you know you can. Tell me anything at all. For example, why you're wearing those clothes."

"Are you going to explain why you're wearing a Barry Manilow T-shirt?" he challenged. "Also, did he *sign* that? Is that *signed*?"

"My most valuable possession," Jenny said. "He writes the songs that make the young girls cry. The middle-aged ladies, too. Did you know that once your grandmother sent me a link to a ridiculous piece of fan fiction about Barry Manilow Potter? He grew up and became a pop star and got together with Ron at the Copacabana, like the song, only with a happy ending and much weirder Voldemort. Her name was Vola. She was a noseless showgirl."

"I'm glad you're here," Mo said. "I don't know what I'd do if you weren't."

"She loved you," Jenny said. "Better than anything in the world. And she knew how much you loved her, too." She kissed Mo on the top of his brand-new head and went off to whichever bedroom she was staying in. She left behind the faintest trace of lavender scent, a dirty pan upon the stove, and a boy who shouldn't have been alive.

The kitchen was warm and cheerful. Anyone should have felt safe and protected here. Mo opened the refrigerator door. Here was the lime marmalade only his grandmother used. Still half-full. Here was a carton of organic free-range eggs from the farmers market. While Mo had been dead, they had been laid by plump, well-fed hens. Someone had collected them. Packed them. These eggs had more claim on being in the world than Mo did. Didn't they? No one had had to magic the yolk into the albumen, the albumen into the shell. Which came first, breakfast or death? He was having a nervous breakdown about eggs. Perfectly normal eggs. Nevertheless, Mo took the carton out of the refrigerator and put it down on the kitchen table. Here were twelve brown eggs. Inside the twelve shells would be twelve albumen rinds, twelve bright yolks. There was a riddle song about eggs. A love song. The house without any doors. There hadn't been any doors in that place. But it was easy enough to crack an egg. You broke it against the top of a table. Like this.

And there was the yolk, spilled out on the table. Coating his fingers. No darkness inside. No Bogomil, welling out like ink. But Bogomil was cunning. You couldn't expect to find him in the very first egg.

Mo swiped down the tabletop with a wet sponge. Examined his fingertips. White chalk dust and bright, gummy yolk. Both of them quite ordinary substances, really. Whereas the fact he had fingers at all was extraordinary. For example, his nails. One of them was broken. Had he done that since he'd come back from the dead? Or was Mr. Anabin particularly fond of the grace note? Or, consider this: as he made Mo, bereft, a body, had Mr. Anabin pulled various bits of information from the wispy noncorporeal thing that Mo had been reduced to? Did the broken fingernail represent something about the way Mo unconsciously (and therefore Mr. Anabin also) saw himself?

Because he didn't want to make a mess, Mo got two bowls out of the drawer below the microwave. Then he cracked every single egg. Shells went into one bowl and contents in the other. Each time, Mo braced himself. Surely one egg would explode black fur like a firecracker. Teeth. Perhaps an eye, firm jelly brimming over with ill will.

But Bogomil wasn't in any of them. He was somewhere else.

When every egg had been broken and emptied and its parts separated, Mo stuck his finger into the bowl of yolks and swished it around. He needed to be sure.

There was a noise as he scried in the bowl, and Mo threw up his hand. But it was Jenny again. She'd washed her face.

"I was going to make an omelet," Mo said.

"Okay," Jenny said. "I was just, um."

They both stared at the bowl.

"I could grate some cheese," Jenny said finally. There was still a small blue fleck by her lip. By morning it would be gone, wouldn't it? So many things he knew now about Jenny Ping that he hadn't known before. Barry Manilow, weird face masks, so much kindness. And here Mo was, reconstituted like a dish of mashed potatoes from woe and mysteries most sinister. No one ought to have to deal with his mess, not even him.

"No," Mo said. "I don't think I'm hungry after all." He gave Jenny the bowl because he couldn't think what to do with it. "Sorry. I'm wearing this because it's stupid. It's just a stupid costume left over from last year. I had this idea, this stupid idea, that it might cheer me up to go for a walk wearing something so, so stupid." It almost didn't seem like a lie. It seemed, almost, like something that could have happened. On the other hand, Bogomil hiding inside an egg—waiting to do what, exactly, Mo, you idiot?—had also seemed like something that could happen.

"Did it help?" Jenny said.

"No," Mo said. "Not really. Good night, Jenny."

He looked at her to see if she was buying this. Her face held so much sympathy, he almost felt bad about lying. But there were so many other things to feel bad about. And no doubt there would be plenty of stuff in the very near future that he'd have to feel even worse about. So this? Was barely a blip. World's tiniest tuba, or whatever they played when you had the feeling you should feel bad about your own behavior.

He went up to his room.

Here was a suitcase on the floor. Here was a passport with a recent photo inside. Look, he was smiling as if no one had ever died. A copy of *Finnegans Wake* with a bookmark a hundred pages in. He didn't remember reading a word. *Finnegans Asleep*.

Here was his Yamaha keyboard. Here was the key that stuck. A sticky note that said, simply: *Listen to more Perotin!* Here, spread out on his stand, one of the projects he'd been working on. For how long? Felt like forever. In that place, he'd thought about it sometimes. The folders full of samples on his laptop. The sheets of paper on which he'd printed out pieces of the score. During the period of time he'd been . . . dead, he'd imagined a full orchestra. It had been so dark. So he'd imagined a curtain rising, house lights coming up. So much light. All that mouthwatering, longed-for light pouring down on a stage with the orchestra just marinating in it. All musicians. No Genevieve. Well, she could sit in the audience. Sorry, Genevieve. He'd conjured up, in his mind, each instrument in turn. The first flute with a black mole clinging to her long neck. Full lips. A good embouchure. A gnome-like man, hands splayed on the neck of a cello twice his size. Channing Tatum (well, why not?) with an oboe. Looking a little puzzled about it but game. Mo had pictured the audience, too: their rapt attention, tears on their cheeks. Take that, Barry Manilow. But the darkness had crept in no matter how much Mo fought it back. More light! Shadows came twining around the ankles of the musicians. Muffled their strings, welled up beneath the keys, the stops. They caked in the corners of the musicians' eyes, their nostrils. Their ears. And in the audience, look. Here was Bogomil at last. As if a crack had opened in some part of you that you had always thought was whole, and here was what had always been there if you had known to see it: Bogomil crouched there, dirty bare feet on the cushion of the seat, hands on his knees. Eyes partly closed but the weight of his full attention bearing down on Mo. On the music that Mo had made out of himself. And, slowly, with Bogomil's will upon it, the music began to change and went on changing until it wasn't Mo's at all. And that was bad enough, but even worse was how beautiful Bogomil's music was, the music that wasn't yours anymore, so beautiful that you realized there was no point in fighting. The music dragged you under and worked upon you. Until you belonged to Bogomil, too. Really, didn't you belong to Bogomil? In the end, you belonged to Bogomil.

"Fuck that!" Mo said.

When he raised one of the windows beside his desk, a breeze came right in. He sat on his window seat until he was so cold he could hardly feel his fingers.

He could see all the way down to the empty street just past the long rectangle of lawn. There was plenty of light outside. The moon was very low. It floated just above one of the chimneys of the Guzman house's extravagant roofline like an accidental magic trick. *Oh, the first kiss it was sweet. The next kiss made you cry. And if again we ever meet. The third kiss I might*—and here Mo realized he was singing out loud. He stopped. They were his lyrics, the ones to "The Kissing Song," the audience-participation song that My Two Hands Both Knowe You played at every show. Susannah had written the original version, but that had only one lyric: *I don't want to live forever, I just want a kiss from you* sung louder and louder until she was screaming it. This wasn't the kind of song Laura wanted to do, and so she'd written her own lyrics and the two sisters had fought about that for weeks until, listening to Susannah fume, Mo suggested a compromise. He would help Susannah write the most saccharine, the most basic rhymes and Laura could sing those while Susannah sang her original lyric with increasing force. A duet, more or less. Stupid, but the kind of stupid that was fun and led to performative kissing.

All the Guzmans were asleep. Mo had had a crush on one of the Guzman uncles for a few years. He arrived every Thanksgiving and Christmas in a red roadster. He had gold hair that was always just a little messy and broad shoulders and went running every morning at six A.M. His name, disappointingly, had been Buddy. And the vanity plate on the roadster had been BUDSTER. That had been the beginning of the end of Mo's crush, although he still woke up in a kind of holy expectancy, like some knight holding a vigil, every holiday morning just before six to sit with a book in the window and watch for Buddy to exit the house in his canary yellow gym shorts and then return, forty-five minutes later, wet curls plastered to his neck. How Mo would have liked to lick his neck.

He put his mouth near a pane of glass and blew out, making a cloudy patch. He watched the moisture of his breath evaporate, and as the glass grew clear again, he saw someone standing in the very middle of the street, face upturned to the window where Mo sat looking down.

Mo flattened himself against the narrow side of the window seat. The casing dug into his back. There was no possibility the person in the street could see into his room. Mo in the window seat was in shadow. There was no light behind him. And after all, book lovers came to look at his grandmother's house all the time. Sometimes, yes, even at night. Mostly women. Mo studied the figure. Not Bogomil. He would have known Bogomil. And not Mr. Anabin. Too slender. Not the Budster, either. Barry Manilow, perhaps? The face was upturned, in shadow, and something suggested infinite patience. Longing and resolve. Weren't those two things what patience was made up of? How Mo had longed for the Budster, just once, to look up and see Mo in his window. See *him*.

They stayed that way for what seemed a very long time to Mo, Mo looking down from his perch and the other looking up. And then just as Mo began to wonder if he was asleep and dreaming, he was so very tired, this night so very strange, the figure raised its hand. Was it waving? No, Mo thought. It was beckoning. Come down, said the gesture. Come down to me.

"Fuck, no," Mo said. Something in the petitioner's stance changed subtly. Had it seen him? The hand continued to conduct the air. Come down, oh come down!

"How stupid do you think I am?" Mo said. Before he had died, it was true, he had been very smart. He had been smart and he had been good and he had been careful.

And where did that get you? the waving hand communicated to Mo. Come down to me! The hand had a point. Mo went down.

Jenny must have gone like a sensible person to bed at last, because all the lights in the house were off. And of course Mo's grandmother was dead. She was dead. He could do whatever he liked. The front door was locked, but it was easy enough to unlock a door. To go through a door. On the threshold itself, he stopped. What was he thinking? He hadn't even put on his shirt, his shoes. But there wasn't time. Like a coin dropped into a purse, the last bit of moon was slipping into the mouth of the Guzmans' chimney. The street was all in shadow. He stepped through the door.

THE BOOK OF LAURA

Laura slept long and late. She would have slept even longer, except downstairs someone was banging things around in a furious and provocative manner. Susannah. Was she knocking down an interior wall? Putting dishes away with a trebuchet? Knowing Susannah, both the means and the ends would prove mysterious comma stupid. By the time Laura had brushed her teeth, smoothed out her hair, and dressed, the banging had stopped and Susannah was dragging a vacuum around. Since when did Susannah vacuum?

Laura went down the stairs, checking her phone. There were texts from Daniel and two DMs from Mo on Facebook. Evidently, in between the first and the second, he and Daniel had talked, because the second just said, Ok so see you at 3 at your house. See if you can get rid of Susannah otherwise she'll think its weird I don't want to hang out. Not that I don't wanna hang out Susannah is the best but you and me and Daniel have things we need to talk about before tomorrow. Whereas Daniel's last text said: Something's wrong. I'll come over before Mo gets there. Check out your war.

Whatever that meant. Laura texted back: What's NOT wrong

Almost immediately her phone buzzed again. Daniel again. Fart's dead. He died while we were dead.

That sucks. You ok?

No. Don't know. See you soon

Downstairs, Susannah had headphones on and her back to Laura. Her usually unruly hair was in a neat braid. Since when did Susannah braid her own hair? Most of the time she didn't even brush it.

Laura went over and snatched the headphones right off Susannah's head. Susannah shrieked, her eyes comically wide. Had she plucked her eyebrows, too? Yes. Not well, but yes, definitely yes, she had.

"What the fuck?" Susannah said.

"That was my question, actually," Laura said. She had to yell to be heard over the vacuum cleaner. "What the fuck, Susannah? Are we expecting company? Is the queen stopping by?"

Because the place was weirdly spotless. And the couch was new. Had Mr. Anabin done that? When had Ruth gotten a new couch? Had it been there the previous night and Laura just hadn't noticed?

"Oh shit," Susannah said. Something was rattling around in the cylinder of the vacuum cleaner. "You forgot. You really actually forgot?"

"Forgot what?" Laura yelled. God, Susannah was annoying. You could swap out Susannah and Bogomil and instead of scaring people, her sister would just go around annoying them until they shriveled up into a handful of dust. She could almost picture this. Susannah stinking of roses and death. Vacuum in hand. In you go.

There must have been a look of horror on Laura's face, because Susannah turned off the vacuum cleaner. She said, simply, "Dad. Dad? Remember? He's coming by to take you out to lunch. He's going to be here any minute."

Laura sat down on the new couch. "Dad? Lunch?" she said. "I forgot. I guess."

Susannah sat beside her, hunched over in that way Laura hated so much. Like, if you were going to be freakishly tall, just be freakishly tall. "I didn't mean to wake you up."

Laura said, "Why are you cleaning everything like a fiend? If we're going out for lunch?"

Susannah looked a little shy. She said, "I guess I wanted everything to look really good. So he would be impressed."

"You're trying to impress him?"

"No," Susannah said. "I just wanted him to think that our life is completely awesome. So he wouldn't get the idea we miss him too much."

"Well," Laura said. "We don't. Where is he taking us, anyway? Do I have to get dressed up?"

"Not us," Susannah said. "He's just taking you. I've got work. Anyway, I've been to lunch with him already. Like, *three* times. Super casual, although if you want, he'll take you for Thai. He wanted me to come over for dinner at his rental place last weekend, but, yeah, I'm still too mad at him to do that. Anyway, it would have been too weird to hang out with him like that while you were in Ireland. You suck, but he sucks more."

"Thanks," Laura said. "You suck, too."

That made Susannah smile. She leaned over and hugged Laura so hard that Laura made an "oof" noise. But she hugged Susannah back. Her sister smelled warm and cleanish, which was cleaner than usual, and unpleasantly of roses. But that was just Susannah's shampoo. Laura preferred strawberry.

"Okay," Susannah said abruptly.

She let go of Laura with a final bone-crushing squeeze. "I have got to go or I'll be late. Say hi to Dad. But don't believe anything he says. He's all 'promise you the moon, Susannah,' 'I'm so here for you and your sister,' and I'm like, Yeah, I remember how it went last time when you left Ruth holding the bag."

She lugged the vacuum cleaner off to the closet where it lived. Of course she didn't empty the cylinder, even though she should have. Someone was going to have to do that. Dump out the dust and bunnies. The forgotten coin.

"Bye," Laura said. But Susannah was already out the screen door. It was banging on the hinges. Laura went to figure out what to wear to lunch with a father she hadn't seen in twelve years.

The Book of Daniel

Daniel ate his stepfather's pancakes until he began to worry he might burst. Peter Lucklow said things like, "Didn't they feed you in Ireland?" But he kept making more batter. He was good at pancake shapes. He served Daniel nineteen little pancakes that spelled out W E L C O M E H O M E L A R G E S O N. Which was corny, but Daniel kind of liked it, too. He made a bunny rabbit. Then a guitar. Then a crocodile. Daniel ate them all.

Daniel's siblings cheered him on. They sliced up bananas and washed blueberries, brought out the container of maple syrup tapped and boiled down last year from the trees in their yard. They shouted out shapes for Peter to make. A pirate ship! A pumpkin! A scary ghost! Harry Styles!

That last one was Carousel. Peter turned around, pointing his spatula at her. "Above my pay grade," he said. "I make an ugly Harry Styles pancake and what happens? You cry. On the other hand, I make a real good Harry Styles pancake. Daniel eats him. And you cry. My pancakes don't make people cry unless it's from joy."

Carousel looked like she wanted to argue, but Dakota said, "The moon! Make a moon!"

At this, Lissy opened her mouth as if she was about to point out how dumb her twin's request was, but Daniel kicked her gently under the table. So Peter made a perfectly round pancake, and Carousel carried it over to the kitchen table on the serving plate. When she picked it up between her fingers to place it on Daniel's plate, it was still hot and she dropped it on the floor.

"Way to go, Carousel," Lissy said. "You dropped the moon!"

"It's okay," Daniel said. "Fart can eat it. Where is he, anyway?" Because Fart was always around at mealtimes to hoover up whatever fell from the table.

"Fart's dead," Oliver said. "We put him in the ground because that's what you do when something dies."

Everyone had been looking at Daniel with horror and perplexity. Now they turned those looks on Oliver, who said, "What? That's what you *do*."

Lissy said, "We had a funeral and everything. And then Davey and Oliver tried to dig him up because they wanted to know what happens after you die."

Dakota made gagging noises.

Daniel said, "Fart's dead?"

His mother said, "Oh, honey. Don't you remember? We called to tell you when it happened." All during breakfast, she had been in the kitchen alcove at her desk, organizing some kind of New Year's fundraiser for the community center where she was the director. Now she came over and bent down to give him a hug.

"He had a good long life full of love," she said. "And we'll always remember him. That's about as much as anybody, dog or person, can ask for."

"Yeah, of course," Daniel said. "I guess it just didn't seem very real. Because I wasn't here." He hoped his mother couldn't feel how he was trembling. Because if it hadn't been Fart last night, skittering around on those long white legs, then who had it been? He thought he knew.

"Here," Peter said, bringing over another round pancake. His mother tousled his hair as if he were just a little boy. All of his siblings were watching him carefully, as though they knew that something was wrong with him. Oh, there was, there really was; there was something wrong with him.

Peter said, "Have a new moon."

The Book of Lovesend

In the town of Lovesend, there were many statues. One was a statue of Ernest Everett Just, a Black marine biologist born in the nineteenth century. One was of Lewis Howard Latimer, the Black inventor of, among other things, an early air conditioner, lightbulb filaments, train toilet systems. The other statues—artists, scientists, inventors—were all Black women. You came across them in odd corners as well as in front of the town hall and the library. In parks. These had been commissioned by Maryanne Gorch. (Paid for by Caitlynn Hightower's books.) Maryanne had never regretted her decision to buy a house in Lovesend, but it was painful to see her daughter grow up in a community that was, more or less, white. There was a smattering of the descendants of Portuguese fishing families, a restaurant run by a young Thai American couple, and so on. But there were no Black children in Cara's class. Very few Black children in the entire school. Only one or two Black children in the playgrounds or on the beaches. The public school Cara attended had been named after an individual called Hugh Hall, and Maryanne Gorch was dismayed, if not surprised, to discover this was a person who had grown rich from the slave trade. There was even a statue of Hugh Hall down the street from the school.

Maryanne Gorch, who was action-oriented, approached the town council. She told the council (all white) that her work as a writer meant she was naturally attracted to research, and as someone who had ended up in Lovesend and planned to stay there, she had been researching the history of the town. It was true Lovesend had not been a stop on the

Underground Railroad. It was not the birthplace of any Black historical figures generally considered of note. However, the small public beach at Lovesend had never officially had a policy of segregation. It was hardly even a beach. In the '50s, there had been a boardinghouse across the street from Little Moon Bay that rented rooms to colored families in the summer. And colored families had therefore come to Lovesend and Little Moon Bay. There had been many letters to the paper protesting this, and yet rooms were still rented. Families still came. Black children went swimming with the children of Catholic Portuguese families and Irish families who fished and caught crabs and dug up long-necks at Little Moon Bay. After desegregation, the boardinghouse's clientele fell off. Black families went elsewhere. Little Moon Bay was not a pretty beach or a long one, and the marsh behind it was buggy and smelled of decay.

Maryanne Gorch wished, she said, to erect a statue in honor of Ernest Everett Just, the Black marine biologist who had spent every summer at Woods Hole but had on a number of occasions stopped off at Lovesend to swim across Little Moon Bay and collect specimens from the rock pools that ran along the sea cliff. Maryanne proposed that the council let her put up other statues, too. She wished to celebrate Black artists, Black scientists, Black figures of historical note. Ernest Everett Just and Quock Walker, and others. And in return, she would fund Lovesend's library, its parks, and its public school, which badly needed a new roof.

The Lovesend town council had put together a committee at once, with Maryanne to sit at its head. They were not averse to philanthropic gestures. Maryanne could not magically fill up her daughter's class with Black children. But she could populate the town of Lovesend with public statues of Black Americans who had done remarkable things. Her preference became, specifically, Black women. She hoped her daughter would grow up to be remarkable, too. And she had. Cara had been remarkable.

Lovesend was not as white as it had once been. Hugh Hall Public School, after a sustained campaign by Maryanne Gorch, was eventually renamed for Lewis Latimer, though the statue of Hugh Hall remained. There were enough Black kids in the upper grades to fill a table at lunch. There were Theodora and Natalie Thanglek, whose parents owned Thai Super Delight. Mo and Theo and Natalie were all friends. But Susannah, on her way to work, thinking about the lunch her father would take Laura to, was pretty sure that while Mo actually liked Susannah for some reason, Theo and Natalie only tolerated her for Mo's sake. And because being in a band had made Susannah slightly cooler. Whatever. She didn't want to think about the band.

Today was walk-to-work day because Susannah's last bike had been stolen a while ago. She hadn't bothered to replace it while Laura was gone. Laura's bike was nicer, anyway.

The route to What Hast Thou Ground? took Susannah through two neighborhood parks, past four statues and one frieze. Susannah's favorite was the frieze. She'd done a whole project in fifth grade on its subject, Leonta Carter, and it hadn't even felt like homework. Maybe that was because Leonta Carter wasn't actually real. She was a character in *Ashana's Heart,* one of Mo's grandmother's books. Of all the statues in Lovesend, she was the only one who was entirely imaginary. Which meant Susannah had only gotten a C, even though she'd worked pretty hard. Apparently you were supposed to pick a real historical figure.

Carter lay in the foreground of the frieze, back to the viewer. Her head, turned slightly upward so you could see she had exactly the sort of leonine profile you would have expected from her name, was pillowed on her arm, and her long skirt was spilling out on the floor. Her hair was in a queenly turban. Her cat lay across her hip, wide-awake, guarding her sleep. Susannah had assumed when she was younger that Leonta Carter was a princess under some kind of spell. In the background of the frieze was one of Carter's paintings. In *Ashana's Heart,* Carter had been one of the figures of the Harlem Renaissance, a painter who incorporated African patterns into almost medieval-style renderings of Black men and women. She worked days and nights on her canvases without eating or sleeping, until her fingers cramped so badly she could no longer use them and her eyes grew so tired she could no longer see the canvas in front of her. When she could work no more, she'd lie down on her studio floor and sleep like the dead right in front of her painting, so that when she woke up, it would be the first thing she saw. And then she'd start again.

In *Ashana's Heart,* Leonta Carter died when she was a very old woman. A friend came into the studio and found her on the floor. He'd thought she was just sleeping. But she was dead. Which was tragic, sure, but in the novel, Mo's grandmother had made it sound kind of amazing, too, to find the thing you loved and wanted to do and then just do it right up until the moment you died. So many people did things they didn't want to do and then died. Some people never figured out what they were supposed to do. Or maybe some people weren't supposed to do anything? What if that was Susannah's situation? She thought it might be.

Like, sure, there were things Susannah wanted to do. For example, singing was not boring. Drums weren't precisely her thing—she'd gotten about five pages into the copy of *Stick Control* Laura gave her before giving up—but she didn't have to be good. She just had to keep a basic beat going. Make a lot of noise. Making noise had seemed like a thing she could keep on figuring out. You could yell, you could make your voice all sireny and electric. You could stretch a note out so far and long it was like you were sending an important message into outer space. Well, she could. Susannah could do that. Mo said she was just showing off, but Mo was weird about music. A little bit like Laura, actually. They had ideas about what you were supposed to do and what you weren't supposed to do.

(Daniel had said, "Do it the way you want to. Do it whatever way you need to do it. You'll figure it out as you go." Susannah said, "What if I want to go do something else?" He said, "Do you?")

It shouldn't be this warm in December. They definitely didn't have enough iced coffee prepped.

Last night, Susannah had gone to sleep so angry with Laura (and Daniel) she'd thought she might just burst into flames. Didn't people sometimes spontaneously combust? Wouldn't it serve Laura right if Susannah did? *Typical Susannah,* Laura would say. And get to work cleaning up the mess. Susannah could just picture it, the whole frieze. Laura scrubbing the stain that Susannah had left behind. Whereas, when Laura had disappeared—

Susannah became aware she was leaning against the slab of marble to which the frieze of Leonta Carter was affixed. Her forehead was right up against a particularly nobbly bit. When she pulled away, she rubbed her head and found the mark. It ached faintly, and there was a sore place in her left heel, too, as if a blister was coming up. Some kid on a picnic bench was staring at her. He was dressed like he'd come straight from the '50s and then forgotten where he'd parked his Tardis or whatever. Black leather jacket, white aviator scarf. Was rockabilly seriously a thing people were still into? Time travel seemed more likely.

He was the second person she'd seen in a weird costume recently. Wasn't he? Daniel, stepping over the fence. Why had he been wearing whatever he was wearing?

Susannah gave the time traveler the finger and he looked even more confused about that, so she decided to just ignore him.

Honestly, she felt better than she had in months. Now that Laura and Daniel were back from their fancy music program, she could stop wondering if they were having a good time over there. What they were doing. Whether she should have gone, too.

It had been a busy summer. A busy fall. So much going on! There was work. There was her father showing up like a bad penny, wanting to go out to lunch and talk about her plans for college or whatever. Her *dreams*.

It wasn't like Susannah had ever thought there was some cosmic destiny pointing its finger down to ensure she and Daniel were going to get together in their last year of high school and then spend the rest of their lives having awesome sex, being magic and happy and together. She was going to keep her head down and avoid him and figure out what she wanted to do next. Did she want to stay in Lovesend for the rest of her life? No. When she was ready, when she understood fully what had been keeping her here this year, she'd take all the money she'd been saving up and she'd go someplace more exciting.

Let Laura go find some other poor sucker to boss around while she lived her perfect, shiny life. And Daniel? He could go live in a deep, dark hole for all Susannah cared. She hoped he'd be happy there.

Down the street, the town square clock began to chime. She was going to be late for work.

The Book of Daniel

WHEN DANIEL CLIMBED over the fence and into the Hands' backyard, it was seventeen minutes to three. He practically fled from his family, which was a puzzle, considering how happy he was to be back home with them in the first place. It was just the thing with Fart. It was freaking him out. And he felt so guilty, too, about having died. Even if they didn't remember him being gone, he shouldn't have been gone. The idea that he would ever have gone to Ireland on some kind of music scholarship was ridiculous. Daniel didn't know how anyone bought that as real. Look how lost they'd been without him.

He'd spent the morning sorting out everyone's clothes situation. He'd taken a look at the laundry, put in another load. The start-of-the-school-year shopping appeared to have been haphazard to say the least. He'd come up with a budget, asked for and been given his mother's ATM card, borrowed Peter's car, and driven Lissy and Dakota over to the Marshalls at Paradise Point, where he made them try on leggings, winter coats, and fleeces. Picked out some things for Davey and Oliver, a little big so they could grow into them. Carousel would get Lissy and Dakota's hand-me-downs. Then to the dollar store for the rest of what they needed. On impulse he bought two badly dented cans of blackboard paint. He bet his parents would let him put it on one of the living room walls. In the back of his head, he kept thinking that there were a lot of things he had to do. There were so many things he had to take care of. Because he might be back only for a little while. So he had only so much time.

He felt guilty, too, about blowing off friends—there were a bunch of people checking in, DMs—but it wasn't as if he'd be much fun to hang out with right now. He couldn't just be who he normally managed to be.

Carousel had a bad teacher this year, his mother had said. When she mentioned the teacher's name, Daniel groaned. Ms. Fish. He'd had Ms. Fish. Couldn't she just retire already? But, his mother said, she was even worse now. Or else she'd taken against Carousel for some reason. Not that she called her Carousel; she insisted on calling her Caroline.

On the way back home from Paradise Point, they'd passed Susannah on her way to work. She looked exactly the same but different somehow in some way he felt sure he wouldn't be able to figure out, even if he had all the time left in the world. Which he was pretty sure he didn't.

He knocked on the Hands' door and then went ahead and opened it and went in, only to find Laura sitting on a blindingly white couch having a conversation with a man he didn't recognize.

"Daniel!" Laura said. "Dad, you remember Daniel, don't you?"

"Oh," Daniel said. "Hey." He awkwardly shook Mr. Hand's hand. The last time he'd seen him, Mr. Hand had seemed like a giant. Now, Daniel realized, he was taller than Mr. Hand by at least three or four inches. Well, good. He loomed over the couch more deliberately. "Have you been in town long?"

"A few months," Mr. Hand said. He gave Daniel a rueful smile, the kind that was no doubt supposed to communicate hard-learned lessons. Better intentions. "Trying out the whole telecommute thing."

"Right," Daniel said. "You still doing ocean stuff?"

"Offshore drilling tech," Mr. Hand said. "Very cutting-edge."

"Dad took me out for lunch," Laura said. "He and Susannah have been hanging out the past few weeks, apparently."

"Susannah," Mr. Hand said fondly. "She's a real kick. There's nobody like her."

Susannah had Mr. Hand's green eyes and his unruly hair. They had the same rangy build, too. Hard to see Laura here at all, except for maybe the determined chin.

"Good to see you, Daniel," Mr. Hand said. "Laura, are we on for dinner? Sometime later this week?"

"I guess so," she said.

"See if you can get your sister to come, too," Mr. Hand said. "I want to have a meal with both my girls." He stood up, and when Laura stood up, too, he held out his arms for a hug and Laura went into them awkwardly.

When he was gone, Daniel said, "He's back?"

"Yeah," Laura said. "And more importantly, Mom and Susannah got a new couch. Like, did they buy that when we were dead? *Oh, too bad about Laura vanishing like that. You know what we should do? Buy a new sectional couch.*" That last she said with real venom. Then, "I can't handle this. New couches. Dad being here. Like, he's apparently being all smooth with Ruth again, too. He showed up with flowers. Not for me, for *her*. What if she decides to get back together with him? Why is everybody so, so stupid?"

Daniel plopped down. "Plush," he said. "But it's firm, too."

"Daniel!" Laura said. "You did not come over here so we could discuss whether or not this is a good couch!"

"No," he said. But oh, he wished he had. "I came over so we could talk before Mo got here."

"Is this about the war?" Laura said.

"The what?"

"Your text. You said something about I should check out the war. But Dad talked a lot about politics and stuff at lunch, but nothing ever came up about a war. So I was going to look online."

Daniel pulled out his phone and looked at it. "Oh," he said. "No. That's a typo. Never mind. I should tell you about Fart first."

Laura said, "He died. You texted me."

"Yeah," Daniel said. "But I didn't know he was dead when I got home last night. And I saw him. Kind of. He went under the kitchen table and wouldn't come out. And then when I was trying to sleep on the couch, he kept waking me up. You know, licking my face and stuff."

"Why were you sleeping on the couch?"

"That's not the important part!"

Laura said, "So you think you saw his ghost?"

"Or maybe it wasn't Fart at all," Daniel said. "You know? All I saw was a big white shape that growled at me and then licked me."

Laura took this in. "You mean it could have been Bogomil," she said at last.

"I don't know," Daniel said miserably. He could see Laura think about Bogomil, Bogomil licking his face. She looked appropriately appalled.

He said, "But if it was, if it was Bogomil, then it was my fault he was there. And I just kept sleeping, and what if he did something?"

"Like what?"

"Like who knows?"

Laura said, "Poor old Fart. And last night I unpacked my suitcase from the trip to Ireland that we *did not take,* and there was this stuffed animal. A black lamb. With the name Bogomil on a ribbon around the neck."

"At least he didn't lick you," Daniel said. He'd been trying not to think about what Fart had made of his disappearance, what it had been like for his family, Daniel disappearing and then Fart dying.

"Yeah, well, I had to go to sleep knowing there was a stuffed animal named Bogomil in my closet. Which I think is pretty bad. You didn't even *know* it was Bogomil."

"Is that supposed to make me feel better?" Daniel said. "Here's the other thing. Take a look at my ear."

"Your ear?"

"Yeah. That's what I was trying to text you. Ear, not war." He bent down and Laura leaned over.

She said, "When did you get your ear pierced?"

"I didn't," Daniel said. "Take a closer look."

"Okay. It's an ear. A little small. Very nicely shaped. You don't have that thing where there isn't any lobe."

"Thanks," Daniel said. He was beginning to find this kind of funny, although he was fairly sure Laura wouldn't when she put it all together. He'd already checked out his own ear, the one that was now on Laura. It was a perfectly good ear. He wasn't tempted to rhapsodize about it or anything, though.

But he did want it back.

"So, what?" Laura said. "Do you think Bogomil pierced your ear? He came back and pretended to be your dead dog and also pierced your ear while you were asleep? Why would he do that?"

"No," Daniel said. "I think it's not my ear. I think it's yours. Mr. Anabin got some stuff mixed up when he put us back together." From his pocket, he produced Laura's butterfly earring.

She snatched it from him. The expression on her face was one of absolute horror. "Wait," she said. She felt one side of her head and then the other, the side with Daniel's ear on it. "Oh no, oh no."

She got up off the couch, still holding onto the side of her head where the wrong ear was. She backed all the way out of the room, still staring at Daniel. He heard her go into the bathroom next to the kitchen and close the door. After that he heard a lot of muffled unhappy noises.

Disconcerting, of course, to wonder what other details, what other bits Mr. Anabin had mixed up or gotten wrong. What if there were things in Daniel's head now that hadn't been there before? What if some of Laura was in there now? Or Mo?

Also disconcerting to wonder what else was wrong with how Mr. Anabin had made them. Like mitochondria. Were those little guys okay? After the trip to Paradise Point, before coming here, he'd gone into his bedroom and checked out some other stuff. Okay, he'd masturbated. That had gone pretty much the way he remembered it, which was to say it was pretty great even given the circumstances, which were 1) having to lock his door, 2) having to be very, very quick, because Lissy and Dakota were kind of communists about private property and they knew how to pop open a lock with a wire hanger like nobody's business, and 3) being behind a locked door, even one he had locked for his own reasons, made Daniel feel weird.

There was a video online he'd seen once, one Susannah had shown him, actually. It was just some girl lying on her side on a bed, the camera pointed at her face. You couldn't see anything else, but you could tell she was playing with herself. Or maybe you were supposed to think that. Then she came, or maybe you were just supposed to think she had. Susannah had said, "That's the hottest thing I've ever seen and I have no idea why." And Daniel wasn't sure if it was or if it wasn't, but Susannah saying that, Susannah showing him the video, Susannah lying down on his bed with a smile on her face, touching herself while Daniel watched, that was what was in his head when he jerked off.

Afterward, he'd lain there on his bed, messy dick still out, sunlight collecting like dust around the lines of the blinds. Once his brain was fully back online again, he'd realized the ear mix-up was, on balance, a good thing. It meant Mr. Anabin wasn't infallible or all-powerful or all-knowing. And therefore Bogomil wasn't, either.

After Laura had come out of the bathroom, her hair fluffed up over both ears, he'd related all of this to her. Well, not the jerking off bit.

"So we're just supposed to go around with the wrong ears for the rest of our lives?" she said.

"Which may not be all that long," Daniel said. "Remember?"

"Right," she said. "This game thing." The way she said it would have made anyone who didn't know her think she hated games. But Daniel had known Laura all his life. There wasn't an uncompetitive bone in her body.

"Gonna suck if it's Monopoly," he said.

"Twister," she said. "Bet you anything that fucker Bowie is superflexible."

"We don't tell him any of this," Daniel said. "Right?"

"Right," she said.

"And what about Mo?" He couldn't look at her as he said it, and then he wondered if he'd said it at all, because she was silent. Finally he looked up and saw that her eyes were burning into him. Sometimes (sometimes?) he found Laura a little scary.

Laura said, "We don't tell him, either."

The Book of Mo

Jenny had turned Mo's bowl of egg yolks into a breakfast casserole. His grandmother had once called Jenny the fifth rider of the apocalypse. The one who makes sure all the other riders actually go in for their dental appointments. And that they're getting enough fiber in their diets. In the *Ping*calypse, the world ended not with a whimper and not with a bang. Instead Jenny helped you check every item off the to-do list, and then the whole world, surprised and gratified and more than a little exhausted, ended with a ping.

There had been bacon *and* sausage in the casserole. He'd eaten almost half the tray, but by the time he was on his way down to Laura's house, he was so hungry again he'd stopped off at the good bakery and bought a dozen doughnuts, half a dozen bagels, and three different kinds of cream cheese.

There was one awkward moment when he'd meant to dump the handful of change into the tip bowl and instead had reached inside it. Pushed coins around with his finger.

"What are you doing?" the kid behind the counter had said, and that jerked Mo out of his fugue state.

"Thought I saw something in there," he'd said.

"Like some tip money?" the kid had said sarcastically.

"Like, uh, a roach," Mo had said. "A really big one." Then he'd dumped his change into the bowl that the kid was now looking at in great dismay.

He was on his mountain bike, which meant he had to balance the doughnut box on his handlebars, messenger bag loaded with bagels slung over his shoulder. The afternoon was sunny and warm, in the seventies at least, which was the least freaky thing about this day. When Jenny had asked where he was going, he'd said, "To see friends." And she'd looked so happy about this he'd almost felt happy, too. Because she'd seemed so happy he had plans. And that his clothes were normal clothes. Meanwhile, he was happy he didn't have to look at the Barry Manilow T-shirt. So they were both happy, and that seemed important because he was so, so very sad. Everywhere he looked, his grandmother wasn't. And she never would be again.

And now he was about to spend quality time with Laura Hand and Daniel Knowe while his actual friends, people like Theo and Natalie and Rosamel, were messaging him, asking when they were going to see him. Theo and Natalie were back in town as of yesterday; Rosamel was arriving today. They were up for whatever! They were so sorry about his grandmother. And if he needed cheering up, they had a lot of great gossip, really good stuff. Rosamel, who had started off more or less a friend by default because she'd been the only other Black kid in the high school at Lewis Latimer who was also gay, was sad about some girl she'd met at Oberlin. Even Vincent Grove, who after clandestinely fooling around with Mo for half of last year had decided he was definitely not gay even though he really liked sucking dick—and who Mo had not broken up with because they were never really going out in the first place—even Vincent had DM'd Mo to see if he wanted to go hiking. For someone who didn't want anyone to know he *definitely wasn't gay*, Vincent had a real thing for performing acts of public indecency.

The point was, there were a lot of people he would rather be hanging out with, under normal circumstances. But of course, these were paranormal circumstances. And Vincent was a hot/cold kind of guy anyway. The colder you were, the hotter he got.

When Laura came to the door, he wasn't sure at first if she was being weird because of how they'd been dead yesterday or if, like Mo, she had been thinking about this situation with Bogomil. How Mr. Anabin had called it a contest. A game. Because Mo had been thinking about that.

The Hands' house was clapboard, one of the un-prettied-up, unrenovated houses you still saw in this neighborhood. Natalie and Theo lived around here, too. You could tell the long-termers from the people who had moved in over the past ten years because the shingles on their roofs were asphalt, the siding, if it was wood, a little scabrous. There was a small kitchen with an old dinette table, and in the living room, a monstrosity of a couch so enormous there wasn't room for much else. White, too. Mo felt like Captain Ahab coming over for a dinner party at a coworker's house only to spot Moby Dick in the living room. *Wait. Guys. You invited* that *asshole,* too? *You know what I'm going to have to do.*

Laura took the doughnut box from Mo and said thank you, a little unenthusiastically in his opinion. Daniel seemed more genuinely interested in Mo's arrival. But then, Daniel always *seemed* interested in other people so it was hard to know how genuine any of it was.

He said, "I've been hungry since I woke up. Are you weirdly hungry right now?"

"Yeah," Mo said. "I am."

Laura said, "I went through the buffet at Thai Super Delight three times. I ate so much rice they had to refill the rice cooker."

Mo watched her cram a salted-caramel doughnut into her mouth. Now there were two caramel doughnuts left. He grabbed one just in case. There was something about Laura's posture, the way she had her head tilted, that he found peculiar. Her hand kept going up under her hair.

"What's up with your ear?" he said.

"What?" Laura said. She clapped her hand over the side of her head.

Mo said, "You have an earache or something?"

"What do you mean?" Laura said quickly, but now Mo could see it in Daniel's face, too. Something was up.

"Look, assholes," he said. "Tell me what's going on or I'm out of here."

When neither of them said anything, Mo said, "Fine. Also, I'm taking the doughnuts." He stood up. Stuffed half the doughnut he was holding into his mouth.

"Wait!" Daniel said. "Wait. Mr. Anabin put us back together a little wrong. I got one of Laura's ears and she got one of mine."

"Daniel!" Laura said. She looked mortified.

Mo ignored her. He thought he might burst out laughing. "That's your secret? Really? Got anything else? Should we do a mole check? Birthmarks? I've got one right on my left ass cheek. It's shaped just like a—"

"Bogomil was in my house last night," Daniel said.

Mo sat back down. He put the doughnuts on the dinette table, first taking the last salted caramel even though he hadn't finished the one in his hand. He took the basil strawberry, too. "You saw him? What did he do?"

"He licked me," Daniel said. Then, "I thought it was my dog. Fart."

"Okay," Mo said. "And?"

"Fart's dead," Laura said. "He died while we were dead."

"My grandmother died, too," Mo said. He took another bite of doughnut and began to chew ferociously. What did it taste like? Ashes and rose petals. He almost gagged, forcing it down.

"Oh," Laura said. "Oh no! Your grandmother is dead?" She and Daniel both looked horrified.

Mo remembered Laura was a romance fan. A fan of Caitlynn Hightower, specifically. He felt his teeth grind together. Had he put his mouth guard in last night? No. He'd probably been grinding his teeth ever since he'd come back from the dead. "Yeah, but don't worry. I bet her publisher has at least another two Lavender Glass books in the pipeline."

"Are you okay?" Daniel said.

"No," Mo said. "But I'm not dead, either. Tell me everything else."

"You first," Laura said, and Mo, having been rude about the romance thing and having had some time to think about game strategy on his bike ride down from the Cliffs, told them about all the questions Mr. Anabin had refused to answer. This sparked a frustrating and somewhat heated conversation, of course, about *that place*. What they remembered. It wasn't that they couldn't remember. It was that it was almost impossible to articulate what they remembered. Mo thought they would have been better off with scrap paper and crayons rather than trying to put it into words. Or maybe just one crayon. The black one.

At last he said, "Look. We're all in agreement this is really happening, right? We died and now we're back, and these two assholes are going to make us play some weird game, and if we lose, we have to go back to that place none of us wants to go back to. So we're all going to do whatever it takes not to go back. Right?"

Daniel and Laura both nodded. Nobody, apparently, was going to bring up the whole thing about how only two were going to be okay, the other two truly fucked. Laura said, "Did Mr. Anabin say anything else?"

Mo told them about the car hanging in the air over the collapsed road and how apparently Mr. Anabin using magic in turn gave Bogomil more magic to use.

"So maybe the opposite is true?" Laura said. "When Bogomil uses magic, Mr. Anabin gets more?"

"Who knows?" Mo said. "But those guys definitely don't like each other. Maybe we can use that? Somehow?"

"We don't think Mr. Anabin should know about the ear thing," Daniel said. "Because it means they get stuff wrong occasionally. Maybe that's a good thing. We watch and wait for them to screw up and see if it helps us at all when they do."

Mo thought about this. "And we report back to each other what we observe. *Everything*. Just like I'm telling you everything."

He saw Laura and Daniel look at each other across the table. "Okay," Daniel said at last.

Laura said, "Fine. We tell each other everything."

Did Mo believe them? Of course not. Laura was sneaky, and Daniel was whatever he was. Tall. Not particularly bright. But fine, if they thought he believed them, that was good enough for now. And maybe there would be a way out of this for all three of them. He realized he was rubbing his fingertips together. As if there were still chalk dust pressed into the whorls and the ridges.

"Are you there in your house all by yourself now?" Daniel said. He looked as if he couldn't imagine anything worse.

"No," Mo said. "Jenny's there. My grandmother's secretary. She's pretty much been a part of the family since, I don't know. Forever. She has an apartment in Bridgetree, but she's been going through my grandmother's stuff, and now that I'm back from 'Ireland,' I guess I'm her responsibility. Until I turn eighteen, which is in March."

He told them about the egg carton and the feeling he'd had that Bogomil had been hiding in one of the yolks. "But then I just had a bowl full of yolks. And, in hindsight, that's okay. I mean, what was I going to do if I cracked open one of the eggs and Bogomil jumped out? Make a delicious Bogomil omelet?"

"So you didn't ever see him," Daniel said.

"Yeah," Mo said. "Apparently you're his favorite."

Daniel looked appalled at this notion, which irked Mo. Wasn't Daniel's whole thing that he liked to be liked? Letting people punch him. Kissing girls and making them cry when he broke up with them, then making them feel better again, just by being so persistently nice and understanding, such a good listener, such a good *friend*. All those half brothers and sisters following Daniel around, like a parade, all over town. Like Mo was supposed to like Daniel because his siblings were biracial like Mo. Suck it up, nice guy. Of course the scary thing wants to be your friend. Everyone else does.

"Wait," Laura said, and grabbed the last doughnut. Cayenne blueberry. Rats. Mo had wanted that one. Doughnut in hand, she went running upstairs and then a minute later was back with a stuffed black lamb and no doughnut.

"Okay?" Mo said.

"Look at the name on the ribbon," Laura said, and so Mo looked.

"Are you shitting me?" He took the Bogomil lamb from her hands. Gingerly. But it was just a stuffed animal, knitted black wool around some kind of squishy foam stuffing. Squish, squish. Button eyes. "Do you have a knife? Should we cut it open?"

Laura snatched it out of Mo's hands. "I don't think we have to do that. It's just a stuffed animal."

"What about Bowie?" Daniel said.

"First things first," Mo said. He reached into his messenger bag and pulled out a notebook and a pen. He wrote down "GOALS" and underlined it. Then he wrote:

STAY ALIVE
FIGURE OUT HOW WE DIED. DON'T DO IT AGAIN
WHAT DO ANABIN/BOGOMIL WANT? FIGURE OUT. THWART
 THEM?
FIGURE OUT HOW THEY DO THIS CREEPY STUFF
MAKE THEM STOP IT
LEARN TO DO MAGIC (BUT IS THIS ACTUALLY A GOOD IDEA?)
BE CAREFUL AROUND ALL ANIMALS BECAUSE THEY MIGHT NOT
 BE
DON'T SCREW EACH OTHER OVER. SERIOUSLY

BOWIE???????
DID SOMEONE MURDER US? WHO?
WHY ARE WE HUNGRY ALL THE TIME?
FIX D & L'S EAR SITUATION (LOW PRIORITY)
NEVER THINK ABOUT ANY OF THIS AGAIN

He went back over the list, underlining every item. "Anything else?" he asked.

Daniel said, "Give me the pen." On the side of the list, he wrote in very large letters:

KEEP SUSANNAH OUT OF THIS

"Agreed," Laura said.

Mo wouldn't have minded if Susannah had been a part of this, considering she was the only one out of this crew he actually liked. But then again, he liked her. "Okay," he said. "Agreed. I have one more thing I need to tell you."

"What?" Laura said.

"Wait," Mo said. "I forgot I brought bagels." He pulled them out of his messenger bag. "They're all everything bagels. Because I want you guys to have everything."

There was a pause. And then Daniel said, "I know you're being sarcastic, but you actually did get us bagels and stuff. So go ahead and be sarcastic, although it seems weird since you're also being nice. Thank you."

"You're welcome," Mo said. He felt a little abashed. But also as if he probably would go on being sarcastic.

It turned out that three kinds of cream cheese had not been excessive. When the bagels were finished, they dug cream cheese (chive, salmon, blueberry) out of the containers with their fingers.

Laura was still covering that ear up with her hair. Her non-cream-cheese hand kept going up to touch it. If she was still doing that on Monday, Mr. Anabin was going to be suspicious right away. There were no flies on that guy. As he thought this, he unwillingly and vividly pictured flies crawling on a dead body. Laying eggs. Rubbing their little legs together. The body, he suspected, was his own. Fuck you, Mo, he thought. Fuck you for dying and getting me into this whole situation.

Fuck you, too, dead Mo said right back. Flies crawling out of his ears and mouth. Little wriggling eggs under the fingernails. On his tongue.

Mo put down his bagel.

He'd taken a long look, earlier, at the side of Daniel's head. It wasn't obvious that it wasn't Daniel's ear, but once you gave it more than a cursory look, it did kind of stand out. Laura had a nice ear. A good lobe. The one on the other side of Daniel's head wasn't half as sexy. But hadn't Mo read somewhere that most people had uneven ears? One bigger or smaller or whatever?

"Stop looking at my ear," Daniel said. Then, in a total non sequitur: "Maybe we're pregnant. Magically pregnant. That could be why we can't stop eating. Magic babies." He said the words "magic babies" with such satisfaction that Mo raised his eyebrow.

"Not funny," he said. "But we can't rule out the possibility that there are unknown consequences to all of this. We're weirdly hungry, but we're eating bagels and doughnuts, not human flesh, so maybe this is more of a psychological side effect than a magical one. On Monday if we're still this hungry, we can just ask Mr. Anabin about it."

Daniel said, "Does anyone know where Mr. Anabin lives?"

Nobody did. Mo said, "Actually I looked him up online. To see what I could find."

"And?"

"Not much," Mo said. "An article from when he was hired. A piece about the production of *Bye Bye Birdie* last year. A quote in another article about when the grocery store opened. Kind of a 'man on the street' quote. He said he was excited about 'the terrific selection of yogurts.'"

"None of this is how I pictured my life after graduation," Laura said. "I didn't even get to graduate."

"I didn't even get to submit applications," Mo said. "A real shame. Think of the application essays we'll never write! How Being Dead Taught Me to Be an Angrier Person. The Time I Wondered If I Was Magically Pregnant. Why I Am Upset About My Ear. Who Was That Guy I Saw and What Did He Want?"

And then he told them about the mysterious person who had stood in the street and looked up at Mo's bedroom window. He told them how the person had beckoned to him to come down.

"Bogomil," Daniel said.

"It wasn't Bogomil," Mo said. "I would have known if it were Bogomil."

"Then it was probably Mr. Anabin," Laura said.

"It wasn't Mr. Anabin, either," Mo said. "It was someone else." Even as he said it, he felt such a strong wave of yearning, longing, that all the hair on his neck stood up. He picked up his half-eaten bagel, appetite restored.

No one, he felt quite convinced, had ever felt like this in the presence of Bogomil, the way Mo had felt looking down at the person who looked up at him. No one had ever yearned for anything other than Bogomil's absence.

Oh, why hadn't Mo just been quicker? It had been like one of those scenes where two people run toward each other in a beautiful field. Except Mo hadn't moved fast enough. Anyway, Mo was a little dubious about what happened after those commercials cut away and also about what had been happening before. Probably it hadn't been good or else the people wouldn't feel the need to run at each other like that. They could just sort of stroll. Or they'd already be walking side by side and probably not in a field, either, because why did two people who clearly loved each other that much and had been cruelly separated for some reason just happen to be in the same field at the same time? Had there been a kidnapping? A *Children of the Corn* situation? Some terrible and dispiriting music festival in the middle of nowhere with no phone reception? How happy he would be right now to be at a dispiriting music festival instead of here.

Daniel said, "But you don't know for sure. It could have been Bogomil or even Mr. Anabin trying to lure you out by making you think it was someone else."

"Why would they do that?" Mo said. "Why would they bother? Mr. Anabin gave me a ride home and was a huge supernatural jerk the whole way. And Bogomil can apparently just show up disguised as a dust bunny or a dust gerbil and nibble on my ear and if I were you I wouldn't even realize it until later because I'm an intellectually incurious extra-large bran muffin."

Daniel looked sadly at him and Mo glared back. He had never, ever liked this guy. Not the first time he'd ever seen him, not at any point ever since. And Daniel couldn't stand it, not being liked. It was kind of insane how good it felt, not giving Daniel what he so clearly wanted.

Laura said, "Good guys don't just show up creepily outside someone's house in the middle of the night and wave at them and expect that they'll just come outside. And bad guys would be more cunning."

Mo grimaced. "Actually, uh, I went outside."

Daniel said, "You went outside?"

"In my defense," Mo said, no doubt defensively, "it had been a really terrible day. Night. Whatever. I probably wasn't thinking, you know, clearly."

"And then what?" Laura said. "Mo, you went outside *and then what?*"

Mo said, practically shouting, "And then I got out to the street and there wasn't anybody there. Whoever it was wasn't there anymore. So I went back inside and went to bed."

"Sorry I asked!" Laura said.

"No," Mo said. "Sorry for yelling. I'm just a little freaked out about everything. That's it. That's the whole box of doughnuts." He looked sadly at the table, where the box of doughnuts was, indeed, still empty.

"So now what?" Daniel said.

"Now nothing," Mo said. "Tomorrow we show up and do magic for Mr. Anabin. I have no idea how we're supposed to do that. Either of you do anything magical since last night when we got back from the dead?"

"No," Daniel said.

Laura said, "No. Maybe we're supposed to try to do it together?"

"Like Light as a Feather, Stiff as a Board?" Mo said. "Sure, I'm game." Though he wasn't. This was where it all went wrong for Black people, sitting around a table with two white people, fooling around with magic. But what else was he supposed to do?

Laura said, "Let's all concentrate on something. The saltshaker. Mo, you try to turn it into something else. Like a pepper shaker."

"No way," Mo said. "Go big or go home. Let's turn it into a hairless cat."

"A hairless cat?" Daniel said.

"Yeah," Mo said. "I've always wondered what it would be like to touch one of those." He concentrated on the saltshaker. Tried to imagine a totally bald cat there in its place. When that didn't work, he thought of Mr. Anabin flicking his finger. Flicked his finger. Be a cat, he thought. Be a weird cat. Come on.

"Let's all try," Daniel said. "Everyone at the same time."

"Do they have whiskers?" Laura said. "I want to make sure I'm imagining it the right way."

"I don't know," Mo said. "Hold on." He looked up sphynxes on his phone and showed them the picture. "How about this one?"

They all stared hard at the saltshaker. Tried flicking their fingers at it one at a time and then all together on the count of three. The saltshaker remained a saltshaker.

They tried to change it into a pepper shaker. That should have been simpler, but it wasn't.

In the end, Laura said, "Well. We can keep trying. What about how we died? We're supposed to figure that out, too."

Mo said, "We know it was Daniel's birthday."

Laura and Daniel nodded.

Mo said, "So that's a clue, right? You guys did a show. See where I'm going?"

Daniel said, "Yeah, okay. We ask around. I'll ask my parents. Because it was my birthday. And Laura can ask Susannah. And we can go up to the Cliff Hangar."

"Exactly," Mo said. "Scooby-Doo around. I was there with Rosamel Walker, I think. I think there was something I was supposed to do with Susannah. But I have no idea what. I'll talk to Rosamel."

Laura said, "Okay, but we keep trying to do magic, too, right?"

"Do whatever you want," Mo said. He checked his watch. "But I think Mr. Anabin's messing with us. Whatever it is that he wants us to do, he wants us to fail first. So we'll pay attention on Monday."

"We could just not show up," Daniel said.

"Sure," Mo said. "Do that and see how it goes. Okay, I've got to run. Got places to be."

"What places?" Laura said suspiciously. "Where are you going?"

Mo said, "Why? You wanna come along, bestie? We gonna sync our Google calendars? I was thinking I'd go for a quick hike. Clear my head."

"Be careful," Daniel said. "Even if that wasn't Bogomil last night, he's still out there. And if it wasn't Bogomil, then that's someone else we should probably be concerned about. Plus Bowie. He's out there, too."

"I'll be careful," Mo said.

He grabbed his messenger bag and was already halfway out the door when Daniel said, "Hey, Mo? I'm really sorry about your grandmother."

"Me, too," Laura said. "I'm so, so sorry, Mo."

Mo said, "You should come see this. Both of you."

Laura and Daniel joined him on the porch. The roof of the porch, the railings, the exterior walls of the house, Mo's bike in the driveway, every blade of grass in the Hands' yard, were carpeted with moths. There must have been thousands of them. Hundreds of thousands, in diameter no bigger than a nickel. They were dusty white until their wings lifted, the undersides velvet blue.

The Book of Susannah

Not being in a band—Susannah had been telling herself all summer and all fall, too—had meant she was free to do whatever she wanted. Not going on some weird scholarship program to Ireland had meant this summer she'd been able to pick up more shifts at her other part-time job. This was at the Seasick Blues, which is what everyone called the Seaside Views at Lovesend. A fancy name for a run-down motel that no one was ever going to Instagram themselves at. There were nicer places to stay, and probably nicer places to work, too, but the hours fit with Susannah's schedule at What Hast Thou Ground?, and the owner, Portia, who had gone to high school with Ruth, paid Susannah under the table. And none of the families and couples who stayed at the Seasick Blues seemed to care how clean the rooms were as long as Susannah swiped down the toilet seats, left some persuasive vacuum tracks on the damp, scruffy carpet, and spritzed the bedspreads with a little lavender water and vinegar. The owner's own recipe. Portia's other trick: a sand dollar or a seashell left on every pillow. She bought them in bulk. Mail order. Forget cleanliness being next to godliness. Ambience, she informed Susannah, was next to repeat business. Ambience was magic.

Portia closed the Seasick Blues every year between November and February and went down to Florida to spend a few months in the sun. Hopefully she stayed somewhere nicer than her own motel. Sometimes she came back with new ideas about ambience. Mostly she came back with a deep tan.

What Hast Thou Ground?, on the other hand, was by design ambience-free, and yet it did a terrific business in lattes, frappuccinos, peanut butter mocha fudge hot chocolates, and plain hot coffee to go. Billy, who owned What Hast Thou Ground?, had explained to Susannah when she first started working there that atmosphere was the enemy of the good. Atmosphere meant people wanted to nurse their flat whites or free coffee refills and hang out forever. Too much atmosphere and you might as well accept that you had declared you were a habitable planet and people should just come and live there and raise their families. They got territorial about chairs. Regarded you, the original inhabitants, with hostility and suspicion.

The trick was to make the coffee strong enough that people kept coming back but to make sure one or two legs of each table were just a little short, the chairs uncomfortable and a little rickety, so no one ever wanted to stay longer than they had to. For this reason, the lock on the unisex bathroom door was untrustworthy and the toilet paper of a poor grade. Whenever anyone asked when the café was going to get WiFi, Billy shrugged and said, "We're looking into it. For sure." Susannah thought Billy was one of the smartest people she'd ever met. Plus he never asked the baristas to smile or be cheerful. He felt it would have raised the tone too much.

On one of Susannah's first days at What Hast Thou Ground? some out-of-town asshole had brought her fat-free latte up to the counter three times: first because she said the foam tasted like whole milk and then that Susannah had over-frothed it. The third time, she'd finished off the latte, then come back to the counter to reach into the tip jar and scoop up a handful of coins because, she said, "tips were for good service" and she was going to take hers back. Billy had watched the whole thing, could apparently see that Susannah was seriously contemplating leaping over the counter and taking this lady down to the ground. "Time to go," he told the lady. "While you still have legs." Then he handed Susannah a bunch of chipped plates from under the sink. "Go out back and throw them at the wall next to the dumpster," he said. "Just sweep 'em up afterward." It was the first time anyone had ever given Susannah permission to destroy anything, and she'd loved Billy ever since.

The walls of What Hast Thou Ground? were a sticky, nicotine beige. Dead flies lay on their backs like dreamers in the corners of the windows.

The ceiling fans worked only intermittently in the summer. Nevertheless, What Hast Thou Ground? had a small but devoted sit-in clientele that Billy had never managed to dislodge, no matter how much Air Supply and Lionel Richie, how many syrupy Broadway medleys from *Cats* and *Phantom* and *Hello, Dolly!*, how much late-period Coldplay and early-period Céline Dion he pumped out over the tin-can sound system.

Kids brought their notebooks, because there were no plugs for laptops, and wrote poetry or Korrasami AU fan fiction or very sad and secret thoughts in their most beautiful penmanship. Young adults met clandestinely in corners so everyone would know who they were thinking about having sex with while the middle-aged came in on their lunch breaks and imagined that they were young again, only this time around with the money for a daily flat white. Even Mo came to sit on the lumpy, smelly armchair in the window for hours at a time, working slowly and surreptitiously on whatever it was he was always working on. Earplugs in, presumably so he didn't have to listen to the terrible music. Whenever Susannah tried sneaking up to look over his shoulder, he clutched his notebook to his chest and gave her wounded looks until she went away again. Susannah showed him her songs whenever she was trying to figure something out, and she enjoyed the faces he made. His suggestions were almost always improvements, and she felt no loss of ego in taking them.

Mo was one of the few people in the world besides her mother and her sister and Daniel whose company Susannah genuinely enjoyed, and sometimes she liked him better than anyone, if only because he didn't seem to want anything from her. And she didn't want anything from him except for a better rhyme or lyric once in a while.

They'd never talked about anything important. Susannah figured that Mo, like her, knew you had to keep the stuff that mattered to yourself. Because if you made the mistake of sharing it, you were just going to find out that it actually didn't matter all that much after all. That had been the mistake she'd made with Daniel.

MO WAS BACK in town, Susannah knew. But there was the thing with his grandmother, his grandmother dying, and so he was probably dealing with all of that. What would it be like to have someone you loved just be gone like that? Be dead? Susannah couldn't imagine. But she couldn't stop thinking about it, either. When it had happened she'd tried to write Mo a sympathy email a couple of times, then given up. Maybe it would be easier to say something in person. Or maybe Susannah just really sucked.

She served people drinks with whipped cream and banana syrup and caramel drizzles. She sold coffee sodas and scones with salmon and cilantro, mint and dried cranberries. People were suckers for novelty scones, novelty drinks. She tried not to estimate the money in the tip jar because then you just had feelings about the state of the world. There were the regulars: The homeless guys Billy let her give cups of coffee to, on the house. The women with retail jobs or who worked in real estate offices, who ran on triple shots of espresso and orange poppyseed scones. The moms with their tired eyes and workout bags and Death Star–class strollers, with sleeping future Darth Vaders or angry Wookiees in every one.

A little after four, one of the Lewis Latimer teachers came in and got his usual drink, which was steamed milk and a shot of espresso on the side. Mr. Anabin. He'd been an okay teacher, but the drink order had always made Susannah think there must be more to him than met the eye. He'd take the shot of espresso and, using a spoon, remove a minuscule amount. Maybe an eyedropper's worth. Then he'd tip that into the to-go cup of steamed milk. It was his regular order. He did the whole ritual every time, then handed the rest of the shot back to Susannah. She'd never asked, but once he'd said, "Too much caffeine and one becomes too aware of the passage of time," ruefully, almost wistfully. On the other hand, some people just ordered a cup of hot water with a slice of lemon.

Mr. Anabin asked for his change in coins. But when Susannah gave him ten quarters and the rest in dimes and nickels, he smiled and then held his hand out high above the tip jar. He dropped every coin in, one by one.

"Thanks?" Susannah said. Mr. Anabin had on one of his dorky T-shirts. ARE YOU ASKING YOURSELF THE RIGHT QUESTIONS? THEN THE ANSWER DOESN'T MATTER. "Nice shirt."

"One of my favorites," he said, but he always said that. "You must be glad to have your sister back."

"Laura?" Susannah said. "Yeah. I guess she had a great time in Ireland. I guess I really screwed up, not going."

"Not to worry, Susannah. Ireland is still a possibility. Everybody gets there eventually."

"I guess?" Susannah said. She'd never known Mr. Anabin had a thing about Ireland, but Mr. Anabin clearly had a lot of things. "You have a great day. Bye, Mr. Anabin."

She knew a secret about him, which was that for some reason he lived out of an ocean-view room in the Seasick Blues. Even during the off-season when Portia went south. He took care of his room himself, but once or twice, Susannah had had to drop off a new remote or lightbulb. The two beds were always made, the room always tidy. A keytar on the shelf beside the wall-mounted flat-screen and a couple of other things that were clearly instruments but none Susannah recognized. Mo probably would have. No other personal effects, with the notable exception of two mirrors in elaborate frames, the largest mirrors she'd ever seen. Definitely not original to the room and honestly kind of amazing that Portia had let him hang them up, one on either side of the two beds. You had to figure Mr. Anabin had some notable kink. Or was under some kind of weird curse. Either way, Susannah didn't judge.

She heard Billy sigh from over by the roaster. He hated when the baristas pretended they enjoyed talking to people.

Because nobody needed anything, Susannah went around What Hast Thou Ground? wiping down tables and clearing cups and plates just to annoy Billy. As she did this, she couldn't help but notice someone was watching her. She knew him, didn't she? Thomas somebody. The sensation of being watched was not entirely unpleasant.

This guy had been around during the summer, maybe longer, and of course Susannah had noticed him. He'd gone to parties down at the beach. He was the kind of person you noticed, especially when you noticed them noticing you. But they'd never talked. Or hung out. Which was just another window of opportunity Susannah had failed to jump out of.

Maybe he was one of the rehab kids from over in Silverside, the ones who came from families with money, who treated their time at the Silverside Clinic as if it were a vacation? Maybe, like her, he wasn't in college. Maybe he was figuring some stuff out about life. Hadn't she seen him around town in a car? A really gorgeous car, someone else driving: a woman, older but not old enough to be his mother. A stepmother or a sister.

The longer Thomas sat there, the more peculiar it seemed to Susannah that she knew so little about him. They had to be around the same age. Under normal circumstances, a guy who looked like this, who was looking at Susannah like this, well, they would already have hooked up at a beach party or someone's barbecue during the summer. Following that, they'd have mostly ignored each other around town. Or maybe they would have hooked up a couple more times, and then he would have found a new place to get coffee. But this summer had been weird. Susannah had been . . . distracted. Maybe a little out of her head. Which could have just been the fact that Laura and Daniel were off having fun in Ireland and here she was like a loser, but the feeling had seemed bigger than that, less containable. And now Daniel and Laura were back home and everything was where it ought to be, everything was the way it ought to be, at least for a little while, and Susannah still felt it, whatever it was, like a wound. Like someone had stabbed her but she still wasn't sure where. And okay, Susannah, wow. Quel drama.

Maybe once she saw Daniel face-to-face she'd be able to get over him. She'd feel like herself again.

Thomas whatever-his-last-name-was sat in What Hast Thou Ground? all afternoon. At one of the precarious, too-tall tables. On a too-low chair. Let us now praise Billy Mean, formerly of Special Ops (he said), master of the psychological stress test and the perfect dark roast.

Susannah, who had nothing better to do, went on observing Thomas. She snuck glances that were in no real way sneaky. He didn't have a notebook so he wasn't a poet. He wasn't here to meet anyone as far as Susannah could tell. He had headphones on, and he drank iced coffee after iced coffee. He put so much sugar in he should have been spinning in his chair by the second glass. But most of the time his eyes were closed, his head against the wall. When his eyes were open, Susannah often found them on her. She felt like an exhibit at the Boston Museum of Science.

Maybe a diorama of a twenty-first-century barista in her natural habitat. Or a small pressed leaf. But somehow his gaze was never creepy. There was no judgment there. Only curiosity.

Long before the end of her shift, Susannah made up her mind. Here was a boy who, without saying a word, had made it clear he was interested in her. Here was a boy who was not Daniel. So why not? Why not have fun, Susannah? Fun is not a crime.

Susannah, turning her head, found Thomas staring out the window. And in that moment, two women came stumbling through the door. One of them was slapping the other's head while her friend, half laughing, half shrieking, said, "Get it out of my hair! Get it out!"

"It's gone, it's gone," the other woman said. "Wait, there's another one. Hold still! It's just a moth."

Susannah, staring like the rest of the café, saw that at least a dozen moths had come fluttering in with the two women. Outside there were hundreds and hundreds of them, landing on cars and trees, flinging themselves at the window at the front of the café. People outside took pictures or ran down the street, hands over their heads. No one in the café spoke, but even the kids with their notebooks were watching. The guy, Thomas, was as still as a cat. Susannah watched him watching the moths. How electric his interest. A few minutes later, the moths, like a flurry, were gone elsewhere. People began to discuss the weather; in the summer there had been cicadas.

Customers let in a few straggler moths each time the door opened, and for days afterward, Susannah would come to work to find wings and moth dust in clean coffee mugs. Ground into the linoleum like nacreous eye shadow.

Billy took off just before five. He'd spent all afternoon flicking through profiles on Grindr, so, go Billy. Susannah hoped he was nicer in bed than he was when customers asked for venti instead of large drinks, but some people were into people who weren't nice in bed. And Susannah enjoyed closing. It wasn't as if What Hast Thou Ground? ever had a last-minute rush. By five to six, it was just Susannah and one other. Thomas. She looked over as she went to flip the sign on the door. Neither of them had yet said a word to the other. He still had half a glass of iced coffee, so she locked them both in and went on closing.

Susannah emptied the cylinders of decaf and caf, rinsed them, bagged up the pastries. She stuck the cow milk and the goat milk, the coconut and the almond and the oat milk, the 0 percent, the 2 percent, the half-and-half, into the fridge. When she counted out the drawer, she was short $2.16. She made it up with change from the tip jar. Thanks, Mr. Anabin, you weirdo.

She counted out change and bills and went on thinking pleasurably about what might happen afterward. She banded the bills and put them in an envelope. The envelope went in the safe. Good-looking. A good tipper. Possibly a stoner, because who else could sit like that for hours in an uncomfortable chair and drink high-octane coffee after high-octane coffee and never fidget? He was a little strange, but who wasn't? Shorter than Susannah, but who wasn't?

Susannah went into the bathroom to make sure it wasn't too gross. Checked her lipstick, but that was okay, too. A year into working as baristas, she and Laura had run a sort of experiment on the clientele of What Hast Thou Ground?, trying to establish the minimum effort, makeup wise, that would produce the maximum tip amount. Lipstick did the trick. You didn't really need anything else.

"All good things," Susannah said when at last she went over to take Thomas's dirty glass. He took off his headphones. "Also, time flies."

Thomas said, "But is Time any good at karaoke? Does he know how to party?"

"You tell me," Susannah said, putting her hand on her hip and allowing the feeling of pleasurable anticipation she felt show in her eyes. It was in his eyes, too, the way he'd looked at her all day long: A little hungry. Appreciative. Was this, as it was for her, a whim? Or had he showed up today at What Hast Thou Ground? because this had been some sort of plan of his, the plan being to finally have a conversation with Susannah? Perhaps he'd walked by the window a week ago and thought, She looks nice. Well. That probably wasn't what he'd thought, but that was why it was a good thing you couldn't read other people's minds.

Thomas said, "Time and me, we're not really on speaking terms. Haven't been for quite some time."

Susannah said, "Well, you know. Some dimensions are just like that. Assholes. Space. People are always saying, Can you believe that asshole

Space?" There was still a little iced coffee, minus the ice, in the glass she held, so she took a sip. Ugh. This boy really liked sugar.

"Exactly," Thomas said, not smiling. She really liked this whole not smiling at each other thing. Daniel, for example, smiled way too much. "Name me one personification of an abstract concept you would want to hang out with. Basically they're all petty fuckers with an inflated sense of their own importance. Kardashians and Osbournes."

He looked past Susannah, out the window. "You're closing up," he said.

"You don't want to go home for some reason?" Susannah guessed.

"I can wait outside," he said. "My ride hasn't texted, but she'll show up. She always shows up."

Susannah said, "Stay if you want. I'm going to turn down the lights and then make myself a chocolate frappuccino. We can hang out or something."

"Or something," he said. "I'm Thomas."

"I know," Susannah said. "I'm Susannah."

"I know," Thomas said. When he stood up, he was at least six inches shorter. Which was the way it always went. Oh, Daniel. Why did you have to be such an asshole?

Susannah hadn't really been planning on making blender drinks, which was fortunate, because about ten minutes later, they were in the small and not particularly clean bathroom and Thomas had already gotten her bra not exactly off but at least out of the way. His pants were down around his ankles, but he wasn't in quite the hurry you would think this signaled. Instead they were kissing. Oh, he was a good kisser. His mouth was sweet from all of that sugar. Susannah's butt was pressed up against the sink, her hands teasing the insides of his thighs, and if she hadn't been so distracted, she might have noticed how three, four, half a dozen moths were swooping around the ceiling fixture, dipping down and alighting first on Thomas's ear and then on Susannah's shoulder. Throwing shadows. On the mirror behind them, momentarily on Susannah's neck. There was a moth in a curl of Susannah's hair, frantic, and then it was dashed down. Not intentionally, poor moth, but Susannah and Thomas were frantic, too.

Bigger things, engaged in their own affairs, their own concerns, never notice when in consequence smaller things are made to suffer.

Not long after that, Susannah heard someone unlock the front door of What Hast Thou Ground? Before Thomas could be made to understand what was happening, the bathroom door popped open (that lock really ought to be fixed) and Billy peered in. His gaze met Susannah's. She saw him evaluate the situation. Thomas, his face turned into Susannah's hair, might as well have been a statue.

Billy closed the door gently. He said through it, "Five points for spontaneity. But my date stood me up and I'm feeling a little pissed off about that, so gonna kindly request you take this elsewhere. Plus, we have to consider the café. The problem of ambience. I'm concerned you may be providing it. Pheromones and so on. Also, the fuck is up with this moth situation?"

Susannah began to giggle. Thomas kept his face buried against her neck.

"Billy?" Susannah said. "Uh, sorry. We are so, so sorry."

"Nah," Billy said. "Don't be sorry. Just take your piece of ass to another location. I'm gonna be in the stockroom for the next ten minutes so I don't have to look at your faces."

Susannah and Thomas pulled their clothes back on. Stepped out into the dark café and grabbed their bags.

"Are you in trouble?" Thomas said. "Did I just get you into trouble with your boss?"

"Don't be a dumbass," Billy yelled from the stockroom. "Casual sex is the only true, good thing in this unjust and fucked-up world. See you tomorrow, Susannah."

"See you," Susannah yelled back. Then she and Thomas were out on the sidewalk, and there was that beautiful old car, lustrous as a shucked oyster, idling across the street.

"I told you," Thomas said. He gave her a rueful look. "She always shows up."

He didn't offer Susannah a ride. So she walked instead, the blister on her heel throbbing. Oh, Daniel. There were dead moths all the way home, on the sidewalk and in the grass. It was cooler than it had been but still balmy. You could almost imagine summer was just ending. Only all the light was gone. It had been for hours.

When Susannah got home, she could see a light on in Laura's bedroom window. So she didn't go in. She left her bag on the porch and went down to Little Moon Bay. You could sit on the rocks there or walk your dog if you had a dog. There was a raised walkway that took you through the dunes into the marsh, and the wind set the small lights above to swinging. The air was full of brine, and rubbery streamers of seaweed lay on the sand like a message, but perhaps not a message for you. The message was never for you.

The tide was some distance out but would be coming in soon. If you looked to the north end of the beach, the soft lines of the dunes turned to long cicatrices of black rock, the rocks rising into a vertical cliff. If you looked out to sea, you could see the haloed shapes of faraway ships. Nearer, bioluminescent threads wrote messages (oh, not for you, why would you ever think so?) in the waves. If you looked up, there were headlights, like ghost lanterns, gliding down the Cliff Road.

A white dog was running up and down the beach. Where was its owner? Who knew? Susannah could keep an eye on this dog in the meantime. There was no danger. She sat down on her usual rock, the one where someone had painstakingly carved the initials *PE* into a smooth place. Either initials or they had begun to write *PENIS* and then given up. A lot of people gave up on things too easily.

Here, too, were moths, translucent with moisture, pressed like sugar glaze into the granular sand, bits of blue wing like scraps of illuminated manuscript on the rock. Susannah took off her shoes and dug her aching heel into the satiny coolness of the sand. She began to sing, very softly, "The Kissing Song." Not her part, but Laura's. When was the last time she had felt like singing? She couldn't remember. When she got to the chorus, she thought of the taste of Thomas's mouth and Billy's face in the door and, like a lunatic, burst out laughing.

Well, it was not a great song. There was one Ruth liked, a folk song. Susannah remembered enough just to get it wrong. Something about the wind blowing onto the floor. And *said our good man to our good wife get up and bar the door o.* That was how it went. She sang, "*If it be barred this hundred years it will not be barred by me o.*" Then she had to go back to humming. They made a bet about who would shut the door. She remembered that. But she couldn't think how it went. Besides, it was a better song with someone else to do the harmony.

The white dog was sitting quite near her rock. When had it come up the beach? Its ears were pricked forward at Susannah, and it stretched out its front paws in a play bow. Oh, what a very large dog it was. Rangy and lean and a little wolfish. Its tail swept back and forth.

"Good boy," Susannah said. "Such a good, big, handsome boy!"

She held out her hand and the dog came obediently to her and ducked its enormous head under the hand, bumping against it the way a cat would. She scratched around its ruff, looking for a collar but finding none.

"Whose dog are you?" she said. Though she didn't expect an answer, and she didn't get one. "If you were mine, I'd feed you better. Yes. Lots of meaty bones. I'd give you a bath, too. Lots of bubbles. You stink."

The dog darted its long white neck out and snapped up a dead moth from the sand.

"Gross," Susannah said. "But whatever. I used to know a dog who ate cat poop. Also, his name was Fart. Poor old Fart. The one he loved best went away. And so he died. But not me. I'm made of sterner stuff."

There was a piece of driftwood near her foot, and she threw it down the beach. The dog did not even look up. It picked up another moth daintily between its black lips and ate it. Then lay down upon the sand and rested its muzzle on its paws, gazing at Susannah.

"I should go home," Susannah said. "I'm avoiding going home. But I can't just sit here in the dark with strange dogs."

The dog sighed.

"You should go home, too," Susannah said. "Wherever that is. I bet someone is missing you."

She allowed herself to imagine what might have happened in the bathroom at What Hast Thou Ground? if Billy had not come back. Or if the car had not been waiting outside for Thomas, if they had left together, gone looking for another place. Beaches were never an ideal place for a hookup, but the ideal is the enemy of the hookup. She allowed herself to imagine Thomas here, someone here with her.

The dog closed its eyes. There were fragments of song in Susannah's head. They kept turning up in the bed of her mouth just under her tongue so that she wanted to spit them out. She wanted to spit them at someone. But she wasn't in a band, and Laura and Daniel had gone to Ireland, and there was no audience here, only dead moths and a dog, asleep, with no owner. No sweet-mouthed stranger. Even the moon hadn't shown up yet. So Susannah sang to the dozing dog.

She was singing "17 Pink Sugar Elephants" when someone said from behind her, "Susannah?"

The white dog at her feet looked up. It laid its ears flat to its skull and began to bark. All its teeth and black gums were exposed. All the coarse ruff of fur along its neck and shoulders bristled, and it stood, stiff-legged and martial, still barking.

"Thomas?" she said, and willed herself to turn around as the dog continued to growl. Of course it wasn't Thomas who stood there. Hadn't she recognized the voice even as he said her name?

Daniel.

The Book of Vincent

Halfway up the Cliff Road, there is a turnoff where dog walkers and joggers, adulterers and bird-watchers, have worn a trail into the hillside. It's public land. Lightly forested. Well up and just off the trail, there is a kind of picnic area where no one ever picnics. There is no view, and there are more inviting spots. It has always seemed to Vincent, who has lived in Lovesend all his life and knows many of its secret places, that this picnic area is hardly a real picnic area at all. There isn't even a grill. The unreality of the place lends itself by extension to everything that happens there. None of this is real. Not the text he sent suggesting Mo meet him here and not the text Mo sent in reply. Certainly not Mo, nor the part of Mo that is currently in Vincent's mouth. It's a warm day for the fourteenth of December. It is never this warm in December. Hence this cannot be real. Not the fact that this has happened before. Not the possibility someone may discover them. Not the chance someone's dog may investigate the noises that Mo is certainly not making. Vincent did not miss Mo while Mo was in Ireland, and he hopes Mo did not miss him, either. He does the thing that he is not doing with even more enthusiasm.

"Oh, fuck," Mo says. Which they certainly are not.

Afterward, Vincent does not let Mo jerk him off. Certainly not. This isn't about Vincent at all. They lie on the grass and Vincent closes his eyes and does not think about anything at all.

When he opens them again, he sees that Mo is crying silently. Not even bothering to wipe the tears away. Vincent says, "It was that good, huh?"

Mo says, "What? Oh. Sorry."

"You okay?" Vincent asks, turning to face him.

"Yeah," Mo says. Then: "No. I'm sad. I'm just sad. Because I died."

Vincent thinks about this. Then feels like the world's worst idiot. "You mean your grandmother. She died. I'm sorry, man. I didn't even say anything."

"Yeah," Mo says. He has stopped crying. "That's what I said. Isn't it?"

"Sure," Vincent says. He wants to touch Mo's face but the problem with afterward is how everything always gets real again. Eventually it gets so real Vincent will have to come up with a good excuse to take off, and everything always just snowballs from there. Once you're back down on the trail with the dog walkers and the bird-watchers, you eventually end up where all the cars and bikes are waiting at the side of the highway, and then you have to go home. Where else can you go?

"I was thinking about biking out to the Point next weekend," he says to Mo. "If the weather's good. Maybe I'll see you out there?"

Mo leans forward and kisses him on the mouth. Gently. The way you might kiss someone if you were actually in a relationship with them. The way you kiss someone if you've kissed their mouth before and they've kissed you and you are one hundred percent used to kissing, so accustomed in this habit that kissing someone like this doesn't mean anything at all. You do it when you say goodbye and when you say hello again. Oh, it's such a real kiss that Vincent knows when it ends what Mo is going to say before he says it. Why does he even bother to say it?

"That would be nice," Mo says. "But I don't think so."

"Maybe some other time," Vincent says.

"No," Mo says. "I think we're done."

Mo goes down the trail first. Vincent stays on the grass. He lies there with his eyes closed until he feels little touches on his face, his nose, his lips and arms and hands. When he opens his eyes, there are moths everywhere. In the air and in the grass and here, too, adhering to his skin as if caught on little painless hooks. He holds perfectly still, watching moth wings lift and fall. They measure passing seconds, little clocks. The undersides of their wings are midnight blue, and the tops are white. When Vincent sits up they go fluttering away, the whole cloud of them gone so quickly it seems likely they were never there at all.

The Book of Laura

Everyone in Lovesend over the age of two had a bike. Even the people who lived up on the Cliffs who could afford to buy their children cars when they turned sixteen. The rich people just bought fancy bikes to go with their fancy houses. You could even get a bike now that had a little electric battery so you didn't have to do all the work of pedaling uphill. Oh, how Laura would have liked to be rich. For so many reasons.

Every time there was a party up on the Cliffs, Laura had thought of graduation and her better, more interesting future adult life in which she would never have to do anything she didn't want to do. She thought she might try living in a place without bike paths and rail trails and bike lanes. Where people didn't spend an hour at dinner discussing the merits of the Campagnolo groupset versus the Shimano. Where people got in their cars to drive two miles to the grocery store.

Her bike had two flat tires, which might have been because Laura had been dead for so long but more likely meant Susannah had been using it. No doubt Susannah had been riding Laura's bike because Susannah's had been stolen again. She never remembered to chain up her own, but to be fair, she was pretty good about remembering to chain up Laura's.

To be fair, while Laura was dead, Susannah would have had no reason to believe that her sister was going to end up annoyed about the flat tires. Susannah might have even been too sad to refill the tires due to Laura being dead. But Laura did not feel like being fair. Her sense of fairness had never been properly inflated.

The moths had dispersed or moved on to do whatever moths got together to do. The day was warm, and the ride to the Cliff Hangar was going to be sweaty. Laura sent Daniel to fill up their water bottles while she got her bike ready.

The Cliff Hangar was up on the way to the Cliffs, out on a promontory. Someone had hauled all the pieces of a plane hangar up there and made a club out of it where you could get bar food and sing karaoke and listen to mediocre bands like My Two Hands Both Knowe You. You could get there going straight up the Cliff Road, which had a bike lane and was steeper but more direct, or you could take a more roundabout route, which offered a slower climb. Laura and Daniel took the Cliff Road. People they'd known all their lives went by in cars or on bikes in both directions. Possibly one of these people had murdered Laura and Daniel.

Taking the Cliff Road meant Laura and Daniel could not talk as they rode, except when they came to traffic lights. At the first, Daniel said, "So how's Susannah?" His voice was too casual.

"You know," Laura said. "Totally normal, by which I mean she's a morose bitch."

She took off pedaling. At the next light, Daniel said, "Maybe I should text her."

"Probably a bad idea," Laura said. "But what do I know? I'm just the person who knows her best."

They pulled over at the next scenic view to take a breather. The sweat ran down Laura's back. Daniel said, "You kissed me before we died. That was to make Susannah mad, right? Or do you like me?"

"Ew," Laura said. "No."

They both stared out at the ocean.

Laura said, "I'm gay."

Daniel said, "Okay. I kind of wondered."

"You wondered?" Laura said. "Never mind." Then, a little maliciously, "But look. If you wanted, we could pretend we were together. You know, to keep Susannah out of everything. Because whether or not she hates your guts, she's going to know something's going on with us."

Daniel took a swig of water from his canteen. "We could just say we had band stuff to do. Practice. Now that she's quit. Right?"

"Sure," Laura said. "That would work."

AFTER THAT, THERE weren't any more lights, which was good because Daniel would have wanted to talk about being dead. Or to congratulate Laura on finally coming out. Or he'd go on talking about Susannah. Instead Laura had a little time to think about how her father was back in her life again.

Was it bad that she had grown used to not having a father? He'd left when she was six. Poof. Gone to California, then farther. New Zealand. A few phone calls, once in the middle of the night just before Christmas. "Call at a more sensible time," Ruth had said, Laura in her pj's in the hallway listening. "Send a check and I'll buy the girls something." But he hadn't called again. She'd thought about him, sometimes, when she and Susannah went down to the beach where he had taught them to swim. Did he miss this? Did he miss them? Which ocean could he see, did he go swimming in?

It troubled her how easy it had been to sit in a booth across from him at Thai Super Delight and talk about school and Susannah and music and all the things that had not belonged to her when she had been dead. He'd known about the band. Looked at their Bandcamp profile. Knew about Ireland. Did Laura know he'd played guitar once, too? Yes, of course she did. He'd left the Harmony behind after the divorce. But if he wanted it back, he could have it.

He'd been in New Zealand, then Australia for a while. Working on a rig. Nova Scotia. In Louisiana, then California because he'd come up with a way of mapping undiscovered underwater oil reserves and he'd sold it to a tech start-up. And now he was here. He'd never stopped thinking about his girls. Sometimes he thought about calling or writing an email, but he'd always figured they wouldn't want to hear from him.

Laura had eaten plate after plate of food. Answered his questions. Asked him her own. All these years, she'd missed her father and hated him and now here he was and he wasn't awful at all. He *cared* about her. He was sorry. He was going to try to make it up to her. So maybe she would let him try. It wouldn't work, but he ought to try.

God, Cliff Road was horrible. Almost worse than being dead. No. Of course it wasn't. She could feel the muscles in her calves becoming little hard knots. Had her father come back to Lovesend because Laura had been missing? Because she had been dead? Had he come back while the search had been going on? Had he blamed his ex-wife for not taking better care of Laura, or himself for having left?

He'd been so easy to talk to. So pleased Laura was willing to share a meal with him. Also easy: to lie to him. He wanted to hear all about Ireland. Laura had showed him pictures she'd known would be there. Looking at her phone, she'd had the peculiarly dual sensation of knowing none of it had happened and yet the smallest part of her remembered the things in the pictures as if they had. But that was true of her childhood, too.

For years, all she'd had of her father were photographs. Stories Ruth told. The time he'd taught Laura and Susannah to swim and Laura's sunburn afterward was so bad she'd run a fever of 101. The time Susannah was five and had drunk two glasses of Baileys, thinking it was chocolate milk, and then thrown up in his underwear drawer where she'd gone looking for the Reese's Peanut Butter Cups he'd always kept hidden there. The time he'd kissed their hamster on the mouth because they'd begged him to, and it had bitten him on the lip. And now here he was again, restored to her. To her and Susannah. As if he, too, had been in Ireland.

RUTH HAD CALLED while Laura was getting her bike ready. "So how was it?" she asked.

"It was fine. Weird," Laura said, setting aside the air pump. She thought she might have to find the bike kit and put on a patch.

"When he showed up at the door, I thought, He hasn't changed one bit. He looks exactly the same. How is that possible?"

"Good genes?" Laura said. "Salt air?"

"He was always vain," Ruth said. "Probably dyes his hair. I hoped he'd gone bald."

"He wants us to come over to his place for dinner sometime. You and me and Susannah."

"We'll see," Ruth said.

"Are you back for dinner tonight? I can't remember."

"Not until ten," Ruth said. "What are you up to?"

"Going to go for a bike ride with Daniel."

"Are you two together?" Ruth said. "Can I ask that?"

"No," Laura said. She was going to have to talk to her mother, too. Ruth wouldn't be surprised, but she was going to want to ask Laura all about her feelings and when she knew, and she'd want to know, how could she be supportive? Well, Mom, I figured it out while I was dead. Not that I didn't already know, but you know. It all just seemed so complicated. Once I was dead, things were a lot more clear.

Laura said, "You know, there's the band. Which is kind of on hold, but maybe not entirely? We're trying to figure out if we're going to keep that going. You know, with or without Susannah."

Ruth said, "Tell Daniel hi."

"Will do," Laura said. "Oh, wait! I forgot! There were these moths."

"Moths?" Ruth asked.

"Yeah, like all of a sudden. All over the place, little ones. I think they're mostly gone. Now there's just a lot of dead ones. I swept them off the porch, but they're all over the driveway, too."

"Did any get in the house?"

"I don't think so," Laura said, and repressed a shudder at the idea.

"Because if they're the kind that eat clothes," Ruth was saying. "Or pantry moths!"

"I didn't let them in the house!" Laura said, exasperated.

"Good," Ruth said. "Good. Because the moth is no friend to man." And then hung up.

WHEN THEY GOT to the Cliff Hangar, Daniel said, "Why did you kiss me, exactly?"

"To make Susannah mad," Laura said. "She kissed Rosamel. Who I sort of had a crush on, which Susannah knew. Sort of."

"She and I had had a fight," Daniel said. "Before we went on."

"About what?" Laura said.

"I told her I was going to quit the band," Daniel said.

"You were *what*?" Laura said. "Why?"

"I don't really remember," he said.

This was clearly a lie. "What if we died because you quit the band, and you're hiding some piece of crucial information?"

"I was thinking about the future!" Daniel said. "I just didn't see myself in a band in the long run."

"What about you and Susannah in the long run?" Laura said.

"What do you mean?"

Was his brain carved out of soap? Rock candy? "Daniel," Laura said. "I know about the two of you. I always knew, okay? That whole fooling around behind my back thing? Exactly the kind of thing that ruins a good thing."

"It wasn't serious!" Daniel said.

"Not to you," Laura said.

"*She* told *me* not to take it seriously!" Daniel said.

"And that is exactly the problem with Susannah," Laura said, aware she was not having this argument with the person she wished to have it with. "She never takes anything seriously that she ought to be serious about. Come on."

But Daniel only stood there.

It wasn't as if Laura didn't understand what he was feeling. What he was imagining. He was imagining a birthday in which My Two Hands Both Knowe You had finished up their performance and had a good time and no one's feelings had been hurt. No one had mentioned quitting. Everyone had been happy. Daniel liked people to be happy. He liked making them happy. Which was probably why he had kissed Laura back when she kissed him. A kiss was a kiss, whether it was for love or out of spite. Wasn't it? Laura didn't regret kissing Daniel. She'd had both things in her heart. And wasn't it better to live in truth than amid confusion and misunderstanding? Having outed herself to Daniel on impulse, Laura hoped sincerely that it was better to live in truth. She hoped, sincerely, to live. To keep on living.

Wasn't this what they were supposed to be discovering? What had been true? But Laura's motivations for kissing Daniel could not be the clue explaining how they had died. It was only one thread pulled loose from a whole tapestry.

Even though it was Sunday, there was just one car in the parking lot of the Cliff Hangar. The most beautiful car Laura had ever seen, an artdeco brooch of a car.

"That's the car from last night," Daniel said. "The one that drove past. Unless you think while we were dead everyone started driving Bugattis."

Laura said, "It's kind of weird, though, if it's the same one. Right?"

"Not really," Daniel said. "This is exactly the kind of place people who own a Bugatti would come."

"They've booked the whole place," Laura said. There was a sign in front of the entrance: CLOSED FOR PRIVATE EVENT.

In the early '80s, the Cliff Hangar had been a tourist draw for its views and for people who were into old planes. Hanging from the ceiling were kit replicas of the Miss Los Angeles and a Pitcairn Autogiro. There was a real Curtiss Robin. There were plaques on the wall for each plane and autographed photos of pilots. The bar was made from the actual aileron of a commercial jet. Lafcadio Santos, the owner, had also installed a carousel, ostensibly as a gift for his daughter, Hannah, on her sixth birthday. But Santos had then had four dining tables built and bolted onto the carousel's platform. You couldn't expect to keep a whole carousel for yourself. There were still six horses and two tigers. He'd gotten the carousel at a bargain price.

Santos had gone to jail for tax evasion in the '90s and the Cliff Hangar shut its doors for almost two decades. It reopened when Santos died and his daughter inherited what remained of her father's estate. She'd once told Laura she wasn't really interested in the restaurant business, but the Cliff Hangar was the only place she'd ever been happy. Now there were open poetry mics on weekdays as well as trivia nights, live music, and wine tastings. You could book children's birthday parties, bachelorette nights. Hannah Santos was game for anything that might keep the Cliff Hangar open.

A warm wind came through the open French windows along the far wall, scented with brine and decaying seaweed. The carousel, seashell pink and banana yellow, rotated as if spun by the breeze, its mirrors throwing out long columns of reflected light. The six horses (Hannah Santos's father had named them after the first six apostles he could remember) and the two tigers (Mary and Martha) went up and down their poles to a tinny recording of "The Blue Danube."

Hannah Santos was behind the bar reading a book on her phone, a half-finished basket of fries in front of her. Laura's mouth began to water. "So sorry," Hannah said without looking up. "Closed for a private event."

On the carousel were three people. Two were strangers to Laura: a middle-aged couple seated at a table. They picked in a desultory way at their soggy fish and chips. The food at the Cliff Hangar was not good. People came anyway for the views. And to get drunk while riding the carousel.

The third person Laura recognized. As Laura and Daniel had walked home last night, she'd driven past. Her candy-red hair was fixed in a heavy coronet roll and she wore the pointiest cowboy boots Laura had ever seen. They were lilac and came halfway up the calves of her plump, bare brown legs.

The carousel went gaily round. As she came back into view, the driver of the Bugatti said something and extended one leg. The woman at the table leaned over awkwardly and kissed the tip of the cowboy boot as it rose, the snarling tiger slinking up its pole.

"Hey, Hannah," Daniel said. "Good book?" He didn't seem to notice the people on the carousel.

Laura had once had a long conversation with Hannah about her favorite genre. Male/male baseball erotica, even though Hannah was single, sixty-ish, and, as far as Laura knew, straight. Then again, Laura could read historical romances about straight couples for fun all day long, so whatever. Maybe it was just simpler that way. Peering over the fence at the guaranteed narrative arc of the utopian sex life, the love story that you yourself did not aspire to, had no stake in. Once during setup, Susannah had elbowed Laura in the ribs, nodded at Hannah tucked over the spectral glow of her Kindle, her long white braid dangling like a safety rope over one shoulder, and said, "You. In forty years." Which was just mean. Although Hannah had always seemed happy enough to Laura.

Hannah said, "Daniel? Laura! But you're in Ireland!"

"Home for Christmas," Laura said. "What's going on here?"

"Lawyers," Hannah said. "I think. Anyway, they drink like professionals. Been up there most of the afternoon and gone through four bottles of wine. Expensive wine."

"Sorry for just dropping in," Daniel said. "We were wondering if you had any kind of recording from the show we did about a year ago. In January? Audio or video, either one."

"Don't think so," Hannah said. "I can barely remember last week, let alone last year. But if anyone tagged the Cliff Hangar on Facebook, I liked the photos. Did you check?"

"Yeah," Daniel said. "There were a couple. But Laura and I have a bet. She says that was the show where there was a fight in the audience. But I think the fight happened at a show in the fall. The show we did in January was my birthday. So I think I'd remember if there was a fight."

"Your birthday," Hannah said. "That was right after New Year's, wasn't it? Yeah, I remember. Because Eddie flaked like he did today and I had the bar. So mostly I was doing that. And then at one point everyone started yelling, so I looked up and you two"—she gestured at them—"were kissing. Susannah walked off the stage. And usually she's the only one doing the kissing, so that's two things different. It was near the end of the set, so you two did the last song without her. Hold on a sec. Looks like they want another bottle of cat piss." Which is what Hannah called sauvignon blanc. She was a whiskey drinker.

"What was our bet for?" Laura whispered to Daniel. "Because I think I just won."

"Shut up," Daniel said. "What was I meant to say? *Hey, Hannah, remember anything weird happening the night we died?*"

"Whatever. Check out the lady on the tiger," Laura said. She couldn't help herself—she reached over and grabbed a handful of Hannah's fries from the basket, cramming them into her mouth.

Daniel had turned and was looking over to where Hannah stood waiting for the carousel steps to come around. As they did, she climbed up and walked around the painted horses until she came to the table and the tiger with the woman on its back.

"Yeah," Daniel said. "I remember her."

The carousel rotated. When the private party came around again they were looking back at Laura and Daniel. Hannah waved emphatically. "Come over," she yelled over the calliope music. "Come over and meet somebody."

"Do we want to meet somebody?" Daniel asked Laura.

"No," Laura said. "We do not. But nobody cares what we want. If that isn't obvious to you by now, it should be." She took another few fries.

"What are you doing?" Daniel said.

"She clearly wasn't going to finish them," Laura said, "and I'm starving."

"So am I," Daniel said. "But I still wouldn't eat those."

"Give yourself a prize," Laura said. She licked the greasy salt off her fingers.

Once on the carousel, Laura could see that the two people sitting at the table were at that stage of drunkenness where you didn't really have bones anymore. Like everything was now just turned to wine, all of it sloshing around inside the loose skin.

Hannah said, "This is Malo Mogge."

"Laura Hand," Laura said.

Daniel said, "Hi."

The woman on the tiger inclined her head. She wore a sleeveless yellow suede minidress and a necklace spelling out I'M WITH STUPID in cursive purple rhinestone letters attached to a thin chain. Her pointy lilac boots were definitely alligator. She wore the glossiest, pinkest lipstick Laura had ever seen. She imagined it would be sticky like cotton candy—and as chemically sweet—and as her mouth filled with saliva, the woman smiled at her. She looked like she knew exactly what Laura was thinking.

Hannah said, "I mentioned you used to play here. Ms. Mogge was wondering if you'd play something for her."

Daniel said, "Oh, dang. We don't have our instruments. You didn't bring your guitar, did you, Laura?"

"No," Laura said. "Left it in Ireland."

"You could just sing," Hannah said. "I'm sure that would be fine."

The tiger went up and down. The man put his head on the table. The calliope music went galloping on, every person on the carousel rotated in stately fashion around its orbit, and all the while Malo Mogge's eyes remained on Laura and Daniel.

"There's music on already," Daniel said. Laura glanced over, although she really didn't need to. Like his voice, his face was full of unhappiness.

"I wish you'd sing something," Hannah said.

Daniel said, "I don't see any point to this." He went over to the edge of the carousel and jumped off. But Laura stayed where she was.

There was a martial feeling in her breast. She was displeased to be, once again, in the presence of a person who she suspected was not a person at all. Malo Mogge! What kind of name was that? You might as well call yourself Bad Intention Reptile Shoes. Laura was annoyed this curvy and improbable person was asking something of her when Laura did not understand why they were asking it. And she was angry with herself that she wanted, very badly, to sing.

"Any song in particular?" she said.

The tiger, varnished black snarl and chipped red tongue, came down the pole. The lady on its back said, "Surprise me."

Laura shut her eyes so she wouldn't have to see Malo Mogge's face. Sometimes it was better not to see the faces of your audience. Not to see what was before you. It was one thing to imagine your future and another thing entirely to be told what your life would be. Its limits. The last time she'd sung here, she'd died. She'd had a guitar strap around her neck. Susannah had been here. She hadn't known there were places without doors. She thought of that place and sang. She thought of Susannah.

WHEN THE SONG was done, Laura's eyes opened. Her ribs were aching, her throat scraped raw. She had the sensation she'd been shouting at the top of her lungs for hours. But she hadn't been. The man's head was still on the table. A strand of drool glued his lower lip to the tablecloth. Light was still streaming through the windows and "The Blue Danube" still played.

"Well," Hannah said at last, when no one else spoke. "How about that? That was really something. Wasn't it?"

"Fuck, yeah," the woman at the table said. She finished the wine in her glass and picked up the new bottle Hannah had brought. But that bottle, too, was empty.

Malo Mogge, descending, said, "Childish nonsense. I was expecting something more."

But Laura saw her grip on the pommel of the tiger's saddle, how her knuckles were white.

"I'm out of practice," Laura said. "Next time maybe you'll be more impressed."

By the time she had gotten off the carousel, Daniel was already outside. She saw he'd unchained both bikes. "Come on," he said. "Let's get out of here."

"That was kind of amazing," Laura said. "I was amazing. Did you hear me? Wasn't I?"

Daniel shoved her bike at her. "We came here to see if we could find out how we died. We didn't. Instead some weird lady who looks like bad news wanted a song. Which you sang for her. What's amazing about that?"

Laura said, "Oh, come on. I was good, right?"

Daniel scratched his head. He said, "You were good. You sounded like Susannah, actually. You know how she makes every song sound like a murder ballad? You sounded like that."

"Maybe Susannah sounds like *me*," Laura said, bristling a little. "Anyway, when we get home you're gonna help me write it down. The song I sang. I think it could be something good."

Daniel said, "Exactly what is it that you think you were singing?"

Laura thought about it. Some of the good feeling went away. She said, "Um. Okay, so this is a little weird, but I'm not actually sure what I was singing."

Daniel regarded her from his great height. He said, gently, "You sang 'The Lady with the Alligator Purse.'"

The Book of Hannah

As the day wore on, it became less easy to pretend that it was summer, which is what Hannah had been doing. That she was in California, rather than in Massachusetts in December. Maybe Santa Cruz. But she was on the wrong coast, and the day was already turning to night at only five P.M., which was as long as these people had rented the Cliff Hangar for. They'd paid the deposit up front, but there was still the matter of the wine. They'd drunk a lot of nice wine. Hannah had brought the bill up with the last bottle. It had never been clear to her what, exactly, these people were celebrating. At first she'd thought maybe old college friends. And then, some kind of tech start-up? Something on the kinky side. Sex robots?

Kyle was in the kitchen, setting up for the dinner crowd. Tonight was salsa dancing and a live band. It was the kind of music she actually liked. My Two Hands Both Knowe You was cute, and you could tell Laura was someone who would go places, and Susannah sure could make a lot of noise, but the kind of music they played wasn't Hannah's thing.

Marissa, who was usually front of the house, was out with the stomach flu, and Eddie wasn't answering his phone, so Hannah had handled service. That was fine with her. She'd wanted to keep an eye on these people. You never knew what evil lurked, etc. Hannah was perfectly comfortable in the role of killjoy.

The man and the woman at the table were familiar, and she thought at last she'd figured it out. The man was semiconscious, so she said to the woman, "You have a kid, right? Rented us out for a birthday party once. A few years ago?"

"A kid," the woman said, nodding. "Oh yes. Yes, we have a son. His name is Garrett."

"Garrett," Hannah said. "What's Garrett up to?"

The woman smiled. Put her hand up to cover the smile. "I have no idea," she said. "Isn't that awful?"

Hannah looked up at Malo Mogge. "Maybe I should call the three of you an Uber," she said.

"Wake up, honey," the woman at the table was saying. "She wants to know what Garrett's up to."

The man lifted his head. He saw the bill on the table. "Here," he said. "On us."

Hannah took his credit card. When she came back, he was sitting cross-legged on the edge of the carousel with his head in his hands while his wife walked alongside, urging him to just get the fuck off. They went around twice like that, and then the man stumbled off onto his hands and knees.

"Such a beautiful carousel," his wife said. Their peculiar friend had wandered out on the balcony to admire the ocean. "Garrett had such a good time on his birthday. He loved the airplanes. Whoosh! Such a beautiful carousel. So unusual! Wolves and rabbits. So many wolves."

"Horses," Hannah said automatically. "Six horses and two tigers. Mary and Martha." But when she turned to look at the carousel, she saw she was wrong. It was rabbits and wolves. Six white wolves and two black rabbits.

"What just happened?" she asked. "How did you do that?" She wasn't asking the man on his knees. Not his wife. Those two had never done anything remotely interesting in their entire lives, she was pretty sure about that, except bring the woman in the purple boots here. What kind of name was Malo Mogge, anyway? "Put them back. Hey! You hear me? Six horses! Two tigers!"

As soon as the words left her mouth, she thought, I have made a very bad mistake. Malo Mogge was turning to look at her. The air around Hannah grew so thick with her mistake she found she could no longer move. She could not do anything at all. She could only look at Malo Mogge as she left the balcony.

The carousel went round, and the wolves chased the rabbits. The rabbits held goblets between their paws, the wolves' eyes were coins. Knives were clenched between their teeth.

Malo Mogge disappeared behind the carousel, counterclockwise to the wolves and rabbits. The wife was fumbling in her purse. Looking for a car key, maybe. Hannah tried to speak, to ask for help. But she could not move and she could not speak. The man on the floor was still on all fours, grimacing at something just over Hannah's shoulder.

"Such a shame," the wife said. She dumped her purse out on the floor, and there were the keys. "It was such a good day, too. Everyone was having such a good time."

"Not me," Malo Mogge said at Hannah's back. She was much too close. Hannah had the sensation that behind her was not so much a person as an immense and very old thing. A mountain wreathed in clouds. A crevasse at the very bottom of the ocean. Out of the corner of her eye, she could see just the knife-tip of a boot.

The voice behind her said peevishly, "I wasn't the one who made them change. But if you like, I'll see what I can do. In return for your hospitality."

"Six horses," Hannah got out. When she had been a little girl, she'd had everything she ever wanted. A mother and a father who loved her. Friends at school. A carousel of her own. Six horses and two tigers. "Two tigers."

"Two tigers I can do," Malo Mogge said.

And then the air around Hannah was pressing her down, stretching her and reshaping her until she was on her hands and knees just like the man had been. She opened her mouth to scream, her jaw stretching wider than it ought to have, every hair on her muzzle bristling. A roar came out instead.

The wife said, "What a pretty tiger! Is it tame? Can I pet it?"

Malo Mogge said, "Do as you like. Only don't ask me for new fingers. Go let it out."

The woman did as instructed while Malo Mogge regarded the tiger. She crouched, holding out her hand, palm up. Ran her palm over its skull, its long silken flank. The tiger lashed its tail. When the door was open, it sprang up and went running through, out and into the dusk.

"Don't close it yet," Malo Mogge told the woman. And here, through the swinging door to the kitchen, came a second tiger who had, only a few minutes before, been a short-order cook in his forties named Kyle. The tiger snarled at Garrett's parents. But when Malo Mogge snapped her fingers, he went out through the entrance like a shot.

The man on the floor stood, heavily. Tigers were so much more graceful. "Shall we?" he said. And held out his arm to Malo Mogge.

The Book of Daniel

At bedtime, Daniel was in demand. Davey and Oliver shared one bedroom and Lissy and Dakota and Carousel were in another, so there was the question of which room got Daniel at eight P.M. and which room was going to make do with a parent. Never mind that thirteen and ten were plenty old enough to put yourself to bed. It was, Daniel supposed, that he'd been away. Everyone wanted to be babied just a little.

His mom suggested a coin flip and the girls won. The boys would get Daniel the night after. But even with that sorted out, there was still the question of who got to choose what Daniel would read. Davey and Oliver, though they had lost the coin toss, wished Daniel to know that Davey currently preferred books about dinosaurs and Oliver liked Sandra Boynton. Who didn't like Sandra Boynton? Or dinosaurs?

Dakota lost the second coin toss to Lissy; then Carousel flipped and Lissy called. Lissy won but said graciously, "You can pick, Carousel. If you want."

They'd already brushed their teeth. Lissy's and Dakota's pajamas had white rabbits on them. Carousel was wearing an old pair that had been either Lissy's or Dakota's. Probably Dakota's, because Lissy was harder on her clothes. That, of course, was the tragedy of being a younger sibling. Even if you won a coin toss now and then, most of your outfits would be hand-me-downs.

Daniel tried to remember which book he and Carousel had been reading before he died. *Runaway Ralph*? Or had it been folktales? Here on the shelf was *The People Could Fly*. No, they'd finished that.

"Tell me the story of me," Carousel said.

"What?" Daniel said.

"I want the story of how I was born," she said. "Instead of a book."

Daniel went to sit on her bed. "Okay," he said. "If that's what you want." But when he tried to begin, he found he had a lump in his throat.

Carousel prompted him. "I was three and a half months early."

"Yes," Daniel said. "You were early. You were very little. You were the size of a bag of sugar."

"A pound and a half," Lissy said. "You probably should have died."

"You had the tiniest diapers," Daniel said. "The nurses fed you with a syringe. Susannah and Laura's mother, she was your nurse in the nighttime. She called every morning so we knew whether you'd had a good night or not."

"And then one day I was big enough," Carousel said. "And I came home to be your sister."

"You're all my sisters," Daniel said. "And I love all of you very much."

"You love all of us, Davey and Oliver, too," Carousel said. She pulled him down and whispered into his ear: "But you love them all slightly less than you love me."

Daniel kissed her on the forehead, and she said, "You shouldn't have gone to Ireland."

"I know," he said. "I won't do it again."

DOWNSTAIRS HIS MOM was watching some TV show while Peter read to Davey and Oliver. The last basket of clean laundry was on the floor beside her, and she reached down and selected things to fold by touch, sorting these into various piles, only needing to look sometimes to see what belonged to whom. She smiled and patted the small piece of couch unoccupied by her neat stacks and said, "Want to watch?"

"This thing about Carousel and Ms. Fish," Daniel said.

"Ugh," his mom said. "I've emailed. We'll see. Come watch bad television with me. We can start this episode over if you want. The murder weapon was a poisoned hair dryer!"

"I was going to walk down to the beach," Daniel said.

"Poor old Fart," his mom said. "He loved it when you took him." And then: "Have you seen Susannah since you got home?"

"No," he said.

"Ruth's worried about her," his mom said. "Who turns down a free scholarship in Ireland?"

"Susannah, apparently," Daniel said. "And nobody can ever figure out why Susannah does anything. Not even Susannah."

BUT HERE SHE was, unmistakably Susannah, sitting on a rock and singing the way sirens were supposed to. And he saw why it worked. You would hear someone singing, be curious, think you ought to wander over. See what she wanted from you. An apology? An audience, company, an explanation? Give her what she asked for. Wasn't that how it ought to be? Hadn't it always been like that? Only when Daniel said Susannah's name did he see the dog at her feet. It showed all its teeth, snarling.

Not a dog.

"Thomas?" Susannah said.

Who was Thomas? Daniel picked up a handful of sand and pebbles and threw it at the dog. It wasn't a dog, was it? It sure as hell wasn't Thomas, whoever that was. "Scram!" he said. "Leave her alone!"

"What the fuck?" Susannah said.

The white dog—Bogomil—shook itself, scattering sand. Now it looked as if it were laughing, white head cocked and ears up playfully.

"That's not a dog," Daniel said. Realizing how this sounded, he said, "You don't know whose dog it is."

"How do you know what I know?" Susannah said. "How do you know I didn't get a dog while you were gone?"

"What's its name?" Daniel said. And then was afraid she would say it.

Susannah stared at him and then at the dog. "This is ridiculous," she said. "It's just some dog."

"Exactly," Daniel said. "You don't know where it came from. It could be vicious. It could have rabies."

The dog yawned and then began to amble away, slowly, in the direction of the sand dunes.

"Clearly!" Susannah said.

"Who's Thomas?" Daniel said. Bogomil was now just a white plume of tail above a rise of sand. What was Daniel supposed to do here? Mr. Anabin had said this would be a game, and clearly it *was* a kind of game to Bogomil. Bogomil appeared to be enjoying himself a great deal, but Daniel wanted to throw up.

"Thomas is a *friend*," Susannah said. Her face was a closed door. "Not that it's any of your business."

When Daniel didn't reply, Susannah's face changed again. Now she just looked miserable. "Anyway, welcome home. Thanks for saving me from the very scary dog. See you around." She scooped up her shoes and without putting them on began to walk up to the road.

Over in the dunes, Bogomil might be waiting. Or he could be swiftly running, black pads throwing up sand. There was a way you could go through the dunes that took you up to Little Moon Street. You could wait there for someone walking home in the dark.

Daniel said, "Wait! I'll come with you."

She didn't stop or even slow down, so he jogged after her. Caught up and then walked alongside her. She said nothing. Her hair was down around her face. She and Laura both did this. Hid in plain sight. They weren't as different as they wanted you to believe. He kept stealing glances at her, but the only piece of her face showing was her nose.

How he had missed her nose. Bogomil could have been behind any tree or bush, but suddenly all Daniel could think about was Susannah's nose. And all the rest of her, the parts he couldn't see. Had he felt this way before he'd died? Yes. He thought maybe he had.

He said, "I missed you. When I was in Ireland."

The nose disappeared entirely. She began to walk faster. They were going to arrive home much too soon, and home wasn't really any safer than anywhere else. Bogomil had made that clear. Once again, Daniel entertained the fantasy of hitching a ride out to California. But that was what Susannah's dad had done, wasn't it? More or less.

"So your dad's back," he said.

Susannah said nothing.

"That's got to be weird," Daniel said finally, and Susannah's head jerked once in agreement.

"Like this," Daniel said. "This is weird, too, isn't it?"

"Yes," Susannah said. "This is weird, too."

Daniel said, "I'm sorry. I don't know how not to make it weird."

"Maybe I should have gone to Ireland," Susannah said finally. "Then this wouldn't be so weird now. Right?" But she still wouldn't look at him.

"No," Daniel said. "It's good you didn't." He said it without thinking, and then they were home and he wished Bogomil would just leap out of the oleander bush and eat him because, dear God, that had been a stupid thing to say.

Susannah fled up the steps of her house and was inside, the door slamming shut, before he even thought to say anything else. And when Daniel got to his house, Bogomil was there, leaning against the screen door. This time he was a man.

The Book of the Second Night

No one slept well. Save Bowie, asleep in a strange bed. He no longer looked entirely like his namesake, although the face he wore still had a starved look to it. His hair was still blond, but his nose was longer, less sharp. One eye still blue but the other was now green, though he did not know this. He had a small scar on his chin. He was still handsome but more conventionally so. He knew none of this, though if he had seen his face in a mirror, he would have found it hauntingly familiar.

Bowie had spent the first half of his first day watching people. Everything he saw was of great interest to him. At first, he, too, seemed to be of great interest to people. But over the course of the morning, he learned how to tell them otherwise. I am no one, he told them. There is nothing here to wonder about. There is nothing here. He found he could do this, too, with various items, bottles that had sweet drinks in them. Bread and meat wrapped in a kind of clear cloth one punctured easily with a fingernail. People sat down beside him on his bench, then left behind their belongings. They'd forgotten them entirely.

In the afternoon, he began to experiment. He let people see him again. He selected individuals, drew them into conversation. When he grew bored or hungry, he let them forget him again. In this way, some time passed and he learned many things about the world and the people who lived in it now. Then Bowie became aware that someone was watching him.

Bowie was on the main thoroughfare of the town. He'd found another bench across from an establishment where people came and went, carrying out food and drink. Many of them, after they encountered Bowie, went away empty-handed but untroubled. It had been such a long time since he'd had a mouth. A stomach. A body.

The person watching him was inside. At first he was not sure who it was, and then through the window he saw a boy at a table. They were perhaps thirty feet from each other. The boy looked at Bowie, and as Bowie looked back, he was riven through as if struck by a mortal blow. In that moment, he was blown into nothingness. There was no Bowie at all. Only thousands and thousands of white moths. They sailed away on the warm air, scattering through the town of Lovesend, the beaches, the Cliffs, the parks, and all the empty places.

WHEN BOWIE CAME back to himself, he was once more in the park where he'd woken up in the early morning. Now his leather jacket was white and his silk scarf was black.

The day was growing dark. A woman not much older than he was talking on her phone. She had a baby in a kind of sling printed with pink skulls and bones across her chest. When she saw Bowie in her path, she gasped and dropped her phone. Bowie picked it up and gave it back to her. He said, "Take me somewhere I can rest."

And she did.

ON THE PORCH, before Daniel could speak, Bogomil said, "You may be wondering why I called this meeting." This time he was not dressed as the Mayor. Instead he had on jeans and a black T-shirt. Daniel could have sworn that the shirt and jeans were his, but if that were true, how did they not swallow up Bogomil?

"Meeting?" Daniel said.

"Kidding," Bogomil said. He peeled himself away from the door. A clot of darkness moving in a queasy wash of darkness. That white, knowing face. Bogomil went over to the porch swing. Picked up a stack of comic books and dropped them on the porch.

"Come and sit," he said.

"No," Daniel said. He looked at the door, wondering if he could get through it before Bogomil snatched him away.

"Suit yourself," Bogomil said indifferently. "Isn't free will great. Choose your own miserable path. And I shall hear, though soft you tread, et cetera, et cetera. I'm sure it will go somewhere interesting."

"Why were you with Susannah?" Daniel said. "Why did you pretend to be Fart?"

Bogomil sat down on the swing, pulled his feet up so no part of him was touching the porch. Other than that, he made no movement. The swing remained still. Everything was perfectly still and yet Daniel felt a sense of vertigo so great he had to grab the porch railing. Lean against it.

He said, "What do you want?"

"What do I want!" Bogomil said. "How much time do you have, Daniel?"

How terrible it was to have his name in Bogomil's mouth. Daniel said, "Stay away from Susannah."

"No," Bogomil said. "I have plans for her. But don't worry. I have plans for you, too. In any case, that's not why I'm here. I came here to give you a piece of advice, Daniel."

"I can guess," Daniel said. "We shouldn't trust Mr. Anabin." The night was growing cooler but sweat ran down his back. He could smell his own fear. Bogomil's ill will. Bogomil's pleasure in Daniel's fear.

"Trust Anabin or don't trust Anabin," Bogomil said. That white face moved forward in the darkness and then receded. It was hypnotic. Was the swing moving? No. But still Bogomil came closer, was nearer. And then sank farther into darkness. "Be foolish or be cunning. Do your best or do nothing at all. It makes no difference to me. Anabin is Anabin. You know him now. There are dangers closer to hand, my Daniel. Do you think any of this is happening by accident?"

"What does that mean?" Daniel said.

Bogomil said, "I was not the only stranger in your house last night. And you are not the only one in your house who is in peril."

"Are you threatening my family?" Daniel said. "Because I will kill you. If you hurt Susannah, I will kill you. You understand?" He tried to step forward, to go to Bogomil so he could smash him, so he could get his hands around that white neck, but he could not move.

Bogomil got up from the swing. He came to Daniel since Daniel could not come to him. The night grew colder. The door of his house was closed against him. Daniel saw only Bogomil. He saw how small he seemed to Bogomil.

Bogomil said, "Do you think you could kill me, my Daniel?" He looked up at Daniel with enormous, calm interest.

Daniel swallowed twice before he could speak. "No," he said. "But that wouldn't stop me from trying."

"Brave Daniel," Bogomil said. "Foolish Daniel. I wish you a restful sleep, my Daniel. No one in your household is in danger from me this night. One more piece of advice. Don't believe anything my dear friend Anabin says. Tell Susannah nothing. And beware the greedy moon."

"That's three pieces of advice," Daniel said.

"True," Bogomil said. "But not all of them are useful." And then he went down the steps of the porch. Before he had reached the lawn, he was a dog again. The clothes he left in an untidy heap for Daniel to claim. They were his clothes after all, the right size once more, but now they stank of Bogomil. Someone would have to wash them. To see if that stink would come out. But then, Bogomil knew Daniel. Daniel was an older sibling. He was used to cleaning up after others.

MO SPENT THE evening with Jenny looking through his grandmother's correspondence files. Mo cried a few times, but there were some amazing things, too. His grandmother had been pen pals with *everyone*. There were letters from so many other writers, and it was clear they all adored his grandmother. There was gossip, there were complaints about editors, publishers, tours, Goodreads reviews. Mo knew a lot of the correspondents. Their books were on the shelves in his grandmother's library: Beverly Jenkins, Leticia Peoples, Nora Roberts, Zane, Laura Kinsale, Sandra Kitt, Alyssa Cole, even Michelle Obama. "If we published a book of these," Jenny said, "The whole industry would go up in flames." There was a paper clip holding two pieces of fan mail together. One said, *TOO*

MUCH SEX IN THESE BOOKS, NO ONE HAS THIS MUCH SEX. The other: *Tell your publisher to stop marketing these as romance, please, if you aren't going to have any real sex scenes.* There was an envelope from some charity auction with a receipt and a gorgeous square of embroidery with female peacocks, cardinals, wrens, veeries flocking around the phrase TRANS WOMEN ARE WOMEN with a note stuck on it saying *To take to framers.*

"I'll do that," Jenny said, setting it aside.

Mo's grandmother had been in the habit of printing out her own emails for her files, too. In one she'd written, *So many questions, always, about Lavender Glass, her beauty, whether she is more beautiful than another character, or less. Nearly as many as questions concerning redemption, UGH. All the describing I must do in the books, over and over, I wonder sometimes what readers would think if I were to give the Glass Lass a cold sore all through one book. A sebaceous cyst on her forehead. Imagine! But there are conventions to all genres, I suppose, and beauty remains a marker of worth in the genre I have loved all my life. I have come to believe, though, that beauty is not so much a quality as it is rather a temporary state through which we transit, as if stepping in and out of a sunlit room. How tiring to have to be beautiful at all times, to remain only in that one room. Much like happiness, I suppose, though the happy ending must be more like a house into which we romance writers move our characters and all their baggage and boxes when at last we're done with them. Poor Lavender Glass, the happy ending just always over another hill. In real life, of course, happiness is a room, too, like beauty. If we're lucky we stumble through its doors every now and then.* She'd highlighted this in yellow, written *Use?*

Mo said, "She said that to me once, but it wasn't about beauty. It was about love. I asked her why she wasn't married when all of her books were about love, love, love. She said romantic love, the kind she wrote about, was just one room and there were lots of others. So then I asked her why she didn't write other kinds of books, and she said it was a very beautiful room and anyway it paid the bills. And then laughed and laughed."

"God, I miss her," Jenny said.

Mo wiped his face with his sleeve. His grandmother had said something else to him, too. She'd said lucky people found the work they were meant to do. Unlucky people found love.

There were a few letters she'd apparently never sent, one to someone Mo didn't know, probably some baby writer. His grandmother was commiserating over language, over how terrible all the words were for body parts and how fast you used them up. Rod, manliness, womanliness, soft mounds, staff, nub, pleasure bud, stiff peaks. All terrible, his grandmother agreed. But, she wrote, you wouldn't believe how bad the contemporary slang was, either. Sugar stick, cranny hunter, fornicating engine, plug tale. That was just the penis. Cat heads or Cupid's Kettledrums for breasts. For the vagina you had names like tuzzy muzzy, dumb glutton, crinkum crankum, Venerable Monosyllable. "What?" Mo said.

There was another letter she'd only just begun. *I hope you'll come see me soon. We have so much to catch up on!*

That's as far as she got.

Now Mo is in his bedroom, sitting in his window seat, face turned to the dark street. He has a Caitlynn Hightower novel in his lap. He isn't reading it. But it's the first one his grandmother ever dedicated to him. So it's special. He was seven when she wrote it. She put a Black pirate captain in it for him. He holds the book in his lap and looks out the window and waits. He has a new theory about the figure who stood and beckoned. He has a hope. I hope you'll come see me soon! So he waits and waits longer, and, still waiting, without meaning to, he falls into a restless sleep. In his sleep, he throws up an arm to ward off the terrible thing that is coming and the book slides off his lap and onto the floor. He wakes with a start, looks out his window.

The world is dark, and the street is dark. It takes time for his eyes to pick out the person who is standing there. Like last time, they are perfectly motionless. They are looking up. Longing emanates from them.

Mo raises his hand and waves tentatively. He feels like an idiot. But his heart is welling up.

Down on the street below, the figure waves back.

Come up! Mo beckons. Come up to me!

The figure beckons him down. Come down to me.

So Mo goes down.

I hope that you

oh
please oh I
oh I hope

SUSANNAH CAME IN from the beach feeling all sorts of things. Chief among them, a kind of white-hot fury so luxurious she could have wrapped it around herself like a cashmere blanket. Kissing a boy in the bathroom at What Hast Thou Ground? had been extremely enjoyable, but what were small pleasures like a stranger's lips on your neck compared to the hate she felt for Daniel Knowe?

Her mother, still wearing her scrubs, was in the kitchen eating peaches out of a can. She said, "Your father gave Laura flowers to give me."

Susannah looked. There were the flowers on the counter. Gladiolas and pink daisies. Ruth went on, "Is he for real?" And laughed and shook her head.

And here was Laura in the living room, with her crabby old acoustic. Susannah listened to Laura tune the Harmony, and the cloud of her anger began to seep away. Not until this moment had she realized how much she'd been missing Laura. Had she really missed her horrible sister this much? But she had. It was as if some piece of herself had been returned to Susannah with the restoration of Laura. And how good it had been to be angry with Daniel not in Ireland, but Daniel face-to-face.

She went and curled up on the other end of the sectional couch and listened to Laura play. In a little while their mother came into the room, and there was room on the couch between Laura and Susannah for her as well.

Ruth leaned her head against Susannah's shoulder, her eyes closed, and Susannah closed her eyes, too. Laura played song after song. You could hear in her playing what she'd learned in Ireland. Susannah should have gone. Not to learn anything, even. Just to see what it was like there, a place that wasn't Lovesend. And then she thought of Daniel again and made up her mind not to think at all. She could just sit on the couch with her mother and sister and listen to what Laura was saying with her guitar. Hello, dear sister. Dear sister, hello. I'm home. I'm home. Don't be angry, Susannah. Dear sister, I've come home.

They all went up to bed long after midnight. Ruth had to be woken up. "My girls," she said. And kissed them on their foreheads as if they were children, though she had to draw down Susannah's face to do it.

"You want the bathroom first?" Susannah said, unsure whether she was being generous or just too lazy to get up just yet. The couch was so very comfortable.

"Go ahead," Laura said. She was looking at her phone.

But Susannah had been thinking about some things all night long. And here was Laura, and you could always count on Laura to be honest about telling you how badly you'd fucked up. "Are you and Daniel friends with Mo now?"

"Yeah," Laura said. But she wouldn't quite look at Susannah. Which meant it was worse than Susannah had thought. "He's pretty cool."

It figured. Laura had Ireland and Daniel, and now she had Mo, too. "Is he okay? It sucks about his grandmother."

"He's okay," Laura said. "I mean, he's as okay as you'd expect." But she still wouldn't look at Susannah, and so Susannah went on.

"I should have emailed him," she said. "When she died. But I couldn't figure out what to say and so I guess I never said anything."

Laura put her phone down and folded her hands in her lap. "I don't really think he wants to talk about it."

"Yeah," Susannah said. "That makes sense." And then guiltily remembered that Laura might be sad about Mo's grandmother, too. She blurted out, "I know you really liked her books. So, sorry!" And then, before Laura could say something snippy, she got off the couch and went upstairs.

When Susannah was finished in the bathroom, she knocked on the connecting door to let Laura know she was done. Then she lay in her bed, listening to her sister take a shower. Afterward Laura slid the pocket door open and came into Susannah's dark room, smelling of her disgusting face cream. She stood in the bathroom doorway, arms crossed, and said, "Don't you miss it at all? Making music?"

Susannah thought about it. "No," she said. "I don't miss it at all." She was pleased with how she sounded as she said it. Mo, music, Daniel. She had moved on to smaller and more achievable projects. Like cleaning bathrooms and then making out in them with carefully selected customers.

"I don't believe you," her sister said.

Susannah pulled the blanket over her head. But did Laura take the hint? No, she sat down on the bed and said, "Sorry I was such a bitch last night. I was really jet-lagged."

Susannah stayed under the covers. She said, "It's fine. We're cool."

Laura said, "Clearly it isn't fine. You're not fine. Look at you. You going to spend the rest of your life making coffee and stripping beds at the Seasick Blues? Living here? With Mom?"

"Maybe," Susannah said. "What do you care?"

"I care because you're my sister!" Laura said. There was a strange quaver in her voice. Like this actually mattered to her. She said, "And one of us, at least, ought to go out and live their life."

"What the fuck are you talking about?" Susannah said, exasperated. "That's you. You're the one who's out there living their life. Good for you. Meanwhile, stay out of my business. Like, you think you can come home and, oh hey, poor Susannah, let's get her sorted out over the holidays before you and Daniel go back to Ireland?"

Laura was silent. Susannah lay there stewing until Laura said, "I'm not sure if I'm going back to Ireland or not. But either way, I'm going to keep on your ass until you quit moping around and figure out what your plan is. Consider it this year's Christmas present."

Susannah bit the blanket so she wouldn't scream. "Why wouldn't you go back?" she said.

Laura said, "Well, you know. Ireland's great, but I guess I missed this place. I missed my old life. You and Ruth. Even my poor old Harmony."

Again, there was something in her voice that troubled Susannah. Although, wasn't this typical Laura? Let's ignore all my little old problems, my medium-sized issues, and the large, obvious ones, too, because Susannah is the real catastrophe, am I right? There was a twinge in Susannah's heel; it had been there all day but was so negligible she kept forgetting it was there. She concentrated on the little ache because that way she didn't have to think about what to say to Laura. She knew if she said anything, Laura would just pounce on her again.

Laura said, "Also your blanket smells. Your whole room smells funky. When was the last time you washed your sheets?"

Susannah stayed still and quiet. I am at the bottom of a pond, she thought. A smelly pond.

At last Laura said, "Good night, Susannah," and when Susannah didn't say anything to that, either, she got off the bed and Susannah heard the connecting door to the bathroom close again. She resisted the impulse to chase after Laura and continue the fight. They would just both end up shouting and then Ruth would wake up, and Susannah already knew whose side Ruth would be on. And anyway, Laura was only here for the winter break. Susannah could wait her out. Susannah curled on her side and wiped furiously at her face. Why she was crying, she didn't even know.

Sometime much later, she woke up in darkness as someone climbed into her bed. "Laura?" she said.

Someone said, "No. Sorry. It's me."

Daniel.

Susannah said, "What are you doing here? Get out!"

"Davey's in my bed again," Daniel said. Susannah's mattress remembered Daniel. It sagged under the extraordinary burden of him. "Let me stay, Susannah. I just want to sleep."

There had once been a time when Daniel slept over at the Hands' house and no one found it strange. They were little then. Later, there had been nights when he used the Hands' spare key and snuck into Susannah's room to get high and laugh at horror movies. Or they ended up in Laura's room, watching band documentaries and eating grilled cheese sandwiches. Not that long ago there had been nights when Daniel woke Susannah up by kissing her neck or her toes or whatever part of her wasn't under the blankets. Right now, oh right now, it was as if everything was the way it had always been. Wouldn't that have been nice? Oh, it was nice. And after all, Susannah could go back to being angry with him in the morning. She decided he could stay.

She said, "I have to be at the coffee shop at seven thirty. You better be gone when I wake up. And I'm going to put on something. You can sleep here but not if I'm naked."

"Here," Daniel said. He sat up and took off his T-shirt, handed it to her. She put it on under the covers and then turned on her side, glad not to be able to see him.

Daniel turned on his side, too. She couldn't see him, but she felt the warmth of his breath on her ear, the warmth of his body where they did not quite touch. She really ought to get out of bed and put on underwear.

"I missed you," he said.

Susannah said, "Turn over."

So Daniel turned on his other side, and Susannah turned over, too. She put her palm against Daniel's long back, ran it down his spine. He shivered but didn't move. Good. It wasn't an invitation. His Dickies jeans were coarse against her bare legs. Susannah put her arm around Daniel's rib cage and tucked her knees into the back of his knees. She found his hand with her fingers.

Daniel said, "Susannah—"

"Shut up," she said. And was relieved when he did not say anything else. There was just the sound of his breathing as it came into time with her own breathing, the rise and fall of his chest, the warmth of his broad back against her face. They fell asleep holding hands.

They slept so deeply that if, as they slept, there had been a thing like a white dog trotting up and down the upstairs hall, they would not have heard it. Even when it stopped just outside Susannah's bedroom door and lay down with its head on its paws, they did not wake. They slept and the dog outside Susannah's door slept, too.

But Laura's sleep was troubled. She was so very hungry.

OH, NEEDY HEART.

Daniel dreamed the most astonishing dream. His brothers and sisters were secure and happy and grew up loved and loving and successful. They had everything they needed. Their achievements were noted, their endeavors rewarded. They had children of their own, and Daniel's parents were frequent visitors, as happy as their children and their grandchildren. There was no lasting shadow. But Daniel was not with them in this dream. He was elsewhere. In other places. He opened a door and went back and forth upon the earth. He had great powers at his command and had many marvelous adventures. He was much admired and (feared) celebrated, and if there was a thing he wanted, he stretched out his hand and (took it) it was his. Although he was often lonely, he understood that this loneliness was the cost of his ascension and this cost was not too much to bear. And though he was alone, so alone he could almost not bear it, sometimes in his moments of greatest loneliness he sensed there was another with him. Susannah was with him, although Susannah, too, was changed. They were bound together in some way for all the remainder of time. In Daniel's dream, he and Susannah went on together through the door and through all of eternity, and because Susannah was with him, he could bear it. He could not bear it. He went on.

IN FIFTH GRADE, Susannah had made two new friends. One was a boy in her math class, Mo Gorch. He was a year younger but advanced. Mo had lots of friends already. Susannah had Laura and Daniel. But there had been a Friday when both Laura and Daniel were at home with chicken pox. Susannah had been sent to the principal's office for painting a pair of eyes on the back of Mr. Ditmar's bald head (when he fell asleep during art) and now she was free again. There were only twenty minutes left of geometry, so what was the point in even going? She snuck into the auditorium and sat on the stage in the dark before the grand piano. She began to play a song that had been stuck in her head for the past few days.

It was unclear to her whether this was a song that had already existed and she was trying to remember or whether it was a song in the process of making itself inside her head. But she felt being alone in the dark would help her figure it out. You didn't have to feel bad about playing the wrong keys if you couldn't see them in the first place. It didn't matter if there wasn't sheet music. And if there were words, she didn't know them, but there was the illuminated red of the exit sign. "Exit" was a satisfying word, and so that was what she sang, very softly.

The darkness of the auditorium had an echoing, listening quality, as if the space might have been full of the sort of people who would be most interested in and encouraging of the thing you were trying to do.

Still, it had been a surprise when a voice had said from the front row of seats, "Go on. That's interesting."

Susannah had almost fallen off the piano bench. "Who's there?" she said.

"Mo," the voice said. "Mohammed Gorch."

It turned out Mo, like Susannah, was having a not-good day. At lunch, Timothy Norris had called him a fag. Said Mo had been staring at him in the locker room.

"As if I would," Mo said. "No one will ever check out Norris. I hear his guinea pig averts his gaze whenever Norris gets undressed. I hear once he was scheduled for his yearly checkup but instead his pediatrician called his mom and said he was sure Norris was in perfectly good health and they didn't need to come in."

"Nice," Susannah said in the dark. She could hear Mo settle back into his seat.

"Anyway," he said, "keep playing. It's cheering me up."

"You like it?" Susannah said.

"No," Mo said. "But it's cheering me up."

After that, some of the time they were friends, even though Mo was younger. Some of the time they talked about music. Mo didn't have anyone else to talk about music with because his mother was dead. And Susannah didn't know anyone who talked about music the way Mo did.

She made the second friend later that year. The second friend was not exactly real. She only ever saw him in dreams. Sometimes he was a wolf and sometimes he was a man. The man was so handsome she felt a little bad for him. It looked like it hurt. She liked the wolf better. Sometimes he changed her into a wolf, too, and they ran through a dark forest, chasing little things. Sometimes they were both rabbits, and they ran from something that was both terrifying and exhilarating. As the rabbit, she longed to be caught. If the thing that was chasing them ever caught her, she would be ready. Something would happen and then she would be changed forever. It was like a song. You knew the shape of it by how it began. You knew the ending, but also you didn't know it, because you could improvise the ending as you went on. A song went on if you wanted it to.

Her friend the wolf promised her when she was older, he would teach her all the things he knew. She would be able to run in the dark forever. She would be like him.

This friend's name was Bogomil.

The dreams were infrequent by the time Susannah was in high school, although she had them still. She no longer believed Bogomil was real, but what did that matter? He belonged to her dreams and her dreams belonged to her. But then Laura and Daniel and Mo had gone to Ireland, and Susannah had not, and the dreams had stopped. She'd felt almost superstitious about this, as if somehow her imaginary friend was disappointed in her.

But now Laura and Daniel and Mo were home again and Susannah (holding Daniel's hand in hers) was fast asleep and here was Bogomil in her dream again. No doubt it was the encounter with the dog on the beach. Her brain had seized upon the white dog and given her back her old dream.

She bent down to wrap her arms around the wolf's neck. He smelled like a bonfire. "Bad Bogomil," she said. "Where have you been?"

"Be quiet," the wolf said.

And then Susannah became a wolf, too, and she and Bogomil were both in the forest.

THE WOMAN WITH the baby had a car, but Bowie did not want to ride in it. "Here," she said, offering him the keys. But Bowie did not want to drive, either. He did not want any part of the car.

"We could walk," the woman said. "But I don't really know how long it will take. I'm over in Silverside."

"Take the car," Bowie said. "I'll follow you."

The woman looked doubtful, but she did as Bowie suggested. He had not particularly enjoyed being thousands of moths, and it had taken some time to reassemble himself afterward. So he became a gull instead. And then a person again once the woman's car had stopped in front of a tall building.

She did not seem surprised this time to see Bowie become himself. The baby again was asleep on her chest. It had a plump, discontented face, as if it had tasted enough of the world already and knew how disappointing its life would be.

Bowie followed the sleeping baby and its mother up an outdoor stair onto a long breezeway. The woman said, "If I had known I was going to have company, I would have cleaned up some."

Bowie said, "It doesn't matter."

They passed many doors, and as they went by, each one opened behind them, although neither Bowie nor the woman nor the baby noticed. At last the woman stopped in front of one.

Bowie did not particularly want to go through this door or any door at all, but neither did he want to be outside. Ever since he'd seen the boy looking through the window at him, he had felt the need to be hidden away. Though, how could anyone here know him? He didn't even know himself.

He said, "Can I come in?"

The woman said, "Of course you can. You can have whatever you want. What do you want?"

"I want food," Bowie said. "I want something to eat."

"It's lucky I love to cook, then," the woman said. "I've always wanted to be on one of those shows. A baking one, or the kind where somebody yells at you that you're doing it all wrong but then finally you cook something and it comes out tasting better than anyone thought it could. Sometimes I plan out a whole dish and imagine I'm making it on TV and everyone who's watching wishes they could try it. Do you have any favorite foods? Are you vegetarian?"

"I eat everything," Bowie said.

HE ATE LEFTOVER fish pie while the woman made an omelet with herbs and three different kinds of cheese. She made him drop biscuits with homemade jam and heated up a Hungry-Man Salisbury Steak in the microwave. Bowie ate a gallon of chocolate ice cream and two packages of bread.

The baby woke up and began to cry. The woman said apologetically, "I ought to feed him."

She was making a stir-fry with rhubarb, hot dogs, and canned tomatoes because Bowie had eaten almost everything else.

He said, "Give me the baby."

"His diaper needs changing," the woman said. "And I really ought to heat him up a bottle."

The baby was screaming as she gave it to Bowie. It was heavier than

Bowie had expected, its limbs rigid with anger and frustration. Its face was wet with tears.

Bowie put his face close to the baby's face. "Stop crying," he said. And the baby, astonished, stopped crying. Its cheeks were chapped and bright red, its wrists creased with fat. Its fingers were glazed with saliva.

"You have a real way with babies," the woman said. She brought over a plate of the stir-fry and then began to warm up a bottle of formula in a pan, testing the water with her finger. But when the bottle of milk was ready, it was Bowie who drank it. The baby watched and did not cry.

When at last Bowie was no longer hungry, he got up from the table. The woman said, "You should go clean up. Give me your clothes and I'll wash them."

"Clean up?" Bowie said.

"You smell awful. When was the last time you had a bath? I'll run a bubble bath," she said. "Peppermint bath oil or rose vanilla?"

"Not rose," Bowie said. "The other." And so she ran him a bath and he stayed in it, full and drowsy and warm, until his clothes were dry again. His body was strange to him but also familiar. He felt a kind of tenderness for it, the same tenderness he had felt toward the baby. As if he'd been entrusted with something that had once mattered to someone. He listened through the bathroom door, which was not fully shut, as the baby was given its own bottle and fell asleep in its crib while the woman hummed an unfamiliar song. Afterward, she read a magazine article about making the most of a small living space, then played *Candy Crush* on her phone and did not even remember there was a boy in her bathtub until the dryer went off and the baby woke up crying.

After Bowie was dressed, the woman said, "It's very late. After midnight. I was going to go to sleep. Do you need anything else?"

"Do I need anything else?" Bowie asked her.

"You could take my credit card," she said. "And I think I still have a Snickers bar in my purse. Do you want it? Do you want to stay here? If you like, you can have my bed. I can sleep on the floor in the baby's room."

"I need to know who I am," Bowie said, and the woman looked distressed.

"I wish I knew," she said. Tears came to her eyes. "You know I'd do anything for you. But I've never seen you before today."

Bowie took the woman's bed. He slept deeply and dreamed of the boy in the window staring out at him. His name was Thomas. When the name Thomas came to him, Bowie shouted it. But he had become a gull, battering at the woman's bedroom window, crying out over and over until the woman woke and came into the room and, screaming at him to go away, threw the window up.

Bowie flew out. There was an hour left before dawn.

The Book of Thomas

After he'd sorted out all of Malo Mogge's complaints and reported to her the events of his day, they took their nightly drive through Lovesend. Sometimes, at Malo Mogge's request, he took the wheel of the Bugatti, but it was not something he enjoyed. He'd never quite learned to enjoy cars, neither as the driver nor, truthfully, as a passenger.

Tonight Malo Mogge drove and Thomas sat in the back reading *Us Weekly*. WHO WORE IT BEST? STARS—THEY'RE JUST LIKE US! (But the moon is quite, quite different.) Malo Mogge had the usual sorts of plans for the night. She was attending a murderer's wedding in a chalet in Zermatt, walking the red carpet as the confidante of an actor at the Mumbai launch of a musical, then running with a pack of foxes in Brittany. Every once in a while, she asked Thomas a question and he had no choice but to answer. The trick was to answer in such a way that you directed subsequent questions toward areas of safety. You didn't want her to be bored or to ask you what you thought. Steer the topic away from you, back to the things she wanted. Long ago, Thomas had realized Malo Mogge was single-minded in pursuit of what she wanted—or thought she wanted. She might want, sometimes, to be distracted, but distractions were also, eventually, irritations. But Thomas understood her single-mindedness. He was much the same.

He told Malo Mogge about the moths and about the girl in the café, the sister of the one who had come back. Anabin had been there, too, briefly, but had either not seen Thomas or else had not considered him of any interest. Every part of Thomas told the world that he was of no interest when he did not wish to be seen. He revealed himself as he chose. Though, surely, Anabin by now knew they were here, Thomas and his mistress.

Thomas let Malo Mogge mull over the moths. Like the weather, the moths were a strange thing in a time when many things were strange and would soon grow stranger. Malo Mogge discoursed upon other things she had seen, that she had been the cause of, many marvels, and then she fell silent. She was imagining the pleasures of the night that lay before her. Later she would recount these adventures and triumphs and tricks to him, whispering them in his ear as he tried to sleep.

Thomas concealed within the storehouse of himself only one portion of the day, which was the boy in the white scarf. What he had seen was not possible. A boy could turn into moths, yes, that he knew to be possible. But the boy he had seen could not be the boy he had known.

Though Thomas had lived in the world too long not to know that the impossible could be possible. Thomas himself was proof of this.

Had he seen what he had seen? His head like a cupboard crammed full of enchantments, instructed by Malo Mogge in the various costs and consequences of magic until he could have rented himself out as a kind of magic-calculating abacus, said what he had seen was not possible. But his heart said that it was. He had seen his brother, though his brother was dead.

MALO MOGGE AND Thomas had taken up residence in one of the glass-fronted modern houses that faced the ocean on a street just above the marsh at Little Moon Bay. It pleased Malo Mogge to see and to be seen, if never truly known. The house belonged to a prosperous couple from Boston who stayed there over long weekends and in the summer. They had initially been surprised to find Malo Mogge and Thomas in their home, but Malo Mogge had been so very appreciative of their taste in art and home décor, their wine cellar—Malo Mogge had been so very charming—that in the end, the couple had begged them to stay. Thomas found them dull. But they did the cooking now, and when Malo Mogge could not be troubled to go out, they watched old movies with her, or read favorite books out loud to her, played cards or hide-and-seek or whatever game she suggested. At the beginning of the summer, they had given their resignations to the law firm where they had been employed. Their ambitions were stranger now.

There was a ten-year-old son. He'd been sent to a private school in Maine. A boarding school. Malo Mogge had very little time for children. They required much more effort.

The woman's name was Giselle. Her husband was Malcolm. Malo Mogge had promised to take one of them with her to Zermatt and then on to Mumbai and Brittany. There had been some sort of contest, none of the details of which Thomas had paid much attention to. Both Giselle and Malcolm still had all of their fingers, and nothing was burnt up or broken, so there was nothing he needed to clean up or replace. Giselle had been the winner. Thomas hoped, sincerely, that she would enjoy being a fox. She was beginning to look used up. Being something other than human, even if it was only for the space of a few hours, was restorative. And it was always nice when Malo Mogge took an interest in a new friend. It meant Thomas had a night off.

In his long time of servitude to Malo Mogge, Thomas had received many gifts. Everything he required or desired was within his reach if he had patience enough. There were only two things denied him. His brother, who was lost to him. And the other, that there was no one to whom Thomas could now say "I have seen my brother" and know they would share his bewilderment, his joy, and his terror. There was only Malo Mogge, who would consume these emotions greedily and then put this information to her own uses.

There was only, eternally, Malo Mogge. For Thomas, it had been this way for more than three hundred years. He did not feel pity for Malo Mogge, but at times he understood how she had become the thing she was. Time pressed in on you from all sides and there was no door you could go through to escape what you became.

MALO MOGGE AND Giselle came downstairs, arms around each other, modeling for Thomas and Malcolm the very pretty dresses Malo Mogge had picked out. Then Malo Mogge and Giselle—feverish with excitement—went away to attend the wedding and to be admired some more. Malcolm stood at the floor-to-ceiling window in the open-plan living space, looking out at the moon and the ocean. It was a very pretty view. He wandered over to the very expensive stereo. Searched for something. He said, "Bruce Cockburn. You ever listen to his stuff?"

"No," Thomas said. Then, "Music's not really my thing. There's just so much of it."

And the president said to Kit Carson, "Take my best four horsemen please."

There was a cutting board on the kitchen island with a very good knife on it. Various ingredients. Thomas had a sudden desire to pick up the knife, draw it across Malcolm's throat, and drink from the fountain that would make. Malo Mogge could find another house. One with fewer windows for once.

Malcolm said, "I was thinking I could make eggplant Parmesan. You hungry?"

"You've made your offer sweet / I'll accept this task you've set for me."

"Starving," Thomas said. Eggplant Parmesan was almost as good as blood and made less of a mess. "But I have plans with a friend." He said good night to the disconsolate lawyer.

Thomas was humming as he went out into the night. It was another song, a different song, but still the kind of song Malcolm liked. *The desert's quiet, Cleveland's cold / and so the story ends we're told.* As if stories ever ended. And Thomas, of course, would never grow old. He thought he would go up to the Cliffs to see if the sad boy in his mansion was still awake.

The Book of the Second Morning

Susannah left the house early, headed off to What Hast Thou Ground? The porch door banged shut and Laura woke up with a shout. Bogomil the lamb was beside her ear. Susu the dog was on the floor.

She threw Bogomil at the door. A nasty trick, but only that.

The idea of the day ahead was so hideous, Bogomil the lamb against the door so ominous, that Laura could not bring herself to get out of bed. She stayed there, watching videos of musicians younger than she was and already YouTube famous and reading music reviews of bands that hadn't even existed when she died until Mo texted just after nine.

Everyone make it through the night ok?

Laura texted back. Had bad dreams

I got some sleep. That was Daniel. You?

Mo didn't text back for a few minutes. Then: Saw that strange person again outside my house

Laura didn't even bother to wait for the rest. She called Mo. "Tell me you didn't go outside," she said when he picked up.

"It doesn't matter anyway," he said. "He was gone by the time I got out to the street. Hold on. Daniel's calling me."

"Ignore him," Laura said. "What are you doing, Mo? What are you thinking? *Are* you thinking?"

"I guess," Mo said, sounding subdued, "I guess I was thinking maybe it was my grandmother. Like, her ghost."

"Your grandmother's ghost?"

"Why not?" Mo said. "It could be. Why couldn't it be her? Who else would want to see me this badly?"

"Not bad enough she sticks around to actually talk to you, though," Laura said.

"Yeah, well," Mo said. "I haven't finished telling you what happened. I went out on the street, and there was no one there."

"Good!" Laura said. "That's good!"

He'd stood there in sweatpants and no shirt, feeling like an idiot. Maybe this was how he had died the first time. Lured out to a location by a mysterious figure and then disappointed. So very disappointed he had expired on the spot.

Disconsolate, unnerved, he turned around to go back inside. Had he left a light on in his room? No, he had not, but now a light was on in his room. And fuck, no fucking way, there stood a figure in his window. That indistinct figure that had previously stood here in the street where he was now standing, it stood in his room now, looking at him from his fucking window.

"Wait," Laura said. "So you went outside and it just came into the house? It was in your house?"

He'd stood on the dark street, looking up at the person in his window.

It was cold outside, although of course not as cold as it should have been. Was anything the way it should have been? Mo's arms and legs, all of his skin, prickled with gooseflesh. All the dark houses and trees holding their breath. That conducting hand. That unmistakable refrain, that irresistible refrain. Come to me, oh come. Won't you come?

Mo thought, I can't believe I'm doing this. Fuck. I guess I'm doing this.

There was a small spark of rage, though, in his heart. Here I am, cast out into darkness, and there you are, whoever you might be, in my bedroom. Do you think this is a game?

But there was hope, too. I came back to you. Have you come back to me? He went back across the lawn, through the front door, closing it after him, up the dark stairs, across the dark landing, and into his bedroom.

There was no one there.

The light was on, yes, but there was no one at the window. There was no one under the bed or in his bathroom. In the closet. He looked out his window: the street in front of the house was empty.

He was going to write a letter. He was going to write a fucking stern letter. What the fuck? Nobody ever mentioned how fucking annoying ghosts were. Showing up, making you do shit. Come outside! No, wait, never mind. Come back in! I'm here! And then when you came inside they'd fucked off again, like ha ha funny, you fell for it again, Charlie Brown. Fuck this, fuck everything, but especially fuck that ghost. Whoever he or she was. Unless it was the one he longed, more than anything, to see.

Telling this to Laura, Mo thought, Fuck you, too. Why am I talking to you? Why don't I have anyone else I can talk to?

Lying on the floor beside the window seat, right where he'd left it, was his grandmother's novel. *Come to Me Beside the Sea*. Nothing surprising about that, but then he saw how a piece of paper, folded over, was now sticking out of it. Mo took it out and unfolded it. It was a sheet of staff paper from his desk. He read what had been written on it.

"What did it say?" Laura said. "Mo?"

YOU SHOULDN'T TRUST THEM

Then, a PS down at the bottom. **I LIKE THE ONE ABOUT DUCHAMP AND THE ROCKING CHAIR.**

Mo didn't tell Laura about the PS, though. Because the idea that someone (his grandmother?) had looked at the sheet music on his desk? His songs? Everything, of course, was terrible. But his music was private. His music was his.

Fuck ghosts. Unless.

"Maybe that was the best she could do," Mo said. "She left me a message."

"She was talking about them, right?" Laura said. "Bogomil and Mr. Anabin."

"Or else she was talking about you and Daniel," Mo said.

"She never even met me," Laura said. She sounded hurt. "Besides, how can you not trust us when we don't know anything? We're all in the same boat!"

"So far," Mo said. "Bogomil and Mr. Anabin seem more likely, but it isn't like we trust them right now, so as far as advice goes, it isn't very helpful, is it?"

"Did it look like her handwriting?"

"Not really," Mo said.

"Then, Mo, why think it was her?" Laura said.

Mo was silent.

"Did it look like Bogomil's handwriting? On the blackboard?"

"No," Mo said. "It wasn't his writing. Fuck. Daniel's calling again."

"I'll hang up," Laura said. "You tell him what's going on. Okay?"

"I will," Mo said. "Okay."

So then Mo had to tell the same story all over again to Daniel. And then Daniel told Mo about Susannah on the beach with Bogomil, and afterward, Daniel called Laura and went over it all again. When Daniel was done, Laura said, "Susannah was fine last night. Anyway, I can't handle this right now. I haven't even had breakfast yet!"

Daniel refrained from saying he knew Susannah was okay or mentioning the reason he knew this was because he'd slept most of the night in Susannah's bedroom. It wasn't relevant. He said, "It's not like we can do anything about Bogomil right now anyway. It's fine. It's going to be fine."

The Book of Laura

When Laura came downstairs, Ruth was in the pantry. She said, "I thought there were Honey Nut Cheerios."

Laura said, "I finished those yesterday."

"The whole box?" Ruth said.

"No," Laura said. She was so ravenous she could hardly think. "I remember. Those moths? So, because of what you said, I took a look just to make sure, and we had weevils. I had to throw out the instant oatmeal and the Oreos, too."

Ruth made a face of disgust. She said, "We should probably go through everything. See if we have to throw anything else out."

"I took care of it," Laura said. "Everything weevilly is gone."

"Heroic child," Ruth said. "How did I manage while you were in Ireland?" Then, "Have you heard from your dad today?"

Laura said, "He texted. There's a call with a big investor he has to prep for. Yesterday he was telling me all about this new ocean-mapping project, some VR thing. He's going to give me and Susannah some goggles or something. Are you okay with all of this? Him being back here?"

"Well," Ruth said. She lifted a jam jar off a shelf, put it down again. "Sometimes people show up long past the point you think you'll never see them again. I guess I'll figure it out as we go. I did love him. He left. And it was awful, but I got to a place where I was okay with that, we got to a place where we were okay, you and me and Susannah, and I got on with my life. We got on with our lives the way you have to."

"I used to be so mad at him for leaving," Laura said. "But then I mostly just stopped thinking about him. Except for once in a while."

"Oh, honey," Ruth said.

"What does he want?" Laura said. She'd found some smoked almonds and crammed a handful into her mouth. "From us?"

Ruth said, "I don't really care what he wants from me. He wants to spend some time with you and Susannah. Good for him. But I don't need anything from him anymore, and I don't expect anything, either. Maybe for him to pay for your school. For Susannah, if she goes to college. But me? My life is good. I've got my two sweet girls home for Christmas."

Laura said, "I love you, Mom." She hadn't said it since she got home. She resolved to say it every day from now on. Twice a day, even.

"I know. You're my good girl. The one I never have to worry about," Ruth said, and for a moment she looked confused, almost frightened. Then she shook her head.

"What?" Laura said, her mouth full of almonds again.

"Nothing. Here's a bag of dried apples. Want one? There's rice, too. I could make us steamed rice for breakfast. We could have sriracha with it. Or we could go over to What Hast Thou Ground? and get coffee and muffins and bug Susannah."

"Rice sounds great," Laura said. "I'll make coffee."

They had breakfast and Ruth asked Laura to tell her about Ireland. Was Professor Annam still giving her a hard time? Were her suitemates still fighting about the broken toaster? Was her dorm room as cozy as it looked? Laura found she remembered Professor Annam. Who was a hard-ass but good at explaining theory. The dorm room was lovely. Her suitemates were not. Nobody ever wanted to share living space with brass instruments. Answers came to her as long as she didn't think about the fact that none of this was real. She had three helpings of rice and most of the coffee.

Ruth said, "If the mothers in the NICU could see you put away food, they would weep with envy."

"Jet lag. My body's all messed up." Laura lifted her hand to tuck her hair behind her ear and then stopped, remembering. "I was thinking about going to the grocery store if you want to make a list."

"Yes, please!" Ruth said. "We seem to be out of everything. Even the condensed milk. I was going to make peppermint-candy fudge, but I need condensed milk." She gave Laura her ATM card.

Today was Ruth's teaching day down at the community college in Silverside. The pay wasn't much, but she liked her students. She was a Silverside graduate. Even after she'd gotten her nursing degree and started rotations at the hospital, she'd continued to take classes at Silverside and, later, teach. Today was the day she co-taught a class on home care with her good friend June, a respiratory therapist, and then she and June would sit in on a course they were auditing on financial security in retirement.

She said, "Talk to your sister, okay? When she gets home."

"About what?" Laura said.

"About her future," Ruth said, sticking her head out the porch door to check the weather. "She's the one who should be in college. Not me. This weather! I ought to be in the backyard on a towel. Getting some vitamin D."

It was true Ruth had the unmistakable pallor of a night nurse. But she was still very, very lovely. She'd always dated, discreetly. But it was hard to find quality men who were free for romantic dinners at three P.M.

Laura said, "I already gave it a go with Susannah, and it went about how you would expect. Besides it's not like my career plan is particularly sensible. At least Susannah's making money right now."

"Don't be silly," Ruth said. "You're doing what you love. Laura, I don't care if you make a go out of music or not, I just want you to not be afraid of what you want."

"Well," Laura began. It hurt more than she would have thought to hear her mother praise her for being brave when, in fact, she had merely been dead.

"Meanwhile, Susannah won't even look at a college application," Ruth went on. "She's sleepwalking through her life. She goes to work, comes home, and watches TV. Well, as far as I can tell. She does dishes! She doesn't cause any trouble. Remember the time she found the baby opossums and brought them home and put them in the bathtub and forgot to tell anyone? The time she decided to cut down the apple tree in the backyard because there were evil elves living in it? The volcano cake that actually exploded?"

"I remember when she cut off my bangs in fourth grade," Laura said. "I remember she cut off her own bangs, too, to apologize."

"Oh my God, that was terrible," Ruth said. "I almost killed her. But we would have had to have a closed coffin."

Once again, something in her expression changed. She shook her head.

Laura said, "Remember when she wanted to make all the babies in the NICU joke tombstones for Halloween?"

"The time we found out she was saving up to have surgery to make herself shorter," Ruth said. "The time for my birthday she decided to make me a red velvet cupcake for each year I'd been alive and then wanted me to eat at least one bite from every single one. I miss that Susannah. This one is just so sad. And she won't tell me what she's sad about. If it was just you and Daniel going to Ireland, if it was just her wishing she'd gone, too, I'd understand. But I think it's bigger than that. Something happened, something happened to her, but I have no idea what. Maybe she doesn't even know. You know?"

"Yeah," Laura said. "I know."

"My ride's here. Enjoy the sunshine!" Ruth said. And then was gone.

Laura texted Daniel. Wanna go to the grocery store with me? I ate everything in house.

He texted back immediately. Can't. Painting living room. Will be ready to head over to school around 2. You OK?

Laura texted: Of course not

She texted Susannah: Aren't you tired of Billy's shit yet

Susannah's reply was two photos. The first was a boy sitting at a table in the window of What Hast Thou Ground? Blond, nice shoulders, long nose. The second was a selfie, Susannah behind the counter, a smirk on her face.

Laura took her mother's car and went shopping. She bought everything on Ruth's list, and then she used her own debit card to buy two hundred dollars' worth of hamburger meat, canned tuna, Skippy peanut butter, and an economy pack of off-brand energy bars, the cheapest she could find. What was the point of having a savings account when things were the way they were?

→→→ ←←←

SHE PUT AWAY groceries and tried not to think about her ear. Not to think about all the rest of it. She tried, again, to turn the saltshaker into something other than a saltshaker. Then another saltshaker, a slightly smaller one. But she couldn't even manage that. Because it wasn't even noon yet, she read the newspaper, poked around online, liked a couple of Rosamel Walker's posts on Facebook (Was Rosamel back home for Christmas? Was the other girl, smiling in two pictures, just a friend? A roommate? Had Rosamel been sad when Laura went missing? Not because they knew each other that well, but in the general way you were sad when someone you said hey to in the halls at school suddenly disappeared and the assumption was something terrible had happened to them. Which it had.), and made hamburger patty after hamburger patty. The last three patties she didn't even bother to cook. She pinched off blobs, forming them into little balls like cookie dough, and ate them ravenously. Afterward, she licked her fingers clean.

FOR THE MEETING with Mr. Anabin, Laura put a notebook and a good pen in her bag. A dozen energy bars. Then she went through her closet, eating spoonfuls out of a peanut butter jar, trying to decide what she ought to wear. Was she supposed to wear something practical? Something to show she understood the gravity of the situation? A T-shirt with a funny slogan to try to suck up?

In the end, Laura went with her favorite blue jeans and a fitted black poplin top printed with small white flowers, which she'd never worn. It had a sash that tied in the back in a big jaunty bow and was the kind of thing you would wear if you were being interviewed at SXSW about the success of your band by someone from Stereogum and there was a photographer. She'd been saving it for something like that, anyway. She decided to leave her hair down. All this time she did not think about her ear. The only reason she was leaving her hair down was because styling it would have been too much. You didn't want to look like you were making an effort. Ears were ears. If they were on your body, they belonged to you. She didn't have to wear earrings if she didn't want to.

She told herself that if she could just make it through the afternoon with Mr. Anabin without thinking about her ear or touching her ear, she'd take all of her money out of the bank and go get a new guitar. She'd buy the Epiphone. Screw the Gretsch. Someone else could save up for it.

Nothing is wrong with your ear, she told herself. So stop thinking about it.

The spoon scraped the bottom of the peanut butter jar, but that was okay. She wasn't particularly hungry anymore.

The Book of Mo

Jenny went around the house singing.
 "*When I first came to this country in 1849 I saw many fair lovers but never saw mine.*"

Mo was messaging with Rosamel because Theo and Natalie were stuck doing family stuff and couldn't meet up and Rosamel had left him a really sweet condolence message on his page a while ago. Fuck Susannah, really. All she'd done was favorite the post where he said he was back.

"*And me a poor stranger and a long way from home.*"

Rosamel was not enjoying her break. Her mom was giving her grief about her first-semester grades and the fact that Rosamel had shaved her head and also stopped shaving her legs. She didn't understand why Rosamel hadn't gone to Spelman like she had. Just because you're a lesbian, Rosamel, Rosamel wrote, doesn't mean you have to make yourself unattractive. Like, please. Mom. I can still get it if I want it. I'm in college now. Lesbians everywhere. Can I just tell her that?

She will high-five you so hard your hand will fall off, Mo wrote.

"*Well, I wished I was a turtle dove, had wings and could fly.*"

Tru but u only need one. Anyway, we're just fighting a lot because this weather is freaking me tf out. I want to wear ugly Christmas sweaters and drink hot chocolate but global warming. You home later? I still have your John Cage book. I could bring it by. You can rub my shiny lesbian skull for luck. Next year I'm going to come home with devil horn implants and my mom will implode.

Jenny Ping is singing folk songs. Found out she looooooves Barry Manilow.

Is she singing Barry Manilow?

Tragic love songs. Got a pretty good voice. I have to go do something boring at 2. Could text you after that?

Rosamel's response came back a second later, a thumbs-up. Tell pretty Jenny I say hi and is she going to make her banana bread if I come over because they don't feed me at college jk they do i am getting sturdy

When Mo passed on Rosamel's request, Jenny said, "I always liked her. She's at Oberlin, right?"

"Could you make two loaves?" Mo said. "Yeah, Oberlin. You doing anything fun today?"

"Christmas shopping," Jenny said. "You want to come?"

"Can't," Mo said. "Have to go see Mr. Anabin. Check in about Ireland. Let him know how it's going."

"Tell me you love it," Jenny said. She was already putting ingredients together. It was a good thing Mo hadn't eaten all the bananas. "You love it, right? Your grandmother was so excited about you getting in. She was so proud."

"Was she?" Mo said. He knew, of course, his grandmother had not been excited about the music scholarship. She had not been so proud of him. She'd thought Mo was dead. And yet, he longed to hear Jenny tell him about his grandmother, even if nothing she said was true.

"She was going to come visit you," Jenny said. "But she wanted you to have time to get used to being over there. She was going to buy a first-class ticket and fly over in style in the spring. Wait until you finished your classes and then take you everywhere. Paris. Egypt. Lalibela. Go all the places your mother went. Go to concerts in cathedrals, museums, vineyards. Eat schnitzel. Injera."

There was a lump in Mo's throat.

"She was having so much fun with the planning," Jenny said. "Had me look up hotels and train schedules. She was going to visit her foreign publishers, too. The whole Grand Tour."

Mo said, "That would have been fun." He couldn't stand to think about any of this. None of it had happened, would ever happen.

He opened the refrigerator and took out a block of cheddar cheese. "Gonna make some grilled cheese sandwiches," he said. "You want one?"

Jenny said, "Do we have bread? I thought we had bread, but this morning I couldn't find any."

Mo said, "I don't think we have bread."

Jenny took the cheddar cheese from him. "I'll make mac and cheese," she said. "You still like that?"

"Make a lot," Mo said. "I'm a growing boy."

HE GOT TO Lewis Latimer early because who wanted to be late to the class with the guy who could raise the dead? Clearly Daniel had the same idea. Here he was, sitting outside on the playground with one of his sisters, the one with the funny name. Carousel. She was a cute kid. Hair in twists, black-and-white zebra leggings, and a black sweater covered in neon stars.

"What's up, Roller Coaster?" Mo said.

"Carousel!" she said in great disgust. "It's like nobody even knows who I am."

"Hey," Daniel said, ignoring Mo. "One day you're gonna be so famous, people will forget there ever was a ride with horses that went around in a circle."

"What will I be famous for?" Carousel said.

Daniel paused, then said, "That's a great question and I can't wait to find out."

Mo squatted down beside them. "Sorry. I didn't know it was a sensitive topic."

"Ms. Fish insists on calling Carousel Caroline," Daniel said. "So Carousel stopped responding whenever Ms. Fish said anything to her. Also Carousel called her 'Ms. Fisholine' and asked her how she liked being called that. I was already on my way here, so I just came a little early to hang out with Carousel. Mom's on her way. She and Carousel are gonna go for ice cream."

"Fish," Mo said. "Now there's a name. You know I had her." He didn't look at Daniel.

"I had her, too," Daniel said. "Everybody gets the fish."

"Everybody gets the fish," Mo said. "But the fish doesn't get everyone if you know what I mean."

"I don't want to talk about her," Carousel said. "Did you know that some people eat asparagus and their urine smells funny?"

Mo said, "Uh, yeah. I think I knew that."

"But some people eat asparagus and their urine doesn't smell funny. And some people can't smell asparagus urine," Carousel said. "Even if their own urine is the smelly kind."

"Huh," Mo said. "I'm not even back inside the school yet and already I'm learning stuff. Thanks, Mad Teacups."

"Carousel," Carousel said. But she was smiling.

"Okay," Daniel said. "There's Mom. Don't worry, Carousel. Mom and Dad are on this."

"I'm not worried," Carousel said. "I'm mad. Like the teacups."

She and Daniel went over to Mrs. Lucklow's car, and Daniel stayed there for a few minutes, talking to his mom. Mo found a Sharpie beside the steps and wrote in very small letters on the underside of the red painted railing, IF ANYONE IS SLEEPY LET HIM GO TO SLEEP.

When Daniel came back, Mo said, "Where's Laura?"

"On her way."

"Bowie?"

"Haven't seen him," Daniel said. He didn't sound that sad about it, either.

Mo went into the school office to get a pass while Daniel, who already had one, waited. When Mo came back out, Ms. Fish was there, speaking to Daniel. God, Mo had hated her. That feeling bubbled up even now, like a low-grade nausea.

"Mohammed," Ms. Fish said. "I was sorry to hear about your grandmother."

"Thanks," Mo said. Thinking, She didn't like you much, either, you unpleasant child-eating troll. It wasn't just me.

"Mr. Anabin is waiting for us," Daniel said, "and we really can't be late. Sorry, Ms. Fish. I understand Carousel can be a handful. But what's the point of insisting on calling her Caroline when nobody else calls her that?"

Ms. Fish patted Daniel on his arm. She had to reach up to do it. She said, "If I give Caroline her way on this, I'll have ten other kids in the classroom telling me that they want to be called Batman or Lightning Bolt or Moon Princess Pony. She's not going to want to be called Carousel all her life."

Daniel said, "But—"

Ms. Fish said, "It's a phase, Daniel. I remember you at her age, lashing out, throwing tantrums. Your mother had remarried. Your sisters were small. You were looking for someone to set boundaries. It was clear to me even then you had greatness in you."

"It was?" Daniel said.

Mo did not roll his eyes. This forbearance, he felt, was an indication of even greater greatness on his part than Daniel would display in his entire life. But of course Ms. Fish, looking up, saw only Daniel.

She said, "Caroline's testing boundaries. I'm setting them. I'm going to tell your parents the same thing when we have our meeting. Good to see you, Daniel. Mohammed. I'm so proud of you both."

Once she was out of earshot Daniel said, "I just don't get it. She wasn't the greatest teacher I ever had, or the most fun, but she wasn't awful. Let me be in charge of the pencil sharpener even after I knocked over Liz Perry's block tower. Once I apologized. But Mom says she just won't give Carousel a break."

"Gee," Mo said. "I wonder what the difference is." He walked off and left Daniel looking after him, open-mouthed. So Daniel's father had been dead for years and Ms. Fish had understood he had issues? What about Mo? His mother had died. He'd come to Lovesend, been put in a new school. What had been unclear to Ms. Fish when, in the second week he'd been in her class, Mo had used a green marker to color in all the *o*'s in a Dr. Seuss book and cried when she took it away? She'd put him in the closet. He'd been in there, with the lights off, until the end of recess. It had happened twice more over the course of the year, and the third time, he'd peed himself after the first five minutes, not because he was afraid but because he needed to go and Ms. Fish wouldn't let him out. That had been awful, but afterward, Ms. Fish and his grandmother had a sit-down, and after that, Mo wasn't put in the closet again. He bet being dead was the first time Daniel had ever been shut away in the dark by some asshole authority figure.

It was three minutes to two. So they weren't late yet. On to the next encounter with a teacher, this one a lot scarier than Ms. Fish. And here came Laura marching down the hall, looking like magical butter wouldn't melt in her reconstituted mouth. But then, magical butter probably didn't melt. That would be the whole point.

"Let's do this," Laura said.

Mo groaned. "When they make the tragic movie of our return from the dead," he said, "I hope someone writes you better dialogue."

The Book of Daniel

When Daniel thought about fourth grade, he didn't have a lot of feelings about it. Sure, Ms. Fish had been Ms. Fish. Which is to say, there had been a lot of rules, and she didn't seem to like being a teacher all that much. Or kids. In fact, he wasn't really sure he knew what Ms. Fish liked, come to think of it. Which was awful. Everyone should have something that made them happy, even Ms. Fish.

Fourth grade had not been a great year. Lissy and Dakota were toddlers, his mom was pregnant again and told him, and all he could think was that he'd have even less of his mom. He'd been so angry at Peter, even though Peter had been so kind, so good to Daniel, but Daniel couldn't get it straight in his head that they were a family, that Peter wasn't going to leave, to die like Charlie Knowe had. He'd even been afraid that his mom and Peter would kick him out, that with Lissy and Dakota and this new baby, there wasn't going to be space for Daniel, too.

God, he'd been an asshole to his mom. And to Peter. All Carousel wanted was to be called by her name. Daniel had wanted to pick a fight with the whole world.

And then his mom had a miscarriage, and she'd been so, so sad. Carousel had been early, too. Twenty-four weeks. Four months in the NICU. Daniel had been old enough by then to know how worried his mom and Peter were. He'd gotten to visit Carousel just once in the NICU, a few weeks after she was born. She'd had an infection, gotten over it, but he could tell by looking at Peter and his mom they were trying not to think about how she might have died. Ruth Hand had been there, too, and they'd all stood around Carousel's Isolette. There were wires and tubes everywhere. Her whole chest went up and down when she breathed, like squeezing an underinflated balloon. She had a little knitted green hat pulled down over her eyes.

His mom had opened one of the port doors and said to Daniel, "Put your hand inside. Let her hold your finger."

Daniel wasn't sure he wanted to, but he did. He'd put his index finger against Carousel's unbelievably small fingers, and she had grabbed it and held it tightly. One of her legs kicked like a skinned frog's. He thought he could have fit her whole body in his palm.

Daniel loved all of his siblings, but he knew he loved Carousel most of all. She was called Carousel because she'd fallen in love with a pink elephant on the carousel at the dinky little fair that came through Lovesend every fall.

She'd loved the elephant, but she couldn't remember the word "elephant." When the fair left, she asked for "carousel" and cried herself to sleep every night for at least a week. She'd cried so much they'd had to make her use her inhaler because she couldn't catch her breath. It was funny. She'd called herself Carousel, but she'd never really cared about the one up at the Cliff Hangar. Not any more than any of the other kids.

This morning when Daniel woke up, the pillow under his head, the blankets, the whole room was redolent of Susannah. Her arm was around his waist and he extricated himself carefully. He didn't want to wake her. He resisted, too, the impulse to study the expression on her face. She looked, what, happy? Well, if she looked happy, that didn't mean it had anything to do with him.

Last night he'd dreamed he was a magician. Something like a magician, anyway. And today he knew three things. That he was never going to get his old life back. That the cost of magic wasn't anything he could afford. And the third thing was about Susannah, about the way he felt about her. He thought maybe it was something he'd known a long time ago. And now it didn't matter.

One of Susannah's hands was tucked under her pillow, and the other was outstretched, turned palm up, as if she were holding something out to him that he couldn't see.

He got out of the house without seeing Laura or Ruth, and after he stuck his head in the door of his own house and ascertained everything there was as it ought to have been, he walked down to the beach wishing he had Fart with him. The day was warm again. He thought, This is what it was like when I was alive. When I'm dead again, I'll remember and that will be enough.

EVERYTHING IN MR. Anabin's room that had once been familiar to Daniel now was overlaid with strangeness and dread. Like the nightmare in which you find you must take a test for which you have not prepared. Here, previously, was where you learned some really basic music theory and waited while everyone around you found the right page of sheet music. Daniel was a percussionist, which meant mostly he daydreamed while everyone else did their setup, tuned their instruments. Found the key. Before a song started, it was always kind of exciting. Maybe this time everybody would get their shit together. Maybe you could just play the song. Maybe the rhythm you heard in your head and the music on the page and the noise everyone made when they started playing would be congruent. It wasn't that Daniel minded rehearsal. Learning something new. It was just, he really liked music, and not everyone else did. And by the time you knew the score, you'd rehearsed it so very often that the mistakes were sometimes the only interesting parts left.

He'd liked playing bass in My Two Hands Both Knowe You so much more. Though he played the drums, too, whenever Susannah was doing the kissing thing. For Daniel, picking up instruments was easy. Like being in the ocean and just floating; the current carried you off.

Which was true of other stuff, too. Daniel could look back now and see he'd mostly just floated. He'd gotten decent grades. He'd played football because people thought you should play football if you were a big guy. He'd ended up in a band with Laura and Susannah because Laura had wanted it so much. And he'd hooked up with girls who never asked him for too much; he'd never ever tried to start something serious with any of them because that would have been work. He'd never tried to figure out what was happening with Susannah because that would have been work, too. Like, a lot of work. They were friends, and friends should have been enough. They were in a band together, and that should have been enough. They'd slept together a long time ago, and that should have been enough, but then they'd started sleeping together again and it had all blown up because it turned out it wasn't really enough after all. And now it was looking likely that not enough was all he was ever going to get. Call it a presentiment. Here was another thing that wanted to carry him away, but for once he was not going to do what other people wanted him to do. Screw magic. He would spend as much time as he could with his family. He would stay away from Susannah.

Mr. Anabin was over by the window, looking out. Maybe he would rather have been anywhere else, too. When he turned, Daniel saw that his T-shirt today was extremely on topic: YOU ARE MAGIC.

Mr. Anabin said, "Laura, Mo, Daniel. Have a seat. Anywhere. Has anyone seen Bowie?"

"No," Laura said. "Not since, you know. The last time we were here."

"Disappointing," Mr. Anabin said. But he sounded more thoughtful than disappointed.

Mo and Laura and Daniel all sat down in the front row. Mr. Anabin sat behind his desk. Over on the blackboard, there was Bogomil's warning.

2 RETURN
2 REMAIN

On Daniel's right, Laura produced a notebook and a pen from her bag. The look on her face was expectant.

Mr. Anabin said, "I believe you were given two tasks. So, the first. Have you remembered anything about your deaths? No need to raise your hand."

No one said anything at first. Mr. Anabin waited placidly. Finally Laura shook her head. "No," Mo said.

"No," Daniel said. Someone had been carving into the desk he'd chosen. He could feel the shape of the heart under his index finger. When he looked down, he saw there were initials inside the heart. *D&S 4EVA*. Had he ever seen them there before? He was sure neither he nor Susannah had ever carved anything like this into a desk. But there were plenty of other *D*'s and *S*'s in the world.

"Very well," Mr. Anabin said. He didn't look particularly disappointed, but then neither did he look like someone who brought people back from the dead. "Let's leave that for the next time. Though time is shorter than you think. The other assignment, then, was magic. What feats of magic have the three of you accomplished? Tell me."

Again, no one spoke.

Mr. Anabin at his desk still regarded them blandly. "Mo," he said. "Tell me what you have done since returning."

Mo sat back in his chair and folded his arms. "Thanks for asking," he said. "Found out my grandmother died. Got laid, broke up with my not-a-boyfriend, and later on, I have plans to see my girl Rosamel. Oh, and I made a whole tray of macaroni and cheese disappear."

Mr. Anabin said, "Laura?"

Laura said, "Excuse me, but can I just say that this is ridiculous first? Just because we came back from the dead, which, sure, I will admit has to be magic, whatever magic is, doesn't mean that we're suddenly able to do magic. How could we possibly know how to do magic when nobody has ever taught us how to do magic things? And I can't believe we're even having this conversation. I can't believe I now have to believe that magic is something that exists. With all due respect, the only reason I'm here is because you and Bogomil are scary."

Mr. Anabin said, "Fair enough. Daniel?"

Daniel said, "Do I look like I do magic?" Because, did he?

"No," Mr. Anabin said. "You do not. But tell me: do I look like I do magic?"

"You don't," Mo said. "But we've all seen you do it. So, kind of, you do. I guess? That other guy, Bogomil, by the way, absolutely looks like a guy who does magic."

"I have a question," Laura said.

"Go on," Mr. Anabin said.

"Why am I hungry all the time?"

"For the same reason that the days are too warm," Mr. Anabin said. "Because you are alive. Let this be your first lesson in magic. You should not be alive, but you are. You do not know how to manage the magic that is keeping you housed in these bodies, and so you pay the coin in appetite. Others pay the coin according to their nature and their will."

"So," Mo said, "what you're saying is that we're already doing magic?

Kind of? We can eat whatever we want? Or if we didn't do that, what? What are you saying our choices are here?"

Mr. Anabin looked down at his hands, turned them palms up. He said, "Tell me, Mo. What do you think magic is?"

Mo shrugged. "Not an expert. But, something happening that shouldn't happen."

"Laura?" Mr. Anabin said.

When Daniel looked over, he saw Laura was writing everything down. "Oh!" she said. "Cool. My turn. It's control. Being able to make things happen. Or not happen. Maybe?"

"Daniel?" Mr. Anabin said.

"Candlepin bowling," Daniel said. He held up a finger. "Magic is like candlepin bowling. Or no. It's baseball cards, collecting baseball cards. Right? No? Okay, then it's like asparagus. Like asparagus pee. Some people can do it. Some can't. Some people can do it and don't even know that they're doing it."

"Oh boy," Mo said. Beside Daniel, Laura had put down her pen. Her shoulders hunched as if Daniel's answer was causing her actual physical pain.

Mr. Anabin said, "Actually . . . that's not the worst description of magic I've ever heard. The comparison to asparagus. But I know you meant only to be entertaining."

"I didn't mean that," Daniel said.

Mr. Anabin said, "You would be making a mistake to think of magic as something that I am going to teach you, and there is very little room here for mistakes. I am not teaching you. I am providing you with an opportunity. What you do with this opportunity is up to you."

"But if we get it wrong, then we die again or something," Mo said. "Two of us are going to go back where we were before, and this is some kind of game or contest, but you're not going to explain any of it to us."

"You say you're not going to teach us," Laura said. "But clearly there are rules. Or principles! Guidelines? Because you ought to tell us what they are. You could at least do that. You're not the greatest music teacher ever, I don't think, but in band you didn't just sit there and ask us to play things we didn't know how to play on instruments we'd never seen!"

"Very well," Mr. Anabin said. "Let's try another tack. Laura. What is music?"

When he asked this, Daniel felt a certain sense of déjà vu. He remembered the first day of band back when he'd been alive. Mr. Anabin had asked them the same question.

He was pretty sure Laura's answer had been the same then as now. She said, "It's about making someone feel something. It's about making a shape that is the right shape for a certain kind of feeling. It's the only thing that matters. At least that's what I think."

"Daniel?"

"Asparagus," Daniel said. What had he said the first time, back when he was alive? Well, it didn't matter. "It's like asparagus."

"I'll allow that. Mo?"

"Any sounds in any combination and in any succession," Mo said.

"Debussy," Mr. Anabin said. "Does not the death of someone we love bring sorrow? Emotion takes place in the person who has it. And sounds, when allowed to be themselves, do not require that those who hear them do so unfeelingly."

"John Cage," Mo said. "I take my emotions and make art out of them."

"Kesha Rose Sebert," Mr. Anabin said. "But what is music to you?"

Mo said, "That's personal."

In the silence that followed, there was a battering at a window. The largest gull Daniel had ever seen was buffeting the glass with its wings. "Look," Daniel said. "Music!"

As abruptly as it had attacked the window, the gull took off again, arrowing up into the cloudless sky until it was a blister-white speck. They craned their necks to watch, and Laura went to the window, her hand shading her eyes. The gull came diving back down at the glass, talons first. Laura threw herself sideways, away from the window as it shattered.

The gull beat its wings, spattering the floor with blood.

Daniel looked around for something to throw over the gull, to contain it, but the gull, wingspan fully extended, ran in a lurching motion toward the back of the room, toppling chairs and making the most terrible, abrading noise. Mr. Anabin did nothing at all. Only watched.

The gull cried out its pain, its desolation over and over. The sound pierced Daniel, and also he recognized it. He had heard it again and again in that place.

"Oh, come on!" someone said. The sound of Mo's voice cut through the clamor like a piece of wire. He said, "Stop that! You're not even a real bird!"

And this was true. When Mo finished speaking, there, crouched on the floor, was Bowie. There was blood on his white scarf, and when he was himself again, he held out his hand. They could see where he had cut himself on the glass.

"Magic," Mr. Anabin said. "Thank you, Bowie, Mo, for the demonstration. Laura, Daniel, the two of you have some catching up to do. There is a first aid kit in the closet. Someone fetch it."

Laura brought it to him.

Mr. Anabin applied antibiotic ointment to the gash on Bowie's hand and taped a heavy layer of gauze over it. "There you are," he said. "Lucky, I suppose, not to have broken your neck."

Bowie endured all this in silence, though Bowie the bird had screamed and screamed. If all of this was magic, now Daniel was even more sure he wanted no part of it.

"How did you know it was him?" Laura said to Mo. Which Daniel supposed was a less interesting question than how Mo had done what he had done, or how Bowie had turned himself into a seagull, but perhaps the easiest to answer. Despite himself, he was interested in what Mo would say.

"I don't know," Mo said. He sounded slightly embarrassed. "I just did."

Laura looked at Daniel. He shrugged. Later on, he could see she was going to give him a pep talk about how they were a team and they both needed to pull their magical weight. And he was going to have to explain he had no intention of ever doing anything that anyone like Bogomil or Mr. Anabin asked of him.

But now, for Laura, he said to Mr. Anabin, "So what's next? What are you not going to teach us now?"

"Now you go home," Mr. Anabin said. He went over to his piano and sat down on the bench. He put his hands on the closed lid. "I'm weary of you, and you are, I am sure, weary of me. Come back to me tomorrow. At midnight. Come and tell me the cause of your death. You will also bring something to me. Each of you."

"So, tomorrow, Tuesday. Midnight. Bring you something?" Laura said, her notebook out again. "Can you be more specific?"

"My birthday falls in the hour before midnight," Mr. Anabin said. "I ask that you use magic to bring me a thing I might desire. You may bring it to me here tomorrow night in the span of time between midnight and one A.M."

"Sucks to have a birthday so close to Christmas," Mo said. "Right, Daniel?"

Daniel shrugged. Yeah, sure, but he didn't expect it was ever going to be a problem for him again.

Bowie left first. He had said nothing, but Daniel supposed he had shown he had some grasp of magic. As Laura and Mo and Daniel stood up to leave, Mr. Anabin said, "Wait. Laura. Come here."

Laura gave Daniel a look full of alarm. "You don't have to," Daniel said, not bothering to lower his voice. "You don't have to do everything he says."

But she went. Daniel saw how she gauged her distance from Mr. Anabin, coming close enough that it was clear she had done as he had asked, but staying far enough away that he would have had to stand up to reach her.

"What?" she said.

Mr. Anabin said, "I see what you have accomplished, Laura. I'm sorry I missed it earlier."

"What?" Laura said again, an edge to her voice. "I accomplished what?"

Mr. Anabin said, "Only a small thing, but a thing nevertheless. I was wrong to be disappointed in you."

"Oh," Laura said. "Okay." Her hand went up to touch her hair and then dropped again. "Have a good day!" And then she was bolting past Daniel and Mo, saying, "Come on, oh, *come on*."

The Book of Anabin

When the children were gone, Anabin remained seated before the piano. The day was warm and the room was sunny and he had no particular place he required to be.

He lifted the piano lid and began to pick out, with one finger, a song. There were so many songs. This one, like many others, had been forgotten. He played it, fairly certain as he did so that he was unintentionally remaking it. And so, the song he was playing, could it even be said to be the same song? There were only one or two besides Anabin who would have the knowledge to correct him where he substituted one note for another. It was not a song that had been meant for a piano.

There had been words as well as a melody. He did not sing the lyrics, though those he remembered.

It had been a song meant to summon a lover. Anabin played all the way through and then began it again. No one else was in the room. No one came into the room as he picked out the melody, meandering, cajoling, never resolving. There was only Anabin and the piano and the window where the broken glass was beginning to fit itself together again.

Well. If someone wouldn't come for the sake of a song, there were other ways. Anabin deliberately played a wrong note. Then another.

No one came into the room. The door was shut and remained so. But now someone stood behind Anabin. He felt them there. He felt their terrible agony as if it were his own, but he disregarded it. He played the wrong note again, and now a white hand came down on his own, fingers on top of his own fingers. Dirt and grime beneath those fingernails, as if

Bogomil had never heard of baths. Anabin waited until he felt Bogomil's index finger exert the faintest of pressure on his own index finger. In this way they finished the song.

Bogomil's hand moved from Anabin's. Now it rested on Anabin's shoulder so lightly it might not have been there at all.

"I know what you hope for," Anabin said. "What you still hope for. But it would not be right for you to have it. And I do not want it."

When he turned around, Bogomil was no longer there.

The Book of Laura

Laura had envisioned, sometimes, what it would be like to come back to Lewis Latimer once she had graduated and gone out into the world. Once she'd seen what the world had to offer. Once she'd conquered the bits of the world worth conquering and was duly celebrated for her talent, her style, her charm, her generosity, her beauty, and her modesty. Ha! Only one or two of those were things that mattered. No doubt she would be asked to speak at a graduation ceremony. To address a school assembly. To play a concert that would benefit the school or the town or something important.

She'd imagined that on returning, everything would seem a little smaller, a little dingier. She'd thought she'd feel a sense of relief: Here was a place she'd escaped. Here were the doors she'd walked through. Here were the teachers who had once had such power and authority over her and who, she would realize, were just people with small dreams and small disappointments and small hopes, who had nonetheless recognized in her a potential greatness that she had now fulfilled. Though not for them, of course.

She would have done it for herself.

Of course what had happened instead was she died. Which was admittedly a setback. And Mr. Anabin was slightly less pathetic than she'd always assumed. That was probably a useful lesson. Always be nice to people, especially when it doesn't cost you anything. Really, it doesn't cost you anything to be nice.

"What the hell is wrong with you?" she said to Daniel.

"Nothing is wrong with me," Daniel said. "I just don't want to do magic."

"But you're okay with being dead again, quitter? With going back there? To that place? What's in that enormous skull of yours? It's like a Pez dispenser of terrible ideas."

Mo was a few steps behind them. "Here I thought all white boys secretly wanted to be wizards," he said. "I thought all they wanted was to go to magic school and have a hat tell them it really got them, like, the real them."

"It works out okay for you two," Daniel said. "Less competition. Not to change the subject, but what did Mr. Anabin mean? He said you'd been doing magic, Laura."

"We're not done talking about your attitude problem," Laura said. "Not by a long shot. But sure. Let's discuss me."

Mo rolled his eyes. But he also looked interested.

"Let's," Daniel said.

"So, I saw something online just before I left the house. It was about the Cliff Hangar." She had very deliberately not been thinking about it for the past hour.

Now that they were outside the school, she wondered: Was the day even warmer? Was that because of Bowie and Mo? Their expenditure of magic? If so, it sounded pretty good to her. Do magic and go lie on the beach. She couldn't understand why Daniel couldn't see the positives here. On the other hand: "Nobody can find Hannah. Or the cook at the Cliff Hangar, Kyle. You remember him, right, Daniel? Used to sell you weed? He was in the kitchen yesterday, but they both disappeared at some point before the Cliff Hangar was supposed to open for dinner service. Left the entrance unlocked. Carousel on. Burners on. Everything on."

"Like I said," Daniel said, "none of this is good and I don't want any part of it."

Mo said, "What did you guys do?"

"Nothing!" Laura said. "We talked to Hannah. And I sang a song for the scary woman with the weird name."

"Malo Mogge," Daniel supplied. "Also there were some lawyers."

"Scary lawyers?" Mo said.

"Drunk lawyers," Daniel said. "Drunk, sad lawyers."

"Drunk, sad, *magical* lawyers?" Mo said.

"Fuck the lawyers!" Laura shouted.

She fumbled her bike lock. Got it open on the third try and then almost dropped it on her toe.

Daniel caught it. "You okay?"

"Of course not," Laura said. "You're a loser and Hannah is missing. And Mr. Anabin thinks I did magic. What if I did it? What if I made Hannah and Kyle disappear?"

"Like, you made them disappear by singing 'The Lady with the Alligator Purse'?"

"Girl," Mo said. He was on his bike but walking it along on tiptoes instead of pedaling.

Here was the public park where, on one end, a statue of the sculptor Augusta Savage regarded with satisfaction a sculpture by the actual Augusta Savage on the other end. Laura let her bike fall and sat down on the grass. "I felt strange while I was singing, okay?"

Mo kicked out the stand on his bike. He crouched down next to her, picked up a gull feather. "Strange how?"

Laura thought about it. She said, "I guess I felt kind of powerful. Like during a show. But more so? And also pissed off. Like I was having a fight with her. Malo Mogge."

Mo said to Daniel, "You were there. Did it feel strange to you?"

Daniel looked down at Laura. She made a face at him. "Yeah, it felt strange. But it already felt *strange* or whatever before Laura sang. If something bad happened to Hannah, it was that lady, Malo Mogge." There was absolute certainty in Daniel's voice, and Laura could have wept with relief to hear it. It wasn't that she didn't want to do magic. It was just she didn't want to do it without knowing that she was doing it.

"So what did he mean?" she said. "What did I do?"

"Here," Daniel said. "Stand up." He hauled her to her feet.

"What?" Laura said.

Daniel tucked her hair behind her ear. "Come see, Mo."

But Laura didn't need to wait for Mo to confirm it. Daniel stood close enough that she could see for herself how both of his ears were the same now. She touched her own ear to confirm it was back where it ought to be, on her own head. Well, now she could wear earrings again. She said, "I guess I can do magic."

"Not only can you and me both do magic, but apparently we can do magic without even learning how to do magic!" Mo said. "This is either very good news or else the opposite. Either way, it's all very interesting, but in about half an hour, Rosamel is due at my house. We're going to hang out and I'm going to stealthily interrogate her about the night we died, because she was there, too."

"Rosamel Walker?" Laura said. "Say hey for me." And then felt stupid because there was no reason Rosamel would ever care that Laura Hand said hey.

"After Rosamel leaves, you two should come over, okay?" Mo said. "To continue this discussion. How about seven?"

Daniel didn't say anything. Mo and Laura exchanged a look and Mo shrugged.

Laura said firmly, "Seven is fine. We'll be there."

"Great," Mo said. "In the meantime, let's try not to do any more magic and then we'll see if not doing magic is a thing that we can also do."

"On it," Daniel said.

Mo gave him a thumbs-up and then rode off on his bike. Laura turned to Daniel. "So," she said. She felt as if flames were shooting out of her face. "Talk."

"Thanks for switching our ears back," Daniel said.

"Will you shut up about ears?" Laura said. "What the hell is going on with you? Don't you like being alive? You remember that place, right? Remember how much it sucked?"

"I remember," Daniel said. "But let me ask you something. You think Mr. Anabin and Bogomil aren't up to something? Because they are. And whatever they're up to, why do you think whatever happens to us next is going to be any better than that place was?"

"How could it be any worse?" Laura said. "Be a little glass-is-half-full, Daniel!"

Daniel said, "Sure, but half-full of what?" He got on his bike. "Let's go home."

They rode their bikes in silence most of the way, Laura formulating arguments she did not speak aloud. Finally she said, "But you're still going to come tonight, okay? Even if you're one hundred percent sure you don't want to do magic, you at least have to help us. Me and Mo. Okay?"

Daniel said, "I can do that." He hesitated in front of the Hands' driveway, and Laura said, "Do you want to come in? Susannah's still at What Hast Thou Ground? You don't have to worry about running into her."

Daniel said, "No. Thanks. Got some stuff to do at home before we go up to Mo's house."

"Tell everybody over there hi," Laura said. "We should do a board game night before, you know, whatever." And then felt ridiculous for suggesting they do something so normal.

Her mother was still over at the college and Susannah was at work. Bogomil the lamb was exactly where she had left him on the floor. Laura put him in the bottom drawer of her dresser before examining both of her ears in the mirror. "Good job, me," she said to the Laura in the mirror, who looked a little anxious about the whole thing. "Gold star."

She put on a pair of plain hoops and brought her guitar downstairs, where she sat cross-legged on the couch, tuning it in between eating scoops of Velveeta cheese off a spoon like ice cream. Her phone buzzed, and when she looked down, there was a text from her father. Around for dinner tonight?

She texted back Can't. Plans with friends. Tomorrow? You, me, Susannah?

Sounds good. Having a good day?

Yeah. Pretty good. Sitting here playing your crappy old guitar

Bring it when you guys come over tomorrow. 8 pm

And then: Tell Ruth she's welcome too

Yeah, right, Laura thought. Build your own bridges, Dad. I've got stuff of my own to deal with. She ate another spoonful of Velveeta. The Harmony was high up enough on her lap that the tips of her hair brushed the strings. Her fingers stung where once she'd had calluses. She'd get them back. After all, she had returned from the dead. She had done magic. She felt like a queen. Although a queen deserved a better instrument than her dad's old Harmony. Tomorrow she'd go over to Birdsong Music in the mall at Paradise Point and buy herself the Epiphone Casino Coupe. Maybe she'd pick something out for Susannah while she was there. For Christmas. There was no good reason for Susannah to give up on music: she was just being a pussy. The last time they'd gone to Birdsong, Susannah had hung out over by the selection of vintage mics. It wasn't that hard to figure Susannah out. You just had to watch her like a hawk. Maybe there was something at Birdsong that might work for Mr. Anabin, too.

All the Velveeta was gone. A fly perched on the foil wrapper, rubbing its limbs together briskly.

"Gross," Laura said. She was tired of things that flew. Things where they shouldn't be. She played a chord and then another. Began a jaunty, inconsequential progression, the kind that suited a fly so jaunty, so inconsequential. Collected all of herself to bear down, to persuade. The fly twitched. Did flies have any sense of musicality? Laura played the progression of chords again, and the fly flew. Go to the television screen, Laura thought. And it did. Good fly, Laura told it. Now make a circle. Walk in a circle. And the fly began to walk a circle. Flies, of course, do not know what a circle is, but Laura told it with the guitar how to go, and the fly went. It was a stupid little song as far as songs go, but even stupid little songs have some magic in them. Anyway, that was what Laura had always thought.

The Book of Susannah

There is the desire (completely reasonable) to wake up in sole possession of one's bed and there is then the moment in which you wake up and discover this is the case. You are alone. And then the only one available with whom to pick a fight is oneself. Susannah lay in her bed until the alarm went off. Now she could go to work and be miserable there and then come home and perhaps Laura would be annoying and Susannah could bite *her* head off. And perhaps Daniel would show up in her room again. Or he wouldn't.

This had been how it often was between Susannah and Daniel before he went to Ireland, and in this brief interlude while Daniel was home, Susannah had no reason to think things might go differently. Daniel had not been magically altered by the gap of several months, and Susannah was still Susannah. When Daniel went away again, Susannah would still be Susannah then, too. The feeling of wrongness that had swallowed her up some time ago had no cause. There was no magical door through which she could walk into a life where she understood how to fix things or even what needed to be fixed.

At least she made pretty good lattes. So she made lattes and listened to every customer make the same jokes about the weather. Sales of iced drinks were way up. Billy listed a new special on the board, Frosty the Snowman, which involved a lot of peppermint syrup and ice cream, and Susannah made those until the peppermint syrup ran out. So they switched to Ice, Ice Babys, which used both nutmeg and lemon and were freakishly tasty. Really, Billy should have been running a bar and not a coffee shop, but then again he was in AA.

Susannah had been at work only two hours when she looked up and saw that Thomas was sitting at a table in the window. Mo's usual place.

She'd messaged Mo on Facebook while she was still lying in bed. I'm sorry, she said. I'm sorry about your grandmother and I'm sorry I didn't write to say I was sorry earlier. But I really am sorry. He didn't write back, and that was fine. He didn't owe her anything.

People she'd gone to school with at Lewis Latimer came through, home for the holidays. Asked after Laura, asked if she'd seen Daniel yet, if he was going to this hangout, that party. She wasn't Daniel's social secretary. She decided if Thomas was still at Mo's table at the end of her shift, she would invite him home. And he is and so she does.

SHE TOOK HIM through the small park and into the neighborhood of bungalows and triple-deckers wearing their necklaces of colored bulbs, their wreaths on doors, inflatable snowmen, and wicker reindeer. Thomas stopped to look at the house with the mansard roof, where every year at Christmas the owners put out the world's gothest Santa. The Santa was fat, dressed in black velvet with snowy trim. It had a grinning skull for a face and a white beard, and it sat on a black coffin being pulled by eight reindeer spray-painted black and done up in bondage gear. A black-and-white banner streaming behind him read OH OH OH!

"There's a whole story there," Susannah said. "Romeo and Juliet–level stuff."

"You've lived here your whole life?" Thomas said.

"Yeah," Susannah said. "Well, so far."

Thomas said, "It's a nice town." There was something derisive in the way he said it. Like he was delivering a punch line to a joke he'd never let you in on.

In every way, he was unlike Daniel. Although she, of course, was still Susannah. She said, "What about you? Where'd you live before you ended up here?" He didn't have the kind of accent that told you anything.

"Lots of places," Thomas said.

"The interview subject was reticent," Susannah said. "Or possibly just a secretive jerk."

"Or both," Thomas said.

"Or that," Susannah said. "Here's my house. And these are my favorite neighbors."

On the Lucklows' lawn, Lissy and Dakota were on their hands and knees, crouched over something.

"Hey, guys," Susannah said. "What's up? Daniel around?"

"He and Laura went off on their bikes a little while ago," Dakota said. "We're making Spoonhenge."

"Shut up," Lissy said.

"You shut up," Dakota said.

"Spoonhenge," Susannah said. Now she could see the excavation better, the circle of silverware sticking up out of the grass and dirt. "Groovy."

"Gonna do a rite," Dakota said.

"Shut up shut up," Lissy said.

"I won't and you can't make me," Dakota said. "Because we need all the help we can get. We need dark energy. I mean, look at her."

Lissy gave Susannah a hard stare. Susannah crossed her arms and tried to look as sinister and also as helpful as possible.

"Fine," Lissy said. "Susannah, you can help. But not you. I don't know you."

"I'm Thomas," Thomas said.

"All right, Thomas," Lissy said. "I'm Lissy. Good to meet you. You're still not invited to help. Magic is complicated enough without introducing unknown factors."

Dakota nodded in agreement, not even looking up.

"Can't argue with that," Thomas said. "I'll just wait on Susannah's porch."

Once he was out of earshot, Lissy said to Susannah, "It's almost Christmas. We want snow. Among other things. So we're going to do some druid magic. Summon winter."

"Sure," Susannah said. "Happy to help. When?"

"Two A.M.," Lissy said. "This very night."

"Isn't that kind of late?" Susannah said.

"It's when high tide is," Dakota said. "I looked it up. Wear something witchy."

"I'll set my alarm clock," Susannah said. "Catch you later."

On the porch Thomas was checking his phone. Shoved it in his pocket. "Nice kids," he said.

"Nice town, nice kids," Susannah said. She unlocked the door and stood there wondering when the last time was that she'd brought a guy home. You couldn't count the boy next door, especially when he knew where the spare key was, just showed up uninvited. "Have you hit your nice overload or do you want to come inside and hang out with me and have a nice time?"

Thomas smiled. It was a very nice smile. Susannah took his hand and pulled him inside. It wasn't like she was embarrassed or anything. The house was clean and, yeah, it was a nice house: old, a little run-down, and you could smell the damp. But when you were quiet, you heard the ocean. The ocean wasn't always a great neighbor. But who'd want to live anywhere else?

"Hi, neighbor," Susannah said, getting two beers out of the fridge. "Have a 'Gansett."

"A what?" Thomas said. He was looking around with great interest: the battered wicker chairs Laura and Ruth had painted orange one summer, the impractical white sectional, Christmas cards featuring former NICU babies tacked up on a corkboard by the fridge, one of Laura's stuffed animals at the foot of the television cabinet.

"Just something my mom says," Susannah said. "Cheers."

Thomas sat down with his beer on the long foot of the sectional couch, while Susannah took off her boots, turned on the TV, and then stretched out on the perpendicular. She admired Thomas's profile as he fastidiously wiped the edge of the can on his shirt before taking a drink. He had an elegant nose. A small, white scar just under his eye. She bet girls liked to kiss it. She wouldn't mind. She stood up again and sat down nearer to him. "I bet you're wondering why I've brought you here," she said.

"Not really," he said, and kissed her. He really was a good kisser. Better than, well, better than lots of people. There was something hungry about his mouth.

Ruth wasn't due back for hours yet. It was, of course, possible Laura would come back at any moment. Or even Laura and Daniel. Susannah hadn't even locked the front door. She took off her shirt and bra.

When they were both naked, though, she said, "Wait. Wait, the couch."

Thomas said, "The couch?"

"Just," she said, "you know. It's still brand-new."

He had a condom on already and his hand between her legs. It felt so good she could hardly stand it. "Sometimes people have sex on beds."

"Ohhhhhh," she said. "Keep doing that. My room's a mess."

"I don't mind. I like messes."

She half-pushed, half-rolled him onto the floor. Got on all fours above him. Laura's stuffed animal was facing them.

Thomas said, "The floor's fine, too."

"Wait," she said. "Wait." And turned the black lamb's head toward the wall.

AFTERWARD, WHEN THEY had their clothes on again, Susannah went to get two more beers. When she came back, Thomas was putting his phone away. He looked absolutely at home, self-contained and prim as a cat.

Susannah sat down and poked her toes into his thigh. "Who is she, anyway?"

"Who is who?" he said.

"The fancy lady with the fancy car."

"Malo Mogge," he said. Shifted so he could take Susannah's foot into his lap. "She's kind of the worst."

"Nice car, though," Susannah said.

"Even terrible people have to go places," Thomas said. "At least with the Bugatti you know when she's around."

Susannah waited to see if he was going to say anything else, but instead he took a long gulp of beer and then laid the Narragansett against Susannah's instep.

"Cold!" Susannah said. "Is she your stepmother?"

He moved his fingers up to her ankle. "What? No, she's an old family friend. She's in imports and exports. I'm her personal assistant currently."

"Huh," Susannah said. She wanted to ask what kind of job entailed hanging out in a coffee shop and drinking mocha lattes because she thought she could handle that. How different, *how nice,* it was to sit here with Thomas. A little while ago, he'd had his mouth between her legs. She hadn't expected a guy who looked the way he did to put in so much enthusiastic effort. And now he was rubbing her foot.

He said, "There's this team in Lovesend, associates of hers, they were supposed to be coordinating with us, but something went wrong with their setup and now we're kind of chasing them around. Trying to figure everything out. I've got some time while that happens. So I guess I've sort of been thinking about my life. About what happens next."

Susannah said, "Me, too. Maybe I could apply for your job." She was half-serious.

"Trust me," he said. "You don't want my job. Someone like you could do a lot better."

Susannah examined his face to see if he was making fun of her and decided he was not. She said, "I'm a high school graduate and the former singer for a moderately shitty amateur band. Last year I was offered an all-expenses-paid music scholarship to Ireland and I flaked on that. I slept with my best friend and when he told me he didn't think we should be together anymore, I made out with my sister's crush in front of her and a few dozen other people. Oh, and I just hooked up on my mother's living room floor with a guy whose last name I don't even know."

"See?" Thomas said. "Things are already looking up. I could give you a list of all the terrible decisions I've ever made and truly you would be amazed, but let me just summarize. If I had any other options, I wouldn't have anything to do with Malo Mogge. Dead Santa on a roof would be a better job."

"Seasonal work," Susannah said. She wouldn't have minded hearing Thomas's list. "You have to supply your own costume."

"You were going to tell me a story," Thomas said.

"I was?" Susannah said. "Right. The family who lives in the goth Santa house. So, okay, they had a son who was sixteen or seventeen and he was in school with the daughter of their neighbors. The son and the daughter dated for about two years, and then the daughter cheated on the son, he found out, and it was like World War III. Both families got involved, and there was a lot of yelling on Facebook and, like, dog shit being thrown on the lawn. Anonymous phone calls to the police about domestic violence. Other stuff."

Thomas said, "Which house was the neighbor's?"

"The house to the left of the dead Santa house," Susannah said. "They actually moved a few years ago. Their daughter, the one who'd cheated on the son, she got some kind of aggressive cancer. While she was going through chemo, someone signed her up for all these funeral home magazines and catalogs. Everyone knew who did it. And she was really into Christmas, and so that year her family did their big Christmas display but even bigger, like even more lawn figures and lights. To cheer her up. That was when their neighbors put up the skeleton Santa riding in a coffin on their roof."

"Assholes," Thomas said. But possibly there was admiration in his voice.

"Total assholes," Susannah said. "She died in October the next year and the neighbors put the skeleton Santa up again. They kept on doing it every Christmas until finally the other family moved away. And they still do it even now that they're gone." She and Daniel had written a song about it: "Fight Christmas," the world's saddest, angstiest Christmas song. "I can't even imagine hating somebody that much."

Thomas said, "Lucky you." He pressed his thumb hard into her heel.

"Ow," Susannah said. She yanked her foot back.

"Sorry," Thomas said.

"No, it's okay, I just have a blister or something."

Thomas put his beer down and picked up Laura's stuffed lamb. "Who does he belong to?" he said. "Is he yours or Laura's?"

Susannah said, "Laura's." Then, "Wait, how do you know Laura?"

"I don't," Thomas said. "Bogomil."

"What?" Susannah said.

"Bogomil," Thomas said. "His name is on the ribbon."

"That can't be his name," Susannah said. "That isn't a real name. Bogomil isn't real."

"Are you sure that's a blister on your heel?" Thomas said. "I thought I felt something. Here." He picked up her foot again. "A splinter. You got a pair of tweezers?"

Susannah stood up. "I think you should go," she said. "I don't know how you know Laura, and I really don't know how you know the name of some imaginary friend I used to have. But, you know, thanks for the fucking foot rub."

Thomas stood up, too. "You're welcome. Here," he said and handed her the black lamb. "See? Bogomil."

She saw the name on the ribbon. Felt blood rush to her head. "I don't like any of this," she said. "I want you to leave."

When she looked into Thomas's eyes, he was regarding her with actual sympathy. "I'll go," he said. "But first you ought to let me take out that splinter. I can't imagine how much that must hurt."

As he said it, she became aware that it was true. Her heel was throbbing. It had been for some time. It was very kind of Thomas to want to help.

"You sit down," he said. "Are the tweezers in the bathroom?"

"I think so," she said. "In the bottom drawer in the bathroom upstairs."

Thomas said, "It's going to be fine. I promise."

He went upstairs while Susannah sat on the couch holding the black lamb whose name was Bogomil. Everything was fine. It was all going to be fine. She felt so relieved she could almost have burst into tears.

The Book of Laura

Daniel and Laura knew where Mo lived, although neither of them had ever been inside his house. They went by the Cliff Hangar on the way, and Laura, who was in the lead, could feel Daniel's eyes on her back as they passed it. The shape of the Cliff Hangar in the darkness felt ominous. Normally all the lights would have been blazing.

A mile on was where the cliff fall had happened. They turned onto Maple. The houses got bigger and the lawns longer the closer they got to Mo's street. Mo's house was the largest, his lawn the longest.

"He lives here all by himself?" Daniel said.

"Well, he lived here with his grandmother," Laura said. "But she's dead now."

"You really liked her books," Daniel said.

"I really fucking did," Laura said.

A green cruiser was already leaning against the porch. They left their bikes with it and went up the stairs to ring the bell.

Rosamel Walker opened the door. She'd shaved her head, and the shape of her skull was so very beautiful that Laura, already warm from the long uphill ride, felt a wave of heat go through her.

"Oh hey," Rosamel said. "Laura. Daniel. What's up?"

"Great question," Daniel said. "I've been asking myself the same question for the past few days."

Rosamel looked at Laura.

"Ignore him," Laura said. "You're in Ohio, right? How's Ohio?"

"There are a lot of cows," Rosamel said.

"There are cows in Ireland, too!" Laura said enthusiastically.

"Interesting," Rosamel said. Which, clearly, it wasn't, but it was nice of her to say it. "You guys hear about the tiger?"

Laura looked at Daniel, who shook his head. "No?" she said.

"Someone got a picture of a tiger on one of the hiking trails this afternoon. Off the Cliff Road. It's kind of blurry but definitely a tiger. They think maybe somebody was keeping one as a pet and it escaped. There was a news crew in town earlier."

"It was a tiger? Not a wolf? Like, a white wolf?" Daniel said.

"Definitely a tiger," Rosamel said. "You heard about the Cliff Hangar? The owner and the cook?"

"Yeah," Laura said. "They're missing."

Rosamel said, "My mom says there's going to be a community night at the Cliff Hangar, karaoke and food. Tomorrow night, cover charge goes to a fund for the cook's family. For Christmas, you know? He has two little kids."

"I didn't know that," Laura said. Whatever had happened, it hadn't been her fault. She hadn't done it.

Rosamel said, "So maybe I'll see you there, yeah? Bye, Daniel. Bye, Laura. Hey, Laura, like what you did with your hair."

Laura's hand went up to touch her head. "I haven't done anything to my hair."

"Right," Rosamel said, not smiling. "I know. It's what you were supposed to say to me. See you tomorrow night."

Then she was going down the stairs of the porch past them. Laura turned to watch her go. Even the old green cruiser took on a borrowed beauty under the glow of the streetlights with Rosamel Walker seated regally upon it.

Daniel, meanwhile, had stuck his head inside the door. "Mo? Hello? Oh, um, hey."

He was talking to a woman Laura thought maybe she'd seen once or twice in What Hast Thou Ground? She said, "You must be Daniel and Laura. I'm Jenny. Mo's upstairs. If you don't mind, take off your shoes before you come in."

Oh, the house was beautiful and there was a smell, too, of good things. Cinnamon and pine. How often had Laura dreamed of being invited inside? Surely the author of her favorite books was here somewhere, sitting in a comfortable chair and writing in a notebook, or at her desk, a cup of tea beside her laptop. Lavender Glass must be here, too, somewhere. Recovering from being stabbed, or reading a letter from one of her lovers, or both. Up in a high place, looking out at the sea through a window. Up in a high place, dreaming of Rosamel Walker.

The floor of the foyer was an inlaid pattern of stars and squares in dark and light wood, so glossy Laura slid her socks along it as if skating on a pond. The wallpaper was dusty green and midnight blue: owls peeping out of bowers of branches. Paintings and photographs of Black men and women hung from picture rails on the walls. Just down the hall in front of them was a doorway with a legend painted in gold above the door: EVERYTHING WOULD HAVE BEEN FINE HAD THE FOLLOWING EVENTS NOT OCCURRED.

When Jenny saw Laura looking she said, "Maryanne's office. I don't know what it means. A private joke, I think."

They passed another room, a library all in blue and gold with glass-fronted bookcases on every wall. Jenny led them up the staircase where, above the landing, a stained glass window showed Adam and Eve, a serpent between them. Adam and Eve were Black. The serpent's round head was a golden coin of light. All around the perimeter were other Black faces, light shining through, and Laura paused on the landing for a better look.

Their guide, Jenny, said, "It was designed by one of Alma Thomas's students. Library on the first floor, bedrooms on the second, and music on the third. Maryanne thought that was ideal, falling asleep suspended halfway between her books and music. So you've been with Mo over in Ireland? I've never been. Are you hungry? There's pizza and sodas and banana bread up in the music studio already."

"He has a *studio*?" Daniel muttered.

The woman on the staircase above them—wasn't one of the Lavender Glass books dedicated to a Jenny? Maybe *Turn Your Back to the Sea and Marry the Sky*—looked over her shoulder. "It was Cara's," she said. "His mother's."

LAURA HAD READ the first Lavender Glass book when she was twelve years old. She'd found it in the quarter rack at a library sale. If her mother had seen her buy it, maybe she would have raised an objection, but Laura bought it when she wasn't looking and stuck it in her backpack. Anyway, she'd skipped all the sex stuff. It wasn't what she was interested in. There were pirates and castles and lots of descriptions of clothes that seemed much more fun than anything that Laura ever got to wear. People went to feasts and also murdered each other. Lavender Glass kept a little dagger called a dirk in her worsted stockings, which Laura thought sounded itchy, and she had a loyal wolfhound who always knew when someone meant her harm. She was an orphan but very brave. She had no mother, no father, no sister. She always tried to do the right thing and even though this frequently led her and those around her into disaster and ruin, Laura loved her for it, as did everyone else in the books. Well, if they didn't, then either they were secretly evil or else eventually they realized their error and learned to love Lavender Glass the way they ought to have loved her in the first place.

There is a moment in the fifth Lavender Glass book, *Marry a Grave at Midnight*, when her dear friend Yvette confesses that she has always loved her. There is even a kiss. Lavender Glass feels a kind of strange thrill in the softness of her friend's lips. She can feel Yvette's breasts pressing against her own. Of course, nothing comes of it and Yvette dies after drinking from a poisoned glass of wine meant for Lavender Glass. But when Laura read that scene, she realized something about herself. She wanted to kiss girls, too. Of course, fiction and television had made it clear to her that girls who loved girls usually came to tragic ends. If you asked her, she would have said this has had no bearing on her own life. The reason she's never kissed a girl is because she has always been waiting for the right moment and the right moment has never yet presented itself.

Lavender Glass played the harp, and her playing was of such unearthly beauty it was as if an enchantment fell upon everyone who heard her play. Laura had no access to harps, but her father's acoustic guitar was in the hall closet. Even an old Harmony Sovereign Marveltone can be a serviceable instrument for a beginner, but her father had treated this one poorly. Nevertheless Laura bought new strings and began to learn how to play. Susannah, who never had any ideas of her own, except for ones that were either impossible or bad, made fun of Laura at first and pretended she was in physical pain whenever the Harmony went out of tune, which it did at all opportunities. It was unlovely, temperamental, warped, scarred all down one side. No wonder their father had left it behind.

And then Laura had bought a Squier electric at a garage sale. When she played, Susannah listened, sometimes. By the time they were in ninth grade, Laura had the Yamaha, and sometimes when she made up songs, Susannah sang them with her. Made up her own songs. See? An enchantment.

The summer before tenth grade Daniel said, "You guys could do this for real." And the thing was, they really could. So that was the start of the band. Laura had the Yamaha Pacifica PAC112J. Someone was going to have to play bass, and Susannah didn't want to, so they made Daniel take it up instead. He got a Squier four-string bass on Craigslist. One of Ruth's co-workers gave Susannah her son's Ashthorpe five-piece. She wouldn't even take money for it. She said now that he was in college, she just wanted it out of the house. Laura didn't know where it was, currently. Maybe disassembled and stowed away in the closet under the stairs. Or maybe Susannah had carried it down to the shore, thrown it into Little Moon Bay.

AFTER SHE FINISHED the first book about Lavender Glass, Laura acquired all the other Caitlynn Hightower books at the library. When Ruth caught her reading *The Sea Is Not Deeper Than My Love,* she'd said, "Are you sure you're old enough for those?"

Laura said she had already read the first three, so she thought she probably was, and Ruth laughed. "Fine. I guess. Half the nurses are die-hard fans of hers. She's a nice lady. Always sends the NICU cookies at Christmas."

Laura said incredulously, "You know her? Caitlynn Hightower?"

"That's just a pen name," Ruth said. "Caitlynn Hightower is Maryanne Gorch, Mo's grandmother. I thought you knew his grandmother was a writer."

"Yeah," Susannah said from the kitchen table where she was using

Ruth's laptop to look up the Wikipedia page for Eleanor Roosevelt. She hadn't even started her report yet, even though it was due in the morning. "Didn't you know that, Laura? Everybody knows." Laura's report was already in her backpack.

LAURA DIDN'T KNOW much about Mo's mother, other than that she was dead. When she looked at Daniel, he shrugged.

The stairs came through the floor of a renovated attic space where Mo was sitting like a supervillain in a chair shaped like an egg. He put down his book and said, "Oh, good. You're here."

"Oh, good," Daniel said. "Pizza. Oh my God, you got Love Sends Pizza pizzas." This was extravagance: Love Sends Pizza was where you went for birthdays or graduations. He went straight for the long plank table where there were four large pizzas in their boxes, and Laura followed. Mo had made a head start on what smelled like LSP's fennel Parmesan with preserved lemon and roasted garlic.

"Enjoy!" Jenny said. "I'll be downstairs refreshing Twitter and reading Facebook posts about how global warming isn't real from people I shouldn't be friends with. Yell down if you need anything."

"Thanks, Jenny," Mo said. "Oh, hey, you should take a couple of slices."

"No, no," Jenny said. "I'll just eat whatever's left over when you guys are done."

Mo and Daniel and Laura looked at one another. "You should probably take some now," Mo said.

The Book of Daniel

Before Laura came by to collect him, Daniel spent a while playing catch with Davey and Oliver, while Lissy and Dakota had a long conversation around the corner of the house. When he went over to ask if they wanted to join in, they looked full of regret. No, they were too busy. There were too many things they had to do. No time for catch. The world needed mending.

"Anything I could help with?" he asked.

Again, Lissy and Dakota regarded him with pity tempered with fondness. It was so nice of him to offer, these looks said. But he'd been away for so long. Everything had changed while he'd been gone.

Carousel hadn't wanted to play catch, either. She had gotten hold of his coin collection again, and she was arranging them on the kitchen floor in small stacks while their mom sat at the table paying bills. "Which one comes from farthest away?" she said.

"That one's from Korea," he said.

"What about the moon?" Carousel said. "What kind of money do they use on the moon?"

"Everything's free on the moon," Daniel said. "You don't have to pay for anything there. You can just have whatever you need because you need it."

"Com-moon-ism," their mom said, but nobody paid her any attention.

Carousel said, "They should have money anyway, because money's pretty. Can I have your coin collection when you die?"

"What if I need it when I'm dead, though?" Daniel asked.

Carousel dumped more coins out onto the floor. She said, "Then get a job."

At least Oliver and Davey were deliriously happy to have Daniel. He could just reach out and pluck the ball out of the air, no matter how much force they put behind their throws. That's how tall he was. They threw the ball over and over, and he tossed it back as many times as they yelled at him to throw it. Every time he threw it, a feeling came over him that he could have thrown the ball even farther and even farther still. He could have thrown it up so high in the air, it would never come down again. He could have used magic to do that, and wouldn't the twins have been amazed? He could have done other things, too. He could have turned the whole yard into Disney World, maybe, or all the grass to silver. Daniel could have summoned every dog in the neighborhood so his brothers and sisters wouldn't miss Fart. He could have gone back to Lewis Latimer and made Ms. Fish *understand* why Carousel ought to be called by the name she'd chosen for herself. He could go tell Susannah how he felt, and if she didn't feel the same, well, he could make her feel differently. He could make her happy. Daniel had potential, a thing he'd never been sure he had before. He had the potential to do things that other people couldn't. He had come back from the dead, and wasn't it kind of a waste to stand here in the yard playing catch with his brothers? Wasn't it kind of a waste to die again when there was still so much life he could have? Yes, and that was okay, too. He would be wasteful. And then he would be dead.

Right now Davey and Oliver wanted as much time with Daniel as they could get. But they were twins. When Daniel was gone, they'd have each other. And when Daniel was gone, he'd have nobody. So he was going to make the best of the time he had now and catch that ball every single fucking time. You didn't need magic to catch a ball.

The afternoon was fading when he and Davey and Oliver went inside again, his brothers flopping down on the floor in front of the TV to play a video game. Carousel and his coin collection were gone, and his mom was cutting up eggplant and salting the slices, laying them down on a plate.

"Eggplant Parm for dinner," she said.

"You need help?" he said.

"I got it," she said. "Don't think I don't see everything you've been doing since you got home. Taking care of everyone. Honey, it isn't that I don't appreciate it, but you know you don't have to do it all."

"No," Daniel said. "I know. It just seemed like you and Peter had a lot on your plate and I wanted to help some."

She looked at him ruefully. "I will admit that we let some things slide in the last couple of months. This year, I don't know what it is. It's just been a hard year. Nothing big. I don't think. Just, life. You know?"

"I think so," he said. "Sorry."

"Why?" his mom said. "Daniel. You don't have to feel responsible for everything."

He said, "Okay."

"You around tonight?"

"Going out soon," he said. "Not really sure when I'll get back."

"Mysterious," his mom said.

"Mom? Did Dakota or Lissy ever have any problems in Ms. Fish's class? I was trying to remember. She was fine with me, but Mo said some stuff and I was wondering—"

His mom put her knife down. She said, "If she has trouble with Black kids?"

"Yeah," Daniel said.

"I've been asking myself the same question," his mom said. "Lissy and Dakota were such sunny kids when they were Carousel's age. They could have had an actual troll as a teacher and neither one would have noticed as long as there were crayons and glue sticks and enough construction paper. But you, you were a handful, and Ms. Fish adored you. Carousel on her worst day isn't even close to you, and Ms. Fish suggested we look into therapy. So your dad and I are going to have a talk tonight. We'll figure this out."

"Okay," Daniel said. "Good. Hey, Mom?"

She was slicing up eggplant again. Vigorously.

"You know how sometimes you feel like you can do anything you want? Anything at all?"

His mom said with finality, "Everybody feels that way when they're young."

The knife came down again.

On the blackboard paint in the living room, someone had written 2 RETURN 2 REMAIN. But unlike in Mr. Anabin's classroom, it came off when Daniel wiped.

THE ATTIC RAN the length of the Gorch house: a long open space with a pitched ceiling and soft carpets in blues and scarlets scattered on the floor. A glass partition at the far-right end separated a recording studio from the rest of the space, and all along one long wall, alcoves had been carved out of the eaves. In each alcove there were instruments on various stands and in display cases. Some of them were unlike any instrument Daniel had ever seen.

On the other long wall was a row of tall casement windows: through them there was a rose garden and small lights along a spiral path of crushed shells; beyond the white path, a low rock wall grown over with more rosebushes, climbing roses; beyond the roses and the wall and the path, the vertiginous drop and then the lustrous seam where the eye insisted sky and ocean met.

Daniel stood before the windows. He didn't wish to talk about magic with Laura and Mo. He didn't want to be here at all. It would be an easy thing, in fact, to unlatch the window and go flying out. To use his human fingers for one task and then to become a bird and fly away. What would it feel like?

In the garden down below, a white shape moved upon the white shell path. It raised its head and looked up at Daniel through the locked window.

He must have made some noise because Mo said, "What? Is someone out there?"

"Is it the tiger?" Laura said.

They joined him at the window, but the wolf was gone again.

"There's nobody there," Mo said. He sounded disappointed.

"Sorry," Daniel said. He went and sat at the piano and pressed the middle C key down so lightly it made no sound at all. Perhaps the wolf had not been there. He played the note again, more decisively this time, and then began to pick out some pop song Lissy had been singing all afternoon. "Nice piano," he said. How did you get a baby grand up those stairs and into the attic anyway? He would have liked to watch. Of course, if you could do magic, you could just float it up. Or shrink it down to the size of a walnut and put it in your pocket. Carry it up that way. The urge came upon Daniel to see if that was something he could do, turn the piano into a walnut, and so he got up and sat down in an armchair instead.

"It was my mom's," Mo said.

Laura said, "What's the deal with your mom anyway, Mo?"

Which was just like Laura, to just get in there and ask all the awkward questions. Everyone should have a Laura, although if you had a Laura, you had to accept that you were also going to get questions.

Mo said, "She died when I was nine. Bad heart." As he said it, he looked at Daniel with a kind of absolute loathing. Daniel looked away.

"That sucks," Laura said.

"All of this"—Mo gestured at the room full of instruments—"These belonged to my mom. Cara. She grew up here, but she was younger than your parents, I think. By the time she was fourteen, she was commuting once a week to Boston for classes at the conservatory at Berklee. But she didn't like performing. She just liked instruments and so she got a degree in ethnomusicology and went all over the world researching rare instruments. Historical instruments. Things people still play but play differently now. Instruments archeologists find in tombs that nobody's ever seen before. She came home with a lot of weird shit. She stored most of it here in my grandmother's house because she had this tiny apartment in Manhattan. I don't really remember it, but I do remember it was tiny."

"And now it's all yours? All of this?" Laura said.

"Yeah," Mo said. "Jenny says there's a trust or something. When I turn twenty-one it's all mine."

"If you live that long," Laura said.

"I'm planning on living a lot longer than that," Mo said. "Got a lot of stuff I want to do. So let's talk about today. What we learned. What we're going to do next."

"Excellent," Laura said. "I made a list. Feel free to add anything I left out. Okay, one, Mr. Anabin is a terrible magic teacher. Two, it's his birthday tomorrow and we are all supposed to magically acquire presents for him. Also we still don't know how we died. Three, Bowie is a lot more advanced at magic than we are. Four, the Malo Mogge person is clearly a part of all of this, and maybe the tiger, and Hannah disappearing, and five, Daniel."

"What?" Daniel said.

Laura crossed her arms. She said, "You're problem number five."

"Because I don't want to do magic?" Daniel said. "Doesn't that make me the opposite of a problem? Only two get to remain, remember? I stay out of the competition and then you and Mo just have to figure out how to be better than Bowie."

"Fine by me," Mo said.

"No!" Laura said. "We agreed we were going to stick together. Which means Daniel is going to do his best to keep on Mr. Anabin's good side. Right?"

"Fine," Daniel said. "I'll think about a birthday present."

Mo said, "Tell me about Malo Mogge again."

They ate the last pieces of pizza while Laura described Malo Mogge in as much detail as she could summon up. Daniel had very little to add.

"We could ask Mr. Anabin about her," Mo said. "Or I guess we could ask her about Mr. Anabin, if any of us run into her again."

"Maybe she was the person you saw last night," Laura said. "The one who waved at you."

"No," Mo said. He sounded very certain.

"What about one of those tie pins shaped like a clef symbol? Aren't music teachers supposed to like things like that?" Daniel said.

Laura said to Mo, "Did you and Rosamel talk about the night we died?"

"Yeah. We did. What I remember is Susannah kissing Rosamel during 'The Kissing Song,'" Mo said. Laura made a face. "And you kissed Daniel. And that's pretty much what Rosamel remembers, too. She said she went home after that because she was already in trouble with her mom for missing curfew the night before. She said when she left I was over on the carousel with you guys."

"With me?" Laura said.

"Yeah," Mo said. "You and Daniel. I don't remember that, either."

"This is pointless," Daniel said. "Even if we remember something, how can we be sure it's a real memory and not just like all of this Ireland stuff?"

He went over to the window again. Here was the moon on the spiral path, the low wall, the shadowed rosebushes. There was no wolf.

Laura and Mo joined him at the window.

"Even if it's pointless, we still have to try," Laura said. "We died and we came back. How many people get a second chance like that?"

"How many people get a chance after they die to come back and say goodbye to their family?" Daniel countered. "Glass half-full, glass half-empty, you're acting like it's glass free refill."

"My grandmother loved roses," Mo said, and Daniel remembered Mo had no family left to say goodbye to.

"It must be incredible when they're all in bloom," Laura said.

"Yeah," Mo said. He unlatched the window. The night was still far too warm for December, though colder than it had been. Daniel watched as Mo opened his hand, extended his fingers. He reached through the window, fingers describing a motion like pulling something out of the air. As Mo did this, the rosebushes began to rustle and quiver. On the bushes, bare branches began to send out new shoots, then the small, dark curls of leaves. Buds appeared and unfolded themselves into yellow and pink blossoms.

"Oh, let me try!" Laura said. She held out her right hand, palm up, and lifted it in an abrupt motion. Every white fragment of shell upon the path rose into the air and became a cloud of white moths beating their wings, churning the air. The smell of roses climbed up to the window and began to seep into the attic room, overpowering and familiar. It was the smell of darkness and death and Bogomil. Daniel looked at Laura and Mo, but they were staring out at the garden, enchanted by their own magic.

Didn't they remember?

"Shut the window," Daniel said. "Before the moths get in."

When neither paid any attention to him, he did it himself. As he pulled the window shut, Laura turned the cup of her palm down. Every white moth fell back to earth and became shells in a neat spiral again. But the bushes still blazed with roses.

"Come on, Laura," Daniel said. "We should head home."

Mo said, "Isn't there stuff we still need to talk about?"

"Not tonight," Daniel said.

Laura said, "We could stay a little longer. I want to check out the instruments. Look, there's a harp. I've never played a harp." She disappeared into an alcove. "Is there anything she didn't collect? This is everything I can think of, every single instrument."

"Everything but a Katzenklavier," Mo said. "No Apprehension Engine, either."

"Stay if you want," Daniel said. He'd never heard of either of those, and he bet Laura hadn't, either. "I'll text you if I see a tiger on the ride home so you can take a different route."

"Who cares," Laura said. "It's probably just Bogomil anyway. Not a real tiger." She had begun to produce a series of rippling, watery chords on the harp. It seemed to Daniel it was not precisely in tune, but that only added to the otherworldly effect.

"Oh, well, if it's only Bogomil!" he said incredulously.

"Stay as long as you like, Laura," Mo said.

"No, fine," Laura said, emerging. "I'll go. Thanks for the pizza, Mo. Talk tomorrow?"

Mo said, "Tell Susannah hey. Be careful out there."

Daniel hesitated on the stairs after Laura was already gone. "You want any help cleaning up? With the pizza boxes and everything?"

Mo raised his eyebrows. His look said: from you?

"I know you don't like me," Daniel said. "Look, if it's because of Ms. Fish, I get it."

"It isn't because of Ms. Fish," Mo said. "And, really, my reasons for not liking you, *should* I not like you, are not going to matter a whole lot if you keep this shit up and Laura and I are the two who get to stay and you end up back there. Just a thought."

"Okay," Daniel said. "I get it. It's not like you owe me anything."

"No," Mo said. "I don't."

The Book of Susannah

It was a while before Thomas came back downstairs, but Susannah didn't mind. Perhaps the tweezers weren't where she'd thought. Perhaps she should have gone upstairs to help him look, but she was very comfortable where she was. And how funny that the stuffed animal's name was Bogomil. She found if she listened very carefully, she could hear the black lamb's voice. It sounded just like Bogomil in her dreams. It was saying, "Well, this is a pickle, Susannah. I never liked that boy. He's a creature of Malo Mogge's, which would be bad enough even if it wasn't clear he has his own agenda. If you aren't careful, you'll end up like him. Though it may be useful to see what he wants of you."

"Are you real?" Susannah asked the black lamb. "If you're real, then help me. I can't get up. He told me to stay here."

Thomas came down the stairs again. "Let's get that splinter out."

Bogomil was still whispering.

Thomas frowned. "Don't listen to him," he said, and took the black lamb away from Susannah. "Whatever he told you about me is doubly true of him."

Susannah said, "Is he real?"

"As real as I am," Thomas said. He shoved Bogomil under the couch. "Here. Let me see your foot."

"Why?" Susannah said.

"You have a splinter," Thomas said. "But you can't remember that you have a splinter, probably because Bogomil or Anabin has been messing with your head. This would be some mechanism of theirs."

"Mr. Anabin?" Susannah said. "The music teacher?"

"Yeah," Thomas said. "That guy."

He took Susannah's foot in one hand and, startled, she said, "What are you doing?"

But then he had the splinter out and Susannah began to feel a kind of vertiginous strangeness pressing on and seeping into the bubble of calm Thomas's voice evoked in her, as if the comfortable white couch they sat upon was perched on some precipice, high and precarious.

"There," Thomas said. "Nasty thing. I wonder where it came from."

"I smashed Laura's guitar," Susannah said. "I stepped on a piece and it went into my foot."

"You smashed a guitar?" Thomas said.

"Into bits," Susannah said.

"Where is it?" Thomas said.

"In Laura's room. I'll go get it." But of course the Harmony was fine, unsmashed and perfectly serviceable. She brought it down to show Thomas. She couldn't even get a simple act of destruction right, apparently.

"Why'd you smash it?" Thomas said. He sounded only mildly interested, the way you would be if someone was trying to explain why they didn't like carrots.

"Because they disappeared. They were gone and no one knew what had happened to them. I realized they were never going to come back and so I smashed Laura's guitar."

"Stop crying," Thomas said absentmindedly. "It does no good."

Susannah, who had not been aware she was crying, wiped her eyes. She said, "They were in Ireland? They were in Ireland the whole time?"

"No," Thomas said. "They weren't in Ireland. That's just something Anabin came up with, spur of the moment."

"Why do you keep mentioning Mr. Anabin?" Susannah said.

"Not important," Thomas said. "Focus on your sister and the other two."

"Daniel and Mo," Susannah said.

"Mo's the guy who lives in the big house up on the cliffs, right?"

"He's great," Susannah said.

"Yeah, cool." There was something wistful in his voice. "So he and

Daniel and your sister ended up someplace they shouldn't have. They went through a door."

"A door?"

"To get through this door in the first place, they had to have something. A token. A key. A coin."

"A coin?" Susannah said.

"Locked doors require something to open them," Thomas said. "A key. A coin. Think of it as a door charge. Have you seen such a thing?"

"Why do I feel so strange?" Susannah said.

Thomas patted her knee. "Because a lot of very weird shit is going on. It would make anyone feel strange."

"Then why aren't I freaking out more?" Susannah said.

"Because I don't want you to. There's no point in freaking out. It wouldn't accomplish anything. So, the coin. I need to figure out how your friends got it and where it is now."

Susannah said, "Daniel collects coins."

Thomas said, "If it were just lying around, Malo Mogge would have found it by now. But very well. Tell me about Daniel's coin collection. Ever seen one like this?"

All this time he'd been holding the bloody splinter that had been lodged in Susannah's foot. Now it became a small coin black with age.

Susannah recognized it at once. "That was his birthday present. It was Mo's, but he didn't want it. He was going to bring it to the show and I was going to give it to Daniel. It wasn't valuable, just old. Mo didn't want money for it. He said I could just give him free cappuccinos for a while."

The coin became a splinter of wood again. Thomas said, "So Mo gave it to you and you gave it to Daniel."

"Bogomil," Susannah said. "Bogomil knew about it. That Mo had it. He told me Daniel would like it. He said if I gave it to Daniel, we would always be together. Like a lucky coin. But then Daniel and I broke up before the show at the Cliff Hangar and Laura could tell, because Laura can *always* tell, and she was like, I told you so, and so I kissed Rosamel Walker during 'The Kissing Song' and Laura kissed Daniel. I walked off the stage. I went home. That's pretty much it."

"I don't really understand anything you just said," Thomas said. "Except for the part about Bogomil. That part is uncomfortably familiar. What happened when you gave Daniel the coin?"

"I didn't," Susannah said. "I never got the coin from Mo. I just went home. Why do I feel so bad about not being able to help you more?"

"Because I want you to want to help me," Thomas said. "I'm very persuasive when I want to be."

"Did you make me want to have sex with you?"

"No," Thomas said. "Why, do you regret it?"

"No," Susannah said. "I don't think so. But I don't want to have sex with you again. I thought you were a good guy. But you're not."

"Fair enough," Thomas said. "In the spirit of complete honesty, I didn't sleep with you because I wanted information. I slept with you because I wanted to. I don't get to do a lot of things I want to. But I hoped as well that you might be helpful. More helpful. Malo Mogge is not going to be a happy camper."

"Sorry," Susannah said. "I'm always letting people down."

"Not your fault," Thomas said. "Although there's one more thing."

"What?"

"I thought I saw someone the other day," Thomas said. "A boy. About my age. Maybe you've seen him, too? He looks like me."

Susannah thought about it. "No," she said. "What's his name?"

Thomas rubbed his head. It left a piece of his hair sticking straight up in a particularly ridiculous fashion, and Susannah thought with a pleasure she didn't entirely understand that she wouldn't tell him. Unless he asked her.

"Kristofer," he said. "His name is Kristofer."

"He's your brother," Susannah said. She knew this without knowing how she knew. Maybe it was the way he said the name. It was the same way she said "Laura."

"Not important," Thomas said. "Just a trick of Malo Mogge. Or Bogomil. It couldn't have been him anyway. He's been dead three hundred years."

"I'm sorry," Susannah said.

"I know," Thomas said. "But it isn't your fault. Not everything is your fault, you know."

"I think it might be, though," Susannah said. "I didn't do what I was supposed to do. Bogomil told me what I was supposed to do and I didn't do it."

"No use crying over spilled blood," Thomas said. "Bogomil ought to have known better. It didn't go particularly well the last time, either. Give me your phone."

"What's going to happen?" Susannah said, handing it over. She had a lot of questions, but this one seemed most important.

"And now you have my number, should you need to call me. What's going to happen is nothing you can prevent," Thomas said, "so what's the point in worrying about it? Sorry about this, but it's for the best."

"What's for the best?" Susannah said, but Thomas had put down her phone. He took her foot in one hand and with the other, he drove the splinter back into her heel. He did it so quickly it hardly hurt at all.

"Now everything's all tidy again," Thomas said, although Susannah had no idea what he meant by saying that. He was rubbing her foot and it felt absolutely fantastic.

She saw Laura's guitar lying beside the couch and said, jokingly, "You going to play me a love song?"

"What's a love song?" Thomas said.

"Funny," Susannah said. "What time is it? There was something I was supposed to do. But I don't remember what it was."

Thomas stood up. "Time I should be going," he said. "Whatever it was, you'll figure it out. But if I don't get back to Malo Mogge soon, she'll come to fetch me. And we don't want that."

He reached under the couch and pulled out the black stuffed lamb. What was its name? Something funny, but Susannah couldn't remember.

"I'll deal with this. It will be as if it was never here. Take care of yourself," Thomas said. "You at the coffee shop tomorrow?"

"Lissy and Dakota!" Susannah said, remembering. "That's it. I'm supposed to do magic with them later. Two A.M. They're going to conjure up some snow."

Thomas watched her.

"But that isn't for a long while yet," she said. "Is it?"

"No," Thomas said. "Do they need any extra help? With their magic?"

"All the help they can get," Susannah said. "Or they wouldn't have asked me. Why? You offering?"

Thomas smiled at her. He looked much older, suddenly, as if he found the idea of magic ridiculous, a thing for children. "If I knew how to change this weather for snow, then, yes, absolutely I would help you do so. But no doubt the three of you will suffice. Good night, Susannah."

When he was gone, Susannah got another beer out of the fridge and drank it in the shower. She stuck Laura's guitar back in her room because Laura didn't like people messing with her things.

Her father called, but she didn't pick up. It was kind of nice to have him back in her life, but part of what was nice about it was ignoring his calls. Let him wonder where she was and what she was up to. Let him see how it felt.

She was watching some movie about a heist gone wrong and not thinking about Daniel (she was so very conscientiously not thinking about Daniel—she shouldn't be thinking about Daniel when she'd just had sex with another guy on the living room floor of her mother's house, not that there was any reason why she shouldn't do what she wanted—that eventually she gave up on trying to understand the mechanics of the heist and instead just watched people as they did things that made other people increasingly unhappy) when Ruth got home from class, and not long after that Laura came in, with a look on her face Susannah recognized. It was the one where Laura was very pleased with herself and displeased with everything and everyone else, and the admixture of these two emotions was giving her mild psychological dyspepsia. It was how Laura had almost always looked after a My Two Hands Both Knowe You show.

"Mo says hi," Laura said, running her hands along the top of the couch as if checking for dust. Susannah wanted to say, *Check the floor while you're at it, Laura. I may have gotten some sex on it.*

"Mo?" Susannah said.

Laura was giving her a considering look. She said, "Yes, Mo. Is that a hickey?"

"Yes," Susannah said.

"That guy in the picture you sent?" Laura asked.

"Maybe," Susannah said.

"Is it something serious?"

Susannah didn't even have to think about it. "More of a one-time thing. You were with Mo? Is he okay? That's where you went?"

"Me and Daniel biked up to his house. He's about how you would expect, but nice try at changing the subject. So you and Daniel aren't going to start hooking up again? Because that's what usually happens. You guys are the three-time Olympic champions of poor decision-making in relationships. Like a figure skating pair who does the same routine every time: one Ina Bauer, curve lift, spread eagle, two make-outs, one breakup, one makeup, followed by a messy-ass dismount."

"Dismounts are gymnasts, not figure skaters," Susannah said. "Why are you of all people lecturing me about my love life? You've never couple-skated in your life. Maybe while you guys were in Ireland, I got my life together. And maybe I can see now how me and Daniel don't really work."

"Yeah, well, he's in a weird place right now," Laura said. "I think he needs someone to give him a kick in the ass, and maybe you guys were terrible together a lot of the time, but you were good for each other, too. Some of the time. I'll concede that."

"You made a rule for the band specifically so Daniel and I would stop hooking up!" Susannah said, astonished at her sister's hypocrisy.

"And now there's no band," Laura said. "So scrap the rules. Daniel needs to be reminded that the people he loves want him around. That it's okay to want to want things."

There was something grim about how Laura said this. Susannah said, "You're making it sound like he's suicidal or something."

"All I know is that he was miserable the whole time we were in Ireland," Laura said. "And right now he's still miserable and maybe if you and he were at least on speaking terms, he'd cheer up some."

"Because it's my job to make Daniel happy," Susannah said.

Laura said, "Fair. But, you know, I guess I thought maybe you were unhappy, too."

Susannah drew herself up, attempting to look as happy as possible. She said, "I'm figuring stuff out, okay? You hung out with Mo at his house, did he show you his mom's music studio?"

"Yeah," Laura said. "Crazy thing is, it was full of guitars and instruments and all this stuff, and instead of appreciating it I just kept thinking I'd kill to see where his grandmother wrote the Caitlynn Hightower books."

Susannah said, "Did Mo say anything to you about me? Like, he's not pissed off at me or anything, right?"

"What?" Laura said. She appeared genuinely confused. "Why would you think that? What did you do?"

Susannah said, "I guess it's that we haven't talked since you guys went to Ireland, and then his grandmother died and I didn't check in on him or anything. And he hasn't texted me, so."

"God, Susannah," Laura said with relish. "Not everything is about you. I bet you haven't even heard about Hannah. Or the tiger. Are there any leftovers? I'm starving."

The Book of Thomas

Thomas has spent much of his long life in various shapes and forms. Once, Malo Mogge, vexed by some failure or impertinence of his, turned him into a star-nosed mole and kept him in a box of dirt for eight years. You would have thought it would be a relief to not be at her beck and call, but such was not the case. When she turned him back again, Thomas fell to his human knees before her and wept from his human eyes with gratitude. Even as hatred burned, restored, in his human heart.

He prefers, now, to remain human. The human body is nourishment to the hatred that sustains him. A star-nosed mole or a bat or a fox, all things he has been at times, is too easily distracted. Sensation blots out reason and unreason, too. He isn't Bogomil, who reeks of human vindictiveness and bad humor as an animal and as a human exudes animal wildness. Feralness. Whatever Bogomil was before, now in all of his aspects and appetites he is changed into something both less and more.

Thomas wonders sometimes about Anabin, who, Malo Mogge says, greatly perplexed, is always only himself. All of these centuries unchanged. What thing can he not bear to give up? That he changes not lest he risk it being changed as well?

Though even Anabin must be something other than what he once was. Not to change is also to change, of course.

Yesterday Thomas had thought he saw his brother. And if what he'd seen was some revenant portion of Kristofer, then what did Kristofer see, looking at Thomas? An abomination. Thomas knows what he is.

All these years Thomas has spent hunting his enemy, perhaps the one he loved was instead within his reach. If Kristofer is here now, if he has been in the world these three centuries, then Thomas has squandered his hard-won time. He has been a fool.

The toy lamb knows what Thomas is afraid of, knows what Thomas knows, and as Thomas carries Bogomil away from the house where Susannah lives, Bogomil is speaking. He says, "He is dead. You know he is dead. But what if he is not dead? You saw him dead. But what if he is now alive again? You saw him and you knew him. What if he is not dead?"

This toy lamb is not really Bogomil, of course, but he has invested some small piece of himself in it.

"He died," Thomas says. His heart is calcified, a stone. That is a thing that never changes.

"What if I caught him up?" the black lamb says. "What if he has been in my realm all this time? What if now he has fled my realm with the others?"

"Has he been with you?" Thomas asks the lamb. He did not mean to speak at all, but this is how it goes with Bogomil. "All this time?"

But now it is the black lamb who is silent. Thomas carries it down the beach to the ocean, where he ties its ribbon to a rock. Then he throws it out as far as he can, which is very far indeed. One day—soon, perhaps—Bogomil will be human again, and if Malo Mogge permits it, Thomas will reenact this moment.

If Thomas walks along the beach, then takes the boardwalk inland, eventually he will come to the house where he and Malo Mogge live with Giselle and Malcolm. Though perhaps for not much longer. They have no bargain with Malo Mogge. There is nothing that protects them. Malo Mogge does not mean them harm, but she does not count the cost.

It is not that Thomas is not grateful to Malo Mogge for his long, strange life. He will never go hungry unless she wishes it. His time is at his disposal when she does not require it, and he has had so very much more time than he ever imagined. He has taken as lovers women and men with kind hearts and gentle hands, and when they do not have those things, Thomas has abilities and the discretion to deal with them as they best deserve. He has a purpose. He has magic.

As Thomas walks, he begins to work the change Susannah's two young friends desire. The temperature drops. Thomas is aware, as he walks, that someone is traveling with him. It may be Bogomil again, or perhaps Anabin wishes to pay his respects. It will not be Kristofer. He must not think his brother has come to find him here. The magic that he is doing is complex enough, this part of it; he must not be distracted by unlikely hopes. He must hold many things in balance: the girls did not request a great storm, and therefore the change must be carefully handled; he is not Malo Mogge or Bogomil to grant a wish by causing greater harm. There is only one he wishes harm upon. If his brother is here in this place, then she must be here, too. Everyone is here for the same reason: once again, there is the possibility of change. Malo Mogge's token, stolen so long ago and secreted away, has been found. No matter that it's gone to ground again. Someone will find it soon, and then Malo Mogge will act.

Malo Mogge will have her coin again. The door will open. Bogomil and Anabin will be released from their contract at last. Thomas will find his enemy before she finds him. Malo Mogge has given him the power and the right to do as he wishes with her. That is the bargain he and Malo Mogge made when he entered into her service.

The Book of Bowie

Bowie spent most of the day as a bird. It was as a bird that he felt the pull toward the building where the one called Anabin was waiting.

He hadn't meant to smash through the window. He had, in fact, forgotten that windows may be opened, not broken. But once he was inside the room and in the body of a boy again, he'd felt a kind of great calmness. Here was a place where doors opened and windows could be smashed and bodies bled. Pissing, too, was marvelous.

Anabin wanted a birthday present. Bowie felt sure both of these were things he had once been familiar with. Presents were things you made for someone. Out of cloth or carved from wood. Ribbons or even a sharp thing like a knife. You gave someone something because it was pretty or because they had a use for it. Birthdays were for the children of the rich so they knew their birth had value to those around them. Their life had value. There were many days for the living, and some of them belonged to the harvest and some belonged to holy saints. On some days there were feasts. The idea of a birthday drew out these random scraps of knowledge Bowie had once possessed, as if joined each to each like a chain of paste jewels. Even though Bowie was quite certain he had never had a birthday, it made sense the birth of one such as Anabin had been marked. Now Bowie must discover what might be of use to Anabin. He wanted very badly to be allowed to stay. He did not want to go back where he had been.

To this end, he spent some of the evening as a crow, following Anabin. By doing this, Bowie acquired more information about grocery stores and ATMs, if no better sense of what Anabin might desire as a present to mark his birthday. There was even a theater where many people including Anabin sat in pews as if in church and watched a story about people fighting in a style Bowie had never seen before, projected like a shadow play but all in colors and at a monstrous size. There had been words on the screen, too, telling what the people said to each other, though Bowie found that even though the language they spoke was gibberish to him, he could nevertheless understand because he desired to understand it. He could read the words on the screen, too, although before his death he thought perhaps he had not known how to read. Reading was a thing like birthdays. Whereas being a witch had been something that anyone could lay claim to, but most likely it resulted in the church imprisoning you or hanging you by the neck. Bowie, who was now a witch, had seen people hanged by the neck. Sometimes a cut was made in their belly first, and their entrails drawn out. This screen was better entertainment.

Had Anabin known Bowie-as-crow was there, at the back of the theater? No doubt he had.

When the entertainment was ended, Anabin went home, Bowie following. But he did not wish to go into Anabin's dwelling place. After his experience with the woman and her baby, he preferred to enter no more dwelling places.

He spent some time coasting on the warm currents of air that rose and fell high above Lovesend. There were no doors in the air. He was a nightjar now, plucking insects out of the air. Bats flitted around him, half choir, half dance. The ocean, stretching, creeping, stitched itself to the rotten fabric of the shore, and there was something else as well. The boy whose face he knew. There he was at water's edge, fumbling with something that reeked of Bogomil. As Bowie watched, he threw the Bogomil thing into the water.

Having done this, he began to make his way along the beach. Bowie did not know who he had been. But this other did. Bowie had seen it in his eyes. And this boy, like Bowie, could do things he shouldn't. He was turning the weather. Drawing the cold out of the water and from somewhere else, too. He was drawing cold from the moon, pulling it down.

Bowie could almost see how he went about it, like reeling in a net. You could see that this person and the moon were old acquaintances. The moon condescended to do his bidding as he did hers.

Bowie became a boy again, accepting as he did so that these actions were those of a fool. Had he been such a fool when he was alive?

He stood barefoot on the sand in front of the other one, his poor human legs prickling with the cold.

"Who are you?" he said. "Do you know me?"

"Who am *I*?" the other one repeated. He looked as though Bowie, suddenly appearing, had driven a knife into his side. "Do you know *me*?" The thing upon his face was a mirror to the thing that Bowie felt.

There was enough moonlight that he could see how much they resembled each other, he and this other one. A name came to him. "Thomas."

The boy said, "Kristofer?"

"I know that name!" Bowie said. "Am I he?"

Thomas clasped Bowie's hand in his own. With his other, he turned up Bowie's face and examined it carefully. The moon was bright enough that Bowie could see the moment the other's expression changed. He pulled his hand back from Bowie's as if the touch burned.

"Avelot," the one called Thomas said.

That name, too, he knew. Grief welled up in him, thick and cold and endless. "Avelot is dead," Bowie said.

"My brother Kristofer is dead," Thomas said. His look of astonishment had become something watchful and avid. "And Avelot who killed him stands before me in his shape wearing his face, but I know you by your eyes. Avelot. One blue and one green. For three hundred years I have hunted you. Do you truly not remember yourself?"

Bowie said, "I have been in Bogomil's realm. There is not much left of what I might have been. When I required a body, this is what Anabin made of me. Bowie was the name I chose for myself. Avelot I may have been, Bowie I am now. What were you and Kristofer to me that I know you when I do not know myself?"

The night was growing colder, a wind beginning to blow. Part of Thomas's concentration had slipped, Bowie saw. Cold air poured in syrupy currents around them, the sand growing slick as grains of ice congealed beneath Bowie's bare feet.

Thomas laughed. He shook his head. "All this time," he said. "I sold myself to the devil so however long it took I might find you and make you render payment for what you did to my brother and me. And all this time I have no doubt Bogomil has made you suffer a thousand times more than ever I would have managed, and now I am to kill you when you do not even remember what you have done."

"Tell me first what I have done," Bowie said. "Let me remember."

"No," Thomas said. "But I will not kill you while you wear the body of my brother."

He made a gesture, and Bowie felt how she was now transformed, both slighter and heavier. Poised to change and flee again, only Thomas held her fixed in place.

"God curse you, Avelot," Thomas said, and raised his hand.

Power collected around them both, squeezing Bowie like a vise. But as she struggled to breathe, Bogomil was suddenly there. He was neither a wolf nor a hare but a man not much taller than Bowie.

"Hold, Thomas," Bogomil said.

Anabin, too, stood nearby, his back to them. He faced the sea and did not speak.

"It is my right," Thomas said. "I am the agent of Malo Mogge, and this is the thing she promised me. Shall we bring her here to make a judgment?"

Bogomil looked at where Anabin stood, facing away. He said, "When I realized in this last short while what was about to transpire, I came to your mistress and we had a conversation. It's been some time since we talked. I'm so very bad at keeping in touch with my friends. Much like Avelot here! But I'm afraid Avelot is once again a candidate in the trial you and she and your brother failed so spectacularly the last time round. We all hope this time she colors within the lines."

"It is my right to kill her," Thomas said again.

"Take that up with Malo Mogge," Bogomil said. "In the meantime, understand I am just as vexed as you. This one did no small amount of mischief to me, brought to nothing all my plans, and then, to add insult to injury, hid under my nose in my own realm in the dark like a flea! All I felt was the slightest itch. Remarkable girl, really."

He flicked his fingers at Bowie dismissively. "You should go," he said.

"Before your old friend here does something and then Anabin and I must do something, too, and it all gets very boring."

Bowie (who was Avelot?) found she was free to move again. She became a gull and flew away crying, "Who am I oh who am I I I I—"

When she circled over the shore because she could not help herself, Anabin and Bogomil were both vanished and the one named Thomas stood alone with the tide running over his shoes and back out into the darkness. A sodden black stuffed lamb rolled in and then was carried away in the surge, dragging a rock along with it. All the shore of Little Moon Bay was white with the water that ran down the sand and became the sea again, and whoever Kristofer had once been to anyone, he was dead and a long way from this place.

The Book of Laura

Ruth was always exhausted on nights when she had class. Slide lectures, she said, were the NyQuil of adult education. She went to bed before eleven, even though they all knew it meant she'd be up again at three, eating yogurt in front of the television and cursing herself. Laura and Susannah stayed up, playing Mario Kart companionably, not talking.

Laura discovered that being magical had made her significantly better at video games. As good as she wanted to be. Beating Susannah in race after race was almost too easy; however, that didn't mean it wasn't delightful.

Every now and then, Susannah's phone chirped. At first she checked it, but then she turned it facedown on the floor.

"What?" Laura said.

"Dad," Susannah said. "He keeps texting about this tiger. First just to let me know, and then when I didn't answer, it's like he really thinks I might have been eaten. Or that I'm walking around outside at midnight with a big sign that says 'Tiger Snax' around my neck."

"That sounds like something you might do," Laura said.

"Yeah, well, he's been texting you, too."

Laura paused the race and got her phone out of her bag. She'd left it on silent by accident, but there weren't any texts from Daniel or Mo. Just a long string from their father's number. "It's actually kind of sweet," she said. "Think he's been worried like this about us the whole time he's been gone?"

Susannah's eyebrows shot up. "Absolutely," she said. "We were his every waking thought. And don't text back! Revenge is sweet. Like breakfast cereal."

"You wanna play something else?" Laura said, feeling a little guilty but also aware that whatever else they played, she would probably win that, too.

"No," Susannah said. "I am one hundred percent going to kick your ass at this stupid game. Eventually."

"That's the spirit," Laura said. And then, inspired, she put the controller down. "Hold on."

She went up to the bathroom they shared and pulled open the communal makeup drawer, the stuff they'd always used for shows. Here were the Tupperware containers of colored glitter mixed into Vaseline: white, red, blue, pink, and black. She went down the stairs carrying all of them. Susannah could pick whichever she liked.

But, when she saw what Laura had, Susannah groaned. "What? No."

"Come on," Laura said. "For old times' sake. Remember after that show that one time? We stayed up all night playing Mario Kart. It was a blast. And you kicked my ass. Daniel's, too. It's not like I'm making you get up on a stage or anything."

"Fine," Susannah said. "But I get black and blue. If any of it gets on the couch, you're explaining it to Mom."

Laura knelt in front of her sister and opened the first container. She laid her left hand on top of the black and pressed down. Then she lifted her hand up and pressed it across Susannah's face: right cheek, forehead, mouth, bridge of her nose. Then, with her right hand, she left an overlapping print in blue on the other side of Susannah's face.

She examined her work. "Not bad," she said. "Now you do me. Red and pink."

It had been Laura's opinion, back when they started the band, that it would be smart to have a persona. Something to step into when they were going to perform. They didn't even have a name at that point, but when they came up with My Two Hands Both Knowe You, the appropriate gimmick had been clear. It was cheap, a little punk, showed well under stage lights, and entirely solved the question of makeup.

Laura had brought down makeup wipes as well so they could get the glitter off their hands. "How do I look?" she said.

"Like someone whose ass I am going to kick," Susannah said very grimly. Susannah's hair was out of control, and she had on dingy, threadbare sweats. Nevertheless, she looked like a rock star, Laura noted with satisfaction. They might have been only a not-bad-verging-on-kind-of-interesting high school band, but their look had been fantastic.

The next three games, she let Susannah almost win. "I could text Daniel and see if he wants to come over," she said. "It's only midnight."

Susannah made a face.

Laura said, "Fine. If I win the next five games, you have to be nice to Daniel when you see him."

"What?" Susannah said. "No!"

"Why, because you know that you're going to lose?" Laura bumped her car, temptingly, into a wall and then again. Susannah won.

"Ha!" Susannah said. "Okay, sure. Beat me five times and I won't be an asshole to Daniel."

"Deal," Laura said. She won the next three games and they'd begun another when there was a knock on the door.

Susannah said, "If that's Daniel, tell him to go away. I've still got at least two games before I have to be nice."

But when Laura went to the door, it wasn't Daniel.

"Dad?" she said.

"Hey, kiddo," he said. Then a hurt look came over his face. "Did you two play somewhere tonight? Why didn't you tell me?"

"What?" Laura said, and then remembered the glitter handprints on her face. "Ha ha, no. No! We were just fooling around. Playing Mario Kart. Uh, you want to come in?"

"Well, for a minute or two." He stepped inside. "I know it's late. It's just I've been texting you and your sister. I started to worry when I didn't hear back."

"About a *tiger*?" Susannah said from the couch. "You were worried about a tiger?"

"It attacked a woman around nine tonight. Down at Little Moon Bay. They think it may still be in this neighborhood."

"I guess you missed the update," Ruth said. She was standing halfway down the staircase. "Somebody ran it over on the Cliff Road about a half hour ago. It's dead."

"Poor tiger," Susannah said.

"Well," their father said uncertainly, "I guess you're all safe. I should probably go."

Susannah and Laura looked at Ruth, and Ruth sighed. She said, "Stay if you want to. I was going to make popcorn."

The Book of Kyle Mylynowski

He knows this body he finds himself in is wrong in some way, but the world has changed more than he. It is painted over in scent. Drenched in stinks bright and thick as egg yolks. The speck of blood in a yolk from an egg cracked between his fingers. He has no fingers. The first night he travels over thirty miles, through the neighborhoods and sports fields and along the shorelines of Lovesend, the county of Wake. But a tiger has no sense of miles. He investigates with his tongue the place between the pads of his paws where broken glass has cut the tender skin. The taste of his own blood is delicious. He kills and eats a raccoon and then a small, elderly dog escaped from its yard, incontinent, scrofulous, and full of bravado. Some of the next day he spends sleeping in a drainage pipe. Once near the Cliffs he encounters another tiger, a female, but she snarls and lashes her tail, warning him off. He does not even recognize her. He does not know himself. He is dreaming of a man in a kitchen cracking eggs in a pan, his long new body draped along a tree branch, when a jogger passes under him and looks up. The jogger takes several pictures with his phone and then backs away. The police show up, but now the tiger is miles off, stalking chickens in a neighborhood where several families keep coops. He kills six plump Buff Orpingtons and eats one. He eats three eggs, still warm. Blood in the yolk.

It's not quite midnight when a woman driving a secondhand Celica does not brake quite in time on the section of the Cliff Road where almost everyone forgets to pay attention to the speed limit. She is driving at fifty miles per hour and the tiger is running across the road. She hits

its hindquarters, breaking its spine, and her back wheel crushes its heavy head like an egg. Oh, tiger! Two miles from the Cliff Hangar. But tigers know nothing of miles.

The woman thinks at first that she has hit a deer or a dog. When she pulls over on the side of the road, she sees the tiger's body and is overcome with shame and horror. She's been a vegan for twenty-seven years and donates five hundred dollars to the World Wildlife Fund every year at Christmas. If Kyle Mylynowski the man could know any of this, he would roll his eyes in disgust. Twenty years in the restaurant business and he always hated vegans.

The Book of Daniel

When Daniel got home, Peter Lucklow was in the kitchen doing the dishes. Daniel loved his mom. She never lost her temper, did her best to remember the things that were important to her children, loved slasher movies and murder shows but never ate meat. She worked all the time, but she still made time when you needed her to. But Peter, Peter was special to Daniel, because there had never been any reason Peter needed to love Daniel. Daniel was just part of the deal, the deal that came with Daniel's mom. But then Peter made Daniel understand he was willing to love Daniel, too. Even though Daniel, for a while, was a nightmare. Peter just waited him out.

No doubt if Daniel tried to tell his mom and Peter what was going on, they would listen to him. If he made them understand that this was real, they would do their best to help. But they already had so much to do, and they couldn't help, anyway.

Peter said, "Maybe tomorrow we could go pick out our Christmas tree."

Daniel said, "I'll get down the boxes of ornaments later tonight."

Peter said, "Or we could just draw a bunch of trees on the blackboard paint. Nice job, by the way."

"You may not feel that way when Davey and Oliver start trying to figure out how to spell swear words," Daniel said. "I'm so sorry I haven't been here, to help with things."

"Oh, kid," Peter said. "Don't feel bad. You know we miss you, right? We miss you like crazy. But we get by. You head back to Ireland, we're all going to miss you like crazy again. But you're doing what's right for you. You're doing the right thing."

"Yeah," Daniel said. "I am. Thanks. I think I needed to hear that."

"Good," Peter said. "Let me know if you need me to say it again."

Daniel went to bed a half hour later; neither Davey nor Bogomil visited him while he slept.

He dreamed Susannah was sitting on the bed beside him. She was humming something under her breath and smiling at him. There was something in her hand, and when he took it from her, it was a key. But she wouldn't tell him what door it opened.

The Book of Mo

Earlier in the day, Rosamel Walker had been stretched out on the floor of Mo's room, sucking cannabis through a fancy new vape designed to mimic a highlighter. It even worked as a highlighter, she said. Best study aid ever.

They'd already gone over the night at the Cliff Hangar, and of course there was nothing useful there. He'd been there to see Susannah or tell Susannah something. But that hadn't happened, as far as he remembered. What had happened, he didn't remember.

Rosamel threw the vaporizer at him. "Catch. They legalized it in Ireland yet?"

Mo consulted his fake memories as he waited for the red light to appear. "No?" he said. "But gay marriage is looking like it might come up for a vote in a year or two, so. You wanna tell me about this girl? The one in Ohio?"

"It was a thing," Rosamel said. "But now it's done. Did she put a dent in my heart? Yes. Do I want to talk about it? No. It's all very boring. What I want to talk about is you. Is Ireland as racist as the Internet says? Please say no. Please tell me you've hooked up with some Riverdancing guy named Seamus."

Mo said, "More racist than Ohio?"

"I wanted to see what it was like to live somewhere you can't see the ocean," Rosamel said. "Like, as far away from the ocean as you can get."

It was interesting. Mo had memories of Ireland but no memories of Irish people being particularly racist or being particularly anything at all.

How depressing it would be if Mr. Anabin had given him that kind of memory. For the first time he was almost grateful, and then mad to be grateful, for something like that.

"Seamus," Rosamel prompted him. "Red hair. Freckles. Big—"

Mo said, "Aren't you the one always telling me to find a nice Black boy?"

"I'm not holding my breath," Rosamel said.

Mo said, "Mostly I've kind of been focusing on my music. Writing my own stuff. You know."

"No," Rosamel said. "I don't. Because you never let anybody see any of your shit." She sounded genuinely put out.

"I am a vault of unheard sounds," Mo said. He really was. As it turned out, deciding never to talk to any of your friends about the music you wrote had been great training for other stuff. "I have nothing to say and I am saying it."

"For a guy with nothing to say, you sure run your mouth," Rosamel shot back.

So then they were silent for a while. Sunlight decorated the ceiling in slabs of brightness. Mo took another hit. He flipped through the book Rosamel had returned. Here were favorite sentences he'd highlighted: *The composer (organizer of sound) will be faced not only with the entire field of sound but also with the entire field of time.* And *Composing's one thing, performing's another, listening's a third. What can they have to do with one another?* And *Will Boulez be there or did he go away when I wasn't looking?* Only someone had crossed out *Boulez* and written *Bogomil* above it. He hadn't done that. He put the book down.

Rosamel said, "You remember that thing my mom had with that Mrs. Sangovich over at her church?"

Mo said, "The one who cheated at bridge and your mom caught her, right? They have that feud."

"Yeah, her," Rosamel said. "So the weirdest thing since I got back, Mr. Sangovich died a couple months ago? And my mom took her over a tray of cinnamon rolls and now they're, like, friends. They go everywhere together. Movies, lunch, now they're even bridge partners. My dad can't get over it. He keeps saying, 'But how can you trust her? She's a cheat!' But, you know, I think he's mostly just jealous. She and my mom are on the phone all the time. Mrs. Sangovich calls after dinner, and she and my mom sit on the phone and watch television together."

"That's a whole romance novel," Mo said. "I'd read it."

Rosamel said, "Just saying. My mom hated that old bitch. But she got over it. Maybe she'll get over me, eventually. We might even be friends someday. Maybe. Maybe I'll come over and visit you in Ireland, though. I always thought there was kind of a thing between me and that Laura girl. Whenever I looked over at her in homeroom, she was always looking at me."

"You hooked up with Susannah," Mo said. "Aren't sisters off-limits?"

"We didn't get past the meet-and-greet portion," Rosamel said dismissively. "You really friends with those two now? With Daniel? Never thought you had any time for him."

"We're not friends," Mo said. "We've spent some time together, but we're not friends."

"What's she like? Laura?"

"Motivated," Mo said. "A little sneaky."

"Both excellent qualities," Rosamel said. She rubbed her head. "Haven't gotten used to this yet. If I'd been smart, I would've waited until summer."

"It looks good, though," Mo said. It really did. Maybe he should shave his head, too. No, he had a weird ridge in his skull. His fingers sought it out. "You look like you're just back from some sex vacation on the moon."

Rosamel said, "Please. Moon couldn't handle me. You up for some time with me and Natalie and Theo tomorrow? Theo said her mom will make us mango rolls."

Mo heaved himself off his bed and carried the vaporizer back to Rosamel. He dropped down on the floor and lay on his back beside her.

"You okay, friend?" Rosamel said. She had turned to look at him, to really look at him. He allowed it.

He said, "Don't know. Missed you and Natalie and Theo something bad. And now, you know, uh."

"I'm sorry about your grams."

"Yeah," Mo said.

Rosamel studied his face. Then she sat up. "Oh, Mo. The state of your ends. Sadness is good for nobody's hair. Here."

She went into his bathroom and came out with his pomegranate oil.

"It's okay," Mo said. "I can take care of myself."

"Yeah, you can," Rosamel said. "But let me. Let me do something for you. Remember when Theo and I broke up and I was afraid she'd make everybody choose between us? Remember how you made it right? You were so nice to both of us. And so we figured out how to be nice to each other. Let me, Mo. A little thing. Because we're friends, and friends ought to take care of each other."

Mo sat up and she poured oil in her palm. "Nice stuff," she said and began to work it into his hair.

When was the last time someone had done this for him? Mo closed his eyes and he was a little boy again. His grandmother's fingers were patient. But he could feel their strength, too. The things they knew. His mother's hands would have been careful. Deft. They had been a musician's hands. He thought he remembered this: how every touch had told how much she loved him.

HIS ROOM STILL smelled faintly of weed and pomegranate oil. Daniel and Laura had left and he'd said good night to Jenny and gone to bed, but now the round moon was in the window, gushing light, and Mo, too, was fizzing with a kind of radiant electricity. He didn't even bother to turn on his bedroom light. He could see in the dark. He could see everything. It hadn't been a fluke, the thing he'd done in Mr. Anabin's classroom. He was magic. He could do magic. He had made the roses bloom. If it was his grandmother who had left him the message, who had come to him, then when she came back she would see her roses blooming. And who else would it have been? Who else in this whole world loved him enough to stand in the middle of the night outside his window, waiting for him to see and come down? Surely she would come again. She had an epigraph from Rumi in one of her books. Mo had always loved it, even when, after doing some digging online, it became less clear whether it was actually by Rumi or by someone called Abu Said Abul-Kayr. The past was a confusing place, full of bad information and mysteries. Mo loved the epigraph so much that in sixth grade he'd set it to music, and he still thought the composition was one of the best things he'd written.

Come, come, whoever you are,
Wanderer, worshipper, lover of leaving.
It doesn't matter.
Ours is not a caravan of despair.
Come, even if you have broken your vows a thousand times.
Come, yet again, come, come.

He said it to the moon in the window. He said it with his whole being. He said it twice more, and then he sang it in his disappointing and wholly inadequate alto, very softly so he wouldn't wake Jenny up. But he let that new part of himself, that new ability, shape what he sang and extend it out into the night, as far as he could, as loudly as he could.

Far down below the Cliffs, Daniel and Laura heard the song and wondered who was singing it. Bogomil pricked up his ears, and Mr. Anabin put down the T-shirt he had been folding. Bowie, now an owl tucked inside the hollow of the oldest tree in Lovesend, a two-hundred-year-old sycamore, drew that yet more ancient pocket of suspended time that exists at the heart of all trees more tightly around himself (older even still) and slept on.

Mo's phone buzzed with a text from Rosamel. Tiger's dead some lady hit it with her car

Mo texted back a sad face.

Rosamel sent back a whole string of them, then Poor tiger

But there had been two tigers.

And there were two beings who heard Mo's song. One was the tiger still living. She'd had a night full of adventures. Earlier she'd attacked a woman almost exactly the same age as she (when she'd been a woman and not a tiger) on the boardwalk. But the woman had been walking her two chows and the chows were not afraid of a tiger. She got one of them by the shoulder, though her teeth did not get much past the fur and loose skin. The other chow locked its jaw around her back leg as its owner screamed and began to strike the tiger's muzzle with the stick she'd been throwing for her dogs earlier. As the tiger ran away, the woman threw a bag of dog shit after her. Later, this was the triumphant highlight of the story the woman told at cocktail parties.

The tiger was standing on her back paws, head inside a dumpster outside the back door of What Hast Thou Ground? when she heard Mo singing.

She began to make her way back to the familiar terrain of the Cliffs.

MO FOUND HE was not entirely satisfied with one piece of his song after all. There should be something to differentiate that last repetition of the word "come." Should it signal command or invitation? Did it seduce or did it beg? Some of that should be in the interpretation, but some, too, should be there already, suggested in the composition. Or perhaps the power was in the sameness, the repetition of the note, and he should be reworking the "yet again." Anyway, the song needed work, but the magic part did not. He'd asked the night a question and soon he would have his answer. Mo stretched out on his window seat on his side. He put one hand against the glass, feeling coolness and sweetness and possibility seep through, and fell asleep at once.

The Book of Susannah

She and Laura stood in the bathroom side by side, washing glitter off their faces. It was almost one in the morning, and Ruth had already taken an Aleve and gone back to bed. Their father had hugged everyone before he left, and it had been clear from Ruth's face she didn't know what to think about that. But she'd seemed okay with his company as they sat around the living room, eating popcorn and playing Mario Kart. She'd even teamed up with him in one of the races.

"You think there's any chance they'll get back together?" Laura said.

"That would be weird," Susannah said.

They were both silent, contemplating that possibility.

"But he did seem kind of flirtatious," Susannah said at last. "And ingratiating."

"And she seemed like she kind of liked it," Laura said.

"It doesn't really seem like it's real," Susannah said. "Remember how we used to make up stories when we were kids about how he was going to come back, and he'd be sorry and everything, and he'd have presents for us? And Ruth would take him back? But we're not kids anymore, and she has dates whenever she wants, not to mention Martim over at the furniture place is always asking about her when he comes in for coffee. Ruth is a hot night nurse commodity. If she'd ever wanted to remarry, it's not like she wouldn't have her choice." Susannah had a soft spot for Martim. He'd given them a great deal on the white couch, practically wholesale. There was no reason for him to do that, except he'd always had such a huge and obvious crush on Ruth.

"Gonna go to bed," Laura said suddenly. "I'm tired of contemplating the love lives of my family members."

There was, tentatively, a plan they would all meet at the Cliff Hangar tomorrow night for the karaoke benefit. The awful possibility that their father would dedicate some terrible song to their mother had occurred to both Susannah and Laura, although neither said it out loud. That would be too much like wishing it true.

"We could talk about your love life," Susannah suggested, evil in her heart. "If you had one."

"Rude," Laura said. But she didn't sound at all fazed, which was an interesting development. It wasn't as if she'd ever confided anything in Susannah at all, but Susannah was not entirely in the dark.

"And you have to be nice to Daniel from now on. Because you never, ever won, except when we teamed up and that doesn't count."

Susannah didn't even bother replying. She'd figured the bet was off once their father walked in the door.

"You working at the coffee shop tomorrow?"

"Day off," Susannah said.

"Want to go to Birdsong Music?" Laura said.

Susannah made a face. "Definitely not." She could be not a jerk to her sister. She could even be not mean to Daniel. But that didn't mean she wanted to be part of a band again or even think about music. Even if now, her face washed clean of Laura's handprints, she felt a pang of nostalgia. It had been nice to be part of something that made so much noise.

"You know what's weird?" Laura said.

Susannah waited because what Laura found weird or not weird was almost always a mystery to her.

"I'm not hungry!" Laura said.

"You had a lot of popcorn," Susannah said.

"No, I've been eating like a horse ever since I got home, unbelievable amounts of food. And all of a sudden I'm not starving."

"Maybe it's being home again," Susannah said. "Like, maybe you really missed American food while you were gone."

Laura said, "I guess I missed a lot of stuff. Even you."

"Mushy," Susannah said. She caught Laura's eyes in the bathroom mirror. "But yeah, okay, maybe I missed you, too."

"And maybe you missed Daniel," Laura said, not even missing a beat.

"Maybe I did," Susannah said. She knew better than to look away or down. "But maybe then I got over it."

SHE CHANGED OUT of her sweats and into the witchiest black dress she owned. She put on the flaky metal crucifix pendant and both of her bird skull rings. The cheapest, most DIY shit had always seemed the gothiest to her. Susannah could have, she supposed, asked if Laura wanted to go help Lissy and Dakota out with their spell, but maybe she and Laura had had sufficient quality time for one night. Besides, it was just as likely that Laura wouldn't take it seriously. That she'd say something snippy and piss off the Lucklow girls. Laura didn't have much patience for things that weren't real. And it was nice to be the one who got to do something. Maybe Laura got the fancy school in Ireland, but Susannah had this: a middle-of-the-night trip to the next-door neighbors' middle school mini coven. She went downstairs and made cocoa, put it in a thermos, and got some cookies out of the pantry. Because only people with no manners showed up empty-handed when there was dark magic to perform.

Only, when she snuck out the door at two A.M. and maneuvered her inconveniently hem-dragging dress over the chain-link fence, there was no sign of Lissy and Dakota. Which figured. Thirteen-year-old girls were big on plans but not so great at follow-through.

She sat down on the grass and drank out of her thermos and looked at the stars. Anyway, it was definitely colder. A lot colder than it had been. No magic necessary at all.

The night sky above her was clear, but you could feel the turn in the air. Like someone sweeping out the old season, cleaning the house of heaven.

Susannah could hear the sweeper's song. High and sweet and far away. She closed her eyes, and when she opened them again, a man stood looking down at her. "Go away, Daniel," she said.

But it wasn't Daniel. Instead it was her old imaginary friend Bogomil. The man and not the wolf, and she was not dreaming but awake. He said, "Susannah, how fortuitous. I was hoping we could talk."

"You?" she said. "You're not real."

Bogomil said, "Am I not? Did you have a pleasant evening with your family?" Bending down, he held out his hand and left it there until Susannah took it.

He pulled her up.

She could smell him, something burnt and musky and sweet, like a fire that had gone out. His nails were longer than hers and blackened as if he had been digging in soot. No, she thought. It's the dark. He tears at it with his claws. No matter how incredibly, carefully goth you get yourself up to be, someone out there is always gothier.

She said, "It's real? All of it, everything? All the things that I dreamed?" The forest, the path, the way it had felt to become a wolf. The things the person standing here had promised her, which she could not quite remember, but which she'd yearned for. "I remember—" Susannah started, and then fell silent. She dropped his hand.

"Tell me what you remember," Bogomil said.

"No," she said. "I don't want to remember." Not turning away, she began to move slowly toward her own house, her own yard.

"You're limping," Bogomil said. "Is something wrong?"

"I have a splinter in my foot," she said.

Bogomil said, "Why don't you take it out?"

"Maybe I will," Susannah said. "But you're not the boss of me."

Behind her, she heard her front door open. The porch light came on. "Susannah?" her sister said. "Who are you talking to?"

"No one!" Susannah said. But she didn't turn around. She kept her eyes on Bogomil.

Bogomil was already changing. She remembered this. He drew in on himself, falling to his knees, shuddering. He said, "Careful, my Susannah. Don't trust them. Mo and Laura. Be careful or your sister will take away the thing I promised to you. They'll steal what should be yours if they can."

"What do you mean?" Susannah said. "Steal what? Steal it how?"

But Bogomil was a wolf now and had a wolf's mouth. He slunk away around the corner of the Lucklows' house. Susannah turned at last and ran, tripping over the hem of her dress. The hem tore and then tore again when she went over the fence. Was she changing, too? She did not want to be a wolf. This was not like her dreams at all. Laura, coming into the yard, caught her by the arm.

"What's wrong?" Laura said. "What are you doing? Why are you dressed like that, Susannah? Why aren't you in bed?"

"Bogomil," Susannah said. "I saw him. He's real."

"Calm down!" Laura said. "You saw Bogomil? Here?"

Susannah caught the slip. And she saw that Laura had caught it, too. Laura said, "Whoever that is! Some bad dream. That's all. You've been sleepwalking, Susannah. Come inside. It's too cold to be out here. When did it get cold?"

"Maybe Lissy and Dakota did their spell early," Susannah said. "Or I got the time wrong. How do you know Bogomil?"

"Okay, now I know you were sleepwalking," Laura said. "I've never heard that name. I have no idea who you're talking about."

"Liar," Susannah said. "You're lying!"

Laura said, "Look at me. There is no such person as Bogomil. You've been sleepwalking. You might even still be asleep, Susannah."

And now Susannah could see it in her sister's face, how Laura had not been lying. Laura was, instead, concerned. Susannah could see a kind of patience and love that Laura only rarely allowed herself to exhibit, much less feel. And what Laura had said felt truer and truer the longer Susannah looked, as if Susannah's brain was a pancake and Laura's concern was a glaze of warm syrup, Bogomil in the yard only a dream. He was someone who came in dreams. He wasn't real. And so, if Bogomil had appeared to her, if he had spoken to her, then all this had been a dream.

"Laura?" Susannah said. "I'm sorry. I woke you up. I must have been sleepwalking."

"You *were* sleepwalking," Laura said, again with the loving intensity that was both Laura- and un-Laura-like. "Come inside with me and we'll get you back to bed. In the morning, you'll wake up and you'll barely remember this. You'll remember you had a weird dream. It will be just like any other dream."

"What else would it be?" Susannah said. "A dream is a dream. They don't mean anything." She'd had dreams about Bogomil before. This one was just another.

She stopped, though, on the porch. "He said I had a splinter in my foot."

"Take it out, then," Laura said. "But not tonight. You're so tired. If you really have a splinter in your foot, I'll help you with it tomorrow."

She and Susannah went up the stairs to Susannah's bedroom and Laura waited while Susannah got beneath the blankets, still in all her witch finery. "Do you need anything?" Laura said.

"No," Susannah said. "Yes. But I don't know what it is that I need."

"That doesn't surprise me in the least," Laura said. "Go to sleep, then. Oh, and Susannah? You really need to do some laundry, okay? Normal people wash their sheets at least twice a year." She sounded completely exasperated.

"Okay," Susannah said. "I'll wash my sheets tomorrow." She was asleep before her sister left the room.

The Book of Malo Mogge

THERE WAS NOTHING better than a knock-down, drag-out fight in Malo Mogge's opinion. It got the cobwebs right out.

She let Thomas shout and throw things and take his puny swings at her. Sometimes she even let them land. He was a little tetchy about the Avelot thing, which seemed fair enough. On the other hand, it turned out he hadn't been entirely truthful with her. If he'd said earlier that he'd seen his brother, she would have known something was up. The brother's bones were turning to dust in a grave in the parish of Harnevi. Thomas knew that. He'd been the one to bury him.

"Should I call the police?" one of her lawyers said to the other. "What if he hurts her?"

"He's breaking things," the other said. She made a much better fox than she did a person, but a fox was only so much fun.

"Nobody here cares what you think," Malo Mogge told them. "So sit tight and keep your mouths shut or I'll take your mouths away entirely. And then you'd look very funny."

The lawyers were both silent after that. But they stayed because Malo Mogge enjoyed an audience. No doubt it pained them to see everything they owned broken into pieces. But nothing lasted forever, except for Malo Mogge and those things she kept with her.

When she judged that Thomas's tantrum had gone on long enough, she pinned him by the neck to the floor facedown, the small vertebrae creaking between the pincers of her fingers. "Be quiet now," she said.

He lay on the floor, his whole body heaving like bellows. She could feel the grief and the anger pouring off him in waves, seeping into the floorboards and flavoring the air. All of it vinegar bitter.

"I have served you all this time," Thomas said to the floor. "And in return I was to be given Avelot so I might kill her."

"And so you shall," Malo Mogge said. "But good things come to those who wait. You've waited so very long, why not wait a little longer?"

"Because," Thomas said, and then did not say anything else. She knew he was being very careful in what he said. He knew how long Malo Mogge had been waiting, after all. It would be impolitic of Thomas to say he did not wish to wait anymore, and Thomas was rarely impolitic these days. She'd taught him manners early on and then again whenever he required it, until at last, mostly, he did not require it at all.

Malo Mogge released her grip. "Get up," she told him. "Go change your clothes. Wash yourself. You stink of misery. You'll curdle the milk with that face."

Thomas stood up, rubbing his neck. "As you wish," he said. He sounded very meek, but the air still crackled around him.

"And then go for a walk," she said as he went past. "Don't come back until morning. See what else you can discover about these children and whether or not Bogomil is playing us straight this time. How I loathe him! And don't worry about us! We can do very well without you for one night, can't we?"

Her lawyers nodded at this when she looked to them. You could practically see the strings attached to their heads.

"One last thing," Malo Mogge said. Really, she was saying this for his own good. She was as fond of him as she could be. "If you turn against me, it will be the end of you. You remain under the terms of our compact. Be faithful and I will give you Avelot and much else that you desire."

He stopped on the stairs, his back to her. The full weight of her regard was upon him, pressing down lovingly. He was strong: he could bear her love.

"As you command me," Thomas said, not turning. "I am yours."

"Well, that's a relief!" Malo Mogge said, clapping her hands. She turned to her lawyers. "Let's have a fire tonight. Thomas has kindly provided us with both a change of weather and plenty of kindling. And let's have some music while we tidy. Gram Parsons or Britney Spears? Surprise me."

The Book of Mo

When Mo woke up, the moon had moved from her station, though he had not. His hand, still resting on the window, was stinging with the cold. When he lowered it, he saw that a figure stood once more beneath the streetlamp. Like Mo's hand, its was outstretched and empty.

He sat up. Lifted the window. "Wait," he said. "I'm coming."

Had he been heard? His visitor waited silently, but by now Mo knew how this went. He went running down the stairs and out onto the lawn. The sky was very low and the grass beneath his feet shone with ice. He stumbled as he ran and fell onto his knees. Picked himself up, but when Mo looked, the street was empty and the streetlamp flickered and went out, a small pool of darkness in the greater darkness.

There was a wetness on his knees, down his shins, a slime of crushed grass. He was chasing a ghost who would not stay, and it was very cold.

When he looked up, his window was dark and no one stood there looking down at him.

Mo's breath came out in a small cloud and dissipated. Which was too much. Why did everything go away? He began to sing under his breath, making magic, collecting the moisture and warmth until he had his cloud of breath back again. He kept it in front of his face with his will. He wanted to cry, but he could do magic now and he was sure magicians didn't cry. They did stuff instead of crying. He thought about his grandmother, and he thought about the things she loved, that she must miss if she were dead. Him, of course, and good tea. Figuring out her next book. Her rose garden.

The idea, when it occurred to him, was as solid and shining as a gold coin in a video game. A series of gold coins, leading him to where he would find her, in the garden upon the shell path. She would be admiring the roses Mo had made bloom for her and wondering what was taking him so long to figure this out.

He crossed the lawn, and his little cloud of breath went with him as if it could not bear to be alone. He hadn't been outside more than a minute or two, but his feet were so cold he could no longer feel the ground. Was she cold? She'd hated winter. Now that he was about to see her, he began to wonder whether or not he was prepared.

What if she were changed in some way? What if she were bloated, rotting, changed from how she had been into something like a living corpse in a horror movie? What if she were in her burial clothes, with sutures underneath? She hadn't let him see her yet, and maybe that was because of how she looked now. He would have to pretend it didn't bother him. And he had magic, so he could fix it. He could make her beautiful again.

But when Mo came into the rose garden, the roses rebuked this notion. They were shriveled and dead, closed up in caskets of ice. Mo's friendly cloud of breath became frozen crystals and rained down on the spiral path.

He looked behind every bush in the garden in case someone was crouching down low, but no one was hiding from him. No one was there in the blighted garden. He might be a magician, but he was also the world's biggest sucker. He'd been right the first time. This ghost was an asshole.

He returned to the front lawn, rubbing his arms, and saw a tiger a dozen feet way. It was between him and the house.

"Fucking Rosamel and her tigers!" he said.

The tiger snarled. It looked about as mad as he'd felt a minute ago.

The tiger took one step forward. When Mo took a step back, the tiger took another liquid, rippling step toward him.

Unlike Bogomil, this tiger did not seem other than a tiger. It had not come to speak to Mo, or scare him, or take him away to another realm. It did not have any purpose, only appetite. It did not even occur to Mo to use his magic.

He turned to run, knowing as he did so that tigers ran faster. But a voice said beside him, "Stop being an idiot. You have power and it has none."

Mo looked and saw a boy only a few years older than him. He'd never seen him before in his whole life, but nevertheless, he knew this was the one who had stood in the street gazing up at him.

"You!" he said.

"Me," the other said. He said to the tiger, "You don't belong here. Shoo before I turn you into something less alive."

Poor tiger! It gave Mo and the other a resentful, golden stare and then wandered away in the direction of the street in a casual manner. They watched it go down the street, and Mo never thought to call the police.

And the tiger? She made her way to the Cliff Road and into the parking lot of the Cliff Hangar, for no reason she understood. There she fell asleep on top of a car whose driver, an out-of-towner, had planned to meet up at the Cliff Hangar with a woman he'd met on Jdate, only to discover the restaurant was closed although the woman was game for adventure. They went off, him on the back of her motorcycle, to her cottage on the shore, where they played two rounds of Betrayal at the House on the Hill with her teenaged son, who'd come home after a fight with his father, her ex. Eventually the son went to bed, and then they did, too, and had quite a satisfactory time. By the time she returned the out-of-towner to the parking lot of the Cliff Hangar, the tiger had been captured by Animal Control working in tandem with a specialist from the nearest zoo, in Winchester, and the out-of-towner never did find out what had left the rather large dent on the hood of his car.

"WHO ARE YOU?" Mo said. "I didn't call for you. I don't want you. But you keep coming and giving me the bat signal. Every night, the bat signal! And then poof!"

"I'm sorry," the other one said.

How had Mo ever thought this white boy was his grandmother? The idea was laughable.

"Don't care about sorry," Mo said. "Why do you keep bothering me? Why do you keep running away? Who the fuck are you?"

"I didn't run this time," the other said. "My name is Thomas."

Mo folded his arms, making himself compact and hard. "Think I'm gonna thank you for saving me from a tiger, you can rethink your sorry ass right out of my yard. I wouldn't be out here in the first place if it wasn't for your bullshit."

"I'm sorry," Thomas said. "I'll go."

"No!" Mo said. He was shivering violently. "No way. No way you're gonna go without telling me why you're here in the first place."

"It's cold," Thomas said. "You should go inside. Get warm."

"Not until you tell me," Mo said.

Thomas was silent. At last he said, "Because I was watching you. You were lonely. You wanted someone to come back to you. And—"

"And what?" Mo said, blinking furiously.

Thomas said, "And I understood what that was like."

"Huh," Mo said. "You think you know me?"

"No," Thomas said. He took a step closer. It was exactly how the tiger had moved. Another step, and now Mo could have laid hands on Thomas if he'd wanted to. There was a cut on Thomas's lip. One eye was swollen nearly shut. The other eye was a shocking blue.

"Look at you," Mo said. "That face doesn't look good."

"I heal fast," Thomas said.

"Sure disappear fast when you want to, anyway," Mo said. He gave in to an impulse and reached out, touching Thomas's lip as gently as he could.

"You're like them," he said. "Aren't you?"

"No," Thomas said. "I'm like you."

"Oh," Mo said. He couldn't think of anything else to say. His grandmother was dead. He was all alone. This person was one more piece of the terrible predicament he was in, and Mo had had just about enough mystery and magic for one evening. He gave another convulsive shudder.

"Go inside," Thomas said. "I won't bother you again."

"Not yet," Mo said. "First tell me why you're here. Why you were watching me."

Thomas lifted his hand, and Mo flinched, thinking of Bogomil. But

Thomas only touched Mo's lip the way Mo had touched his. His fingers were warm. He leaned forward, and Mo knew this strange person was going to kiss him.

But instead what Thomas did was put his mouth close to Mo's mouth and breathe out. Warmth streamed through Mo, through his entire body. Beneath his feet, the grass grew warm, too. No part of Thomas was touching Mo, except for Thomas's fingers, Mo's mouth. Mo shivered though he was no longer cold.

"I want to, uh," he said and swallowed. "Can I—"

"Yes," Thomas said.

And so Mo kissed him.

Mo had kissed boys before. Four boys, in fact. Every one of them a keeper of their own secrets. Didn't everyone keep secrets? Kissing was weird and gross and fun and fantastic and didn't mean all that much if you didn't want it to. Sometimes Mo had wanted it to and sometimes he hadn't. He kissed Thomas gently, because Thomas had that cut on his lip. He kissed him tentatively. A hello kiss. He tasted Thomas's lip, the bottom one, and then the upper one. He traced the place where the skin had split and tasted old blood. Then inside the lip, between the swollen place and Thomas's teeth. He began to draw back then, to see Thomas better, but one of Thomas's hands snaked around Mo's back, grabbed hold of Mo's shirt and pulled him all the way in. If Mo was warm, Thomas was a fire. But Mo was magic now. Fire didn't hurt him unless he wanted it to.

They kissed until Mo pulled away to take a breath. Thomas let go of him at once. He took a step back, looked at the street and then at Mo. He said, "It's going to start snowing soon. I should go."

"Go where?" Mo said.

Thomas said nothing.

"Don't go," Mo said. "Come inside with me."

Thomas looked down at the ground. Rubbed his face. Already his eye was a little less swollen. He said, "Okay."

Mo held his hand out until Thomas took it. Warm vapor rose up from every footprint they left in the frozen grass. They went through the open door of Mo's grandmother's house together, never bothering to shut it (doors will shut themselves if you want them to), up the stairs in the dark, and by the time they were in the hallway outside Mo's room, they were kissing again.

"Never done this before," Mo said in between kisses. Thomas was stripping off his own shirt. Mo was in his boxers.

"Had sex?" Thomas said.

"Had sex in a bed," Mo said, although whether he'd ever had sex depended on how someone defined it. Mo was very interested in definitions but much more interested presently in sex. He sat down on his bed and kissed Thomas's stomach. A rib. There were bruises here, too, growing fainter. Mo kissed every bruised place and left it unblemished.

"You know what I am," Thomas said.

"You're a magical individual of some kind," Mo said. "Like Bogomil or Mr. Anabin. Or a unicorn or a vampire. Maybe we could discuss the details later."

Thomas said, "And you still want to do this."

"Who hasn't wanted to have sex with a vampire?" Mo said, and pulled Thomas down onto the bed.

It was snowing when he woke up. Thomas was asleep in the bed beside him, head buried under a pillow, his hand beside Mo's cheek.

For a moment, Mo felt a sensation of loss so terrible, the room rearranged itself around him. It became a place that he had never been, just as the person beside him was a person he did not know. His grandmother was dead. She had not tried to come back to him. She never would.

HE WENT DOWN to the kitchen in sweats. He had an idea he would make something and bring it up for Thomas's breakfast. Toast and eggs were simple enough, or maybe just toast. People were weird about their eggs.

And coffee.

He ate a banana while he was waiting for the water to boil for coffee and looked out at his grandmother's garden. Snow had made of the rosebushes a collection of polished marble shapes, made the wall at least a foot taller. Later, people would go cross-country skiing down the street.

He almost ate a second banana, but it occurred to him he wasn't starving right now in the way he had been for the past few days. Instead he was hungry in a completely ordinary way.

That was probably not a bad thing, right? He bounced on his toes experimentally. He felt fine. In fact, he felt better than fine. He felt terrific.

Jenny came into the kitchen as Mo was coaxing another minute out of the finicky toaster.

She glanced at the tray where Mo had already placed a glass of orange juice, a glass of water, a napkin, and a knife. "Bringing yourself breakfast in bed?" she said.

"Um," he said. "Actually I have some company."

"Anyone I know?" she said.

"This guy Thomas," Mo began, and then wasn't sure what else to add. "We've been having this thing. Kind of." Which was true.

"Thomas who?" she prompted.

"Uh," Mo said. "Just Thomas."

He saw the look on Jenny's face and realized it would have been smarter to come up with some last name. Any last name.

"Just Thomas," Jenny said slowly. "Got it. Just, please tell me that you're using condoms."

Mo nodded. They had not, in fact, used a condom. The thought had not even occurred to him. "Of course," he said.

"Go take him his breakfast," Jenny said. "Otherwise the toast will get cold, and nobody likes cold toast. I'm going to go shovel the driveway."

"Hey, I could do that," Mo said. The kind of guy who had definitely been responsible enough to use a condom last night would also offer to do something about the driveway.

Jenny said, "You've got company. And I am going to go shovel and redo this conversation in my head one hundred times until I'm less embarrassed about the fact that we just had it."

"Cool," Mo said. "Me, too."

THOMAS WAS AWAKE. He was sitting on the floor, back against the window seat. He had on a pair of Mo's boxers and was flipping through some book. He smiled at Mo.

Mo did not smile back. In the daylight he could see the bruises had returned, were everywhere on Thomas's body, greenish-blue and yellow.

"Good morning," Thomas said. "There's a person on your lawn and I think she saw me through the window. So I borrowed these."

"Poor Jenny," Mo said. "She went out to shovel the driveway."

"No good deed goes unpunished," Thomas said. He didn't smile.

"Your bruises came back," Mo said.

"It seems the one responsible doesn't want me to forget why she gave them to me," Thomas said. "Not yet."

Mo brought the tray over and bent down to kiss Thomas, carefully. From the taste of his mouth, he'd borrowed Mo's toothbrush and toothpaste. And then Mo saw Thomas had been looking through one of his old notebooks.

He snatched it away. "No!" he said. "Absolutely not!" He remembered the note Thomas had left him. "Don't you have anything better to do than poke around in other people's private stuff?"

Thomas said, "Those are your lyrics, though? Your melodies? You write songs."

"Yes," Mo said. "But not for other people. They're just for me."

"Why?" Thomas said.

Mo said, "How is my business any of your business?"

"Very well," Thomas said. "But I still really like the one about Duchamp. And the list one. 'Things I Haven't Done.' Can I have the toast? I'm starving."

"The list one," Mo said. And then he blushed.

The list song was a conceptual piece. About two years prior, Mo had come up with an idea. As was the case with almost everybody his age, his knowledge of the things that people did in bed with each other was almost entirely theoretical. He'd watched some porn. He had a vocabulary he hadn't yet put to use. And so the song was a list of things he thought one day he might have a chance to try if he was lucky. He wasn't sure he wanted to try all of them, but they were at least of theoretical interest. The song was a list of all of these activities. A liturgical song. And as Mo became sexually active, items would be struck from the list. From the song. The absence would be given formal weight.

Mo still liked the idea of this song. He was interested in the autobiographical element. He was interested in the way it would make the audience complicit in his choices and experiences. He was interested in the way the song would change and continue to change. Eventually it would just be the singer standing on the stage and not singing anything at all. Perhaps.

Over time he had crossed out a handful of items but in such a way that you could see what had been crossed out. And, of course, he had never performed it. The line between the personal and the public was something he was not quite ready to explore. The line wasn't even on the list.

He said to Thomas, "I'll tell you about that song if you tell me who you are and who did that to you."

Thomas said, "As you wish."

The Book of Kristofer

Thomas said: "I was born in 1691. My parents were prosperous farmholders in an area just outside the city of Uppsala in Sweden. When I was seventeen years old, my older brother Kristofer, who was the black sheep of the family, fell in love with a prostitute named Avelot. She had some skill as a singer, and my brother composed music that had some repute, though he made his income primarily as a card sharp. Kristofer heard her singing one night as he walked home, and he became infatuated. After that, Avelot was often in his company. I will admit I, too, found her voice extraordinary. She had not been trained in any way but had a kind of natural gift. She had as well one green eye and one blue eye, which was considered a mark of witchcraft, and there were many who treated her cruelly. But my brother said it was God who had given her a rare beauty. He loved her beyond reason and behaved in all ways toward her as if he found her remarkable, though she could not read and knew nothing of the world outside Uppsala. To be honest, I knew not much more than she.

"I believe she loved him, too. For his kindness and because he treated her as if she were a great lady and not a whore.

"Meanwhile, I was studying theology. My brother and I were members of an esoteric society that dabbled in mystical practices. I'll confess I mainly attended because the beer they brewed was very good.

"Then one day a member of the society much more senior in the hierarchy took an interest in my brother and me. He said he had in his possession a magical token that gave him immortal life. He said this token came with certain responsibilities and that over the centuries he had grown tired of these. He told my brother and me that the two of us struck him as likely candidates to take over the role he and his fellow Anabin played.

"You recognize the name Anabin, of course. The one who we had dealings with was Bogomil.

"I thought Bogomil's claims were nonsense, but it was true he had power of some kind. He demonstrated inexplicable abilities and was both wealthier and more well read than any other man of my acquaintance. I had run through most of the money my parents had set aside for my education, and Bogomil was very generous. He put us up in lodgings more pleasing than we might otherwise have afforded, and he paid for the most extravagant meals. He let me borrow freely from his library, and he and my brother spent many evenings making music together while Avelot sang for us.

"I could carry a tune well enough and play the latfiol. Bogomil encouraged me to join in, and I did. I even took pleasure in the music we made. He said our gift for music was a good indication my brother and I would be capable of working magic. A grasp of music gave one an understanding of the kind of structure and invention and harmony that magic also required."

Mo said, "I don't know what the latfiol is, but there's this bit in a book by John Cage where he quotes this other lady, this musician who says music quiets the mind so it is susceptible to divine influences."

"A latfiol is a kind of fiddle. And, yes, music is a framework for many purposes, I think. Bogomil did not introduce us to Anabin, although he talked of him with great affection. He said Anabin was much taken up with his work and when he was not so engaged he was too weary for company.

"Bogomil spoke of a cup he said was essential to the ritual. This was the magic token. He said that when the time was right, my brother and I would clasp it together in a spirit of acceptance, speak words that he would give us, and then drink, and the thing would be done. Twice he asked if we were ready, and twice I demurred. The third time, I was intoxicated. I said I would participate in the ritual in order to prove it nonsense.

"What I did not realize was that Avelot had been observing for some weeks and thinking how to gain her own advantage by this token. When we set a time and a place for the ritual, she made her plan. She hid herself in a cupboard in the old dyer's hall before we arrived, and when Bogomil produced the cup and my brother and I clasped hands around it and spoke the words, she burst out and gripped my brother's hand as well. She lifted the cup and drank from it.

"I think she hoped she, too, would be given the power and immortal life Bogomil had promised to us. But instead, the ritual was disrupted, and the hall grew so cold and airless that I could not breathe. I knew myself to be at the point of death.

"I saw my brother was dead already. Avelot and Bogomil were fled. The cup was gone. As I lay there I saw a woman of great puissance—power—was in the hall now. She asked what had happened and even if I had not wished to tell it, still I would have told it because it was what she willed.

"When I was done with my story, she grew even more angry and icy than she had been before. She said Bogomil was a poor and deceitful servant and he had done this thing without her knowledge or consent. She said, too, that I was mortally injured and would die soon unless she gave me succor. I said that if my brother was dead, I, too, wished to die. But then I thought of Avelot, and I asked what had become of her. The woman said Avelot was not here. She said perhaps Avelot had indeed gained some part of the power and the immortality she had desired.

"Then, I said, I wished for her help. I wished not to die until Avelot, too, was dead by my hand. And so I entered into Malo Mogge's service.

"We stayed in Uppsala for the better part of a week, hunting for traces of Bogomil, Avelot, and the cup, but then plague came and Malo Mogge took me away because she dislikes decay and disorder. I think it is because the changes that occur when the human body decomposes disquiet her. She finds it a great waste. Had my brother and I not attempted Bogomil's ritual, I have no doubt one or both of us would have been struck down by plague. Many died then.

"Bogomil slunk back to Malo Mogge a few decades later. He'd been nursing his wounds in the realm between Life and Death, into which Malo Mogge, having lost her token, can no longer pass. Once it was her realm, but now only Bogomil may come and go through the door that leads to it. It seemed Bogomil had planned in some fashion to be free of his responsibilities while keeping his immortality. He had found the cup that Malo Mogge had lost long ago, wooed us, and disarranged the ritual he wished us to perform in order to accomplish this freedom for both himself and Anabin, but without consulting Anabin, who only wished to be mortal again. Avelot's actions had been a great blow to Bogomil, but Bogomil's actions a greater blow still, I think, to Anabin.

"Malo Mogge punished Bogomil by almost entirely banishing him from the day. He did her great harm and he survived her temper only because without her cup she might not make a new covenant and replace him. Ever since, under her stricture, he lives until nightfall on one side of her door. Should he come by day he suffers great agony to be here. I believe that even when he comes by night it pains him to be in our world. This is his punishment.

"Bogomil and Anabin fell out over Bogomil's treachery, though my understanding is that they loved each other once above all others. They are still Malo Mogge's servants, though she no longer trusts them. I have served Malo Mogge faithfully in all things to this day, though, and one day I will kill Avelot, whom you know as Bowie.

"As for the cup, it could not be found. It is contrary and secretive and changes its shape, sometimes a cup, sometimes a coin. Malo Mogge and the others have pursued it all this time, and only in this past year did we have any sense of it in the world. It was here. And now it is not, but the four of you have touched it. Its traces remain on you. Anabin and Bogomil depend upon you to restore it to them in some way, and whoever does that, I suppose, will win their favor. It was in their keeping and Malo Mogge will not release them until they have it back again."

Thomas finished speaking. He took a bite of toast.

Mo said, "What does this thing do? Malo Mogge's cup, or whatever?"

"It opens a door," Thomas said. "But forgive me. You asked for my story and not the story of the cup. Can we speak of other things?"

"Okay," Mo said. "I guess I was wondering why I'm less hungry than I was. Mr. Anabin said that we were hungry because magic needed fuel. That being alive again was affecting our appetite? But I'm a lot less hungry now."

Thomas said, "You're learning to manage what you're made of. How to regulate what must be regulated."

"So, like electricity? But magic? I'm becoming more energy efficient?" Mo said.

"That," Thomas said, "and there are different kinds of appetite. Hunger. Different ways of replenishing or maintaining your magic. One may draw upon sex."

He was not looking at Mo and his posture did not change, but Mo was suddenly much more aware of Thomas's body, bruised but beautiful. The lustrousness of his lower lip from eating butter. And then, too, came thoughts of the things they had done the night before.

Thomas seemed to know what he was thinking. He said, "Eventually I will have to go back to Malo Mogge."

"Like, how soon?" Mo said. "Really soon or in a few hours soon? She's the one who beat the shit out of you, isn't she?"

Thomas took Mo's left hand, turned it up, and traced the longest crease in Mo's palm. Stroked the pad of Mo's thumb. He said, "We have a little space of time. Enough to cross a thing or two off your list."

"Sex in a shower," Mo said. "And then you can choose. Just let me lock the door."

"How long have you known her. Your Jenny?" Thomas said.

Mo said, "Most of my life?" He didn't want to talk about Jenny Ping. Thinking about Jenny meant thinking about his grandmother. "She doesn't know about any of this Bogomil-Anabin stuff. She's just a really good person. I don't know what I would have done if I'd come back and she hadn't been here. But if we only have a little time, let's not talk about Jenny."

Thomas opened his mouth as if he was going to say something else, and so Mo dropped down beside him. He fastened his mouth to Thomas's neck and got his hand inside Thomas's boxers. As a result, the sound that came out of Thomas's mouth wasn't a question at all. It wasn't even a word. Thomas wrapped his arms around Mo, and they didn't make it to the shower for quite some time. When they did, they used up all the hot water and then poor Jenny had none.

The Book of Anabin and Bogomil

Two mirrors the height of a man hang in Anabin's room at the Seaside Views, one on each side of the beds. In the dark they give the impression of doorways into other rooms, other places where some other one lies alone. There is some comfort in this, knowing that there are doors, even if Anabin may not yet step through them.

He woke just after dawn, Bogomil beside him on the bed, his body at Anabin's back. He was naked, cooler in temperature; he had evidently not been there long.

"Felicitations," Bogomil said. There was nothing in his voice to indicate suffering, and yet Anabin knew what it cost Bogomil to be here. Knowing, he did not tell him to go. There was little point in telling Bogomil anything these days.

In darkness, mirror Anabin met mirror Bogomil's gaze. "How long has it been?" Anabin said. "How many years?"

"I don't keep count," Bogomil said. "Not of inconsequential things."

"Says one who keeps a museum-caliber collection of grudges and grievances," Anabin said.

"Oh, but truly my patience is admirable," Bogomil said. "Your pupils cluttering up the great matter and mystery of our lives like some cloud of gnats and I have not swatted one."

"If they master this matter and mystery, as you call it," Anabin said, "then all the inconvenience and mess will be nothing to me. They are in a trap, and we will not let them out of it nor tell them the shape of the trap. No wonder, then, if they are flustered and insolent. They are, after all, children."

"And which one of these children might we hope will achieve this mastery?" Bogomil said. "Do Nothing, Say Anything; Miss Eyes Bigger Than Her Stomach; or Barely There at All?"

"What they are is not what they might yet become," Anabin said. "Even you and I are not yet what we might be."

"I have said this a thousand, thousand times," Bogomil said. "And now you say it back to me?"

"What I say and what you mean are yet at odds," Anabin said.

Bogomil said, "I did not come to talk of what might be. I came to see what you might like for a gift this night."

"Nothing you can give me." Anabin closed his eyes so he would not see Bogomil's face.

"Some might think life without end in the company of the one who loves them would be enough," was what Bogomil said.

Anabin said, "Some might. For a while."

They lay there in silence, then, and gradually Bogomil grew warmer, his breathing slower. He was asleep or pretending to sleep. Anabin slept, too. When he woke again, there was no one in the mirror except himself.

The Book of Daniel

Lissy and Dakota woke Daniel up in the traditional Lucklow manner on snow days: they threw open his door, jumped on his bed, and rubbed his face with a snowball. "Guess what, guess what?" they chanted. "We made it snow!"

Daniel sat up roaring like a bear and they fled the room. He could hear them giggling in the hall.

When he looked at the clock, he saw it was 9:30, which meant they'd let him sleep in and also that school must have been canceled.

Downstairs was chaos. The house was too small for snow days. There were Lucklows yelling about broken zippers on snow pants, that they couldn't find their boots, that they didn't want to go outside, that they wanted to have hot chocolate with marshmallows.

Daniel's mom still had work; Peter had already gotten the day off.

"Tonight's the benefit at the Cliff Hangar," Peter said. "Figure you're going to want to go to that. Did you hear about the other tiger?"

"Poor tiger," Carousel said. "Daniel, help me put on my snow pants. Then come outside so I can throw snowballs at you."

"Sure thing," Daniel said. "Just let me check my phone first. And eat some breakfast. Hear how my stomach's growling?"

Carousel stuck her head against his stomach. "Whoa," she said.

"Yeah," Daniel said. "I'm under a magic spell. My appetite can never be satiated. I roam the earth eating all in my path."

Peter said, "I remember being under a similar spell when I was your age. There's oatmeal on the stove."

Daniel ate two bowls and then made a peanut butter and banana smoothie and drank it out of the blender. Then, while Carousel watched, fascinated, he ate six hot dogs straight out of the package without even microwaving them.

When he checked his phone, he didn't have any texts at all. So he sent a question mark to Mo and Laura. Laura simply texted back Busy here, quitter and eventually Mo responded, too. Lots to talk about but not right now. Tonight

Sure, Daniel wrote back. Because even if he wasn't going to learn magic, it didn't mean he couldn't help solve the mystery of how they had died. Not many people got to do that.

When he went outside with Carousel, his brothers and sisters were in the middle of an all-out war, Peter in the role of war correspondent. Next door, a car was pulling out of the Hands' driveway. Laura was in the passenger seat and her dad was driving.

As they went by, Laura rolled down the window and gave Daniel a look. The look said, I'll deal with you later.

"Where you off to?" Daniel said.

"The mall," Laura said. And was gone.

A snowball hit Daniel in the back of the head. Dakota yelled, "Turn and face your doom, varlet! Your great height will not save you."

He turned away and got another snowball in the face, and all of his siblings cheered. Susannah was standing there in a T-shirt, black leggings, and an old pair of boots he knew had once belonged to her father. Her long hair was stuffed under a red hat. "Gotcha, sucker," she said.

When everyone was satisfyingly soaked through, they went in for hot chocolate.

Susannah followed only as far as the door. She said, "Are we friends?"

Daniel said, "Do you want to be?" and then felt incredibly stupid. She was going to say, "Do you?" It was like they were six years old.

But instead she said, "Yes. So, good. That's settled. I missed being friends."

He couldn't help it. He said, "What if I wanted to be more than friends?"

"Seriously, Daniel," she said, "if you ever figure out what you want, let me know. Send me a postcard from Ireland. I'll put it on the fridge."

"Come inside," he said. "Come have some hot chocolate with us."

Susannah shook her head. "I have to go home and do laundry," she said. "My sheets smell like poor decisions."

The Book of Ethan

"It's really, really nice of you to take me to the mall," Laura told her father.

"My pleasure," he said. "But I'll tell you, this is one thing I didn't miss in California. All the snow."

The roads had been plowed and the snow was supposed to stop by noon, but on the other hand, it hadn't been supposed to snow at all. In tenth grade, Laura and the rest of her class had taken an aptitude test meant to give them insight into careers they might enjoy or something. Laura had gotten meteorologist, as if she wanted to spend the rest of her life telling people things that usually turned out not to be true.

Daniel had gotten funeral parlor director, which was apparently because he was good with people. And Susannah had refused to take the test entirely. She said what was the point when she already knew what she was going to do with her life? What that was, exactly, she refused to say.

Which, look at her now. Wandering around in the middle of the night, dressed like Stevie Nicks's sexy pet bat and talking to the worst kind of strangers. What business did Bogomil have with Susannah? Couldn't he be satisfied with ruining Laura's life and Daniel's and Mo's?

Her father said, "You okay over there?"

"Fine," Laura said. "Just, everything's complicated right now."

"Gotcha," her father said.

Laura hadn't known, exactly, what she was doing the previous night until she'd done it. She'd woken up because of the cold. The last few days, no one had ever turned on the heat—it was so warm they hadn't needed to. But when she woke, the house was so cold it reminded her of the time Ruth had taken them to Miami over winter break and how, when they got home, the old boiler took so long to heat the upstairs they'd all ended up sleeping in Ruth's bed with glass jars of hot water wrapped in towels at their feet.

The thermostat in the hallway was at fifty degrees; she bumped it up to sixty-five. When she went downstairs, the lock on the porch door was open, and a familiar stink was seeping in through the keyhole and all around the frame. That was Bogomil.

When she stepped outside, she heard voices. Saw someone standing in the Lucklows' yard, back turned. Susannah. But who stood there with her?

She called to Susannah, and then her sister was running to her, Bogomil loping away in the opposite direction. She'd never seen Susannah afraid of anything before, so Laura had done her best to calm her down. She'd also, somehow, made Susannah forget that she'd encountered Bogomil at all. She'd made her think that it had all been a dream. It had been like making the fly walk in circles.

This, too, was something Laura could do with magic, apparently. Maybe it wasn't as spectacular as turning white shells into moths had been, but it was definitely a more practical application. This morning, Susannah had seemed entirely normal for Susannah. When Laura asked her how she'd slept, Susannah had shrugged. She'd said, "Bad dreams." But sounded almost cheerful about it, as if she enjoyed having bad dreams.

In hindsight, before fixing the situation maybe Laura should have asked Susannah to tell her exactly what Bogomil had been talking to her about. She had a feeling Bogomil wasn't going to say.

She could, too, have impressed upon Susannah the need to be nice to Daniel. To be his friend. But it was undoubtedly wrong to make people be kind to each other, even if it would solve a lot of problems. Laura was a respecter of free will, even if other people's poor decisions and petty, shortsighted grudges were causing them (and Laura) nothing but grief.

But she hadn't been able to resist mentioning laundry. Susannah could be a real pig sometimes.

WHEN THEY GOT to the mall, her father said, "You mind if I hang out in the food court? I've got a couple of work calls I need to make."

"No problem," Laura said.

"Whenever you're done, just call or come down and find me and we'll have lunch. What do you think, you need more than two hours here?"

Laura said, "An hour and a half, tops."

Her father said, "Take as long as you need. Need any cash? I've got a couple of spare fifties in my wallet."

Laura almost said no, because did he think he could buy her affection? Her forgiveness? But that was stupid. It didn't matter what he thought. She was willing to spend time with him right now to figure out what kind of relationship she wanted to have with him in the future. In the end it was up to her. And if her father wanted to spend money on her, well, she'd spent a lot of years wondering why he didn't love her or Susannah enough to send them Christmas cards, let alone presents. So this was a nice change.

She held out her hand. "Hand it over," she said, and when her father grinned at her affectation of brattiness, she grinned right back.

On the way out of the food court she examined the tips of her fingers. If she was going to look at guitars she wanted her calluses back. She used her magic to do this and found the results quite satisfactory.

THE FIRST THING she did when she got to Birdsong Music was check to make sure the Gretsch Electromatic was still hanging on the wall. This was habit.

On a stand on the floor was the Epiphone Casino Coupe, which she'd already tried out many times. She'd never quite had the nerve to ask the guy who was always behind the counter if she could play the Gretsch, though she'd watched a ton of videos on YouTube. He had intimidating facial hair and a surly glint in his eye. He was the owner, so he didn't have a name tag, but Laura and Susannah had spent quite some time coming up with possibilities. They'd settled on Ethan.

Laura went over to the Epiphone and then realized that she was being the old Laura. Maybe the new Laura was going to walk out of here with the Epiphone, but this didn't mean she wasn't bold enough to ask if she could play the Gretsch.

"In the market for a new guitar," she informed him. "Like, the Casino Coupe is really sweet and I'm definitely leaning toward that. But maybe I ought to try out the Electromatic?" She hated how her voice made it a question.

The asshole behind the counter didn't make it easy. "You come in here a lot," he said. "But you never buy anything except a pack of Ernie Ball Nickel Plain every once in a while."

Laura crossed her arms. "Yeah, well, I've been saving my money. But if you don't want it, I could go buy it somewhere else, I guess."

He gave her a sour look. "Everybody comes in here and plays around. Then goes and buys their guitars at Walmart or online. You think I don't know how it works?"

Laura said, "Ever think maybe they don't buy a guitar here because you're mean?"

At this, he almost looked hurt. "Okay," he said. "But keep it down. I was listening to Clapton this morning and I don't need to get some shitty version of an Avril Lavigne song stuck in my head."

"Avril Lavigne?" Laura said incredulously. She'd died last year, not in the '90s.

The guy got the Gretsch Electromatic down off the wall. It was not the biggest axe out there, but then Laura wasn't a giant like Susannah. It was pearly white, and all the hardware was gold. The weight of it was so very satisfying that when Laura held it she almost wanted to cry. Was this what some women felt like when they held a baby? Maybe, but nobody liked to hear a baby cry. When a guitar made a lot of noise it was the opposite story.

Laura plugged it into the amp and played an open G as quietly as she could, but still the guy's eyebrows shot up. The Gretsch was horribly out of tune.

"Sorry," Laura said. She turned around and, hunching over, her foot on the bottom rung of a stool, began to tune it. Once she had it in tune, she began to play.

She had no sense of how much time was passing. It was like having a conversation with someone who loved the same things you loved. It was like finding a part of yourself you hadn't known was there. It was so perfect and so expressive and so anxious to be played that even when she flubbed a chord or a line, the Gretsch accommodated her. It spoke nimbly, with joy and heart and power.

Laura played the kinds of things she knew guys like Ethan thought were good songs. Some Mike Campbell, some Neil Young. Then she thought, Fuck it, and did St. Vincent's "Cruel." She sang along very quietly.

When she was done, the guy behind the counter cleared his throat. During the last song she'd forgotten he was there. She'd forgotten everything but the discovery of what she and the Gretsch could do.

She turned around. She knew she hadn't been, like, out-of-this-world amazing, but she knew she had sounded good. She knew he hadn't expected her to be any good at all.

"You write that?" he said. He sounded like he was trying not to sound impressed.

"Seriously?" she said. "You should listen to more contemporary stuff."

He shrugged. "We should all do a lot of things. But life is short. And I'm a snob."

Laura didn't want to like him. But even Ethans were real people. And it was nice when they treated you like you were real, too.

"Not bad, right?" he said. He sounded, for the first time, almost friendly. "It's a good little guitar."

"Yeah," Laura said. Then she handed it back to him. "It's amazing. But I think I'm going to get the Epiphone."

He said, "Your choice, sweetheart. Leave the Gretsch for people who are actually serious about their music."

Laura, who had turned around to grab the Epiphone, looked back. The sneer had returned to his face. It was almost as unappealing as the facial hair around it.

She said, "You know what? I'll take the Gretsch. But let's talk about discounts. Because I think you want to give me a major one."

By the time she'd finished speaking, his whole face had softened. It took at least five years off his age. See? It was good for people to be nice.

To be generous. In the end, she paid him the same amount for the Gretsch as she would have paid for the Epiphone. While he ran her debit card, she looked covetously at all the other guitars up on the wall. There was one she'd always wondered about, in a special glass case hung on the wall. It was vintage, flamboyantly strange in its shape. It had an extravagant curve like something that might live under the sea, patterned like a labyrinth in coral and black.

"Tell me about that guitar," Laura said.

"The Glory?" he said, clearly pleased to have been asked. "This guy Andy Beech made it. He's a legend. Made guitars for Prince and a bunch of other people. Used to tour with Ozzy Osbourne, too."

Laura gave in to her curiosity. "What's your name, anyway? I used to come in here all the time, and we've never talked once about anything."

"Jackson," he said. "Like Jackson Browne."

Laura shuddered. "From now on, you're only going to respond to people when they call you Ethan, okay? Like Ethan Frome."

"Sure," he said, looking puzzled. "Okay."

Laura said, "Also, from now on you're only going to listen to women guitarists."

"Female guitarists?" he said.

"Women guitarists," Laura said. "Only women. There's a lot of stuff I think you're really going to enjoy. A whole new world."

"Yeah?" he said.

"Oh yeah," Laura said. "It will change your life."

In the end, she left with the Gretsch in a molded Gator case, the Glory in its custom-made case, and an Orange Crush 12. She also got a Jodi Head Voodoo Jessee strap for Susannah's Christmas present—she had an idea she would give Susannah the Harmony as a sort of, kind of joke—and she picked up three packs of D'Addario NYXL Nickel Wound strings. Ethan threw in half a dozen picks with "Birdsong" emblazoned in hot pink on blue.

Afterward Laura stopped off at the fancy chocolate place and got Ruth the biggest box of chocolate truffles they sold. She bought her father a bag of chocolate pretzels and a canister of hot chocolate mix. She had a vague memory of being small, watching him make hot chocolate for her and Susannah. The next year he was gone. Remembering this, she was suddenly convinced that she would look for him now and he wouldn't be there. He'd be gone again.

But when she got to the food court, there he was, staring off into space, thinking about Ruth, maybe, from the goofy look on his face, and eating Chicken McNuggets. He said, "Get everything on your list?"

"Yeah," Laura said. "I did."

The Book of Mo

"I REALLY HAVE TO go soon," Thomas said. But he was lying beneath Mo and showed no sign of moving.

Mo said, "Why? You're immortal." He didn't want to move, either. He liked the way it felt to lie naked with someone. He liked Thomas's sharp hip pressing against his own stomach, the way Thomas's stomach, then his chest, rose and fell with his breathing. He liked the way Thomas's breath felt against the side of his neck, warm and slow. He'd liked listening to Thomas before, the strangely formal register in which he'd told his story. Why hadn't he put any of these things on his list song? Because he hadn't known. And now none of these things would even be a pause in the performance of the song because they'd never been there in the first place. That was a real shame.

~~Orgasm denial. My own.~~

He'd said to Thomas, You can tell people things, right? Tell people things and then they have to do them. I can, Thomas said. As infrequently as possible, but I can. Then tell me, Mo said. Tell me not to come until you decide I can. That's on the list. My list song. He hadn't thought it would be that big of a turn-on, really. But Thomas's voice in his ear: Not yet. Not yet. You may not come, not yet. And so he hadn't come, as badly as he'd wanted to, as badly as he'd needed to. Not until Thomas said, at last, Come now. And then Mo had spilled out of himself in such a rush he'd felt disembodied once again, Thomas pressed against him, the body he was rushing out of.

The things he crossed off the list song would get a pause while the performer said them in their head. Everyone at the performance would try to guess what they had been. Supply their own list of acts. Things they'd done or had done to them. Maybe by the time the song got a performance Mo would have crossed every single thing off the list and no one would ever know anything except that Mo had had a lot of fun in his day.

He said, stalling, "I thought of another question."

Thomas said, "Of course you did." He was drawing patterns on Mo's back with his fingers. Magical patterns, maybe. Mo kind of hoped they were. Give him wings.

But he didn't object, so Mo asked it. "So the sex thing is like the eating-all-the-time thing? Because we should be dead, but we're alive? Like, I'm a sex fiend now? Like a zombie movie, but instead of brains I need sex?"

Thomas said, "Brains would probably work, too, actually."

"Ew," Mo said. "Gross."

Thomas said, "There are myriad ways for ones like us to sustain ourselves. You can draw from an item that someone has stored their magic in. Like Malo Mogge's cup. Once she had a knife, I believe. You can draw from living things, like animals or people. There are different ways of doing that, which is why you get so many stories about vampires and succubi and witches sucking cows dry and so on."

Mo said, "Vampires are real?"

"No," Thomas said. "But drinking blood is real."

"For the blood is the life of the party," Mo said in his best Dracula voice. "Uh, what about periods? Period blood?" Rosamel and Natalie and Theo were always complaining about vampire stories, about how they never dealt with that. Natalie had even written *True Blood* fan fiction about it, but the comments had been so negative she'd taken it down. Natalie hated it when people didn't realize she was being funny.

"Of course," Thomas said. "Magic is all about patterns and secrecy and taboos. Menstrual blood ticks all the right boxes. Cum, too."

"Oh," Mo said. "Wow. Cool. Okay. How about earwax?"

Thomas was silent. Then he began to laugh so hard his whole body convulsed. Mo lay on top of him feeling as content as he ever had. He was naked, made of magic, and someone thought he was funny. When

Thomas was finally able to stop, Mo put his mouth right up to his ear. He flicked his tongue inside and whispered, "Bite me anytime you want, sexy vampire boyfriend."

Mo thought this would make a pretty good song lyric, actually. But not one he'd ever use.

The Book of Susannah

While their dad took Laura off for their mall expedition and Ruth went to water aerobics at the Silverside YMCA, Susannah pulled on snow boots and went over to apologize to Lissy and Dakota about missing the ritual. They forgave her, of course. As it turned out, they hadn't needed to do the ritual at all, they told her. They'd slept through their alarm, too, and the ritual hadn't happened. All they'd needed to do, it turned out, was to make the demand of the universe and go to bed. That was how powerful they were.

Basically they were now one hundred percent convinced they could do magic, and Susannah decided she was one hundred percent going to be there to cheer them on. Maybe, she said, they'd even give her a lesson or two. Maybe, they said. They'd have to think about it. She'd have to ask nicely.

After that Susannah threw snowballs and she even said the thing she needed to say to Daniel. Then she went back to her house and wasn't even sad, because was there anything better than having a whole house to yourself while it was snowing? The hush of the trampled snow outside was a held breath, as if something extraordinary had happened, was about to happen again.

The electric feeling was no doubt knowing that Christmas would be here soon, and even if Christmas wasn't a big deal once you were Susannah's age, you couldn't help but be a little excited it was on the way. And she'd had one of her weird dreams about Bogomil again, and she always woke up from those feeling as if she were special. As if she'd been chosen to be queen of a dark forest. As if she could run forever and ever and never get tired. Her feet never sore. She couldn't remember everything that had happened in her dream, but Bogomil had been very interested for some reason in her foot. Which made no sense but was typical of dreams.

Bogomil wasn't real, and she and Daniel were friends again. Her sheets needed washing.

When Susannah started the machine, though, she had the trouble she usually had with laundry, which was she began to have an idea for a new song. It was Pavlovian. This was why, a while ago, she'd stopped doing laundry. She'd been tired of having ideas.

At last, greatly exasperated, she sat down on the white couch with a piece of paper and began to write down bits of lyric. She hummed a little as she wrote because the melody had come to her first and she didn't want it to escape.

And then, by the time the laundry buzzer went off, she had a song. More or less. It wasn't very good, and maybe it wouldn't ever be good. But if Susannah kept working on it, it would get better. That was how you knew it was a song and not real life.

She ran the dryer and went on working on the song. It still wasn't particularly good, but Susannah thought it was getting interesting. She forgot to eat lunch, and she forgot, too, that there was a sore place in her heel. She forgot there had been something wrong for a very long time, and she didn't even know what it was.

When there was a knock on the door, Susannah didn't recognize the sound at first. She came up from the song like a swimmer from the sea. There was another knock, but still Susannah didn't get up. She didn't want to go to the door. She knew it wasn't a person standing there on the porch. It wasn't anyone who ought to be there. It was a wolf, and when she opened the door, the forest would be there, too, and it would always be night. She would go and live there, and no one would ever know what had happened to her. She would just be gone. Part of her wanted this badly, but part of her did not.

And Bogomil wasn't real. Susannah went to answer the door expecting a Lucklow emissary, come to entice her outside again.

But instead it was a girl Susannah had never seen before. She had pale yellow hair sodden with melted snow, a pale and anxious face, lips bluish with cold, and eyes that didn't match.

Susannah said, "Hello?"

The person at the door said, "Who are you?"

"Susannah," Susannah said. "Who are you?"

"Bowie," the girl said.

Susannah, unable to help herself, said, "Because of the eyes? Did your parents name you that or is it like a nickname?"

"It isn't my real name," the girl said. "But I like it better. Does another girl live here?"

"Maybe," Susannah said. She was more than a little annoyed because there were one or two more things she wanted to try with her song. "Who are you looking for, exactly?"

"I don't remember her name," the girl said.

"In that case," Susannah said, "maybe I know who you mean and maybe I don't. And even if I did, I'm the only one here right now."

"Oh," the girl said. Bowie. "In that case, I'll come inside and wait. I'm hiding from someone."

Not quite sure why she did so, Susannah stepped aside and let her visitor in.

Once inside the house, Bowie looked around as if she'd never seen anything like the Hands' kitchen. She wandered over to the white couch, bent down to smell the upholstery as Susannah watched in amazement, and said, "Is he here? You said you were alone."

"I told you I was the only one here," Susannah said. "Who are you talking about, or don't you know this person's name, either?"

"Thomas," Bowie said. She looked extremely uneasy. "I don't want to be found by him."

"You know Thomas?" Susannah said incredulously.

Bowie said, "I know that he was here."

"Okay," Susannah said. "But I have no idea where he is now, and I doubt he'd come back without calling first. That's not a thing that normal people do."

Bowie didn't catch the sarcasm. Instead, mollified, she said, "Do you have anything to eat?"

It was the least strange question she'd asked so far.

"Probably," Susannah said, giving up any hope of getting back to her song. "Sit wherever, person from Porlock. I'll make us both some lunch."

And so they were both at the kitchen table, eating a stack of peanut butter and jelly sandwiches in companionable silence, when Laura got back. Their father poked his head through the door and said, "See you at the benefit tonight, Susannah," nodded at Bowie without much curiosity, and was gone again.

Susannah had not thought Laura would actually buy a guitar. Usually she came back from the mall mooning over the Gretsch Electromatic, which she could not yet afford, too much in love to buy a guitar within her budget. But Laura came through the kitchen door carrying not one guitar case, but two. You'd think she would have been radiant with happiness about this, but she stared at Susannah's visitor as if Susannah was sitting and eating sandwiches with an apparition.

Susannah said, "Laura, this is Bowie. Bowie, this is my sister, Laura."

"Bowie?" Laura said. "But . . ."

She carefully put her two guitar cases down on the kitchen floor. She stared hard at their visitor for a long moment, and then said, her voice strangled, "You're a girl now?"

Bowie said, "Laura? Is that your name? I forgot. I forgot my name also, for a time. If I could I'd be rid of it again. Laura. I know you. From that place. You're the one who is afraid of what you want. The one who is angry because you are afraid."

"I was afraid because that place was scary!" Laura said, practically spitting. Her fists were clenched. Susannah had seen Laura angry many times before, but she'd never seen her frightened before. Laura was frightened now. "And I'm angry because you're in my house and I don't want you here. Get out!"

How could anyone be afraid of a girl who didn't even know enough to wear something warmer than a biker jacket and a T-shirt when it was ten degrees outside, tops? Susannah said, "Laura, it's snowing. Bowie doesn't have a coat."

Laura said, "Zip it, Susannah. What did you do to my sister, you asshole?"

"Nothing you haven't done," Bowie said calmly. "I can see the marks of it on her. You and Bogomil both."

Susannah perked up. "Bogomil!" she said. "Do you guys know him, too? That's so weird!"

Laura ignored her. She said, "You messed with her, didn't you? She should be freaking out right now, not sitting there like she's had three Xanax and a massage."

Bowie said, "I have done nothing you did not do first."

"She's my sister, though," Laura said. She looked flustered. "It's different. She was so scared, and she doesn't need to be mixed up in all this. I told her something so she'd be safe."

Susannah said, "She also told me to do my laundry. Laura's very bossy. Do you want another sandwich?"

"No," Bowie said. "I had some business with your sister, but I will come back when she's had time to think over why it would be to her advantage to listen to me. Thank you for the meal, Susannah. If you should see Thomas again, refrain from mentioning you gave me aid. He must not find me. Better: when I depart, forget that I was ever here."

"No problem," Susannah said. "And there are coats in the closet right there. Take whichever one you want."

Laura said, "Thomas? The guy you hooked up with, Susannah? What's he got to do with any of this? Wait, not that coat. That's mine. Here. Take this one. Or this one."

Bowie chose their mother's old coat, the fake fur that was in no way fashionable anymore. It was so large Bowie's hands disappeared entirely. The hem came nearly down to her ankles. "Buttons!" she said happily.

"Ruth is gonna be sad you picked that one," Susannah said. Their mother had an unholy love for it despite its awfulness. "Give her a hat, too, Laura. And some gloves."

"I'll give her a hat if she tells me why she's worried about your fling," Laura said, folding her arms and speaking through her teeth.

"He is a servant of Malo Mogge, like Anabin and Bogomil," Bowie said. "And he wishes me dead."

"The second part I totally get," Laura said. She rummaged through a shelf of knitted hats, pulled out a pink one with a silver pom-pom Susannah had given her for Christmas the year before last. Laura had never worn it. "But what do you mean Anabin and Bogomil are her servants? Who, exactly, is Malo Mogge, anyway?"

At last Bowie seemed surprised. She looked at Susannah and Laura as if startled to discover there were people in the world who were less informed than she.

She said, "Malo Mogge is the Moon. I thank you for the coat. One day I will do you a good turn for the gift of it." And then, while Susannah could see Laura beginning to formulate her next question, Bowie abruptly departed. She left the door open behind her so that Laura, shivering, had to go to close it.

"So what did you get at Birdsong?" Susannah said. "Can I see?" She felt quite sure they had been talking about something just before, but she hadn't really been paying attention. She'd been too preoccupied with thinking about her new song.

THE BOOK OF LAURA

As far as Laura could tell, there was nothing wrong with Susannah. She looked happy and well rested. Here was vindication. Laura had done nothing wrong when she'd made Susannah forget about Bogomil.

There was all the stuff about Thomas, and Malo Mogge being the moon, whatever that meant. Not to mention the fact that Mr. Anabin and Bogomil were apparently in thrall to her, but this was something Laura would need to talk about with Mo. And Daniel. Not Susannah. As for Bowie, if Bowie had a mortal enemy now that she was back in the world of the living, wasn't that a good thing? So far Bowie appeared to be much better at magic than anyone else; it wouldn't be the worst thing if someone did something about her.

"You got the Gretsch?" Susannah said, opening one of the guitar cases on the couch. "Holy shit!"

"Yeah," Laura said. "Dad gave me some Christmas cash."

She'd come up with that story on the way home. "See?" she said to Susannah. "You should've come, too."

Susannah said, "Does it sound as badass as it looks?"

"Yeah," Laura said. "It does. But wait till you see what's in the other guitar case." She laid it down on the coffee table and undid the catch. "Take a look."

The look on Susannah's face was truly gratifying. It was like the scene in *Raiders of the Lost Ark* when the Ark of the Covenant was opened and all the angels started flying around and smiling at people.

"What is that?" Susannah said. "Is it real?"

"Sure is," Laura said. "It used to hang on the wall behind the counter, remember? Some guy called Andy Beech made it. It's called a Glory."

Susannah said, not even joking, "Did you steal it?"

As if Laura would do such a thing. She said, "Ha ha. They were having this raffle. Every purchase meant you got a couple of tickets and the drawing was today at noon, and so I got my tickets and then it turned out I won. Like, it was just luck." Not as good as the real story, of course, but not bad, either.

"No way," Susannah said.

"Yeah way," Laura said. "And guess what? It turns out that guy's name? We were totally right, his name is Ethan."

Susannah said, "Sorry, but this is the best day of your life. From now on it's all downhill."

Laura said, "I prefer to think of it as a harbinger of things to come. One day I'll look back and I won't even remember I once owned this Gretsch because I'll have bought so many excellent guitars. I'll have so many guitars I'll have to buy another house to keep them in."

She saw the pad of paper on the coffee table, Susannah's notations, and said, "Are you writing a song?"

"None of your beeswax," Susannah said, snatching it away from her. "Play me something on your new guitar."

"Which one?" Laura said. She knew exactly how smug she sounded.

The Book of Daniel

He was not going to get Mr. Anabin a birthday present, he decided. But that didn't mean he didn't have to get other people Christmas presents. When he'd taken the kids to the dollar store the other day he'd gotten some fun stuff on the sly. Stocking stuffers like Play-Doh and emoji erasers and toy cars and lip gloss and fuzzy slippers. He'd gotten a Darth Vader union suit for Peter at Marshalls because he couldn't resist ("Daniel, I am your father," Peter had liked to intone when Daniel was about twelve and super into all things *Star Wars*). For his mom, who was always losing hers, he'd gotten a phone charger and a couple of Scandinavian thrillers. She liked it best when people got murdered in far-off places.

The best present was the one he'd gotten for Carousel. There was a place online that printed anything you wanted on lots of stuff, so he'd ordered a thermos with her name on it. She could take it to school and Ms. Fish could suck it. He'd gotten her a hat with her name stitched on it, too. These should arrive in plenty of time for Christmas, and he'd paid extra for gift wrapping just in case he wasn't around when they showed up.

He wasn't sure how much longer he would be around. He'd eaten almost a bag of sliced bread's worth of sandwiches and a plate of scrambled eggs, too. But it was as if he hadn't eaten for days. Since before he'd died. He was hungrier than he'd ever been in his whole life. He was so very hungry he thought that if he didn't figure out what he needed, he would go flying out his bedroom window. All he would be was appetite, wings and a beak and a gullet. Crying loudly as he swallowed the whole world down to fill himself.

He was going to give Laura all the photos he had from when they were kids. Susannah, though, he had no idea what to give Susannah. What did you give Susannah when you were Daniel? Everything he came up with seemed inadequate.

Susannah was the problem he was interested in. Not Mr. Anabin.

The Book of Mo

Before it was quite noon, Thomas again began to talk about leaving, despite Mo's best efforts at distraction. "Fine," Mo said. "I'm supposed to meet some friends. You could come if you want?"

Thomas shook his head.

"Okay," Mo said. "But what about later? I have to get Mr. Anabin a present and I could use some help. It's apparently part of our magical education. Finding something for his birthday. Any idea what he's into?"

"I know Anabin no better than you," Thomas said, "though it is true I have known him longer. But he has been your teacher where Malo Mogge has been mine."

"You must know something," Mo said.

Thomas thought. He said, "Once he loved Bogomil. And he uses magic sparingly. Bogomil is appetite, but Anabin is an empty cupboard shelf."

"They do say opposites attract," Mo said. "He wears T-shirts with corny slogans on them. But that's super obvious. Maybe an audiobook? Self-help?"

Thomas said nothing, only looked out the window at the snow that was still falling.

"If you were Mr. Anabin, what would you want?" Mo asked, poking his toes into Thomas's calf.

Thomas didn't answer. Look at him, and he looked like any moody boy staring out a big window at some pretty snow. But he was unbelievably old. Like, Declaration of Independence old give or take a century. Mo had always been a little fuzzy on historical dates.

Mo went on. "Come on. Pretend it's your birthday. What do you want? New headphones? A ferret raised since birth by a man named Sylvester? A—"

Thomas kissed him. It was a kiss that said what Thomas wanted was to kiss Mo and keep on kissing him.

"Hey," Mo said at last. "I get it. You're really old. You don't like talking about birthdays. Lots of old people feel the same way."

"Give me your phone," Thomas said. When Mo handed it to him, Thomas typed in a number and handed it back. "Should you need me."

"Couldn't I summon you magically?" Mo said. "More fun."

"Harder to share memes and cat GIFs that way," Thomas said. "Not to mention the whole point of emojis is you may use them to cover up the way you're feeling. Whereas, if you use magic to summon me, I'm going to know how you're actually feeling."

"What was I feeling when I summoned you last night?" Mo said. He had felt powerful. He'd felt like magic.

Thomas was closest to the window and he turned his head away from Mo and looked out again. Every time he did that, Mo wondered if he was expecting something more interesting than snow. Tigers, maybe.

"Desolate," Thomas said finally. "Alone."

Mo did not recoil. He remained composed. He smoothed out a small wrinkle in his T-shirt. He said, "My two most attractive qualities. So before that. Why were you spying on me? Why did you stand outside my window?"

Thomas said, "Because Malo Mogge wanted to know about you. You and the others. I do her bidding."

"Oh, man. Maybe we should be having this conversation via text," Mo said. One arm was around Thomas's shoulder, one knee hooked over Thomas's legs. He took his arm back. "Slightly freaking-out face. Frowning face. Row of question marks."

"Do you want me to lie?" Thomas said. He turned his head at last, looked directly at Mo. Their noses were practically touching.

Mo said, "No! But if you slept with me because it was a way to find out things for Malo Mogge, maybe you could just not say anything at all. How about that?"

"I sleep with many people for many reasons," Thomas said. "I slept with Laura's sister because it seemed possible she knew a thing Malo Mogge would find of interest. And because I had an appetite and she was not only convenient but interesting in her own right. I didn't mean to sleep with you at all. But you're alone. You have no one, and I am alone, too. And when you called, I thought you were calling me. But you weren't, were you?"

Mo said, "You slept with Susannah?"

"Yes." Thomas met his gaze. Mo could see no trace of shame. "But neither of us had any expectation of the other."

"That's great, I guess?" Mo said. He got up and went over to make his bed. He always made his bed. His grandmother had been very big on chores like washing dishes and making beds and being polite even when you didn't want to be. "I think I need to think about all of this. This is all kind of fucked-up."

"Who were you calling?" Thomas said. "It would be strange, Mo, if you were calling me. Since we'd never actually met."

"Fine," Mo said. "Fine. This is so stupid. I am so stupid. I thought I was being haunted. I thought you were a ghost. My grandmother, she died while I was dead. I came back. So I thought maybe she had come back, too."

"But it wasn't her," Thomas said. "It was me."

Mo said, "Yeah. It was you."

Thomas said, "Last night I thought I saw my brother. But the one I saw was Avelot, whom you know as Bowie. I tried to kill her, but Bogomil and Anabin prevented me. And Mo, I will do everything I can to help you in the game Anabin and Bogomil are playing with you. Because if Avelot wins, then I will never be able to kill her. Malo Mogge will not permit it."

"Ugh!" Mo said. He let himself flop back down on the half-made bed and covered his face with his hands. "I'm sorry you didn't get to kill somebody, I guess? And thanks for the offer of help but, sorry, I don't know if I want help from a person who goes around spying on people and sleeping with people and plotting to murder people. Like, apparently you aren't even that good at the revenge and murder part? How long has it been? A couple hundred years? But, hey, dream big. Time plus tragedy equals none of my business. Good luck with your thing."

Thomas listened to all of this attentively and then stood up. He gave Mo a long look that Mo felt in the palms of his hands and the soles of his feet. He felt it in every place Thomas's mouth had been on his body.

Mo set his chin.

Thomas said, "I understand. I thank you for your honesty and for your hospitality."

"Hospitality!" Mo said in great disgust.

But Thomas had picked up his clothes and left the room without bothering to put them on first. Mo sat there, scratching his head and feeling like the first name in the comprehensive list of notable dumbasses. Yes, he was still young and had a lot to learn about sex and guys and relationships, but even babes in the wood knew hot guys came with issues. Just look at Vincent. And Thomas? He was so very much hotter.

Of course, Mo was magical now. Maybe he could turn himself into a small green turtle and marinate inside his own shell for the rest of all time. That seemed a sound plan. Instead, unable to help himself, he went to his window. He could see the driveway Jenny had shoveled and the snow that was still coming down. She'd have to do it all again pretty soon. Mo could see, too, the marks where someone had walked across the lawn down to the street. But there was no sign of the person who had made them.

His phone buzzed, and when he checked it, it was Rosamel. Hey rope-a-Mope still coming? Natalies got a romantic crisis like always situation requires all friends on deck

On my way, he texted.

JENNY CAME OUT of the kitchen as he came down the stairs. She'd clearly been lying in wait. Like a moray eel in a cleft. A purple-haired, Manilow-loving eel.

"So," she said. "Mo."

"'S'up," he said. "Just going downtown. Meeting Rosamel. Okay if I borrow the car?"

"Yeah, fine," Jenny said. "No, wait. Okay if I give you a ride instead? I need the car for errands."

"Whenever you're ready," Mo said.

"Great," Jenny said. "I'll get my coat and my purse." But she didn't move. Instead she said, "So, he's pretty fine."

"Thomas?" Mo said. "Yeah."

"I was about to send up a search party."

"Ha," Mo said.

"Yeah," Jenny said. "Look, I'm not going to get up in your business, Mo, but maybe next time he comes over, we could all have a cup of coffee or something? Would that be weird?"

"No," Mo said. He gave her his sunniest smile. "Yeah. If he comes over again we can for sure do that."

"Great!" Jenny said. "Is he somebody you knew at Lewis Latimer or . . ."

"Or," Mo said. "Definitely or."

"Okay," Jenny said. "Got it. Sounds like we'll *all* have a lot to talk about next time. Looking forward to it."

Mo said, "Not to change the subject or anything, but I have to get someone a birthday present and I don't really know them all that well but I want to make an impression. Without looking like I tried too hard. What kind of present do you get somebody like that?"

"Who is it?" Jenny said. "Sorry. I don't mean to keep prying."

"No, it's cool," Mo said. "Uh, Mr. Anabin? The music teacher at Lewis Latimer, the one who drove us back from Logan the other night?"

"Oh," Jenny said. "How thoughtful! What a nice thing to do, Mo."

"That's me," Mo said. "A nice boy. Who needs to buy a present. The kind of thing that really blows somebody's mind."

"No pressure then," Jenny said. "So not a gift certificate to What Hast Thou Ground? Wait, I know. You can go online and pay to have an organization name a lemur after him. Or a star. That would be pretty neat."

"Yeah, it would," Mo said. And Jenny wasn't wrong. A star or a lemur would be a pretty neat present for a cool music teacher but a less neat present for a scary immortal who had caught you breaking out of Death and now was teaching you magic and you really needed to get a passing grade because if you didn't, you weren't sure what would happen, but there was no fucking way it was anything good. "Thanks."

"Anytime," Jenny said, looking pleased.

"When's your birthday, anyway, Jenny?" Mo was suddenly drawing a blank. "Sorry."

"Not for a while," Jenny said. "June. June second."

"You want a star named after you? If you got the best present ever, what would it be?" He was actually curious. Did Barry Manilow still tour? What did a person like Jenny want? She'd been his grandmother's secretary for years and years, and she'd always seemed pretty happy with her job, but that didn't mean she didn't have bigger dreams. And now she was stuck looking after Mo, and Mo didn't really know anything about her. He knew she had family in Colorado, and maybe she was wishing she was there instead of here, but Mo wasn't going to ask her. She'd just lie to make him feel better.

"Oh boy," Jenny said. "I don't know. Wait! I do know! A parade. A parade in my honor."

"A parade," Mo said.

Jenny said, "Yeah. A parade. You know, not because I did anything important or spectacular or anything like that. But a parade in my honor anyway because I was a person who mattered. Because I was a person who had an impact on other people's lives and on the world. A parade."

"I was going to get you a fuzzy hat for Christmas," Mo said. Actually he hadn't been thinking about Christmas presents at all, but he thought Jenny would be cute in a fuzzy hat. "And something practical. Like a phone charger."

Jenny patted his shoulder. "Those are good, too. Let me get my coat and I'll drive you into town."

THAI SUPER DELIGHT wasn't busy, it never was in the winter, so the Thangleks were okay with Natalie and Theo and Mo and Rosamel staking out a booth in the back for as long as they wanted. When was the last time Mo had been here? With his grandmother, of course. Before he'd died. Before she'd died. She would have ordered pad kee mao because that's what she always got. But then given all the broccoli to Mo. She didn't like broccoli, but she was too shy to ask if it could be left out.

There was a lump in his throat. His eyes burned. But also, he was angry. He hadn't just died. Someone had done this to him, and that was one thing he was angry about. And he was angry, too, because he'd come back and it had seemed as if she were still there, somehow, trying to get back to him, but it hadn't been her at all. Mo's grandmother was just gone. How was that even possible? Why couldn't she have waited just a little longer?

He held on to his anger. Clung to it. Otherwise what would he have? Only sadness and fear, and what were their gifts? Bad skin and a feral stink.

Natalie and Theo said all the stuff your friends should say when your only living relative has died. They embraced Mo carefully, tenderly, and he wondered if this was because his body felt different to them, not because he had been dead and was now remade, but because they could somehow tell how small he felt himself to be inside it again.

Once they'd said hello to Genevieve from band, who was working part-time at Super Delight over the holidays, and ordered food, Rosamel pulled out the old, worn deck of cards with the picture of Leonardo DiCaprio on the back that she'd stolen years ago from Mrs. Paulsen's desk in homeroom, and they played Hearts and ate lettuce wraps and dumplings. Natalie shot the moon twice and only cried once. The day before she'd been looking at Instagram and seen someone who looked like the guy she'd been dating at college. He was in the background of another friend's picture, and he was not only dancing with someone who wasn't Natalie, he was full on touching a boob. And not in a tentative way, either. It looked like he was planning on taking it home with him when the party was over.

"It's kind of blurry, though," she said. "Like, maybe it isn't actually him? I can't believe he would actually do this. Last week he drove out with me to Wat Nawamintararachutis. We were going to take a Li-khe class together."

Theo sighed heavily. Her look at Rosamel and Mo said, quite plainly, You see what I have to deal with?

Finally Theo said, "Doesn't he have a tattoo? Look, you can see the tattoo right here. It's him." She blew up the picture on Natalie's phone.

"It might not be a tattoo," Natalie said. "It could just be a smudge on the lens."

"You could text him the photo," Rosamel said. "Just send it with no comment. See what he texts back."

"But then it doesn't matter if it's him or not," Natalie said. "Because if I send it to him, he'll think I'm jealous. I think I should go back to the dorms early. Just show up at his door like a surprise present. He's studying too much. He said he couldn't go back home for Christmas because he had so much work to do."

Natalie was at Tufts, and Theo was at Boston College, both on full scholarships. They hadn't wanted to go to the same school, but they hadn't wanted to be too far apart, either. They'd had a meltdown during college applications, Mo knew, because they couldn't figure out what they'd do if they both got into Harvard. They couldn't figure out how to decide who would get to go. But neither had gotten in, so they'd had literal twin meltdowns about that, then happily sent in their acceptance letters to their top backup schools.

Theo said, "Great idea! You catch him in the act, we won't have to talk about whether or not he's cheating on you. Bless. Anyway, it's not like men are ever short on the ground for you. Men love a sad girl. They think if they just try hard enough, they'll be the one who finally makes her happy."

"I can't help how my face looks! I look sad even when I'm perfectly fine!" Natalie said. "And that's not why men love sad girls. Men love sad girls because it works out in their favor when they screw up. They think, Well, she was already a mess. How can anyone accuse me of making things worse?"

It was a mystery, truly, how Natalie and Theo could have the same face and yet Natalie was the picture of woe, while Theo always looked ready to party. Mo thought in this case they both had made good points. This was usually the case.

"Anyway, how about you?" Natalie said, poking Mo in the side with her elbow.

Rosamel said, "Yeah, so I was poking around on Facebook late last night and saw Vincent, remember from band? He wrote this long poetic thing about the human heart and how he ran into an old friend the other day and it brought back a lot of very pent-up feelings. And then he said that this was his official coming out. And then he said maybe love would return to him again one day because he thought he would be ready for it this time."

Mo ducked his head down. Fucking Vincent. For about five minutes, once, he'd thought maybe he and Vincent might be something that actually meant something. That was the time Vincent had taken Mo's hand out of his pants and said, "Maybe we could talk for a little while first?" And so Mo had said he'd like that. And then Vincent had started talking about this bicycle pump he'd read about online, and after four minutes of that, in desperation, Mo had gone down on him just to shut him up.

"Vincent?" Natalie said. "That guy? Wait, Mo, did you and he ever—"

Mo had no intention of speaking about Vincent, not ever again. So he sidestepped, said, "As it so happens, there is a guy. Kind of."

Rosamel said, "Come on, man. You and Vincent? For serious? I was pulling your leg."

"Nah," Mo said. "Not him. Just, somebody. A guy."

Theo said, "Is he nice? Did you meet him in Ireland?"

"What's he like?" Natalie said. "Let me be very shallow for a minute. No, wait. Let me be shallow my whole life. Being deep sucks. Is he hot?"

"Actually, yes," Mo said. "Actually he looks kind of like that guy."

On the street outside, Thomas was standing in front of Thai Super Delight. He was with a woman in a voluminous turquoise fur coat. She wore cat-eye sunglasses, and her cartoon-red hair was piled up in a beehive. She came inside the restaurant and Thomas trailed sullenly after her.

"Seriously," Natalie said. "You're seeing someone who looks like that?"

Rosamel said, "Who hangs out with people who look like that?"

"More or less," Mo said. He couldn't help but feel a little smug. Mainly he felt a dim foreboding, but the human animal is a complex organism. There was space for smugness and some foreboding, too. Even some annoyance. Whatever Thomas was up to, Mo would have preferred it if he was up to it somewhere Mo wasn't. He would also have preferred it if his own body wasn't so aware of Thomas, of its proximity to Thomas's body. Little hairs were standing up all over. His pulse was up and his mouth was dry. He reached for his water glass and almost knocked it over.

Genevieve showed Thomas and the lady to a window table. Thomas didn't even look over at the booth where Mo was sitting, but the woman turned and smiled as if she'd heard Mo and the others talking. As if she could hear Mo's heart beating too quickly. She still had her sunglasses on.

"I've seen that guy around some," Theo said. "But *she* is something else. I can smell her perfume from here. Bet you she's from L.A."

"Girl," Rosamel said. "No. Definitely San Francisco."

"Yeah," Natalie said. "And she's an actress. A TV actress. No, wait, a porn star. My mom is going to flip if she sees her. She'll be like, That porn star better appreciate my food."

She and Theo both cracked up. At least Natalie was out of crisis mode. Rosamel would be pleased about that. She hated when her friends were sad. Rosamel was the best person Mo knew. He hoped the whole state of Ohio got it together and realized it'd won the best-person lottery when she decided to go to school there.

The woman with Thomas let her fur coat slip off her shoulders, Thomas catching it and draping it across the back of one chair, then pulling another out for his companion to sit. Like the coat, the dress was outrageous in a way you usually didn't get in Lovesend in the afternoon: a bosomy sheath resembling a tall glass of Pepto Bismol someone had set down accidentally on top of a small upside-down flamingo. Some people just didn't seem to feel cold. Or shame. You could see why Natalie had thought of porn stars.

When the woman sat down, her bare, dirty feet were visible under the slush-crusted feathers of the hem.

"Oh wow," Rosamel said. "The hell is she doing, going around in the snow with no shoes on?"

And here came Natalie and Theo's mom, because clearly Genevieve wasn't going to be able to handle this. She began to say something. The woman said something back, and Mrs. Thanglek shook her head. Then nodded. Thomas stood up and took off his black boots. The woman slipped her feet into them and then smiled back up at Mrs. Thanglek.

"But now he doesn't have any shoes on," Natalie said.

Indeed, Thomas had only a pair of socks on. There was a sizeable hole in one heel.

When Mrs. Thanglek passed by their table, Natalie said, "Ma?"

A short conversation in Thai followed, and then Mrs. Thanglek vanished into the kitchen.

"My mom says she'd like to draw her," Theo translated. "Also that she's trouble. But even trouble gets hungry. Even if trouble doesn't feel cold." Natalie and Theo's parents spoke English perfectly well, but as Natalie and Theo liked to point out, it was useful to have a separate language to be judgmental in.

"Tell me about it," Rosamel said. "You should see Ohio. Blond beardy boys in board shorts smoking bongs on their porches in the middle of snowstorms. Little pipestem legs going blue."

"You guys know Mom has been taking life drawing, right?" Theo said.

Mo had not known this. Previously Theo and Natalie's mom had been into pottery and before that into macrame. But Rosamel nodded.

Theo said, "So Dad's taking her to Paris in January. Planned this whole big surprise romance vacation. Taking her to the Louvre and stuff. She thinks he's getting her a new bike. Meanwhile, she got him some socks and stuff like that."

"Nothing wrong with socks," Mo said.

Natalie said, "They're pretty nice, actually. Little white elephants. He's worried 'cause she keeps coming home with these drawings of a hot naked guy from the life drawing class. She's even getting one framed. Anyway, there goes our inheritance. Thanks, hot naked guy."

Rosamel shuffled the Leonardo deck and they went on playing Hearts, while Mo, keeping an eye on his supernatural hookup and his hookup's boss lady, made up things to tell them about the cute boy he had met in Ireland. His name was Thomas. Yes, he was white, and yes, there were queer Black guys in Ireland, but not, like, throngs. No, Mo didn't have any pics. They weren't officially dating or anything like that. No, Mo didn't think Thomas was on Instagram. (Instagram? Had that even been a thing before he died?) Thomas wasn't really on social media. Mo didn't think it was anything serious. But, you know, not everything had to be life or death or even good for you. Sometimes a thing could just be fun.

While Mo went on inventing a relationship as tidy and short as a pop song, Mrs. Thanglek brought out dish after dish from the kitchen, and the woman in the pink dress ate helping after helping of papaya salad, beef salad, pad Thai, sticky rice, duck lollipops, and the house specialty, a whole salmon wrapped in spinach and steamed with basil and mango. Mo couldn't help noticing Thomas didn't eat at all. He drank hot tea and sat there, not looking at the table where Mo and the others sat. There was still a hole in his sock. Mo wanted so badly to hold Thomas's heel in his hand. To see if his foot was cold. To warm it with his breath.

"Hey, hey," Theo said. "Look over there. Does *he* know *them*?"

Mo saw that Mr. Anabin had come in, was sitting down across from Thomas.

"Maybe before he came here to teach he lived out in L.A.," Natalie said.

"San Francisco," Rosamel said.

"Maybe he had a porn career, too," Theo said. "No, wait, he composed the score for her porn movies."

"Always knew there was something off about him," Rosamel said.

"You did?" Mo said. "Mr. Anabin?"

"No," Rosamel said scornfully. "That was a joke. He wasn't any weirder than any other teacher we had. Look, here comes Lady Gatorade."

The pink dress was headed in their direction, all those dirty feathers vibrating around Thomas's untied boots like flagella. Their booth was on the way to the bathroom, but Mo's phone buzzed and when he looked, there was a text. BE CAREFUL

Mo shoved his phone back into his pocket just as Natalie or Theo kicked him under the table. He straightened up.

The woman stood just at his shoulder.

She said, "You like games."

"We do!" Rosamel said with straight-faced enthusiasm. Theo began to crack up. She covered her mouth with her hands and kicked Mo again under the table.

Natalie said, "You know how it is, when you get to hang out with old friends after a long time. It's just sooooo nice to have everybody together again. Is Mr. Anabin a friend of yours or something? We were in his class last year."

"Oh, I agree!" the woman said. "It's been longer than I care to mention since Anabin and I broke bread in one another's company. Do you know, it just happens to be his birthday. Today! We'd completely fallen out of touch. But a little while ago I found myself wondering what exactly it was about your town that drew him here so far from my orbit, and so I decided I would come find out for myself."

"Sweet," Rosamel said. "I hope I'm not being rude, but would you settle a bet for us? We were wondering if you were from L.A.? Or San Francisco?"

"Dear heart," the woman said, "I'm from a place much farther away than that. How about you, Mo? Are you looking forward to going back to Ireland?"

All of his friends looked at him. "Sorry?" Mo said. "Do we know each other?"

The woman patted him on the shoulder, left her hand there. The weight of her hand was cold and heavy, and he could feel her gaze on him like two blobs of mercury. Her nails dug into the meat of his arm. He reached out, found Rosamel's hand, and gripped it. Didn't look at her.

"My old friend Anabin was telling me about you," the woman said. "He says you're quite bright. Thomas, on the other hand, is not in a confiding mood. Or perhaps he doesn't agree with Anabin that there's anything interesting about you and is too polite to say so."

"Him?" Rosamel asked Mo. Under the table she squeezed his hand quite hard. "That's him? The one sitting over there, the guy you said looked like the guy you're dating? You're seeing that guy?"

"They were fucking like bunnies this morning," the woman said. "But I suspect my Thomas is out of Mo's league. What do you think, Mo?"

"I think you're an actual monster," Mo said. Because this was Malo Mogge. Who else could it be? "And I think maybe Thomas is a monster, too, but he's a sad monster and you wouldn't recognize a human emotion if it brought you breakfast in bed after it had pissed in your orange juice. But mostly I've been thinking about what sort of birthday present to get for Mr. Anabin. I've been thinking about that, really, and not thinking about you or Thomas at all."

This was bullshit and bravado, and Mo knew it and he knew Malo Mogge knew it, too, but it wasn't like he had anything else on tap at this particular moment. And what was Malo Mogge going to do, anyway? Dip him in sauce and eat him like a fresh roll? He clung tightly to Rosamel's hand beneath the table.

"Little dead boy," Malo Mogge said. "You know who I am and still you speak to me this way? Anabin and Bogomil have been poor friends to have not schooled you better. Was it your eyes or your tongue or your cock that Thomas found so charming? Tell me and I could offer it to him as a souvenir to remember you when I leave this place and he goes with me."

Mo heard Theo gasp. He said, "It would be easier to get a puppy, wouldn't it? You can't make a puppy give you its shoes, but it's easier to house-train, surely. And a puppy will love you even if you're an awful person."

Malo Mogge said, "I don't give up the things that belong to me. Thomas can cause a great deal of trouble, yes. But Thomas is mine."

"Maybe you should leave then," Mo said. "And take your puppy with you."

"In my own good time," Malo Mogge said. "And once I have retrieved another thing that belongs to me. Do you think I have any desire to be here? In this small place? Though perhaps improvements can be made, now that I come to think of it, and coming here has given me the opportunity to meet you, Mohammed Gorch. Your grandmother was very proud of you, I'm sure. It's a shame she never found out what happened to you. How she must have grieved. Though perhaps it's a mercy she won't see what becomes of you. Your mother is dead, too, isn't she? What extraordinary bad luck, that the people who care about you, Mo, die so easily."

He couldn't speak.

She patted his shoulder, then removed her hand. "Anabin is fond of confectionary," she said. "He has a sweet tooth. Are you going to the Cliff Hangar tonight? I understand there's going to be karaoke."

Mo said, "Are you?" His tongue was clumsy in his mouth, as if those two words weighed too much to be properly articulated. His shoulder, where she'd held it, ached. The cold ache radiated down his arm until he couldn't feel his fingers.

She said, "It's a delightful place. In fact, the whole town is charming though smallish. Full of charming and delightfully stupid, self-satisfied, reasonably attractive people of adequate nutritional value. Did you know suffering tenderizes the meat? More towns should let citizens keep free-range tigers. And build temples where flowers can be laid in my honor.

As I said, improvements can be made to almost any place. Or to any person! But I don't know how long we'll be here."

She went back to her table. When Mo craned his neck, he saw Thomas staring down at the plastic tablecloth. Mr. Anabin was checking his watch. He gave Mo's table a small salute. Then he stood up and began to help the woman put her coat on.

"Mo?" Rosamel said, pulling her hand away. "What the fuck?"

Mo said, "I am so sorry. I am so sorry. I have no idea." He could not think of a persuasive or reasonable story. He couldn't think of a story at all.

"Now *he's* coming over here," Natalie muttered. "Don't make eye contact."

Mo regretted, fervently, sitting on the outside of the booth. First Malo Mogge and now Thomas, both invading his personal space. He was eye level, more or less, with Thomas's waistband. He knew what Thomas's skin felt like, the grassy smell of it. How soft it was. He had held Thomas's uncircumcised penis in his hands earlier this morning. Rubbed it against his cheek. He'd knelt behind Thomas, put his own cock into Thomas's well-lubricated asshole and listened to Thomas swear in a foreign language. Thomas was still wearing the same clothes he'd been wearing the night before, and so Mo suspected if Thomas was wearing underwear it was the pair he'd borrowed from Mo. His face was unbruised again.

"Afternoon," Thomas said. His look said he knew everything Mo was thinking. That he was thinking about it, too.

Everyone else was looking at Mo. No one said anything.

Thomas said, "You guys are probably wondering about the woman over there. She's a little excitable and she doesn't have a good sense of boundaries, which is why she came over and talked to you about sustainable fashion and the environment. She's passionate about environmental issues. You probably want to avoid her in the future, though, because she's kind of intense and also she farts constantly. She's like an active volcano. I call her Smello Smogge. She's a distant cousin of Mr. Anabin or something, but even he doesn't like her much. As for me, apparently I look somewhat like some guy your friend Mo here had a thing with, except I'm much hotter."

When he finished, Rosamel and Natalie and Theo all looked relieved and a little grossed out. Like everything now made sense.

"What did you just do?" Mo said.

"Fixed things," Thomas said. "You could have done it but you didn't. So I did."

"Excuse me," Rosamel said, butting in. "Is she from San Francisco or L.A.?"

"What?" Thomas said.

"Is your friend from L.A. or San Francisco?"

"Neither," Thomas said. "But she's pretty fond of L.A. Also, I'm not her friend."

There were still a few dumplings on the table. They were cold, but Thomas reached over and took one. He ate it, licking his fingers, and then picked up two fortune cookies. He gave one to Mo and kept the other.

"See you around, maybe," he said, and then followed Malo Mogge and Mr. Anabin out of the restaurant in his socked feet.

Natalie said to Mo, "He was super into you."

(Thomas, this morning, saying, "Like that. Do that again, Mo.")

Mo willed every unwanted thought out of his head, stuck the fortune cookie into his pocket. "Not really sure I'm in his league," he said, and meant every single word.

"He should be so lucky," Rosamel said. "So, karaoke at the Cliff Hangar, are we going? I was thinking I might do 'Eye of the Tiger.'"

"Poor tigers," Natalie said. "This town didn't deserve them."

"So," Mo said. "Are you all on Instagram? I should be on there, too, right?" But as it turned out, Mr. Anabin had gotten there first. Mo already had an Instagram.

THE BOOK OF LAURA

Of the two guitars, Laura decided she preferred the Gretsch. It wasn't that the Glory sounded bad, per se. It sounded amazing. It was just she wasn't sure it sounded like her. Susannah agreed, and she actually did agree. Laura wasn't doing anything to make her agreeable.

"Come on," Laura said. "Let me see what you wrote."

"No," Susannah said. "It's not done yet."

"Well," Laura said, "when it is done, can I see it?" She made the Gretsch beg Susannah, too. *Dear sister, let me see your song. Dear sister, I fear I won't be here too long.*

Susannah folded her arms behind her head and lay on the floor with her eyes closed. "Just keep playing," she said. "It's nice."

But Laura stopped. "Hold on," she said. She went to the kitchen and rummaged around in the bag from Birdsong Music, passed back through the living room. "Keep your eyes closed, okay?"

When she came downstairs again, she had the Harmony with the new guitar strap attached. "Open your eyes," she said.

Susannah said, "Yeah, I know. Now you have three guitars. Neat."

"No," Laura said. "I'm giving it to you. Just fool around with it. I got you the strap at Birdsong. Isn't it pretty?"

Susannah closed her eyes again. "I don't want to play guitar," she said. "I don't want your old hand-me-down. Okay? Music was something I used to do with you and Daniel and it was fun, but now I'm not doing it and it's fine and I'm happy and it would be great if you would just accept that."

Laura said, "If you're done with music, then why are you writing a song?"

Susannah took the piece of folded paper out of her bra strap, where she'd tucked it for safekeeping, and ripped it into pieces. "There," she said. "I'm not."

"Great!" Laura said. "So you're completely happy? Living with Ruth and taking coffee orders and flirting with inappropriate guys?"

"Why the fuck would I flirt with appropriate guys? Where's the fun in that?" Susannah said. "I'm having fun. I'm happy. Sorry if I'm doing it the wrong way or something."

"Happy," Laura repeated.

Susannah got up. Stood in front of Laura with her hands on her hips. "Yeah," she said. "Completely. Why? You don't believe me?"

"No," Laura said, all of her blood boiling. "I don't."

Susannah sneered. It was a real rock-and-roll sneer and Laura felt a prick of envy. How did you make your face do that? She said, pressing with all of her will, "Tell me the truth. Tell me if you're happy."

The sneer wavered. Susannah looked down at her feet. Her gaze returned to Laura slowly, as if dragged there. Her eyes began to well over. "I'm not happy," she said. She spoke so softly Laura could barely hear her. Tears were running down her face now. "I'm sad. I'm so sad. I'm afraid. I'm sad and I'm afraid."

"Why?" Laura said. "Why are you sad?"

Susannah said, "Because you're dead. Because you're gone. You and Daniel and Mo are gone and nobody knows what happened. You're dead and gone and you'll never come back and I don't know what to do. There's nothing I can do."

As Laura listened, it seemed as if blackness were gushing out of Susannah's mouth, out of her fingers, out the ends of her hair. Laura had never heard anything as desolate as her sister's voice. She shrank back against the couch.

Susannah stooped down, raising her hand, and Laura thought her sister was going to strike her. But what Susannah did instead was grab up the Harmony by the neck. She brought it down so hard on the coffee table it splintered into pieces.

Then Susannah turned and went up the stairs. She came back down again in her winter coat while Laura was gathering up the broken guitar with trembling fingers.

"Susannah, stop!" she said. But Susannah had her old boots on and was out the door.

The Book of Susannah

W HY HAD SHE done what she'd done? Why had she said those things to Laura? Poor old guitar, poor Laura who had to put up with the things that Susannah said and did.

When she was sure her sister wasn't chasing after her, Susannah slowed down to a walk. Her left heel throbbed as if she had a blister there. No, a splinter. It had been there for days.

She came to the neighborhood park where Leonta Carter slumbered in bronze. Susannah brushed snow off a bench and sat down. If she sat long enough, she could just disappear beneath the accumulating snow. Ruth would be at the hospital. Would Laura call to tell her what Susannah had done? Too much to hope Laura would keep it secret. Ruth and she would discuss how worried they were. How they didn't know what was wrong with Susannah. Well, Susannah didn't know, either.

A girl sat down beside her. Susannah had never seen her before, but the coat and hat she knew.

She said, "Where did you get those?"

"You gave them to me," the girl said. "Susannah. That's your name. You can remember mine now. But don't let it make you anxious or fearful. I mean you no harm."

"Bowie," Susannah said. She couldn't understand why she hadn't known Bowie before.

"What a great, lanky thing you are," Bowie said. "I wonder what you have in you that Bogomil spied."

"Bogomil isn't real," Susannah said. "So he doesn't care whether I'm tall or not."

Bowie said, "Oh, but you're wrong about that. He's as real as the devil and twice as bad-tempered. Do you have a temper, too?"

"Yes," Susannah said. "A bad one. How about you?"

"I don't know yet," Bowie said. Then, "What is wrong?"

Susannah had been wriggling one foot out of her boot without knowing she was doing it. She said, "I think I have a splinter in my foot."

Bowie looked at her with great sympathy. "Then you should take it out."

Susannah couldn't think of a reason not to do so. She took off her sock and held her foot turned in her hand so she could see. The end of the splinter was right there, large enough that she could feel it like a matchstick head between her thumb and forefinger. It hurt a great deal. So she did as Bowie had suggested and pulled it out.

IT WAS LIKE going through a door. On one side of the door was the world you'd always lived in, where your sister and your friend and the guy who was sometimes more than a friend had all gone to another country and you had stayed behind. On the other side of the door was where Susannah found herself now. On this side, her sister and Mo and Daniel had returned from Ireland but she knew that they had never gone there in the first place. They had disappeared and now they were back, and there was no explanation for what had happened except for a thing that she knew had not.

There was this, too: She had not meant to do laundry. She had not dreamed of Bogomil the night before. She had seen him. Bogomil was real. The laundry and the dream, these were things Laura had told Susannah. Everything Laura had told Susannah, Susannah had believed, Susannah had done.

"I broke Laura's guitar," Susannah said. "I broke it twice."

"Did she deserve it?" Bowie said.

"Yes," Susannah said with feeling. But it wasn't just the breaking of the guitar that had happened twice. "Thomas! He took the splinter out. He asked me questions. Then he made me forget. And you said he was hunting you, but he didn't ask me about you. He asked me about a boy named Kristofer."

"That is why he is chasing me," Bowie said. "Because of Kristofer. He will never stop chasing me until he catches me. When he catches me, he will kill me."

"Do you deserve it?" Susannah said.

Bowie did not answer for a long moment. Then she said, "Yes. Can I see that?"

Susannah handed Bowie the splinter. It was more than an inch long, dark at the end where it had drunk up her blood.

"It's from the first time I broke Laura's guitar. But later on it wasn't broken."

"Some part of you remembered and so you broke it again," Bowie said. "Here. Put it someplace safe."

Susannah found an old Kleenex in her pocket and wrapped the splinter in it, then tucked the Kleenex back into her pocket. "I don't understand anything that's going on," she said. "Can you explain it to me?"

"Yes," Bowie said. "But first you must take me somewhere else. Thomas and his mistress are near and drawing nearer."

Susannah said, "We can't go back to my house. Laura's there. Look, here's a bus. We could take it to Silverside and then get on the 84 to the hospital. My mom works in the NICU. But I don't have any change. I've only got a twenty."

"I can manage that part," Bowie said.

So they got on the bus.

The Book of Avelot

"Bogomil keeps one side of the door and Anabin the other. We are on the side that Anabin watches over. When your sister and the others died, it was because the door opened and they fell through. Then the door shut."

"They did die! We didn't know, but I knew. I *knew*. Oh shit. Oh shit, Bogomil's real? He knows Mr. Anabin? The music teacher?"

"Will you please listen? I am trying to be helpful. Yes, that Anabin. He and Bogomil are very old and very cunning. You shouldn't trust them. Is this where we disembark?"

"No. Not for another dozen stops at least. Sorry. The second bus ride is longer."

"I will survive it, may it please God. I have survived many other things."

"Okay, but if you think you're gonna puke, let me know. We'll get off the bus. I don't understand any of this."

"I will begin with the Moon then."

"The moon. Okay. Why not."

"Once there was a goddess who was not from our world but from another place much more beautiful and marvelous. This is what she told Bogomil. She opened a door there and came through to our world and although our world was less beautiful, less marvelous, she found charm in its novelty and in the people who worshipped her for the things she could do and they could not. In our world there was something she had never seen before, which was death. And so she decided to stay for a time.

"She had great power over many things: the moon, the sea and its tides, and death, where she kept her provender. Those who worshipped her thought it impolite to refer to a god such as she as the god of death and so she was known as the Moon instead. She had many houses in our world, and in these houses she came and went through many doors she had wrought. Through these doors were other lands, other worlds. Each door was the responsibility of two priests who stood on either side of the door's thresholds. When she wished it so, her priests would hold a particular door open and she would pass through.

"The work of the priests required a great sacrifice on their part, and in return for this, the goddess gave them the power to extend their lives so long as they held her door. She gave them other powers, too. When they grew weary of keeping their door, they found and trained others to do their work and became mortal again. She was not one who was easy to serve, and her priests grew discontented. And although her people loved her, they also feared her. She was capricious and quick to wrath. Eventually their fear was stronger than their love.

"In the end, two of Malo Mogge's priests rebelled. They destroyed the door over which they had been given charge. These doors were not made of wood or stone or cloth but were areas where one place pressed up against another.

"Malo Mogge was enraged by the perfidy of the two priests, and she slew them both. The city where the door had been, she overwhelmed with a great wave, and when her wave receded there was not a stone of it left.

"After that, she grew crueler and asked more and more terrible sacrifices of her priests and her people. But they rose up against her in place after place and destroyed her doors. In the end, only one door was left to her, which was the door through which is her sustenance and, also, Death.

"The goddess could no longer go back to the place of her origin, which had been so beautiful and marvelous. Why? Perhaps those on the other side had barred it to her. She was trapped in this world, where so much of her power had been invested in doors now destroyed. I do not think she could create new ones. She was too diminished. The only priests who remained were the two priests who stood on either side of that last door. To destroy it would have been a great evil. Any may pass through it into Death so long as they do not return."

"Hold on. This is our stop. Now we have to wait for the 84. Sometimes you have to wait for a long time."

"What is long to you may not seem so to me."

"That is a very weird humblebrag. Look, you just said nobody returns, but Daniel and Laura and Mo died and they came back. And Bogomil and Mr. Anabin, they're the priests, right? Because that's the only door, according to you, and you said they stand on either side of the door. Here's the bus already. So you didn't have to be supernaturally patient after all. Or regular patient, even."

"How long will we be on the bus this time?"

"A while. There are a lot of lights."

"Then I wish to sit by the window."

"Fine by me. Just, try to be less confusing."

"Anabin and Bogomil kept the door open so the goddess they served could pass back and forth and draw strength through it. Her magic was great but not inexhaustible. What was beyond the door replenished her. Those who passed through it became her meat. Only now she may not restore herself because the key she must use to move between this world and that other realm was lost to her in some way, I do not know how or when. It came into Bogomil's possession and he kept it in his realm, hidden from Malo Mogge. He devised a plan by which he meant to kill his mistress and take her place and power and immortality. He meant two brothers, Thomas and Kristofer, to become his priests. But I interfered with the ritual. I wished for what Bogomil had promised them, and Bogomil's plan failed because of my interference. This is how Kristofer died and how I was lost and why Thomas hates me. The key, too, was lost again. For many centuries this is how matters stood. While the key was lost, nothing could change. Anabin standing before the threshold on one side, and Bogomil lurking on the other where it is dark and no one may stay, save him."

"But Mr. Anabin is a music teacher. And Bogomil is from my dreams.

And you aren't lost anymore, and my sister is doing weird stuff to my head, and Daniel is just the same as he's always been, and Mo isn't even talking to me on Facebook, and I thought he was pissed off because I hadn't been keeping in touch, but the reason I wasn't keeping in touch was because he was dead. They were all dead."

"They were like me. They must have attempted the ritual and fallen through the door. They remained in Bogomil's realm between Life and Death. Where I have been. To attempt the ritual, they must have found the key. Perhaps they found the key by chance, but once it was found and used, Anabin and Bogomil and Malo Mogge would have felt it."

"Isn't Malo Mogge the woman Thomas works for?"

"Yes. Malo Mogge is the Moon. She is the mistress Thomas serves. Bogomil and Anabin are terrible, but she is worse. All the time I spent upon the threshold in the darkness with Bogomil, I listened to him. His stories. I listened when he did not know what or who I was. I learned much of Malo Mogge and what she is. I forgot myself but I did not forget the things he said. Why does that man keep looking at us?"

"Because you're talking in a normal voice and he can hear us. Talk more quietly. Like me. So where is the key now? The key was what Thomas was asking me about. He thought I knew where it was."

"You say you have dreamed of Bogomil before."

"For years. Since I was in fifth grade? He was my imaginary friend. He promised me one day, if I wanted to, I could live in his realm and rule over it. I didn't have to stay here in Lovesend. In *this* world. When I was older, he said that if I loved Daniel, he knew a way Daniel and I could be together forever."

"Did he tell you how you could do this?"

"He said I had to give Daniel a coin. It had to happen when we were alone and at night. Not during the day."

"How did you find the key? Where did you find it?"

"It was a coin, not a key! And I didn't have it. Mo did. He showed it to me years and years ago. It was in a glass case with a latch. We took it out when we were kids. When we were older, I asked if I could see it again. Bogomil kept asking about it in my dreams. So I went to Mo's house, and Mo got it out of his grandmother's closet again. He let me hold it for a second. That was two years ago, maybe? And last year, I asked Mo if I could buy it from him. I was going to give it to Daniel for his birthday. For his coin collection. Mo said sure. I think it kind of creeped him out actually. He didn't even want money for it. You keep saying it's a key, but it isn't. It's a coin. And I didn't really believe anything that Bogomil said, either. But if a wolf told you to give the person you loved a coin, wouldn't you do it?"

"I see you are very stupid. It isn't always a coin. It might be a key. It has been a knife. When Thomas and Kristofer were to do the ritual, it was a cup. Thomas drank first, but I ran out from my hiding place then and stole the cup from Kristofer. I drank from what was in it. Thomas had not offered me the cup. And his brother had not drunk from it. I took what had not been given, and the one who had been given it did not. And so the ritual went wrong and the cup was lost."

"Well, whatever! Mo was going to meet me on Daniel's birthday. We had a show at the Cliff Hangar. But before we went on, Daniel and I broke up. He broke up with me. Laura pissed me off during the show and all this other stuff happened, so I walked off the stage and I went home. I never got the coin from Mo and so I never gave it to Daniel."

"Mo, then, had the coin."

"I guess? What happened to the cup when you drank from it?"

"Ask Avelot. Maybe she knows."

"Who is Avelot?"

"No one who matters. She died long ago. Is this our stop?"

"Next one. Tell me the rest."

"Malo Mogge desires her key back and two new priests to keep the door for her. Anabin wishes to be mortal again, but Bogomil imagines he can be free of Malo Mogge and yet keep his immortality in some way. He found you here when you first touched the key. That is what I think. That would be when you began to dream of him."

"I don't know. Maybe."

"Then when you touched it the second time, Anabin came to your town."

"He came because our school was hiring a music teacher. Okay. Maybe."

"And when, somehow, the ritual went wrong again, Malo Mogge and Thomas felt this and descended upon this place. And then your sister and your friends and I came back through the door. And now here we all are."

"Hold on. Press the cord. Never mind, I'll do it. We're getting off here."

"What are we going to do?"

"I don't know. Go see my mom. But don't say anything about Laura. Or anything weird. You know what? Don't say anything at all."

The Book of Mo

He was supposed to call Jenny when he wanted a ride home, but first he was going to find a present for Mr. Anabin. He went into a shop he was fairly sure hadn't been there before he'd died. It had handblown glass newts and salamanders wearing crowns and top hats, tea towels and pillows embroidered with book quotes. That sort of thing. It was the pillows that made him go in. They made him think of Mr. Anabin's T-shirts. Was the acquisition of this present supposed to require some magical ability? Should Mo feel magically drawn to one thing or another? That, too, seemed likely. DON'T PANIC seemed like a good choice, a solid choice. If Mr. Anabin really needed a throw pillow, these were a possibility. That quote he recognized. There were weirder quotes, too: THE YOUNGER PEOPLE, WITH THE ACHE OF YOUTH, WERE EATING ALL THE CHEESE. Was that really from a book? Who went to all the trouble of embroidering something like that on a pillow? Or LOOK AT THAT MOON. POTATO WEATHER FOR SURE. He liked that one. But not in a magical way. At least he didn't think so.

There was a display of polished stones on a shelf. Feldspar, striated rose quartz, granite. Mo picked up one that was perfectly palm-sized and realized it wasn't a stone at all. It was porcelain, glazed so texture and color gave it the appearance of a stone, but so light it must have been hollow. Mo turned it over and saw where the artist had signed their initials.

There was no meaning to something like this, except that it was not the thing it seemed to be. It made Mo want to go straight home to work on a new piece of music. But instead he put the porcelain stone down and picked up another. He held this one up to his ear and listened. All objects collected and organized sound and silence and whatever lived in the uncanny territory existing between those two states, but a hollow object collected and organized silence around itself in a way that was different from a solid object. There was the silence inside the shape, which neither listened nor spoke. Nothing dwelled there. Mo was not held a prisoner inside it, he was free. His silence was not silence: it was made up of his breath, his stillness, his busy thoughts, and his steady heartbeat. Listening, he became aware that in the silence someone was observing him. This, too, was a sound.

When he turned his head, he saw a woman behind the counter. She was in her forties, he thought, a white woman. She wore a stack of hammered silver bangles, the kind that would make noise when she moved. She had her hand on the counter beside her cellphone.

"Hey," Mo said. He put the stone back down. "Cool stuff."

She said nothing so Mo tried again. He said, "I'm looking for a birthday present."

"I saw what you did," the woman said.

"What I did what?" Mo said.

"You put one of those in your pocket," the woman said. Her tone was not friendly. "I saw you."

Mo said, "What? No. Seriously? Look." He patted his pockets, pulled out his own cellphone. His wallet. He made his face as open as he could while inside him everything was closing up protectively. "Nothing else in there, okay?" He backed toward the door.

"Where are you going?" the woman said.

"Taking my business elsewhere," Mo said. He went back out into the snow. White retail ladies had not been a problem while he was dead. Somebody embroider that on a pillow.

To his dismay, the woman followed him outside. She said, "What a fool you are. Back from the dead for not three days and already with Malo Mogge's breath on your neck."

"What?" Mo said.

The woman wasn't wearing a coat, and snow powdered her shoulders, her hair. She said, "Give it to her. Or you'll be sorry."

"I don't have it! And I didn't steal anything. I just wanted to find a present for my music teacher so he won't send me back to hell! You know?" Mo said. He turned and began to go swiftly down the street. Wind spat snow into his face, into the gap of his unbuttoned coat. There was too much whiteness in the world. It did not love him, but he would not leave it. When he turned around, the woman had gone back inside her shop.

Mo walked briskly until he came to the tiny Lovesend bookstore where the black cat slept all day long in the window. He could go into the bookstore, he could get Mr. Anabin a book. A self-help book. But in the window, yes, here was the cat; here, too, were his grandmother's books. Here was Lavender Glass in the arms of the man who loved her and tormented her and left her and returned to her and saved her. The Lavender Glass series had been repackaged three or four years before Mo died. The new male model was handsome enough, but Mo preferred the old design. Before he was old enough to read his grandmother's books, he'd been entranced by their covers. He'd thought the man on the cover was the most beautiful person he'd ever seen. Hair painted by an artist who had used at least eight different shades of yellow and gold, a face that conveyed yearning so consuming there was no energy left over for a morning shave or even putting on a shirt all the way, and the kind of six-pack that required a personal trainer and an unpleasant (though unlikely in the sixteenth century) diet.

Of course, Mo had only had these realizations later on. For many years, he'd only imagined what it would be like to be held by someone as the man held the woman on the cover. He still had a thing for blonds who let their hair get a little too long. He still imagined what it would be like to be held so tenderly by a hot, kissy-lipped guy with sleepy eyelids and big hands falling out of the shirtsleeves of an unbleached linen lace-up shirt.

The guy on the new covers was also hot, kissy-lipped, and protective. No one cared that Mo missed the way things had been.

In the corner of the window was a copy of *Ashana's Heart*. That, too, had been repackaged in the 2000s after Avon released Beverly Jenkins's *Night Song* and publishing realized that Black women, too, bought romance novels. Wanted romance novels with Black heroines. Thank you,

Beverly Jenkins, thank you, *Night Song*, fuck you very much, publishing. The new edition had had a modest success. But Mo's grandmother never wrote another book like it, and Mo had never asked her why. He'd always thought the girl on the repackaged edition of *Ashana's Heart* looked a little like his mom did in the framed photo his grandmother kept on the bureau in her bedroom. He'd never asked his grandmother about that, either. He'd always thought one day he would.

On the back of *Ashana's Heart* was a photograph of his grandmother. There was no author photograph on the back of any of the Lavender Glass books, not even the reissues.

Mo stood in the snow outside the bookstore. He thought, If the cat wakes up and looks at me, I'll go in.

But the cat remained asleep and his grandmother was still dead and Mo's grief surged up from whatever low, interior space it had made its home. He could have fallen over right then, only you shouldn't just lie down on the ground and give in to misery, no matter the relief such an action would give you. Even the man who carried the terrible burden of loving Lavender Glass managed to get his shirt halfway on most days. Mo had been set a magical errand, and therefore he would accomplish it. Magic, like grief, could come welling up. The difference was how grief slammed into you without any kind of ceremony or invitation. Magic you could use. Grief just used you up. So Mo thought of what it had been like in the music room when he'd named Bowie into boy from bird. What it had been like to make roses bloom at night. He drew on magic, asked it, What should I give to Mr. Anabin? What does that asshole want for his birthday?

Magic didn't answer him. No book knocked against the window or suddenly caught fire. Instead, as Mo stood in the street, a heavy wet snow falling down, he saw how in the bookstore window there were two cats now, not one. The second cat was perched on a high shelf. It was the largest cat Mo had ever seen. The tip of every white hair bristled with menace. Its tail swung slowly back and forth, and its eyes were fixed on Mo.

Here was magic. The cat stretched languorously and began to stroll along the shelf.

Its eyes never left Mo, but when the white cat came to the edge of the shelf, it leapt from its high perch, falling upon the sleeping bookstore cat.

It buried its teeth in the other cat's neck and shook it like a rag, staring still at Mo.

Mo fled into the slushy street. The day was growing darker fast: the snow as it fell was mixed with bits of black soot. He could not see the source of the fire, but ash continued to fall with the snow as if something invisible and very large was burning and could not be put out.

The Book of Daniel

By midafternoon, not a single Lucklow offspring had a dry pair of snow boots to their name and the front yard was a battlefield of decapitated snowmen and crumbling snow weaponry. Peter had gone to help shovel an elderly neighbor's driveway, so Daniel made grilled cheeses and hot chocolates, even though this meant that no one would be hungry for dinner. He was no longer interested in long-term planning. Then he sat everyone down in front of the television in their pajamas to watch *Gravity Falls* while he went to his room to read the five thousand texts Laura had fired off in the past ten minutes. As he finally began to understand what she was saying, that Susannah remembered they had been dead, she called.

"Where is she?" Daniel said.

Laura said, "I don't know. She just took off."

"I'll try calling her," Daniel said.

"She didn't take her phone," Laura said. "I kind of had a fight with her. That's when she remembered."

Daniel rolled his eyes. Laura and Susannah fought all the time. "Why would that make her remember?"

Laura said, "So, it's complicated." She began to explain: Bogomil the previous night, Susannah in the yard, Susannah's terror, and then the rest.

"Bogomil visited last night?" Daniel said. "She saw him? And you made her forget?"

"I just told her to go back to bed, which she did."

"And that was all," Daniel said. He could tell it hadn't been all.

"Yeah. Well, I also told her she should do laundry."

"Laundry?"

"Oh, come on! It's not like I told her to stand on her head!" Laura said. "Just, she's been depressed and not doing stuff she should. I was being helpful. Like you've never wanted to tell Susannah to knock it off. And also, I mean, it was kind of a test. We need to know what we can do."

Daniel said, "No! We don't! We shouldn't be doing stuff like that. You're not fixing Susannah, you're just messing with her. Did you even ask her what Bogomil was doing there?"

"Okay," Laura said, "maybe in retrospect I was taking a shortcut but, I mean, it didn't really work. It didn't take. What if she's remembering stuff she shouldn't because I tried to make her forget stuff? Shit. What if Ethan starts getting his memory back?"

"Who's Ethan?" Daniel said.

"Nobody," Laura said. "I'll call you when Susannah gets back, okay? We're all supposed to go to that benefit at the Cliff Hangar, her and me and Ruth and my dad. She'll be back."

"Wait—" Daniel began, but Laura had already hung up. He'd found Susannah at the beach the last time, so he'd start there. When he turned around to grab another layer from his chest of drawers, he saw that a white cat was watching him lazily from his unmade bed.

"How did you get in here?" Daniel said.

The cat yawned. It said, "Through a door, you great big pudding. There are very few doors that can keep me out. And none of them are in this house."

"Get out!" Daniel said.

"Keep your voice down," Bogomil said. "Unless you want your family in here. I'm not very good with children, and there are so very many of them in this house. One might even say too many."

"What do you want?" Daniel said.

"Many things," Bogomil said. "But the time is short and I find daylight uncomfortable. So let me get to the point as quickly as possible. Anabin has given you some instruction on how magic may be used, and I see your friends Laura and Mo have taken to it. Like ducks to quicksand! But you, you won't even dip your toe in the stuff. I'm curious as to why."

"You've been watching me?" Daniel said.

"Of course I've been watching you," Bogomil said. He raised one hind leg and began to clean the pads of his paw. There were rust-colored stains along the leg and around his muzzle. "You're a very boring individual. But even if I hadn't been watching you, I would know you weren't using magic. The state of you is shocking."

"It is?" Daniel said.

"Magic brought you back," Bogomil said. "And magic gave you a shape. A body to inhabit. If you've been made of magic, have magic inside you, you must learn a thing or two about it. Learn how to use it, to manipulate it. You can't just hold magic inside you like you're a piece of Tupperware. Magic is volatile. It ebbs. It expands. It spoils. Sooner or later, magic unused, unregulated, will overwhelm you and then you'll just explode or shrivel away, melt into goo or become a shower of pennies or expired condoms."

"I don't want to use magic!" Daniel said. "I don't want to be a magician or whatever you are."

"Very well," Bogomil said. "What do you want, then?"

"I want you to leave me alone," Daniel said. "I want you to leave my family alone, and I want you to leave Susannah and Laura and Mo alone, too."

"What do you want besides that?" Bogomil said.

"Nothing," Daniel said. He folded his arms. He thought, I can be Tupperware if I want to.

"What did you want when you were alive?" Bogomil said.

When Daniel remained silent, Bogomil said, "Do you think I don't know you, Daniel? After all the nights you spent sheltering in my realm? Let's see. What do I know? Your father's untimely death left your poor mother in terrible debt. You found that out by eavesdropping when you were thirteen. There are two mortgages on this house, and your mother and your stepfather have been paying them down for years now, but there are just so many bills! It can't be easy for your parents. You came up with a plan when you were fourteen. You would get a scholarship to the best college you could and then go to business school. You would make enough money so that by the time your siblings thought of college, you would be able to contribute. So noble, Daniel! You applied early decision to the University of Pennsylvania before you died and you got in. Full ride, very impressive. Yes, and there's a drawer in your desk over there full of lottery tickets. When you were alive you bought two scratch tickets every month. If any of those tickets had ever been a winner, you were going to give the money to your parents. But the most you ever won was sixteen dollars. How much did you spend, over the past two years, on tickets? Oh dear. Not a great return on investment. Are you really sure you have a head for business?"

The white cat did not use its mouth for speech. It spoke directly into Daniel's head and continued to groom itself. Once this had been accomplished to its satisfaction, it opened its mouth even wider and began to swallow its own hind leg. It went on swiftly swallowing itself until its entire body had disappeared, impossibly, its mouth stuffed full of white fur. The mouth opened farther, the head turning itself inside out, rosy wet gullet snapping together like a fanged coin purse, the voice continuing to speak until there was no cat at all. Only Bogomil's voice.

"You should do as your conscience tells you, of course. I only find it interesting that you have at last been given a winning ticket and what do you do? Turn up your nose. Turn up your toes. All the things you could do if you chose magic as I chose it. As I *choose* it. You and my dear friend Anabin make a fine pair. Oh, Daniel, money to pay off a mortgage is the least of it! Imagine everything you have ever wanted. Only then refuse the gift that has been offered you. Starve and dwindle and die all over again. Well, let me do you a good turn so you might think better of me in the short span you have remaining. Should you decide not to use magic, then you may open that drawer again, the one where you keep your lottery tickets, and you will find some there I have acquired for you. So when you die, your family might find all of their needs provided for. But, Daniel, is there nothing else in this ripe and astonishing world you might want?"

The voice fell silent. The cat might never have been there, and of course it hadn't ever been a cat at all. Daniel sat down on the bed and tried not to imagine that someone, somewhere, minutes later, was still waiting to hear his answer.

Carousel popped her head around the door. She said, "We're going to watch *Lilo and Stitch* now. But Lissy says we should ask you first because we've already watched so much TV."

"Today is for breaking rules," Daniel said. "As long as you all agree on what to put on, watch whatever you want. As long as you want. Hey, Carousel? You know that when Ms. Fish calls you Caroline, that's her problem not yours."

"I know," Carousel said. "But she still shouldn't call me Caroline. That's not who I am."

"I know," Daniel said. "But she's spent her whole life being Ms. Fish. She's never realized she could have been someone else if she wanted to be. I bet she's never met anyone quite like you."

"That's because there isn't anyone like me," Carousel said. "We're going to make popcorn. You want some?"

"Hope you make a lot," Daniel said.

The Book of Susannah

About fifteen years ago, consultants had been paid a great deal of money to rebrand Cresthill, the hospital where Ruth worked. They'd run ad campaigns showing smiling women holding sleeping babies, and older men looking on calmly as their blood pressure was checked. The cafeteria had been remodeled, the menu adjusted. There was a lot of quinoa now, and you could get sweet potato fries that were actually tasty. But the nurses and the therapists in the NICU hadn't had a pay raise in ten years, and the premature babies didn't notice that the lobby now had banquettes instead of benches and sofas. Susannah's mother loved her job, and she liked several of the doctors she worked with, but she had dark things to say about management, consultants, and banquettes, which were designed to be sleek rather than comfortable.

On any night of the week, Susannah knew there were likely to be between two and a dozen babies in the NICU. There were so many things that could go wrong with babies. Every nurse knew this. You could even be born with all of your organs on the outside, though Ruth had explained to Susannah and Laura that fixing this was actually a fairly simple procedure. Complicated babies went by ambulance to Boston Children's Hospital. But Ruth and her team of nurses were quite capable of handling most preemies.

A woman in a hospital gown, pulling an IV stand after her, came down the hall toward them. She was holding a bag of Doritos in the other hand, and Avelot stopped her. She said, "I'm hungry. Give those to me," and the woman handed them to Avelot without hesitation.

"What?" Susannah said. "No!" She took the Doritos away from Avelot and gave them back to the woman, then hustled Avelot farther down the corridor. "You can't just make people do things."

"But I can," Avelot said.

"Well, it's an asshole move," Susannah said. "You're not going to do that stuff while you're hanging out with me, okay?"

"But I'm hungry," Avelot said.

"Then I'll buy you something in the cafeteria," Susannah said. In the end she bought Avelot three slices of pizza and two brownies (because Avelot did not know what a brownie was). While Avelot ate, Susannah thought about the problem of Laura. She had been pissed off at Laura many times in her life. It was, in fact, possible she'd spent more time being pissed off at Laura than otherwise, but the state had been comfortably mutual. And now? She had no way to describe what she was feeling. How could Laura have done what she had done?

"She fucking made me do laundry!" she said out loud. "That secret-hoarding bitch!"

Avelot, her mouth full of pizza, said, "Malo Mogge is a harsh mistress."

"Not Malo Mogge," Susannah said. "I've never even met Malo Mogge, and if I did I'd punch her right in the mouth. I mean Laura."

Avelot said, "There are others who have done worse."

"Yeah, but they're not my sister," Susannah said, brooding. Laura had been dead, and Daniel and Mo and oh my God that was so awful and she remembered, she remembered how awful it had been.

She said, "Are they going to be okay? Laura and Daniel and Mo?"

"Probably not," Avelot said. She had finished both brownies and two pieces of the pizza. Susannah had met dogs who ate more slowly.

"What's going to happen to them?" Susannah said.

"Anabin and Bogomil, and Malo Mogge, too, wish to see if your sister and your friends and myself may discover the key while they go on looking for it themselves. By the time the key is found, Anabin will have determined which two are best suited as replacements for himself and Bogomil, to take up duties on either side of the door. He will make his suggestions to Malo Mogge and either she will go along with them or she will not. The two who are not chosen to keep Malo Mogge's door will die again and return to the realm from which they escaped, to wait for Malo

Mogge to devour them, and Malo Mogge will be free at last to punish Bogomil however she might choose.

"Your sister and the others know only a small part of this, and you will not tell them, either, unless I decide that you may. It is to my advantage that they do not hold all the pieces, and I must take what advantage I can. Unless I am chosen to guard the door, Malo Mogge will offer my death to Thomas and then she will have me for her meat once I am dead."

"You seem very calm about it all," Susannah said. "But I'm kind of freaking out. How can we stop it? What can I do?"

Avelot stopped chewing. "You? Nothing. There is nothing you can do."

Susannah said, "This is what Bogomil was trying, last year. With me. And it didn't happen. He didn't get what he wanted."

"No," Avelot said. "Instead everyone died."

"Well, I can help. I'll figure out how to help," Susannah said. "No more dying, and definitely no getting devoured. But first I'm going to make Laura sorry she ever came back from the dead. Make me do laundry, my ass."

But she could tell Avelot wasn't thinking about Laura or any of this predicament at all. She was thinking about getting more pizza.

"Come on," Susannah said, before Avelot could ask. "Let's go see my mom. And just, don't say anything. To anyone."

Maude at the check-in desk waved Susannah and Avelot in, and Susannah stuffed both their coats in a locker and made Avelot wash her hands at the bank of sinks for the requisite minute and a half. Avelot did as she was told without asking why.

The first person they saw was a respiratory therapist, Paula. A huge oversharer, according to Ruth. But Susannah liked the pink streak in Paula's hair.

"Your mom didn't tell me you were coming by," Paula said.

"Spur of the moment," Susannah said. "This is my friend Ava. We do yoga together?" This, the first thing that came to mind. Yoga? What the fuck, brain? "She's thinking about applying to med school. I thought I'd show her who the real heroes are."

"Hope your grades are good," Paula said to Avelot. "Your mom's in Bay 4. Tell her I'll be back with the blood gas results ASAP."

"Come on," Susannah said. When she looked to see if Avelot was following, she saw Avelot was now sporting a pink streak in her own hair. "Seriously? What is Paula going to think if she comes by and sees that?"

Avelot stuck out her lip mulishly. The pink streak remained.

"Fine," Susannah said. "But it looked better on her."

"Why are these babies encased in glass?" Avelot asked. "And how are so many so small? What is that uncanny light?"

"They were born too early," Susannah said. "The Isolettes keep them warm and safe, and the purple light is ultraviolet. For jaundice. How are you going to get into medical school if you don't know anything? Paula would be very disappointed."

"I had a babe born too early," Avelot said. "It slipped from me like a fish from a hand."

Susannah said, "Oh shit. I'm so sorry."

"Why?" Avelot said. "It would not have had a good life. In its short life no man ever hurt it and neither did it cause any injury to another. Before you feel pity for me, you should know I have been thinking all this time about whether or not it would be right and meet to kill you."

"Kill me?" Susannah said, then looked around to see if anyone had heard. But the NICU was mostly empty at this time of day. Various alarms sounded, shrill or soothing, as a baby's heart rate rose or dipped, an oxygen saturation went below the level some doctor had determined to be reasonable. But these were small ripples in the calm of the NICU. No real crises were occurring presently. Here was the break room, with its beat-up sofa and shelf of romances and young adult novels, because nurses liked to know their happy endings were guaranteed, even if only in fiction. Here was the small closet where lactating parents went to pump breast milk and cry. In the fourth bay, Ruth, in one of her cheerful animal print scrubs, was holding a baby Susannah estimated to be about three pounds, joggling it against her chest with one hand while she unfastened an Isolette from its berth. She hadn't noticed Susannah and Avelot yet.

"Why?" Susannah said. She was trying to understand what this peculiar person had just said to her.

"Because I don't understand your part in this," Avelot said. "You have been Bogomil's tool, and he may still have some use for you. Why else would you still be living when you failed him previously? You may yet do great harm. I would take no pleasure in it, but your death might be a fitting gift for Anabin's birthday, which is the task he has set me."

Susannah knew she should have been afraid; instead she began to lose her temper. "You think my old music teacher wants my head in a box for his birthday for some reason. Okay. So why spend all this time hanging out? Why not kill me earlier? Did it seem like it would be more fun to wait and kill me in front of my mom?"

"I did not say I was going to kill you," Avelot said. "I said I was thinking about whether it was the thing I was meant to do."

Susannah said, "Can I make a counterargument? What the fuck is wrong with you?"

Avelot said, "I am trying to stay alive. One day perhaps I will not need to cause harm to do so. But I have no magical box—no Isolette—to hide myself in where I can remain safe. And if I am not safe from the world, why should the world be safe from me? You have been in danger since the first time you saw Bogomil, and you are a fool if you do not see that you, too, are dangerous. That woman is gesturing at us."

Ruth was waving them over, still joggling the baby. "Okay," Susannah said. "Can we talk about this later? That's my mom. Can you please be normal around her?"

Avelot gave her the kind of look that didn't promise anything, and Susannah felt her first uncomfortable flicker of fellow feeling.

"Susannah," Ruth said. She looked pleased to see her daughter and also a little anxious because Susannah didn't usually show up at Ruth's place of work without calling first. "Is everything okay? Who's this?"

"Everything's fine," Susannah said, lying through her teeth. "My friend Ava and I went to the mall—this is Ava—and then I thought maybe we should come say hi. She really likes babies."

"Good news for me," Ruth said. "Ava, this is Hector. Hold Hector for me. Yes, good, just like that. Hector is a bad, bad baby. He pooped so explosively I have to go grab him a new Isolette. How do you and Susannah know each other?"

"The coffee shop," Susannah said. "She loves muffins!"

Avelot, cradling Hector so tenderly within her arms that it astonished Susannah, said, "What is a muffin?"

"Ha ha ha!" Susannah said. "Ava does stand-up, actually. She's always trying out new material. Go deal with the Isolette. We'll hang out with Hector."

Then, when Ruth had wheeled the Isolette away, to Avelot: "If you kill me, I hope you never ever find out what a muffin is."

Avelot said, "Maybe if you tell me what a muffin is, I won't kill you."

"It's another word for kale," Susannah said.

"What's kale?" Avelot said.

Susannah said, "It's delicious. You should definitely try it. Just go ask for a big plate of plain steamed kale the next time you're out to eat. Look, do you want to sit down in the lounger or something? I keep worrying you're going to drop Hector on his head. Why don't you get comfortable?"

"You think if I get comfortable then perhaps you may get away from me," Avelot said. "I do like this. Holding Hector. He's very warm and I like, too, the smell of the top of his head. But it would be easy to catch you again."

"Then I'll conserve my energy," Susannah said. "Anyway, I don't think you should kill me. I can think of practically a dozen presents that would be better. Like a thoughtfully selected book! Or chocolate!"

Avelot said, "Perhaps I could give him Hector. He seems like a delightful baby." She didn't remark upon the wires and cords that connected Hector to his monitor, the feeding tube taped to his nose, the cannulas in his nostrils, the tangerine Binky plugged into his mouth. Susannah felt that unwanted sympathy again. How strange it must be to find oneself arrived in the future. You wouldn't even know the right questions to ask. What is a muffin? Should I kill this girl?

She said, "You're forgetting the explosive pooping. And if he's in here then he needs to be here. These guys have all sorts of issues."

Avelot said, "Yes. I know. His heart was bad. But I have fixed it."

"You fixed his heart," Susannah said.

Avelot said, "Also his lungs. So there is no reason why he would not make a pleasing gift."

Susannah said, "What about the other babies?"

"You think that I shouldn't give Hector to Anabin, but instead I should give him every baby? Is one baby not enough?"

"No, I mean, could you fix all of the babies in here?"

Avelot closed her eyes and then opened them again. Hector was now awake. He squirmed in Avelot's arms, beginning to cry. The movement dislodged his sat probe, and an alarm dinged. The Binky fell onto the floor. "I have fixed them all," she said. "To the best of my ability."

"How?" Susannah said.

"When we came out of Bogomil's realm, Anabin gave us each a body. He made them part by part out of his magic so we could remain in this world. I felt what he did as he did it, and I remembered," Avelot said. "That is how. But now I am hungry again and tired and I still don't know what gift should be given to Anabin. Shhhh, baby. Don't cry. It doesn't help."

Susannah said, "You fixed the babies? What if you did something wrong? Holy shit. The nurses are going to freak out. We should go. As soon as Ruth gets back we should leave. Just, I have to do one thing first. Don't do anything else. Just sit there and don't do anything."

When Avelot nodded, Susannah went over to her mother's workstation and tore a sheet of paper off the scratch pad. She tried to compose herself. Pretend she had come alone. There was no horror show of a girl who could, in the blink of an eye, solve the problems an entire NICU full of doctors and nurses and specialists and therapists spent all of their energy and time and focus on. A girl who was making up her mind on the subject of whether or not she should murder Susannah. She wrote on the sheet of paper: *Dear Susannah, don't freak out. But also, this isn't a joke. If you're still alive and Avelot hasn't killed you, long story, there's some stuff you need to know. Stuff you may not remember, because someone might make you forget. Laura can do magic. Also she and Daniel and Mo used to be dead. NOT IN IRELAND!!!!* This she underlined. *If none of this seems like it can be real, it means Laura has been messing with your memories. She can make you do stuff and you have to figure out how to stop her. Unfortunately you also have to help her because she and Daniel and Mo are in a lot of trouble. Some goddess named Malo Mogge wants to eat them. Also Bogomil is real???? Mr. Anabin is not a music teacher! Love, Susannah.*

She put the date on the piece of paper, folded it up into a little rectangle, and stapled it. Her sister had been dead, and Mo, and Daniel. The other night she had fallen asleep in his arms and never known he had ever been dead. She wrote her name on the outside of the paper and said, "Hey, Avelot?"

"Yes?" Avelot said.

"Never mind. It's a stupid idea."

"Tell me," Avelot said.

"It's just, Mr. Anabin's a music teacher. Whatever else he is, he's that, too. So, can't you get him something that you'd get for a music teacher? Like, what about a music box or something? He must have a favorite song."

Avelot gazed down at Hector, who was still screaming out all of his rage or sorrow, whether or not it helped anything. Her hair hid most of her face, the stripe of pink looking like an attempt to be trendy, an area where Avelot had several irredeemable disadvantages. She looked as if she were whispering a secret to Hector. Probably telling him the world was a terrible place and even if he never meant to, he'd hurt people and people would hurt him. But as Avelot whispered to him, he stopped crying. And it was now that Ruth came back with a fresh Isolette.

"Mom?" Susannah said. She knew she sounded manic. Ruth was going to think she was on drugs. "We have to go. But first, can I give you something? I want you to hold on to it for me, and in a day or two if me and Laura are really getting along, like we aren't fighting at all, I want you to take me aside and give me this note. Okay? If Laura and I are, you know, in a super awesome place and you're just like, Wow, I can't believe my daughters are getting along like this, you have to give me this. But you can't read it. It's private."

"Is everything okay?" Ruth said. "Susannah?"

There was a fifty-fifty chance Avelot was going to try to kill her as soon as they left the NICU. Definitely once she tasted kale. And if Avelot didn't kill her, then Laura was going to make her forget everything, and that made Susannah so angry she wanted to kill Laura. Basically murder was going to happen at some point, it was just a question of how soon. "Everything's great!" she said.

"Then I'll see you in a couple of hours," Ruth said. "We're all going up to the Cliff Hangar, still, for karaoke? Your dad texted. He says he's in."

Avelot said, "Here. I didn't drop him." She gave Hector back to Ruth.

Ruth, looking at the monitor, said, "One hundred percent! Hector, you overachiever! Let's turn you down a bit."

"Bye, Mom," Susannah said. She grabbed Avelot by the arm.

Once they were in the corridor again, she let go. "Okay," she said, pulling on her coat. "Let's get this over with. Are you going to kill me or is there any chance we could just go to Paradise Point and get Mr. Anabin a gift card?"

Avelot said, "I have arranged for a gift. I think he will find it acceptable."

"You got something for him while we were in there?" Susannah said, and then: "Never mind. Don't tell me. I'd hate to ruin the surprise. So, I guess, goodbye. I think you're doing the right thing not murdering me."

But when she looked at Avelot's face, Susannah saw Avelot was still thinking about killing her. Every muscle in her body grew ready. She imagined shoving Avelot, running down the corridor. And Avelot getting back to her feet, inescapable as any monster in a slasher movie.

"I should kill you," Avelot said. "It would make my path simpler. But there is your sister, Laura. And Daniel. Your friend Mo. If they discovered what I had done, they would require payment from me. And I do not know if I have the strength to stand against them. Already Thomas desires my blood."

"Plus you can always decide to kill me later," Susannah said. "If you change your mind. Right?"

"There is that, also," Avelot said. "But for now, I will be your ally if you will be mine."

"Like I need your help," Susannah said scornfully. "You didn't even know what a muffin was until I told you."

Avelot grabbed Susannah by the lapel of her coat. Her hand dug into Susannah's pocket and pulled out the Kleenex-wrapped splinter.

"Hey!" Susannah said.

"Take off your boot and your sock," Avelot said. And though Susannah did not mean to do so, she found she was taking them off anyway. People passing by gave them curious looks. But none stopped.

Avelot knelt down. "Lift your foot," she said. "No, the other one." And

Susannah did. Avelot drove the splinter up into the meat of Susannah's heel, a hot, bright flare of pain.

Avelot, standing back up, said, "It's better if you don't remember this for now."

"Oh," Susannah said. "Oh no. You asshole! Don't you dare!"

But Avelot went on and so Susannah had to go on listening.

"You and your sister had a quarrel about something very small. Nothing that followed was out of the ordinary, and in the future, should she attempt to work any magic upon you, she will find it has no effect. She may not command you nor may any other of your friends besides myself, though you will not remember I have said this. You do not remember any of the strange things I said or did. But you know I am your friend. This afternoon you enjoyed my company as I have enjoyed yours."

"We should hang out more often," Susannah said, meaning every word.

"It's curious," Avelot said. "I believe you have some access to magic, still. I feel it in you, pushing back at me. Some door you or some other opened by chance has not yet closed all the way. And yet you cannot find your way through to use it. What are you going to do now?"

"I should catch the bus home," Susannah said. "I guess. You coming?"

"No," Avelot said. "I find I am hungry. Perhaps this place will serve me kale."

The Book of Laura

Laura walked into town because she couldn't stay at home and not do anything at all. After she'd hung up on Daniel, she put her two new guitars in her room. The busted Harmony she almost threw away, but she could not quite bring herself to do this. Surely here was one thing she could fix by magic. And it was so much easier than you would think. The simplest puzzle in the world, and when it was a guitar again, Laura sat down to tune it and found that this, too, had been accomplished. And since the Harmony was already tuned, she found she wanted to play it one last time.

"Terrible old guitar," she crooned to it over the most carefree progression of chords she could summon. *"This is a lullaby for a terrible old guitar. My sister broke you, but here you are. I replaced you but I fixed you, you old, terrible guitar."*

Then she returned it to its case and went out into the snow.

It had grown bitterly cold. Snow caught in her eyelashes and hair, melted, and then refroze. As she went by the window of What Hast Thou Ground? she looked inside, but Susannah was not there. She recognized some of the regulars, and one or two looked up and met her gaze in a way she did not like. Passersby on the street, too, turned as she went past; they seemed to know something about her she did not know herself.

It was with enormous relief that she recognized Mo on the next corner, taking shelter against the marble plinth where Alice Ball, cast in bronze, stood holding her beaker out, promising the cure for leprosy, her arm never growing weary, her face never losing its serene and joyful air of accomplishment.

"What's up?" she said, drawing near, and Mo flinched. Then he said, "Oh. Hey. Today is a *day*."

"You, too?" Laura said. "Susannah knows stuff. Like, she remembered. She yelled about us being dead and then she ran off. You haven't heard anything from her, have you?"

"Oh shit," Mo said. He seemed genuinely surprised. "No, but I met Malo Mogge earlier."

"Malo Mogge!" Laura said. "Why didn't you call and tell us?"

"I don't know," Mo said. "I guess for the same reason you didn't call to warn me about Susannah, right? Anyway, I'm telling you now." He told her about Malo Mogge, about Bowie who was Avelot, and Thomas, who served one and hated the other.

Laura was pretty sure he wasn't telling her everything, but she would get more details later once Susannah had been found.

Mo's orange fleece was flecked with black blotches. Laura reached out to brush one off, and the black smeared into the fabric of her glove.

"Ashes," Mo said. "Someone got a little enthusiastic with the old yuletide log somewhere."

"You trust this guy? Thomas?"

Mo was silent for long enough that Laura knew two things. One, Mo had no idea whether Thomas was trustworthy. And two, he wanted to believe that he was. Finally he said, "I trust him more than I trust Mr. Anabin. Put it this way. Thomas's agenda seems pretty easy to understand. He wants revenge on Bowie because a long time ago Bowie killed his brother. And I don't think we have any idea what Mr. Anabin wants, except it's probably the same thing as Bogomil and Malo Mogge. To find this cup."

"Have you told Daniel any of this?" Laura said.

"No, I haven't talked to Daniel," Mo said. "Talking to Daniel is never high on my list of things to do. Tell him they're looking for a cup. Or a coin."

"Mo!" Laura said. It came out as kind of a scream. "You keep saying things as if they ought to make sense. But they do not make sense!"

"Calm down, rock star," Mo said. "You think I understand any of this business? But here's the gist, in bullet points. One: Malo Mogge is bad news. Two: She wants us to find something for her that a bunch of people with magic haven't been able to locate in hundreds of years. It's either a cup or a coin. It's been both of those at various times. Three: Bogomil and Mr. Anabin and Malo Mogge all hate each other and if we do turn up this thing they want, they're going to tear each other apart trying to claim it. Four: So, you know, we're fucked."

"And Susannah," Laura said. "Five."

"Yeah," Mo said. "What do we do about that?"

"I can use magic to make her forget," Laura said.

"Is that a good idea?" Mo said.

"Do you have a better one?" Laura said. "Either way we have to figure out where she is."

Streetlights were coming on, cones of falling snow strobing out from bowls of yellow light. A plow passed, flinging silver slush. A middle-aged woman, bundled up in a puffy coat, stopped. She was no one Laura knew.

"Here we go again," Mo said, but before Laura could ask him what he meant, the woman was speaking.

"Shame on the pair of you."

"Excuse me?" Laura said.

The woman went on. "The sight of you disgusts me. Insignificant fly-specks on the hem of her least garment! Give her back what you took."

"Ignore her," Mo said. "This has been going on for the past half hour. People coming up to tell me they know I have the thing Malo Mogge wants. And her least garment? Like, what's a least garment?"

"An exercise bra," Laura said. "One you haven't washed in like two months."

Mo said, "Sure. A pair of tighty-whities you leave in a gym locker until it's old and mildewy and the elastic goes rotten."

"Her name in your mouth should reduce you to cinders and ash!" the woman said.

"Malo Mogge," Mo said. "Nope. Nothing."

"Give her back her cup," the woman said. "Then fall on your knees and pray she will show you mercy."

"Oh, leave us *alone,* you tiresome, weak-minded sycophant!" Laura said.

Their tormentor took a step back. She gave Laura a fearful look, then hurried away. They watched her disappear around the corner of Dolphin Street.

Mo said, "How did you learn how to do *that*?"

"Practice," Laura said, feeling smug. Because it was such a relief to have someone she could actually talk about this with, she said, "I guess I don't really know? You know how sometimes you're talking with someone and they're wrong and they just aren't listening to you and the conversation isn't going anywhere and it's pointless? So now I'm in their brain and they're actually listening to me, and Mo, it feels good when I do it. It feels amazing." She told him about Ethan and Birdsong Music.

Mo said, "Seems kind of messed up, by which I mean extremely unethical, but whatever. Have you figured out a present yet? For Mr. Anabin?"

"Yes," Laura said.

"But you're not going to tell me," Mo said. Laura shrugged. It wasn't really any of his business, was it? You couldn't do everything for everyone.

"Well, I got nada. Nothing. Every time I went into a store, somebody told me to give Malo Mogge back what I'd taken." Mo pulled his phone out of his pocket. "Jenny's here to pick me up. Want a ride anywhere?"

"I need to find Susannah," Laura said. "And I'll call Daniel. Tell him what's going on."

A car pulled up beside the curb and Mo said, "Good luck, I guess," and got in.

Laura stamped her feet, trying to get warm. She didn't blame her sister for this, for making her come out into the snow. The fault was Laura's. It had been reasonable to make Susannah forget Bogomil. She'd been trying to keep her sister safe. But making Susannah do laundry had been an unnecessary flourish. She could admit that. It was one thing to teach a lesson to an asshole in a music store. It was, perhaps, another thing entirely to push your sister around with the force of your magical will. Laura resolved to do better—once she'd made Susannah forget that she'd done anything in the first place. Once she'd found Susannah.

Only a few people were on the street, none of them her sister. A gray-haired man in a black parka tramping down the street stopped when he was a foot away and began to swear. "Give it back to her! You nothing. You slut. You child of dust. Did you think you would get away with your meddling, a worm like you? Give back what you have no right to!"

Ordinarily it would be pretty fucking alarming to have some random guy on the street start yelling about sluts and worms, but the past few days had clarified some stuff for Laura about what you ought to be afraid of and what you should just deal with. Laura said, "Oh, shut up. If Malo Mogge has a problem with me, she can come and tell me herself. But this? She's not going to scare me with some stupid game of magical telephone. Okay? I'm doing my best to do what everybody seems to want me to do. You want me to figure out where your cup is, maybe you should have come and told me to look for it earlier. Now I know, and now I'll do my best. And we don't have to be best friends, but can't we all be reasonable?"

The man licked his lips. Looked, for a minute, as if he were listening to something very far off. "Okay," he said. Laura watched until he disappeared around a corner.

There were black specks mixed in with the flakes of snow, just as Mo had said. She held out her palm and one landed on it. She rubbed it between her thumb and middle finger. Ash. But she could not see what was burning. Everything Mo had said about Malo Mogge was, in equal parts, troubling and interesting to her. If Malo Mogge was at odds with Mr. Anabin and Bogomil, didn't that mean she might be an ally? Maybe there could be some kind of bargain. The enemy of my music teacher, etc.

Laura went all the way down Main Street looking for Susannah, wondering what she would do if she encountered Malo Mogge instead. No one else stopped to shout at her, and once she looked down and saw a glint of something in a snowbank that glittered so attractively she thought perhaps it might be the coin or the cup they were meant to be looking for. But it was only a Susan B. Anthony dollar. As for Malo Mogge, evidently she had other business. And Susannah was nowhere to be found.

The Book of Mo

"Fun day?" Jenny Ping said.

"The funnest," Mo said. He'd taken off his gloves and was rubbing his hands together, trying to get warm. Being this cold reminded him unpleasantly of what it had been like in Bogomil's realm. Jenny had the heater turned all the way up, and still Mo was a lump of ice.

She reached over and squeezed his two cold hands in her small warm one. "Let's get home and pig out on mac and cheese. You going to this thing at the Cliff Hangar?"

"Yeah," Mo said. "Maybe. First I want to go up to the cemetery. Will you take me? I need to see where she's buried."

"Oh, Mo," Jenny said. "I know we're hardy New Englanders and we're not supposed to care about cold, but frankly that's bullshit, winter sucks, and so does snow. It's like one degree out there."

"I know," Mo said. "But I need to do this anyway. Okay, Jenny? Please?"

"It really needs to be now?" she said.

"Yes," Mo said. "It does."

Mo didn't spend a lot of time hanging out in cemeteries. That wasn't his thing. But the old Lovesend cemetery up on the Cliffs was pretty, and once in a while he'd go and sit under the hemlock beside his mother's grave. Wonder what she would have said about the problems he was having with some boy. Vincent. He really needed to stop hooking up with weird white boys. Find someone Black, boring, and fine.

The cemetery was a short bike ride from his grandmother's house, twenty minutes if you walked. It was small, only a few acres, and on one end was a steep drop-off. Markers warned visitors away from the far end, the iron fence that now tilted oceanward. But the view was spectacular.

It was so cold today. He couldn't get the idea out of his head how cold he had been when he was dead. How cold his grandmother must be now. His mother. Maybe it would warm them a little to have him near.

Jenny parked just inside the gates. "Do you want me to come with you?"

Mo shook his head. Took off his seatbelt. He began to open the door and then said, "I don't have any flowers. I should have flowers."

"We could get some," Jenny said.

Mo thought about it. "No," he said. "I want to just get this over with."

Jenny said, "I'll wait in the car."

"No," Mo said. "You go on home."

"Mo," she said, and before she could go on, he said, "I'll walk. It's okay. I just want to be alone for a little while."

She reached over, squeezing Mo's wrist as if to see whether or not he had grown warmer. "You have your phone. You promise you'll call? If you want a ride?"

"I promise," Mo said. He got out of the car. The wind, which was always stronger on the Cliffs, threw fine grains of snow into his eyes.

Wind had carved strange signs into the snow that lay over the cemetery grounds, scouring it away from the face of one tombstone, heaping it in a perfect dome upon another. Loaves of snow lay upon the flagstone paths, sat in sleek caps upon the tops of crosses. The grandiflora hydrangea standing at the top of the Gorch family plot was bare and starred with ice on the side that faced the Atlantic. Here was the small stone house where Cara Gorch was buried. When Mo had first seen it, he'd thought it was a real miniature house, with its stained glass windows, its wrought-iron gates, and two stern angels—one on each side—carved out of Nero Marquina marble, one holding a broken flute palm up as if asking you to take and repair it, the other sitting with its back against the mausoleum, wings folded protectively over the guitar it was cradling to its chest. Maryanne Gorch's grave was hardly anything by comparison. A plain stone with her name on it and the dates of her birth and death. Under these: **LOVE IS AS STRONG AS DEATH**.

"Well," Mo said. "I guess you really are dead, then." He touched her name, recognized the font, Freight. It had been her favorite for display text. Because he was very tired and he thought he should say something else and yet couldn't think of anything, he sat down in the snow beside the grave. He was glad Jenny wasn't there. Though it would have been nice if she had been there. He was so alone.

How long he sat he didn't know. The snow continued and the last light drained from the sky. A gull landed on a nearby tombstone and watched him, its head tilted.

"Bowie," Mo said. But the gull stayed a gull, and so Mo gathered up his will and said instead, "*Avelot.*"

The gull, grumbling, became a girl with a pink streak in her hair. She had on a ridiculous coat much too large and Bowie's white scarf.

"Nice hair," he said. "I met someone who wants to kill you."

Avelot said, "Once I thought Thomas was kind. But kindness is soft. It wears away eventually. I wonder what Kristofer would be like now, had he not died. Had he been given the immortality Bogomil offered him."

Mo said, "Thomas's brother. What was he like?"

And suddenly Avelot was Bowie again, only with two blue eyes. Straw-colored hair. The face a little thinner and foxlike. The expression more confident than Avelot/Bowie had ever looked. Mischievous.

The person who was now wearing Kristofer's face said, "Like this, or so I remember him. He loved to hear me sing. He loved his brother. I did not love him, but neither did I wish him harm. And yet I was the cause of his death and now I wear his body more easily than ever I wore my own."

The boy who stood before Mo wavered, became a girl again, and then Bowie again, his expression now empty, a pink streak appearing and disappearing in his hair until Mo wanted to yell, Pick one and stick!

The boy said, "Avelot I never chose to be. Her life was hard. If Thomas does not kill me, still I would not choose to be Avelot again."

Mo said, "You do you. But do it somewhere else. It's late and I'm sad and I wasn't looking for company."

"I have a message for Thomas," Bowie said. "I am sorry. I will be sorrier still if I am the cause of his death as I was his brother's."

"You want what now?" Mo said, incredulous. "You want to deputize me? To go say all that to the brother of the guy you killed? No thanks. I am not getting in the middle of that."

"I think there are many things to live for," Bowie said, "and after all this time he might choose something other than revenge."

"And I can see how it might be in your best interest to say that to him," Mo said. "But come on. True or not, it's hard to give up on a plan when you've been carrying it around for such a long time. Even I know that, and I'm young and only a middling planner. You know Thomas better than me, so tell me, does he seem like a quitter to you?"

"This grave," Bowie said, indicating Maryanne Gorch's headstone. "Was she someone to you?"

"My only one," Mo said. "My grandmother. She would have been fascinated by you. Your life, what you did, what happened to you. She would have carved a love story out of it somehow. That was her whole deal."

Bowie said, "There was a graveyard in my city I liked to walk in. Those who visited their dead placed stones upon the graves."

He held out his hand to Mo, and Mo saw there was a stone in it. He took it; it weighed hardly anything. When he looked more closely, he saw it was one of the porcelain stones from the store on Main Street.

"Where'd you get this?" Mo said. But Bowie was no longer there. A gull rose up, its wings beating snow into clouds of shining powder so Mo had to take a step back. That was one way to leave a party.

On his grandmother's grave he placed the porcelain stone and the fortune cookie Thomas had given him, still in its wrapper.

The Book of Susannah

Had she spent the afternoon in a dream? When had it begun snowing? Susannah rode the bus back to Lovesend, her throbbing head against the twilight glass. She'd had an idea for a song earlier, and that, too, seemed dreamlike somehow. She was done with all that.

When she got off the bus, she thought she saw Laura far down the street, but she wasn't in the mood to deal with her sister. It kind of spoiled a day off hanging out with your sister if your sister's idea of hanging out was to demonstrate her chops on the two brand-new guitars she'd just bought while reminiscing about what a fuckup you had always been.

She hadn't thought to bring a hat, and her jacket had no hood. Her nose began to run. What had she and Laura even been fighting about? Laundry? Could it have really been that stupid? Why couldn't she ever let the little things go? When Susannah tried to untangle the fight in her head, she felt as if she were unpicking a knot on a long strand, the thinnest strand, the only thing holding her suspended over a great black nothingness. She was knocking and knocking against a door through which she would fall forever if she ever got it open.

When she got home, the house was dark.

I am drowning, she thought, and they know it and they won't save me. They can't save me because they're dead. They're all dead and it was all my fault.

"I'm going crazy," she said out loud. "It was a fight about laundry."

Here was her phone on the floor beneath the couch, filled up with texts from Laura. One from her father. Tonight was karaoke at the Cliff

Hangar, the fundraiser, and they were all supposed to go to that. There were texts from Daniel, too, asking if she was okay—and even one from Mo. *You around? Know we haven't talked in a while but it has been some heavy shit around these here parts and I am in it. You know?*

She texted back *Been thinking about you. Im around. Come by the coffeeshop if you want tomorrow. Drinks and pastries on me. So so sorry about your grandmother.*

That was a good thing, wasn't it? Mo was okay. And maybe he didn't hate her after all.

The front door banged opened, Laura home at last. But when Susannah turned around, it was Daniel.

The Book of Daniel

Not too long after he got back from looking for her at the beach, he saw Susannah come walking slowly up her driveway. She stood on her porch for a long moment before she squared her shoulders and went through the door, as if something dreadful was on the other side of the threshold. He should have texted Laura, but instead he told his siblings not to burn the house down, and over the fence he went. He didn't even bother to put on his coat.

Susannah turned when he opened the door, and he tried to see in her face what she knew, what she remembered. But she didn't draw back in horror or point an accusing finger. She didn't even look surprised to see him.

He said, "Laura's been looking everywhere for you. Are you okay?"

"I'm fine," Susannah said. "I don't know why everybody's so worried about me. It's just, sometimes Laura is a lot. Sometimes she's a lot and sometimes I'm a lot. We take turns. We fought; I left. Ended up hanging out with this girl I know." She took a step toward him. "Are *you* okay? Daniel?"

"I was just worried about you," he said. Whatever was going on with Susannah, it didn't seem to be what Laura thought it was. It seemed like the usual Susannah/Laura stuff. "I'm fine."

Susannah came closer. "You're fine?" she said. "You look like shit. What's going on?"

Did he really look that terrible? He said, "It's fine, Susannah. Really. Everything's fine."

She said, "If everything was fine, you wouldn't have to say it five thousand times." She took another step toward him. Her eyes were full of worry.

"Susannah . . . ," he said. Then could think of nothing to say.

She said, "Let's make a deal. I'm going to admit that I'm not sure I'm fine, and then you're going to tell me what's going on with you. What's going on with me is I think maybe I'm going crazy. Do you ever imagine that everyone you know is dead? Because sometimes I do."

He did not know how to answer.

"I know it sounds crazy," she said.

"No," he said. "It isn't."

"I'm alone," she said. "You left me, all of you. And now I'm alone."

If Mo had been there, he could have shown Susannah magic. Mo was spilling over with it. If Laura had been there, she would have told Susannah not to worry. She would have taken away everything Susannah was in despair over. He could tell Susannah everything was going to be okay. She would believe him when he said it.

Instead he said, "I'm sorry." And then, because he would not use magic on her, he kissed her.

THE SUMMER BEFORE sophomore year, Susannah had stolen one of the romance novels off Laura's bookshelves. *Meet Me Beneath the Wanton Stars, My Love.* She and Daniel snuck off to the beach to read it by flashlight. You could discover where the sex scenes were by holding the book by the spine to see where the pages fell open. Daniel had been glad it was dark and Susannah couldn't see his face. He'd needed desperately to know what she thought of what she was reading out loud. He knew how sex worked, he understood the mechanics, and surely Susannah did, too. But it was different, sitting on a blanket in the dunes, listening to her read. The way Caitlynn Hightower described sex, it seemed like a magical act. Like a magical act that everyone should be doing all of the time. A combination of mountain climbing, going to church, dancing, a practical joke, and sitting down to a meal of all of your favorite foods. Yes, the sex in the book was ridiculous. Probably. He didn't know for sure. It was also making his dick hard. Did people do these things? Did they feel this way?

Susannah read sex scenes as if she were reading a school essay. Her voice was matter-of-fact, unembarrassed, and even a little amused. She read through a scene in which the heroine discovered how much she enjoyed receiving oral sex in a hot-air balloon, and then a scene in which some people had sticky sex in a vat where grapes were being crushed to make wine. Later on, the lovers drank the wine. Susannah was halfway through a scene in which the heroine and hero were having sex on horseback when she put down the book. She looked over at Daniel, and then she placed her hand on his stomach, just above his waistband. When he didn't say anything, she stuck her hand down his pants and took hold of his dick and began to stroke it.

It was the first time he'd ever been touched in this fashion by someone other than himself. He couldn't help it. He made a noise.

Susannah took one of his hands in her free hand, never stopping what she was doing. She put his hand on her breast, his fingers between the material of her shirt and her bra. "I have a condom," she said. "We could do it if you wanted to."

It wasn't the way the characters in the book talked, but Daniel didn't care. It was the best thing anyone had ever said to him. What happened next wasn't like the sex scenes in the novel, not for him and he knew it wasn't for her, either. But afterward Susannah said, "If we keep doing that maybe we'll actually get good at it. Right?"

"Okay," Daniel said. He wasn't sure what to do with the condom now, but Susannah took it from him and tied a knot in it.

She said, "Do you think people really have sex on horseback? It just doesn't seem like a good idea."

Daniel said, "I bet people have it everywhere." He sat up and kissed her collarbone. There was sand in her hair and crusted on her neck, too, stuck there with sweat and his saliva. She had a mole underneath one breast, and she had had his dick inside her vagina. He'd had his head down there, too, and his tongue and his mouth, and everywhere she had been so soft. She'd been ticklish, too. She'd made noises, too.

"Would you want to do that?" she said, shivering beneath his mouth.

He could feel all the little hairs on her skin standing up. He wanted to kiss her under her knee. And so he did.

"What?"

"Have sex on a horse."

"No," he said. Was this disappointing to her? Was he being too practical when he should be romantic? "Would you want to?"

"We should probably get the sex part down first," Susannah said.

As it turned out, Daniel's favorite place to have sex was Susannah's bed.

Over the next few months, they had a lot of sex. They got better at it. They never said they loved each other. They were friends. Of course they loved each other even if it wasn't in the romance novel way. Sometimes they fought. Sophomore year they broke up without breaking up. After all, they'd never gotten together officially, either. While they were broken up, they both had sex with other people. But they had never been great at staying broken up, not even when Laura had the idea for the band, which made everything more complicated.

Daniel had never imagined he and Susannah would stay together forever. There were things he planned to do, that he needed to do. He'd loved being part of My Two Hands Both Knowe You, and he loved being with Susannah. But music had never really felt like real life. It had just been messing around. Anyway the band didn't really need him. Susannah didn't really need him. She might think she did, but she didn't. Sometimes he was surprised she hadn't figured that out yet.

The night he'd died, he and Susannah had broken up for good. No, he had broken up with Susannah. He remembered pieces and bits. But he remembered the way she'd looked when she'd said she loved him and asked him how he felt. What he felt. He remembered, too, the way she'd looked when he'd said he didn't think they should keep doing whatever it was they were doing. And then whatever had happened had happened, and now here he was with Susannah again as if everything in between had been erased.

"Wait," he said. "We shouldn't do this. You don't want to do this."

Susannah said, "Don't tell me what I don't want to do. Why does everyone keep telling me what to do?"

By the time they'd made it to her bedroom, he'd already shucked his pants and his boxer shorts. He dropped them on the floor. His arms were out of his sweater, the sweater bunched around his neck because Susannah wouldn't leave his mouth alone. When he pulled back she said, "Oh shit. The sheets. I was washing them. I don't even know if I got them in the dryer."

Daniel had both hands on the marvelous territory of her ass, pushing her jeans down, her underwear. She was biting his neck, making noises in his ear. He picked her up and waded forward through the tender, yielding air until he could drop her on the unmade bed. "Who gives a fuck about the sheets?" Daniel said.

The Book of Susannah

She lay on her side, staring at Daniel. The room was too cold to lie there naked without even a comforter, but she felt so relaxed and boneless she couldn't imagine moving just yet.

She and Daniel had had a lot of sex. They'd had mediocre figuring-stuff-out sex, and they'd also had spectacular figuring-out-some-other-stuff sex. They'd had sex when they were pissed off at each other, and they'd had sex when they were both pissed off at Laura and supposed to be at rehearsal. They'd had sex when they were broken up and single; they'd had sex while they were technically seeing other people. They'd had sex because Daniel wanted to see how many times he could get an erection in a twenty-four-hour period and when Susannah wanted to celebrate because her least favorite contestant had been kicked off *RuPaul's Drag Race*. They'd had sex in Ruth's car, on the make-out ledge beneath the balcony at the Cliff Hangar, and once in Boston on a field trip to the Arnold Arboretum beneath a Glauca Pendula. They'd had sex when they were drunk and horny and didn't want to have to talk to each other and sex while Susannah was waiting for the time limit on *Candy Crush* to be up, sex when they were bored and there was nothing better to do. Something this time had been different. Susannah wasn't the shiniest apple on the highest branch of the tallest tree, but she was smart enough to have figured out that sex wasn't always the same even when you were having it with the same person. For one thing, Susannah had been taller than Daniel the first time they had sex. It wasn't that he'd become someone new while he was in Ireland. He wasn't more handsome, and he hadn't grown weird facial hair, either. He didn't seem more grown-up. He seemed, somehow, the worse for wear, insubstantial in a way she couldn't quite put her finger on. And maybe it was just because this was how he was around her now, but he didn't seem happy.

"What?" he said.

"Nothing," she said. "Just, sorry. I know you don't want this. It just always happens anyway."

"I do want this," Daniel said. "Don't you?"

"Yes," Susannah said.

"That's why it happens," he said.

She said, "We won't keep doing this forever. You're going to meet other people. I'll figure out what I ought to be doing with my life."

He didn't say anything.

She said, "When we broke up, you told me you had a whole plan. You'd gotten into college or whatever. You were quitting the band. Giving up music."

"Yeah," he said. "I remember." He sounded a little surprised as he said it.

"But you didn't quit. You went to Ireland," Susannah said. "I'm glad. You didn't give up music after all."

He said, "You said you keep thinking about death."

"Yes," Susannah said. Though at the moment it was hard to remember what she had been so upset about.

"Do you ever wonder what happens when we die?"

"No," she said. Did she? It would be weird not to, wouldn't it? It was just that it was hard to think about things like death when everything was like this, with Daniel here next to her. It was like thinking about a forest at night when it was the middle of the day and you were floating in the ocean. "Yes. Maybe, sometimes? When we were kids, I used to have these dreams about this person. Bogomil. He was a little scary and kind of awesome and he did magic. I never told you about any of that. Never told anybody. It just seemed stupid, I guess. They were just dreams."

It was getting late and Laura wasn't home yet. Susannah couldn't remember if they'd locked her bedroom door. Well, Laura would get an eyeful if she suddenly burst in, and it would serve her right.

"Are you sure you never told me?" Daniel said. "I feel like I've heard that name before. Bogomil."

"He was a man sometimes and a wolf sometimes," Susannah said. "He was ridiculously attractive. Like someone in one of Laura's romance novels. And I was his only friend. He ruled over this whole kingdom, and I would go there. We'd both turn into wolves and we'd just run. It was always night, and it was this endless forest, and it felt amazing. Like I belonged there. In those dreams, I knew I was exactly how I was supposed to be; I never felt that way when I was awake. He told me one day his kingdom would be mine. If I wanted it."

"Did you?" Daniel said. She could feel the tension in his body, see all the little goosebumps rising.

"I don't know," Susannah said. "Maybe? Who wants to have to live in this world? Not me. Bogomil's realm was pretty great. And when I started feeling stuff for you, he knew that, too. He said in his kingdom, I would never have to grow old or die. He said I could live forever. He said you and I could be together forever. When you broke up with me I stopped having those dreams. I hadn't had one in such a long time, but I dreamed about him last night. He was in your yard. He wanted me to find something for him, I think. You never have dreams like that, I bet."

"No," Daniel said.

"Yeah, so I guess that's why I never wanted to tell anyone," Susannah said. "Because it's weird and it's stupid and when you try to explain it, it doesn't make any sense. Just a stupid dream I used to have. Eternal night, dark realms, eternal love, wolves. None of it was real. Well, except for wolves. And love. I do love you. I will always love you."

She saw the look on his face. "Can you please not?" she said. "I mean, can you please not look at me while I'm telling you all this? It's so much easier if you don't look at me."

Daniel said, "But—"

She cut him off. "You don't look at me and I won't look at you, and that way I'll manage to say everything I need to say to you. Okay? Please let me say it."

"Okay," Daniel said finally. He turned his face away from her and looked up at the ceiling. Susannah did the same. She took a breath and began again. "I just want to say that it's okay. I love you and I'm always going to love you, but it doesn't mean anything. It isn't epic. I don't love you in an epic way. It's just the way it is. I know we're not going to get back together or anything, but you know what? It's okay because I know you love me, too. Whether or not we ever do this again. One day you'll be this fifty-year-old banker at Goldman Sachs with three ex-wives and a couple of kids, because let's be honest, you're probably going to give up on music eventually because music isn't sensible and you are too fucking sensible and instead you'll just splurge on expensive tickets for summer festivals or stadium concerts or you'll have a season pass to the opera, and you'll come home for the holidays to see your parents and I'll have gotten my shit together and figured out what I should be doing and I'll be doing it and I'll come home to hang out with Ruth, and we'll say hi when we see each other in the driveway. Maybe it won't feel awkward and maybe it will. It's okay if it does. Because I'll still love you and you'll still love me even though we haven't seen each other in years."

Daniel said, "What about Laura? Where's she?"

She snuck a look at him. He was still staring up at the ceiling. He was such a good guy. "Paris," she said. "Rio de Janeiro. The moonbase. First concert on the moon. Headlining in Las Vegas."

"Yeah. Her comeback tour," Daniel said. He rubbed his eyes and then turned on the pillow so he was looking directly at her. "I do love you. I'm glad you know. Whatever love is. It's asparagus, I guess. Or music. But I should have said it before. I wish I'd said it a lot."

Susannah's heart was full. She said, "Every time I was ever on stage and we did 'The Kissing Song,' I was singing it for you. Every time I kissed someone, I wished that I was kissing you."

"You did?" he said.

Well, it would have been nice if it were true. But it would also have sucked. She said, "Okay, no, I didn't always wish it was you. Sometimes I kissed someone and it was pretty great. I was pretty into it, sometimes. Stand on a stage and pick out somebody and kiss them in front of everyone? Knowing you were watching, too? Sometimes it was hot. A lot of the time." It hadn't been a hardship, most of the time, kissing people who wanted to be kissed. "But every time you kissed someone else at a party, I wished you were kissing me. Every single time. Next time you kiss someone else, you should think about that. You should think about this."

She began to kiss Daniel again, then to kiss down his chest. You couldn't just give a big romantic speech and expect someone to remember it forever. First you gave the speech and then you gave the blow job. After that, there was no fucking chance they'd ever forget. But Daniel said, "Wait. Someone's here. I hear someone."

Susannah said, jokingly, "It's probably just Bogomil. Dropping by in case we changed our minds and we want to rule eternal night. Ow! Hey!"

Daniel had jackknifed up in bed, his knee knocking into her ear. "Sorry," he said.

Someone tried the door. Found it locked and rattled it vigorously.

"Don't say anything," Daniel said into Susannah's sore ear. He was holding her arm too tightly. "Be quiet or he'll hear."

"Who? Hear what?" Susannah said. There was really only one person it could be. "Laura?"

"Susannah?" Laura said. "Let me in."

"Go away!" Susannah said. She felt the tension leave Daniel's body.

He got up and began putting on his clothes. Susannah didn't bother. She sat on the bed totally naked. It was her room. She was allowed to be naked in her own room. Daniel had his boxers on and his jeans in his hands when Laura came through the connecting door of the bathroom. She saw him, looked over at Susannah on the bed, and threw her hands up over her face. "Oh my God! And you didn't even make the bed first!"

"What the fuck is it with you and my laundry?" Susannah said. "Get the hell out of my room!"

Daniel said, "Everybody calm down. Everything's fine, Laura. Just, give us a minute." He'd finally gotten his pants on.

Laura, her hands still up over her eyes, retreated into the bathroom. Daniel pulled the door shut behind her. He turned to Susannah. "Maybe one of us should go talk to her," he said.

"That never goes so great for me," Susannah said. "But you do whatever you want." All of her feelings of charity toward Daniel, all of her grown-up realizations about love and about herself, all of it had evaporated at the sight of her sister coming through the bathroom door. She might finally be in a good place with Daniel, but there could be no good place with Laura in it as far as Susannah was concerned.

Daniel came over to the bed. Susannah fixed her gaze on his hip bone. "Hey," he said.

She would not look up. He bent over and kissed her on the top of her head. "I should go anyway," he said. "But can I come over tonight? After dinner?"

"You're not going to this karaoke thing?" Susannah said.

"I don't know," he said. "Are you?"

"Fuck no," Susannah said.

"So," he said. "Can I come over? Or are you sick of me already? We could watch a movie."

Susannah laid her head against his stomach. Wrapped her arms around his waist, then reached lower and slapped his ass. Once, twice. Finally looked up and saw him grinning down at her. "Or we could just fuck," she said.

He said, "We could do that, too."

She shoved him back so she had room to stand up. Her left heel ached when it took her weight.

"What's wrong?" Daniel said.

"Nothing," she said. "I have a splinter or something." She could hear Laura in the hallway, then clomping back down the stairs.

"Then you should take it out," Daniel said. "Look, I'll go deal with Laura. Okay?"

"Okay," Susannah said. She threw on a T-shirt and went to the bathroom to find the tweezers, but by the time she'd turned on the light over the sink and opened the drawer, she'd forgotten what she'd come to look for.

The Book of Laura

She waited with as much patience as she could muster for Susannah and Daniel to come down the stairs, but then it was only Daniel.

"What the hell are you doing?" she said.

Daniel rolled his eyes. "Your sister," he said.

Was he twelve? "Fuck you," Laura said. "I have been out in the snow for like two hours looking for her and you couldn't even text to say she'd come home?"

"Sorry," Daniel said. "I don't know what was going on earlier, but she seems completely fine. She mentioned Bogomil, but just to tell me that she used to have dreams about him when she was a kid. And she thinks you and she were fighting about usual stuff. Laundry or something."

"She had Bogomil dreams?"

Daniel lowered his voice. He said, "She says she used to dream about him all the time. He told her if she wanted, one day she could rule over his realm."

"Susannah?" Laura said. The idea was so implausible she almost felt blind with panic for a minute. That place. The trees that reached for you. The clearing where something was waiting. The door that could not be opened. But she had. She'd pried it open and she'd gotten out. And she wasn't going back. "Susannah couldn't rule over a plastic bag full of ants. I *knew* she had something to do with this. Thinks this world isn't good enough for her. Typical Susannah bullshit."

She headed toward the stairs, but Daniel got in her way. "Where are you going?" he said.

"To find out what she did," she said. "We don't remember what happened, but I can make her remember for us."

"By messing with her head again?" Daniel said.

"What are we supposed to do, ignore this? An actual clue?" Laura said. She told him what Mo had said about Malo Mogge and the cup. "They all think we can find it for them for some reason. Because we got away from Bogomil. That place. But I don't remember having a cup. Do you?"

"No," Daniel said.

"Or a coin," Laura said. "Mo said it could be a coin."

"There's my coin collection," Daniel said.

Laura said, "Sure, we can check, but I highly doubt some stupid nickel your mom let you buy on eBay is going to be this extremely magical thing everyone is looking for. I feel you don't understand the situation here, Daniel. Do you think I want to go poking around in Susannah's lumpy oatmeal brain? Do you think she'd want us to die again? Just because you'd rather give up than figure out how all of this works, and by the way, you reek of sex and it is really grossing me out, but the point is, maybe *you* don't plan to do anything about not dying but that doesn't mean that I'm going to do the same. I'm going to go ask Susannah what she knows, and you can come back upstairs with me or you can stay down here."

"Fine," Daniel said. "But we should tell her everything."

That was Daniel for you. You could be pursued by a car full of murderous clowns while a troupe of sentient fire tornados was enacting *The Nutcracker* in your rearview mirror and he'd suggest taking the scenic route down Good Intentions Boulevard. "You want to tell her everything *everything*? Go ahead. But then you're going to have to explain the whole magic thing and why you won't do it even though you could. Even though you have to. Explain how you're going to let yourself die. See what Susannah does then."

She went around him and up the stairs, and Daniel followed right behind her. And this was also Daniel for you. Unlike Susannah, he eventually came around when you explained things to him.

Susannah was in her room, dressed now, thank God. A look of purest rage crossed her face when she saw Laura. "What?"

Laura said, "Calm down, okay? Be mad at me later, but we have to talk about what happened last year. You have to tell me what you did. And about Bogomil. You have to tell me everything you know about Bogomil." She said this, pushing at Susannah with her will. She pictured it flowing from her like a net, catching Susannah up and holding her gently but firmly.

As she did this, Daniel came into the room behind her. "Laura," he began.

"Shut up," she said just as Susannah said, "What the fuck, Daniel. You told her about Bogomil? I tell you my embarrassing childhood wish-fulfillment fantasy and you immediately sell me out to *her*?" To Laura, she said, "Can you just lay off? I had weird dreams. Big deal. And frankly it's none of your business if Daniel and I sleep together!"

Laura felt a flicker of unease. She said, drawing that invisible net around Susannah again, "Tell me what happened at the Cliff Hangar last year, the last time we performed there."

"Why?" Susannah said. "What's the point of this? You were there, you were both there! Daniel broke up with me, I kissed Rosamel, you kissed Daniel. I left. I went home. You guys celebrated Daniel's birthday or whatever. I got drunk by myself. Here. It was *great*."

Now there were tears in her eyes.

"Don't be sad," Laura said. She could feel the net still, but somehow Susannah was slipping through it. "You shouldn't be sad. Everything's fine."

"Don't you tell me what to feel," Susannah said. She got up and shoved Laura hard in the chest. Laura staggered back, falling against Daniel. "Get the fuck out of my room. Both of you."

"Laura," Daniel said. "Stop. Just stop."

Heat rose up Laura's neck, into her cheeks. "Fine. Let's go. Come on, Daniel."

But Daniel stayed in Susannah's room. She heard him say, "Are you all right? Susannah?"

Which just went to show how thoroughly he had missed the point. Susannah, in typical fashion, was now somehow impervious to magic as well as logic. Susannah would be fine, though. They were the ones he should be worried about.

Laura fired off a quick text to Ruth and her dad, telling them she would see them at the Cliff Hangar. She still had two errands. She grabbed the Harmony in its traveling case and set it down on the kitchen table while she put her coat back on and went to the bathroom, where she discovered her period had started. "Seriously?" she said. "Now?" And used her magic to stop it.

Checking her phone as she went out into the night, she found a message from Mo. Everything ok with Susannah? She shoved the phone back into her pocket.

Her first stop was the Lucklows' house. Daniel's mom let her in. "Laura!" she said. "So good to see you. If you're looking for Daniel, I'm not sure he's here."

"He's at my house making cookies with Susannah. He wanted me to grab something out of his closet for him." Laura gave Mrs. Lucklow the biggest, most open smile she could currently manage.

"Don't let me stop you," Mrs. Lucklow said.

Daniel was not the most organized person in the world, but his room wasn't that big, either. Laura found some weed under his mattress. The tacklebox containing his coin collection was on the middle shelf in his closet. There were maybe a hundred coins in it, each in its own individual sleeve. Laura ran her hand over them. She would be able to tell, she thought, if anything here was other than ordinary. Then she texted Daniel Your collection sucks. No magic coin or whatever

Not really surprised, Daniel texted back at once. I hate magic & feeling is mutual I suspect

"Ha," Laura said.

It was still snowing. There was maybe half a foot of accumulation since the last time anyone had plowed, and this was the worst kind, granular and wet. She slipped now and then but always managed to right herself. The guitar made a good counterweight.

There was no reason to expect Mr. Anabin to be at Lewis Latimer. It wasn't the appointed fucking hour. If he wasn't there, she'd leave the guitar in the music room. She even had a birthday card she'd bought at the CVS while looking for Susannah.

Someone was sitting on the steps in front of the school.

"What are you doing here?" she asked.

"Nothing," Bowie said. "Admiring the night. I came to offer my gift to Anabin and now I may do as I please."

"Your butt is going to get wet," Laura said. "Sitting in the snow like that. Aren't you cold? What did you give Mr. Anabin? Is he in there right now?"

Bowie said, "I may be colder yet than I am now."

"Did you do something to Susannah?" Laura said.

When Bowie said nothing else, only looked at her with his one green eye and one blue eye, she marched up the steps past him, resisting the urge to bowl him over with the guitar case. Unlike her sister, she did not give in to every childish impulse.

The doors were locked and bolted, but what are locks and bolts to someone who'd opened the door that cannot be opened? Laura made her way up to the music room and there was Mr. Anabin looking exactly as he always did, which is to say Laura found him disappointing even knowing what she did now. His T-shirt tonight said I CAME HERE TO KICK ASS AND CHEW GUM BUT NOW I JUST FEEL LIKE DANCING.

"Here," Laura said.

Mr. Anabin took the card from her and placed it on the desk. "Is that for me as well?" he said.

Laura put the guitar case down. "Yes," she said. "But first you have to answer some questions."

He said, "Questions come first. Answers must come after."

"Happy birthday, pedant," Laura said. "Something's going on with Susannah. I've been experimenting or practicing or whatever, and I can do things. I can make people do things or believe things I want them to believe. Which, I know, isn't very moral, but whatever. The point is, I can't do it to Susannah. I did it once, but for some reason now I can't. Last night I found her talking to Bogomil in our yard. And it turns out she used to dream about him? But she never told anyone and now she won't talk about it at all and I can't make her talk about it, either? She had something to do with how we died, like, that's completely obvious, and that's one of the things that we're supposed to figure out, right? And now there's this Malo Mogge person, and I don't think you can be trusted."

Mr. Anabin said, "Show me what you have brought me."

Without meaning to, Laura handed over the guitar case. She said, "You made me do that!"

Mr. Anabin said, "As you made others do your will. Though it is harder to make those who have their own magic do one's bidding. I am very old and my will is strong. If Susannah will not yield to you, it may be she has magic of her own."

"From Bogomil, I bet," Laura said. "I know what you're looking for, what you want us to find. A coin or a cup. A magic token."

"Do I want you to find it?" Mr. Anabin said. "I suppose it must be found, either way." He opened the guitar case and took out the Harmony. "What is this?"

"My first guitar," Laura said.

Mr. Anabin turned the guitar over in his hands, brought his knuckles down on the body as if he were testing a melon in the grocery store. He did not attempt to play it. "It was broken?"

"I fixed it," Laura said. "Magically. So, happy birthday, hope you like it. If you're not going to answer any questions, I should take off." She would call an Uber and head up to the Cliff Hangar.

Mr. Anabin didn't say anything to this. He was still contemplating the Harmony with greater interest than Laura thought a crappy old guitar merited. But he'd been like that in band, too, always paying the closest attention to everything. Giving in to curiosity, she said, "What did Bowie give you?"

But this, too, was a question that Mr. Anabin was not going to answer. And apparently there wasn't going to be a magic lesson, either.

Laura was nearly out the door when Mr. Anabin said, "I'm afraid there is yet one more task I must set you."

The Book of Mo

There were a lot of people at the Cliff Hangar whom Mo hadn't seen since he'd come back from the dead. They all wanted to tell him how sorry they were about his grandmother. They asked how he liked Ireland. One or two had harassed him earlier in downtown Lovesend thanks to Malo Mogge, but now they didn't seem to remember that, so Mo pretended he didn't, either.

"She was so good to this town," a white woman was saying to Mo. He didn't know her. Someone's parent, maybe, or a member of one of his grandmother's thousand thousand committees. "So community-minded, such a good speaker. She visited our book club once; we had the hardest time getting her to come, but eventually she did. I don't read romance novels, generally, but all the research she did, it was so interesting. She was just so articulate."

"Articulate, absolutely. But you know, writers are. Even the Black ones. Writers have to know a lot of words," Mo said. He couldn't help himself. His poor grandmother. "Romance writers especially. You can't just keep using the same boring old words for sex organs. Cock, plenipotentiary instrument, raging dragon of his desire, turgid love weasel. You got to mix it up or else it gets boring. Excuse me. I have to go see a girl about her voluptuous, womanly secrets."

Rosamel, too, was getting her fair share of attention. She'd used some kind of glitter spray on her freshly shaved scalp, and you didn't get a lot of that in Lovesend, at least in this crowd. It wasn't a dead grandmother or a missing cook, but it was still something different.

Mrs. Walker took Mo's hand. She'd never known what to make of Mo, but like everyone else, she had nothing but good things to say about his grandmother. He stood beside Rosamel and endured her mother's tribute because it was no less than his grandmother had deserved. It was all true.

Despite the snow, people had come out. There were plenty of kids from Lewis Latimer—graduates, too, back for the holidays like Rosamel and Natalie and Theo. People kept asking about Daniel, if Mo knew whether or not he was showing up. Mo most certainly did not. He caught sight of Philip, the only other Black guy from his year, regrettably straight. They'd gone over to each other's houses a few times when they were younger, but Philip, too, had never known what to make of Mo. Philip had been into D&D and Frisbee golf, and Mo hadn't known what to make of that. Philip nodded and Mo nodded back.

Up on the carousel, draped over an oversized rabbit with frightened, goiterous eyes, was Vincent. Every time Mo looked in that direction, he caught Vincent looking away. Basic Vincent-in-public behavior.

Beyond Vincent, sitting over at a table against the French windows, was Mo's third-least-favorite person, Malo Mogge. Tonight she wore a golden half mask and heavy gold armbands that spiraled up all the way to her biceps. Her dress was a deep green in complicated, sculptural pleats. Best policy, he decided, was to ignore her as long as possible.

Someone Mo recognized from some of his grandmother's committees got up on the stage and made a brief speech about Hannah and the missing cook, Kyle. She thanked everyone for coming out and then announced the sign-up sheet for karaoke could be found at the bar. Natalie and Theo took off at speed. There was some Taylor Swift song they needed to be sure no one else got first.

Jenny had brought along a tray of brownies, and Mo snagged two. He already knew Jenny was planning to sing Barry Manilow's "Mandy." There was no chance anyone else wanted to do it. Or, if they did, that was that. That person and Jenny had to get engaged on the spot.

The last time Mo had been up here would have been to see My Two Hands Both Knowe You. He didn't remember much. He'd been planning to meet up with Susannah. Which wasn't usual—he usually hung out with Susannah at What Hast Thou Ground? and sometimes at school.

A couple times she'd come over to poke around in the music studio. He'd seen her sing, of course, but afterward she was usually up to something or other with Laura and Daniel, and sure, Mo would have been welcome, he just couldn't take that much Daniel.

That night Susannah had asked a favor of Mo. Something small. He couldn't recall what, exactly, but had it been horseshoe-nail-level shit?

He had a nagging feeling if Susannah were here now, it would have come back to him. But Susannah wasn't around, and he hadn't seen Laura yet, though their mother was over at the bar with some guy Mo didn't think he'd ever seen before. But their father was back in the picture, right? Not everyone was magic.

Rosamel slid up behind Mo and wrapped her arms around his shoulders. There was a drink in each hand. Ginger ale, because no way was the bartender not carding tonight, but when Mo took one of the drinks, he could smell the tequila.

"Got a flask in my pocket," Rosamel said into his ear. "Drink up, my unloose goose. Eyes on you."

"Vincent?" Mo said. "Yeah, I know. Ignoring him."

"Poor old lost gym sock," Rosamel said. "As if he'd ever have a chance with you. Nah. It's the guy from the restaurant. Over there, sitting up on the stage. Don't think he's taken his eyes off you once. Nat and Theo are making me sing 'This Love' with them, and if you don't go talk to that guy I'm gonna make you get up on stage with us."

Mo looked over. Unlike Vincent, Thomas didn't look away. He didn't smile or make any big thing out of it. He just looked back. Mo felt as if he were going up in flames. How did Thomas *do* this? Was it supernatural? Or was this just what it felt like when you really, really wanted to sleep with someone? Did Vincent feel any part of this for Mo? If so, well, good. Fuck Vincent.

Mo was already halfway across the room when he realized Rosamel had still been talking to him. He imagined she'd have plenty more to say later on.

"Didn't figure you for a karaoke aficionado," Mo said when he was close up. Thomas's legs dangling off the stage, an extrovert's throne.

"I go where I am sent," Thomas said.

"And you do what you're told," Mo said. "All good boys deserve favor, right?"

"There is what I deserve and there is what I want and there is as well what I desire though I should not."

"Oh snap!" Mo said. "I also like being fucking oblique but also totally obvious. Another thing we have in common."

Someone was positioning a microphone at the center of the stage. The speakers and the screen were already up. Some beardy loaf of a middle-aged white guy in a flannel shirt was waiting on the side of the stage. If they were lucky, he was going to sing "Paradise by the Dashboard Light."

Thomas said, "Will you sing tonight?"

Mo said, "I don't sing in front of people. And I'm not here for the karaoke anyway. Came with some friends, gonna meet up with Laura, then I have an errand to run. Magical homework."

"An appointment with Anabin," Thomas said. "At what hour and place?"

"The school," Mo said. "Around one in the morning. Oh. Ohhhhhh. You wanna know because you know Bowie will have to be there, too. But I thought you couldn't kill him. Her. Avelot." He didn't mention his earlier run-in with Bowie in the graveyard.

Thomas said, "I might yet strike a blow. You could help me were you willing."

"Oh, my dude, murder, grievous bodily harm, no," Mo said. "Those're even further out of my purview than karaoke. Come on. Off the stage. They're starting it up." He held out his hand and Thomas took it. The man on stage began to sing "Heartbreak Hotel." He had a surprisingly pleasant tenor.

Off to the side of the stage, there were Rosamel and Natalie and Theo, all watching Mo and Thomas with great interest. At a table near the front was Mrs. Walker with her best friend, the widow Sangovich. Mr. Walker was over by the bar, looking over at his wife with an expression that suggested love triangles could strike at any age, any moment, in any configuration. And back near the buffet table on his big sad rabbit was Vincent, who did not and maybe would not ever understand that tragedy was not always a decision you made for yourself, sure, but at least you could choose a carousel wolf and not a bunny. Even farther out on the periphery of the event was Malo Mogge, a marzipan scorpion on a green cupcake. And here came Laura, not nearly as neatly put together as she usually was. Mo could see, for once, how much she and Susannah resembled each other after all. *Well, they're so lonely,* the man sang.

"Who's this?" Laura said to Mo.

"Right, you guys haven't met," Mo said. "This is Thomas. And, by the way, in case you hadn't noticed, Malo Mogge's here. So, Susannah. What's up with her? Spill." Laura turned in a circle until she'd located Malo Mogge. "Oh good," she said. "I need to talk to her."

Mo grabbed Laura's arm. "Hold up. Susannah? Is she okay?"

Laura said, "No. Apparently she's been having dreams about Bogomil since we were kids, but that's all I know, because magic doesn't work on her or something. She couldn't tell me anything useful, or she wouldn't, and also she and Daniel are sleeping together again and Daniel is still refusing to do magic. So that's the situation. I know we said we were going to help each other get through this, but I feel like I'm pulling all the weight here. Maybe I should start looking out for myself."

Thomas said, "You would be best to have no dealings with Malo Mogge."

"Whatever, decorative minion," Laura said. "Stay away from my sister, okay? If you think I'm going to just let Mr. Anabin and Bogomil run me through their weird grudge maze, think again."

Mo, ignoring that, said, "Wondered how long it would take you to give up on Daniel. You going to Mr. Anabin's birthday party after this?"

"I'm not giving up," Laura said. "But I'm not going to let Daniel drag me down, either. I'm taking care of things in the necessary order. Anyway, I already gave Mr. Anabin his present. Went by the school early. Not that I was that early, apparently. Bowie was there first."

Thomas said, "Trust that one even less than you do Malo Mogge."

Laura said, "Right! You and Bowie have some kind of story. I'm sure it's really interesting but I'm kind of starting to think Bowie's not real."

"What's that supposed to mean?" Mo said.

"Never mind," Laura said. "Just something Mr. Anabin said. More magic homework stuff."

Before Mo could ask her anything else, she was off, headed in the direction of the buffet table.

"So that's Susannah's sister," Thomas said.

"They were in a band together and everything," Mo said. "Yeah. She had big plans for that band before she died. Believe it or not, she's actually a pretty good guitarist even if she's a little intense, by which I mean an asshole. Oh, hey, it's my friends."

He turned his attention to the stage, where Theo and Natalie were belting out "This Love" as promised. Rosamel, Mo decided, was just mouthing the lyrics. But the lights sure looked pretty on her glittery head.

Mo was entirely too aware of Thomas beside him. There were things he needed to be doing. He still hadn't gotten Mr. Anabin a birthday present. And maybe he should be up on the stage with Rosamel and Natalie and Theo. He could have lip-synched the way Rosamel was doing. What he shouldn't have been doing was wishing he could take Thomas's hand. He shouldn't have wanted to lean against Thomas, shouldn't have wanted to feel Thomas's arm come around his neck, to rest his head against Thomas's shoulder.

He'd never done any of these things in a place where anyone else could see. Yes, he was out, but yes, he was also someone who liked to keep the important things to himself. Had liked. Maybe it wasn't Thomas at all. Maybe it was only the possibility Thomas represented, the things Mo had never been or done. This thought gave Mo the courage to do these things. He leaned into Thomas's side, wrapped his arm around Thomas's waist, stuck his finger through a belt loop. And Thomas did exactly the thing Mo had hoped he would do, as if he had seen the picture in Mo's brain. His arm went around Mo, and he pulled him even closer.

Up on the stage, Rosamel stopped even pretending to sing. Her eyebrows shot up. *"This love is alive back from the dead oh,"* Natalie and Theo sang, and Mo thought, Oh, if only you assholes knew. Without having to turn around, he knew Vincent would also be watching, and Mo knew he shouldn't luxuriate in the pettiness, the pleasure this idea brought him, and yet, in this moment, Mo was, at last, utterly content.

Like John Cage said, composing was one thing, performing was another thing, and listening was another thing again. But in this moment Mo felt he was engaged in all of these simultaneously.

When the song was almost over, he said, "Do you want to get out of here?"

Thomas said, "And go where?"

"I don't know," Mo said. "But my friends are about to come down off the stage and ask a bunch of questions, and unless you want to do that magic mind-control thing again, which in theory is extremely useful but also I am not entirely comfortable with the idea of using it for the sake of convenience, especially on my friends, maybe we could just go somewhere?"

Thomas looked back toward the tables by the windows. He turned back to Mo. He said, "Sure."

The Book of Susannah

She had zero regrets about skipping karaoke. It wasn't as if someone was going to get up on stage and sing a song explaining what had happened to Hannah and Kyle. Sometimes people disappeared, and sometimes people showed up again. Susannah's father, for example.

If she'd gone to the karaoke thing, Laura and Ruth would have made her sing with them, as if Laura hadn't been yelling at her an hour earlier. Even minus the yelling it would have been a whole Family von Trapp, Family von Partridge situation and Susannah was just not in the mood. Had never been in the mood, honestly. Singing with your sister was one thing. Lots of people did it. Haim, Heart, First Aid Kit, the Pierce Sisters, plenty of others. But the whole family? That was either country music or a whole horror movie with Wes Anderson directing.

And karaoke was such a weird scene, anyway. People got up there thinking the goal was to hit the right notes. You could tell how much time they'd spent practicing, trying to perfect the song the way the original sounded. But performing was about a point of view, about how you felt. It was better to get up and yell the whole way through a song and really mean it than to try to get all the notes right. You knew it when you heard it.

She lay on the white couch zapping through television shows, not in the mood for any of them. Daniel had gone away when she'd refused to talk to him through her bedroom door. Probably he was up at the Cliff Hangar, too. Fuck him, whatever. Susannah went and got all the clean sheets and her blanket and duvet from the laundry room. She made her bed.

Ruth texted a couple of times and Susannah responded to each with a series of randomly chosen emojis. Ruth could interpret these however she wanted. Snake plane crying-face rainbow rainbow rainbow 100.

How had she ever come up with a name like Bogomil? Bogomil her magical wolf friend and his spooky midnight kingdom. It probably had something to do with the divorce, her father leaving. What a sad kid she'd been. How much better her life was now. Ha!

She had a bowl of cereal for dinner and a bag of gummy bears, and then around eight the doorbell rang. When she turned on the porch light, Mr. Anabin was standing there.

"Mr. Anabin? What are you doing here?" She pulled her hair back, tucking it down the neck of her sweater.

"Susannah," he said. "Your sister left this in my classroom." He held out a guitar case.

"Laura?" Susannah said. "When?"

"No matter," Mr. Anabin said. "But I thought I would return it. It would be better in your keeping, I think."

Susannah said, "Laura's out right now, but when she gets back—"

"Or you could put it somewhere safe and not mention it to her," Mr. Anabin said gently.

He was still holding out the guitar so Susannah took it. The handle was warm from Mr. Anabin's grasp, but the old cracked case was freckled with snow. The Harmony would be horribly out of tune. "I guess so?" Susannah said. "But—"

"Wonderful," Mr. Anabin said. "And Susannah? Take care of yourself."

"Yeah, absolutely," Susannah said. "You, too. Still snowing out there?"

Mr. Anabin said, "Still it snows. But is this music?"

"Okay," Susannah said. "Um, good night." She closed the door, trying to figure out where she should put Laura's guitar. How kind of Mr. Anabin to return it. Next time he came into What Hast Thou Ground? she would make his weird drink for free. He seemed down.

The upstairs hall closet, she decided. Laura couldn't even reach the top shelf. But first she took it out of its case. Ran her fingers over the strings, and then sat down cross-legged in the hall to tune it. Poor old guitar. Everyone kept leaving it behind.

She sang a little song to cheer it up.

"*Oh you weren't ever as good / as we wished you were / my sister has boughten new guitars / so much fanci-ar / but a piece of you remains with me yet / like the smallest splint-ar / and I'll wash my sheets again before I forget you / you old guitar / may that day come oh never / oh nev-ar—*"

As she was singing the doorbell rang again. She laid the Harmony back in its case, put the case up on the high shelf, and closed the door to the closet.

The Book of Bowie

Avelot was no fool, until she was. She gambled on one throw and lost everything she had, everything she was. She went down into Bogomil's realm, and most of her is still there now. Now Avelot is Bowie, and Bowie will not make the same mistakes that Avelot once made. Bowie will be cautious where Avelot was bold. There are wolves in the marsh. A saying when Avelot was alive. Now Avelot is dead but there are still wolves in the marsh. Bowie will be one of them. Thomas hunts Bowie at his peril.

Bowie wears the face of Thomas's brother. He watches Thomas with his brother's two blue eyes. He knows this will make it harder for Thomas to kill him, should Thomas discover him. Bowie lies on his stomach on the roof of the Cliff Hangar, snow falling all around him, and listens to everything that goes on inside. There is pleasure in this, in being alive and secret and wearing a shape that pleases. When Thomas and Mo come out through the door, Bowie watches them go hand in hand down the plowed and salted road. There's a turnoff a few hundred yards on. It leads to a steep trail that goes down to a rocky beach. Snow has made it unusable. Bowie, before he chose his perch above the Cliff Hangar, spied out the terrain.

Thomas and Mo pause before the turnoff. Does Thomas sense Bowie is near? But Thomas has only stopped to embrace his companion, and Bowie watches with great interest, only the smallest part of it prurient. How greedy Thomas is to want more than his own survival.

The embrace is lingering. But all things come to an end, and so one shape becomes two, two alter into black specks and go laddering up the air. Bowie's preference is a gull. Never a songbird. If the crows take flight toward the Cliff Hangar, he will become a gull and flee them. But the crows dive down, plummeting over the guardrail. No need for stairs when one has wings.

Bowie who was once Avelot knows fucking can take as much or as little time as one wants. Will they fuck as birds or boys? Let them, please whatever god never cared for Avelot, dally long. He stays some time upon the roof, but there are good smells below and he grows hungrier. He will go in. And if Thomas returns and catches Bowie inside, well, Bowie must depend upon Malo Mogge, who has said in this space of time she will not permit his death. Perhaps Bowie may make his own bargain with her.

As he passes through the door, Bowie becomes aware something is happening. Some great work is happening. Malo Mogge is summoning her power.

The Book of Laura

Laura has always been good at compartmentalizing. You have to be if you want to get things done. Your father leaves? Well, that sucks, but your mother is barely holding it together and your sister has always done whatever the opposite of holding it together is. Someone is going to have to get her own breakfast. Make sure she has enough clean underwear to get through the week. Keep track of her own homework assignments, pack her own lunches, wash her own hair, and remind Susannah when Susannah forgets to do these things for herself. Susannah is ten months older, but Susannah has always been the dreamer, the sleepwalker, Laura the one who lives in the future. Music is the path that leads there, music is the future where she is going, music is the house where she will live. When she gets there she will unpack all the carefully labeled boxes in which she keeps the things she won't let herself feel yet, want yet. Think about yet. *Be* yet.

But even Laura, who keeps her feet upon the path, has a heart and eyes. She knows she's made a mistake with Susannah. She marks it down on the chart where she keeps all of her grudges, all of her love for her sister, and the tally of the wrongs they have done each other. Are the wrongs that Laura has done larger because Susannah acts from impulse and Laura thinks first? Laura has good reasons for everything she does. This is not an excuse. Laura knows that. Put that knowledge into a box.

Susannah is on her mind. And Daniel, too, who will not choose himself. And then there is Rosamel Walker, up on the stage with Mo's other friends. Before she died, Laura thought of Rosamel quite often. If there wasn't so much at stake right now, Laura would do different things than she is doing now. She wishes, now, that she had done things differently before. Rosamel is on Laura's mind.

Ruth and Laura's father, too. She saw them when she came in, up at the bar. Ruth was drinking wine. She looks as if she is enjoying herself, despite herself. Perhaps Ruth does not remember how it was when her husband left, but Laura does. How it was is on Laura's mind.

There's the thing that Mr. Anabin told her in the music room. There's someone near her who shouldn't be. Who isn't real. When they came back from the dead and agreed to Mr. Anabin and Bogomil's game, Mr. Anabin placed someone into their lives, each of their lives, who is not real. Whose flesh and biography and place in this world are made of magic. This is her assignment. Discern the unreal person and send them away. Of course Laura thought first of Susannah. Wouldn't it make a kind of terrible sense? Susannah wasn't with the rest of them in Bogomil's realm, and Laura's magic earlier had had no effect on her when it should have. And so little that Susannah does seems to Laura like something a person should do. But Laura's heart and her head agree it cannot be Susannah.

Most likely it is Bowie, who is hardly a person at all. How convenient if it is Bowie. But Bowie, too, can wait. Right now Laura is going to have a discussion about her future with Malo Mogge.

Before she can do this, Ruth intercepts her.

"You look happy," Laura says, hoping she doesn't sound censorious.

Ruth says, "Laura! What a day! Every baby in the NICU, every single one. No one can understand it. They're all thriving!"

"Wow," Laura says. "Awesome!"

"I'm celebrating," Ruth says. "Your dad signed up for a song and we're next. You have to help."

Ruth sings in the shower and sometimes when she's doing dishes, but she's never liked performing in front of other people. Laura feels a surge of animus toward her father for putting Ruth on the spot. But here he is, smiling and joking about how they are going to kill this and Ruth actually seems excited and Laura realizes Ruth just wants her family up on stage with her. She wants to do this as a family. And maybe it's a good thing Susannah isn't here because she'd say something and make it weird.

So Laura goes up with them, and the song starts and it's Mariah Carey's "Always Be My Baby." Oh, the worst possible choice; you couldn't pick a worse karaoke song if you tried. What was her father thinking? But with karaoke, there's no point unless you really commit, and so Laura commits, even though she's always said melisma is a party trick, melisma is for people who lack conviction. She concentrates on stripping out all the goofy, thrilling frills that belong to Carey and sings the lyrics as simply and sincerely as she can. Her parents provide backup. And for the space of a song, there they all are, really pulling this off so much more successfully than Laura would ever have expected. Her mom has a nice voice—it's a shame she doesn't sing more—and Laura's father is an honest-to-God countertenor. She doesn't remember him singing at all when she was little. Even the Harmony, as far as she can remember, just sat in the corner of the living room. He didn't play it. But no wonder Laura loves music so much. It runs in the family.

It goes down big with the crowd at the Cliff Hangar, and, oh, Laura has always loved this. You sing and an audience gives you the coin of their love, their attention, their interest. Not every time, but sometimes, like this time. Even Malo Mogge, oh, even Rosamel is paying attention to Laura on the stage. Maybe it's magic how Laura can feel the attention of a particular member of the audience upon her, how she feels the current of attention rising from each member of the audience like a heady and delicious vapor. She opens her mouth and song pours out, emptying her. All the doors and all the boxes fly open so that she may receive admiration, adoration, veneration. Catch what comes. Store it away safely. You'll need it in the dark, eventually.

All songs end. If they didn't, why then, Laura would stay here all her life.

When they're off the stage again, Ruth is as bubbly and girlish as Laura has ever seen her. Even Ruth, who does her work in a place where everything is twilight dark and twilight hushed, can be raised up by song and praise. Laura loves seeing her like this.

Ruth asks her ex-husband to go get her another glass of white wine and then she hugs Laura and says wistfully, "I don't suppose Susannah is going to believe how good we were."

Laura says, "Karaoke really isn't her thing. Or me. Or even singing, right now."

"She's a mysterious creature," Ruth says. "And you know how to push her buttons."

"I may have pushed a few buttons," Laura says. "But I'm going to do my best to make it right."

Ruth says, "Good." Then, "Maybe I'll get myself a karaoke machine for Christmas and Susannah can suck it. I'd forgotten how much fun it is to make noise. Want to stay a little longer?"

"Yeah," Laura says. "Is it okay with you? I mean, is stuff okay with him? With Dad?"

Ruth makes a face, as if she knows what she's about to say is ridiculous. "I'm not looking for a do-over. But in my wildest dreams? I used to imagine him crawling back, groveling at my feet, telling me what a huge mistake he'd made. I never had any idea what was supposed to happen after that. For him to stay? To go away again? But we used to have so much fun. And I'd forgotten that. How much fun he could be."

"Sure," Laura says. Honestly, she's glad her mother is happy, and she is not going to think about the long run. About whether or not her father is going to fuck everything up again. Put that thought in a box.

Here he is with a glass of wine for Ruth. And he's obviously glad Laura is here, but his attention, his focus, is on Ruth. Laura stands next to her parents and listens to people enthusiastically butcher songs she's never liked, while occasionally wandering back to the buffet table to load up another paper plate with cold pizza or deviled eggs. She's putting off a difficult and potentially dangerous conversation for as long as she can, but eventually she can no longer eat another bite, or listen to another terrible song, and so she goes to find the person she needs to talk to.

Malo Mogge is sitting in the shadows, as far from the stage as one can get, and although no one seems to notice her, neither has anyone claimed any of the tables in her vicinity.

Laura sits down opposite Malo Mogge. She says, "Why do you dress like that?" She can't help herself.

"Like what?" Malo Mogge says. Her dress is ridiculous. Her arms have snakes made of gold going up them like two fat Slinkies with fangs. Her half mask looks like something you would wear to a Roman orgy and then regret because everyone else just went with togas and sandals.

"Like *that*," Laura says.

"Why do you dress like that?" Malo Mogge says.

Laura is wearing waterproof boots, blue jeans, and a red cable-knit sweater. She'd planned to change outfits before getting here, but then everything happened with Susannah. She says, "I'm wearing perfectly ordinary clothes."

"I am not ordinary," Malo Mogge says. "And neither are you."

Laura accepts the compliment. Already the conversation is headed in a promising direction. She says, "This thing you want, why do you think we have it?"

Malo Mogge says, "My key. You or one of you had it once. I came when I felt it turn within the lock."

Laura says, "When we died. Why can't you or Bogomil or Mr. Anabin find it now? Why do we have to do it for you? And is it a key or a coin or a cup?"

A goddess shouldn't look like a teapot, but that's what Laura thinks of when she looks at Malo Mogge. Or maybe a watering can. Shiny, decorative, a little bulbous. If you tried to tip her little spout, though, what you'd get is a lot of snakes. Malo Mogge says, "Why should I explain myself to you?"

"Because I'm trying to help you," Laura says earnestly. "Because I'm not stupid. I know it would be better to be on your good side. If it's your key, then it's yours and I have no idea why you think I would even want it. Trust me, I have a very long list of things I want, and a key that gets me into that place with that guy Bogomil in it is one hundred percent not on my list."

Malo Mogge nods. All the watchful snakes settle down inside their teapot. She says, "Very well. A long time ago I used my power and severed a piece of myself. I took that part of me and fashioned a tool from it. When I knew thirst, it was a cup I drank from. When I was threatened by enemies, it was a blade and I slew them. When I wished for new worlds, it was a key that made many doors for me. But the first door I made here was a door into Death and I set guardians on each side so I might travel back and forth through it to take my due and increase my power. When my priests made sacrifices to me, the dead departed through that door. I consumed the life that remained upon its threshold."

Laura says, "They used to sacrifice people to you? Bogomil and *Mr. Anabin*?" She tries to picture this, cannot. What T-shirt would he wear?

"They sang me songs of praise. They held open the door to Death while I wielded the blade. They held the cup while I drank from it."

"I hope they also held your hair whenever you drank too much and puked in the toilet," Laura says. "That's how you know somebody's an actual friend. I still don't understand why you can't find your key yourself."

"Because when I made it from myself, I invested it with my power," Malo Mogge says. "Just as I used some of my power in every door to every world I ever opened. But those were mere scraps set against what the key required of me. And because so much of me was invested in the key, I warded it with many protections and gave it agency to protect itself against my enemies. I gave it abilities that, as my strength has waned, now hide it from me."

"You can't find your key because it doesn't want to be found," Laura says. "So why do you think we can?"

"I believe it is using one of you to hide itself," Malo Mogge says, "without your knowledge. You must work to discover how. And if you cannot find it then not only will you suffer when Anabin and Bogomil are done with their game, but this place will as well. Though I am diminished, I remain myself. The air itself catches fire if I ask it. On our first meeting, you sang when I bade you, but you do not yet know me."

"And the people up on stage right now singing 'Tubthumping,'" Laura says, "are they singing for you, too?" She recognizes the guy on the left. Jordan Bass. He comes into What Hast Thou Ground? on Saturday mornings and always leaves a huge tip. In Laura's opinion, big tips count for more than a mediocre rendition of "Tubthumping."

The golden mask turns toward the stage, and then Malo Mogge stands up. She claps her hands once, softly, but every head in the room turns. On stage, Jordan Bass and the other singer fall silent.

Laura hears someone say, "Who the hell is that? Why is she wearing a mask?" Then, "Are we on TV?"

Malo Mogge says, "You have not known I was among you, but now you will know Malo Mogge is with you." She doesn't raise her voice, but Laura can see it carries. Everyone in the Cliff Hangar can hear her perfectly well. "Now you will know me. I will remain among you, and you will not depart from me. No one shall leave Lovesend and neither will any enter until I have been satisfied. Until I have my cup to drink from again. Until all doors are open to me. But do not be afraid. Love me and worship me and I will raise you up as I raise my temple."

Laura sees the faces of the citizens of Lovesend all turned toward Malo Mogge. How they all look at her, now, with adoration and awe and perfect trust. Malo Mogge waves her hand and the French doors along the hangar wall all fly open. When she goes out the crowd follows and so Laura does, too.

Snow is falling. Out in the darkness, down in the water out past the shoreline at Little Moon Bay, something begins to happen. The people standing on the balcony of the Cliff Hangar hear the noise first, a roar as if pieces of the cliffs are tumbling down. But instead, the water in the bay begins to froth and boil around the temple Malo Mogge is raising from the ocean bed. It is massive—at least twice as big as the Bank of America building on Main Street and three times as gaudy. Dark green stone, big steps leading up to a slab of a porch with towering columns and above this a portico with carvings that at this distance Laura can't make out, all of it glowing lividly.

Laura's parents are on the balcony with everyone else. Ruth says, "That's something you don't see every day." She doesn't seem troubled at all. No one is. People are talking animatedly, cheerfully, as if they're watching Fourth of July fireworks. A guy Laura knows from Lewis Latimer is filming the whole thing on his iPhone. Other people have theirs out, too.

Once again flecks of black are falling, mixing with the snow, and Laura can smell something burning. She thinks the smell is emanating from Malo Mogge's temple. The char creeps into Laura's nostrils, down into her lungs. It has the tired reek of something that has been burning for a very long time, and quickly Laura's red sweater is dotted with smuts. They leave greasy streaks when she tries to pick them off.

She makes her way through the crowd on the balcony, looking for Mo, for Thomas. She needs to see she isn't the only one who understands that none of this should be happening. Instead, back inside the Cliff Hangar she sees Bowie calmly stuffing his stupid stolen face with donated pizza.

Malo Mogge in her golden mask claps her hands again. She says, "Please, go on with the festivities. Sing for me. If I am pleased, I will show you favor."

Why do supernatural beings have to be like this? Give any high school art teacher enough power, and they'd probably dress exactly like Malo Mogge. Make you go to their weird underwater art project opening.

Rosamel brushes past Laura. "Laura," she says. "You were good up there. But I like your original stuff better." Smiles and walks away before Laura can think of what to say. She looks back once. Put that into a box. Rosamel smiling.

Malo Mogge links arms with Laura. Her skin is warm. Laura feels the heat through her sweater. "There," she says. "Now I feel more comfortable. More at home. But where is Thomas, I wonder? He will be devastated to have missed our friend over there."

"Mo said you have a deal with Thomas," Laura says. "The deal was you would help him kill Bowie when he found him. Right?"

"Yes," Malo Mogge says.

"But now you won't let him kill Bowie," Laura says.

"Bowie is a piece of all of this," Malo Mogge says. "So for now I will stay my hand."

"Well," Laura says, "I see your point, but it doesn't seem very fair to Thomas." She carefully extricates her arm from Malo Mogge's.

"And what do you care for Thomas?" Malo Mogge says. "Has he seduced you, too?"

"No!" Laura says. "Wait, what? Never mind. What I was going to say is I don't trust Mr. Anabin and Bogomil. At all. And so I started thinking maybe I should make a deal with you instead. But if you don't keep your bargains, then why would I ever do anything to help you find your key?" She still isn't sure whether Bowie is real or not. But if he is, he's competition.

Malo Mogge turns her head. Beneath the gold mask, Laura can see Malo Mogge's eyes, the skin around her eyes. Is there a little red bump just below the eyelid? Or is she imagining it? Do goddesses get zits?

Malo Mogge says, "Bring me my key and you may have your heart's desire of me. Life forever. Wealth. Power. A safe harbor for the ones you love."

"What I want is to be a rock star," Laura says. "But I have nothing against wealth and some of the other stuff."

Up on the stage, a guy Laura used to see every day in What Hast Thou Ground? shouts out, "Hey! This is for Malo Mogge!" Then he launches into "Your Body Is a Wonderland."

Right in front of the stage is Bogomil. Oh, this doesn't seem like good news. Is he here because somehow he knows what Laura is up to? That she's sucking up to Malo Mogge? But he isn't paying any attention to Laura and Malo Mogge. Instead he's watching the singer on the stage. He looks bemused. Maybe he's never really listened to the lyrics before. Susannah used to sing "I'm not wearing underpants" instead of "Your body is a wonderland" when that song came on. Honestly that was a better lyric. Surely Mr. Anabin didn't conjure up Susannah. He doesn't have a sense of humor as far as Laura can tell.

Bowie is watching Bogomil. Bowie's expression gives nothing away. He picks up another piece of pizza, folds it in half, begins to stuff it into his pocket. He heads for the door just as that person Thomas comes through it.

"And if you want love we'll make it," sings the guy on stage. Thomas lunges forward, faster than humanly possible, but as he does so Bowie disappears. The slice of pizza falls on the floor and a cloud of moths explodes into the crowd. People swat at the moths as a crow cries out just above their heads, snapping moths out of the air with its beak one by one. Then the moths are gone and a bat darts high, higher, over the carousel and out the open windows. The crow shoots after it, a black arrow.

The Book of Rosamel Walker

Coming home, she had goals. If you don't set goals for yourself, you might as well be water in a bucket someone else is carrying. All of your feelings just sploshing around while your mom says, "Why are you in that bucket? Is something wrong? You're so different from the way you used to be. You used to be so happy in that other bucket." Goals didn't even have to be big goals. Small achievable ones were preferable. For example, Rosamel was going to hang out with her friends. She wasn't going to stress out about her grades or think about the thing she'd had with Veronica and how that had ended. And she was going to appreciate all of the good things about her mother. There were so many, many good things. Her therapist had had her write them down. Good boundaries: that was the last of her goals, what she was going to give herself for Christmas. Good boundaries make good parents. Like that poem you had to read in high school and then when you got to college you read it again in freshman comp. A booster shot of Robert Frost. Or was Frost the *"sorry I could not travel both* but even more sorry that I couldn't, in my day, talk openly about wanting to fuck ladies but also other guy poets" poet?

Her dad hadn't said one single thing about Rosamel's lack of hair. But then he was bald, too. She'd taken a great father/daughter selfie the first day she was home.

Rosamel had come up to the Cliff Hangar with Natalie and Theo, and she would have been having a pretty great time making fun of other people's karaoke choices if it wasn't for the fact that her mother was here with all of her church friends and whenever Rosamel turned around, there she was, giving her the saddest looks. Love the sinner, hate the hairstyle.

She was tempted to give her mother something to be actually sad about. Maybe, if there was dancing later on, she'd pull that Laura girl out onto the floor. Laura had always given off a certain vibe: Not now, but maybe tomorrow. Maybe someday. Some girls maybe-somedayed their whole way through high school. But high school was over and done, and now here was Laura, here was Rosamel.

And then everything had happened with the lady in the golden mask, and a temple rose out of the ocean, and Rosamel realized she was going to be stuck in Lovesend with her mother indefinitely. A little medicinal marijuana was required. She had her vape pen. She was in the bathroom, trying to get to a place where she could deal with all of this, when she suddenly got a look at herself in the mirror and, stupid move, she decided to try to see what it was her mother was seeing when she looked at Rosamel. What was it that was so terrible? Was glitter a crime?

She wet a paper towel and began to wipe some of the glitter off. Her mother wouldn't stay. She liked to be in bed no later than eleven. Rosamel could just stay in here and wait her out.

The problem with using a paper towel to remove glitter is mostly you just move it around. Her eyes were stinging. She'd gotten some of that shit in them. And that was when Someday Laura opened the door to the bathroom and then just stood there, staring at her.

Laura said, "Sorry. Uh. You okay?"

Rosamel said, "Glitter incident." She ran the tap, bent over, and splashed water onto her face. When she looked up again, Laura was still standing there. Girl was awkward as hell.

"You need something?" Rosamel said. She dried her face on her T-shirt. Waited.

Laura said, "We never hung out when we were in school."

"True," Rosamel said.

"But, you know, I always thought you seemed really cool. Really interesting?"

"Still am," Rosamel said.

Laura looked down at the floor. Mumbled something. Rosamel said, "Sorry? I didn't catch that." It was hard to be flirtatious when you had glitter in your eyes.

"We used to do that," Laura said. "Me and Susannah and Daniel, for shows. Such a pain in the ass afterward."

"I remember," Rosamel said. Her eye was streaming, but the speck of glitter was finally out. "Came to your shows once or twice. You guys were pretty good. But you're better now. You sounded amazing up there tonight. I don't even like Mariah Carey. But that was magic."

"Oh wow," Laura said. "Thank you. I mean, I guess I've just been going through some stuff? But it felt pretty good to be up there." She looked down at the floor, then back at Rosamel. Opened her mouth and then closed it again.

Rosamel sighed. Someday Girls never knew how to get a thing started. It was never enough to show them the path they were looking for, the one that went to the place they wanted to go. You had to take their hand, lead them down it. Rosamel reached out, said "Hey," and took Laura's hand in hers. Rubbed her thumb over Laura's fingers. A fleck or two of glitter discernable against the smoothness. Now Laura could see the path and the place, Rosamel knew. She lifted her other hand, brought it to Laura's waist, just over her hip. Let it rest there.

"This day," Rosamel said. "It's been weird, right?"

"Pretty weird," Laura said. Her fingers twined with Rosamel's. Her free hand rose, a magic trick, levitated. Finally it tentatively came down to Rosamel's waist. Rested so lightly it might have been a moth.

"Okay," Rosamel said. "That's good. But maybe you could take the next step, Someday Girl."

"What?" Laura said.

"Kiss me," Rosamel said. So Laura did.

After they had been doing that for a while, Rosamel pushed Laura—ravenous, devouring—back.

"Sorry," Laura said. Her T-shirt was wedged between them. Her sweater was on the floor.

"For what?" Rosamel said.

"I haven't ever done this before," Laura said.

"But you want to, right?" Rosamel said.

"God, yes," Laura said. Real enthusiasm there. That was a relief. "But..."

"First time for me," Rosamel said, "I was so into this girl. I couldn't believe it was actually happening. And somewhere in there, when everything was going pretty great, I looked up and saw she had this huge crusty thing in her nose. And she was making all these noises and we were doing stuff and she was into it, and I was like, This is the most amazing thing ever, but I also just couldn't stop checking out her nostril. This monster booger. It was so bad. So, relax. And if it's too weird, just say something. Deal?"

Laura nodded. She went and locked the door. The Cliff Hangar had two other bathrooms. But they were lucky here: this was the biggest one. "Who was it?" she said.

"Who what?" Rosamel said. And then, "Oh no. I don't tell tales."

"Angela Freitas," Laura said.

Which, good guess. Either that or Laura had noticed a lot more than Rosamel would ever have known. "Come here," Rosamel said, and Laura came willingly.

Things went well for a little while, very well indeed, but Rosamel became aware once again that Laura was distracted. It wasn't what you wanted when your mouth was around a nipple. "Hey," she said. "You still okay with this?"

"So very okay," Laura said. "Extremely okay. It's just, the song, this guy is really not pulling this off."

Rosamel stopped. Listened. It was true someone was absolutely butchering "I Miss the Misery." "Poor baby," she said, suddenly glad she'd lip-synched earlier. "I got earplugs. You want them?"

"It's fine," Laura said. "I'm fine."

"Good," Rosamel said. "That's good. Here. Put your hand here. Now pinch. Just a little." She put her mouth against Laura's ear and breathed, "They're playing our song." Laura began to laugh and could not stop until Rosamel was kissing her again.

Things got more serious, and then Rosamel had to stop again, reluctantly. "Hold on," she said. "We have to deal with the glitter situation. On the fingers at least, okay? Otherwise glitter gets in places you don't want it." She turned on the faucet, took Laura's left hand and began to carefully, thoroughly, rinse it, smoothing her own fingers along Laura's. Then the other hand. When the glitter had been dealt with, she didn't bother with a paper towel. She took Laura's hand, wet and smelling like soap-dispenser soap, and sucked each finger one by one. Laura's other hand, Rosamel's other hand, Rosamel slid them down the unbuttoned waist of Laura's jeans. "Buddy system," she said.

Later on, Laura said, "Things keep happening I didn't expect to happen."

She sounded a little plaintive. Rosamel, on the other hand, felt pretty smug. Wow, sex was great. Girls were great.

They didn't really know each other, but now they knew at least a couple of things about each other that they hadn't known before. For example, Rosamel had suspected Laura was an uptight control freak. But now she knew Laura was also a straight-up freak. She said, "Come here. I have to tell you something."

Laura, whose whole posture and demeanor had changed over the past little space of time, drew up and into herself. It was like watching a windup Harlequin go back all by itself into its box when the song was over. "What?" she said.

It was a terrible idea but Rosamel couldn't help herself. She pulled Laura close, wrapped her arms around her. She said, lovingly, softly, "You got something in your nose. I didn't want to say anything, but oh man. It's huge. Huge and green."

Laura gave her a look of absolute, wide-eyed horror. And then she figured it out. "You are an asshole!"

Rosamel, feeling better than she had in a long time, kissed Laura right on her prissy little booger-free nose. "I know," she said. "But you still like me. You even liked me back then. Back at Lewis Latimer."

Laura put her face against Rosamel's shoulder. "I do," she said. "I did. I really did."

"What's your number?" Rosamel said. She was stuck in town until that Malo Mogge lady got whatever she needed. It sucked, but maybe there were things that wouldn't suck. This wasn't going to be anything long-term, but it didn't mean she and Laura couldn't hang out. See what that felt like.

There was some more kissing, lazy and sweet and still experimental. And then Laura arranged her hair so you couldn't see the hickeys Rosamel had given her. That was what you did when you hooked up with the girl you used to wonder about when you were in high school. You gave her hickeys, the way you used to think about doing when you were in AP English and she was sitting a couple of desks in front of you. Laura had the softest skin. There was glitter in Rosamel's mouth. Probably glitter in the places they'd tried to avoid getting glitter. And Laura, too, she'd wake up tomorrow and there would be gold on her sheets. Gold in her hair and in all the creases of her clothes. Under her nails and, inevitably, all over her thighs.

"So, okay, bye," Laura said, smiling and flustered and then gone.

When Rosamel left the bathroom a few minutes later, the crowd had thinned out. There was Laura, heading for the exit with her parents. Theo and Natalie were up at a table on the carousel. Malo Mogge in her golden mask was sitting at another, and as Rosamel watched, a crow swooped through one of the French doors and landed on the saddle of a carousel rabbit. It shook itself, all of its feathers fluffing out, and then there was a boy instead of a bird, the boy who kept showing up when Mo was around. Rosamel might be stuck in Lovesend indefinitely, but Lovesend was a lot more interesting than it had been.

She climbed up on the carousel and went to sit with Theo and Natalie, who probably wondered what Rosamel had been up to. But Theo and Natalie were cunning. They'd ambush her later on when they thought she wasn't expecting it. Even though they'd all been friends long enough that, of course, Rosamel would be expecting it.

They took selfies, which was what you did when you were up on the carousel, while some guy on the stage did a pretty great version of "Umbrella." He wasn't anyone Rosamel had ever seen in town before—he wasn't the kind of person you'd forget. He was so good-looking it kind of hurt to look at him. The whole time he was on stage, he kept his eyes fixed on the bar, and finally Rosamel turned so she could figure out to whom he was singing. And that turned out to be her old music teacher, Mr. Anabin, sitting on a barstool with his back to the stage, paying absolutely no attention to anyone or anything.

Surely no one had ever looked at Mr. Anabin like this. And yet, when the song was over, the singer went straight for the bar and sat down on the stool right beside Mr. Anabin. He didn't look at Mr. Anabin, and Mr. Anabin never looked at him. Someone else got on stage, and then when Rosamel looked back, Mr. Anabin and the mystery guy were still not looking at each other but they were holding hands.

A couple more people sang. The guy who owned What Hast Thou Ground? did Blondie's "Heart of Glass." Terribly. It was kind of great how terrible his voice was because it didn't even matter. His conviction sold it anyway. And when he was done, Malo Mogge summoned him over. She asked his name, and he said "Billy," and then Malo Mogge asked him what his heart's desire was. He said he didn't really know but he wished he could get just one good night's sleep. So Malo Mogge said she could give him that, and she beckoned him a little closer. Rosamel and Theo and Natalie watched her stretch out her finger and touch him on the forehead. He immediately fell over on the floor of the carousel, under one of the wolves, fast asleep.

Rosamel whispered to Theo and Natalie, "Hey, so maybe we should do another song. Sing for her. Ask her for something."

Natalie whispered back, "Genevieve got up there earlier, believe it or not. She was really awful, but she put her whole heart in it, and then Malo Mogge asked her what she wanted, and she said she wanted to actually be good at music. But it didn't go that great for a bunch of other people, and some of them were not bad at all."

"Besides," Theo said. "Last time you just lip-synched. That's not gonna fly."

"Fine," Rosamel said.

Anyway, it looked like maybe that was it, no one else was around who wanted to sing.

Malo Mogge said, "Thomas. You haven't sung yet."

The crow boy gave Malo Mogge an extremely not-happy look. "Or perhaps I should ask these three here," she said, meaning Rosamel, Natalie, and Theo.

Crow boy got down off his rabbit and made a little bow. He jumped off the carousel.

"Five bucks he sings some old Green Day song," Theo said.

Natalie said, "No, it'll be the Killers. Or Lorde. Or something *really* old-school. Toto. He'll bless the rains down in Africa."

Rosamel was starting to feel concerned about Mo. Did he know his friend could turn into a bird? And this guy seemed to have some weird deal with Malo Mogge. Rosamel wouldn't ever say it, but Malo Mogge seemed kind of high-maintenance. Also pervy.

Natalie was close. Mo's friend picked an old Rod Stewart song, "Maggie May," and he started out on the quiet side but got into it eventually. And when "Maggie May" was over, he launched straight into "Goodbye Yellow Brick Road" like he was really feeling it.

Next he sang "Rolling in the Deep," and that was when Rosamel realized he was picking songs with a theme: these were all break-up songs, songs about leaving. He was singing his heart out by the end, and you could hear how fed up he was. And then he was done.

He came back to the carousel. Then he just stood there, looking at Malo Mogge and not saying anything. Finally Malo Mogge said, "Would you leave my service, then?"

Rosamel couldn't imagine that. Who would ever leave Malo Mogge unless she made them? But Thomas was silent.

Malo Mogge waited. When Thomas still said nothing, she sighed. It wasn't the kind of sigh Rosamel was all too familiar with. This was real sorrow, real disappointment. If Rosamel's mother had ever sighed like this, Rosamel would have died of shame. She and Natalie and Theo all sat holding their breath. How could this guy be such an asshole? Couldn't he see how sad Malo Mogge was? And pissed off? Because she was. She was in an absolute rage. Next, a noise came out of her mouth that sounded like a dog. Like John Wick's dog if you killed John Wick. Any minute now and Malo Mogge was going to do something terrible to this guy, Thomas, and really it was his own fault. But instead Malo Mogge said, "Ask me what is in your heart and I will grant it."

"Avelot's death," Thomas said. "As I am your servant."

The mask made Malo Mogge's face hard to read, but Rosamel could see her mouth draw tight. She said, "You would have me break the arrangement I have with Anabin."

Thomas said, "I would have you keep the promise you made to me."

Malo Mogge made that horrible growling sound. Rosamel would have done anything for her.

"The thing you have sought all these years is finally close to you," Thomas said, clearly unimpressed. "Soon it will fall into your grasp. For me, it is the same. All this time I have searched for the one who caused my brother's death, and now, at last, I have found them. How should I stay my hand? But how can I strike the blow when you tell me hold? Yet Avelot must die."

At last Malo Mogge said, "Done. As you are my faithful servant."

She held out her hand and Thomas took it. He raised her up from her chair and they left the Cliff Hangar. When Rosamel looked over at the bar, Mr. Anabin was gone and so was his fine friend.

After that, Rosamel and Natalie and Theo went back to Natalie and Theo's house, Natalie driving very carefully in her mom's old Prius because the roads were bad, the snow accumulating. When they got to the house, Mr. Thanglek was sitting on the bench beside the door, putting on his boots.

"Dad?" Theo said. "Are you going somewhere? Where's Ma?"

"Asleep," he said. "I won't be gone long. But Malo Mogge's key is missing. If it isn't found, how will your ma and I get to Paris? Ma said she came to our restaurant. Maybe she lost it there. I'll go over and look for just a little while. I've always been good at finding things."

"He really is," Theo said. "You really are."

"You want company?" Rosamel said. "We could all go look, I guess."

"No," Mr. Thanglek said. "It's late. *Mai pen rai.* The three of you should sleep. Look in the morning. But maybe I will find it first!"

"Okay," Natalie said uncertainly. "But don't stay out too long."

They shed their coats and shoes and got coconut waters out of the fridge. There was a sketch of a buff naked guy stuck up on the side. "Your mom did this?" Rosamel said.

"Yeah," Theo said. "Not bad, right?"

"He kind of looks like your dad," Rosamel said, studying it. "Like, she made him look like your dad, don't you think? The mouth, the face?"

"What the hell, Rosamel," Natalie said. "Shut your stupid mouth!"

Theo began to laugh so hard she almost fell over.

"Sorry," Rosamel said. But she didn't think she was wrong. They took the coconut waters to Natalie and Theo's bedroom. Shared a little weed and talked about the old days. They texted Mo because he should have really been with them, he was missing out on all the fun, and eventually they heard Mr. Thanglek come home. Had he found the key? Probably not, they agreed; they would know if he had found it. There were no texts from Mo. Or Laura. Maybe she was out looking for the key, too. They got Natalie's sleeping bag out and Rosamel fell asleep on the floor.

And what does Rosamel dream of? She dreams she is chosen to be sacrificed to a goddess in some esoteric and beautiful ritual, and before it happens she is kind of terrified and she's kind of excited and a little turned on, tbh, and the moon is hanging over the temple, and then the moon turns out to be a booger in someone's nose, Laura's nose, and Rosamel realizes Laura is the goddess and the moon belongs to her, and Rosamel is just not sure about any of that. She keeps saying, "But you're not the moon, you're just some girl. You're just some Someday Girl."

But that was what you got when you indulged in too much weed before you fell asleep.

The Book of Mo

There had been a moment when he was flying when he realized: He did not have to change back, become Mo again. He could remain a bird. Maybe not a crow—a golden eagle, perhaps. Or a duck. A fruit bat. Navigate the world by sound. Live in sound. Eat bugs. Okay, maybe not.

Who would miss him? Rosamel and Natalie and Theo. Jenny. Susannah, but he'd already sort of ghosted her. Twice. Once literally. *Ha caa,* the crow called. *Ha caa haa ca haaaa.*

They skimmed the waves. Spray rose up to bathe them, droplets clinging to their throats and ventral feathers, snowflakes catching and melting on the glossed armature of their wings. His companion fled before Mo, mocking him continuously. Mo did not even realize they were above land again until the other crow dropped abruptly onto a bit of jutting rock and became Thomas once more.

Mo circled him, and Thomas held out his hand, a perch. Mo settled instead upon Thomas's shoulder. He nibbled an ear, muttering all kinds of things that he would never have said in human language, until Thomas flinched and Mo saw he had drawn blood with his beak.

He flapped up, ungainly and light as a drunk, and settled back down upon the ground. Became Mo. Wondered what had become of his clothes while he had been a bird. Was magic like a gym membership? Did your things go, heaped or folded, into some sort of uncanny locker?

"Sorry," he said.

Thomas touched his finger to his earlobe. "I've done worse," he said. "Come here. We won't have much time."

"Before what?" Mo said.

"Before your friend Laura annoys Malo Mogge sufficiently," Thomas said. "Or, worse, gives her an interesting idea."

Mo clambered up onto Thomas's rock. Saltwater mixed with snow and sand had made a slick, gritty paste. Thomas steadied him. Kissed him with a cold and slippery mouth under Mo's jaw, on his chin, his lips.

"Really," Mo said. "You really want to do it here? On a wet pointy rock in the middle of a snowstorm?"

Thomas said, "We can do as we please wherever we please in this short span of time. Tell me you desire it, and I will suck your cock on the stage at the Cliff Hangar in front of the audience of your choosing."

"Okay, yeah," Mo said, unable to not picture this, "that's super hot, but why not head back to my house? Unless you have something against beds?"

"Very well," Thomas said. He began to take off his shirt.

"Don't do that!" Mo said. "It's snowing. You're gonna freeze." It was what his grandmother would have said. Though, of course, not what she would have written. Not in a Caitlynn Hightower novel.

"Look," Thomas said. He balled up his shirt and tossed it onto the sand behind Mo. Mo looked: the shirt had become a pavilion of dark blue silk. Thomas took his arm and drew him off the rock and inside his former shirt. Here was a lacquered platform heaped with blankets and a red ceramic stove with a fire already lit inside. "This seems very . . . Instagrammable," Mo said. "Imagine the post: *Oh my God, you guys, my magical boyfriend ate my ass in this culturally appropriative Orientalist fantasy tent. Afterward we had hot chocolate and some baklava!*"

"Come here," Thomas said.

MO SAID, "I don't care that this isn't real." He was proud of how it came out. He was sitting up with his head against the headboard of the ridiculous bed. The ocean rushed busily in and out of the pavilion. The tide was coming in. The fire in the stove was guttering out.

Thomas said nothing. You could barely see his nose over the blankets. Maybe he had fallen asleep. Mo poked him. He said, "Hey."

"What?" Thomas said.

"When we were crows, I wondered if we were going to fuck."

"We just did," Thomas said. "Didn't we?"

"No, I mean I thought we might fuck as crows. I know I said I'm not particularly kinky, but could we do that? I mean, if I became a crow, would I even know how to have crow sex? Do crows have gay sex? Have you ever had sex while you were a crow?" Bestiality hadn't ever been on his list. Closest was quite a long way down: have sex in a room where there's a parrot in a cage; say some things during sex that a parrot might repeat later.

Thomas said, "I had sex with a badger sow once. It seemed like the thing to do at the time. A courtesy. Oh, and I had quite a long-term affair with a vixen. I was a fox for many years. Malo Mogge banished me into that form, but eventually she called me back into my body. I was almost sorry. I was happy being a fox. Or, I wasn't happy but I was content. It was a pleasing thing to be, hardly a punishment at all. I went to find the vixen afterward so she could see I had not chosen to leave her, but she wasn't having any of me, even when I turned myself back into the shape she knew."

"I think I'd like that," Mo said. "Being a fox."

"Done and done," Thomas said. And then wasn't Thomas. Instead, he was a reddish fox, squirming out from under the blanket and into Mo's lap. Only Mo didn't have a lap. He was a fox as well.

THE PILLOWS ON the bed were full of feathers. And there were fish washing in and out of the pavilion as the tide came in. The foxes tore up the pillows with their sharp teeth until there were white feathers everywhere. They stuck their muzzles into the salty water and snapped up the fish. They raised their legs and wrote in piss on the silk walls of the pavilion and then fucked on top of the gutted pillows. They were dozing in the ruin of the bed when Malo Mogge's temple rose from the bay.

Mo in his fox form, calm and alert, watched the temple rise. Around the temple, water turned to boiling clouds, and the not-unpleasant smell of heated rock was sharp in his nostrils. Dead fish, their eyes cooked white, began to float into the silk pavilion.

Thomas became Thomas, standing shin-deep in the foaming tide, so

Mo changed back, too. He had not been a fox for that long, but even so, he vaguely resented his clothing. It was far less comfortable than his fine fox skin had been.

Thomas wore pants again but presumably his shirt was still doing duty as the pavilion. "Now that is a thing I have never seen," he said.

"What's that?" Mo said.

"What it is is what I'm going to go find out," Thomas said. The bed and the stove and the pavilion all disappeared, although feathers were still drifting in the water around their feet. Thomas's shirt looked a little the worse for wear.

"Sorry about the piss," Mo said.

"Magic means you never have to be sorry about the piss," Thomas said. He smoothed a hand down his shirt and, indeed, it was as good as new afterward. "You shouldn't go back to the Cliff Hangar. She's already out of sorts with you."

"But my friends are there," Mo said.

Thomas said, "I won't let her do anything to anyone you care about." Before Mo could ask if he was including himself in that category, Thomas became the crow again, disappearing against the wet black face of the cliffs.

Mo estimated the temple to be half a mile from shore. Even at this distance, it seemed monstrously large. He did not like how it sat in the bay, sullen as a toad. It looked exactly like the kind of temple where parents threw their babies into fires, where terrible things happened and everyone just thought this was the way it was supposed to be. Malo Mogge in her couture dresses and her bare feet had seemed comical—well, no, she hadn't, but her pettiness and her gluttony and spite had seemed recognizably human—but the temple was of another scale of magnitude. It was, Mo felt, like seeing Mount Doom rise up in your backyard. He tried to imagine what his grandmother would have thought, looking out at it from her rose garden. Would she have shrugged, gone inside to work on another book? He didn't think she would have but the temple seemed to say otherwise. Go about your business. I am here to stay.

Mo did not want to go back to the Cliff Hangar where Malo Mogge was. Not even if Thomas was there with him. Even knowing Rosamel and Natalie and Theo were there. Did that make him a coward? Probably. His second life so far was turning out to be nasty, brutish, and somehow even more complicated than his first. He wished he could be a fox again. But foxes could be hunted and killed. He thought, I will be water. No one will think to look for me in the ocean, and if they did bother to come and look, they would never find me.

And so, for some space, Mo was water. It was very restful. He might have stayed that way until the end of time, except at last a hand drew him out of the ocean and onto the shore.

Back once again in his body, he felt only heaviness and discomfort.

"Stop that!" a voice said.

Mo realized he was dissolving again. "Sorry," he said, and then looked to see to whom he was apologizing.

Bogomil stood there, looking extremely put out. "That was the least intelligent thing any of you have done since coming back to life," he said. "And considering some of the things some of you have been doing, I congratulate you."

"How long was I in there?" Mo said, gesturing at the ocean. He tried to gauge the tide, but he wasn't sure he was anywhere near the rock where Thomas had first landed.

"Twelve years," Bogomil said.

Mo tried to take this in. "Really?" It was still snowing. But maybe it wasn't still anything.

"No," Bogomil said, "you exasperating, foolish child. It's long past midnight. And you are late for your appointment with Anabin. He is waiting for your gift, and I am tired of waiting for all of this to be over. If you do not fear me, then rest assured you should fear Malo Mogge. Give Anabin the thing we are looking for so we may appease her or we will all suffer."

"How?" Mo said. "*How*? I can't give him a thing when I don't know where it is! Or even what it is. Is it a cup? A coin? A rare Pokémon? We're just kids, we shouldn't have to clean up the messes you guys made in the first place. That *you* made."

Bogomil said, "Go to Anabin. Maybe he will give audience to your complaints. I will not. Go to Anabin. Or don't. Become water."

Then he was gone.

Mo found his phone in his pocket. Amazing how you could drop your smartphone on your sofa (as Mo had once done) and have it bounce off in such a way that the whole thing shattered when it hit the floor, just a foot below, but the translation from human to crow to fox to ocean water had not even scratched the glass.

There was a text from Rosamel. Whatever take off and miss all the weird shit but we're heading out. gonna crash with N & T & spec-U-late about whether or not you hooked up with that guy. anyway had some fun of my own and then an emoji of a peach, a taco, and a winky face.

"Gross," Mo said involuntarily. He considered and then sent her back a text of a bird, a fox, two eggplants, and a wave. Let her wonder about that.

He knew where he was now. Little Moon Bay, at his back the boardwalk—a long shelf of snow on the perpendicular—pointing out to Malo Mogge's temple. That was going to be popular with the boating community. And probably with kraken. It was like bird feeders and bears. You put a creepy temple up and you get some large guys you hadn't really anticipated or planned for.

"Shut up, Mo," he said. He didn't need to be thinking about bears or kraken or even Malo Mogge. What he needed to be doing was thinking about a present. Maybe he could find a nice shell? Why, oh why, hadn't he bought one of those pillows? But of course what Mr. Anabin wanted was Mo's grandmother's coin, the one he'd forgotten all about, the one he'd agreed to give to Susannah. Who had been going to give it to Daniel on his birthday. The rest was a blur, but at least Mo remembered this much now, even if he had no idea where the coin might be.

And did Mr. Anabin really deserve any kind of birthday present?

At last he set off for the school.

"So Malo Mogge has raised her temple and sealed off Lovesend," Mr. Anabin said. "None may enter or leave now until she has what she wants."

Mo's old music teacher lay on his back on the floor at the front of the classroom, arms folded behind his head, shoes left neatly beside the piano.

"The party never stops," Mo said.

"Bowie who was Avelot and Laura have each given me their gift," Mr. Anabin said. "What do you bring?"

"Come here and see," Mo said.

He went to the window, Mr. Anabin following. "There," Mo said. "Look."

His present wasn't really for Mr. Anabin at all. Instead, as Mo and Mr. Anabin watched from the window of the classroom, the parade he had arranged for passed by on the street below. The parade was made up of every statue in Lovesend, all of his grandmother's gifts to the town, each one imbued with life as Mo had willed it. Some of the women were splendidly naked and some wore the costumes of their time. They were not bothered by the cold. They were not made of flesh. They were carved out of marble, cast in bronze or copper. Those they were modeled on were dead, and some of the artists who had sculpted them were dead now, too. Mo's grandmother, too, was dead. But this company was not mortal. It was made up of scientists, artists, composers, singers, and writers. Some were larger than life and some were not more than a foot tall. Leonta Carter carried her cat, Alice Ball her beaker. Here, too, were the two angels who had spent so many years keeping watch over Cara Gorch's grave, the one whose flute Mo had mended at last and the other with her guitar slung over one shoulder. It was the angels who, as Mo and Mr. Anabin watched, tore down the slaver Hugh Hall where he stood in bronze and rent him into fragments. One figure bent down, plucked something from the road—a red knit cap—shook off the snow, and placed it on her head. Mo knew her: Edmonia Lewis. The parade did not linger or speak, but as each statue looked up at the window where Mo and Mr. Anabin stood, Mo felt the weight of their regard. They continued heavily down the dark road, and no one except for Mo and Mr. Anabin saw them as they passed by.

The last statue was Marcenia Lyle Stone, who had always been Mo's favorite of all of his grandmother's statues. She stopped suddenly, bent over, and scooped something out of the road. When she stood up again, she drew her arm back and threw a snowball with such force it smacked into the wall just beside the window of the room where Mo and Mr. Anabin stood. She lingered a moment longer, looking up at Mo, and then turned and ran down the street after the rest of the parade.

When the road was empty again, Mr. Anabin said, "Where are they going?"

Mo said, "I don't know. Wherever they want, I suppose."

"One need not fear about the future of music, I see," Mr. Anabin said. Mo recognized the reference and accepted it as his due. Then, "It is an impressive piece of magic. I will accept your gift."

"I did it for my grandmother," Mo said. "Not for you, even if you were the occasion. My grandmother gave them to the town. I gave her a parade. If they want to, they can come back and be statues again. But there are other places, hidden places, maybe better places. They'll find them. So, anyway, good night. I'm going home."

Mr. Anabin said, "There is the matter of your final assignment first."

"Can it wait?" Mo said. "I'm beat." Though, in fact, he felt fizzy with energy. It seemed the more magic he did, the more alive he felt. He was water again, but the water was magic. He was an entire ocean, all of it power, all of it living magic.

Mr. Anabin said, "You know now what it is that Bogomil and I are looking for."

"Yes," Mo said. "A cup. But it doesn't always look like a cup. When my grandmother had it, it was a coin. But she didn't know what it was. I don't know why you couldn't have explained all of this right at the start."

"It is a cup, sometimes," Mr. Anabin said. "Or a coin. A key. It has many times been a knife, though I hope it will not be again."

"There are a lot of cups in the world," Mo said. "And a lot of knives. And so on. How are we even supposed to know it if we find it?"

"It will make itself known to you," Mr. Anabin said. "As you have acquired magic and used magic, so you have been acquiring the abilities necessary to find and handle Malo Mogge's coin. I did not tell you your purpose because until now there would have been no point."

"And when we find the coin and give it to you," Mo said, "what exactly is going to happen? You return it to her? Malo Mogge powers up? Is that actually a good thing? She may be the only goddess I've met so far, but

I'm guessing she's not anywhere near the top of the curve when it comes to generosity of spirit. Or table manners, or even running with scissors."

"She has closed Lovesend," Mr. Anabin said. "And she will do worse as time goes on. Now that she is so close to having what she desires, she is in a frenzy to acquire it."

"Good luck with your thing, I guess," Mo said. "That's the last assignment? Find Malo Mogge's token?"

"No," Mr. Anabin said. "That is the thing you must do. But listen and I will give you your final task. When you came through the door from Bogomil's realm, I used magic to give you a body. I gave you a history that filled the gap in which you were dead. I gave each of you, as well, a double. A companion made of magic. Just as those around you remember that you went to Ireland and have now come home for Christmas, you yourself remember things about this double that are only invention. What is required of you now is this: that you discover the one whom I made by magic and that, by magic, you send them away. Your doppelgängers are not malevolent, but they are parasitical. They feed on sources of magic. If you do not send your companion away, it will leech upon you until it has drained both magic and life from you. But you are powerful enough now to unmake what I have made."

"So," Mo said slowly. "My assignment is to murder someone who isn't really real but who is real to me?"

"An adequate summary," Mr. Anabin said. "Thank you for my present, Mo. It was very interesting."

The Book of Daniel

Some people he knew from Lewis Latimer were hanging out at a house, pregaming the Cliff Hangar. Daniel figured if he stopped by, said hey, he could see some friends, see what it felt like to inhabit his old life. Maybe he'd feel more like himself.

Ten minutes at the party and he knew he'd made a mistake. Here were Torrey and Margret, both of whom he'd hooked up with in the past at other parties, and so now he had to make small talk, answer questions about Ireland, feeling as if he were the prize in some weird competition they'd decided to have the minute they saw him here. Torrey and Margret hadn't been part of each other's friend group back in high school, but now they were both at Boston University. They'd driven down to Lovesend together for the break. Clearly at some point during the past year, while he'd been dead, they had compared notes.

Everyone wanted to say hi. Everyone was happy to see him. Everyone had—or at least wanted everyone to think they had—cool things going on. And then Barb Gilly, whom he hadn't had a thing with, walked over and punched him in the stomach before he knew she was going to do that. It actually hurt. "I never did that in high school," she said, "but I always wanted to."

So maybe this was why Daniel had come back from the dead, so Barb Gilly finally got to punch him. He ducked out before anyone else decided to punch him. Honestly, he didn't understand much about the person he'd been before he died, except for the way he'd felt about Susannah. So he went to see her.

Susannah's face when she opened the door was pretty much what he expected. It wasn't as if Daniel had never seen this expression on her face. Before she said anything, he said, "I'm sorry."

She crossed her arms over her chest. "For what?"

"For all of everything before," he said. "With Laura. She said something and I guess I wondered if you'd ever said anything about those dreams to her. The Bogomil ones. So I asked her. And then, you know. You know Laura. She doesn't like it when people don't tell her things."

"Yeah, well, I don't like snitches, I don't like Laura," Susannah said, "and I don't like you."

"I know," Daniel said. "I know you don't like me right now. But I also know you love me."

"Who said I love you?" Susannah said. Her expression changed, just a little.

"You did," Daniel said.

Susannah said, "Is that everything?"

"No," Daniel said. "There's a lot of stuff I should tell you. But this is the important part. I love you. And I wish you'd let me come in. There are things I'm supposed to do tonight, but I don't want to do any of them. I just want to see you. I want to be with you while we can be together."

"Before you go back to Ireland," Susannah said.

"Yes," Daniel said.

"Okay, fine," Susannah said. "But you keep showing up here unexpectedly, and I think it means it's only fair if one day I show up in Ireland on your doorstep. Deal?"

Daniel said, "As long as I have a doorstep, you're welcome to show up on it. Deal."

"I made the bed," Susannah said.

LAURA AND RUTH and Mr. Hand came home at some point. He and Susannah heard everyone come stumbling in. Clearly the adult Hands had had a pretty good time. Laura was sheepdogging them, telling her father she'd bring bedding downstairs, coaxing her mom up the stairs.

"Are they gonna get back together?" he asked Susannah.

"Don't know," she said sleepily. "I'm thinking about moving out anyway."

"Where would you go?" Daniel said.

"California," she said. "Or Canada. Someplace starting with a *C*. Community college."

"Really?" he said.

"No," she said. "I don't know. Just someplace. I can't live with Ruth forever. I wish I knew what I wanted to do."

"Laura would be happy to make some suggestions," Daniel said.

"Laura is never happy," Susannah said. "Which makes her suggestions a little dubious."

His arm was under Susannah's neck, his hand falling asleep. He didn't want to move, though. "I was supposed to head out to a birthday party," Daniel said. "But I'd rather stay here."

Susannah said, "Whose? Yours is coming up. What do you want?" Then, startling him, "Go away, Laura. Stop being a creep."

There was an exasperated sigh from outside the door, then Laura moved on down the hallway.

"Your birthday," Susannah said. "Tell me what you want."

"Nothing," Daniel said. "I don't want anything."

"Liar," Susannah said. "What did I give you last year? I keep trying to remember. All I can remember is I was really excited about it. That I got you something I thought for once didn't suck. But if it was something awesome, I would remember it, so it must not have been awesome after all. I didn't give it to you, did I? Maybe I could find it. It has to be around somewhere."

"Maybe it's better if it never turns up," Daniel said.

"Why would you say that?" Susannah said.

"I don't know," Daniel said. "Just, maybe I wouldn't have liked it. And then you would've gotten mad at me because I was being a jerk."

"And then you would have gone off to Ireland and by the time you came back, I would have forgotten why I was ever mad in the first place," Susannah said. She began to hum something.

"That's nice," Daniel said.

Susannah said nothing, only kept humming. He fell asleep. He woke up briefly when Laura came upstairs again and banged around the bathroom. He could almost hear her trying to make up her mind whether or not to open the connecting door. But eventually she turned off the bathroom light and everything got quiet again. Susannah snorted in her sleep as if someone had told a joke.

Daniel got dressed in the dark, but he didn't leave. He had several messages from Laura on his phone. It was now almost one A.M. At some point Mr. Anabin would realize Daniel wasn't coming and something would happen. Daniel lay back down on Susannah's bed and tried not to worry about what that might be.

He did not think he would fall asleep. But the next thing he knew, something sharp was tickling his nose. There was a smell of dirt.

He swatted it away and opened his eyes.

"Daniel," Bogomil said. "Large lump. Boy toy. Were you really asleep? Didn't think to set an alarum? Boys like you never think the rules apply to them. Why is that?"

Daniel fell out of the bed, scrambled across the floor away from Bogomil's sharp fingernails. When he looked over, Susannah was still sleeping.

"Don't worry," Bogomil said. "She won't wake up. She's a wolf right now. Running around in a forest. Maybe once you're back in my realm, I'll let her chase you. She wants to catch something so badly."

"I'm out of the game," Daniel said. "I'm done. Do you haul me back now? Go ahead." But he could hear the tremor in his own voice.

"First things first," Bogomil said, and took Daniel's shoulder in his cold, sharp hand. He flung him forward so Daniel went flying at the bedroom window. Daniel threw out his hands, but instead of hitting the window, he fell into a brightly lit room. Mr. Anabin's music room, and here was Mr. Anabin, Bogomil nowhere to be seen.

"No," Daniel said. "Send me back! He's in her room! Bogomil's in Susannah's room."

Mr. Anabin said, "Susannah is fine. I do believe she will be fine no matter what. Your concern should be for yourself, Daniel."

"How do you know he won't hurt her?" Daniel said. "And I don't care what you do to me. I don't want magic."

Mr. Anabin said, "Brave Daniel. So you have no gift for me?"

Daniel thrust his hand into his pocket. Closed his fingers around a quarter. "Here," he said, and slapped it down on Mr. Anabin's desk.

Mr. Anabin picked it up and turned it over. Looked back up at Daniel. "Acceptable," he said.

"Seriously?" Daniel said.

"If I accept your gift, then I do not have to send you back to Bogomil's realm just yet," Mr. Anabin said. "And believe it or do you not, I have no desire to send you back."

"Send me anyway," Daniel said. "I'm not going to do magic. I accept the consequences, whatever they are."

"It is quite an act of will," Mr. Anabin went on. "To be so full of magic and yet refuse it. The natural inclination of magic is to be used so that by use it may make itself a better channel as water does. And in this place, where Malo Mogge's key has already charged the ground itself, and now Malo Mogge has raised her temple, magic is increasing tenfold. Already your friends are working great feats. They believe they have a talent for magic, but it is both less and more complicated than that. The magic in them desires to be used. If you continue to refuse your magic, eventually it will overrun you. It will undo you to be free of you."

Daniel said, "Then that's what happens."

"Or, instead, this," Mr. Anabin said. He made one of those small, terrifying gestures at Daniel.

"No!" Daniel said. But it was too late. Mr. Anabin's magic caught him up just as it had the first time. His outraged protest became a growl, became a roar. Then it was a bear who stood on its hind legs before Mr. Anabin. It dropped to all fours, shaking its heavy head.

Mr. Anabin said, "This will bind your magic a while. And should you wish your human body back, you may use magic to do so and that will keep you longer. When you are human again, remember this, the final task I set you. When first you returned to life, I made you and I made one other who is bound to you. It has seemed to you that this other, this parasitic double, is a part of your life. But this is false. It is only magic makes them seem so. Discover the thread that ties them to you and sever it. Send them away. You do not want anything to do with magic. This last task should be one you find easy."

The bear moaned.

"Now go," Mr. Anabin said. "It has been a trying day. And I doubt tomorrow will be less trying. Or so has been my experience for quite a long time."

It is no easy thing for a bear who will not do magic to escape a locked school. The main entrance was chained shut. The bear blundered along the ground-floor hallway, testing now and then to see if a door to a classroom would give. At last it found its way into the farthest girls' bathroom, where a smoker (Addy Peart, eleventh grade) who hadn't yet switched over to vaping had broken a latch so she could hold her cigarette out the frosted window.

The bear scrambled up onto the sinks and pushed its long snout out into the night. The window was small and the bear was not, but once its head and one paw were through, it scraped and heaved its whole bulk out. It left behind tufts of fur and long scrapes where its claws had dug in.

Then it was loping down the road, its paws sinking into the snow already marked by the feet of the parade who had passed that way before it.

The Book of Bowie

AND WHAT HAD Bowie given Anabin?
There is a song that Anabin knows and Bogomil knows better. He sings it often down in his realm. Even when Bogomil is singing other songs, he is always singing this one.

Bowie has heard this song many times. He has heard Bogomil sing it, and he has spied, too, upon Anabin as Anabin played it on his piano.

When Susannah took Bowie with her to visit her mother, a memory came to Bowie, a piece of memory, how women sang songs to their infants. Maybe once someone had sung lullabies for Avelot. Someday the infants in the NICU would go home. Or they would not. They would grow up or they would not. The world was full of music either way. But Bowie put the song into the heads of every infant in the NICU. He impressed the pattern into their dreams. They would know the song all their lives without ever knowing how they knew it. One day many years from now, some would have children of their own and they would sing the song to their children, and in this way the song would replicate itself.

Songs are doors, too.

When Bowie had finished telling some part of this to Anabin, Anabin did not say anything for a long time. But Bowie saw his gift had been acceptable.

Finally Anabin said, "I have set a task for the others I could not set for you. They had lives here and you did not. I embroidered upon their lives but you I could not give a companion. I did not know you because you did not know yourself."

"I did not know who I was," Bowie said. "Now I know, but I am not that person now. I do not wish to be."

"Avelot's life was hard," Anabin said. "I know only a little of what she was before she died."

"Avelot knew only a little of herself before she died," Bowie said. "If Thomas kills me, it will not be Avelot he kills, though Bowie is all that remains of Avelot. And half of what is left of Kristofer."

"In my experience," Anabin said, "some people are harder to get rid of than others."

The Book of Laura

Oh, Laura felt brand-new. She was desirable. She had magic. She had power, and she had ideas. Good ideas. Even Malo Mogge had recognized this.

She drove her tipsy parents home in Ruth's car. They sat in the back seat, and there were reminiscences, some giggling. They were suddenly children, Laura the adult. Laura drove carefully, responsibly.

All the way down the Cliff Road, Malo Mogge's ocean temple hung in the car window on the passenger side like a second moon. Or, Laura thought, a casserole dish left to soak in a sink. Her nostrils were full of the smell of something burning, but her parents did not seem concerned.

"Malo Mogge must have done it," Ruth said suddenly.

"Done what?" Laura said. Malo Mogge had done so many things.

"The NICU," Ruth said, "The babies. I bet she healed them all. That would be just like her, don't you think?"

"Sure," Laura said. She didn't really know what her mother was talking about.

"I'll ask her the next time I see her," Ruth said. "Though if she can just do that, I'm going to need to find another job. Everyone is. No need for a union vote if we're all out of work."

Laura said, "Maybe you could just retire. Become my manager. You know, once I'm famous and need a manager." It wasn't how things were going to go, but it was fun to imagine.

"You were incredible tonight," Ruth said. "Just an absolute star. Not that you don't sound amazing ordinarily, but it was different tonight. Just gorgeous and warm and sweet. I don't know why you don't take lead vocals more often. Not that Susannah isn't incredible, too, but she always sounds so murdery."

"Thanks," Laura said, "I guess? You sounded pretty great yourself, by the way. Do you want me to drop you off?" she asked her father.

Ruth said, "He can crash at our house if he wants."

"Or I could just drive him home," Laura said.

But it was decided he would nap on their couch for a few hours until morning came. When he was sober, Laura or Ruth could drive him back to the Cliff Hangar to retrieve his car. Laura looked into the rearview mirror, evaluating her parents' body language.

Ruth, in her slouchy T-shirt and trendy jeans, hair all tousled, wearing the long dangly earrings Laura knew were her special-occasion earrings, looked barely out of high school: a badass with a good ass who liked to party on the weekends. And her father, he looked like the kind of father you could count on, the kind who wore a Fitbit around the house and drank light beer and smoked an occasional joint on Friday, then got up in the morning on weekends and made pancakes. So, basically Peter Lucklow.

Laura tried to catch her father's eye in the mirror, to give him the kind of look that said, You can sleep on the couch, but don't think this means I trust you yet. Don't think any of this means you're back in Ruth's life this fast, this easy. Don't mess with me. Don't mess with us.

Her father's head was back against the headrest, but as if he could feel Laura's glare, he opened his eyes and gave her the sweetest smile. He reached across the middle of the back seat and took his ex-wife's hand. He closed his eyes again. Ruth looked surprised, but she didn't pull her hand away. Laura looked back at the road.

It was all straight out of a fairly chaste romance novel. A Lifetime movie. All of it, except for the goddess and the temple out in the bay and the fact that Laura had been dead just a few days ago. When people complained about romance novels not being realistic, it was usually the romance part they were complaining about and not that the writer failed to capture the true scope of various supernatural complications.

Laura's father had left them once before. Wasn't it likely he would leave again? Perhaps Laura had a suspicious and untrusting nature, but this was no doubt due, in part, to her father. It would be nice to imagine he was an entirely different person now, and clearly he was doing his best to impress his good behavior on everyone, but something about the whole situation was niggling at Laura. It niggled all the way back to the house, where Ruth proved to be even drunker than she'd first seemed. Laura helped her mother navigate the stairs, peel off the jeans, and untangle the earrings. She got Ruth a glass of water and a Tylenol for the morning and set them on the bureau. She tucked Ruth into bed and turned off the lights.

"Make sure your father has sheets and a blanket. Make sure he takes his shoes off. Don't want shoes on the white couch. Nicest couch we've ever had. He never took his shoes off. Never picked up after himself. God. Such an asshole. Why did he have to be so good-looking? And funny. He was always so much fun. He's still a lot of fun. Why'd he have to come back? I can't deal with this right now. Sorry, Laura. I'm drunk. I'm just drunk."

"It's fine," Laura said automatically. "Go to sleep. I'll take care of everything. It's all going to be fine."

"You shouldn't have to take care of everything," Ruth said. "That's my job." But then she was asleep, and Laura went out and closed her mother's bedroom door. She stood outside Susannah's door for a minute, but Susannah said loudly, "Go away, Laura. Stop being a creep."

Laura didn't want to talk with Susannah anyway. She opened up the linen closet to collect some bedding for her father, but all the joy and power and thrill of the night—the karaoke, the bargain she'd made with a goddess, Rosamel, Rosamel, Rosamel—all of it drained out of her at once, seeping into the towels and folded sheets and dark spaces where the women of the Hand family stored various items they didn't need or want but that might still prove useful one day.

Laura shut the closet door.

Her father was already lying down on the white couch, one arm thrown over his eyes. Just as Ruth had feared, his shoes were still on his feet. You could see marks on the end of the couch already. White was such an impractical color. Laura sat down beside him. She shook his shoulder gently. "Hey," she said.

"Hey, sweetie," her father said. "I was just resting my eyes. Pass me the blanket; I don't need sheets. No point in you having to do extra laundry. But I'd take a pillow if you've got a spare."

"I didn't get a blanket," Laura said. "Or a pillow. I thought we could talk some."

Her father sat up. He said, "Of course. What is it?"

"Not here," Laura said. "Maybe out on the porch?"

"Let me get my coat," he said. Laura followed him out.

"Yep," he said. "Still cold." He rubbed his hands together. "So what's up? Everything okay?"

"No," Laura said. There was a lump in her throat, and it made her angry. There was no reason to be sad. "You shouldn't be here. You don't belong here."

Her father said, "Oh, Laura. I understand. Do you want to drive me home, or should I call an Uber?"

"No," Laura said. "You don't understand. You can't understand. You can't understand because you're not real. You were never real. You're a parasite. I can't believe that asshole did this. He made me believe you were real. But you're not. Of course it was you. Of course you never really came back."

"Laura," her father said. He reached out and touched her cheek. Held up his finger and she saw there was glitter on his fingertip.

"Go away," Laura said. "I don't want you here." She could feel the thread now that connected him to her magic and she broke it. It wasn't hard at all. And then she was alone on the porch with all of her anger and with all of her sadness.

The car left in the parking lot of the Cliff Hangar vanished, too, though Laura never even thought to go looking for it. But the scuff marks on the white couch remained. Laura went up the stairs to bed and slept more soundly than she had since she'd come back from the dead.

The Book of Mo

He did not think that this time Mr. Anabin would have given him a ride home. Even if Mo had asked. Anyway, Mo had all sorts of other options. He could have turned himself into a bird to waft up to the Cliffs on his own damn wings. He could have turned himself into a baby elephant or Céline Dion or a hot-air balloon made out of lettuce and diamond dust. Instead he walked, following the prints his grandmother's statues had left upon the snowy road. He admired the empty plinths and plaques that gave evidence that magic was real. That Mo was made of magic. It might be that being made of magic, having magic, mastering magic, was not a good thing. Probably it wasn't. But Mo would let it be a good thing for now. It felt good and Mo needed that. He was trying to ignore something he knew to be true, or rather that he knew to be too good to be true.

This was hard to do when you suddenly realized the person you knew was too good to be true was now walking beside you. Well. Mo decided he would allow himself to enjoy this, too, at least for a little while. It was nice to have company on the way home.

"How was the rest of your night?" he said.

"Not as satisfying as the first part," Thomas said. "I sang for Malo Mogge. She has closed the town. No one may enter or leave now until her key is found."

"Huh," Mo said.

"I saw your friends," Thomas said. "They left the Cliff Hangar unscathed."

"I know," Mo said.

"Avelot was there," Thomas said.

Mo said, "Did you kill her?"

"No," Thomas said. "Though not for lack of trying."

Mo, too, had been trying. But what point was there? Eventually you had to face up to the truth. Of course Thomas hadn't killed Avelot. Bowie. He said, "You couldn't kill Bowie, Avelot, whatever, because they don't exist. They aren't real. You aren't real, either. You're just a magical tapeworm or something."

"I'm a what?" Thomas said.

"Mr. Anabin explained a bunch of stuff," Mo said. "He explained that each of us have a magic-leeching doppelgänger that we've been thinking was a real person. But they're not. I mean, obviously Avelot isn't real. But Laura or Daniel will figure that out, whichever one of them is supposed to. And you're the one I had to figure out. Because if Avelot isn't real, then you aren't real, either. Right? Of course not. You're too good-looking, and you're into me, and also we hooked up five minutes after we met face-to-face. You're all mysterious and vengeful and my grandmother could have written a more believable you with one hand tied behind her back. You even said you liked something I wrote! I am such an idiot."

"Yes," Thomas said. "You really are. You are astonishingly stupid."

"Shut up," Mo said. "I don't care to be insulted by someone who isn't real. God, I wish you were real. But then again, if you were real, it wasn't like this was ever going to work out."

"No," Thomas said. "We would both be very stupid to think that."

"That's what I said," Mo said. "So now I'm supposed to send you away."

"Do you want to send me away?" Thomas said.

"No," Mo admitted. "I don't."

The Cliff Road was getting steeper. Mo stopped because it seemed humiliating to struggle up an icy bike path, out of breath because you were having an argument with your imaginary boyfriend. Here was the block of granite with a plaque on it marking where Ellen Garrison should have stood, the first of the statues Mo had given life to. Mo brushed snow off the plinth and hoisted himself onto it. Thomas stood at the base. He rested his hand on Mo's calf lightly. "You could kiss me one more time," he said. "Before you send me away."

"I could," Mo said. "But I won't." But he bent down and did it anyway. He meant it to be a polite and valetudinarian kind of kiss, but nevertheless it went on.

Finally Mo drew back. "Goodbye, Thomas."

How magic worked was, he thought, an intuitive process. There also needed to be willpower and focus, both of which Mo had always assumed he possessed a good amount of. But maybe anyone could do magic if they had enough of it, *it* being magic. Animating the statuary, bringing them to life, had been a thing he had wanted to do because he had to do something and he'd wanted it to be impressive. He'd stood in front of the statue of Ellen Garrison and thought about his grandmother. He'd thought of how she'd brought her heroines to life in her novels in an entirely different way. He'd thought of the kind of steadfast purpose his grandmother had always demonstrated, even when the circumstances of her life were difficult, unpleasant, even fucking tragic. Maybe Mo's view of her was lopsided or starry-eyed or just incomplete, but whatever faults she might have had, she'd been kind and loving and accepting and she'd gotten shit done no matter what. He thought of what it had been like to be water, how water moved. He took all of that and poured it into Ellen Garrison until she came to life. The next nearest statue had been Marsha P. Johnson, and Mo poured magic down through her, from her flower crown that would never wilt to those sensible shoes. Next was Fanny Jackson Coppin, her statue so small Johnson extended her palm and then lifted Coppin to her shoulder to sit so she would not disappear beneath the drifts of snow. Then Sissieretta Jones, who had sung at the White House four times, though she had only been allowed to pass through the front door once. *Ad libitum,* Mo told her. Mo expanded his magic, his will, his purpose, until he had felt it coursing through the town of Lovesend, flowing around and up and into every piece of sculpture that had been part of his grandmother's favorite side project. He gave the statues all the love he'd felt for her, all of his admiration. He gave them joy and freedom. His grief and his guilt that he'd left her—no matter that leaving her hadn't been his intention or his choice—he kept.

To send away Thomas shouldn't have been harder. He tried to feel how Thomas was made. How he could be unmade.

"Ow," Thomas said. "Stop that."

"Sorry," Mo said. He was extremely tired. He'd done half the assignment. He could do the rest later. Or maybe simply telling Thomas goodbye, leaving him, would break whatever bond was supposed to join them. He was definitely too tired to walk the rest of the way home, so he changed himself into an eastern red bat.

Goodbye, Thomas. You were too good to be true. Vincents were what you got in the real world. Real life was an all-you-can-eat buffet of Vincents. That was why his grandmother had stuck with novels when she gave up on men.

The Book of Daniel

WHILE THE BEAR was trapped in the school, its only thought had been to escape the presence of Anabin. Once it put enough distance between itself and Lewis Latimer it sat down on its haunches on the sidewalk outside What Hast Thou Ground? and took stock.

It was late, which meant that currently no one should be around to be startled by seeing a bear on the streets of Lovesend. Just as the bear was thinking this, a snowplow came around a corner. The bear flattened itself against the side of the building.

Once the snowplow was far along, the bear went padding down the cleared road until it came to the small park marking the turn home. Magic fizzed furiously around in its bulk. The bear did not care for what had been done to it. It was agitated and afraid and not used to being a bear. It was stuffed full of its own magic that, as Anabin had said, wished to be put to use. The bear could be Daniel again if it chose. But what was Daniel? A tool for Anabin and Bogomil to use. The bear and Daniel were united in their desire to avoid this scenario. On other subjects they were divided.

For one thing, the bear was very hungry. Bears are usually hungry to begin with, and magic amplified this hunger. The part of the bear's mind that was bear and not Daniel was ravenous and red. The bear wished, secondarily, to find a place far from humans. Once it had eaten something or someone.

Eventually Daniel and the bear agreed they would go down to the marshlands beside Little Moon Bay. There would be frogs down in the mud under the ice or perhaps raccoons or birds' nests. There might be fish.

Daniel knew all the ways to Little Moon Bay. The way he knew best was the one that led down past his house, and this was the way the bear went. Bears have their own cunning, but Daniel was cunning, too. He could not go home, but he wished at least to come as near his home as might be safe. And although the magic that animated Daniel and the bear had no cunning of its own, it pulled at both of them. It pulled so strongly the bear came slowly, reluctantly, up the driveway of Daniel's house. Daniel was not unwilling. He told himself he would stay there in the yard for a little while before he went on. He told himself homesickness, heartsickness, explained the pull, the impetus that drew him closer and closer to his family.

Bears do not have good eyesight, though there was a smell that troubled the bear. It drew very near the house before it knew who stood there on the porch. When it did, it turned to flee, but a voice summoned it back.

"Well," Bogomil said. "Who do we have here?"

The bear stretched up to its full height and snarled.

"Enough of that," Bogomil said. "Sit down." The bear sat down on the lawn. It had no choice. "Who did this to you? Malo Mogge? No. Anabin. He's giving you extra tutoring, is he? Some teachers go the extra mile. If it had been me, I would have made you a beetle. Or a shrew. You might learn more from being just a little smaller. What exactly is he hoping to achieve? Yes, I see. He wants you to take up the reins of your magic. What a stubborn and irritating piece of furniture you are. What Susannah likes about you I have never understood."

The bear sat and endured the lecture, imagining what Bogomil's flesh might taste like. Twice in one day, Daniel thought. Two lectures in one day. Three if you counted Laura.

Bogomil said to the bear, "Anabin has his reasons, no doubt. But his methods are squeamish. I can feel how hungry you are. Why don't you go inside? Here. I'll open the door for you."

Once again the bear found it must do as Bogomil said. It went through the front door and Bogomil patted it on its furry rump. He said, "Good bear. Now don't leave your house until you take human shape again. Or, I suppose, until they all wake up like Goldilocks."

The bear snarled again.

"Precisely!" Bogomil said. He sounded delighted. "Let's up the stakes, shall we? You must be extremely hungry. Magic does that. And you are a bear, after all. Why don't you poke around? Find yourself someone to eat? Be a person or eat one. Up to you."

Then he shut the door to the house and left the bear inside.

The Book of Mo

He didn't really want to be himself again; nevertheless Mo changed back under the shelter of his porch and discovered he was barefoot. Somehow he had lost his Timberlands and his socks. He checked, but his phone was still in his pocket. He had his keys, too. He really didn't understand how magic worked at all, and he didn't think he cared enough to try to understand. He was still figuring out music. One thing didn't leave much time for the other. John Cage had written, *The principle of form will be our only constant connection with the past.* That was something Mo was interested in. And now he had been the ocean, so maybe he had a different understanding of form than he'd had before. The ocean hadn't been interested in thinking about John Cage, for one thing. There was that.

Music, magic, either one was preferable to thinking about Thomas.

The house was quiet in a way Mo was not sure he'd ever experienced. Maybe it was the absence of Thomas, or maybe it was the thought of the abandoned plinths and friezes all over Lovesend. Here, too, lay abandoned all the unlit rooms of his grandmother's home, the spaces full of books and art and mugs and bright carpets his grandmother had taken such delight in, had carefully chosen so that she might do so.

Should Mo go on living, he would make his own choices. He would have money and time. He had friends. Right now he had magic, too. Why did none of these things feel sufficient? He didn't bother to turn on the overhead lights when he got to the kitchen but instead opened the refrigerator and found leftover sesame noodles. He poured himself a glass of water, opened a drawer, and got a fork.

He turned to take everything over to the kitchen table and almost dropped it all. Someone was sitting there already.

"Fuck!" Mo said. Then, "Jenny?"

She said, "Mo? What time is it?"

"Were you waiting up for me?" Mo said. He turned on the lights.

"What time is it?" she repeated. She wore a fluffy purple robe over another concert T-shirt. MANILOW LAS VEGAS: THE HITS COME HOME!

"I don't know," Mo said. "Late. Sorry."

"Next time text me," she said. "Everything okay?"

"Yes," Mo said. "No. Not really."

"Want company?" she said.

Mo set the container down on the table. "It's fine, go to bed. Get some sleep."

"You sure?" When Mo nodded, she said, "Don't worry about cleaning up. I'll do that in the morning."

"Thanks, Jenny," Mo said. "Good night."

"Good night, Mo," she said. She got up from her chair and gave him a hug. "Love you, kid."

He said, "Love you, too, Jenny," and for a moment he could not remember if he had ever said this to her before. It seemed important. He was just so very, very tired. As she left the room, Mo looked at her. He really looked at her.

He saw how she was made, not of flesh and bone and blood but of filaments of magic. Pretty Jenny Ping with her Slurpee-colored hair, who loved Barry Manilow, who made delicious food and sang and gave him well-intentioned advice, who had kept him company for many days in his grandmother's empty house.

"Oh," he said. "No." He saw the vertiginous strand that trailed from her wrist, tethering her to his left side. He felt how magic pulsed along it.

"Mo?" Jenny said. She came slowly toward him until he could see the worried crease between her eyes. The crease was magic and so, too, was the concern. None of it was real. "What is it?"

"No," Mo said again, and this time it wasn't only a word. Jenny was magic, but the single syllable Mo spoke was magic, too, and as small as it was, it poured over her in a wave, undoing every part.

Jenny was there in the hallway and then she wasn't. Mo stood holding in his hands a container full of sesame noodles prepared for him by a person who had never really existed. He threw it as hard as he could at the place where she had stood. It hit the doorframe, and noodles and shards of glass went everywhere. Mo sat down on the floor and put his head in his hands. The sun was rising in the kitchen windows before he got to his feet and went to clean up the mess he had made. There was no one else there to do it.

The Book of Thomas

The night had not, in any way, gone as he had expected. He was not sure exactly what he'd expected. Perhaps it was simply that, for so long, nothing much had seemed to happen that mattered in any real way. He had been the creature of Malo Mogge. He had desired the death of Avelot. He had had life. Too much life, by turns interesting, bloody, unpleasant, pleasurable, painful, and tedious in patterns that he found, after some centuries in the company of Malo Mogge, he could predict. Perhaps he had begun to believe Malo Mogge's key would never be found. That Avelot would always elude. That he would go on down the centuries in the service of Malo Mogge until one day she broke their bargain because of some carelessness or miscalculation on his part and took back the life she had given him.

Then they had come to Lovesend, this inconsequential place, and Avelot had been here, and here, too, was the thing Malo Mogge had been in search of all this time, tramping up and down the earth, Thomas dragged along in her wake. In this place, in the span of only a few days, he had found Avelot and tried to kill her. He had disobeyed Malo Mogge, threatened to leave her service, and in the end made his bargain again. He had kept a secret from her. He had dallied with Mo. He had been broken up with. Mo, again. It should have seemed a fine and delicious joke, except that all the fine gloss Thomas had lacquered himself in seemed rubbed away. Underneath, it turned out he was as raw and tender as he had been all those centuries ago.

If Mo had asked, Thomas would have told him about his doppelgänger. He'd almost told him earlier. Malo Mogge sometimes constructed creatures of that sort in the games she played with mortals, but her stamp had not been on Mo's companion. There had been no malice in what Mo's Jenny was made of.

To be sent away by Mo was vexing. Thomas had thought that the first time, and now it had happened again. Perhaps when Mo realized his mistake, he would grovel. Perhaps he would beg Thomas to come back. Thomas thought he would accept even the most basic text from Mo admitting the magnitude of his fuckup. He thought if Mo were to summon him, he might go. Just to see what Mo was like when he apologized. It had been quite some time since anyone had had occasion to beg pardon of Thomas except when they were in fear for their life.

"What do you think?" Malo Mogge said. She wore black silk pajamas and a pair of scabrous flamingo-pink wings, molting and stained with something sticky that by the smell was rum. "Should the conversation pit go here or over by the windows?"

They were back at the Cliff Hangar, which Malo Mogge had decided she would like to live in. The lawyers' house, down beside the sea, was no longer habitable. Thomas did not know exactly what had happened, only that there was a great deal of blood, most contained in the claw-foot tub in the master bedroom, but a fair quantity, too, splashed around on the walls and drying on the hardwood floor and stairs. It seemed to his knowledgeable eye significantly more than the amount of blood two bodies might contain.

Malo Mogge had sent most of the Cliff Hangar's interior fixtures away and was refurbishing it in the style of a house in Malibu they had temporarily squatted in during the 1960s. It was a place Thomas remembered well, though he wished he did not.

Thomas said, "I have no preference. Besides, in the end you will do as you like."

"I shall," Malo Mogge said. "But why so petulant, my Thomas? I thought we were friends again."

Thomas said nothing. There was still a man sleeping on the floor of the carousel. If Malo Mogge wanted conversation, she could wake him up.

"Maybe a daybed over by the windows. Something to recline on while we take in the view. You haven't said anything about my temple, Thomas."

He turned, looked out the French windows, pretended he was seeing it for the first time. "Very nice. Is it new?"

"No," Malo Mogge said. She looked over at it with a fond expression, the way you would look at a favorite mug you'd finally located in a misplaced moving box after you'd spent years thinking it had been lost. "It's actually very old."

"My mistake," Thomas said. "I have no objection to a daybed."

"How boring you are," Malo Mogge said with affection. She was in an excellent mood. "How shall we entertain ourselves?"

"A flat-screen television?" Thomas said. "Or a PlayStation?"

Malo Mogge said, "I wasn't thinking of anything quite so domestic. I was thinking of a hunt. For example, you and I might go hunting Avelot."

"Both of us?" Thomas asked.

"Why not?" Malo Mogge said.

"Because I am to be the one to kill her," Thomas said. "That was our arrangement."

"Yes, yes," Malo Mogge said. "And clearly you are going to sulk until the thing is accomplished. So let us accomplish it together."

"I will do it myself," Thomas said.

"Yes," Malo Mogge said. "That is how you wish it to be, but surely you must know the matter is not settled as easily as that. You are old and strong, but she is just as old and I suspect even more full of magic than you are. Otherwise she would already be dead."

"Perhaps," Thomas said. "But according to the terms of our deal, I am the one who gets to kill her. I worry you are under a misapprehension that you killing her would be just as good. But you don't have my reasons, and so neither would you have my satisfaction. You only wish to kill Avelot for sport."

"If not for her, I imagine my key would have returned to me long ago," Malo Mogge said. Her tone was mild, but Thomas saw that the feathers on her wings were beginning to fluff themselves. "She is the reason why I may not rid myself of the traitor Bogomil. She brought harm to you and your brother, Thomas, but she *diminished* me. She closed the door against me."

"We have a bargain," Thomas said. "I serve you. If you wish her dead, then by killing her, I will serve you still."

"True," Malo Mogge said. "But I worry for you, Thomas. She might do you greater harm than she already has. Let me at least find her for you. Let me be *your* servant in this."

Thomas said, "That is more than I could have hoped for." There wasn't any other answer he could have given.

"Most wise," Malo Mogge said. "Moreover, I will give you a weapon, Thomas, because of my great love for you."

She pulled a knife out of the air. It was small and heavy looking, of some dull metal Thomas did not recognize. The hilt and the blade were all one piece, and the hilt fit perfectly in Malo Mogge's hand. She said, "I had another knife once. When I have it back, you will see me do such things! The streets will run red for days." She pressed the palm of her empty hand against her own side, and then before Thomas knew what she was going to do, she had stuck the knife into herself, just above where she held her side. She grunted, though her face remained pleasant. She cut deeper, angling the blade up.

"What are you doing?" Thomas said. In all the long years of his service, he had seen many things but never this.

Malo Mogge slid the knife out, blood pouring over both it and her hand. She stuck the fingers of her other hand into the wound she had given herself and jerked. When she pulled her fingers out again, she was holding a bloody piece of bone.

Thomas saw she was holding her smallest rib.

"There!" she said. "That was even less fun than I had remembered." She ran the back of the hand holding the knife down her side, and although wetness continued to seep through her pajama top, blood trickling out the leg of her left pajama bottom and onto the floor, Thomas knew she had healed her wound. She wiped her hands against her wings, dark clots sticking to the pink feathers, the rich smell of her blood mixing with the smell of rum.

"You think I do not value you," she said. "But I do. I do love you, Thomas, though you have not always deserved it. Right now you believe the reason you have stayed with me is because I will give you your vengeance. But, oh, Thomas, soon there will be so much more I will be able to give you."

"There is nothing I need beyond Avelot's death," Thomas said.

"Oh, but listen! Bogomil intended you and your brother to be servants," Malo Mogge said. "To serve the purpose he and Anabin perform. He meant to take my place, make you keep his door with your brother. That was treachery. But Bogomil was not mistaken in your worthiness. When the key is found again, I will raise you up as he once promised to do. I have offered the other side of the door to the girl Laura. I believe she has promise. But if you preferred it, Mo would do as well. You and he could serve together. You care for him, I think."

"He does not care for me," Thomas said. He said this lightly.

"No one cares for you as much as I do," Malo Mogge said. "But I could make him care for you."

She, too, spoke lightly, but Thomas could see how she watched him. She was testing the place where he might be vulnerable. Or perhaps her offer to make Mo love him was sincere. Both these things were terrible. But someone who had just casually removed one of her own ribs was not someone you could trust to measure what was reasonable or good. Thomas, of course, could not be trusted, either. He knew that.

He said, "What are you planning to do with that, anyway?"

Malo Mogge turned the rib over in her hand, pinching it between her fingers so it grew thinner, smaller, giving it a keen edge near the point where she'd broken it off. She said, "Once, a long time ago, I fashioned part of myself into a key. That is the key Bogomil lost me. I will have that back again soon, I know, and all my power returned with it. I have been hungry for so very long, and that hunger has made me weak. Once, I feasted as I chose, and, oh, soon I will feast again. You have not known me in my full power, Thomas. But you will."

She held out her rib. "This is a much smaller portion of my power, but it is all I have to spare and I believe you will discover it suffices to kill one such as Avelot easily enough. Since you will not let me deal the blow myself, let me give you this."

When Thomas took it from her, he found it was still warm. It had a point on one end narrow as a needle. He tested the point on his finger and felt the power coursing through it. Every hair on his body was standing up.

"Safeguard this," she said. "The cost to me to make it is not small. Use it and even the slightest wound you deal will be grievous. Strike true, and it is her end."

"I did not ask you for this," Thomas said. "But I thank you."

She inclined her head. "Think on the matter of what I am offering. Think on the matter of your friend. Think on my love for you and all that you and I owe each other after so many years of faithful friendship. And while you think, let us see if we can discover where Avelot is hiding."

Thomas slipped the rib into the back pocket of his jeans. As he did so, he felt his phone vibrate, and when he pulled it out, he saw that Mo was texting him.

I'm an idiot. A real and true idiot.

A second text quickly followed. Why didn't you say anything though and then I'm sorry I'm so sorry so so sorry please

Malo Mogge was watching with a cold eye. "Do you need to take that?" she said.

Thomas said, "No." Before another text could arrive, he blocked Mo's number.

The Book of Daniel

Daniel took up more than his fair share of space as a human, but the bulk of the bear filled the kitchen. The bear shambled past the breakfast table, shoving it toward the refrigerator. A glass with an inch of milk still in it fell over but didn't break. It rolled off the table, across the back of the bear, and onto the floor. The bear lapped up the milk.

There were many stinks, and the bear could not make up its mind which to investigate first. Daniel could not think what to do. The three parts of him were at war. His magic was bubbling up in him, telling him how easy it would be to become himself again. The bear told him there was half a piece of pizza buried under the cushion of the old blue chair. While Daniel tried to think, the bear dug its snout under the chair cushion.

There was no place in the Lucklows' house where a bear could hide. Furthermore, the bear did not wish to hide. It was very hungry. Half a piece of pizza, an inch of milk, would not do. It went rooting around in the mind it shared with Daniel much as it had the seat cushion and was astonished at how many siblings he could lay claim to. Surely, the bear asked, Daniel could spare at least one? It did not have to be a very large one.

Fuck you, Daniel told the bear, but as Bogomil had said, the bear was ravenous. And Bogomil had told the bear to eat. Sorry, the bear said. If you don't pick, then I guess I will. Use me, his magic said. Before it's too late. Daniel argued with both as the bear went up the stairs and along the hallway, snuffling along the floor where someone had dropped a handful of Cheerios. The bear was imagining a small head, the right size to fit inside a pair of jaws. The crunch, the satisfying way bone split, the weight and savor of dangling meat below.

The bear paused in front of the first door. It put its snout to the door, snuffling. Then continued to the next, which it tested, too. It wasn't as if the bear couldn't have broken down a door. But that would have woken the rest of the house, and the bear was cunning as well as hopeful. The next door was Daniel's bedroom, and it was open just the slightest crack.

Aha! the bear said, and Daniel said, That's my room, asshole. There's nobody in there.

Really? the bear said. What about Davey? I think I hear him.

No! Daniel told the bear. We can go back to the kitchen. We'll raid the refrigerator. There's all kinds of stuff. The bear ignored him. It began to gather up the magic Daniel refused to use. It planned to bind Daniel with this magic. It had no intention of becoming human again, and eating someone would mean Daniel had even less reason to do so. It will be better this way, it told Daniel. You'll see. First a snack and then we'll blow this joint.

The bear pushed into Daniel's bedroom, leaned back to close the door. The room was darker than the hallway outside, and neither the bear nor Daniel could see anything, but the bear didn't mind. Two ropes of saliva hung from its jaws. It moved forward until its head butted the bed. It laid one front paw and then the other on the mattress.

"Daniel?" Susannah said from under the comforter. She sounded only half-awake. "Is that you? You reek."

The bear snorted in surprise.

"Stop fooling around, dumbass," Susannah said. "Come to bed, go to sleep. It's late."

Without understanding why it did so, the bear lay down beside Susannah, who was already asleep again. It closed its eyes, despite its hunger. Let it sleep, Daniel thought. I'll stay awake and keep it from doing harm. But as the bear fell asleep, so did Daniel. After all, they were the same. For a span of time, a girl and a bear slept restlessly in a rumpled bed. And in the morning when the sun came up, Daniel woke up to find Susannah's arms around him. She was kissing his ear. He was human again.

The Book of Bowie

High in a stolen nest in a fir tree, Bowie was sifting through Avelot's memories. How vivid these were, and yet how little sense he could make of them. A jet bead dangling from a string, keyhole black. A dry fountain in a public square, a woman picking up her skirts to dance in the dust. He did not remember who she was.

A meal, porridge in a wooden bowl, a child waiting to eat, the porridge cold and skinned with blue. He did not know what she waited for.

The girl child, again, standing beside a woman in an empty room. The smell of shit and sickness. Bowie thought the room had not belonged to either Avelot or the woman. The woman opened a wardrobe where a white dress hung like the moon on a peg. The girl reached out her hand to the dress and moths rose in a frenzy from it, landing on her face, her arms. The girl screaming. The woman slapped her. The medicinal powder of a crushed moth on her lips. The blue dress, in its cloak of white moths, who had eaten it to pieces. Poor dress. Poor moths.

Bowie remembered Kristofer. Kristofer had loved Avelot. He said it often. Only to herself did Avelot ever admit this: that she did not believe love was real. But certainly Kristofer wished to believe what he felt was returned. He had been intermittently satisfied by her pretense of it. And she had felt fondness for him. Only sometimes irritation. She had not meant him harm. It was just that she had not always been kind. She had had so few opportunities to practice kindness. And Kristofer, too, was not always kind. His love was the dramatic sort, with acts of generosity and then storms of jealousy and weeping and accusations. Kristofer should not have fallen in love with a whore. Avelot had not deserved what he felt for her, but she had not asked for it, either.

Thomas, though, Thomas had been unfailingly kind in Avelot's memories. He teased the whores as if they had been his sisters. He played songs for them and cajoled his brother out of his bad moods. He brought Avelot sweets and a peacock's feather and never once had he asked anything of her. If love were something tangible that could be proved or weighed, Bowie might have suspected there had been in Avelot a grain or two of love for Thomas. Her love had not been one that had required anything of her, though, so could it really have been love?

Avelot had valued Thomas for his kindness. She'd had so little of it. Bowie, too, longed for it. Susannah's mother, Ruth, with the baby. How gentle she'd been, and how trusting when she'd given the baby into Bowie's care. Bowie thought he would like to be kind, too. He'd been merciful to Susannah. He had not killed her. But mercy was not the same thing as kindness. As gentleness.

The Thomas of this place and this time was greatly translated. All of his kindness and good humor stripped from him in Malo Mogge's service. One whore recognizes another.

Had Bogomil succeeded in his scheme and made Thomas and Kristofer the guardians of Malo Mogge's door in place of Anabin and himself, Thomas would have had Kristofer for company, but the brothers would be, then, the servants of Bogomil or Malo Mogge. Kristofer would have changed and changed until he was as strange and inhuman as Thomas. As Bowie was. Bogomil and Anabin hated each other. Would this not have happened to the brothers, too?

Though there could be delight in change. Bowie found this so. In the nest Bowie became a gull, a toad, a coiling snake, a beetle the color of an emerald. Avelot had been fixed in her place as if with a pin, even before she fell into Bogomil's realm. Bowie was free, might be whoever or whatever he chose. A boy, a girl, a starling, a fox kit.

When the key was found, Bogomil, no doubt, would make some last throw against Malo Mogge. Bowie thought it unlikely he would succeed. Bogomil had lost the element of surprise.

Laura would end up a guardian, keeping one side of the door. Daniel would not. That left Mo or Bowie to make the other guardian. Were

Bowie to become doorkeeper then Thomas could not slay him. As Avelot had escaped Bogomil's realm, Bowie could escape Thomas. But to keep the door was to lose all chance of any other life. Bowie did not know what kind of life he wanted. He thought he would like to learn how to be kind. What grew from kindness. He wished, too, to remain free. To be as he chose, for as long as he chose it, and then to freely change again.

Perhaps he might yet escape both Thomas and the role of guardian.

He thought of the wardrobe again, how the moths escaped when the door was opened. How afraid Avelot had been of them. Bowie wished he could tell her to rejoice instead. They had been born in transformative darkness, eaten their fill of beauty in their teeming company, and then they had been freed.

The bird shape Bowie had taken should have been watchful. But the night was cold and in its nest the bird had begun to think ravenously of moths when a voice said, "Here she is! See, Thomas, I have found her for you."

There was a crack, then, and the tree split at its base. Half fell to the ground. The half where Bowie hid on his branch shivered. He flew out as another blow struck the tree.

"I see it." That was Thomas, something in his hand.

Thomas threw. Bowie fell like a stone. As he hit the ground, he became a fox and began to flee again. Hot blood streamed down his shoulder and spattered the snow as he went. Something was stuck in the meat there.

"Well done," he heard Malo Mogge say. "You have wounded your enemy. Now hunt her down. Bring me back my rib."

Bowie ran and something came after. He did not look to see what shape Thomas had taken. He ran on.

The Book of Mo

"Oh, fuck you!" Mo said when he saw that Thomas still had not replied to his texts. "It was an honest mistake!"

He was keenly aware he was yelling like a crazy person in an empty house. But there was no one he could talk to. He'd texted Rosamel, he'd even tried calling her, but Rosamel slept like the dead. She'd get his weird texts in the morning, and then what? It wasn't like he would explain any of this to her. He used his magic to delete his message and the texts.

Once he'd mopped up the noodles, he'd gone, against his better judgment, to investigate the bedroom that had belonged to Jenny. The bed was made, and in one of the bureau drawers there was a neat stack of T-shirts, three of them apparently acquired at Barry Manilow concerts. These all were faded from use. But there were no other clothes in the drawers. Nothing hung in the closet. There were no toiletries in the bathroom. Not even a toothbrush.

He sat on the bed and examined both of the pillows up close. He thought he could detect the smell of the shampoo he was pretty sure Jenny had used. It was a familiar smell. He found three purple hairs. In the nightstand drawer, there was something squishy but also firm.

It was a small vibrator. "Ugh!" Mo said, and dropped it on the floor. He didn't know for sure that it belonged to Jenny Ping, but the color made him suspect it had. It was purple striped with white.

None of this made sense. Jenny had not been real. It made him think again about his Timberlands. Where had they gone? Why were Jenny's

T-shirts still here? Mr. Anabin had a lot of nerve pretending he was teaching anyone magic when what he was really doing was just fucking with them. A vibrator but no toothbrush. Really?

How could someone who wasn't real have been so kind? Or should that have been a giveaway? Real people were, by and large, jerks at least some of the time. How could Mo miss someone who wasn't real?

"Come back," he said experimentally.

No one answered him. Perhaps he hadn't said it loud enough. This time he screamed it. "Come back!"

He left the room that had not been Jenny's and went down the hallway screaming. "Come back! Come back! Come back! Come back!"

Jenny Ping did not come back. His grandmother did not come back. His mother did not come back. Thomas was not going to come back and, anyway, Mo didn't want him to.

"I came back," Mo said to the music studio when he climbed the stairs to see if anyone was there. "If I came back, then they could, too. If they can't come back, then why did I?"

He returned to the kitchen, where he ate the last four brownies from the batch Jenny had made the day before.

He thought about calling Natalie or Theo. But what he wanted was someone who would understand, even if they didn't understand. He wanted someone who was in the middle of things even if they didn't know the middle of things was where they were.

A text appeared on his phone. Rosamel. Call me when you're up.

He ignored this and texted Susannah. Everything is terrible and my life is falling apart, he wrote. Come by the house when you wake up. Please come

He put the phone down on the counter, then picked it up again.

If you want

The Book of Susannah

IN THE MORNING Susannah could not remember why she was in Daniel's bed.

She'd fallen asleep in her own bed. Daniel had been asleep beside her. And then, at some point, a conversation had woken her. Daniel's voice and someone else's. But this must have been a dream because the other person had been Bogomil, and she was the only other person in her room. It was almost two A.M. and Daniel had left while she was asleep. It wasn't very polite of him. She decided to go find him and tell him so.

She put on long johns and a sweatshirt, slipped on her old Keds. Grabbed her phone off her nightstand.

Outside it was still snowing. The night sky had an eggshell luster, heavy with the snow that was still to fall. There was a burnt taste to the air. Her Keds sank into the snow and her feet quickly grew wet. The cold numbed the place on her heel where the splinter was. Why did she keep forgetting to pull it out?

She had a sudden memory of sitting on the counter in the kitchen while her father used tweezers to take a splinter out of her palm. How old was she? Four, maybe. He'd held her arm down against her side. He hadn't been hurting her, but she'd been frantic to escape. She'd hit him, hadn't she? He'd gotten a black eye and she'd jumped off the counter and run away. Now Susannah didn't even remember how they'd gotten the splinter out. Maybe they never had. Maybe this was the same fucking splinter.

It wasn't exactly kosher to take the key the Lucklows kept under their fake rock and let herself into their house. But she'd done it in the past. And she wasn't there to do anything bad. She was just there to yell at Daniel.

But when she opened his bedroom door, he wasn't there. She didn't feel like sneaking back out of the house or sleeping in her own bed and so she lay down on Daniel's.

She fell asleep then and at some point Daniel came home. Now it was dawn and Daniel was sleeping beside her once more. She decided yelling at him could wait a little longer. Makeup sex didn't always have to come second. Sometimes you could even skip the yelling and go straight to the sex, especially when the other person never even knew you'd been mad in the first place.

Daniel appeared surprised at first, as if he hadn't realized until now that there was a girl in his bed. Then he was into it with a kind of enthusiasm that suggested he really liked surprises. Not that in the usual order of things Daniel lacked enthusiasm. It was surprises Daniel usually wasn't keen on.

Afterward, Susannah couldn't stop smiling. "We should fight more often," she said.

Daniel gave her a sideways look. "Were we having a fight?" he said.

"Yes," Susannah said. "But I forgot to tell you. Know what's better than karaoke?"

"What?" Daniel said.

"Fighting," Susannah said. "Also sex."

"What would you have sung at the Cliff Hangar if we'd gone?" Daniel said. "If you were singing for me?"

Susannah said, "I would have picked Elton John. 'Daniel.'"

"The obvious choice," Daniel said. "So very obvious." But he was smiling.

Susannah said, "But when it started I would have just started screaming. And kept on screaming."

"So the usual," Daniel said.

"Yeah," Susannah said. "Why mess with a good thing? Want to come to What Hast Thou Ground? with me? I'll make you a fancy coffee."

"It's Wednesday," Daniel said. "Billy doesn't open until noon on Wednesdays."

He held up his hand, examining it. Susannah watched, bemused. He touched his nose, then his ears. Lifted up the sheet and appeared to be checking to make sure that his dick was still there, which of course it was.

"Any place is open if you've got the keys," Susannah said. "I've got keys. Come on. Besides, Billy gets there early, and he'd love to see you." This was true. Billy hated people, but he loved Daniel.

She checked her phone, saw Mo had texted her.

"What?" Daniel said.

"Mo," she said. "Something's up."

"With Mo? What?" Daniel said. "Does he say?"

"Don't know," Susannah said. "Gonna go find out."

"Tell him to come to the coffee shop," Daniel said. "I'll go with you."

"You guys don't even like each other," Susannah objected, texting. She didn't know if Daniel coming along was a good idea. "Unless you became friends in Ireland or something."

"No," Daniel said. "I don't know. Hold up. I'm coming, too."

"Maybe I should just go," Susannah said. "You could come later. It's just, Mo and I haven't seen each other in a while."

"I could walk you into town," Daniel said. "Unless you're sick of me."

"Clingy," Susannah said. "But okay."

Lissy and Carousel were in the kitchen eating Pop-Tarts. They looked at Susannah, then at Daniel.

"Hey, guys," Susannah said. "Just came over this morning to help Daniel out with something."

"Help him out with what?" Lissy asked.

Susannah said, "Oh, you know. Just something. Something really cool." She couldn't think of anything, though. She waited for Daniel to help her out.

But Daniel was staring at his sisters. He looked as if he were suddenly sick to his stomach.

"You okay?" Susannah said.

"I'm fine," he said. "You go. Tell Mo hey. I'll see you later."

"You sure?" Susannah said.

Daniel nodded.

"Someone made a mess in the kitchen last night," Lissy said. "We cleaned it all up."

"It wasn't me," Susannah said, because she really hadn't. Then she wished she hadn't said anything.

Lissy gave her a knowing look. Carousel just went on eating her Pop-Tart.

Susannah would have kissed Daniel goodbye before she left if they hadn't had an audience. He really did not look good. Clearly whatever was going on with him was still going on. Eventually he would come clean, but that was not going to happen in front of his sisters.

She ducked into her house and put on more weather-appropriate clothes. There were black scuffs on one end of the white couch. She was probably going to get blamed for that as well when Ruth saw it. She got a Post-it note from the kitchen and wrote SUSANNAH DIDN'T DO THIS on it. Stuck it beside the scuffs.

When she checked her phone, Mo had texted back. He was on his way.

The Book of Laura

She woke up early with a sensation that something was about to happen. What exactly, she wasn't sure. The discovery of Malo Mogge's missing key. The answer to the mystery of how she'd died.

She had a song in her head. What was it? Halestorm, "I Miss the Misery."

Her two new guitars were leaning against the wall by the closet. She took the Gretsch downstairs with her because that was pretty fucking cool. She had a Gretsch. Perhaps she'd magically shrink it and carry it around in her pocket all day. She made herself coffee in the French press with the busted top that she and Susannah had liberated from What Hast Thou Ground? and sat on the couch goofing around on the unplugged Gretsch while she drank it.

Here was a scuff mark made by a man who hadn't existed. (Susannah's Post-it note she read and then crumpled up.) Mo and Daniel must be trying to figure out the same thing. Who wasn't real. And Laura didn't even know what Daniel had given Mr. Anabin. She was pretty sure he and Susannah were still asleep in Susannah's bed. When they came down, she'd get Daniel alone. Check in, find out what he'd given Mr. Anabin. See if he was finally using his magic.

She took out her phone. Thought about texting Rosamel, decided that this was a bad idea, then texted her anyway. What was the point of being able to do magic if all you did was do magic? You probably have plans. But if you want to come over I'll make you pancakes. If you like pancakes.

Rosamel texted back, a thumbs-up. And then, Have you seen this? and a link.

Someone stirred upstairs, and Laura put away her phone. But it was only Ruth. "Oh no," she said sadly when she saw the couch. "Look at that."

Laura said, "It wasn't me."

"She swore when we got it that she'd treat it like a museum piece," Ruth said.

"You don't know that it was Susannah," Laura said. How did the magic work, exactly? What had happened when she'd sent her father away? Would Ruth wonder where he'd gone? Think that he'd taken off again? Would she remember him at all?

"Who else would it be?" Ruth said. "Do I smell coffee?"

"Help yourself," Laura said.

She sat at the table and Ruth poured coffee for herself and more for Laura and made them both scrambled eggs.

"That was fun, last night," Ruth said.

"I guess," Laura said. Did Ruth remember Malo Mogge? What she'd done? "I don't know about the whole temple thing. Are you going to work today?"

"I think it's nice," Ruth said. "Much more interesting than another seafood restaurant. Or a Starbucks. And I already called in to the hospital and said I couldn't come in this week. I thought maybe I could help look for this key Malo Mogge wants. She just wants it so much. I think she'd be really happy if we found it for her."

"You bet," Laura said. It was fascinating to see how easily Ruth accepted all of it. Creepy, but was it that different from the way things usually worked? It was like weather, or coming down with the flu, or obeying traffic laws. Malo Mogge and Mr. Anabin might have messed with Ruth's life, but wasn't Ruth still Ruth? She didn't seem any different to Laura.

"When Susannah gets up, let's go get a Christmas tree," Ruth said.

"Or we could just make Daniel stand in the corner and decorate him," Laura said.

"Are they back together again?" Ruth asked.

"He's up there right now," Laura said. "I think. How do you feel about that? Them?"

Ruth said, "Far be it from me to pass judgment on young love, but also I think you know it didn't work out so well for me and your father."

She was saying something else when there was a banging on the door. Later on, Laura tried to remember what it was, but right now Laura wasn't paying attention to her mother. When she opened the door, Bowie pushed past her and into the kitchen.

He was holding his shoulder, blood seeping down all of his left side. "Hide me," he said.

"What happened?" Ruth said in her nurse voice. "Was it a car? Did a car hit you?"

"Hide me," Bowie said.

Ruth said, "I'll call 911. No, we can't get you to the hospital. And they won't be able to get here. There's an urgent care over on Strong Avenue. I'll call them. Go sit at the table. Laura, get that coat off. Is that mine? Never mind. I'll get some towels."

Bowie staggered farther into the house. He sat down on the couch.

"Oh," Laura said. "Oh no. You'll get blood on it."

He already had.

She grabbed dish towels and a throw blanket. Helped Bowie take the coat off, then his T-shirt. His arm near the shoulder was black and swollen, and blood trickled from a puncture just above his biceps.

"Where is he?" Laura said. "Does he know you're here?"

"I lost them in the marsh," Bowie said. His face was gray.

"There's something in your arm. How did you do this?"

"I can't get it out," Bowie said.

Ruth came back with a mixing bowl. In it were various supplies. "Let me see," she said. "Okay. That's not great, but it isn't that bad, either. Can you bend your arm? Is anything broken? I know you, don't I? But I don't know how."

Bowie bent his elbow, let Ruth run her hands along his arm. She said, "There's something in here. I should be able to get it out. It isn't bad that it's bleeding. That's good. Will you let me?"

Bowie nodded. "Please," he said. "Hurry."

Ruth swabbed his arm with a sterile wipe. "It's deep. Maybe even stuck in the bone. This will hurt," she said. "Maybe a lot."

Bowie gave her an incredulous look. "I know," he said. He gripped

Laura's wrist with his other hand so tightly she could feel her own bones grind together.

"There," Ruth said. "I've got it." Then, "What is it?"

It looked, to Laura, like a fragment of bone. Too big to have come out of the puncture in Bowie's arm. Was it his? Bowie let go of Laura's wrist.

"First things first," Ruth said. "Let's bandage that." Then, "It isn't bleeding as much now." She put the piece of bone in the mixing bowl. "Get some Advil, Laura."

The door to the front porch opened again, and Bowie said, "Let me go!" though no one was holding him. Laura turned, expecting to see Thomas there, but instead it was Susannah and Mo.

"What's happening?" Susannah said. "Bowie?"

Bowie rose to his feet, then fell back against Ruth, who steadied him.

"Where did *you* come from?" Laura said to Susannah. "What are you doing with Mo?"

"Hanging out," Susannah said. "It's a thing friends do sometimes. You'd understand if you had any."

Ruth said, "I don't understand. Look at this."

Laura saw Bowie wasn't going to need a bandage after all. The wound had stopped bleeding. Already the mark the projectile had left was disappearing as Bowie used his magic to heal himself. Laura could feel how much magic this cost, how much more it cost than it should have.

There was more noise outside on the porch, and Mo turned his head. "Get Bowie out of here quick," he said, but it was too late. Thomas and Malo Mogge were in the kitchen.

Malo Mogge, dressed in pajamas and a pair of bright pink wings, held out her hand. The shard of bone Ruth had set down in the mixing bowl shot through the air to rest upon her palm.

"Well?" Malo Mogge said. She tossed the bloodied projectile and Thomas caught it. "Here is your enemy. Kill him and our bargain is accomplished."

Thomas did not move. Malo Mogge said, "Do you hesitate? Then I will do it." She raised her hand, flicked her finger as Ruth pushed Bowie behind her.

"Don't!" Laura said.

Ruth's mouth opened as if she were going to say something. Instead she fell onto the white couch and her head struck the soundboard of the Gretsch with a crack. Bowie was no longer behind her. A gray cat shot between Laura's feet and through the open door.

Laura bent over Ruth. "Mom?" she said. "Susannah, help!"

No pulse. She kept her finger on Ruth's warm wrist, felt nothing. Ruth was dead. Susannah wasn't going to be able to help. Nevertheless Susannah began to do CPR and Laura let her while she tried to figure out how to fix this.

"There's blood in her mouth," Susannah said, pausing. She wiped her own mouth, then Ruth's. There wasn't much, but how horrible it was to see Ruth's blood on Susannah's chin.

When Laura looked, Malo Mogge and Thomas were no longer there.

"Do something," she said to Mo, who still was.

"What do you want me to do?" he said. But then, "Okay, wait. Just, wait." He left the house, and Laura held Ruth's hand while Susannah breathed into Ruth's mouth and did chest compressions and told Ruth everything was going to be okay. "Call 911," she told Laura, and so Laura pulled out her phone and called. When she told the emergency services operator their address, the operator said, "Oh, honey, that's in Lovesend," and hung up.

Ruth's left arm hung down at an awkward angle, her fingers splayed the wrong way against the floor. Laura picked up her hand again. Held it.

"I don't think this is working," Susannah said. "Should I keep doing it?"

"Keep doing it," Laura said.

Time passed and Mo came back into the kitchen. But he hadn't brought help. He'd only brought Daniel.

The Book of Mo

Mo got to the coffee shop before Susannah. She lived a lot closer to town, but Mo could turn into a bird. He'd never managed to go to sleep. Instead he stayed up in the music studio writing in a notebook, and when Susannah texted back, he slipped a new notebook and a pen into the pocket of his hoodie (this was an experiment, after all, and he didn't want to lose what he'd been working on the way he'd lost the Timberlands). It was the kind of cold outside that made your bones ache. He put on his duffle coat and a wool cap. Then he turned himself into a Eurasian eagle owl (go big or go home) and flapped majestically down the Cliff Road, detouring over the bay where Malo Mogge's temple steamed gently. Fish floated belly-up in the water around it, but the eagle owl did not find these tempting.

Mo had wondered if he'd have some sort of psychic connection to the statues he'd given life to, but apparently it didn't work that way. Wherever they were now, he had no idea. They were off doing their own thing, and he was alone again. Shut up, Mo. Stop feeling sorry for yourself. Just enjoy being a very large owl.

He flew a slow circle over the roof of What Hast Thou Ground? and landed on a dumpster in the alley. When he changed back, he was pleased to discover pen and notebook still in his pocket. He had an idea about the process he might use to determine the structure of the overture and so he stood in the doorway and wrote until Susannah showed up.

"Mo," she said.

He said, "Hey, Susannah. Uh, thanks for coming."

At this, she threw her arms around him and hugged him so violently he staggered back. She didn't let go, and honestly it felt kind of good to have someone hold on to him like that, like they were afraid he was going to get away.

"I'm sorry," she said. "I'm so sorry. About everything. Mo, it sucks so much. She was always so nice, and I always thought you were so lucky to have a grandmother like that."

Mo's eyelids were already swollen from crying. He blinked furiously. He said, "She wasn't just my grandmother. She was the only one I had. How is that lucky? Although, yeah. I was lucky. But now? I don't have anyone."

Susannah nodded. Sniffed. They let go of each other. She pulled a key chain out of her coat pocket and opened the door of What Hast Thou Ground? "Come on inside. I'll make you whatever you want."

"Coffee," Mo said. "I want lots and lots of coffee. And a muffin."

"Sure," Susannah said, going behind the counter. "Looks like we've got lemon thyme and bourbon pecan. Oh, and chocolate lavender."

"Let's start with bourbon pecan," Mo said.

Susannah turned on the sound system and the soundtrack to *Camelot* came on. "Shit," she said. "Billy is such an asshole."

"No," Mo said. "Leave it. It's fine. I've always wondered what the simple folk do." He sat at the table in the window where he and Susannah had always sat. He put the notebook down. It was almost exactly like old times except he had to keep wiping tears off his face. Susannah brought him a muffin, coffee in a French press, and a napkin. He blew his nose on it and began to devour the muffin.

"So tell me what's going on," Susannah said.

"You mean besides my grandmother being dead," Mo said. He couldn't help it. "No, I mean there's other stuff, too. But it's complicated. So complicated I don't even know where to start. Can I have another muffin?"

"They're day-old," Susannah said. "Let's eat them all. I'm starving. Are you really up there in that house all by yourself? That seems awful."

"Do you remember Jenny Ping?" Mo said.

"No," Susannah said. "Did she go to Lewis Latimer?" She came back to the table with a plate of six muffins.

"No," Mo said. "Never mind." It wasn't Susannah's fault Jenny had never existed. "It's okay, I guess. There's a bunch of legal stuff I'm going to have to deal with."

Susannah said, "I hadn't even thought about that part. But you're not staying here anyway, right? You and Daniel and Laura have the program in Ireland."

"I was kind of thinking I might stay," Mo said.

"Really?" Susannah said, her mouth full of muffin. "Here?"

"I know," Mo said. "But I don't want to go back there. There's a bunch of really complicated stuff going on right now."

"Like?"

"Well," Mo said. "For one thing, there's this guy. We hit it off. Like, not just a hookup. I liked him? I think he really liked me? But he's got all this other shit going on, and I told him I wasn't sure it was real, what was going on between us, but I think maybe it was something real. But now he's ghosting me. Plus, you know, he's kind of evil. I think."

"Is he hot?" Susannah said.

"Yeah. Like out-of-my-league hot. Probably out-of-my-league evil, too."

"Like, neo-Nazi evil? Corporate evil? Petty stuff?"

"Corporate evil, I guess?" Mo said. "Petty evil stuff, too."

"Petty evil like petty crime or petty evil like bad tipping?"

"Crime."

"That's okay, then, I guess. What's his name?"

"Thomas."

"Um," Susannah said. She ducked her head. "Mo, so I may have run into a Thomas recently. A hot Thomas. I may have hooked up with a Thomas who was extremely hot. I don't know if he was evil or not. He was a good tipper."

"Oh, right," Mo said. "Fuck. He did say that. I totally forgot. To be clear, though, we got together and then he told me. I didn't know beforehand."

Susannah was still studying the muffin plate. "It wasn't anything serious. Anyway, Daniel and I are sort of back together. At least for the next few days. Until he goes back to Ireland, unless, you know, he decides not to go."

Mo thought about it. "I'm pretty sure he's going back to Ireland," he said. "Sorry." And he was sorry. Mostly for Susannah, but he was even a little sorry for Daniel.

At last she met his eyes. "I know you guys have never gotten along. But he's really not that bad."

"It isn't that we don't get along," Mo said. "I just don't like him."

"Right," Susannah said. "And you've never said why. And the last time I asked, you said not to worry about it and so I'm not going to ask you now, because it's none of my business and you're the one who texted me and said you had stuff going on. Everything with me and Daniel is fine. Everything with me is fine. Me and my mom, fine. Me and work, fine. Me and Laura, it's not fine, but that's nothing new. So it's fine. Now you. Spill. Tell me about you and Thomas. Unless it's weird. Because, you know."

"Huh," Mo said. And then stopped. Why had he thought this would be any better than talking with Rosamel? He couldn't explain anything. "You have to promise you won't tell him," he said. "Okay?"

"Who?" Susannah said. "Thomas?"

"No," Mo said. "Daniel."

HIS GRANDMOTHER HAD brought him to Lovesend after his mom died and he hadn't really understood what was going to happen to him, only that his life had changed forever. He began to have this fantasy that somehow his father would find out what had happened. He didn't know anything about his father, but he had this idea that when your mom died, your dad got a call. Then he had to come get you. Mo was a little worried about what this father was going to be like. What if he didn't like Mo? What if he was mean? Or had a loud voice? But weeks went by, and his father didn't show up, and Mo didn't say anything to his grandmother, but he was still hoping his father would show. Didn't he want Mo?

And then one day he was at the park with his grandmother, and there was a white kid who was about the same age as Mo, and he was just pounding on this Black guy. The white kid was punching the man in the leg and yelling at him, "You're not my dad! I don't want you. You're not my dad! I hate you! You're not my dad!"

Finally the man bent down and picked the kid up, let the kid whale on him all the way back to the car, the kid screaming the whole time. You could see that the man wasn't angry. He was just worried about the kid. Worried other people were going to think something bad was going on. Just, worried. Sad. Embarrassed.

Fuck that kid, right? Didn't he know how lucky he was? You don't want that guy as a dad? Fine. Pass him over, asshole. Then Mo had his first day at Lewis Latimer and there was that kid again, one grade above him. Mo couldn't believe it. He'd hated the other kid with every fiber of his being from then on. And this was okay because everyone else at Lewis Latimer liked the other kid. Older kids, younger kids, all the teachers. Mrs. Fish. That kid didn't need anything from Mo.

"I remember that phase," Susannah said. "Barely. They all went to therapy. So that's why you hate him? Really?"

"I don't hate him," Mo said. "I used to hate him. Now I just don't like him. I don't have to like everybody."

"Sure," Susannah said. "But Daniel has to have everyone like him. That's the tragedy of Daniel."

"Sounds about right," Mo said. "How about you? What's the tragedy of Susannah?"

She didn't even hesitate. "My tragedy is my dreams are much more interesting than my life," she said. "And my sister is an outrageous bitch. How about you? And don't say it's that your grandmother is dead."

"My mom's dead, too," Mo said. "Remember?"

"Shit. I'm sorry. I am so sorry, but your dead mother doesn't count, either. It has to be your tragedy. The tragedy of you."

Mo thought about it. "I want to compose music," he said. "But I don't want to ever have to show it to anyone."

Susannah said, "So you're a coward."

"A huge coward," Mo said. It was pretty great to say all of this out loud. "I'm afraid of everything."

"That's what's in your notebook, right?" Susannah said. "Your music."

Mo nodded.

"But you're not going to show it to anyone," Susannah said. "Not even me."

Mo said, "We haven't done Laura yet."

"Laura's easy," Susannah said. "She thinks she knows how everything should be, and then she gets that mixed up with what she thinks she actually wants."

"What if it turns out she's actually right about everything?" Mo said.

"Well," Susannah said. "That would also be pretty tragic. But please don't make me talk about Laura. I want to talk about the music you're writing. Tell me one thing. Just one."

"It's kind of experimental," Mo said, trying it out. After all, if he decided he wished he hadn't said anything, couldn't he just take it back? He could make Susannah forget. The thought made him a little queasy, but it gave him courage, too. "And really big."

"Something more specific," Susannah said.

Mo said, "It's going to be everything I remember about Jenny."

Susannah said, "You're going to have to help me out here. Who is Jenny?"

"Exactly!" Mo said.

A white lady came up to the door of What Hast Thou Ground? and knocked despite the CLOSED sign hanging there.

Susannah yelled, "We're closed! Come back at noon!" But the lady stayed there until Susannah went and opened the door and said it all again.

"We shouldn't stay here," Susannah said. "It will just be a steady deluge of customers who have nothing better to do than bang on the door now that they can't leave town."

"Can't leave town?" Mo said, wondering what Susannah knew or thought. She hadn't been at the Cliff Hangar. How did Malo Mogge's spell work if you hadn't been there?

"Not like I have anywhere to go anyway," Susannah said as if it weren't even worth discussing. "Come home with me. Ruth will make you scrambled eggs."

"Why not," Mo said. He was fairly certain he was only ever going to be hungry from now on. For breakfasts, for bodily sensation, for love. But it was always best to start with breakfast.

The Book of Daniel

Waking, there was the question of why he was no longer a bear. Had he used his magic after all? Remade himself? He didn't think he had, but Susannah was kissing his human mouth, reaching down to grasp his most definitely human dick. The bear's appetite and anger once again belonged to Daniel and only Daniel, who had not realized they were there at all. He was no longer large enough to contain everything that had come welling up out of him while he was a bear. Susannah would be able to detect the taste of everything he'd been keeping secret from her. She would draw it from his mouth like poison. He pushed her back on the bed, nudged her legs apart. The little pad of fat above the pubic bone, her pubic hair, one of which would inevitably be caught in his teeth, the shine of wetness already on her thighs.

"Just let me," he said, and went down on her.

They lay there talking about nothing that particularly mattered. There was a reek in the room that was either sex or bear, and Daniel was taking lazy inventory of himself to make sure no trace of bear remained when Mo texted Susannah. It was only when he saw Lissy and Carousel sitting at the breakfast table that he remembered the other thing Mr. Anabin had said.

Someone in his life was not real.

Lissy was real. Carousel was not.

There was a Pop-Tart on the plate in front of Carousel, and as Daniel watched, she took a bite out of it. Presumably she would eat the entire thing and then take another. To be made of magic was to be hungry. Daniel knew that.

The Pop-Tart was real and Carousel was not.

Susannah left. His parents and the rest of his siblings woke up and came into the kitchen. They put a plate of something in front of Daniel and he ate it. They said things to him, and he said things back. Carousel ate a second Pop-Tart.

Here is what Daniel remembered about the real Carousel. First, that she hadn't been called Carousel. She hadn't lived long enough to be called anything other than Caroline. Only Pumpkin and Cupcake and Peanut and all the other nicknames nurses gave premature babies. Once at a barbecue a nurse friend of Ruth's had said in an offhand way that babies came and went and nicknames meant nurses didn't have to worry about getting names right when everything was going wrong. It helped when a baby died. A baby might die, but Peanut would be back in the same old Isolette in a day or two. Daniel remembered the stricken looks on everyone else's faces. That nurse hadn't known.

Laid on top of the memory of Caroline who had died were all of Daniel's memories of this Carousel, the one who had never been real. Here was everything that had not happened. She had not spent almost four months in the NICU. One day his parents had not brought her home. How small she had not been, how much he had not been afraid of her, her fragility, that he might accidentally hold her too tightly, and everything since. None of these things had ever been real.

This Carousel, telling Davey and Oliver they hadn't wanted Pop-Tarts anyway, this Carousel did not exist, had never existed. She was a construct made out of magic. And here it was, a ripe, gummy string trailing from Daniel to her. He saw how he could sever it. The magic he didn't want told him how easy this would be. No one would even know it had been done. Carousel would no longer be Carousel though the Pop-Tarts would still be gone. What if Carousel picked up a knife and stabbed Davey with it? What if Daniel made her go away after that? Would Davey still be dead? But, of course, Carousel wasn't going to do that. She wasn't evil. She just wasn't real.

Magic makes her real, Daniel's magic said. Magic can do all sorts of things. If you have magic, magic said, you never run out of Pop-Tarts. If you have magic, you can turn all the snow to amethysts and tourmalines for Lissy and Dakota, who had not been content to share the same birthstone. You could stop Davey from sleepwalking, make Susannah happy. You could kick Bogomil's ass with magic. Well, you could try. You could *live*. Carousel isn't real, but you are. The magic that sustains her doesn't belong to her. It belongs to you.

Shut up, Daniel told his magic, and then realized he'd said it out loud when everyone stopped eating and stared at him.

"Sorry," he said. "Talking to myself. Who wants cinnamon toast?" You didn't need infinite Pop-Tarts. You could improvise.

Lissy raised her hand. And Carousel did as well.

When Mo showed up, pounding on the door, and said Laura and Susannah needed him to come over, it was almost a relief.

Once they were outside, Mo said, "What's wrong with *you*? Never mind. Come on, come on." His face was full of worry and something worse.

Daniel said, "Is Susannah okay?"

"She's fine," Mo said. "Come on. *Hurry*. It's Malo Mogge. She showed up and Bowie was there and she tried to kill him, I think, but Ruth got in the way."

"Ruth?" Daniel said. "Is she okay?"

"No," Mo said.

When they came in, Laura looked up as if she had been waiting. Then her expression closed again. She was beside Susannah on the couch, hunched protectively over Ruth.

Daniel went over, full of dread. He looked at Ruth and then had to look away. He said, "What did she do? Malo Mogge."

"She pointed her finger," Laura said. "That was it."

"She doesn't have a pulse," Susannah said. "I was doing CPR, but maybe I was doing it wrong. Maybe she had a stroke?"

"I can't get her to stop being dead," Laura said. "I tried. There has to be a way to do it, but I don't know what it is. Mr. Anabin knows. Or Bogomil. We know they know how to do it. We just have to find them and ask."

Mo said, "They can't."

"How do you know?" Laura said.

"I asked Mr. Anabin to bring my grandmother back," Mo said. "He said it didn't work like that. They don't bring people back from the dead."

Laura said, "Okay, but your grandmother had been dead for a while. She was buried! This is different, she's right here. She's just a *little* bit dead."

Daniel sat down beside Susannah. "Hey," he said. "Susannah. I'm so sorry."

"I don't understand what they're talking about," Susannah said. "We have to call 911 again. They have to come."

"Take her upstairs," Laura said to Daniel. "She shouldn't be here."

"I shouldn't be here?" Susannah said. "This is my house! You don't even live here anymore! Ruth and I live here. You're just here on your break!"

"Please," Laura said to Daniel. "I can't. I can't deal with Susannah on top of all this."

Susannah said, "Tell me what's happening. Daniel?"

When he said nothing, Mo, that fucker, said, "What's going on is that we all died, Susannah. And then we came back. You don't remember and we all agreed not to tell you, but I think we're way past that now. There's a coin, it's magic and it belongs to Malo Mogge. She thinks we have it or had it and she wants it back. And Thomas keeps trying to kill Bowie, they're both part of this, and Malo Mogge was going to do it instead, but your mom got in the way. Oh, and Malo Mogge is a goddess and Bowie and Thomas are hundreds of years old and Mr. Anabin is even older and he's basically a wizard and there's this other wizard and now Laura and Daniel and I can also do magic but we're in deep shit. Because we died. I am so, so sorry about your mom."

Susannah stood up. She picked up an electric guitar Daniel had never seen before (where had that come from?) and swung it at the flat-screen television. There was an explosion of sparks and the flat-screen fell over onto the floor.

"Okay, wow!" Laura said. "Really helping, Susannah, thank you!"

Susannah raised the guitar again. She began to bring it down on Laura's head.

"Susannah!" Daniel said. "Stop!"

Had he used magic? Again, he didn't think so, but Susannah stopped. Daniel took the guitar from her. "Come upstairs," he said. Laura was glaring at them both. "You can ask me anything you want. Okay?"

Susannah looked at Ruth. Then she turned and went up the stairs.

"I'll go find Mr. Anabin," Mo was saying as Daniel followed Susannah.

She lay down on her bed without taking off her coat. Daniel sat beside her and began to unlace her boots.

"We have to call the police," Susannah said. "Laura needs to do that."

"She will," Daniel said. He put her boots in the closet and looked around the room. There were dirty clothes at the foot of the bed, clean clothes, folded but not put away, on Susannah's desk. He put the dirty clothes in the hamper and began to put the folded clothes into drawers.

"Do you want a glass of water?" he said. "Can I get anything for you? Susannah?"

"I'm supposed to work at What Hast Thou Ground?" she said. "I'm supposed to be there at eleven thirty."

"I'll call," Daniel said.

"Billy won't be there yet," Susannah said. "He doesn't come in until after ten."

"I'll leave a message," Daniel said.

Susannah said, "I'm cold." He sat on the bed again and took her hands in his.

"Get under the covers," he said. "I'll get another blanket."

"No," she said. "Don't. Lie down with me."

Daniel lay down. Susannah said, "Hold me." So he did.

"Is my mother really dead?" she said.

"Yes," Daniel said.

"Mo says you were dead, too," Susannah said. "But you're not."

"It's complicated," Daniel said. "Do you want me to explain?"

"No," Susannah said. "Bogomil is real, though, right?"

"Yes," Daniel said.

"Are you crying, Daniel?" she said.

He had not realized that he was. "Yes," he said.

Susannah was silent for a while. Then she said, "I have a splinter in my foot. I keep forgetting to take it out."

"Let me take a look," Daniel said. "Does it hurt?"

"A little," Susannah said. "I think I just want to go to sleep. Okay?"

"Okay," Daniel said.

"Stay with me, okay?" Susannah said.

"Okay," Daniel said.

The Book of Ruth

One minute she was in her living room and the woman who'd made a temple rise up in the bay was pointing something at the boy who'd been wearing Ruth's old coat. At first Ruth had thought it must be a weapon. But it hadn't been a weapon. It was just Malo Mogge's finger.

Ruth put herself between Malo Mogge and the boy before she realized Malo Mogge's hand was empty. She'd felt extremely silly when she did. And also terrified, though why, she wasn't sure.

And then what had happened? She'd found herself here. Where was here?

Here was a forest. It was also her living room but somehow her living room had become a forest. She wasn't sure it was her living room at all.

Someone said, "This is unexpected." Then, "I know you."

A man was in the forest with her. No, they were in her living room. He was extremely handsome, but Ruth saw that his fingernails were black with dirt. She was afraid, suddenly, that he would sit down on her couch. That he would leave his dirt on it. No, the couch was already ruined. She said, "I don't know you. What are you doing here?"

"You're the mother," he said. "Ruth. I see. You're dead."

"Am I?" Ruth said.

"Yes," the man said. "Can't you tell?"

Ruth evaluated. "Yes," she said finally. "I think I can. But this isn't at all what I was expecting. Are you Death?"

"Not in the ordinary way," the man said. "I'm more Death adjacent. I handle the special cases."

"You're a specialist," Ruth said. She began to laugh.

"I'm sorry?" the man said.

"No, it's just that I work with specialists," Ruth said. "It's not actually very funny."

"No," the man said. "Tell me. There is a coin I think you must have handled once. It would have looked like this."

He held out his hand, which was empty. Then, lying on the dirty palm was a small, tarnished coin.

"No," Ruth said. "Wait, yes. Someone showed it to me, I remember. It was Susannah's friend Mo. I went to pick her up at his grandmother's house. They were up in Mo's room and had taken it out of its case. I told them to put it back. It was too valuable to play with. You could tell by looking. It was too heavy for something so small."

"I'm sorry," the man said.

"Why?" Ruth said. "For what?"

"For many things," the man said. "I know Susannah is very fond of you. I'm a friend of hers. Is there a message you'd like me to give them? Before you go?"

"Where am I going?" Ruth said. She didn't mean to be so full of questions, but it seemed likely this was her last chance to have them answered.

"I'm not exactly sure," the man said. "Where everyone else goes. Most people don't need any help from me, but sometimes someone has come into contact with Malo Mogge's key, and then I have to assist, so to speak."

Ruth said, "You know Susannah?"

"Yes," the man said. "She's very special."

"They both are," Ruth said. "I used to worry about Susannah. But I'm starting to think Laura is the one I should have been worrying about. She was gone, wasn't she? She was missing. She and Daniel and Mo were all missing. And then she came back. They all came back."

"She did," the man said. "They did. Yes."

"You should do something about that woman," Ruth said. "Malo Mogge. I think she's dangerous."

"I'm working on that," the man said. "But as much as I'd love to stand around talking for all of eternity with you, I'm afraid I have a long list of things that need doing and quite soon. And it wouldn't be safe for you to stay here if things go the way they're likely to go. So. Is there anything you want me to tell Susannah and Laura?"

"Yes," Ruth said. Then, "Sorry. I'm not good at coming up with speeches on the spot. I love them. You could tell them that. I'm so proud of them. Tell them to look out for each other. And tell them not to worry about the couch. It was too big for the living room anyway."

"Is that all?" the man said.

"Well, no," Ruth said. "But it's all I can come up with right now. And that's already a lot for you to remember and I don't know whether or not I can trust you to get everything right. If I tell you anything else, you might mess it up."

"I might," the man said.

Ruth said, "Even if there were a lot of other things I wanted you to tell them and you remembered all of it correctly, it could still turn out something was the wrong thing for me to say. That's the problem with being someone's mother. You try to be helpful but it may turn out you were saying the wrong thing in the wrong way at the wrong time, most of the time. I don't want to make it harder. This is going to be so hard on them."

"Yes," the man said.

Ruth thought he could have been a little less honest, a little more comforting. But some people don't have much of a bedside manner. She said, "What do we do now?"

The man said, "Take my hand."

Oh, but it was so dirty. What kind of specialist had hands this dirty? Ruth stood in the forest, hesitating. As she hesitated, she realized she could hear singing somewhere. "Oh," she said. "How nice. I always loved that song."

"What?" the man said, still holding his hand out to her.

"That song," she said. "Don't you hear it?" She hummed a piece of it, kept humming.

"Wait," he said. "Where is the singer? Do you see him?"

But Ruth had already taken Bogomil's hand and so there was no one there to give him an answer.

THE BOOK OF MO

MO WOULD HAVE liked to imagine this was a situation in which he was trying to be as helpful as possible, but really he just needed to get out of that house.

He would have liked to do something, he *wanted* to do something, but there wasn't really anything he *could* do, was there? There wasn't anything anyone could do. Except for Malo Mogge, who could apparently go around doing anything she wanted. And everyone wanted them to find this key, just give it back to her?

Fuck Thomas. It was his fault Ms. Hand was dead now. Mo was too good for him. Susannah was, too.

Mo would go find Mr. Anabin. If he went to Lewis Latimer, to Mr. Anabin's classroom, he was pretty sure Mr. Anabin would be there. Mo would come as a supplicant. A petitioner.

He didn't want to be those things. He kept being things he wasn't sure he wanted to be. For instance, he'd been a bat. Had he ever in his life wanted to be a bat? No. He'd indulged an impulse. And then he'd been an owl, making the decision the way you opened a drawer and decided which T-shirt you were going to wear. It was funny how at first magic was amazing and surprising and then pretty quick you were like, No, I don't want to be a bat or a crow, I've already been both of those. Last night I was the fucking Atlantic Ocean.

He decided to go home. He wouldn't petition Mr. Anabin. He'd summon him.

"Mo?" someone said. And coming up the Hands' slushy driveway was, for some reason, Rosamel.

"What are you doing here?" he said.

She said, looking slightly shifty, "Could ask you the same."

"Just catching up with Susannah," he said. "Hadn't seen her since I got home."

"Right," she said. "Susannah. Forgot she'd be around."

There was something about the way she said this. "Wait," Mo said. Then, "Oh shit, Laura and you? *You* and *Laura*?"

"Not sure which part of this you find so surprising," Rosamel said. "Also not sure which part of this is your business, friendo."

"She did something to you," Mo said, horror coming over him.

"Well," Rosamel said. "Yeah. Kinda hope she might even do it again."

Mo took Rosamel by the shoulder. "I don't know what Laura did or what she told you to do, but you need to get out of here. You need to stay out of this. Okay?"

Thomas was right. It was as easy as pie. A big old slice of hypno pie with delicious whipped mesmerism on top. "Okay," Rosamel said.

Mo said, "You should probably stay away from me, too. I'm part of all this. Sorry, Rosamel."

"Don't be sorry," she said. "Maybe I'll see you later, Mo."

"Yeah," he said. "Oh, Rosie. Be safe. Take care of yourself."

She trudged off through the snow, turning once to look back at him. He waved and she waved back. "Fuck," Mo said.

He became a starling. How easy it was. *They fly into one's head like birds.* But when he arrived home, it was one of the hardest things he'd ever done, becoming human again. Becoming Mo. Every time it got harder.

He couldn't help feeling that Ms. Hand's death was his fault, that if he hadn't texted Susannah, if she hadn't come to the coffee shop to meet him, things might have played out differently. Maybe if Susannah hadn't invited Mo home, if he hadn't been there, maybe Thomas wouldn't have hesitated. There wouldn't have been time for Ms. Hand to get in the way.

It wasn't like anyone cared about Bowie. Sorry, Bowie.

Bad things happened to people around Mo. At least Rosamel would be safe. He'd stay away from her and Natalie and Theo.

How alone he was. How much nicer it had been to share his grandmother's house with Jenny, who sang and baked and wasn't real at all. Mo went up to his mother's music studio and turned on all the lights. Down in the garden, the snow was so deep now the rosebushes were distinguishable only in their exaggerated and simplified shapes, lumps of sugar lying upon a plate heaped with more sugar.

He said, "Mr. Anabin? If you can hear me, I think we need to talk."

And then Mr. Anabin was there at the window with him, looking out at the sugared garden and, past it, Malo Mogge's temple.

"You made quick work of your doppelgänger," Mr. Anabin said.

"Nah," Mo said. "I guessed wrong the first time."

"Wrong?" Mr. Anabin said.

"Yeah," Mo said. "I thought it had to be Thomas. He didn't correct me, either."

Mr. Anabin smiled the smallest smile. "I would have liked to see that."

"Not my finest hour," Mo said. "But Thomas is not what I want to talk about. We need to talk about Malo Mogge. The door and the key. You and Bogomil want to quit. You want replacements. Two of us to replace the two of you."

Mr. Anabin's face didn't change. The text on his T-shirt said THE GREAT FORM OF THE FUTURE WILL NOT BE AS IT WAS IN THE PAST.

What a dork he was, and Mo, of course, was a dork, too, for recognizing the quote. Dorks shouldn't have so much power. Nevertheless, Mo trailed after him when Mr. Anabin went to sit at the piano.

"It will be your choice," Mr. Anabin said. "We cannot make you serve." He began to play something wistful.

"I know that," Mo said. "Um. Julius Eastman. *Gay Guerrilla!*"

"I saw him once," Mr. Anabin said. "A dance piece. He sat in a chair and spoke of God."

"I was super into *Eight Songs for a Mad King* for a while," Mo said.

Mr. Anabin said, "Sweet Thames, sweet Thames, far, far have I followed thee."

Mo would've liked to follow this topic, honestly. Mr. Anabin had seen Eastman? Who else had he seen? But this wasn't school. They weren't hanging out. He said, "You can't make us serve. But if we don't choose to serve, then we die. If we find the key, two of us are going to have to choose to serve Malo Mogge? To be *you*?"

Mr. Anabin went on playing. He said, "I have been me for a very long time, Mo. I do not wish to go on being me forever. I imagine it will be you and Laura. Thomas is hunting Bowie, and I do not think he will stop until Bowie is dead."

"Yeah," Mo said. "About that. Malo Mogge showed up with Thomas about an hour ago at Susannah's house and tried to kill Bowie. But Ms. Hand was there, too, and Malo Mogge killed her instead. Right in front of everybody. Bowie got away."

"I see," Mr. Anabin said. He stopped playing.

"Laura thinks magic can bring Ms. Hand back to life," Mo said. "I said I'd find you and ask if that was true. But I don't really need to. I already asked you that."

Mr. Anabin stood up. He lowered the lid over the keys and said, "Magic is less complicated than you think. There is very little that I or Bogomil can do that you cannot. It is just we have a greater store of magic because we belong to Malo Mogge. And we may use it less freely than you because we belong to Malo Mogge. But not even Malo Mogge may bring back the dead once they have gone through the door. Even when the key was in her possession, and all this world and other worlds besides."

Mo said, "What was it like, back when she ran things?"

Mr. Anabin extended his finger toward the garden. "Like that," he said. "And also like this."

Mo went back to the window to see. The snow was gone, and gone, too, the rosebushes hidden beneath it. Along the rock wall to Mo's left, now there was a city in miniature. Chariots went swiftly past people on foot who drove herds of cattle down long avenues. Tiny people idled in a busy marketplace. There were houses made of clay bricks, marble palaces, terraces, and pavilions. In the middle of the city was a green temple Mo recognized. Smoke rose from it, and people went in and out, carrying offerings of fruit and flowers, platters of meat.

To the right of this city was another, this one in ruin. Palaces and houses reduced to rubble, outlying fields scorched, the ground split, steam coming from fissures a deep red color, like cracks in an animal's hide. It was the same city, Mo knew. There was the temple, but now it crouched crookedly upon the lip of a volcano. Lava spilled down the volcano's sides. Here the tiny people ran about, struggled or wept or lay still. Only the temple remained untouched.

"That does not look great," Mo said.

Mr. Anabin said, "It isn't so different from the way the world is now. Is it? There is order and there is suffering. Is it so much worse that Malo Mogge's hand metes it out? There will still be joy and suffering beyond what she decrees. I suggest you do as I have sometimes done and consider her a meteorological event. A hurricane with a narcissistic personality complex. Currently you might think of her as a Category Two storm."

"And if she gets her key?"

"Category Five," Mr. Anabin said. "But the same is true if she does not."

"Got it," Mo said. "Can you make the garden a garden again? This view is not making a great case for why I should help find the key."

Mr. Anabin said, "There is little I can do that you cannot."

"Helpful," Mo said. "Thanks." He thought of what he wanted to accomplish and then undid the casement lock of the window in front of him. He inhaled, drawing into his lungs the warm, singed air of the small kingdoms that did not belong in his grandmother's garden. When he blew that breath out again, it was transformed by his magic, so cold his lips tingled with it. The breath floated out over the garden, and as it did so, it unmade the cities. Snow covered the garden again, and Mo told himself that under the snow there were rosebushes and only rosebushes now, not temples, rubble, desolation. Rosebushes now, said the temple in the bay. Desolation will come before the snow is gone. Desolation unless Malo Mogge's key is found. Find her key or you will never see roses again.

"Why didn't you just tell us in the first place you wanted us to find some key for you?" Mo said. "Wouldn't that have been easier?"

Mr. Anabin said, "First we needed you to become accustomed to magic. To become adept in its use. That was, in part, the mistake Bogomil made with Thomas and Kristofer."

"What about Jenny?" Mo said. "Why did you make her?"

"To keep an eye on you," Mr. Anabin said. "And because it seemed a useful lesson. The world is full of deception and disguises. You need to learn how to see. To discern."

Mo said, "I know she wasn't real. But she felt real. She felt as real as real."

Mr. Anabin said, "When you were very young, your grandmother had an operation. Nothing serious, but there was a period of two months when she hired a twenty-year-old woman named Jenny Ping to look after you and the house and herself. When Jenny left, you missed her for a day or two. Time passed and you mostly forgot her. I took all of that and sent a facsimile of her to you."

Mo tried to take this in. "Did the real one, the real Jenny, did she love Barry Manilow?"

"Who doesn't?" Mr. Anabin said. It was hard to tell whether or not he was joking. "This is quite a collection of instruments."

"They belonged to my mom," Mo said. "She could play anything. That's what my grandmother said."

"I knew one like that," Mr. Anabin said.

Mo said, "What if we won't find the key for her? For Malo Mogge?"

Mr. Anabin said nothing. In the garden outside the snow caught fire.

"Put it out!" Mo said.

Mr. Anabin looked at him. "There is nothing I may do that you cannot."

Asshole. Mo put the fire out. He said, "You keep setting things up to make me, to make all of us, do the things you don't want to do. I don't like Daniel. But maybe he's got the right idea. Maybe we shouldn't be doing magic. You and Bogomil, you want so badly for us to use magic. But it isn't for us. It's for you."

Mr. Anabin said, "Have you seen Daniel, then? Today?"

"Yeah," Mo said suspiciously. "Why?"

Mr. Anabin said, "Tell Laura I am sorry for the death of her mother. Tell her Malo Mogge will do worse if the key is not restored. I will see if I can discover Bowie."

Then he was gone. Good riddance. Except that Mo was alone again. He did not think he could bear to be alone, not now. But did he have to be? His magic said he could choose whether to be alone or not. Mr.

Anabin had made Jenny out of magic, so Mo could do the same. For materials, he used the snow in the garden below and the rosebushes. He told the rosebushes to bloom, and so they did. He told them to grow until they blocked the view of the temple in the bay. And then he made Jenny again, this time out of snow and rose petals. While she stood there, barefoot in the snow, Mo made his grandmother, too. She was just as he remembered her, even if she wasn't real. And then, though by this time he could feel the cost of the magic and was weak with hunger, he made his mother. Three women stood in a garden, looking up at him. Mo went downstairs to let them in.

The Book of Laura

She tried again and again to find where Ruth had gone. To make Ruth's body obey her and become Ruth again. The fly had done what Laura had told it and so had that jerk at Birdsong Music. And they didn't even love her. Ruth loved Laura. She should have heard her calling. Ruth couldn't go, couldn't leave Laura here all alone with Susannah. It wasn't fair.

Daniel was upstairs with Susannah. Let Daniel deal with her. Laura would deal with this. She just had to figure out what she was supposed to do. She could not think of what else she ought to do. Her mother was dead and time had passed, but she did not know how much time. When she looked at her phone, she saw Mo had texted her.

> Just talked with Mr. Anabin he says there isn't anything he can do to bring your mom back. Not even Malo Mogge can do that. He says dead is just dead. He can't do anything we can't do. Sorry. Tell me if theres anything else I can do

"Not even Malo Mogge," Laura said. "We'll see about that." She went back to Ruth. Stroked her forehead. Ruth's eyes were closed, her mouth open, and the tip of her tongue swollen and dry.

Laura said, "I'm sorry. I'll try to be gentle."

The Hands didn't have a sled anymore. They'd given it to Daniel's family. But Laura thought the Lucklows probably kept it in their garage.

Only, it turned out she didn't have to go looking. It was propped up against the side of the Lucklow house.

Daniel's brothers, Davey and Oliver, were in the yard drawing lines in the snow with a rake.

"I'm just going to borrow this for a little while," she said.

"Are you going sledding?" one twin said. It might have been Davey. Laura could never remember which one was which. It wasn't a race thing. It was a twin thing. Also, they were just little kids. Did it really matter if Laura had never bothered to keep them straight?

"No," Laura said. "Kind of. But not really."

"Can we come?"

"Not right now, sweetheart," Laura said. "Maybe later, okay?"

She left the sled at the bottom step of her house and went in to get Ruth. In the ordinary way, she could not have lifted her mother easily, but magic made all tasks easy. She wrapped Ruth up in the old chenille blanket from the upstairs closet. Why had Ruth gotten in the way like that? Laura should have stopped her, but she hadn't. She arranged Ruth on the sled, then went and got Ruth's good coat and a scarf and some bungee cords they used with their bikes. She laid the coat over Ruth's torso, over the chenille blanket. Once Ruth was fastened securely, Laura draped the scarf over her face. She had an image of Ruth's mouth filling with unmelted snow.

She set off down the street toward Little Moon Bay, pulling the sled behind her. Cars went by, throwing slush on the sled, on Laura, but the drivers did not seem to notice Ruth. Laura had almost made it to the turn-off to the bay when a man walking his dachshund stopped on the sidewalk. He said, "Is she okay?"

When Laura looked back, the dog was sniffing Ruth's head. The scarf had come off her face. Laura thought it was quite obvious to everyone, including the dachshund, that Ruth was not okay.

"She's dead," Laura said. "But I'm going to fix that. It isn't something you should worry about. Everything's fine. It's a beautiful day. Look at all this snow! Isn't it beautiful?"

"It sure is!" the man said. He pulled his dog away from the sled, and Laura went hurrying on to the bay.

It was harder to pull the sled along sand. The tide had been busily dissolving the snow, washing it out to sea, but she got Ruth all the way down to the shoreline without too much trouble. The next part was going to be a little unorthodox, but she didn't particularly feel like turning into a pelican or a seahorse or whatever. Besides, there was Ruth on the sled.

The temple was less than a mile from shore. Laura had gone out that far before in a boat. She'd never swum past the mouth of the bay, but swimming wasn't her plan. She was going to walk.

The tide was still going out and Laura told the rush of water to make a space for her. This was the hardest work of all, dragging the sled along the bottom of the bay while telling the water what she wanted of it, but Laura's magic made her strong. The noise the metal runners made was unpleasant, and the feel of Ruth's body jolting over rocks and then sliding over seaweed was unpleasant, too, but Laura distracted herself by focusing on the green wobble of the water hanging voluptuously to each side. Spray mixed with snow and came down on Laura and the sled and Ruth. The rich, cool smell of the exposed floor of the bay stung her nose, and now and then crabs went scuttling away in front of her, along the damp, current-ridged path.

At last she reached the base of Malo Mogge's temple and was relieved to see there were not only steps but a kind of greenstone ramp with grooves cut into it running up the center. She was quite deep into the narrow canyon she'd carved out of the ocean, and the walls of water rose up on each side more than a hundred feet. The steps in front of her did not seem to be on a human scale. But neither were they insurmountable. Laura went up the steps and pulled the sled alongside on the ramp. As she ascended, she began to imagine human faces, human forms, staring back at her through the walls of water, like doll parts in a Jell-O mold. They kept a distance, sliding out of her line of sight when she tried to confirm they were there. Not all of them were the size they should have been. Maybe it was not her imagination. It seemed possible there might be other impossible things besides Malo Mogge's temple in the bay now.

At last Laura found herself above the surface of the water. There was a concourse here, and she drew the sled up on it, looking back to see the way she had come. There was the path she had made along the ocean bed far below. She admired her work, then let the ocean go slouching back into the gap.

Ruth's coat and hair were soaked with seawater. It dripped off her chin, had dragged the scarf down. There was sand on her lips. Grains on her tongue, on her teeth.

At the other end of the sled, one foot now stuck out from the sodden blanket. Ruth's toes were a livid gumball blue.

Laura's triumph went out like a blown match. She felt it go, let it go. Never mind, never mind. What mattered was she was here, and Malo Mogge could make right the wrong she had done.

The temple had no doors. In a bad storm, the ocean would sluice right through. Ruth hated mopping. Did anyone ever enjoy it? How much better to give it over to the ocean. How marvelous.

The ceiling of Malo Mogge's temple was very high, and in the center, where the ceiling was highest, Laura could see the sky through a place cut in the stone. There was a kind of pit in the floor, directly below, far below, and inside the pit there was a fire. Whatever was burning smelled very bad. Seaweed, perhaps, only rotten, rotten. Light came down, and the smoke went up.

There was nothing else in the temple aside from a beach lounger with a rusty frame. Some of its plastic slats had given way.

The sight of the beach lounger gave Laura pause. What kind of a god lay around on a beat-up beach lounger instead of a golden throne? There wasn't even an altar.

Before she had ever gone inside Lewis Latimer, way back when she'd been in preschool, whenever they'd walked past, Laura had imagined how splendid it must be on the inside. The art-deco façade, the doors that stretched up as if to admit giants, the broad steps that led up to them, were so stately and formidable she'd thought the classrooms inside must be more beautiful than any rooms she'd ever seen. She'd pictured chandeliers, stately murals, desks with claw feet and brass fittings. Ha! The interior of Malo Mogge's temple was somehow even less impressive than Lewis Latimer had turned out to be. Ha ha!

But she'd come all this way and Laura was otherwise out of ideas. When someone you loved was sick, you took them to the doctor's office. If the person you loved was dead, you took them to a (funeral parlor, her brain said) goddess. She sat down on the floor beside the sled. Her phone buzzed. When she looked, there was another text from Rosamel. Girl, you've gone viral. Sent you the link. Go watch already.

When she clicked through, it was a Twitter link. Someone had posted a video on YouTube of Laura and her parents singing on the stage at the Cliff Hangar. Mariah Carey had retweeted it. She'd written, *Seriously! Who is this kid?*

Laura watched the video. Three people singing on a stage: a girl who had escaped Bogomil's realm, a father who wasn't real, a mother who was now dead. There was Ruth, alive, singing. Here, too, was Ruth, a corpse on a child's sled. Laura turned off her phone.

It seemed better not to wait any longer. Ruth shouldn't have to be dead any longer than necessary. Laura went over and peered down at the fire in the pit. She yanked a hair out of her head and then decided that one hair might not be enough. She pulled out a few more and let the strands of hair fall into the fire.

She felt a little silly, but in fact this turned out to have been the right thing to do. Malo Mogge was suddenly standing there on the other side of the firepit, looking somewhat surprised. Her flamingo-pink wings were gone, but she still wore the black silk pajamas. They were stiff with mud up to the knees and elbows, her midriff splattered as if she'd been running on all fours.

"I'm sorry," Laura said. "I didn't mean to interrupt you."

"No apologies necessary," Malo Mogge said. "It gets tedious chasing the same person around and around. Thomas can deal with Avelot, though if he loses the rib I gave him, I will take one of his in its place. Do people think I'm made of ribs?"

None of this made much sense to Laura, but she gathered Bowie was still alive. "I'm sure you'll get them eventually," she said.

"Yes, of course," Malo Mogge said. "Now, what's this? What have you brought me?"

Laura glanced over at the sled, trying not to look too closely at Ruth—her face like a piece of wax fruit, her sandy tongue that Laura had not been able to wipe clean, the slack fixedness of her limbs. "My mother," she said.

"I remember," Malo Mogge said. "She got in the way."

"She didn't mean to," Laura said.

"I'm sure she didn't," Malo Mogge said. It sounded as if she were humoring Laura but Laura went along with it. She didn't mind if Malo Mogge treated her like a child as long as she brought Ruth back. And of course Malo Mogge was very old. Laura could see she must seem like a child to someone like that.

"I brought her to you," Laura began, and then swallowed. She was afraid she would say it all wrong and then Malo Mogge would refuse.

"Yes," Malo Mogge said. "It's very thoughtful. No one else has thought to bring me a sacrifice yet. And a parent! That's a very big sacrifice. Though of course she's dead, isn't she? Usually there is a ritual and they're alive to begin with."

"No!" Laura said. "I mean, that isn't why I brought her. Though of course the next time I come I will definitely bring you a sacrifice. Does it have to be something living? How do you feel about flowers? Or"—she tried to think of nice things—"expensive fragrances? Clean pajamas? Songs? I could sing for you. I'm not a particularly good person or anything, but I'm good at that. I'm good at music."

"I like perfume," Malo Mogge said. "And songs. But why have you brought your mother all this way if it wasn't to give her to me? Why did you call me to my temple?"

"Because I want you to bring her back," Laura said. "I need her back. I don't want her to be dead."

"Oh," Malo Mogge said. She sat down on her beach lounger and produced a comb out of one pocket. She began to drag it through her ratted hair, tidying it. "No. That isn't something I do."

"Is it something you don't want to do or is it something you can't do?" Laura said.

"I fail to see the distinction," Malo Mogge said. "Either way, the answer to your question is the same." She licked a finger and smoothed her left eyebrow. Then the right.

"I made a deal with you," Laura said. "I said I would find the key for you. That I would serve you."

"Have you found it?" Malo Mogge said.

"Not yet," Laura said. "But if I find it for you? Will you bring her back?"

Malo Mogge said, grudgingly, "If it were possible, then so I would reward you. But that is not a thing I can do."

Laura bit her lip to keep from screaming. She said, "I understand."

Malo Mogge gave her a sharp look. "I did not mean to cause your mother's death, you know. And just as I cannot bring her back from death, so you cannot cause harm to me. You must see this. You are grieving presently. But know if you serve me, I will give you succor. I will give you power. I will give you more things than you can imagine."

"And if I don't serve you?" Laura said.

"Then we would not be friends," Malo Mogge said in a perfectly pleasant voice. "But I think you are too smart for that."

It wasn't really as if she had a choice in the long run. Laura thought carefully. Then said, "Okay. Thank you."

"Excellent. Let's be friends," Malo Mogge said. She put her hand to her side and winced. "And I will do your mother a great honor. I've given Thomas my smallest rib, and I don't know when I will get it back."

She went over to the sled, where she pulled the blanket back from Ruth's body. Before Laura understood what was happening, Malo Mogge had lifted up Ruth's shirt and reached deep into the flesh of her side as if she were extracting a piece of jewelry from a jewelry box. When she drew her hand back, there was a piece of red and white bone in it.

"There," Malo Mogge said. She turned Ruth's rib over in her hand and then, grimacing, pushed the broken end into her own side. "Ah. Better. A little better. Now let's dispose of this. Unless you wish a memento of some kind?"

Laura could not speak.

Malo Mogge pointed her finger at the sled, and though it and Ruth both were soaked in ocean water, it burst into flames. There was a smell of burning hair. Laura turned and threw up on the temple floor.

Malo Mogge gave her a severe look.

"Sorry," Laura said. "Sorry."

"You are weeping," Malo Mogge said. "Those who serve me should be joyful."

"My mother," Laura said. And could not go on. Ruth's corpse was burning on the floor of the temple.

"Let me take that pain from you then," Malo Mogge said. And as she had before in Laura's house, she made a gesture. Laura felt the hole it made in her. Where Ruth had been, where the idea of her death had been, now there was nothing. Ruth, dead, had been the worst thing she could imagine. This was something she could not have imagined at all.

"You needn't stay," Malo Mogge said. "Not this time. I will tend the fire."

Laura turned and fled. Once she was on the broad terrace of the temple, she became a tern and beat her way back to the shore. When, human again, she came up the driveway toward her house, the twins were still playing outside.

"You were gone a long time," one said, standing up against the chain-link fence. "Where's our sled?"

"She burned it," Laura said. She went into her house.

The Book of Thomas

Bowie became a squirrel, a wasp, a fleet dog, a cloud of gnats, a hummingbird flicking away through the opalescent snow. Thomas followed, one thing and then another. He pursued Bowie through the marshes, lost him, found him again, a frog no bigger than a fingernail flattened upon a reed. Bowie sprang away, was gone again.

Malo Mogge's enthusiasm for the hunt dimmed. First she fell behind, then she came abreast of Thomas again, a black jackal, grinning, her whiskered snout daubed with crystals of frozen mud. This was play to Malo Mogge; for Thomas and Bowie, life and death. Thomas had never thought Avelot would be so difficult to kill; he had thought the difficulty was in the finding, but this was not the Avelot he remembered. As a girl, the only things remarkable about Avelot had been her voice and Kristofer's infatuation with her. In Thomas's memory she had seemed surprised by these things as well.

When he'd taken his shot at the bird in the fir tree, he'd thought it hit true. The next time he must not miss.

He could not stop seeing the woman moving her body to protect Bowie. Why had she done that? Mo had been there. What if it had been Mo instead?

When he had pictured Avelot's death, there had never been an audience. It had been a private thing.

He had hesitated. Bowie had escaped, was still escaping. Thomas would never catch Avelot, who was now Bowie; only Bowie could be caught and killed. Thomas lost Bowie and hunted until he found him once more.

HE WISHED MO had not seen. The woman's blood was on Thomas's hands now. Like Kristofer, she had died not understanding what was happening to her. Perhaps her daughters would want to take revenge on Thomas. He had not killed her, but all of this was his fault. Avelot had not killed Kristofer, but his death had been the consequence of her action. His blood was on Avelot's hands. If Thomas did not kill Bowie, then the woman would be dead for nothing. As Kristofer had died for nothing.

RUTH. HER NAME was Ruth. He remembered now. You should remember the name of the one whose death you have caused. Bowie had not remembered Kristofer. Bowie had not even remembered Avelot.

Bowie was all that was left of Avelot, just as Bowie and Thomas were all that was left of Kristofer. Thomas's brother had loved Avelot whether or not Avelot had deserved that love. Thomas, for Kristofer's sake, for his own sake, would kill Bowie whether or not Bowie deserved to be killed.

BOWIE WAS A burrowing mole, a snake, a long-legged marsh bird. None of them were the person they had once been, but no matter. If Kristofer had not died, then who would Thomas have been? An Anabin or a Bogomil? A keeper of an eldritch door or a divinity student, servant of another god, dead in a riot or stabbed in a tavern or swollen with some plague or ague, feverish, ranting, old and respectable and content, bitter and grasping still for what he could not find, a piece of apple or meat or a tumor caught in the instrument of his windpipe?

He envied these other Thomases. No, this was rank self-pity. He had had a purpose. He had paid the price. He would yet have some satisfaction.

If Thomas did not kill Bowie, then who was he?

BOWIE WAS A sand louse. Thomas, a wasp, striking fast, then caught in the noose of thread spun by the crab spider his prey had become.

The crab spider said, "Will you never let me go?"

"No," the wasp said, struggling to get free. "My brother loved you and you killed him."

"If he loved me so well, why did he pick you and not Avelot as his companion for the ritual?"

The wasp became still. "I cannot ask him because he is dead," it said at last.

"You hate me because he is dead," the crab spider said. "But if he had lived and the ritual been completed, you would have hated him instead. For what he made of you. You know this."

The wasp broke free. But the crab spider was gone. A pine marten was dashing across the snowy marsh. It held the dart made from Malo Mogge's rib in its teeth.

The Book of Anabin

It was no easy task locating one like Bowie. Thomas, on the other hand, thrashed around in the marsh like some great gothic beast in the most rococo opera, all wrath and bloodthirstiness and self-loathing. You might almost have mistaken him for Bogomil.

Anabin, in a peacoat he'd owned for more than fifty years now, made his way along the snowy boardwalk. As he walked, he hummed softly. It was a very old song, and he did not always remember exactly how it went. But he got it close enough, and in not too long a time a mouse darted onto the walkway and into his path. It was trembling, the way small things did when they fell into the wake of larger events. But it carried a weapon of great power in its jaws.

Anabin held out the cup of his hand and the mouse jumped in. It shook itself, neat and shining and inconsequential as a coin, then ran down the sleeve of his coat. There was a pocket in the lining, and soon Anabin could feel the small adjustments as the mouse made itself at home there.

He said, "I have some sympathy for him, you know. It is hard to live for so very long with the lack of the only thing you know how to desire. And she has made him dance all this time lightly. As if he knew no want at all."

The mouse said nothing to this. Mice do not care about the suffering of cats.

The Book of Bogomil and Susannah

She lay with Daniel's arms around her, her mother dead in the room below her bed. She willed herself to fall asleep, not to escape but to go in search of her old dream, her favorite dream, the one in which she ran freely and forever in a dark forest.

When at last she found herself there, everything was as she remembered it. The black and alluring pools of shadows beneath trees that were also shadows. The paths soft as velvet, exhaling under your bare feet as they led you one way and then another, deliriously, until, drunk with delight, you found you were no longer on a path at all but rather the place you were meant to be. The moon that did not shine because there was no sun and therefore no light for it to reflect and so everything lay in darkness beneath it, waiting to be discovered by whatever light you carried yourself. Everything was quiet and lovely and strange and asleep and awake as if it were her own body. This was the kingdom of Bogomil. This was the kingdom he had promised would be hers someday. Here she could be as ferocious and wild or as lazy and solitary as she wished and no one would ever tell her how else she should be. Here there was no other way to be other than how you yourself decided.

She had never come here purposefully and neither had she ever been here unless Bogomil had brought her. Unless Bogomil was with her.

She called his name and he was with her.

"I'm dreaming, aren't I?" Susannah said.

"Yes."

"I'm dreaming, but this is real, isn't it? You're real. You've always been real."

"The distinction between real and unreal is more slippery than you think it is," Bogomil said. "But yes."

"And my mother," Susannah said. "Ruth. She's dead, isn't she?"

"Yes," Bogomil said. "An accident, I believe. Malo Mogge meant to kill another."

"She's real, too," Susannah said. "Malo Mogge. There was a story someone told me. It was about Malo Mogge and you. And my old music teacher. I don't remember it."

"You are part of the story, too," Bogomil said.

"There was another dream I had," Susannah said. "Where Laura and Daniel and Mo were all dead. But no one knew what had happened to them. A year went by and no one knew."

"Not a dream," Bogomil said. "They came into my realm. I held them near a year. They had upset a great many plans of mine, and I was annoyed. But then by chance they escaped."

"It was my fault they died," Susannah said. "But I don't remember why. I don't remember a lot of things. Is it my fault that my mother is dead?"

"No," Bogomil said. "We can lay that death directly at Malo Mogge's door, so to speak. I spoke with her just before you called me. Ruth. She was sorry she had to leave you. She expressed a wish that you and your sister look after each other."

"You saw her?" Susannah said. "How?"

"One of my responsibilities," Bogomil said. "Sometimes there is one who has been involved in Malo Mogge's affairs. They have come into contact with her key in one of its various forms. These come here upon their death and I make sure no part of them is left trapped in this realm, which is not Death but merely its threshold. When Malo Mogge had her key, this was her larder. The ones who came here would have been her meat. But presently Malo Mogge is trapped in your world. The door will not open for her. She has lost her key and goes hungry."

"Is that what they are all looking for?" Susannah said. She was not going to think about Ruth right now. Her heel was hurting her quite badly. She decided to focus on this instead. "A key?"

"It was a coin when Mo gave it to you," Bogomil said. "It might be something else now."

"No," Susannah said. "Mo never gave it to me. I was going to give it to Daniel. You'd told me to. But I never did. That's why everything went wrong. You said if I got the coin from Mo and gave it to Daniel, then he and I would be together forever. You would give me your realm. There was going to be a ritual. But Daniel broke up with me and I took off before I ever had the chance to meet up with Mo. I never even had the coin. So I never gave it to Daniel."

"An adequate summary of what I understand to have happened," Bogomil said.

"I trusted you," Susannah said. "I thought you were my friend. But I don't think things would have worked out any better if I'd done what you wanted me to do. If I'd given Daniel the key."

"Oh, Susannah," Bogomil said. "I don't think you should trust anyone at all."

"Not even Laura," she said sadly.

"Not even her," Bogomil said. "Is there something wrong with your foot, Susannah?"

"I have a splinter in my heel," she said. "I keep forgetting to take it out."

"That seems like something you ought to remember," Bogomil said, "when you wake up."

She woke. Daniel was asleep, his arms around her. She wriggled out of them and got out of bed. "Susannah?" Daniel said. He sat up.

"It's okay," Susannah said. "I'm fine. Just go back to sleep."

He lay back down, his breathing growing easy. Susannah found she still had on the coat she'd worn out to meet Mo that morning. She was so warm she felt feverish. Her hair clung damply to the back of her neck.

She took off the coat, took off her sweater. She went down the stairs, not sure what she would find, but neither Laura nor Ruth's body was anywhere. The only thing on the white couch was Laura's Gretsch. Stains where Ruth's blood had already dried, scuff marks from someone's shoes.

On the carpet beside the couch was a folded and stapled square of paper. When she bent down to pick it up, she found her name was written on one side. The handwriting was hers.

The Book of Daniel

"Wake up," someone was saying. "Or do you plan to sleep until the thing is ended and it is time for all to change? Wake up, you most stubborn child."

Daniel did not wish to wake, but the voice demanded obedience. He opened his eyes. He was in Susannah's room, in Susannah's bed. Seated at Susannah's desk was Mr. Anabin.

"Where is Susannah?" Mr. Anabin said.

"I was asleep," Daniel said. He remembered Ruth was dead. "She was here with me. Where is she?"

"So we have established that Susannah is missing," Mr. Anabin said. "Where is Laura?"

"Laura's gone, too?" Daniel said.

"Laura is not here. Neither is their mother's body," Mr. Anabin said. "Mo told me how their mother died. That it was by the hand of Malo Mogge."

Daniel said, "Laura was trying to figure out a way to raise Ruth from the dead. Maybe she did? Maybe that's why they're not here?"

"Not even Laura can raise the dead," Mr. Anabin said. "Which is a mercy. But how have you become yourself without using your magic? Was it Laura?"

"The bear thing," Daniel said. "I forgot. Bogomil caught me and made me go into my house. He, uh, he told me to be hungry. To go and eat someone or else to become human again. So I changed back. I didn't mean to, but I did."

"If you had used your own magic," Mr. Anabin said, "I would see it. I would suspect Bogomil of doing it himself, but I don't detect his magic here, either. I am familiar with the particular flavor of Bogomil's magic."

"All I know is this morning I woke up human," Daniel said. "Susannah was with me. I think she would have noticed if I were a bear."

"And now here you are in Susannah's bed," Mr. Anabin said, "and Susannah is missing and you did not notice when she left."

"That's not the same thing at all," Daniel said.

"No," Mr. Anabin said. "But it's perplexing all the same. Especially as, wherever she's gone, I believe she has taken Malo Mogge's key with her."

"Why would Susannah have the key?" Daniel said.

"Because I gave it to her," Mr. Anabin said.

"Why would you do that?" Daniel said. "She doesn't even know what it is!"

"I think she is beginning to put the pieces together, in fact. Would you prefer I had given it to Malo Mogge? Or Bogomil? Now Susannah is hidden from me, and so I suggest you go and find her. Or, if you prefer, I will turn you into a bear again."

"I'll find her," Daniel said. "But not because you're telling me to. She shouldn't be alone right now."

"Good enough," Mr. Anabin said. He stood up.

"Wait!" Daniel said. "We have to talk about Carousel. My sister. You said to look for the person who wasn't real, but it isn't Carousel. It can't be her."

"Here is a little more of your magic at last," Mr. Anabin said. "A little late, but better late than a bear, Daniel. I'm curious: why do you reject what your magic tells you?"

"Because it isn't right," Daniel said. "Because she's my sister, and because I remember what it was like when she was born. When she died. And maybe you made her out of magic, but now she's just as real as you or me."

"Is she?" Mr. Anabin said. "How do you know?"

"I know," Daniel said. "I know there is no fucking way I'm going to use magic to send her away now that we have her back. I'm not going to send her away before she finishes fourth grade and gets a better teacher than Ms. Fish. Maybe Carousel is real and maybe she's magic, but what I do know is it doesn't make things any better if I send her away. Everything you and Bogomil want us to do is horrible or it's for a horrible purpose. So go ahead. Turn me into a bear."

"Magic made Carousel," Mr. Anabin said. "Are you sure then that magic is entirely bad?"

"If magic isn't entirely bad because it made Carousel," Daniel countered, "how does using magic to send away the good thing magic made make any sense?"

"Consider this," Mr. Anabin said. "If you refuse to use your magic, you will fail the last test Bogomil and I have set you. You will return to Bogomil's realm. Do you know what will happen to you there when Malo Mogge at last has her key again? You will be her meat. She will come through the door into Bogomil's realm and when she finds you there, she will devour you. It has been a long time since she has had access to those who were once her sacrifices and she is famished beyond all imagining. She will consume all of you, spirit and flesh and magic, and Carousel, who is made of the magic in you, will be unmade just the same."

"I won't let that happen," Daniel said.

"You will not be able to stop it," Mr. Anabin said. "Not without the aid of your magic."

"It isn't mine," Daniel said. "I'll figure out another way."

"There is something admirable about your stubbornness," Mr. Anabin said. "It's a shame you choose not to use magic. You would be a steadfast guardian of the door. It is work that requires tenderheartedness, and you have that also."

"If the job of guarding this door was all that great," Daniel said, "then why would you want to give it up?"

"Sass!" Mr. Anabin said. "Be careful or I really will turn you into a bear again."

"You can't win every argument by turning someone into a bear," Daniel said, though he wasn't sure that was true. "Is that a mouse? Is that *Bowie*?"

The mouse had crept up to nestle under Mr. Anabin's collar, its fur the color of silver sand, the slender cord of its tail threaded through a buttonhole. Mr. Anabin plucked the mouse from the collar of his coat and held it close to his face, whispering something to it. The mouse became a gull. It shrieked, a noise too loud and desolate for a room to contain. The noise reverberated until Mr. Anabin opened the window so it could fly out.

"What did you say?" Daniel said.

"That he should go before I came to my senses and took from him the extremely useful artifact he has stolen."

"What did he steal?" Daniel said.

"Nothing of any concern to one who does not wish to wield magic. I'm sure I'll be seeing you soon, Daniel." Then Mr. Anabin was gone, the window left open for Daniel to shut. Snow was coming in.

He tried calling Susannah, was sent to voicemail. He hung up without leaving a message.

You ok? he texted. Worried about you. Call me

Ellipses appeared in the text box almost immediately. Then they disappeared.

No one was downstairs. The couch was an object of horror, and outside the light was seeping away, no way to use or keep it now.

Daniel went home, where the Lucklows were all playing Monopoly. Carousel was the top hat. He could see, again, that she should not have been there. But he could not discern how she was any less real than any other member of his family. Why should *he* remain but be made to send her away? They were made of the same thing.

He crouched down and said, "How are you doing?"

"I am not winning yet," Carousel said. "But that doesn't mean I won't win."

"You're going to lose," Dakota said. "Wear a cape and die super mad, carnival ride."

"In North Dakota, it's illegal to fall asleep with your shoes on," Daniel said. "And in South Dakota, you can arrest arm-wrestling pacifists." He had a whole list of these.

"I'm the great state of Neither Dakota," Dakota said. "Only thing illegal here is people named Daniel."

"Want to play?" his mom said hopefully. She had one of Peter's feet in her lap, was pressing her thumbs into the arch. That was his mom, always multitasking. Peter had terribly flat arches. "You can be the iron and I'll go lie on the couch. I've got three hotels on Baltic Avenue."

"I don't really see myself as a landlord," Daniel said. "Though it's a kind offer." He stooped down and kissed Carousel on her cheek. She smelled of baby lotion and magic unmistakable. Up in his room he opened the desk drawer where Bogomil had told him to look.

There were lottery tickets, the scratch-off kind where sometimes you found you had won two dollars. Maybe, sometimes, five or twenty. The top amounts, though, those were just for fun. For imagining what you could buy before you took your coin and scraped off the plasticized film. He brought the tickets back to the living room and gave them to his mom. "Bought these on a whim. I'm going to walk into town to run a couple of errands and hang out with Susannah for a while, but maybe the kids could scratch these off at dinner, okay? Early Christmas presents."

Everyone cheered at this idea, even his parents, who should have known better.

His mom said, "Can you pick up some bread while you're out? And strawberries, if there are any that don't look too ripe and they aren't more than six dollars?"

"Sure," Daniel said. He took one last long look at his family and then went out into the snow.

He wasn't going to ride a bike in this weather. He could have become some sort of beast if he were willing to use magic. But Daniel was wearing winter boots, and the walk might do him some good, and he did not intend to use magic no matter how badly it wanted to be used. He went into town and past the coffee shop, which was closed although it was not even five yet. The plinth where the statue of Sarah Goode (first Black woman to receive a U.S. patent, for the precursor to the Murphy bed; Daniel had done a report on her in fifth grade) should have been was, mysteriously, empty, and as he went on, he saw that every other statue was also absent from its station. Was this something else that Malo Mogge had done?

He went trudging up the Cliff Road, full of doubt, full of dread. He'd made a guess as to where Susannah had gone, and leaving aside everything else, he was going to feel like the world's largest potato if he was wrong. But if she wasn't at Mo's house, perhaps Mo would help Daniel find her. He wasn't going to call Mo, though, because if he did and Susannah was there, Mo might tell her. She might take off if she knew

Daniel was coming. Mr. Anabin had said she was putting the pieces together, all of the things Daniel had been keeping from her.

He was just passing the Cliff Hangar when he realized someone stood there in the unplowed parking lot. They were calling his name.

As he came nearer, he saw this person was not a person at all. It was an improbably colored horse with wings and a horn between its eyes; it called to him in a voice he knew.

The Book of Carousel

The last hour of Carousel's life had been full of surprises and magic, the first a thing she had previously enjoyed a great deal, and the other, magic, something she'd thought was reserved for television, movies, and books. The first surprise was the scratch-off tickets Daniel had given each of them. Underneath the little silver coins of film were three bells that turned out to mean Carousel's ticket was worth real money, a lot of money. This was the second surprise, and the third was it wasn't just Carousel's ticket: it was all of them. This meant the game of Monopoly was over, abruptly. And, yes, it was great how everyone had just won a lot of money, but Carousel thought she'd had a shot at winning Monopoly, only no one else cared about that now.

She went back to the room she shared with Lissy and Dakota because everyone was yelling and jumping around and trying to get Daniel on the phone, and sometimes she just really needed to get away from her family. She loved them, but they were a lot.

The next surprise was the man looking through the bookshelf in her bedroom. He was the whitest man she'd ever seen. She thought about yelling, but something about the man suggested this would not be a good idea.

"You're Caroline," the man said. "Daniel's sister."

"Carousel," she said. "Not Caroline. Who are you?"

"I'm Bogomil," he said. "Truly it's a pleasure to meet you, Carousel."

"I don't see why," she said. "You shouldn't be in here, by the way. You look like a vampire. Nobody invited you."

"I go where I please," Bogomil said. "I'm here because there's something you need to know. It concerns you and your brother Daniel. After I tell it to you, I will go. And after I have gone, there's something you will need to do."

"I don't care for bossy people," Carousel said. She ought to have been afraid of this very strange person, but she felt she knew something about him that kept her from being afraid: that as long as you interested him, you were okay. And he was interesting, too. "But go on. I'm listening."

When Bogomil finished his explanation, Carousel felt no differently than she had before. She felt no less real. "Poor Daniel," she said. But she was also annoyed. Why did people keep secrets like this?

"Poor Daniel!" Bogomil said. "You realize, don't you, that his task is now to unmake you. If he does as Anabin commands, he will undo the magic you are made of. Then you will no longer exist, and no one will even remember that you did."

"Daniel wouldn't do that," Carousel said.

"Then he will die again," Bogomil said. "And you will be unmade anyway."

"That won't happen, either," Carousel said. She said it as definitively as she could.

Bogomil said, "It will happen unless you do as I tell you. You, being made entirely of magic, require magic in order to go on in this world. You need a great deal of it. What you have now is borrowed from the magic Anabin used to make Daniel a new body. You and Daniel have been drawing on the same battery, so to speak. Daniel has been told he must take magic back from you, but you, if you wish to be real, may instead take it from him."

"I'm not going to do that!" Carousel said. Then, in spite of herself, "How would I even do that?"

"You are made of magic," Bogomil said. "You are already using it, without knowing you do so. Not all like you are capable of this, but as Daniel has refused his magic, this abundance has been made available to you, and I see you have made the most of it. Will is a source of magic, but given enough magic, magic may become the source of will. For example, magic maintains you in the shape of what Daniel could imagine, but you, now that you know what you are, might become whatever you desire. A prairie dog. An anteater."

"An anteater?" Carousel said. Much of what he'd been saying seemed like homework or one of the TikTok tutorials on the occult her sisters liked, but the last bit was interesting. "Why would I want to be an anteater?"

"It is a pleasant discovery that you, independent of Daniel, want anything at all. But all I mean to suggest is magic is easier for one like you than you can imagine," Bogomil said. "Anyone can use magic as long as they have a sufficient quantity to begin with. And if you wish to take Daniel's magic, all you have to do is reach out your hand to take it."

"If I can just reach out and take someone's magic," Carousel said, "Why wouldn't I take yours instead?"

Bogomil said, "I don't advise trying. But Daniel's magic is already yours. It would come to you willingly. Magic wants to be used, Carousel; Daniel will not use it. It would be a shame if you, too, refused to use it. Even Daniel ought to be able to see this."

"But you said I'm not even real," Carousel said, working her way carefully through the tangle of hidden motives passing for helpfulness. "If I'm not real, maybe I should do the opposite of what you're saying. Maybe I should give all my magic back to Daniel. From what you said, nobody would care. Nobody would even remember me."

"I would remember you," Bogomil said. "And although you and I have spent less than a half hour in each other's company, I find you far more interesting than Daniel has ever been. I have been alive for a very long time, longer than you can imagine, and although you have been what you are for only a handful of days, you are already more real than many I have met. Why sacrifice yourself for him?"

"I'm not going to do anything that hurts Daniel," Carousel said.

"You are thinking of your family, perhaps," Bogomil said. He sat down on Dakota's bed. If it had been Carousel's bed, she would have objected, but it served Dakota right. "You think your family would be devastated if something were to happen to Daniel. But, Carousel, if you take your brother's magic, he will simply be missing again. No one will remember he ever came back. They've already grieved him. This will be no new source of pain."

Perhaps Carousel wasn't real, but neither was she as stupid as Bogomil seemed to think. Some of what he was saying was true, she could feel that. Maybe the compliments were even sincere. But the way he was looking at her as he said all this was the same way Lissy and Dakota looked when they sent her off on made-up errands so they could do their stupid spells without having to include her. "You want me to get rid of Daniel for you. Why?"

Bogomil stood up. For the first time, Carousel was afraid of him. He said, "Everything I have told you is true. But I will tell you one more true thing. I don't like this brother of yours. It's as simple as that. Make up your mind for yourself. Tell your family you are going out. Use your magic and tell them not to worry. Then use your magic to find your brother. Go talk with him if you like. After talking you must do what you think you ought. But I can tell you, as someone who began as a real person and has become, over time, less and less such a thing, what you are now is not what you may someday become. Real is as real does. But I'm sure your parents have read you *The Velveteen Rabbit*."

"They have," Carousel said. And then realized they had not. It was just another thing she remembered that wasn't real at all.

Bogomil smiled as if he could see this on her face. And then he was gone. A second later the horrible, knowing, delighted smile was gone, too.

Carousel sat down on the floor. She thought about throwing a tantrum, but what good would that do? Someone would show up and think she was throwing a tantrum about Monopoly and she wouldn't be able to explain otherwise.

She turned over and over in her mind what she thought she ought to do until she realized that just because Bogomil had suggested it didn't mean she ought not to do it. She would go find Daniel. And, wanting to find him, she found she knew where he was. He was up in the rocks along the Cliff Road, just below the Cliff Hangar.

HER FAMILY WAS in the kitchen, eating handfuls of popcorn and talking about money. Money! Magic was much more interesting. There the scratch-off tickets were, on the table, and the magic in Carousel recognized that, yes, here was more magic. It smelled like Bogomil.

"I'm going to go run an errand," Carousel said. This was something that her parents, that Daniel, often said. Everyone at the table looked at her. Dakota burst out laughing.

"Don't worry about me," Carousel said. "I'll come right back."

And Bogomil was correct about this, too. Magic was easy. Her family accepted what she said, and when Carousel stepped outside, she used magic again and became a unicorn, because what was the point of having magic if you didn't use it to become a unicorn? Then, because she needed to catch up with her brother as quickly as possible, she gave herself the most beautiful, iridescent, and powerful wings she could imagine.

If only she could be a unicorn all the time. Unicorns were unreal, and everyone loved them anyway. Wanted them to be real. Who wasn't Team Unicorn? Ms. Fish, probably. And in that moment, Carousel made up her mind that she would go on being Carousel. She would go on being. She had done a pretty good job so far. And if Ms. Fish wasn't nicer after the Christmas break, maybe they could see how Ms. Fish felt about being an actual fish. Carousel could keep her in a little bowl.

There was an indent in the cliff face just below the balcony of the Cliff Hangar. Not quite a cave but a sheltered ledge that was clearly someone's excellent hangout space. It was entirely hidden from anyone standing above, and there were colored handprints on the cliff wall like the ones My Two Hands Both Knowe You put on their faces before shows. The outcropping of rocks was covered in frozen snow: Carousel landed, placing her hooves carefully. There were three or four snow-covered lumps sticking up, boulders that would have made good seats for anyone who'd scrambled down to the ledge, but no one was sitting on them. Daniel was here and yet he was not here.

Carousel prodded the nearest lump of rock with her horn, excavating. There was something about its shape that distressed her.

Beneath the covering of snow, like a shape in a cloud, she could see how the rock mimicked the crude shape of a body curled protectively around itself. Here could have been one reaching arm.

Carousel investigated the other lumps. One was, as far as she could tell, just a bit of fallen rock. The other two, like the first, had a shape suggesting they had once been living people. She thought of the library book about Pompeii, bodies caught in the rush of lava.

Here, her magic told her, was Daniel. And two others. But here, too, coming up the Cliff Road was Daniel. Carousel took to the air again, leaving Daniel's poor corpse for the body made by magic that he occupied now.

The Book of Mo

The house was full of women. They sat around the kitchen table laughing and talking. They listened as Mo explained everything that had been going on and all the stupid things he had done. They brushed aside his apologies, told him not to be ridiculous, assured him everything would be fine in the long run. Mo made tea, and as he set it down in front of them, they touched him affectionately. His hand. His shoulder. His face.

But when his grandmother picked up her mug, Mo saw how her fingers began to dissolve.

"Here," he said, taking it from her. He opened the windows, let the cold air in. "We can do better than tea anyway." Possibly snow wasn't the best material to make people out of. The smell of rose petals, chosen because his grandmother had loved them, made him think of Bogomil.

"Always looking out for me," his grandmother said. "He's such a good boy, Cara."

Mo's mother said, "I can't get over it. He's so handsome."

"Oh, stop," Jenny said. "You're embarrassing him."

"No," Mo said. "Go on. Enumerate my charms." He'd located a cache of Brut Rosé that remained from the cases the founder of Romance Writers of America, Vivian Stephens, had sent his grandmother when the new edition of *Ashana's Heart* was published. His grandmother, never a heavy drinker, had nonetheless dutifully opened one bottle each time one of her books listed at number one on the *USA Today* list. There were still three bottles left.

He popped the cork as his grandmother protested she couldn't possibly have a glass now. "How will I ever get back to work if I'm tipsy?" she said.

"What work?" Mo said.

"I haven't worked on my book in I don't know how long," his grandmother said.

"You were dead!" Mo said. "Don't you think you get a day off?"

"Mo," his grandmother said. As if it wasn't even worth thinking about. She got up from the table, stood on her toes, and kissed his cheek.

Cara said, "Let her, Mo. You know she won't be happy unless she gets her pages written. Let's you and I go up to the attic. I want to see all my old friends."

Mo saw that Jenny was confused. "She means her instruments," he said.

"Come with us, Jenny," Cara said. "Do you play anything?"

"Me?" Jenny said. She appealed to Mo. "Do I?"

Maybe it was the work of making the three of them. Mr. Anabin had made only the one. But there was something blurred about the women, something thinner. His grandmother was herself, more or less, but this Jenny was lesser than the one Mo had sent away. And his mother! How would he even know if this Cara was how she ought to have been? He'd known Cara through photographs, his grandmother's stories, the instruments that had belonged to her. Was this a reasonable likeness of her? Mo wanted it to be.

"Only if you want to," Mo said to Jenny. "What do you want?"

"I want to sit here and drink a little champagne and look out at the snow," Jenny said. It was what Mo had hoped she would say. He poured a generous measure into the balloon glass she held out, bent down, and hugged her, his face up against the coolness of her soft hair, which smelled not of Jenny Ping's shampoo but of roses. Then he followed his mother out of the kitchen. As they went down the hall, he could hear his grandmother in her office, settling down at her desk to get her eight pages written. Maybe when she was done she would come up and join them. Maybe later they would all have dinner together and talk late into the night, and then in the morning go on together in just this way. With his magic he opened all the windows in the house, though already he was shivering.

Cara wandered around the attic room, picking up first one instrument, then another. At last Mo said, "Don't you want to play something?"

"It's just so hard to choose," she said. She looked out the open windows at the bay where Malo Mogge's temple gloated behind the rosebushes. "Someone should do something about that," she said.

"Yeah," Mo said. "They should."

"But not you," Cara said. "You stay away from that woman. Let someone else clean up her mess."

"Can we talk about something else?" Mo said.

Cara was more amenable than his grandmother. Or perhaps she was slightly less real. She sat down at the baby grand and lifted the lid; Mo settled himself into the egg chair.

When she began to play, her fingers bore down so lightly Mo could not hear what she played at all. But gradually she increased the pressure on the keys. Mo did not recognize the piece. It was wistful and fragmented and involved frequent key shifts, pauses where Cara appeared to be trying to recall how the next bit went. Eventually Mo began to identify lines of melody, or perhaps it was all the same melody, changing, trailing off, and then reappearing, moving between Cara's left and right hands. Every time it seemed to be about to resolve, Cara took it meandering over into another key, beginning again.

Cara Gorch played for some time while Mo sat listening. Downstairs, Maryanne Gorch wrote and then revised, moving steadily forward in the manuscript abandoned since her death, while Jenny Ping opened another bottle of Brut Rosé. There was someone else in the house, too, going from room to room, wondering at where she found herself. Mo had not meant to make her at all and maybe he hadn't. Magic creates magic and so on.

Cara took her hands from the piano abruptly.

"What was that?" Mo said. "I don't know it."

"Oh, you know," Cara said. "Just one of those things that gets stuck in your head. Did you like it?"

"Yes!" Mo said. "Is it yours?"

Cara closed the piano lid. She went and picked up a squeeze-box and began to draw music out of it. The same melody as before, Mo realized. But now she'd made something infectious out of it. Comical and bouncing.

She played for only a few minutes, then put the squeeze-box down and went over to the spinet. Once again she began the same piece.

"Play something else," Mo said.

"Sure, baby," she said. "How about this one?"

But it was the same song again. Cara stopped playing. She said, "I don't seem to know any other songs. I'm sorry. I didn't want to leave you, Mo. I would've stayed if I could."

"I know," he said. He leaned forward in the egg chair and she took a step toward him. "She took good care of me, though. Wrote her ten pages every day. Eight before lunch and two after dinner before she went to bed. But she always had time for me."

"Still does. Otherwise she wouldn't have come back." She took another step.

"I needed her," Mo said. "I needed you."

"Is that all you need?" Cara said. Now she was so close he could have reached out and touched her. She could have touched him. But she didn't.

"No," Mo said. "Yes. I don't know everything I want, not yet. I want to compose music. I want to live. I want there to be someone who won't leave me."

"You write music?" Cara said.

"Yeah," Mo said.

"How wonderful! Will you play me something you wrote?"

Mo was finding it harder and harder to look at his mother. "I don't really play my stuff when other people are around."

"I wish you would," Cara said, smiling at him. "Just pretend I'm not here. Go on."

Maybe it was that she didn't ask why he didn't let other people hear what he wrote. Maybe the real Cara, too, would have persisted, would have wanted to hear Mo play something. Maybe eventually they would have had a conversation. But it wasn't this, that she was only asking the question everyone always asked and Mo couldn't decide whether he ought to give the answer he always gave. It was that, thinking about whether he would play something for her, Mo realized it didn't matter. Cara wasn't real. He could play something for her, but it wouldn't be real because she wasn't, either. So what was the point, really?

"I'm sorry," he said. "I love you. I'm sorry." And he undid the thing he had done. He undid them all.

It was fully dark outside now. There was a damp patch on the carpet in the music studio and a handful of rose petals. Mo sat down at the spinet. The bench was still warm, though he had made her of snow. She wasn't here, she had never really been here, he knew he was absolutely alone in the house, but he played the stupid song about Duchamp and the rocking chair that Thomas, so long ago, had written he liked. It sounded even stupider than he'd expected on a spinet.

He didn't believe his grandmother would be there still, typing away in her office until she hit her eight pages, but on the other hand, wouldn't that be just like her? To refuse to vanish away until her work was done? He went downstairs, but the kitchen was empty, Jenny Ping's balloon glass still half-full. The study was empty, too, though the laptop had not gone to sleep yet. Well. Mo bent over and saw that Lavender Glass was addressing a minor villain, Lord Torquil Spintorm, on the subject of love. Of course! What else did she ever talk about? What did she have to say this time? Only this:

"But I never meant to leave him, Lord Spintorm. He will not understand I had no choice."

"It is of no concern to me what he understands or does not understand," Lord Spintorm retorted.

"You think by separating us you can put an end to love, that he will believe I will not return to him. But when he was gone, I knew he had not left me by his choice. I knew he would return to me if he could. And I knew if he did not, it did not change love into its absence. Love goes on even when we cannot, Mo. Love is

Here was where the manuscript broke off.

Mo read those last lines of dialogue out loud, to hear it. "Love is what?" he said.

Behind him, someone said, "Who is Mo?"

"Shit!" Mo said, and jumped up. He took in the woman standing behind him. She had long red hair spilling over bare shoulders. There was a whole cleavage situation going on, too. "Who are you?" he said. But as he said this, he knew. Fucking Lavender Glass.

"I am Lavender Glass and those are my words," fucking Lavender Glass said. "I remember saying them. But who is Mo? Why was I thinking of him?"

"Mo would be me," Mo said.

"Where is this place?" Lavender Glass said. "And who dwells here? Whose man are you?"

"Excuse me," Mo said. "This is my house."

"Yours?" Lavender Glass said. Clearly she did not believe him. Fucking Lavender Glass. "Who has brought me here?"

"Again," Mo said, "me. But it was an accident." He couldn't quite figure out how he'd done it, but he could also sort of see how he'd done it. He'd been thinking about his grandmother and bringing her back, all the stuff she'd cared about that had made her who she was and how she'd done what Mr. Anabin could do. She'd made not-real people like Lavender Glass feel real. This was just one last little piece of Maryanne Gorch, even if what it looked like was a racist white lady with extensions wearing the wrong kind of clothes for this kind of weather and also this century.

"I get it," Mo said. "She spent most of her life with you. Thinking about you. Making sure you got out of bad situations and then getting you into even worse ones, all the way to happiness by the end. And if she still had you when I wasn't there, I'm glad about that."

"You know me," Lavender Glass, fucking Lavender Glass, said, "but I do not know you. Should I know you? Should I know this place? Who is knocking at the door? If it is Lord Torquil Spintorm, then I beg you, hide me."

"Will you *please* just shut up, please?" Mo said, and went to see who was at the door. If it was Lord Torquil Spintorm, he would hand her over and let them sort everything out or murder each other somewhere else. Sometimes the story went another way. Sometimes you never even knew how it ended.

The Book of Laura

She went through the house looking for Susannah. Wasn't this just like Susannah! Everything falling apart, and her sister disappeared, leaving Laura to straighten out the mess.

The couch, for instance. What was she supposed to do about that? You could get the stain out that her father's shoes had made, but then there was the blood. Maybe magic would help? Laura regarded her efforts and felt a little better.

You came back from the dead and your mother and sister had splurged for some reason on a white couch. Laura, had she been alive at the time, would have told them it was a mistake. But magic could be useful here, too. She made the couch a velvety green, and then swapped the green for a nice floral pattern in pink and green. But no, she didn't like that. Pink was too much like Malo Mogge's wings. And she had made the green the same green as Malo Mogge's temple, she saw now, and there was a hole in one of the cushions. Smoke rose out of the hole. She wasn't in the right frame of mind. There wasn't a single color that seemed suitable, and so she told the couch not to be a couch at all. It became a small black lamb made out of wool.

"Bogomil," Laura said, and there he was.

"You?" he said. He seemed a little surprised. That was nice.

"I think we should talk," Laura said.

Bogomil's face took on an expression of polite receptiveness.

"I have spent most of the day," Laura said, "trying to figure out how to bring my mother back from the dead, but I haven't gotten anywhere with that. And I'm guessing you can't help, either."

"No," Bogomil said.

Laura waited for him to express his condolences, but he said nothing else. "I need some coffee," she said. The French press was still on the table. It needed to be emptied before Laura made more. Ruth's mug was there, too, half-full. Laura reached out for it, saw lipstick smudged on the rim. She turned back to Bogomil. She didn't really need coffee.

Bogomil was right there behind her, so close she jumped. He said, "Let me get that," and picked up the French press and the mug and carried them over to the sink. Before Laura could say anything, he began to wash them.

"A long time ago," he said, "I made friends with a young musician. Thomas's brother. Kristofer. I made arrangements for Kristofer and Thomas to take on the roles Anabin and I have endured. Anabin would have the freedom he wanted, the freedom to be mortal, to grow old and die, or to go on living in the world with me, forever. If that was what he wanted. And I, I would take Malo Mogge's power from her. I would dispose of her and take her place."

Laura switched the kettle on. "When you say dispose of," she said, "what do you mean exactly?"

"I meant to kill her," Bogomil said. "I had the element of surprise on my side. But as it turned out, it was Avelot who surprised me. And the key hid itself from all. It found mortal protectors, a long chain of them that it forged against discovery. Only when one mortal protector died did that protector come to me. All who have business with the key in whichever form it may assume must come to my realm when they die. I was able to track the key, always one or two or a dozen lives or more behind and unable, therefore, to seize it. I learned it now took the form of a coin, and when it passed from hand to hand, I caught a glimpse of it, though not whose hand held it. Anabin, too, could feel when it made its presence known. And though Malo Mogge could not, still she followed after Anabin and me whenever she grew suspicious of our movements. What a comedy. All of us, in our power, in pursuit of what amounts to a bus token!"

"Sounds like it shouldn't have been that hard," Laura said. "Not if you could see it. Not if you knew where it had been."

"Except the coin did not stay with any person long enough to be found,"

Bogomil said. "Upside, this meant I had visitors to my realm, which, otherwise, can grow quite lonely. And if they grew wearisome, I might send them on their way. To make a very long story as short and to the point as possible, the coin that had been Malo Mogge's key disappeared altogether perhaps two hundred years ago. I no longer had even glimpses of it. It was as though it had been dropped down a well, locked away in a vault. Even more dismaying, sixty and some years passed between its disappearance and the next person to visit my realm. When he did, I discovered that upon taking possession of the coin, he had recognized it for a talisman of power. He'd taken efforts to conceal it, sealing it in such a way as to render it invisible to those looking for it. Though he had some natural talent for magic, he was a remarkably stupid man and bragged to his wife of what he'd done. Shortly thereafter, she ran away, stealing the coin because he had valued it so highly and her not at all. She, smarter than he, never spoke of it to anyone and neither did she dislodge the seal he'd placed on it. I surmise she sold it as a lucky piece, perhaps warning the buyer never to take it out of its casing, lest the luck run out. Or something like that. I kept her idiot husband for quite some time, but eventually, like his wife, I grew tired of his company. And because she had never handled the coin directly, when she died she did not come to me. I hope it was a miserable death, though her husband, it turned out, had loved her, though not well, and missed her still as long as I knew him."

"Do you want milk in your coffee?" Laura said.

"Just sugar," Bogomil said. "Lots of sugar."

They took their coffee over to the kitchen table and Bogomil went on. "That is how things stood for some time. And then the key came into the possession of a woman named Maryanne Gorch."

"Mo's grandmother," Laura said, "who died. Did you have something to do with that? She was my favorite writer."

"I read one or two of her novels," Bogomil said. "Pleasing if predictable in their shape, which is to say I enjoyed her romances more than I do the company of people, who are mostly predictable but rarely pleasing. I did not kill her, no. Maryanne Gorch's part in my story is this: She removed the coin at some point from its casket, having been told it was lucky. She flipped it while making up her mind whether to head west or north when she left her life in Chattanooga, and then she put the coin back. She used it a second time to see if she should settle in Lovesend. These are not things I knew at the time, mind you. I learned her reasons when she died. And, no, you need not ask. I did not torment her or keep her in my realm. She had already suffered enough in her life. I enjoyed her novels, though they were improbable."

"They're romance novels," Laura said. "They're supposed to be improbable. But, unlike you, they make people happy."

"Disappointing to hear," Bogomil said. "The third time the coin was taken out of its sealed casket was when Mo showed it to your sister, Susannah. Shortly afterward, Anabin arrived in Lovesend. He meant to discover and shield the coin so Malo Mogge would not see it. But I was already here. I had set my plan in train."

"And then Susannah did whatever she did," Laura said. "And we died and the coin disappeared again and Malo Mogge finally noticed everything that was going on."

"Correct," Bogomil said, "except for one detail. Susannah did not do anything. I had arranged for everything just so, only for Daniel to reject what Susannah offered without ever understanding what it was she meant to give him. All of this, though, would have been a temporary setback, except for you."

"Me!" Laura said.

"You," Bogomil said. His voice was mild, but he was watching Laura very closely. "Oh, please. Do you mean to tell me that you still remember nothing?"

"I have been trying to remember all of this time!" Laura said.

"Let me aid you then," Bogomil said. He reached out his hand as if he meant to take something from her.

Laura thought, How is it he just washed all of the dishes and yet his hands are still so dirty? And then Bogomil flicked her in the temple, hard, with his forefinger.

"Ow!" Laura said. Here is what she remembered:

SUSANNAH KISSING ROSAMEL Walker, yes. And then Laura, vengeful, had kissed Daniel, and Susannah had stormed off. This, too, was something Laura already knew. But now everything else was restored to her.

She said, "Oh. Oh! Oh, I was so mad! Not just because she kissed Rosamel but because I could tell it was the end of the band. She and Daniel never could keep their hands off each other. Thinking they were sneaking around. That I didn't know. That it wouldn't wreck the band and ruin everything. They'd get together and sneak around, and then they'd come up with some stupid reason to break up and be sneaky about that, too, and then, guess what? Get back together. I hated it. It wrecked rehearsals, and they were always being weird around each other, and Susannah for some reason thought all of this meant she was in love with him. That it was something that was going to last forever and ever. She made this big scene before the show, I walked in on it, and, oh! Okay, I remember. Daniel said he was quitting. He broke up with her and he also broke up with the band. And then we all had to go on stage and pretend nothing had happened. So then Susannah kissed Rosamel during 'The Kissing Song' and I kissed Daniel. She just took off. It was Daniel's birthday and we were all supposed to hang out, but obviously that wasn't going to happen. And okay. Mo! He said he had something Susannah had been planning to give Daniel. We went looking for her down on the ledge under the Cliff Hangar because we hung out there sometimes. We all did, but she wasn't there. I told Daniel he should just open the present. I'd already found this weird note in Susannah's stuff, all the stuff she'd just abandoned. Not a note. Song lyrics! This song she'd clearly written for Daniel. No music, just lyrics. Super dramatic. And, uh, I read it. Out loud. But it wasn't funny. It should have been funny, but it was just weird and super intense. And then I took the box from Mo; he didn't want to give it to me, but I grabbed it and tossed it over to Daniel, and he opened it and took out a—"

"Coin," Bogomil said.

Laura said, "Mo tried to get it back, but then—"

Bogomil said, "The ritual is designed for two people, not three. Anabin and I felt it happen, but we were not present. Anabin, I believe, was at a chamber music festival in Weymouth. I was keeping an eye on Susannah. When you recited the words and Daniel opened the box, we felt it like a blow. Malo Mogge felt it, too. And once again the key hid itself."

"You say that like the key has a will of its own," Laura said. She was still taking in the fact that everything that had happened had been, to some extent, her fault. She didn't like the feeling. Was this how it felt to be Susannah? No wonder she was in a funk so much of the time.

"Given enough time," Bogomil said, "all magic embodied develops a will. Consciousness. And Malo Mogge made her key out of herself. Malo Mogge is not everything she once was. Nor am I. Nor Anabin. But the key is more than it once was."

"I don't care how she used to be," Laura said. Everything she'd been tamping down came boiling out. "She killed my mother. She desecrated her body! She took a part of Ruth and stuck it into herself! Who does something like that? And she took something away from me, too: the way I should be feeling. I can't even feel sad about the fact my mother is dead! I think about it, and I know what I should feel. But what I feel is *nothing*. She thinks she can get away with everything, but she can't. I don't care how long it takes or what I have to do, but I'm going to kill her. You said that she can die, right? Tell me how I can kill her."

"Do you really think one such as Malo Mogge can be killed by the likes of one such as yourself?" Bogomil said. His voice didn't change at all, but Laura drew back. "I came to you because it seems likely you will be my replacement. When you take my place, I will be vulnerable, and Malo Mogge will make me suffer and then she will devour me. I see no way free. But Anabin, too, will be vulnerable. She will have no more need of him and his magic is ripe and would be delicious in her mouth. She may not wish to wait for his life to come to a natural end, and I do not wish him to suffer at her hands before he must. Let him be human as he wishes. And if, when he is human, he regrets his choice, I will not be there to see it. When he dies a human death and Malo Mogge comes to eat him in the realm that was mine, I will not be there to see it. I will have gone before him."

"You really love that guy," Laura said. "Why? He's weird. And boring."

"And you are very stupid to talk about him that way in my presence," Bogomil said. "I have only been able to bear what I have had to bear because Anabin bore it with me. And because no matter what I have become, he—"

"Never mind," Laura said. "It's epic. I get it. I mean, I don't, but clearly you do."

"What I am trying to say is that you must intervene on his behalf when you become the servant of Malo Mogge. I believe she might stay her hand if you asked."

"But I don't wish to serve her," Laura said. "I wish to kill her. I want her to fix what she did to me and then I want to kill her."

"Then serve her first," Bogomil said. "Bide your time and wait your moment. It matters not to me whether you succeed or fail. I will be dead. But if you will promise to do your best to keep Anabin safe, I shall tell you everything I know of Malo Mogge. You will find it useful one day."

Laura said, "I always thought someone would show up and tell me I was special. That I would be chosen. And then my life would change. I even thought there was a pretty good chance the person would be an asshole! And a liar. But I thought it would be a music scout or a producer, someone who came to see me sing. I wasn't expecting you. Or *her*."

"Promise you will intercede for Anabin," Bogomil said.

"Fine," Laura said. "I'll watch out for Mr. Anabin. But what about the key? Don't we have to find it before I take over your job?"

"That's already been taken care of," Bogomil said. "Your sister has it with her now."

The Book of Malo Mogge

TIME DOES NOT proceed directly. Is there anyone who knows this better than Malo Mogge? It hesitates, eddying about one's feet, collects in shallow pools, and then goes gushing and rushing onward in a welter. There is only the smallest drop left before she has the thing she needs, that essential piece that left her so long ago. And yet, this small drop of time stretches out in an expanse as vast and empty as any land she has ever known. Thomas with her rib is still in pursuit of his tedious vendetta, and so Malo Mogge leaves her temple to see what small delights or distractions Lovesend may offer a goddess.

She takes the same path that interesting child, Laura, retraced earlier, making her way through a negligible neighborhood down a negligible street where she sees the house where she struck down the woman Ruth. Next door is the home of another of Anabin's protégés. When Laura and one of these others take up their new roles, Malo Mogge will give them housing more appropriate to their station.

But—her borrowed rib yearns to go to its home. How painful is such ingratitude. Like a stitch in her side.

The snow steams and melts away under Malo Mogge's tread. If only time, too, might melt away at her touch and lay every secret thing bare.

It is growing dark and snow hangs in the air, turns the street into a river of white. People go about their business, some of them already known to her. They have sung for her. She has given them gifts, shared herself with them. These pause as she passes. They nod or bow. One begins to weep, and she knows he will never stop weeping, not as long as he lives. A clock made out of water. She can't help but notice how every plinth she passes is empty where previously a statue stood. Has someone done this, anticipating what should stand there? Is some artist already commissioned to pay tribute to her, to Malo Mogge? How touching. How appropriate. But she has a more amusing idea.

At the next plinth, she waits (a short time, the smallest snip of a snip) until a woman comes hurrying past.

"Do you know me?" she says, and the woman stops.

Says, "I do."

"Good," Malo Mogge says. "And what do you owe me?"

"Whatever you ask of me is what I owe," says this very good woman.

"Then let us change garments," Malo Mogge says. She is tired of what she is wearing. No, she is hungry. She is always hungry, and there is nothing that satisfies, nothing in this small and too-known world. Until she has her key again, she will go hungry.

The woman takes off her coat, her scarf and hat. Underneath she is wearing a red velour tracksuit, quite attractive. Malo Mogge is pleased with this offering. She strips off her pajamas. Passersby see the two women standing there naked, but such is Malo Mogge's numen that no one looks askance.

Once Malo Mogge has put on the tracksuit and the other has put on Malo Mogge's attire, Malo Mogge says, "I will do you a great honor now."

"Thank you," the woman says. "But first put on my shoes and my coat. It's below freezing."

"I do not require them," Malo Mogge says. "And neither do you. Climb upon this plinth and be still. Some little time will pass, and as it passes, you will take on my likeness and my glory. Time will go on passing and you will turn to stone, and all who see you will see me. This is my gift to this town, and this is the honor I will do you."

"Thank you," the woman says. She climbs up onto the plinth and takes up a posture she must suppose does Malo Mogge justice. She is shivering a little. She will not notice the cold so much once she is stone.

"Chin up a little more," Malo Mogge says. "Look toward the horizon. Night is coming, and after that, who knows? You will see it all. Children will lay down flowers, pour out their hearts' blood at your feet. What is your name, dear one? I wish to remember you."

But the woman does not answer. She is not stone yet, but power is already at work upon her. Snip, snip, time lurches forward.

As Malo Mogge progresses through the town, she entertains herself by selecting others to make her statues. She instructs these to go and find empty plinths she has already passed by. In time (kick up your heels, sweet time, and at last go dancing forward) there will be a statue of Malo Mogge upon every one.

The Book of Daniel

"Where, exactly, are *you* going?" the unicorn in the parking lot said as Daniel drew near.

Daniel said, "Who are you?" But he knew, he knew.

"Seriously?" the unicorn said. It tossed its lustrous mane, stamped one purple hoof into the snow. The scent of cinnamon and warm milk wafted toward Daniel. Was she part cappuccino as well? "Why do you suck so much?"

Daniel had never seen a unicorn in a snit before. But he'd seen Carousel in a snit a hundred times. This version of Carousel was somehow even more Carousel than she'd been an hour ago.

"Who did this, Carousel?"

The unicorn did a little unicorn curtsy, looking very pleased with itself.

"You?" he said. "How?"

"Magic," Carousel said. "What, like it's hard?"

"But you're not even . . . ," he began, and then stopped.

"Real?" Carousel said. "And you're dead. Yeah, I know everything. Bogomil told me."

"Bogomil? Carousel, you can't trust him," Daniel said. He had to crane his neck to meet the unicorn's eyes. Carousel taller than he was: it was the smallest part of how freaky this was, but he could see Carousel was enjoying it.

She said, "So he was lying about me not being real and you not being alive? Because I just found your body, Daniel. Down below the Cliff Hangar. It's a big, gross lump of rock, but it's definitely you."

"What were you doing there?" Daniel said. He'd known all this time that he was dead, that he'd died. But the idea of his body here, just a little way from where they stood, he could not take it in.

"I wanted to find you," Carousel said. "And I did. Just, not the new you. But now here you are after all."

"I'll go see," Daniel said. "You should go home. If Bogomil shows up again, come get me. Right away, okay? Don't talk to him."

"I don't know if I want to talk to him again or not," Carousel said. "But he did explain magic to me and how I could use it. I'm not saying he's my new best friend or anything, but he does know stuff."

"Bad stuff," Daniel said. "Can you stop being a unicorn, please? Just, be Carousel. Go home and be Carousel."

"I'll be a unicorn if I want to be a unicorn," Carousel said. "And Bogomil told me *everything*, Daniel. I know you're supposed to make me go away."

"Oh, come on!" Daniel said. "I wouldn't do that! I didn't even know until this morning that you—" Once again he couldn't say it.

"That I'm not real," Carousel said.

"Yeah," Daniel said.

"So what are you going to do?" she said. "Use magic to get rid of me? Not use magic and die? I'm made up of your magic, so if you die, that's the end of me, too."

"I'm going to figure something else out," Daniel said.

"He really doesn't like you," Carousel said. "Bogomil."

"And that is extremely painful to me," Daniel said, driven to sarcasm at last.

Carousel said, "He says I should use my magic and take yours. I could unmake *you*, Daniel."

"Let's get you home," Daniel said. "It isn't safe out here."

"Oh, I know," his sister the unicorn said, advancing on him. "But it isn't me you should be worrying about."

Daniel found he was no longer able to speak. He was rapidly dwindling, shrinking away. He could not move or evade or argue. Carousel stretched out her long golden neck, and he felt the spice-scented steam of her breath warm him. She picked him up delicately between her teeth.

Eaten by a unicorn. Daniel wished he could tell Susannah. She'd think it was funny. Wouldn't she?

The Book of Mo

WHEN HE OPENED the door, Susannah was standing there in a short-sleeved T-shirt, jeans soaked with snowmelt. Her hair was a sheaf of ice and her skin was mottled and purple with cold. She had a guitar case in one claw-like hand.

She said, "Can I come in?"

Mo stepped aside, then closed the door after her. He was about to get her a towel or a blanket or something when he realized she was staring at Lavender Glass, Lavender Glass staring back. You'd have thought the two might feel some kind of kinship in this moment, but Lavender Glass said, "Why did you let her in? She may be an agent of Lord Torquil Spintorm!"

"This is Susannah," Mo said. "She's a friend. Uh, Susannah, this lady is kind of a friend of my grandmother?"

Susannah ignored this pretense. "You're not real," she said to Lavender Glass. "Go away."

And just like that, Mo and Susannah were alone. Lavender Glass was gone.

"The fuck!" Mo said. "You can't do that!"

"Apparently I can," Susannah said.

Which, valid. Fucking Lavender Glass had been the last piece of his grandmother, but then it hadn't really been his grandmother, had it? Mo tamped down one last surge of grief.

"Where's Laura?" he said. "What are you doing here?"

Susannah said, "I don't know where anyone is. Daniel was asleep, but maybe now he's awake. I don't know where Laura is."

Mo said, "I'm so sorry about your mom."

"Why?" Susannah said. Her voice was calm but there was something crazed in her eyes. "It wasn't your fault. Malo Mogge did it."

Mo touched her arm. It was like ice. "Come on," he said. "We have to get you warm." He was cold, too, and then remembered he'd opened all the windows. Easy to shut them all. Susannah didn't even notice.

"Come upstairs with me."

"Why?" Susannah said. Still clutching the guitar case, she let Mo lead her up the stairs and into his grandmother's bathroom, where there was a full-on Jacuzzi tub.

"Get in," he said, and started the water running.

Susannah tried to take off her jeans, but it was clear she couldn't feel her fingers. Mo helped. He helped her with her sneakers, her socks stiff with ice.

She got her T-shirt off herself, left her underwear and sports bra on. Climbed over the edge of the tub and sat in the inch of water.

She said, "I know everything, Mo. I remember."

"Okay," Mo said. This was fine. "Which is what, exactly?"

"You were dead. Bogomil is real. I know Mr. Anabin is not exactly a high school music teacher. I know about Malo Mogge. I know if she gets her key back, it's not going to be good for anybody. Bogomil wanted me to take over for him, and for Daniel, I guess, to take over for Mr. Anabin, but I fucked that up somehow."

"Do you remember how?" Mo said.

"No," Susannah said. "I can't figure that part out. Everything else is pretty clear right now. Did you know Laura has been messing around with my brain, making me forget things? Meanwhile you and Daniel have been helping her keep all of this secret from me. Thanks for that."

"We were trying to protect you," Mo said. "To be fair."

"Laura made me do laundry," Susannah said. "I don't give a fuck about fair!"

"Also fair," Mo said.

Susannah said, "Avelot messed with my memory, too. So did Thomas, who also hooked up with both of us and then just stood there while Malo Mogge killed my mother."

"He did do that," Mo said. "Is the water warm enough? Do you want it a little warmer?"

"I'll do it," Susannah said. She reached out to adjust the dial but the bathtub was complicated. You had to adjust more than one thing.

"Here. And then you can just bump up the temperature. See? But not too much. You want it lukewarm in case of frostbite," Mo said. "So you know the part where two of us, whoever doesn't take over from Bogomil and Anabin, are just going to be dead again?"

"Not just dead," Susannah said. "Malo Mogge eats you. You die, go back to Bogomil's realm, and then she eats you once she has her key again." Under the surface of the water, her skin was beginning to flush bright red. But her fingers were still blue-white. Mo had always thought of his grandmother's bathtub as enormous. Luxurious. But Susannah's long arms and long legs filled it. She drew her knees up and laid her cheek on them, facing away from Mo.

He tried to take in what she'd just said. "How do you know that?"

"Bowie told me," Susannah said. "That's the whole deal with Bogomil's realm. It's where she goes to eat. Only she hasn't been able to get there for centuries."

"Then maybe it's not such a bad thing that we haven't been able to find the key for her," Mo said.

"It's not always a key, though, is it?" Susannah said. "Sometimes it's a cup. Or a coin. Your grandmother's coin."

"Like a Swiss Army knife," Mo said. "Multipurpose."

Susannah pointed over at something. "Right now it's a piece-of-shit Harmony Sovereign Marveltone acoustic."

Mo turned. There was, as far as he could tell, nothing magical about the case she'd brought or what it contained. "That?" he said. "Definitely not."

"Definitely yes," Susannah said. "And maybe if you assholes had thought to include me in any of this, we would have figured it out sooner and my mother wouldn't be dead." Her lip began to tremble as she said this, and then, as Mo watched, the rest of her began to shake. She produced a noise so abrasive it sounded as if she were barking instead of crying.

"Hey," he said. He patted her shoulder. "I know. It's so bad. I know how bad it is."

After a while she stopped crying, though she was still trembling violently. Little waves of water slopped over the lip of the tub. "I'm okay," she said.

Mo waited.

"Okay, I'm not okay," she said. "But we're both going to pretend I am. Because there's something we have to do now."

"Which is what?" Mo said.

"I have a splinter in my foot," Susannah said. "We're going to take it out."

She pulled the plug out of the drain. Mo handed her a towel and his grandmother's bathrobe, ridiculously short on Susannah.

"Tweezers?" she said.

"Here," Mo said, getting them out of a drawer. "You want to or should I?"

Susannah sat on the edge of the bath. She held her foot in her hand. "I'll do it."

Mo could see the splinter, where it had pierced her heel. It wasn't a small splinter. All the flesh around it was raised up and tender. Had she really walked like this all the way from her house to his?

"Can I see the guitar?" he said.

"Go for it," she said.

Mo unlatched the case. Maybe he was a snob—okay, he was definitely a snob—but the Harmony wasn't an impressive guitar. It was out of tune, probably from being lugged at least five miles, most of it uphill, through a particularly wet snowstorm. In no way did it feel like a powerful magical object, and by this point, Mo thought he would probably recognize a powerful magical object. Even in his memory his grandmother's coin, the one that had caused all of this trouble, throbbed like a bad tooth. Back then he hadn't felt it. Or he'd felt it and not known what it was he was feeling.

"Look," he began. "I think if this was it, the key, I would know."

"Hold on," Susannah said. There was a look of great concentration on her face as she drew a long, blood-soaked splinter out of her foot. "Okay. Give me the guitar."

Mo passed it over and she turned it on its side. She stuck her fingers down into the sound box and said, "Here it is." Then she took the splinter that had been in her heel and slotted it into the gap where it belonged.

"Oh," Mo said. "Oh wow."

The crappy guitar wasn't a guitar anymore. It became a coin, a cup, a knife. A key. None of them particularly impressive to behold but, oh, the way they felt, like the deepest note ringing from a bell the size of a room you'd never manage to walk out of again, not in a lifetime. This was not how it had felt before, when Mo held Maryanne Gorch's lucky coin. Now the magic in him rose up and met the magic in the key.

The key became the Harmony again, cradled in Susannah's hands.

"I found it," she said.

"Yeah," Mo said. He wished she hadn't, though. Nothing good would happen because she had.

Susannah stuck her fingers back inside the guitar and plucked the splinter out of its groove. As she did this, the guitar became once more a scarred and modest workhorse, suitable for beginners of no particular talent.

"What about the splinter?" Mo said. "Please tell me it doesn't have to go back in your foot."

Susannah said, "I've got a Tampax in my wallet. We'll stick it in the wrapper and hide it in the drawer with the tweezers. Nobody's going to look there. Now you can call Thomas. Tell him to tell Malo Mogge we have her key."

Mo said, incredulously, "We just do what she wants? And then she eats two of us?"

Susannah said, "Do you have a better idea?"

Mo said, "Destroy it!"

"Already tried that," Susannah said. "Poured lighter fluid on the guitar, tried to set it on fire in the backyard. Didn't catch. Took it to What Hast Thou Ground? and jumped up and down on it and then put bits into the industrial coffee grinder. Result was a heap of powder, but then while I watched, it all just came right back together."

That didn't sound great. Mo said, "There has to be something we can do."

"Probably," Susannah said. "But I can't see what, can you? Give it to Mr. Anabin? He doesn't want it. Bogomil? Why does that not seem like a good idea? Keep on hiding it? How long before Malo Mogge kills someone else? Maybe we can bargain with her. Give her what she wants if she lets all of you stay. She's terrible, but maybe if we give her key to her, she'll go be terrible somewhere else."

"So we let her do whatever she wants to whoever she wants as long as it's not us?"

Susannah said, "I'm kind of a fuckup. You know that, right? I always knew I wasn't supposed to be here. I was supposed to be in this other place, this magical place that definitely wasn't Lovesend. I was supposed to rule over an enchanted kingdom, only now it turns out this kingdom is some fucked-up Death-adjacent sub-basement realm and my friend who lives there is a bigger psycho than I am, and, yes, I could go rule there if I wanted to take Bogomil's place but then I'd be the eternal doorkeeper for the person who just killed my mother and wants to eat my friends. So, yeah, I'm giving up on that. Best-case scenario isn't great, I'll give you that, but I don't know what else we do. What?"

"Nothing," Mo said. He had forgotten what Susannah was like. "I guess I just thought in situations like this, the thing to do was figure out what the right thing to do was. And I may not be sure what that is, but I'm pretty sure it isn't handing the key over to Malo Mogge."

"If you want to be a hero," Susannah said, "go ahead. Tell me the plan."

Mo thought. Susannah waited, her eyes on his face, until at last he sighed. Gave up. "I don't know," he said.

"Okay, then," Susannah said. She shrugged. "So call Thomas. I mean, maybe he'll help us somehow? If not, he can be a go-between. Let's get this over with."

"One problem," Mo said. "Not the biggest problem, but perhaps the most immediate—Thomas isn't answering my texts."

Susannah gave him a disbelieving smile. "Really?"

"I may have . . . implied he might not be entirely real," Mo said. Ugh, ugh, ugh. "He took it the wrong way."

"Tell me some other time," Susannah said. "Here." She passed him her phone.

"Let's get you some clothes first," Mo said.

"Why?" Susannah said.

"Because yours are all wet? And kind of filthy?"

"Why is everyone obsessed with my personal hygiene?" Susannah said. "Did Frodo and Sam stop and do laundry on the way to Mordor?"

"No," Mo said. "But they did take a bath in Bree. Plus, they didn't just hand the ring over to Sauron. I'll text Thomas."

Susannah said, "Can you take the Harmony? I don't want to look at it right now."

Mo didn't really want the Harmony. He said, "What about Laura? Do you want me to tell her you're here? That you're safe?" What he meant was, do we tell Laura about the key, about what we're planning to do?

"I don't want to look at her, either," Susannah said. "You know what? I don't remember the last thing I said to Ruth. I texted her. Not words, though. Just emojis, random emojis."

"I don't remember, either," Mo said. "With my grandmother."

"Sucks, doesn't it?" Susannah said.

Mo went out with the Harmony in its case and shut the door behind him. As he went down the hall, he could hear Susannah weeping in his grandmother's bathroom.

HE WAS MORE than a little tempted to kick the guitar case down the stairs but refrained like a good hobbit. In his grandmother's office he read what was on the screen one more time. Then he saved the document, closed her laptop, and turned off the light. He didn't particularly want to text Thomas, impending doom or no impending doom. Except he kind of also did. In the kitchen he drank the rest of the champagne out of Jenny's glass, though it was flat now and warm and too sweet. "To the time you shoveled all the Barry Manisnow out of the driveway, even though you weren't real," he said, toasting her. Whatever the opposite of celebration was, this was the taste of Jenny's champagne.

He went up to his room, sat down at the window, the guitar case propped against the wall. He didn't actually need Susannah's phone. He could just use magic. Summon Thomas that way. But Thomas could ignore a text if he wanted to, if he felt like it, and then they could just postpone the whole apocalypse or whatever was going to happen.

Susannah didn't even have a password. No wonder she was okay with just passing the guitar over to Malo Mogge. Apparently she didn't care about anything. He scrolled until he found Thomas in her contacts. He thought about what he should say for so long that the phone went dark again.

He tapped it back on. At last he typed

We have to talk. I know you don't want to, but it's important. Come over.

He sent this and then said, "Oh shit!" out loud. He sent a second text. This is not Susannah! This is Mo

Then he waited. He didn't like waiting. He didn't like any of this. To occupy his hands, he took the Harmony out and began to tune it.

Afterward he got out his notebook and began to work on his opera again. This, too, was a mistake. He used his own phone to go on Facebook to look for Jenny Pings. Okay, there were a lot. He didn't think there was much chance the real Jenny would remember him anyway.

Susannah's phone buzzed. Here was Thomas's response.

I can't come over right now. When I can, I'll come over.

"Thanks, Samuel Beckett," Mo said out loud. What he typed was Great. Then: Don't tell you know who ok

Then he waited again. At last Thomas texted back.

Not stupid, ok

Mo blew out a long breath. "Okay," he said. There were definitely going to be text messages in his opera. Lots of them. If he didn't end up being eaten. Here was something he actually wanted to think about: how did you convey an emoji in a score? Not a semantron, but there was something about the sound of a semantron that suggested texting. Birdsong, too. That call and response. If sung, what would the singer sing? Perhaps just the name of the emoji? *CRY-ING FACE. SING-LE ROSE. PUK-ING GREEN FACE.* Maybe sung as clausulae? His grandmother hadn't been a big texter. But there was a thing that she'd said over and over again whenever she'd been on tour and they'd talked on the phone or been texting. *I love you and I sure am proud of you.* He could hear the melody of it even now, and the instrument. An oboe, plangent and steady. And yet the note, once played, decays. Perhaps one instrument to suggest that decay, but something else that would sustain? How much he wanted to write music that would make people feel what those words had made him feel, not just the words but the loss of the person who had been the one to say them. His opera wasn't just going to be about Jenny Ping, it couldn't be. Poor Susannah. It would be cheating to use a visual component for an emoji, wouldn't it? He thought it would be.

SUSANNAH, DRESSED AGAIN in her wet and filthy clothes, came to find him while he was still thinking about emojis. "Did you get him?" she said. "What are you doing?"

Mo said, "He says he'll come over when he can."

"Okay," Susannah said. "And then whatever happens next happens next. Do you have any food? I'm starving."

"Already ordered pizza," Mo said. "Should be here soon. And the thing I'm working on, it's an opera."

"Okay," Susannah said.

Really? Mo opened up, told someone what he was working on, and that was all he got?

Susannah sat down on the window seat beside him. She picked up the Harmony but did not play it. "It's weird," she said. "It's this incredibly valuable magical object. But it has this whole other history. Like, part of me remembers how it belonged to my dad. And then it was Laura's—and I think that's what she remembers, too, that this was hers, that this was the guitar she learned to play on. And, like, seriously? Laura's starter guitar was a Yamaha Studio Lord and she traded that in pretty quickly for the Yamaha Pacifica. Wonder what happened to that."

"Probably the same thing that happened to her and me and Daniel," Mo said. "Nothing good."

"Sorry," Susannah said. "I don't know exactly what I did, but I'm guessing it was me who did it."

"Don't do that, please," Mo said. "Let's assign blame where blame is due. Bogomil was running a con on you so you and Daniel would have to take his and Mr. Anabin's place. And that's what would have happened if Daniel hadn't broken up with you. Basically this is all Daniel's fault."

"Did you just figure out how to blame this on Daniel?" Susannah said.

Mo said, "Did you know he's completely refused to do magic? Won't do it at all. Mr. Anabin is white-hot. You wouldn't think that dude could get angry."

"Can he do that?" Susannah said. "Just not do magic?"

"Sure," Mo said. "If he wants to be dead again."

"Why would he want to be dead again?" Susannah said.

"I don't know!" Mo said. "Because he doesn't want to have to do magic."

Susannah said, "That doesn't make any sense."

"Right?" Mo said. "He's basically the dude who shows up at the party and doesn't want to dance or drink or even just hang out and talk shit. He just wants to stand there and make everyone feel awkward."

"He gets that way sometimes," Susannah said. "Gets an idea and won't budge. But we can't just let him die."

Mo had several things he would have liked to say, none of them particularly helpful or sympathetic. But the doorbell rang. "Oh good, pizza."

"Or maybe it's Thomas," Susannah said. "You want me to come with you?"

"No," Mo said. "But thanks."

On the way down he rehearsed what he was going to say to Thomas if it wasn't the pizza. But it wasn't Thomas at the door. It wasn't the pizza guy, either. It was Daniel's sister, the super-intense little bitty one.

"Carousel?" he said. "What are you doing here?"

"Take him," she said, and stuck out her hand. Mo took what she held and saw he was holding a hedgehog.

"Don't drop him!" she said. "It's Daniel."

Mo lifted the hedgehog up to his face. It was making horrible snuffling sounds. Its little clawed feet scrabbled at his palm. Nevertheless, it was, indeed, Daniel. "Why is he a hedgehog? Why are you giving him to *me*?"

"Because Bogomil wants me to take his magic," Carousel said. "All of it. I don't want to, but if you don't take him, I think I might. Because I'm not real, I'm just magic, and I need more magic to stay here, and Daniel has lots of it and he's not using it."

"You hold him," Mo said. "He's your brother, not mine." He passed the hedgehog back to Carousel, and this time he felt it, what she was. "You're like Jenny! You're like her, but you're not."

"Who?" Carousel said.

"Someone else who wasn't real," Mo said.

"Where is she?" Carousel said. "Can I talk to her?"

"Uh," Mo said. "No. She isn't here anymore." Was he supposed to feel bad about this? Well, he did. Shamed by his least-favorite person's doppelgänger.

"You made her go away," Carousel said. "Why? Didn't you like her? Daniel was supposed to make me go away. But he wouldn't."

"I liked Jenny a lot!" Mo said. "But she wasn't . . ."

"Real," Carousel said. She looked incredibly disappointed in Mo, as if she had expected better.

"I'm going to go home," she said. "It's past my bedtime. Plus, you know, I'm not real. Or whatever. You have to take care of Daniel. Okay?"

"Why a hedgehog?" Mo asked, hedging. Yes, hedging. That was exactly what he was doing. He knew he shouldn't be entrusted with Daniel.

"I needed to turn him into something I could carry," Carousel said, "and hedgehogs are adorable but prickly. It made it less tempting to just swallow him."

"Carousel?" Susannah said. She came down the stairs. "What are you doing here?"

"I don't have time for this," Carousel said, stepping back onto the porch. Before Mo or Susannah could say anything else, she became a unicorn with the largest, most iridescent wings anyone could ever have wanted. They were ridiculous but Mo kind of loved them anyway. Carousel launched herself unceremoniously off the porch, wings like sails. Why did she smell like pumpkin spice?

"She can do magic?" Susannah said.

"Everyone can do magic now, apparently," Mo said. "Except for Daniel. Carousel turned him into a hedgehog for some reason." He shoved Daniel at Susannah. "Take your tiny boyfriend. Go put him somewhere safe."

"Change him back first," Susannah said.

"Absolutely not," Mo said. "If Daniel doesn't want to be a hedgehog, he should just stop being a hedgehog. I am not getting involved."

The hedgehog said nothing. Susannah sighed. "I'll take him up to the music studio."

"Take the guitar up there, too," Mo said. "I'll wait here for the pizza." He didn't see why he had to be responsible for either Daniel or the guitar. He'd ordered pizza and texted an ex. Surely that was enough.

Except that after Susannah had gone up the attic stairs, he went up to his grandmother's bathroom and retrieved the splinter they'd hidden in a tampon wrapper. He wasn't sure about much, but he was pretty sure they should do some more thinking before they just handed it over to Malo Mogge. He stuck it in his back pocket.

The Book of Daniel

Daniel rested peacefully in Susannah's cupped hand all the way up the stairs. When they reached the music studio he uncurled himself and began to lick her palm, making a kind of spit-paste out of her scent that he began to apply to his quills. This was for the purposes of scent camouflage but also because he loved her.

"Ugh," Susannah said. She sat down on the piano bench. "That's gross."

The hedgehog understood what she was saying but didn't particularly care. Why had Daniel cared so much about what other people thought? It went on grooming itself.

"I really want to yell at you," Susannah said, "but I can't yell at you if you're a *hedgehog*. So, you know, can you please just stop being a fucking hedgehog?"

She set him down beside her on the piano bench.

Daniel had no intention of not being a hedgehog. And yet, he found himself human again in the room full of instruments that had once belonged to Mo's mother.

Susannah's eyelids were swollen and her face was blotchy from crying, but she didn't seem to be at all disconcerted that Daniel had been a hedgehog previously or that now he was not. Her long, level look said she knew everything he'd been lying about.

"Where's Carousel?" he said.

"She said it was past her bedtime," Susannah said. "Then she turned into a unicorn and flew away."

"She turned me into a hedgehog," Daniel said. "Who turned me back just now? You did, didn't you?"

Susannah said, "All I did was tell you to stop being a hedgehog."

"You wouldn't believe how easy magic is to do," Daniel said. "Or how hard it is not to do it."

"From what I hear, you're managing that okay," Susannah said. Her tone said she knew what this meant, too.

"I woke up and you were gone," Daniel said. He sat down on the sofa closest to the piano. "Mr. Anabin was there instead. He told me you'd found this thing everyone's been looking for."

"The key," Susannah said. "Yeah. It wasn't a big deal or anything. I could have done it anytime if anyone had explained. I just didn't know I was supposed to be looking for it."

"What are you planning to do with it?" Daniel said.

"Give it to Malo Mogge," Susannah said. "If she wants it so badly, she can have it. Why? You have a better idea?"

"All of my ideas so far have been bad," Daniel said. "I know this isn't the time, but I know I fucked up. You're mad at me. You should be."

"You think?" Susannah said.

"Be as mad as you want," he said. "I shouldn't be here. I'm mad about that. But you can't blame me for dying."

"Can't I?" Susannah said. "I get that Laura thought she was protecting me, and Mo—my God, he doesn't owe me anything. But you came back and you slept with me! You let me think you cared about me! And then what? You were going to be dead again and I wouldn't remember any of this, that you came back from the dead and then fucked off again? Or I would and I'd go through all of it again?"

"I screwed up," Daniel said. "I keep screwing up. And I wanted to tell you. But if I had told you everything, what would have happened then?"

"I would have tried to help you figure a way out!" Susannah said. "I know you and Laura think all I ever do is make things worse, but, Daniel, I'm neck-deep in the middle of this. And you've been keeping me in the dark, all of you. Like, apparently you've all been doing magic—except for you—and escaping death and having weird, scary adventures and all this time I thought I was going crazy. Did you know Bowie was going to kill me?"

"What?" Daniel said.

"And now Ruth—"

Tears began to well up in her eyes and she stopped.

"I'm so sorry," Daniel said. "Come here."

She stayed where she was.

"Please," he said.

She got up. Left the piano bench and came to him. Sat down and leaned against his side. She said into his shoulder, "Ruth's dead. And you and Laura and Mo already died once. What happens if you die again? I won't have anybody."

"Laura will be okay," Daniel said. "And Mo, too. They're good at this."

Susannah said, "Mo says you won't do magic. That you'll die again if you won't do it."

"I'd rather be dead than be like Bogomil or Mr. Anabin," Daniel said.

"You'd rather be dead than be with me," Susannah said.

Daniel said, "I remember it now. For a long time I couldn't, but I think I can now. Some of it, anyway. You wanted to live forever. Be like Bogomil. You were going to do some kind of spell and do it to me, too." Maybe he ought to have been angry about this, but he wasn't. None of this had been Susannah's fault.

He opened his mouth to say this, but Susannah took his hand, looking a little embarrassed. Before he could speak she said, "This goddess-gift I give you, your portion my portion. Your road my road. Oh, do not leave me. As a blade has two sides and a coin two faces, as a cup holds what is poured into it, so you and I will be in our service, our days unnumbered. As I become Life-in-Death upon this threshold, so I give you her gift, which is Life. Take it up."

Daniel said, "I thought it was pretty heavy metal when Laura read it. Just, you know, song lyrics. But it's a spell."

Susannah said, "That night at the carousel, your birthday, before the show I waited until Laura was off talking to Hannah. I was going to tell you about Bogomil, I was going to tell you about my dreams. I was going to ask you if you would try to do a spell with me. I only partly believed, but what the hell? I thought, Why not try to do a little magic? Bogomil gave me the gist of what I was supposed to say. But yeah. You broke up with me. I didn't get to give my speech. I didn't give you the coin. We didn't do the ritual."

"We did, though. Laura and me. Laura read it out loud to be funny, and when she threw me the coin, Mo grabbed it," Daniel said. "And then we all died. Carousel found our bodies. We were down under the Cliff Hangar, on the make-out ledge. I'd gone there to look for you, and Laura and Mo followed me. And we messed up the ritual and we died. It was so fucking stupid, what happened."

"I'm really sorry," Susannah said. "I'm so sorry."

Daniel said, "Did you know Mr. Anabin turned me into a bear?"

"He did what?" Susannah said.

"Yeah," Daniel said. "Last night. You know what? I don't even remember why I thought we ought to break up. I just thought if I was going to quit the band then you and I probably ought to take a break, too. I thought we both needed to figure out some things before we figured out whether we worked together."

Susannah said, "I think I'd like being a bear. I think I'd like it a lot." She took her hand back, stood up, and stretched, cracking her knuckles. And then she was a bear.

Daniel recoiled so violently the entire sofa tipped over.

The attic was large. The ceiling was not low. And yet the bear filled up the room with its bulk, with the fragrance of its fur, sweet and rank and wild. Daniel lay half on the floor, half across the upended sofa.

Then the bear was Susannah again. She said, "Yep. Just what I thought. Pretty great."

The Book of Rosamel Walker

SHE AND NATALIE and Theo went for dinner at Thai Super Delight. It was her favorite restaurant in town, even if Natalie and Theo, long inured to its charms, would rather have gone to Paradise Point in Bridgetree for food-court french fries, Starbucks, and kiosk cookies the size of their heads. But you couldn't exactly get to the mall right now. Mo was apparently off doing his own thing.

They'd all spent some of the day looking for Malo Mogge's key—everyone in town was out looking for it. Tomorrow they'd all go looking for the key again. The restaurant was closed to everyone except family—and Rosamel. The doors were locked, and the food wasn't off the usual menu. It was all the stuff the Thangleks needed to use up. Not that Rosamel had any complaints! Theo invited her back to watch the most recent season of *American Horror Story*, but Rosamel was kind of done with that show. She'd never been a big horror fan.

Instead she thought she'd go home and pick a fight with her mom the way you did when you were stuck at home and a little stir-crazy. Honestly she would have been happy to pick a fight with anyone who looked at her funny, but the first person she met back out on the street was Malo Mogge.

Malo Mogge said, "You. I remember you. Thomas seemed to take an interest, though why I don't know."

"I'm sorry," Rosamel said. "I don't know why, either." She hadn't noticed that he had.

"No matter," Malo Mogge said. "Go and stand upon that plinth. I don't know what future you imagined for yourself, but I will give you one more splendid than you ever might have dreamed of."

And so as Malo Mogge went on her way, Rosamel found herself climbing up onto the ice-slick marble, though why she did this she didn't know. A feeling of strange stillness began to seep through her, and although she was content to do as Malo Mogge had asked, some small part of Rosamel still thought, Must I then stay here in this shit-ass, bougie tourist town forever? Was this why I came home? Really?

People went down the street not even looking in her direction. She could hear them but could not turn her head, could not speak to a one. A gull came swooping and looping past her, circling as if it wished to peer into her face. Then, faintly, she felt a weight settling on her head. What a joke it was going to be, being a statue.

The gull said, "I know you. Mo's friend."

Rosamel could not speak at all.

"What a vain bitch she is," the gull said. "I knew ones like her once, but they had not a drop of her power. But me, oh I do, I have quite a bit of her power now. Why don't you become yourself again?"

As the gull said this, it rapped sharply on the crown of her head with its beak.

"Ow!" Rosamel said. "Crazy bird."

She put her hand up, to shove the bird away.

The gull heaved itself up into the air. "No, really," it said, "don't thank me."

"Shoo!" Rosamel said. She jumped off the plinth and scooped up a handful of snow. She threw it at the gull.

"Go home," the gull said. "It isn't safe out here. Tell those you care for the same."

Rosamel didn't think of herself as someone who took advice from gulls. Nevertheless she texted Natalie and Theo as she went: You still at restaurant?

Home, Theo texted, got a ride with the parents.

Oh good. Stay inside tonight ok? Keep your parents home too.

Theo texted back: Dad wanted to go look for the key again but mom's making him stay home. They haven't watched every single fucking movie on the Criterion channel twice yet. I'm gonna have to watch AHS on my phone. Please kill me before I get that old and cultured

Next Rosamel texted Mo. Stay home, go home if you aren't home, bad stuff is happening not kidding

A few seconds later he wrote back: For sure. Love you you stay safe too

Rosamel thought, When I get home I'm going to ask my mom if she'd like to watch a movie. She'd let her mom choose. But when she got home, her mom and dad were in the living room, arms wrapped around each other, dancing real close. Some old TLC song was on, turned up to eleven, the only lights the ones on the Christmas tree. They didn't even notice her, they were so busy looking into each other's eyes. Romance! Rosamel went to hide out in her room. She decided she'd check out the new season of *American Horror Story* on her iPad after all. Text Theo during the scary bits. She needed a palate cleanser.

THE BOOK OF MO

WHEN THE DOORBELL rang the next time, it still wasn't the pizza. "You texted me," Thomas said.

"I did," Mo said. "From Susannah's phone because you weren't answering mine."

"You said it was important," Thomas said, ignoring that.

"Come in," Mo said.

"Or I could stand here and you could just tell me whatever it is that's important," Thomas said.

"You're mad because I called you imaginary?" Mo said. "Is that really the worst thing anyone has ever called you?"

"I'm not angry with you," Thomas said. He was lying through his teeth, though. It was so obvious.

"It was very rude of me," Mo said. "To call you imaginary. But at least I didn't stand there while the person I work for murdered someone's mother. But maybe that kind of thing doesn't bother someone like you."

"If something like that bothered someone like me then truly my life would be an unpleasant one," Thomas said. "But let's not argue about inconsequential things. We owe each other nothing. Why am I here?"

How nice it would have been to tell Thomas to go away again, then go up to his room and lie on the floor. To call Rosamel, tell her everything, then pick over every word that Thomas had just said. To tell her about the look on Thomas's face at this moment, how it was like a closed door with no clue what was behind it. "Did you kill him?" Mo said. "Bowie?"

"No," Thomas said. "Not yet. Why am I here?"

"Because we have the key," Mo said.

Thomas grew very still. Then he was moving again, so fast Mo hardly understood what was happening. They were inside the house, and Thomas cocked his head as if he were listening for something. Mo knew what he was listening for. Thomas said, "If you had it now, I would know. I would feel it."

"Sure," Mo said. "You would know, except it's in two pieces. One of those pieces is a truly nondescript guitar. The other piece is hidden. Very, very well hidden. Actually not that well hidden. Adequately hidden, let's say."

"Why are you telling me this?"

"Why wouldn't I tell you?" Mo said. "Isn't this what we were supposed to do all along? Because if we weren't supposed to find the key, maybe you could have said something earlier? When we were, I don't know, looking for the key?"

"Who else knows?" Thomas said. His entire aspect had changed. You could see everything he was thinking on his face. And he was really looking at Mo now, too. Mo hated how much he liked this, to be looked at by Thomas, even if it wasn't for the right reasons.

"Susannah," Mo said. "And Daniel probably knows by now, too."

"Anabin? Bogomil?" Thomas said.

"Maybe?" Mo said. "Those two seem to know a lot of stuff. The guitar is up in the studio with Susannah and Daniel. I'm waiting for pizza to show up. You want any before you head out? To go tell Malo Mogge or whatever?"

There was another knock on the door.

"Stay," Thomas said. He went to the door and stood on his toes to look out the little window. He was so much shorter than the guys Mo usually liked.

"Is it *her*?" Mo whispered. "Did she follow you?"

"Pizza," Thomas said. He pulled out a wallet and unlocked the door. "How much?"

"No," Mo said. "I'll get it. Okay, but don't give a tip. I called like an hour ago."

"Excuse me," the pizza guy said, "but the roads are really shitty. I am doing my best."

"Fine," Mo said. "You're doing your best and so am I and possibly Thomas, here, is also doing his best though we've seen no evidence of that. Tip freely, Thomas."

Thomas paid. He said, "I have not really been at my best in some time. I have failed to kill my enemy. Worse, I have lost the tool Malo Mogge gave me."

"Hey," the pizza guy said. He looked alarmed. "I met Malo Mogge the other night at the benefit. She seems cool? Also very powerful? Is she going to be mad I brought you pizza? Can you not tell her I did this?"

"My lips are sealed," Thomas said. "Farewell, coward."

This seemed to hurt the pizza guy's feelings, but Thomas clearly didn't care and neither did Mo. He shut the door.

"So what's going on?" Mo said. "Spill."

"I have been hiding from Malo Mogge for these last few hours," Thomas said. "Twice now she had me but for good chance, and so, before coming here, it seemed best to make sure she was not on my heels. But if she does not find me I will still, in the end, go to her when her patience is gone and she calls me."

"She's chasing you now?" Mo said. "Thought you were buddies."

"She is not chasing me, exactly, but she wonders about my absence. I have been careless with something belonging to her," Thomas said. "Now it's in the possession of the one you call Bowie. For this she will have my skin."

"Let me be the bearer of some good news, then," Mo said. "We have her key! Remember? So maybe we can make a deal with her. She gets her key, you get to keep your skin."

Thomas took Mo's hand and kissed it, a move straight out of one of the Lavender Glass books. Mo yanked his hand back. "Cool it, Masterpiece Theatre!" he said.

Thomas said, "I will summon Malo Mogge if you promise not to trade advantage for me. It wouldn't have been the worst thing not to be real, you know. To have been made out of your magic and then sent away. It might have been preferable than to live as I have lived."

"Oh, come on," Mo said. "Just come upstairs, okay? Let's take the pizza up and eat some before everything gets all terrible again."

He went up the stairs carrying the pizza and Thomas followed. On the first-floor landing, though, Thomas lunged at Mo, pressing him against the wall, kissing him. "Pizza boxes!" Mo said. Thomas took them from him, dropping them on the floor, kissed him again. "Wait, wait," Mo said. "One more thing." He took out his mouth guard, shoved it into his pocket. The one time he'd actually remembered to wear it some and now this. Now his hands were free and he took good advantage of that, getting Thomas's zipper down, wrapping one around Thomas's cock. He couldn't help it; he said, "Did people really call it a sugar stick?"

"What?" Thomas said.

"Your dick," Mo said. "Did you ever call it that? Or a pizzle?"

Thomas said, "We have very little time. And you are interested in what I named my part?"

"Never mind," Mo said, stroking him tenderly.

"*Kukhuvud*," Thomas said. "*Arsle*. That one I am sure I do not need to translate. But more usually, *rovhal*."

"Good words," Mo said. "I like hearing you say them. Are we a thing again now? Even though I called you imaginary? I didn't mean it as an insult. I really did mean you were too good to be true. I don't even know why you like me."

"I like you because you know who you are," Thomas said. "Because you looked out and saw me standing on your lawn." This was corny. His grandmother said that when she was agonizing over confessions of love. It's so horribly corny, she'd say. It's awful. I love it. I hate it but I love it. Mo loved it, too. He wished Thomas would keep on talking to him in that soft voice, keep saying corny things, and keep speaking filth, too, in other languages. He bet Thomas knew how to say all sorts of things, all sorts of words in other languages. But Thomas had stopped talking and was looking at Mo.

"I don't know why I like you," Mo said. "I don't know a lot of stuff, not yet. But I do like you. I really do."

He saw that this was enough for Thomas, at least for now.

They stayed there on the landing, the pizza growing cold, until there was a noise from somewhere below them. It wasn't the kind of noise Mo thought he could ignore.

"Take the pizza up," he said. "I'll go down and deal with that."

"I'll go with you," Thomas said.

"It's fine, just something I did that I need to go deal with," Mo said. "Go up and say hi. I need to get drinks anyway."

He knew who it was. And was it really a surprise? The bad people in his grandmother's books were always thinking they'd gotten rid of Lavender Glass, only for her to pop up again. And there she was, standing in the kitchen, holding the refrigerator door open, peering at the shelves as if the love of her life might be inside.

"You again," Mo said. "I thought Susannah got rid of you."

"I am not here on my own behalf," Lavender Glass said. She set the carton of eggs on the counter and took one out. "A box without hinges, a key, or a lid." She smashed the egg under her palm and yolk oozed out like jam. "Do you know my riddle?"

"Hey," Mo said. Another egg. "Stop that! Just go away, okay? No one wants you here. You aren't real. You were never real."

Lavender Glass picked up another egg, threw it down between her bare feet. "No," she said. "It isn't this one, either."

"Go away!" Mo said. He let his magic go flooding out, discerning the edges of Lavender Glass, pulling apart that remnant of magic animating her.

Lavender Glass, even as she vanished for the last time, picked up the whole carton and dropped it on the tile floor. Every egg except for one broke, painting the floor with yellow yolk and white flecks of shell. The last egg rolled toward Mo, wobbling drunkenly, comically. A crack like a seam ran from the narrow end toward the wide.

It came to rest in front of him, turning one last time so that, improbably, it pointed up, spinning still. The crack widened and something wormlike began to wriggle out. Mo took a step back.

He remembered the feeling when he'd first come back, that every space contained too much shadow. That fear he would crack an egg and Bogomil would spill out. But the person who emerged, first one pointed finger, then a hand, a wrist, a long muscular arm, and then all the rest of her all at once, was Malo Mogge.

"What a pretty kitchen this is," she said. "The granite countertops, these tiles, the cabinets. The fixtures. This charming table. These delightful bits of eggshell everywhere. What a lovely view you must have of my temple. But how lonely you must be. No one here but you. Let's go join your friends."

It was like the first time she'd spoken to him. Like someone finding the softest place in you and setting a hook there. "Let me get a sponge first," he said. "Clean this up some." He wanted the kitchen to be clean. If he died, it would be like this for a long time. Egg yolks got gummy as they dried. You had to clean them up before that happened.

"Don't bother," Malo Mogge said. "You know the saying? If you want something you have to break a few eggs. And I want my key very, very badly. You have no idea. How could you? So?"

"Fine," Mo said. Fucking Lavender Glass.

The Book of Malo Mogge's Key and How It Was Lost

"Imagine you are a being of such vast power you may go wherever you please. There is no one like you in all the worlds." This was Bogomil. He was walking very quickly. Laura was having a hard time keeping up. The sidewalk had not been shoveled, and so they were in the street.

She said, "There are other worlds? She's from another world? Are you taking me to Susannah?"

"Does it matter, Malo Mogge's origin? If there were any others like her, they have never discovered themselves to us. She made a door of herself and came through it into our world and then made many other doors, each with its own guardians. I do not know what lay beyond the doors not in my keeping. She destroyed the faithless guardians all, and with them her doors. In this way she was made to diminish herself."

"But she didn't destroy you," Laura said.

"We did not rebel. Perhaps our predecessors would have. They'd served her long. They knew her better. But the realm beyond our door is not another world. It is a threshold place only, Malo Mogge's larder, which borders the kingdom of Death. I live upon that threshold though I do not cross over it yet."

"If Susannah has the key, can't we use it? Make a new door and go into other worlds, ones where Malo Mogge has no key to follow?"

"All these years and Malo Mogge has made no new doors. It is a task beyond her strength while she may not replenish herself. This temple of hers, the closing of Lovesend, this is all show. For the span of five hundred years, more, she has had to conserve her power. Entertain herself on a smaller scale. Now that she knows her key is near at hand, she is profligate. But this is nothing compared to what she will do when she has it back."

"She won't get it," Laura said. "I'll stop her."

Bogomil halted so suddenly she almost walked into him.

"Hey!" she said.

"Do you think so highly of your talents that already you might surpass her?"

Laura said, "Should I just give up? I think I've done okay for someone who only came back from the dead a few days ago."

Bogomil began to walk again, faster this time. They were on Little Moon Street, nearly down to the bay. He said, "All the magic you have comes from Anabin, and everything Anabin has, has as its source Malo Mogge. You are a match head beside the conflagration of her sun, a bit of chalk beside the majesty of her moon, even diminished as she is. When she has her key back, she will be able to cross to my side of the door again. She will replenish herself on sacrifices and in time she may again be what she once was."

"She said something about sacrifices to me. People sacrifices, right? Why are you always barefoot? Your toes are going to fall off."

"The cold doesn't bother me," Bogomil said. "And when we translate ourselves, peripheral things have a tendency to drift. One of the lesser mysteries."

Like dryer socks, Laura thought. Bogomil went on speaking. "Those like yourself who have been marked by contact with her key in one of its incarnations are her sacrifices. Long ago it would be a knife her guardians used to cut the throats of men and women upon her altar, but that was only spectacle. To make physical contact with any of the key's incarnations means that upon leaving Anabin's realm, one does not go into Death directly but rather enters my realm, where, when Malo Mogge possessed her key, she might follow as she pleased. Once, you and your friends would have been Malo Mogge's meat unless I had shown you kindness and sent you on your way into Death."

"Ugh. None of this seems very helpful," Laura said.

"Helpfulness goes against my nature these days. But here is something you do not know. When, very long ago, Malo Mogge's key was lost the first time, she searched for it and I searched, too. I thought it was my own ability that helped me discover it when she could not. I took it into my realm and studied its nature. I came to understand it is a living thing. Once it was a part of Malo Mogge but, divided from her, it came to have desires that were divided from her desires. It was not lost but fled her. I was allowed to discover it because it is inimical to her. It showed me how she might be undone."

"See? That's actually helpful. Tell me."

"In the moment when new guardians of our door are chosen, Malo Mogge is vulnerable. Both old and new guardians must draw on her magic then, but they draw as well on the magic that the key possesses. The last time I had the key I might have used Malo Mogge's own strength in coordination with the power of the key to strike a blow. Thomas and his brother were to take up their roles, and in that moment, she and Anabin would have been summoned; I thought to wound her, then drag her across the threshold. Once she was on my side of the door, I could have taken more of her power, enough that I might have taken her place and become a god myself. But the one who calls himself Bowie interfered with the ritual, and Malo Mogge, who had not known the key was found and the ritual begun saw in that moment she was betrayed. And the key, too, saw my intention had been to not only strike down Malo Mogge but to become her. So once more the key hid itself."

"Why did it care?"

"I would have had her power. I would have kept her key, too. What a waste it would have been, all that power, to keep none for myself. The key wishes Malo Mogge destroyed, her door destroyed with her, and itself, too. My plan was less wasteful. Here we are."

Bogomil left the road.

Laura knew where they were now. She said, "The Seasick Blues? It's the off-season. Susannah won't be here. No one's here."

"Room twelve. See, there is a light on. Knock."

I am tired of being told what to do, Laura thought. I am tired of doors. Nevertheless she managed a smile when it was Mr. Anabin who opened the door, as if she were genuinely glad to see him. Who had ever been glad to see Mr. Anabin? Well, Bogomil, supposedly, though as soon as the door opened and Mr. Anabin was there, Bogomil turned his back on him. Apparently this was what you did when you really liked somebody. If you were Bogomil.

"Mr. Anabin, hi!" she said, knocking snow off her boots and stepping into the room. "Sorry to bother you, but Bogomil's been giving me a history lesson and now we're visiting you. He hasn't told me why. Did you know my mother's dead? Ruth? Oh, right. You do. Mo found you and told you."

"I'm sorry for your loss, Laura," Mr. Anabin said. As if he were actually her old music teacher. As if her mother had died of cancer or in a car accident instead of being murdered by a god. As if they were just going to have a normal conversation while Bogomil stood with his back to them both.

"Malo Mogge took away my grief," Laura said. "So I'm not particularly sad or anything. I'm just angry."

"I am sorry for that loss, too," Mr. Anabin said.

"Thanks. I guess. Can I ask you a question?" Laura said. "Why do you do that? The thing where one of you spins around like that."

Mr. Anabin said, "This is how it goes when we are together. It is the cost of the magic that made us guardians. He may speak, but I must turn from him. As he turns from me when I speak. In the realm of Life we may look but not speak. Speak but not look."

"What about in his realm?"

"I may not enter it. The guardian whose realm is Life may not pass through the door. Though I still hope one day to see Bogomil's realm."

"It's not that great. Anyway, maybe could you just go sit on the bed and face the other direction? Bogomil still hasn't gotten to the important stuff yet. Thanks."

She watched in fascination while Mr. Anabin went and sat on the left-hand bed. The largest mirror Laura had ever seen hung on that wall, its twin on the other side. A workaround, she realized. Remember that, Laura. There are always workarounds.

Bogomil sat down on the other bed. Laura stayed standing. You never knew with the motel beds. Susannah had told her stories. Susannah must have known Mr. Anabin was here, though. Susannah, full of secrets. As full of secrets as a fucking motel bedspread.

Bogomil said, "I can sum up the rest quite quickly. Malo Mogge made her key out of herself. She still does not grasp how it might now oppose her. She knows I betrayed her, but she does not know her key chose to leave her; she does not know her key once made alliance with me against her. When it is in her possession again, and you take up my place, you may yet make your own bargain with the key. Serve Malo Mogge faithfully until you may strike her down."

"Because that worked out so well for you?" Laura said, exasperated. Mr. Anabin watched them both in the mirror.

Bogomil said, "Serve Malo Mogge faithfully then. Make sacrifices to her and keep her larder. Make your home in darkness as I have done. But should life as Malo Mogge's servant pall and you decide to make common cause with her key, keep the terms of your bargain. My error was not that I betrayed Malo Mogge, but this: I betrayed the key as well, and with it, Anabin."

Mr. Anabin's face did not change as he listened to this: Laura checked in the mirror surreptitiously. It was like being in the room while your weird parents fought without ever acknowledging they were in a fight. Well, that wasn't a situation Laura was ever going to be in again.

"None of this is how I saw my life going," she said. "I had plans. They were so much better than any of this. I don't know that I want career guidance from either of you."

"Just wait until Malo Mogge has her key back. Things are really going to get interesting then. Her appetite will be vast after so many centuries starved of sacrifice. She'll devour this town—everyone in it. Your work will be to serve it up," Bogomil said, not sounding entirely displeased about this.

"Yeah, I got it, your job sucks. Eternal darkness, lots of murder. Betrayal, more betrayal, regret, inexplicable feelings for Mr. Anabin. No offense, Mr. Anabin. Just, maybe don't give me any more advice for a second? Okay? Either of you," Laura said.

"There is one more thing you ought to know," Mr. Anabin said. He wasn't looking at Laura, though. He was looking at Bogomil. Or, rather, Bogomil's reflection.

"What?" Laura said.

Mr. Anabin said, "Malo Mogge is with your sister and the others now. She has come for her key."

Laura found she was raising her hand in front of her face, as if bracing for a blow. Neither of her companions moved from where they were sitting. They only sat looking at the mirrors, at those other versions of themselves. How useless they were! She said, "What are you doing just sitting there? Come on, come on, get up. Get up! We have to go."

The Book of Daniel

It was such a relief to tell Susannah everything. About Carousel, about what it had been like in Bogomil's realm, about his feeling, too, that it would be better to go back there rather than go along with whatever it was that Bogomil and Mr. Anabin wanted.

"Thank you for sharing," Susannah said when he was done. "We are going to have the biggest fight in the world, but not right now. First you have to know some things." She told him about the Harmony, about the splinter, about how Malo Mogge needed her key to go to Bogomil's realm, about how those who went there became her meals. "Still want to go there?"

"No," Daniel said. "But if I don't, then Laura or Mo does. Two return, two remain."

"Or we can make a new deal with Malo Mogge," Susannah said. "I found her key. So she kind of owes me." She put her head on Daniel's shoulder again.

A person Daniel had never seen before came up into the attic carrying two pizza boxes.

"Who are you?" Daniel said.

Susannah didn't lift her head. She said, "That's Thomas."

"Susannah," Thomas said. He put the pizza boxes down on the table in front of them. "And Daniel, I presume. My God, you're monstrously large. Mo will be up in a moment."

"How do you know each other?" Daniel said.

Daniel saw Thomas look at Susannah. "Fine," she said, sitting up. "He and I slept together. Once. But it didn't mean anything. What does mean something is he and Malo Mogge came to my house hunting that person you know, Bowie. Avelot. Then Malo Mogge killed Ruth. Also, Thomas and Mo have a thing. But maybe not anymore."

Daniel couldn't help it, the way he felt. Here was someone he gladly would have let the bear he had been tear apart. He saw that Susannah was watching carefully, to see what he thought, to see how he responded. "Thanks for telling me," he said at last.

Thomas said, "More information than he needed, surely. I am here on behalf of Malo Mogge. Mo says you have her key."

Neither Susannah nor Daniel bothered to respond. Instead they took one pizza box while Thomas took the other. Before Daniel finished his third slice Malo Mogge came up the stairs. Her feet were bare. One sleeve and both legs of the tracksuit she wore were spattered with flecks of something yellow.

Daniel could not look away. Here was the cause of all of their misery looking like a clown on a community cable show.

"Careful," Susannah said.

What exactly did she think Daniel was going to do? But perhaps she was saying it to herself as much as to him. He could feel the tension in her body.

"So you have found my key," Malo Mogge said. "In future centuries this day will be marked with festivities and gifts. And here, too, I see, is my Thomas."

Mo came up the stairs behind her. He looked no better than anyone did, than Daniel felt. This was what it was like to be in the presence of a goddess. Stricken by awe. By her awfulness.

"Well, Thomas?" Malo Mogge said. "Surely you have slain your enemy by now. Where is the weapon you were lent?"

Thomas said nothing.

Malo Mogge's face became even more terrible, then assumed an air of pleasant expectation that was the worst thing yet, somehow. "No matter. These children will return to me my key and at last we will have new guardians for the door. I will replenish myself and then you will know me in my fullness rather than this starveling crescent I have been in all our time together. What a feast I will make of this town! You, sweet Thomas, I will deal with at my leisure. Now. Where is it?"

"Before we hand over your key we need to talk about some stuff," Susannah said. Her voice was steadier than Daniel's would have been. But that was Susannah. She never had stage fright. She just got up on stage and went at it. "Nobody is going back to Bogomil's realm, okay? Not Daniel, not anyone. If you want your key back, you have to let them stay. And Daniel's sister Carousel, too. You get your key and leave town. That seems like a fair trade to me."

"And Thomas," Mo said. "You're not going to do anything to him, either."

So Susannah was right, Mo and this guy did have a thing. How had they even had time to have a thing?

"Bargaining?" Malo Mogge said. "You see the moon in the sky above you and take it for a merchant in the marketplace?"

"I see a murderous bitch dressed up like a gummy bear," Susannah said. "A murderous bitch, by the way, who seems to have misplaced her keys for five hundred years. Took me less than five minutes to find this thing, and I didn't even know it was missing or who you were."

"Susannah," Daniel said. "Be careful. Remember?"

Susannah ignored him. "Anyway, I'm not really asking for a lot."

"Ask and I will show you wonders," Malo Mogge said. "There."

Daniel felt it then. All the power in this person, how it emanated from her like a wind made of cold light.

Thomas said, "What have you done?"

Malo Mogge turned toward the windows that faced the garden. "Come and see," she said.

By the light of Malo Mogge's temple Daniel saw how the water in the bay was heaving itself up. It rose behind the temple, so vertiginously high it seemed almost on the same level as the house upon the cliff in which they stood watching. The wall of water broke into two curving horns and went racing in the direction of Little Moon Bay until quickly it was too close to shore to see, hidden by the cliffs. It would be rushing up toward the town now.

"What are you doing?" Susannah said. "Stop it!"

"Don't worry," Malo Mogge said. "It will do less damage than you think. And now, water is so swift, the damage is mostly done. Now it's finished. Your house gone, little girl, so full of demands, and yours, too." This to Daniel. "Here is my bargain, children. Give me my key and I will not send a wave to smash this house and all in it to a fine paste."

"No!" Daniel said. He threw himself at Malo Mogge to bring her down, but the nearer he came, the farther she seemed to retreat, though she never moved at all. He was contracting, rising up into the air even as a hand reached out and Malo Mogge caught him firmly between her finger and thumb. She brought him so near her face he could smell the sweetness of her breath when she spoke.

"Why fret over the dead?" Malo Mogge said. "Spending in pointless worry the tail end of that little time left to you. You are like a cheese, ripe and stinking with magic unused when you would have been better to employ it in service of finding my key. I might have spared you and your house had you pleased me better. Instead I will send you to Bogomil's realm again. May you please me better there."

He could not get free. He did not even know what Malo Mogge had made of him. He could not speak. He could not defend himself. He could hear Susannah screaming. The pressure of Malo Mogge's thumb and finger increased until Daniel thought he could not bear it. He could not bear it. And then he was dead.

The Book of Laura

ONE MOMENT LAURA was in Mr. Anabin's dreary room at the Seasick Blues and the next she and he were at the top of Mo's house in the music studio, though Bogomil was not. Had they left him there? Susannah was here, her face a rictus of horror for no reason that Laura could discern. Mo and Thomas, too, and Malo Mogge brushing something off her fingers with a look of mild distaste.

"Here you are at last," Malo Mogge said.

"Where have you been?" Susannah said. She practically screamed it.

"Trying to sort out this whole mess," Laura said. "Where's Daniel?" Because he'd said, hadn't he, that he'd keep an eye on Susannah. What else did he have to do?

"Dead!" Susannah said.

"What?" Laura said. She looked at her sister's face to see what she meant by this. But now Susannah was calm again. She seemed to have nothing else to say.

Mo said, "She turned him into a bee. And then she squashed him."

"He will be in Bogomil's realm again," Mr. Anabin said.

"Don't forget what my power wreaked upon your houses," Malo Mogge said. Laura had never seen anyone so horrible and so pleased with themselves.

"What's happened?" Laura said. "What did she do?"

"She sent a wave to destroy our house and Daniel's," Susannah said.

"Give her the key," Mr. Anabin said. "Let us be done with this at last."

"You actually have the key?" Laura asked Susannah. She wouldn't, she *couldn't*, think about their house right now. Daniel. Put those thoughts in a box. She had so, so many boxes.

"It's right in front of you," Susannah said to Malo Mogge. "You asshole."

"Manners," Malo Mogge said. "You dear insignificant speck of dirt. You scrap of flies' meat. Were my key here, would I not know it?"

Susannah bent down and picked up a guitar. It was, Laura saw, her old Harmony, the one she'd given Mr. Anabin.

"That?" Laura said.

"Minus the splinter that has been jammed in my foot this whole time," Susannah said.

Malo Mogge took the Harmony from Susannah. Turned it over. "Where is this splinter?" she said.

"I'll get it," Susannah said. "Just, don't do anything else. Please."

"No," Mo said. "Here it is." He pulled something from his pocket. "Sorry," he said to Susannah. "I thought I should take it, to keep you from giving it to her, but now your idea seems better."

"Better is maybe not the right word," Susannah said.

"Give it to me," Malo Mogge said. She did not move from where she was standing.

Laura watched, astonished. She didn't even understand how her old guitar had anything to do with this. None of this resembled anything she'd ever wanted, ever known you ought to plan for. She seemed to herself to be involved in none of it. Though some small part of her reminded Laura: you did give that guitar to Mr. Anabin for his birthday. Something fluttered near her ear, the one that had been Daniel's, and she raised her hand to brush it away. A moth.

Wait, the moth said into her ear. Don't let them see me.

Daniel, Laura thought. She didn't crush him after all. But the moth said, Not Daniel. Bowie. I have a thing that may aid you. In return for the loan of your mother's coat. I am sorry for her death.

Laura thought of Ruth. Ruth saying, "The moth is no friend to man."

"Give it to me," Malo Mogge said again. Her voice said she wouldn't ask a third time.

"First," Mr. Anabin said from the piano, "There is the matter of who will guard your door."

"Very well," Malo Mogge said. "Laura shall be one. As for the other, this one will serve."

"Me?" Mo said. "I don't want to be a guardian!"

"Would you rather be dead?" Thomas said. "Sent to Bogomil's realm to be eaten?"

"No," Mo said. "I don't think so. But maybe? I don't feel I have enough information to make a solid decision."

"And I am to make my guardians from the likes of these?" Malo Mogge said to Mr. Anabin.

"They have restored your key to you," Mr. Anabin said. "Is that not worth some reward?"

"I do not have it yet," Malo Mogge said. "Bring me that which he holds, Thomas."

Thomas held out his hand to Mo.

"No," Susannah said. "I'll do it. I'm the one who found your key. I should get to be the one to give it to you."

"Go for it," Mo said. He slapped the splinter down in Susannah's palm. Laura opened her mouth to object: Was he really sure Susannah wasn't going to do something stupid? Did he know her at all? Except that Bowie was still whispering in her ear. She has used too much of herself up, given too much of herself away. Here is a weapon. I will distract them when the chance comes, he said. Here is what you will use. Laura lifted her hand up to her hair as if she were pushing it back and felt the moth's wings brush her knuckles. As it did so, it left something between her fingers, smooth, curved, pointed at one end. The rib was Malo Mogge's smallest, but it was too large for a moth to have carried. Bowie had carried it and kept it hidden all the same.

Susannah held out the splinter of guitar to Malo Mogge. She said, "Daniel's dead, but he was dead before. He's in Bogomil's realm now, isn't he?"

"Yes," Malo Mogge said, examining the splinter.

"What happens to him now?" Susannah said.

"I will go there soon and eat him," Malo Mogge said.

"Please," Susannah said. "Let him go. Eat me instead. Let that be my reward for finding the key."

"Such an unworthy reward it would be," Malo Mogge said. "For one so valiant and so demanding. No. You will take Bogomil's place, I think. Your sister Anabin's. And when I come to eat Daniel, you will be there at my side. Ah! I see how it is."

Laura went to Susannah and took her hand. Squeezed it tight. How cold Susannah's hand was.

Malo Mogge bent down and picked up the guitar, tilting it this way and that. She slipped Susannah's splinter into the sound hole. When she withdrew her hand, the guitar became a key, then a cup, then a coin, then the battered Harmony again.

"Oh," Malo Mogge said. "Yes. Here it is." She held the guitar tenderly as if it were her child.

But then her face changed. She said, "Here is my key and yet it is not as I remember it. Do all things grow more stubborn with time? No matter, it has returned to me and it will serve well enough even as it is. Now where is Bogomil?"

"Gone to his realm one last time," Mr. Anabin said.

"And left you here alone again," Malo Mogge said. "Does he not care for you at all? He will not be able to hide himself away from me for much longer. But I will not send you there until I have eaten him."

The Book of Daniel

He was in the forest again, only this time he was alone. The tree-threaded darkness pressed in on him as Malo Mogge's fingers had done. The idea came upon him that he would be alone there forever. This seemed worse by far than being eaten.

But then Bogomil was there, too, looking at Daniel with familiar disdain. "And here you are again. How predictable the shape of your two lives."

"Much of it came as a surprise to me," Daniel said.

"And that, too, predictable," Bogomil said. "Was it your sister who sent you here? I liked that one."

"No," Daniel said. "My sister's dead. My whole family's dead. Malo Mogge sent a wave and drowned them. Then she squashed me."

"A surprising thing at last," Bogomil said. "Are you sure of this? You were there to see it? They are dead?"

Daniel said, "No. Maybe Carousel wasn't there when it happened. She brought me to Mo's house. She was headed home again."

"I ask because the thread of magic that connects you to her has not been severed. Can you feel it still?"

Daniel discovered it, the faint, strange current. "Yes," he said. "So maybe Carousel is alive. But I'm dead. My whole family except Carousel is dead. What happens to her?"

"Malo Mogge will have her key soon," Bogomil said. "If you tarry here, she will eat you. Were I generous, I might offer you another choice. I might release you from my realm. I might send you across the threshold where she could not follow you. Would you ask this of me?"

Daniel said, "If I did, what would happen to Carousel?"

"A good question," Bogomil said. "My answer is, I do not know. She is tied to you by magic. She is made of the same magic that made you. She may prove strong enough to sever the cord. She may follow you into my realm or simply be unmade."

"Then I'll wait," Daniel said. "I'll wait here for her."

"Such patience!" Bogomil said. "Though Malo Mogge will eat you long before."

"I know what's going to happen to me," Daniel said. "You can't make me leave."

Bogomil said, "Apparently no one can make you do anything. But there is yet another possibility."

"What?" Daniel said suspiciously.

"You have been changed by magic already," Bogomil said. "Your body was destroyed, unhousing you, and yet you made your way back into Life. Now you are something more than mortal and have resources others who find themselves here do not. Malo Mogge may have sent you through the door, but you escaped my realm before."

"I don't know how we did that!" Daniel said. "We were desperate!"

"The last time you and your friends fled, I pursued you," Bogomil said. "Were I at your heels, perhaps you might manage once again. I believe your friends are in need of you." Even as he spoke, he was changing, man to wolf.

Daniel fled and the wolf came after him, all helpful teeth and darkness.

The Book of Mary Kenner

Carousel arrived back home, shook off the ice clinging to her eyelashes and muzzle, folded her wings down as if closing an umbrella. She became herself again though it pained her to give up her wings, her size, her silky tail. Her family still sat at the kitchen table, concocting fanciful schemes by which to spend their newfound lottery wealth. Hot chocolate formed a skin in the pot on the stove. And, yes, this was the reason she had put on a human body again, as tempting as it might be to stay a unicorn forever. This was her family, even if they didn't know they had been her family for less than a week. Dakota came over sometimes when it was bedtime and farted in Carousel's face. Lissy just laughed when she did this. Davey and Oliver were younger than Carousel was, and that was annoying. Carousel remembered being the baby, even though, of course, she had not ever been the baby, the real baby. Poor Caroline. And, yes, they'd eaten all the marshmallows this afternoon and there were none left, but so what? Carousel had magic. As she was working out what kind of marshmallows she wanted (real marshmallows, magically summoned; magical marshmallows in whatever flavor or shape she wanted), the wave came.

One instant they were all in the kitchen, and in the next there was a noise so loud Carousel could hear nothing else. The whole house moved forward on its foundation as water came roaring in, smashing everything it touched. Carousel changed in that same moment without even knowing she did so. The other Lucklow children and her parents she turned into six small red stones and she caught each one up in her horny beak.

Then the water was pulling apart the house in a boiling foam of smashed timber, drywall, Monopoly pieces, Daniel's coin collection, dirty laundry and clean laundry, too, six scratch-off lottery tickets, each one a winner.

The wave went back down the street again in a rush. There were six pebbles under the curved plate of Carousel's radula, safe as she could make them. What was she? A squid, monstrous but still frail compared to the deluge of water. The receding wave carried her along briskly, spinning her and ripping at her arms, the rough skin of her terrible head, her beak. The water was so thick, bristling with debris, that it was hardly water at all. She could not breathe in the churn. Bits of herself came away, she felt this without feeling it, the cold an anesthetic. Still she was pulled out, down to the shore and out and out, farther from the shore, so swiftly she had no space to think what she should become. She had magic, but she had only been what she was for four days, and almost everyone who cared for her in this world was, instead, in her care. Dying, she became a girl again, drowning, and that would have been the end of Carousel and the magic she was made of, but strong arms caught her, a woman standing upon the floor of the ocean, braced against the deluge. Once her grasp on Carousel was firm, the woman began to walk along the sandy bottom toward the shore. Once she had been a statue of Mary Kenner, one of Maryanne Gorch's more controversial commissions when it was discovered that her notable contribution to humanity was the invention of the sanitary belt (but does that really merit a statue, said one of the men on the panel, the other arguing it wasn't really something you wanted to celebrate even if it had been a useful invention). Because of this, Maryanne had commissioned a statue of Kenner twice to scale. There should be more celebrations of practicality and problem-solving had been her opinion. Fewer statues of murderers and the rich.

Malo Mogge's great wave had swept the bay clean of everything else: boardwalk, rocks large and small, all dunes, all features. Like shaking a rumpled bedsheet before laying it down quite flat. Once she had Carousel upon this new shore and was satisfied the human child was breathing, Mary Kenner pressed something into Carousel's hand. Then she went back into the ocean. Carousel coughed hard and spat six red stones onto the beach. She began to use her magic to make herself warm again.

The Book of Thomas

"This isn't what I wanted," one sister was saying to the other. "But I'll be with you. Last time I was the one who messed everything up. Not you. This time I'll make sure it goes the way it's supposed to. Though I wish you'd told me what you thought you were going to accomplish."

"You wouldn't have believed me," the other sister said. Then, "I should have told you anyway so you could have told me how stupid I was being. I wasn't doing so great. You know, while you were gone."

"God, I wouldn't have done any better."

Thomas, listening, felt a wave of envy so great it almost dragged him to the floor. He swallowed, felt Mo looking at him again. Here was another thing he did not think he would be able to bear. Who, knowing what Thomas was, would ever look at him the way Mo did? Mo would be Malo Mogge's meat and Thomas could only choose to go on serving her or be the same. It did not seem a hard choice.

"Never mind all that," Malo Mogge said to the sisters. "The two of you will have all the time you can imagine to discuss the truths you have in your heart. But now I have my key and next I will have the ritual and then I will have my rightful meat. Do you and your sister know what you are to say?"

"Bogomil is not here," Anabin said.

"A cur comes when it is called," Malo Mogge answered. "Let the ritual begin and we will have him back. How merry, to be among friends."

"All except one," Thomas said, thinking of Bowie.

"Is that really what you're thinking about right now?" Mo said, sounding exasperated. "Revenge? When Malo Mogge eats me, I hope you manage to maintain that energy."

Thomas did not speak. He tried to convey, with his eyes, everything he would attempt.

"I remember what I'm supposed to say," Susannah said. "I wrote it, after all. Laura, you just have to repeat it. But we need the Harmony, too. Don't we? We hold it and we say the words."

Reluctantly Malo Mogge gave it over. Thomas had never seen her quite like this. There was something childlike in her face, as if she had been asked to share with others her dearest possession, fearing they would be careless. She stood very close to the sisters.

"Put your hand on it," Susannah said. Laura did so. Thomas remembered this, too, the soul-heaviness of the cup his brother had held. How he had given it to Thomas to examine before the ritual began. Thomas had been drunk. It had seemed to him a nothing game, a bit of guild ritual to perform before their benefactor, the kind of thing the alchemists did with great pomp. Afterward, this Bogomil would be pleased with Kristofer and Thomas, and it would be a tale to tell among fellow students, how seriously Bogomil and Kristofer moved in the ruins of the old dyer's hall, roofless but no matter, still suitable, Bogomil said, as any other place and out of the way of prying eyes. And then Avelot, dashing out from a half-toppled cabinet to take her prize, and everything that had happened since.

It would not happen the same way again. But if it all happened again the same way, Bowie bursting forth from some hidden place to break the ritual, Thomas would be ready.

The way it happened was like this, instead: The room began to have the feeling Thomas still remembered all this time later. The moon in the window grew bright, then brighter still, and closer, until it seemed as if it perched upon Malo Mogge's right shoulder. There were points of light around her head like stars and she seemed to grow as tall as a mountain, a mountain range, Bogomil and Anabin, Susannah and Laura foothills where she began. Susannah and Laura, Thomas thought, were not speaking. They were singing. Had he and his brother sung like this? Then Susannah broke off.

"No," she said. "I don't want to do it. It doesn't even want me to do it." She was speaking about the guitar, and Thomas saw that this was true.

"Keep on," Malo Mogge said. Her voice was thunderously loud. It crackled with power.

"Or what?" Susannah said. She did not raise her voice. She did not seem to notice how strange the room had become. "Break it, Laura. It wants you to break it. Just smash it."

Laura lifted up the Harmony and brought it down hard on the floor, Malo Mogge catching her wrist as she began to do it again.

At this same moment a white rabbit came scrabbling out from under a cushion on the strange chair shaped like an egg. And, after him, a gaunt black wolf, toppling the chair over. Susannah called the rabbit by name: here was Daniel shuddering back into human shape, back again from Bogomil's realm, ramming forward into Malo Mogge so she would let go of Laura. The wolf became Bogomil. Anabin at the piano bench did not see this. He was already turned away.

Bogomil was still leaping forward. He wrapped his long arms around Malo Mogge. He dug his face into her neck as if he were nuzzling her, but blood began to run down.

Susannah began to stomp on the pieces of the Harmony in her socked feet. She had better be careful, Thomas thought, or she would end up with another splinter.

"Thomas!" Malo Mogge said. She struck Laura across the face with the palm of her bloody hand. Laura fell to the ground.

There was no chance of success here, and therefore Thomas should have gone to help his mistress. Instead he took the arm Malo Mogge had managed to free and pinned it back behind her. Bowie—of course!—was here now, too, helping to restrain her.

Mo took up a long, thin piece of the guitar's broken body and, as Malo Mogge struggled, he drove it into her eye, so it burst and ran down her cheek like the white of an egg. Daniel had another piece and that one went deep into her stomach. She groaned as if they had actually done her some hurt.

"Now!" Bowie said. "Laura, now!"

And here came Laura with the dart Thomas had so foolishly lost. She reached up and cut Malo Mogge's throat. Blood spurted, drenching

Laura. As the blood ran, Malo Mogge's thin, angry scream grew tinny and shrill, like a kettle telling you it was time to pour it out. Her legs still kicked, but Bogomil and Thomas and Bowie held her arms until they kicked no more.

"Is that it?" Laura said at last. Her hair was dripping with Malo Mogge's blood, the print of Malo Mogge's hand across her face. "Is she dead?"

"More or less," Anabin said from the piano.

"She's gone to my realm," Bogomil said. "I will deal with her there."

"No," Anabin said.

"Then she will find a way back," Bogomil said. "Her magic must be taken from her or she is not done with us."

"Laura will do that," Anabin said. "See, she has already begun."

Laura was licking her lips. Thomas could almost see the magic seething in the blood running down Laura's face, her chin. There were spatters of blood on his own arm, on his clothes, but he would not taste it. He was tired of the taste of Malo Mogge.

"This one?" Bogomil said. "To take her place?"

"And two others," Anabin said, "to take ours."

"Me," Laura said. "You mean I'd be a god?"

"But we destroyed the key," Susannah said. "It let us smash it. Look, it's all in pieces." But it was reshaping itself already. *A coin a cup a key a knife* and then it was the guitar again.

Thomas made his move now for Bowie, but of course Bowie was ready. He was a gull, flying out the window in that very instant, and Thomas another chasing after him.

The Book of Susannah

"Excuse me," Mo said, and then he was a gull, too. He went after Thomas.

Susannah put her hand on Daniel's arm in case he was also thinking of going anywhere. When he did, she was going with him.

"My family," he said.

"First there is the matter of the ritual," Mr. Anabin said from the piano. "And Laura."

"Let the door be kept by Susannah and this other one, then," Bogomil said. "Some small enjoyment for me, I suppose, to see you take up a role you are so ill-suited to play. What will you be, Daniel? Death-in-Life or Life-in-Death?"

Susannah had been perfectly prepared to go through with the ritual if that was the only thing to be done, but now Malo Mogge was dead. Look, here was her body on the floor of the attic. Couldn't they all come up with a better plan? "Daniel doesn't have to be anything he doesn't want to be," Susannah said. "Laura, are you okay?"

"I think so," Laura said. "I feel fantastic, actually." She went over to the toppled egg chair and righted it. This left a smudge of blood on the plastic frame, but Laura saw this and as Susannah watched, her sister licked her thumb, then wiped the plastic clean.

Daniel said, "I need to go see what's happened to my family."

Bogomil crouched down on the floor beside Malo Mogge's corpse. "There," he said, and the corpse was gone, and the pool of blood, too.

Instead there was something small and bright that Bogomil slid into his pocket so quickly Susannah couldn't make out what it was. "What's that?" she said.

"Nothing," Bogomil said. "A souvenir only."

Mr. Anabin, his back to them, sighed.

"Very well," Bogomil said. He held out the thing on his dirty palm and they saw it was a snow globe on a key chain, glittering tinsel stars and moons floating. At the base, wide-eyed and dead, was Malo Mogge's mutilated corpse.

"There's power in that, isn't there?" Laura said. "Hand it over, opportunist."

It was amazing to Susannah how Bogomil did what Laura said and how Laura seemed to accept that this was her due. Laura shook the snow globe and made a face of disapproval. She said, "This is better." The snow globe became a sticker, and Laura picked up the Harmony and carefully applied the sticker to the lower bout. *This Machine Kills Gods.*

Susannah said to Daniel, "I'll go with you. Come on."

"No," Bogomil said. "I will go, then return and make report. Anabin, you may deal with these." And before Daniel or Susannah could object he was gone.

This was what Mr. Anabin told the last three, then.

Magic must be taken from Malo Mogge. Otherwise she might use it to return as they had. Down in Bogomil's realm (not Bogomil's realm much longer) she was weakened and vulnerable but still wily. You couldn't leave her there to torment Bogomil's replacement, to eat the ones who still must pass through the door, to gather enough magic to escape. Laura must go there and take Malo Mogge's magic from her. She would do this by consuming Malo Mogge.

"Gross," Susannah said. She could not see her sister doing any such thing, and neither, apparently, could Laura. Laura said, "I have to eat her? All of her? But she doesn't have a body anymore. She's a sticker. Can't I just turn the sticker into a ham sandwich or something and eat that?"

"What remains of her is in Bogomil's realm, and there is more of her than you imagine. It will take some time," Mr. Anabin said. "But the more you take from her, the easier it will be to consume the rest. Eventually you will have all of her magic."

Susannah took the Harmony from Laura. There was hardly any blood on it, though Laura was drenched. Or perhaps the guitar had drunk it all. "You should sit down," she said.

"I can't," Laura said. "I'll get blood everywhere."

"Oh, who cares?" Susannah said, but of course Laura did, so Susannah reluctantly let go of Daniel. She gave him the Harmony and then tore the lid off one of the pizza boxes. This she put on top of the harpsichord bench. Laura sat.

"Move over a little," Susannah said. She sat down next to Laura. "Do you want this? To be a god?"

Laura said, "What I want is to play music and have lots of people listen to it. I don't know, maybe being a god doesn't necessarily interfere with that, though. It might actually help some. Right?"

"What does that mean?" Susannah said. "You'll use magic like Auto-Tune or something? Or do you mean you'll use it to make people buy tickets? The way you made me do laundry? You'll magically compel good reviews? Punish people if they say mean stuff about you on Twitter?"

"No!" Laura said. "I just mean maybe my shows can be a little more fun and stuff. I don't know. I'll figure it out as I go, okay? But you don't have to jump on my back. I haven't even eaten Malo Mogge yet. And you're going to have to figure all this out, too. You're going to have your own magic. We'll all figure this out together."

Mr. Anabin, ignoring this conversation, took a slice of pizza and began to eat it as if this were band. As if they were at a pizza party. Susannah regretted every time she'd been kind to him at What Hast Thou Ground?

Daniel said, "Why do there have to be guardians or a door at all, if Malo Mogge's dead? If there's stuff that still needs to be done, why can't you and Bogomil be guardians a little while longer?"

Mr. Anabin said, "You say a little while longer and mean a week, but you do not understand what is to come. There is need for a door and keepers as long as there are any who have held Malo Mogge's key. Mo and Thomas and Bowie, Bogomil and I. We must pass through the door into the realm that Bogomil has kept and on into Death."

"All of us?" Susannah said. "We have to wait for everyone here to die?"

"Then there is Laura," Mr. Anabin said. "Who will have magic beyond reckoning. What was Malo Mogge's and what is in Malo Mogge's key. Should she choose, Laura is immortal. If she chooses that the key be her knife, there will be many who will come through my door, as you call it. And remember Carousel, who is tied to Daniel and therefore to the key. Carousel must pass through the door one day."

Laura did not appear to be listening to any of this. She was rubbing at her face, licking her fingers.

"Laura," Susannah said. "Stop. I'll get you a paper towel. A napkin."

"No," Laura said. "It's okay."

Daniel said, "So there has to be a door. And doorkeepers."

Susannah said, "Maybe Mo would do it. You don't have to."

"You're going to do it," Daniel said.

"Yes," Susannah said.

Bogomil was back, suddenly.

"Tell me," Daniel said. Mr. Anabin turned his back.

Bogomil said, "Your sister, it seemed, saved herself and the rest of your family, too. They are making their way home again, though your home is gone. No piece of it left. Has all been decided then? Will they do as they must?"

Daniel opened his mouth as if he were going to say something, but nothing came out. He put his hand behind him, finding the egg chair, and sat down. How wonderful that his family was still living. Susannah thought of Ruth, who was not, and how glad Ruth would be, nevertheless, if she could know Daniel's family had been saved.

Bogomil wandered over to the harp and rested his chin on the shoulder. He patted the strings so they made small discordant ripples of sound. Susannah had liked him much better as an imaginary friend. She thought, One day you will come into my realm and I will make you sorry. Bogomil looked at her, and she saw he knew what she was thinking. He grinned, though.

"Laura must go into your realm," Mr. Anabin said from the window where he stood.

"Only if she wants to," Susannah said. She was practically growling. Laura had only to give the word and Susannah would become a wolf. She would tear Mr. Anabin apart, Bogomil, too, or die trying.

But Laura stood. Susannah could feel the power in her, all the magic Laura had already taken from Malo Mogge's blood. "No," Laura said. "I'll go. I'm ready. How do I go there?"

"I will take you," Bogomil said. And then he and Laura and the Harmony were gone before Susannah could say or do anything at all.

The Book of Laura

So here she was again. Only this time she was not afraid of either the place or the man who walked beside her. (A man, then a wolf, now a man again.) And the shining darkness, the soft, dusty exhalation of the path against her feet, all of this was, she was now able to see, something one might find beautiful. Susannah had found it beautiful, hadn't she? But then she had been Bogomil's guest, while Laura had been his prisoner. Now? She was his equal or perhaps she was something greater. Had she not succeeded where Bogomil had not? Had she and the others not defeated Malo Mogge and sent her to this place? This triumph sustained her until they came to a clearing where something lay, wounded and bleeding.

"Go on," Bogomil said. "Your dinner."

When Laura hesitated, he said, "She must be eaten. If she isn't eaten, if all of her magic is not consumed, then inevitably she will mend herself and come creeping out of this realm. Back into the world. You did so; do you think she is less capable? Less determined? Even Daniel—Daniel!—made his escape. If you don't eat her, then I will and no one will be pleased about that. Well, I will be. Very pleased. But Anabin would not be, and I find after all this time that I would like him to be happy with me again."

"I still don't get the two of you," Laura said. "You suck, but at least you're good-looking and you do stuff. He's got all this power, he could do whatever he wants, and what, he's spent years teaching mediocre kids at a mediocre public school to put on mediocre concerts, mediocre musicals. Wearing stupid T-shirts and living in a shitty motel. Like, I get liking music! It's what I've spent most of my life thinking about, doing, planning for. You wanted to be a god, I wanted to be a rock star. The music thing I get. But Mr. Anabin? I don't get him at all."

Bogomil said, "What I am to Anabin and Anabin is to me is none of your concern. What he was, and what he is, and what he will be, you see only the smallest part. But even that smallest part is dear to me. You think you are interesting and Anabin is not because you are young and stupid and you do not know the value of anything yet. But if you are wise you will take a lesson from Anabin in how to comport yourself."

"Whatever," Laura said. "I am young and stupid and uninteresting whereas you and Mr. Anabin are old and incredibly smart."

"I'm very old," Bogomil said. "I am so very, very old. You will have as many years as you desire, as many years as I have had, perhaps. Perhaps one day you will be wiser than I have been. But I doubt you will be as wise as Anabin. There has never been another like him. Now. Are you ready to do what must be done?"

Laura looked into the clearing, where Malo Mogge lay in her torn red velour tracksuit, head thrown back to show the red rent in her throat. Laura said, "I don't know how, though. How do I eat her?"

"Begin," Bogomil said, "and you will see how it must be done."

"What if I don't see?" she said. "What if I mess it up? Will you tell me if I'm doing it right?"

Bogomil said, "I am not the keeper of your door and I am not your psychopomp. I do not, in fact, much care for you. I am not your teacher and I won't be your audience. She was my mistress for longer than you can imagine. I find that if I am not to be the means of her end, I don't wish to witness you making a mess of it."

"Well," Laura said, "fine—"

But he was already gone. It was only Malo Mogge and Laura, standing above her.

She got down on her knees, turned Malo Mogge fully onto her back. Malo Mogge did not resist her, did not seem to be able to resist her. And, oh, Laura could feel all of Malo Mogge's magic, how ripe and delicious it was down here in Bogomil's realm. Malo Mogge looked up at her, panting like an animal. Air whistled out of the wound in her throat. Her mouth opened as if she were going to speak but Laura said, "No. I don't want to hear it. Whatever it is that you want to say. Whatever you want to promise me, tell me, it doesn't matter anymore. Bogomil keeps talking about how I'm going to take your place, how I'm going to become you, but I'm not. You were horrible! I'm not going to be you. I'm going to be better."

She could feel the blackness of Bogomil's realm clinging to her knees, getting under her fingernails, pressing itself into the pads of her fingers. No wonder Bogomil was always so filthy. Malo Mogge, whatever she had been trying to say, was silent now. Laura had made her silent. Laura could tell her now to say how sorry she was. How sorry she was for killing Ruth. That she had caused so much trouble. Laura could command Malo Mogge to beg for her life. Could ask her to give up every secret she'd ever held. That was tempting. And that was the trouble. Let Malo Mogge speak and she might say something you had to listen to. She might offer something you actually wanted.

Laura decided to skip that part. She didn't want to hear her mother's name spoken by that mouth.

She lifted one hand and put it down on Malo Mogge's shoulder. Her dirty fingers passed easily into Malo Mogge's flesh. It was like sticking your hand into a stick of butter left out on a plate. She had the sense her fingers were sharper now, the palm of her hand like a scoop. There was a smell, too, indescribably delicious. A birthday cake, sugary but also sharp like blood. Like a steak oozing with blood and butter and whipped cream. She reached farther. Here was something different in Malo Mogge's soft body, a thing that was thin and curved and hard. That last bit of Ruth, the rib Malo Mogge had stolen. Laura snapped it right off, withdrew her hand. She stuck her mother's rib into her pocket and then, without thinking, licked the clots of Malo Mogge's blood off her fingers. Oh, delicious. Oh, how strong, how sweet, how rich! How hungry she was!

She reached down and scooped up a whole handful of Malo Mogge's flesh. She crammed it into her mouth. She bent her head down toward Malo Mogge, felt how her own face was elongating, becoming something wolfish and toothy, her tongue becoming serrated, hollow, designed to puncture and suck up sweetness. She thrust her back claws deep into the dirt of Bogomil's realm and her face into Malo Mogge's body and began to eat in earnest. There was no need for manners because there was no one there to watch her eat.

Only when she had finished her meal did she realize someone had come to keep her company.

The Book of Daniel

He had thought everything lost, but it was not, it had not been lost. He couldn't think about what would happen next, not yet. First he would go to his family.

"Can I go with you?" Susannah said.

Daniel took her hand, let her pull him out of the too-small chair.

Mr. Anabin said, "See for yourself no harm has come to your family, then return. There is much that needs to be done. Laura will need some time to consume Malo Mogge's magic, but we must talk while she does so. And Daniel, you must bring your sister back with you. Carousel."

"I won't make her go away," Daniel said.

"Then we must figure out what can be done to help you both," Mr. Anabin said. "Bogomil and I will speak on it."

"I don't trust him," Daniel said. "I don't trust either of you."

"I'll stay here," Susannah said. "In case Bogomil comes back."

"No," Daniel said. "We'll go quickly."

All these long days in which he had had magic and never used it. Perhaps he should have. What were the other things he might have had but had let go to waste? Susannah, who loved him. Music, which he'd had a gift for but he'd only ever dabbled in. Even his height, a thing he'd found embarrassing. If one of his brothers or sisters had scorned their abilities, their gifts, wouldn't he have talked with them? Told them to celebrate what they could do, who they could be?

He had thought his family was dead, but they had been saved. This, too, was no doubt due to magic. Magic, wielded by Laura and the others, had vanquished Malo Mogge. He had not wanted magic but he must now be grateful for what magic had done. He did not want magic but he must learn how to use it. It would be a shame, then, to only use it grudgingly and without joy.

"The roads are bad," Susannah said. "It took me over an hour to walk up here."

"Ride on me," Daniel said.

And so, leaving Mo's house, of his own volition he became a brown bear. It was a kind of exorcism to choose that shape again of his own free will. And how pleasurable it was, he found, to wish to be a thing and become that thing. How pleasurable it was to be alive. It was pleasurable, too, to see Susannah's delight in his transformation. She climbed onto his back, grabbing handfuls of his thick fur.

It was still snowing, and he could feel how the snow, too, was made by some magic still in motion though Malo Mogge was gone. Magic would be required to stop it, but not yet. Let it snow a little longer. Daniel turned from brown bear to polar bear to match the whiteness of the snow, and he ran down the very center of the Cliff Road through the new snow.

He stopped beside the Cliff Hangar and looked out into the bay where Malo Mogge's temple still stood. Snow was falling on it. Let it be hidden from sight. Let it be torn down. But this would not be his task.

He had died here; his body was here still. Here he'd accepted the gift Susannah had meant to give him without ever knowing what he was being offered or whether he might want it. He wouldn't have wanted it. He didn't want it now. But Susannah had tried to explain it to him at the Cliff Hangar that night before their last show, and he'd let Laura make a joke out of it, out on the ledge with Mo.

He was ashamed of that. He was ashamed of the secrets he'd kept from Susannah. If he was in his human body he would have had to find a way to begin to apologize, and then they probably would have had another fight about all the things he'd done, the things she'd done, too. But luckily he was a bear.

Susannah must have come to the same conclusion because she slid off his back and said, "You're an asshole. But I'm glad you're here and that you don't hate me. I'm glad your family isn't dead and Malo Mogge is."

And she became a bear, too. Together they went running down the snowy road.

Once in their own neighborhood they became themselves again. It was hard, at first, to comprehend what they saw. There were the foundations of their homes, scoured clean by water, powdered in fresh snow. No other house had been touched. Here was the tidy path the water had taken back to Little Moon Bay, carrying the wreckage of their houses with it, washing the street as it went. And here, coming back up the street, was Daniel's family, their clothes sodden with ocean water.

"You go talk to them," Susannah said. "I'm going to lurk over here beside some bushes. Become a weasel or something."

"I don't mind if you stay," Daniel said.

"Seems awkward," Susannah said. "What am I supposed to say to your parents? 'Oh, look, your house is gone! Mine is, too. Also, you probably don't know, but my mom is dead. A goddess killed her. Did you hear about Laura? No, she's fine. She's busy eating somebody right now.' Thanks, but I'd rather be a weasel."

"Fine," Daniel said. "Hide in my coat pocket."

"That's me," Susannah said. "Your lucky weasel." She climbed into his pocket and he went to meet his family.

"The house," his mom said. "Daniel, the house—"

Daniel said, "You're okay."

"We were carried out by the water," Dakota said. "But then it carried us back in again. It was like magic. Real magic."

"Tides," his stepfather said. "Strange things happening every day."

His mom said, "The Hands? Ruth and the girls, were they home?"

Daniel said, "Laura and Susannah are at Mo's house. But Ruth was here."

"Oh," his mom said. "Oh no."

"Yeah," Daniel said. He reached down around Susannah, who had become ferociously still in his pocket. She bit him on the finger, hard.

"Poor Ruth," his mom said. "Poor Susannah, poor Laura." She began to cry, and Davey and Oliver began to cry, too. Dakota and Lissy had their arms around each other's shoulders. Daniel could hear their teeth chattering.

"Our house," Davey said. "My toys. My books. My bed."

"No, look," Carousel said. "See? It's fine."

And when Daniel looked back, their house was standing on its foundation again.

Carousel said, "Mom, Dad, remember? We were having hot chocolate next door with Ruth. We went over to show her the lottery tickets. Then everything happened, the freak wave, we got swept out. I don't know what happened to Ruth, but look, our house is fine. It's right there. We're okay and our house is okay."

"We're so lucky," their mom said. "How could we be so lucky when Ruth wasn't?"

"Yeah," Lissy said. "Except for the lottery tickets. I'm guessing those are gone."

"Girls," their dad said, "count your blessings. We're alive. Our house is still here. Ruth is gone. What are lottery tickets compared to a human life?"

Everyone was silent after that.

Daniel said, "I'm going to walk around and see if anyone else was affected by this. I'll be back as soon as I can."

"I'll go with you," Carousel said.

Their mom said, "Oh no, you won't."

But Carousel said again, very firmly, "I'll go with Daniel. Don't worry about it, okay? Don't even think about it. We'll come back when we can."

"Well," their mom said. She still looked unhappy, but she said, "Come back when you can."

Peter, who did not care for miracles or mysteries—didn't Daniel know this?—said, "It's as if no one even saw it happen. No ambulances, no fire trucks. You'd think all the neighbors would be out with their phones. Not a single house touched besides Ruth's."

"Snow muffles sound," Daniel said. "That's the explanation, I bet."

"But everything's okay now," Carousel said firmly. "Except poor Ms. Hand."

Daniel could feel how persuasive she was. How relieved his parents were to believe that this might be true. He picked up Oliver and hugged him hard. "What a night you've had, buddy! Swept out to sea and then home again before midnight." He embraced each member of his family, trying not to squash Susannah in his pocket as he did so.

"Come on," Carousel said, almost whispering, when he hugged her. "Don't be mushy. They're all fine. I saved them all."

She took his hand and led him away from their family and their home.

"Don't leave me hanging," Daniel said. He couldn't get over it. He wanted to find Mr. Anabin and shout in his face, *See? I was right not to do what you wanted me to do. Carousel saved them. If I'd done what I was supposed to do, who would have saved them?* Except Carousel shouldn't have had to save anyone. She was just a child. Younger, even, than that. "What happened? How did you save them?"

"I turned them into stones and kept them safe in my mouth," she said. "The water carried me out into the ocean, and I thought I was going to die. But then a woman caught me and brought me to shore. I recognized her. She was the statue from in front of the post office. I don't remember her name."

"A statue saved you?" Daniel said.

"Is that Susannah in your pocket?" Carousel said. "Hey! Come out! Come out and fight me, Susannah! You were supposed to keep Daniel safe, but you didn't. He died. I felt it when he died."

The weasel's head emerged from Daniel's pocket. Daniel said, "It wasn't entirely her fault. I did something really stupid."

"What about the first time you died, then?" Carousel said. "You want to tell me she didn't have anything to do with that?"

The weasel came flowing out of Daniel's pocket like water. Became Susannah again. "My fault," Susannah said. "Absolutely."

"It's more complicated than she's saying," Daniel said. "But I'm here now and you've put the house back where it ought to be and Malo Mogge's gone. Let's focus on the positive."

"Oh good," Carousel said. "Let's all go back to the house and order pizza. Where's Laura?"

"Eating Malo Mogge's magic-rich corpse so she can take her place," Susannah said. "Sorry, Daniel, I don't know if that goes in the positive or the negative column. But we have to talk to Bogomil and Mr. Anabin about what happens next. They want you to be there, Carousel."

"You don't have to come if you don't want to," Daniel said to his sister.

"If you think I'm going to let you go alone, you're even stupider than it turns out you already are," Carousel said. She was practically spitting she was so mad.

"Susannah will be with me," Daniel said.

Carousel said nothing to this, only looked at both Susannah and Daniel with enormous contempt, presumably for Daniel's great stupidity and Susannah's equal untrustworthiness. "Come on," she said. She became a luxuriantly furred four-legged creature with two heads, one a lion's. The other head seemed to be a goat. Daniel saw on the end of her long, scaly tail was a third head, this one a snake.

"What the hell are you supposed to be?" Susannah said.

"I'm a Chimera!" Carousel said. "Doesn't anyone know anything? You could be literally anything and you picked a weasel, Susannah. I just think that says a lot about you."

"Fair enough," Susannah said, and then Daniel couldn't see her any longer.

"Uh," Carousel said. "Okay. Okay. That's pretty good, actually."

"What?" Daniel said.

"Your girlfriend is a flea," Carousel said. She wriggled her long, furry body, the snake head dipping down as if to strike at her own side. "She's biting me. Daniel, she can ride up on me if she wants, but if she bites me again, I'll make her sorry."

"I don't know what I ought to be," Daniel said. It was such a small decision, and he couldn't make it. He didn't want to make it.

"I could choose," Carousel said. "If you want."

Daniel let his sister choose what he would be.

The Book of Bowie

AND SO HERE they were again, picking up the stitches in the pattern Thomas had determined they were to make. Bowie fled, and of course Thomas followed. So perhaps, then, it was Bowie who set the path. But he could not see how to make a new one. Malo Mogge might be vanquished, but would not Laura assume her shape? Avelot had become Bowie: still the pattern was the same. He and Thomas between them would ensure this. How to choose something new? No one could ever care for Avelot (or for Bowie) as much as Thomas had, all those centuries, Thomas's hatred distilled down to pure and radiant tar. Bowie thought of the woman who had fed him, her baby. He thought of Laura and Susannah and their mother, who had taken the blow for Bowie. Who had tended his wound. He could not remember what manner of person his own mother had been, only the wardrobe, the dress, the moths.

There was delight in this world, there was delight in change, in exploration, in flight. Bowie was not tired, yet, of discovery. A plan came to him as he fled. He would become something new. Perhaps in this way he might change the pattern.

The Book of Susannah

Carousel had turned Daniel into a kinkajou. Susannah wasn't sure if this represented something Carousel saw in him that Susannah could not see or if Carousel simply liked kinkajous. It wasn't the biggest or most important mystery in her life, but would she ever really figure Daniel out? Possibly Susannah was just very stupid, but she was smart enough to know she was thinking about Daniel because she could not bear, yet, to think about Ruth. And maybe this was why she had become a flea. Fleas mostly thought about blood, which was delicious.

Nevertheless, halfway up the Cliff Road, the flea said to the Chimera, "Why do you keep making him so small? First a hedgehog and now this?"

The Chimera stopped. It lashed its tail, said, "Because he wants to be smaller. Can't you feel it? He thinks he takes up too much space."

"Stop indulging him," the flea said. "If he wants to be small and insignificant, then make him choose it."

The Chimera said, "Fine." And Daniel became Daniel again.

"Better," the flea said. "But why not something even bigger? Go big or go home, right?"

Daniel scratched his head. "Go big?" he said. And then he was Daniel, only now he was four or five times larger than he had been before.

"A real giant!" the Chimera said. "Carry me!" And so the giant picked up the Chimera in one large hand, draping it around his neck like a fur stole. Then he went striding up the Cliff Road. It was much better, the flea thought, than riding a bike. Much faster and she didn't have to do any work at all. She hopped from the Chimera to the giant's earlobe and nipped it. After all, he was so very big. Such a small taste of blood would hardly be missed. The giant cleared the gap in the Cliff Road where the cliffside had crumbled away in one step.

Once on Mo's street, Daniel became his normal size again. Mo wasn't home so Daniel opened the door for the Chimera. (The flea hoped Mo wasn't still chasing after Thomas chasing after Bowie, even if she didn't much care whether Thomas killed Bowie or the reverse. Neither of them was worth one of Mo's nose hairs.) Carousel remained a Chimera and so Susannah stayed a flea, too, all the way back up to the attic, where Mr. Anabin and Bogomil waited, Bogomil at the window, looking out, and Mr. Anabin at the piano again, his back turned to Bogomil. This suggested they had either been talking or in a fight. And this was going to be Susannah and Daniel in just a little while. She couldn't quite imagine what it would be like. Well, soon she wouldn't have to imagine.

Susannah became herself.

Mr. Anabin said, "So this is your Carousel, Daniel. All of your fallow magic. She's made extraordinary use of its loan."

"Say all the nice things you want," Carousel said, changing from Chimera to girl. She pointed her chin at Bogomil. "He wanted me to kill Daniel, and you wanted Daniel to kill me. I already know what you're like."

"Where's Laura?" Susannah said. "Why is he back and she isn't?"

"At her meal," Bogomil said from the window. "Before she is done, we must be ready for her."

Susannah said, all of her hackles rising, "Meaning what?"

"Bogomil was once other than Bogomil," Mr. Anabin said. "Malo Mogge not always as you saw her. Imagine what Laura, given unlimited power and days, might become."

Susannah imagined it. She saw Daniel was doing the same.

"Now is the moment for those who will replace Anabin and myself to consider what compact they will make with Laura and the key," Bogomil said.

"So, me," Susannah said.

"And this other one," Bogomil said. "The great lump."

"Me," Daniel said. "And Carousel can go on being Carousel. She can draw on my magic."

"Not like you use it anyway," Carousel said.

"The point Bogomil wishes to make is that the key is a powerful ally," Mr. Anabin said. "Those who have touched the key must pass through Bogomil's realm. But Laura needs only to go through the door one time more, when she wishes to pass into Death herself. Malo Mogge came and went as she pleased, using the key to feed upon the dead in Bogomil's realm. Laura need not do as Malo Mogge did. You need not let her become another Malo Mogge. Make your own bargain with the key."

"You want us to double-cross my sister," Susannah said.

"It will do her no great harm," Bogomil said. "Deny her the realm and she will grow hungry, but what is hunger? One may be hungry and still live."

Susannah said, "Is Laura a pain in my ass? Yes. Am I concerned about Laura having all the power of a literal god? Also yes. Do I want her to go around eating people? Definitely no. But let's wait for her to get back. Then we can hash all this out together."

"Agreed," Daniel said.

"A pretty speech," Mr. Anabin said. "Perhaps Laura, with all of her newfound might and power, will choose to tread lightly, to send no others through the door. Perhaps she will take pity on you and Daniel and choose not to live forever. Perhaps your task will not stretch on as endlessly as it has for me and for Bogomil or perhaps you will find others who will take it up willingly in your place. There are always those who will serve a goddess."

Susannah, looking to Daniel, saw what she felt reflected in his face. His affection for Laura, his knowledge of her. Oh, how unfair it was. Why did they have to make a trap for Laura, as if Laura were some kind of monster? "And what if Bogomil had gotten what he wanted?" Susannah said. "Because that was your whole plan, right? Me and Daniel to replace you and Mr. Anabin, you to replace Malo Mogge. I'm guessing you would have eaten pretty well as a god."

"I would have made a feast for myself," Bogomil said. "But I am not your problem. Laura is."

"Laura is what?" Laura said. She was in the room with them again. To Susannah her sister looked exactly as she had always been. She was smiling a little, as if she were glad to see them, as if she had not been entirely sure she would see them again. There was something terrifying about her, but then hadn't there always been something terrifying about Laura? There was a smear of blood on her lips.

There was a new person with Laura, a girl. She didn't look much older than Carousel, but unlike Carousel, you could tell she wasn't really a girl. She was slight, but she was also tall, even taller than Susannah, so tall her head almost brushed against the peaked roof of the attic. She wore a dress so faded it was impossible to tell what color it had once been; her hair, pulled back into a sleek braid, was gray and her skin was bluish-white. This was the key. Something about her face made Susannah understand this had been Malo Mogge, too, before Malo Mogge had divided her magic and herself.

"Hi," Carousel said to the girl who had been the key.

"Hey," the key said. Gave a little wave.

"What Malo Mogge did, you wouldn't ever do that," Susannah said to Laura. "Cut away a piece of yourself to use it like a weapon. You're nothing like Malo Mogge. I don't know why they can't see that."

"I'm more of a box person," Laura said, which made no sense at all.

Mr. Anabin said to Laura, "You are here in time to settle an argument for us. We are debating whether or not you can be trusted with all of your power or whether you ought to be bound."

Laura said, "You think I could be bound against my will?"

The girl who had been Laura's guitar said, "With my help they could bind you."

"Because they're afraid," Laura said. "Of me." She was speaking to the key.

"They are wise to be afraid," the key said.

"Excuse me," Susannah said. "Do you have a name? Is there something we can call you?"

"Harmony," the girl said. "Call me that."

"Okay," Susannah said. "Harmony. You need to understand some things about my sister. She always puts the lid down when she flushes, and she always replaces the toilet roll. She has a billion stuffed animals. She eats her cereal in the morning superfast because it makes her gag when it gets soggy. I'm not afraid of her."

"That's because you're stupid," Laura said. "I made you forget things you needed to remember because it was expedient. Just as Malo Mogge did to me. I thought once I ate her I would get it back, the way I ought to feel about Ruth, about the fact that she's dead, but I didn't. I still don't feel anything about it at all."

"Good!" Susannah said, absolutely losing her shit. "Fuck Ruth! Fuck her for dying! I am so mad at her. I should get you to take away how I feel about it, too."

"I could do that," Laura said, "if you wanted me to. Look, I can make it stop snowing. I can do almost anything."

Daniel said, "Susannah, don't ask for that!"

Outside the snow was no longer falling.

Susannah wanted Laura to. She absolutely wanted her sister to take away how pissed off she was, how sad she was, all the scraped-raw parts of her. Just for a little while. Then she could ask Laura to give it back. Give some of it back. As much as she could bear. She said, "I do *want* you to do it. But I know you shouldn't. That I shouldn't ask."

"And that's why we should bind my power," Laura said. "I have so much power, so much magic. You have no idea what I could do now."

"And do you? Have some idea of your power?" Mr. Anabin said from the piano.

"I think so," Laura said. "Hey, Mo."

There was a gull perched on the windowsill. It hopped down to the floor, became Mo. And here was another gull. Thomas. This was the problem with hookups in a small town. You kept running into them. Susannah should have known better.

Laura said, "So did you catch him or not? Bowie?"

"Kind of yes," Mo said. "Kind of no."

Thomas did not say anything. His look suggested he would murder anyone in the room who asked any more questions about Bowie.

Mo said, "What did we miss? Who the fuck are you? Sorry, Carousel. Language." He had only just seen the key.

"I'm Harmony," the key said.

"That's Malo Mogge's key," Susannah said. "I don't know why she has a body right now. While you two were chasing Bowie, Laura ate Malo Mogge. We're discussing what happens next."

Bogomil said, "Susannah and Daniel must take up their new roles, and dear Laura must be rooted like a houseplant in a pot small enough that she does not gluttonously overgrow this entire world as Malo Mogge meant to do."

"Seems like a good idea," Mo said. "She already messed with Rosamel. Hey, Carousel, you guys all okay down there?"

"It was horrible," Carousel said. "But I saved everyone. Thanks for asking."

"I did not!" Laura said. "Why would you think I did something to Rosamel?"

You could tell she hadn't. She was completely outraged.

"Well," Mo said, "I thought you had. What about the guy at Birdsong Music? You said you made him give you a discount. And told him he could only listen to women musicians."

At this Laura looked somewhat abashed. "Okay, but he was being kind of a jerk!"

"So only nice people deserve to have free will?" Mo said.

"I'll go back and fix things," Laura said. "I need a new guitar anyway."

"Carousel," Bogomil said, ignoring this exchange, "must be given access to a source of sufficient magic so she may remain here in this world. So why kill only two birds with one stone when we could kill them all? So to speak. That is, if Carousel wishes to remain Carousel."

"I do," Carousel said. "I like being me."

"Then let Laura give up the key," Bogomil said. "If the key and Laura are agreeable. Let Carousel and the key be bound together for the span of a mortal life. For the span of that mortal life, Laura will have all the magic from the meal she made of Malo Mogge. Daniel and Susannah will make a different bargain than the one Anabin and I made so long ago. They will keep the door for those who must pass through, but they will not serve them up as meat for a goddess."

"Like you, you mean," Susannah said. "You and Mr. Anabin."

"Yes," Mr. Anabin said. "Like Bogomil and myself. I would prefer not to be eaten." To Laura he said, "You will be hungry, as Malo Mogge was, but hunger may be endured. At the end of her mortal lifetime, Carousel may pass through the door."

"I will go with her," said the key. "All in this room may go then, too, should they choose to."

"What if we don't choose to?" Laura said.

"Then you will have to make your own way into Death," the key said. "When I am gone, the door Malo Mogge made will no longer open for you."

"Well," Laura said. "I guess we'll see. We were dead once before, and we managed to get back. How hard can it be to 'make our way into Death' or whatever? Anyway, there's plenty of time to decide about that and I probably ought to be bound in some way, I guess. I didn't do anything to Rosamel. I really didn't. But, you know, what if someday I did? That or something worse?"

"You have something in your pocket," the key said to Laura. "May I see it?"

Laura looked, at first, like she would rather die. But then she drew something out. A bone, curved, broken at one end. She gave it to the girl who was the key.

The key took it in her hand, pressed it so it folded in on itself like a piece of putty. Laura made a horrible noise.

"No," the key said. "See? It's yours again." She gave it back to Laura. It had become a guitar pick. "Keep it with you. I've put some of myself in it, too. Now I may be in the world and any may come into contact with me. Unless I am united with the guitar pick you hold, any who touch me may avoid passing through the door."

"Okay," Laura said. She was clenching the pick tightly in her hand. If it were Susannah, Susannah thought, she would lose something like that before she even knew it. But Laura would keep it safe. It wasn't like you ever wanted your sister to become a goddess, but on the whole Laura was being quite reasonable so far. It probably wouldn't last, but it was impressive all the same.

Bogomil said, "You see? Your fate is not so terrible. Anabin and I served a thousand years. You will keep the door for hardly a day by comparison."

Daniel ignored this. He said to Susannah, "You don't have to take over Bogomil's job if you don't want to. I could do it. I've been down there twice. I could get used to it. If you wanted, you could take Mr. Anabin's job instead."

"How generous!" Bogomil said. "What a gesture!"

"Are you making fun of him?" Susannah said. "Stop laughing. It isn't funny."

"Oh, but it is," Bogomil said. "Isn't it, Anabin?"

He turned his back to them as Mr. Anabin said, "Bogomil made the same offer to me. He saw I was afraid and so he took my place. I stayed in the sunlit world; he went to the realm beyond the door. He was tenderhearted then, much more so than I."

"Tenderhearted?" Mo said. "Him?"

They all looked at Bogomil. But his back was turned and no one saw his face.

"Of course I'll do it," Susannah said. "Take over for Bogomil. It's what I wanted. It may not be exactly what I thought it was, but it suits me. Better than this place ever did."

"I'll take up Mr. Anabin's place," Daniel said.

"You don't have to," Susannah said.

"I think I do," Daniel said. The way he said it told Susannah he had made up his mind.

"There's one thing you ought to know," Laura said. "It's about you and Daniel, when you've done the ritual. You'll be like them. Mr. Anabin and Bogomil. You'll still be able to talk and see each other, but, um, not both at the same time. That's why Bogomil has his back turned right now. It's part of the magic."

"Seriously?" Susannah said. "That's the stupidest thing I've ever heard. But whatever. Fine."

Daniel said, "Let's just get this over with."

Mo cleared his throat. He said, "Okay, so I'm not offering to take over for Daniel. Not right now. There are all kinds of things I want to do first. But maybe later. Maybe when I'm old. Like, fifty or whatever. Maybe then I would be willing to do it, to take over. Be Mr. Anabin. If you wanted."

"And what about Susannah?" Daniel said. "She has to just keep being Bogomil?"

Thomas said, "Susannah may speak for herself, I think. But I make her the same offer Mo has made you."

"We'll see," Susannah said. "That's a long time from now and who knows if you'll feel the same way." She wanted to add, And who knows how Mo will feel about you. But that seemed mean.

"Can we please get this over with?" Laura said.

It wasn't even a particularly complicated or impressive kind of ritual. Susannah took one of the girl Harmony's hands, and Daniel took the other. The ritual of the door they knew. And afterward, Susannah didn't say anything at all. Daniel was silent, too. They let go of Harmony's hands and stayed there, looking at each other.

"What do I need to do?" Laura said to the key.

"Not much," the girl said. "Just let me go. Carousel and I will be friends now."

"We can be acquaintances first," Carousel said. "We have to figure out if we like each other."

Mr. Anabin got up from the piano. He went to Bogomil, who had stayed at the window. He rested his hand on Bogomil's shoulder. "Bogomil," he said, "look at me."

Bogomil turned.

Mr. Anabin said, "It's done."

"Susannah?" Daniel said. As he said it, Susannah felt a terrible force spin her on her heels.

When she stopped, she was looking directly at Mo.

"You okay?" Mo said. "That seemed kind of awful. Sorry."

She caught her breath. "I'm fine. It's okay."

"It isn't that great," Thomas said. "But there are workarounds. Texting, sign language, that kind of thing. You'll figure it out. Anabin and Bogomil are—Were! I guess?—just extremely old-school."

"I'm fine," Susannah said. "We'll manage." Was she managing? The room was so full of people, and she felt so strange. She could feel the pull of her realm, the push of Daniel at her back. But she would stay here as long as she could.

Behind her, Mr. Anabin and Bogomil were talking.

"And where will we go?" Mr. Anabin said.

"Somewhere not here," Bogomil said. "Anywhere."

Carousel said to Harmony, "So are you going to come home with me? You could have my sleeping bag."

"I'll go with you," Harmony said. "But not like this."

"You could be a guinea pig," Carousel said. "We have an old cage in the garage. Or a dog! Ours died."

"No," Harmony said. She crouched down, rested her forehead against Carousel's. "You're kind. And so warm! I was curious what it was like, being so full of blood. So soft. I'd forgotten. But another shape suits me better."

To Susannah and Daniel, Harmony said, "The door you keep will stay open for any who require it. Only Laura and Daniel may not pass through, until Laura decides she is finished with this world. It will stay open until Carousel and I are ready to go on. When we have done so, the door will be no more and your task will be complete."

Then she became Laura's old guitar again, only, of course, it wasn't Laura's guitar at all. It never had been. And now it was Carousel's. *This Machine Kills Gods*. Laura's joke, but now, of course, Laura was a god herself.

Bogomil said, "Take good care of it, Carousel."

"It's a magic guitar," Carousel said. "Of course I'll take care of it."

"It's magical," Laura said. "But you can't just go around doing magic. Just because you're made of magic and you have a magic guitar doesn't mean you can go around using magic however you want to."

"But you can?" Carousel said.

"I'm a goddess," Laura said. As if that settled everything.

"Susannah?" Daniel said.

"No more magic for us," Mo said sadly to Thomas. But that turned out not to be entirely true. Susannah said, "I'll be back. I promise." And then she fled, pouring herself out of the world and into that place she had been promised so long ago, dark and lovely and strange.

The Book of Susannah's Realm

When she got to Bogomil's realm—no, it was hers, it was her realm now!—she couldn't help herself. She went to look for Ruth. Hadn't Bogomil said her mother had been here? But in all the shining darkness, in all the shadowed grass, on the silky paths, there was no one, no one at all. No Ruth, no Bogomil. Not even a trace of Malo Mogge; Laura had eaten every bit. There was no one there but her.

The Book of Mo

Later on Mo and Susannah met up for coffee at What Hast Thou Ground? Billy was at the counter; the Broadway cast recording of *Carousel* played over the terrible speakers. Susannah had used magic so no one would notice her. She explained to Mo, almost apologetically, that otherwise, if the customers noticed her, they would ask her for things as if she still worked there. The spell did not seem to have any effect on Billy. He appeared to be under the impression Susannah had a fancy new job in the Boston area, and he stopped by the table three times to ask after Daniel, how he was doing, what he was up to. Daniel was over at the mall, Susannah explained. Hanging out with his friends. The *normal* ones, she said. Billy nodded as if he knew what Susannah meant by this. There was a HELP WANTED sign in the window.

There were muffins, which Mo enjoyed in moderation. His magic was dwindling away but not gone entirely. He'd spent a half hour as a veery on a tree branch the previous morning.

Susannah ate six muffins. Mo kept count.

They talked about Susannah's realm. How it seemed to her, how it had been for Mo. As they talked, it seemed to Mo that the coffee shop grew colder, darker. Just out of his field of vision he knew the dusty path was making its way between the slender trees. Susannah, too, seemed made of shadows now, most discernable in the blackness around her nail beds, under her nails. She was quieter, somehow, but her teeth were sharper. But then, Mo was changed, too.

They didn't talk about Daniel or Laura. They discussed Maryanne

Gorch's will—she'd left a lot of her money to a nonprofit foundation she'd been in the process of setting up. Some would go for grants to artists and writers, more would go to found a publishing company in the model of Odyssey or Arabesque to publish Black romance. This seemed likely, Mo said, to actually make money, and then the foundation would have to decide how best to use it.

He said, "So I think they've left town. Bogomil and Mr. Anabin."

"I know," Susannah said. "Good riddance. I ran into Bogomil, by the way. Well, by 'ran into' I mean ambushed. Kind of fun to turn the tables."

"I bet," Mo said. "How was he?"

"Sunburned," Susannah said. "I told him he better live a long, happy life. Because when he dies I'll be waiting for him. Anyway, you and Thomas and Bowie. Tell me the whole thing and don't leave anything out."

How ridiculous it had all been after Malo Mogge's defeat, Thomas the gull chasing Bowie, and Mo chasing after them like the Three Stooges. Larry, Curly, and Mo. He had never quite caught up, and maybe that was because he didn't really want to see Thomas kill Bowie. Just because someone you liked wanted to eat five hundred hot dogs in one sitting, had wanted to eat five hundred hot dogs for several centuries, and now they were actually going to do it, didn't mean you had to watch them do it.

"Did you really just compare killing someone to eating five hundred hot dogs?" Susannah said. "Also, why wouldn't you want to watch them eat five hundred hot dogs? It seems kind of cool."

"I don't really get the whole revenge thing," Mo said.

And what if what had ended up happening was Bowie killing Thomas? Why would Mo have wanted to be there for that? What had he been thinking he could do? In any case, he'd thought he'd never catch up and by the time he did they would be engaged in their terrible business. He decided he would fly over them and shit on their heads. He would absolutely take a shit on Thomas's head. Have a little humiliation to season your epic revenge. Good luck from your friend Mo.

"But that's revenge, too," Susannah said.

"I guess?" Mo said. It wasn't the kind of thing that happened in the Lavender Glass books. In those books people did the right thing or the wrong thing and then more things happened. There was lots of revenge, plenty of boats and seagulls, but nobody ever got shat on. Not even the people who really deserved it.

Eventually he'd realized they were no longer over Lovesend. They'd gone inland. So that part of Malo Mogge's spell was finished. He'd fleetingly wondered about all the people she'd done unpleasant things to, the people she'd made worship her. What would they remember? As it turned out, nothing. But in the moment Mo hadn't really cared about Lovesend. All he'd been able to care about was Thomas. Even if Thomas killed Bowie, Mo would have gone on wanting Thomas in the same way he wanted music, planned to go on thinking about music and caring about music and the things that music could do. Maybe the way he felt about Thomas wasn't the way he would always feel about Thomas. Sometimes that happened with music, with a song you heard on the radio or with something you were working on. Something you were super into or trying to make work. All that intensity of feeling boiled down into a kind of residue, and then the residue wore away, too, and there was nothing there. Maybe that was Mo, maybe that would be Mo with everything except for music and thinking about music. After all, that was how it had gone with Vincent, all the feeling boiled away. The other way, where all that feeling caught you up in it forever in a kind of hard casing, like amber, that was how it had been for Thomas, wasn't it? With how he hated Bowie. How he'd hated Malo Mogge, too, even as he'd been tied to her for hundreds of years. Hundreds of years!

Mo wanted, though, to know what Thomas would be, who Thomas would be now that Malo Mogge was gone. And maybe, he'd thought, if Thomas killed Bowie, Mo would get that wish. To see what Thomas might become. But Bowie was sneaky, and Thomas hadn't gotten the better of him once yet. If Bowie killed Thomas, what would Mo have done then? Become like Thomas, obsessed with revenge? Give up music? Not that Mo thought he would be any good at revenge. But maybe no one was, at the beginning.

He said, "So then it turned out we were over in Silverside above Cresthill Hospital. Where your mom worked." Susannah looked down at that. Studied the empty plate where muffins had been. "That was where

Bowie was headed. Right for the NICU, straight through a window someone had cracked open."

"They do that when the heating is on too high," Susannah said. "The Isolettes are temperature-controlled, but it gets pretty miserable for the nurses sometimes."

Mo had gone sailing through the six-inch gap, marveling at this precision even as he enacted it. He became himself again at Thomas's side. There was no sign of Bowie at all.

"A nurse came up and wanted to know what we were doing there, but Thomas just sent her away. I figured Bowie had gone out a door or something, but Thomas knew."

"Knew what?" Susannah said.

"Bowie changed himself into a baby. Or babies. He may be babies plural."

Susannah took this in. "Bowie went there with me once," she said. "He told me all this weird stuff about Avelot and talked to my mom and held a preemie. Then he told me he ought to kill me. But he didn't. If he had, maybe my mom would still be alive."

"That's a shitty thing to say," Mo said.

"It feels pretty shitty when I think about it, so that's about right. So what did Thomas do? And what do you mean, babies?"

Thomas had gone from Isolette to Isolette, peering in at each occupant. It had made Mo extremely uncomfortable. It wasn't as if he'd been thrilled about the possibility of Thomas killing Bowie in the first place, but the idea of Thomas killing a baby was so much worse.

"Is it really worse to kill Bowie as a baby than to kill Bowie as Bowie?" Susannah said. "Why?"

"Definitely worse," Mo said. "I feel like most people would agree with me. But Thomas couldn't figure out which baby was Bowie. There were nine babies, and every single one of them was exactly as babylike or as Bowie-like as any other."

"He was all of them?" Susannah said.

"Could he even do that?" Mo said. "I still don't know! I don't know why anyone would even want to become a baby!"

"Or, for that matter, a lot of babies," Susannah said.

"The point is, Thomas couldn't figure out which baby he wanted to kill. And he was wicked mad about it. I could see him thinking about how maybe he should just kill all of them, you know? He thought about it for a while."

He couldn't really explain to Susannah what it had been like in the NICU, all those babies like astronauts in capsules with their science-fiction-movie-style life supports, on their hopeful missions into whatever their future lives would be, Mo waiting to see if Thomas decided he wanted to straight-out murder one.

"I was just hovering there, like an anxious bat or something. I wasn't literally a bat, I mean, but I felt like one. Vibrating all over the place. Waiting to see what Thomas was going to do, trying to figure out what I would do if he did anything. Like, this is not a relationship that is going anywhere if I can't even figure out how to have an argument with him about why you shouldn't go around killing babies. That's not the kind of relationship fight I'm prepared to have."

"Especially early in the relationship," Susannah said. "Do you mind if we go somewhere else? I think I'm affecting the ambience in here."

She wasn't wrong about that. A kind of cold and crepuscular gloom was rising up from the floorboards, radiating out of the espresso cups, the cupcake crumbs. You could hear those trees whispering secret dark things. Mo and Susannah left What Hast Thou Ground? and walked down to the little park. Here, no one was looking, so Susannah became a black squirrel. She ran up the trunk of a chestnut tree and began to tidy her gothic plume of a tail on a high branch. Mo became a common loon and joined her on the branch. He said, "I think Bowie was tired of being Bowie. Third time's a charm, right? Anyway, I left Thomas to do whatever it was he was going to do. I had a slice of really bad pecan pie in the hospital cafeteria. And eventually Thomas came and found me. He hadn't killed any babies."

"Kind of figured you would have led with that," the squirrel said. "If he'd killed a baby."

"I feel a little bad for him," the loon said. "All he's wanted for five hundred years or whatever. To find Bowie or Avelot and kill her. Him. And now what?"

"Wait another sixteen or seventeen years," the squirrel said. "Maybe teenager Bowie will do something obvious. Give himself away."

"Or all of those babies will turn out to be Bowie," the loon said. "And they'll gang up on him and kick his ass. Or Thomas will show up one day with all the babies, he'll have kidnapped all of them so he can have a couple of days or years or whatever to figure it out. Which one he wants to murder. In which case, I'm out. Let him change all the diapers."

The squirrel said, "He waited for a really long fucking time. What's another decade or two?"

"Yeah," said the loon. "Take the long view. How about you? You really like it? Being down there in the dark?"

The squirrel said, "Suits me for now. We'll see how I feel in a decade or two."

"Do you think it suits you and that's why Bogomil picked you? Or do you think it suits you because Bogomil kept dragging you there? Made you into someone who would be the right fit for it?"

The squirrel did its best to shrug. "Does it matter? Don't change the subject. You and Thomas."

"Fine," said the loon. "Okay. I like him. A lot. But do I really want to spend a decade or two or even a couple of long weekends with a guy who is mostly thinking about someone else? The one who got away? Yes, okay, someone else is someone he wants to kill, but that seems intense. I want to be with someone who is mostly thinking about me."

"Mo," the squirrel said. "You have music. You know what you want to do. What you want to be. You have all these ideas about songs, about things you want to do. Whoever you end up with, they're going to have to put up with that. With all the stuff in your head and in your heart that isn't about them. So, yeah, I mean, have a little sympathy for Thomas? Let him have his thing? Even if you don't really get it?"

"Even if his thing is revenge? Murder?"

The squirrel said, "Maybe you give it some time. Give *him* some time. Maybe now that Malo Mogge's out of the picture, he'll find something else to be interested in. Like tabletop gaming. Or cake decoration."

"I really like him," the loon said. "And I want him to like me. I want him to like me a lot. I want him to like me, to *want* me, more than he wants to kill Bowie. But not, like, in an ultimatum way. I don't want to have to make a whole 'it's Bowie or me' speech. I couldn't do it, up at the hospital. I wanted him to choose me without me asking him to choose me."

"Well," the squirrel said, "he did. He chose you. You and your slice of bad pie in the cafeteria. Didn't he?"

The loon lifted one foot, scratched its sleek head thoughtfully. Then it swooped down to the grass and became a boy. "Yeah," Mo said. "I guess he did."

The Book of Carousel

AFTER ALL THE magic has been sorted out in Mo's extremely cool attic and Susannah has gone to her dark realm, Carousel and Daniel get a ride back down from the Cliffs in Mr. Anabin's car. She gets the front seat; Daniel and the Harmony ride in the back. Bogomil has gone ahead of them with Laura.

Daniel's knees are up around his shoulders practically. He should have taken the front, but that's Daniel for you. Very kind, not very intelligent.

First they stop at the Cliff Hangar because Mr. Anabin says there is someone there who needs Daniel's help. This turns out to be the guy who runs What Hast Thou Ground? He's sleeping up on the platform of the carousel, which Carousel has never loved. She's always felt she was in competition with it, whether or not the carousel knew. It's definitely more popular than she is. But it turns out she's more magic.

"Malo Mogge did this," Mr. Anabin says to Daniel. "You might use your magic to undo it. What magic you do here gives Susannah magic of her own. If you do none, she will, in time, have none."

Daniel kneels by the sleeping guy. He says, "Hey. Billy. Wake up. Party's over."

The guy, Billy, opens his eyes, sees Daniel, and smiles. "Danny boy, my good friend," he says, "long time no see. How you been?"

Carousel wanders over to the windows and surveys the night. Laura is out in the bay tearing apart Malo Mogge's temple. She becomes aware that Bogomil is standing there, too, also watching. There's someone else, a boy Carousel doesn't know, the one who flew into the attic with Mo. They all watch in silence.

Mo? Mo stayed home. He said today has been a lot and he could use some downtime.

Carousel wonders what Susannah is up to in her realm. She wishes she could go visit, see this place, but apparently that's another thing she's not allowed to do, even though she's in charge of the key. Most of the key.

Back in the car, Billy gets the front seat and Carousel goes in the back with Daniel and her new guitar. It's all banged up and scratched, and maybe it wouldn't mind if Carousel puts some more stickers on it, something to make it feel more like it actually belongs to her.

Billy keeps dozing off. Daniel is talking about applying to state schools. He asks Mr. Anabin to write him a recommendation. Carousel is perplexed. Her brother is the guardian of a magic door now. He has magic, he can do magic, he *is* magic. Shouldn't he be thinking bigger? Well, he'll figure it out as he goes. Carousel will, too. She sits beside Daniel, the guitar across her lap. She has discovered that she can talk to it and it talks right back. They didn't really ask you if this was what you wanted, Carousel says. *I* didn't ask. Is it okay? What do you want?

To be something other than what I have been, the guitar says.

Fair enough. Carousel has no idea what she wants to be, either.

They have to make more stops on the way home so Daniel can help people step down off pedestals. Help them stop being statues. It's nice to see Daniel using his magic. Carousel is proud of him. She knows how hard it can be to try new things.

When Mr. Anabin finally drops them off it's so very late that time has wrapped back around itself and now it's early. The rest of the house is asleep, but here are Lissy and Dakota. They have their coats on over their pajamas, and they're putting on their boots.

"Where are you going?" Carousel says.

"Where have you been?" Dakota asks. "Do you know what time it is?"

"Don't worry about that," Daniel says. So they don't. "What are you up to, anyway?" he asks, and Lissy says, "We're going out to do a spell. We want it to keep snowing a little while longer. And maybe ask for the lottery tickets back."

"I want it to snow through Christmas," Dakota says.

"Okay," Daniel says. "Just don't stay out too long. And keep your voices down. Don't wake anybody else up. I'll make hot chocolate. It'll be ready when you're done if you don't take too long."

Carousel says, "I think I'll go to bed." She doesn't mention the pearl in her pocket, the one the statue lady put in Carousel's hand when she left her on the shore. It's the size of a chicken's egg, lustrous and perfectly round. Who cares about lottery tickets? But she can show everyone the pearl tomorrow. Or save it for Christmas even.

She doesn't bother to turn on the light in the bedroom. She leans the Harmony against her bed, looks out the window to where Lissy and Dakota stand in the yard, holding hands and chanting, looking up at the sky. "I'm not supposed to just go around doing magic," Carousel says to the guitar. *Her* guitar. Her magic. "But we'll see about that." She calls the snow down.

The Book of My Two Hands Both Knowe You

For Christmas, Laura gives Daniel a replacement bass guitar—a Fender Mustang—and a Gallien-Krueger Combo amp. Susannah gives him a T-shirt that says JACO PLAYED 4. They both watch him unwrap his presents, but Susannah turns her back when he tells them thank you. It still makes her queasy, the push-pull yank that spins her round unless she turns first. Sometimes they sit back-to-back and talk. Sometimes they don't talk at all. Sometimes she comes to him as a white cat or a wolfish black dog. A black beetle.

"Do you know," Laura says, "I think there's another door. Not here, though. On the moon. I've been hanging out up there some. Anyway, I don't know what's behind it or how to go through it. Not yet."

"I can't believe that you just said, casually, that you've been hanging out on the moon," Susannah says.

"That wasn't the interesting part of what I said," Laura says. "But whatever. Merry Christmas, Daniel."

They're in room 12 down at the Seasick Blues. Laura is staying there while she makes plans for what she wants her future to look like. Is Laura still the same Laura? This is one of the things Daniel and Susannah talk about. Will she be like Malo Mogge? Does she seem hungry? As if she might be thinking about what people (well, people like Mo and Thomas and Carousel, Bogomil and Mr. Anabin, all of them ripe with magic) might taste like? Hard to tell. Like Daniel says, Laura's always been hungry. But so far, Laura has used her new power sparingly. She could have put their house back, she could have restored everything the wave destroyed, but in the end she decided she didn't want to. Let it go, let it all go. Susu and the pangolin and the sky-blue owl. The Glory and the Gretsch. Every Caitlynn Hightower paperback. The white couch and the china shepherdess and all of Ruth's scrubs, Ruth's mugs, Ruth's self-help books, every piece of Ruth, every bit of Laura's and Susannah's life from before. Laura is determined to make a clean start. She's writing a song about her mother. She doesn't feel anything about Ruth's death yet, but maybe if she gets the song right she will. And Susannah? Susannah doesn't need couches now, or shoes, or anything much, really, not even the British Drum Company four-piece set Laura picked out for her. Susannah has her realm, and when she is out of it, she has Daniel and Laura.

Daniel's working on college applications. Figuring out whether it's better to stay home where he can keep an eye on Carousel and his family or whether he should get his own place. "The Fender's gorgeous," he says. "But I don't know if music is my thing now."

Susannah snorts. That's Daniel for you. He doesn't ever admit he wants something, not even when it's right in front of him. You have to give him a lot of time and space to get there on his own.

"Okay," Laura says. She sounds impatiently patient in the way only Laura can. "But in the meantime, while you're figuring out what your thing is, maybe we could just play a little? I could take the Fender back to the store, return it, but that would be a shame. To take it back when you haven't even tried it out?" Laura has a new guitar, too, another Gretsch.

"I've been thinking a lot about this genre of super-annoying songs," Susannah says. The first word she says, Daniel spins around, almost topples over, the Fender in his arms. Nice save. "The ones that just keep on repeating at the end, the ones that do the fade-out but it takes forever. I was thinking maybe we could do an ending like that? But just keep it going. Going and going and going and going and going and going and—"

"We get it," Laura says. "Very funny. But do we always have to have a gimmick? Come on, Daniel. Just one song. See how it feels?"

"I guess," Daniel says. "Sure. Why not. You're the boss, right?" Then, "Susannah? You in?"

She is.

The Book of Endings

Here's the thing about endings. Caitlynn Hightower knew this. Mo knows it, too. Even after you finish a book, things go on happening, no matter whether or not you plan to write them down. But romance novels have to end while everyone is happy enough with only the prospect of more happiness and only minor disappointments ahead. Poor Lavender Glass! Every time Maryanne Gorch sat down to write another chapter, another book, it meant more trouble for her heroine. More kidnappings, more misunderstandings, more sea voyages, more wickedness, bad luck, and suffering. Is a handsome man with an impressive dick and a good heart really worth all of the attendant misery? Lavender Glass appeared to think so, but who knows exactly what Maryanne Gorch thought. Natalie's boyfriend *was* cheating on her, it turns out. But the next guy she goes out with is actually perfect. He really is. And not now, but in a couple of years, Theo is going to discover polyamory. Sure, it's a lot of work, but when has Theo ever been afraid of work? Why not have your cake and share it, too? Mo says to Thomas, "What was in the fortune cookie you gave me?" "What?" Thomas says. "In the restaurant, when Malo Mogge was tormenting us. You gave me a fortune cookie." "You didn't open it?" Thomas asks. Mo says, "I didn't *feel* like it at the time. So I left it at my grandmother's grave. But you could just tell me. What was in it?" "Come here," Thomas says. "I'll whisper it in your ear." Everything we do is music. There are many kinds of love, and not all of them are built to last past the span of one romance novel, let alone a thousand years. But let's imagine a rose garden, winter, the sky clear and bright. Snow can't keep falling forever. In the garden, two men. "What happens now?" one man says to the other. Sometimes two lovers meet in a movie theater after the lights have gone down. Imagine them right in front of you. They're tall enough it's annoying, but the theater is mostly empty and you could always move. They never talk, never turn to look at each other, but they are holding hands. There are always workarounds. You can text or write down a message while the other person watches. *I love you, you asshole. Oh, I love you still. Can you bear it? I can bear it still.* Oh, the world is a terrible place and getting worse. Laura would like to fix things. She may yet fix things, once she's sure the best way to proceed. Not every act of Malo Mogge can be undone. Three of the karaoke singers from the night of the benefit at the Cliff Hangar are never seen again. Hannah Santos remains a tiger for the rest of her life. She's happy enough in the sanctuary where a photo of her splendid stripy self ends up on a souvenir postcard. Some of the citizens of Lovesend still dream some nights of being a statue. Standing on a plinth, strange and still and silent as snow falls and others walk past them, gaze up at them in wonder. Some of them want to know what this dream might portend. Will they be famous? Do some notable deed? Be remembered long after they're dead and gone? There are no statues of Malo Mogge in Lovesend. Some nights, when Rosamel Walker is asleep in her cinder-block dorm room, on her narrow bed, the moon comes and sits in her window. The moon comes to Ohio on certain nights. This is what the moon says: "Wake up, wake up! Come with me. Oh, come with me and I'll show you marvelous things. I'll give you whatever you want. We could be together and never grow old. Oh, won't you come with me?" And Rosamel, asleep and dreaming, always says the same thing. "Maybe someday," she tells the moon. "Not today. There are things I need to do! But someday, oh someday, maybe I will." In the rose garden one man is humming a song, a very old song. Carousel is teaching herself to play the Harmony. There is so much magic in her! What she will do, who she will be—all of that lies ahead, in a room so big it contains the whole world and other worlds besides. Every door will open for her. "I figured out how they got out of Bogomil's realm," Carousel says to her guitar. "You let them out, didn't you?" Her guitar doesn't say anything back, but it doesn't have to. It and Carousel have something like a perfect understanding. "Play me something you wrote," Thomas says. He is lying across Mo's bed. And because Mo loves him, and because eventually if you keep on writing music you'll have to play it for someone, Mo does. He plays Thomas a song on his keyboard, gathers up his courage and sings what he has on paper. Before he's finished, he stops. He says, "That was terrible." Thomas says, "It wasn't ever going to be perfect the first time, Mo. Try it again." One day there will be an opera called *The Book of Love*. It will be about Maryanne Gorch, Caitlynn Hightower, Lavender Glass, the two Jenny Pings. On opening night you might recognize some members of the audience if you're lucky enough to be in attendance. Genevieve Cabral, for one, who recently was performing sold-out shows at Bar Thalia. Mo and Thomas don't live in Maryanne Gorch's house beside the sea, but they visit now and then. Thomas is suspicious of the children of Lovesend, the ones of a certain age. Avelot may yet make herself or himself or themselves known one day, and what would he do then? He doesn't know. But the house isn't empty. Occupants come and go. In the house there are marks on the floors where heavy feet have trod. Sometimes in summer, voices can be heard in the overgrown rose garden. Someone tends the rose garden. Imagine it was possible, under cover of night, to climb the cliff face from the rocks beside the shore up to the wall where Maryanne Gorch's roses trail over. Imagine you made a house, too, with many rooms on the floor of the ocean from the tumbled green stones of Malo Mogge's temple. Imagine no one on land or sea ever bothered you or kept you from where you wanted to be or what you wanted to do. Imagine once you stood still as stone but now you move as you please and do only as you please. There are no statues of Malo Mogge in Lovesend, or anywhere else for that matter, but eventually, in the end, there are three statues of Maryanne Gorch in Lovesend because Mo can't choose among the finalists when he and the Committee for the Beautification of Lovesend must make their choice. And, after all, Mo is supplying the funds. He can put up as many statues of Maryanne Gorch as he wants. *I Don't Want You to Worship Me I Just Want You to See What I Can Do.* That's the name of Laura Hand's first EP. By the time her first full-length album comes out, she's playing concert halls. Sometimes she comes back to Lovesend and plays the Cliff Hangar. The band gets back together. Susannah sings with Laura, Daniel turns his back. The audience doesn't particularly care. It doesn't affect the sound. And so on. We may not know every ending, but let us imagine Maryanne Gorch has a hand in it, and every love, though there may be ups and downs to keep our interest, is true and living. Every ending happy when the time must come at last for endings. Two men are kissing in a garden; the snow begins to fall again. Open the door, a voice says, and let them come in!

Acknowledgments

This novel took a long time to write, and I had a great deal of support from various people while I worked on it. One of them is my agent, Renée Zuckerbrot, who signed me on as a client knowing that I was a short story writer. Thank you for your extraordinary patience, and for reading this book so many times. Thanks to Holly Black, who suggested that I write a novel on purpose, rather than by accident, and to Cassandra Clare, who has provided many beautiful houses in which to work, as well as much sound advice. Thanks to all of the early readers who provided encouragement and asked helpful questions: Craig Laurence Gidney, Sofia Samatar, Steve Berman, Jedediah Berry, Emily Houk, Joshua Lewis, Robin Wasserman, Maureen Johnson, Sarah Rees Brennan, Barb Gilly, and Leigh Bardugo. Thanks to Sarah Pinsker for providing much-needed feedback from a musician's point of view and for pointing me at various guitars. Thanks to Steve Ammidown for looking at this novel from the point of view of an archival librarian and fellow fan of the romance genre.

I'm so very grateful to my editor, Caitlin McKenna, for her enthusiasm, her painstaking care with edits, and her patience. This is a much better book because of your attention, and I promise the next one will be shorter.

Thank you to the MacArthur Foundation for a life-changing level of support. Thank you to the creative, solutions-minded, and hilarious staff who have kept Book Moon alive through three very interesting years: Laura, Kate, Jess, Beth, Diya, Jed, Andy, Ruth, Caroline, Franchie,

Amanda, and Joey. It isn't the smartest idea to take over a bookstore while you're working on your first novel, but that's what happened. Thanks to Mary Ruefle for a reading of John Cage that made me think about Cage as a magician. Thank you to Amanda Morrell (again) for tracking down permissions. Many thanks to Noah Eaker for acquiring this novel before I'd even figured out what I wanted it to be.

Love always to Gavin, always my first reader. I wouldn't write books if I didn't write them for you. All my love and gratitude to Jade and Annabel Link, for their good humor and for keeping the chickens and the dog (and me) happy.

There is a whole team of people at Random House that I'm so very glad I have on my side. Among them are the extraordinary Noa Shapiro, Andy Ward, Rachel Rokicki, Erica Gonzalez, Windy Dorrestyn, Maria Braeckel, Erin Richards, Madison Dettlinger, Caroline Cunningham, Benjamin Dreyer, Rebecca Berlant, Richard Elman, Michael Morris, Loren Noveck, Diana D'Abruzzo, Barb Jatkola, and Allison Merrill. Some of you I've had the pleasure of meeting in person, and some of you I've seen on Zoom. Every single one of you is a star in my book.

ABOUT THE AUTHOR

KELLY LINK is the author of *White Cat, Black Dog; Get in Trouble*, a finalist for the Pulitzer Prize in Fiction; *Magic for Beginners; Stranger Things Happen;* and *Pretty Monsters*. Her short stories have been published in *The Best American Short Stories* and *Prize Stories: The O. Henry Awards*. She is a MacArthur "Genius Grant" fellow and has received a grant from the National Endowment for the Arts. She is the co-founder of Small Beer Press and co-edits the occasional zine *Lady Churchill's Rosebud Wristlet*. She is also the co-owner of Book Moon, an independent bookstore in Easthampton, Massachusetts.

kellylink.net
BlueSky: @kellylink.bsky.social